THE MOONSTONE

THE MOONSTONE

Wilkie Collins

edited by *Steve Farmer*

broadview literary texts

Canadian Cataloguing in Publication Data

Collins, Wilkie, 1824-1889
    The moonstone

(Broadview literary texts)
Includes bibliographical references.
ISBN 1-55111-243-4

I. Farmer, Steve, 1957-   . II. Title. III. Series
PR4494.M6 1999   823'.8   C99-30170-5

Broadview Press Ltd., is an independent, international publishing house, incorporated in 1985.

North America:
P.O. Box 1243, Peterborough, Ontario, Canada K9J 7H5
3576 California Road, Orchard Park, NY 14127
TEL: (705) 743-8990; FAX: (705) 743-8353;
E-MAIL: 75322.44@compuserve.com

United Kingdom:
Turpin Distribution Services Ltd.,
Blackhorse Rd., Letchworth, Hertfordshire SG6 1HN
TEL: (1462) 672555; FAX (1462) 480947; E-MAIL: turpin@rsc.org

Australia:
St. Clair Press, P.O. Box 287, Rozelle, NSW 2039
TEL: (02) 818-1942; FAX: (02) 418-1923

www.broadviewpress.com

Broadview Press is grateful to Professor L.W. Conolly for editorial advice on this volume.

Broadview Press gratefully acknowledges the financial support of the Ministry of Canadian Heritage through the Book Publishing Industry Development Program.

Text design and composition by George Kirkpatrick

PRINTED IN CANADA

Contents

Acknowledgements • 7
Introduction • 9
William Wilkie Collins: A Brief Chronology • 35
A Note on the Text • 40

The Moonstone • 45

Appendix A: Early Reviews of *The Moonstone*
    1. Geraldine Jewsbury, *The Athenaeum*
       (July 25, 1868) • 543
    2. *The Spectator* (July 25, 1868) • 544
    3. *Nation* (September 17, 1868) • 548
    4. *The Times* (October 3, 1868) • 549
    5. *Harper's New Monthly Magazine*
       (October 1868) • 556
    6. *Lippincott's Magazine* (December 1868) • 557

Appendix B: Excerpts from Newspaper Accounts of the Constance
    Kent/Road-house Murder Case of 1860 • 560
    The Times (July 3, 1860 to October 2, 1865) • 561
    The Somerset and Wilts Journal (July 21, 1860) • 562

Appendix C: Excerpts from *The Times* Accounts of the Major
    Murray/Northumberland Street Case of 1861
    The Times (July 13, 1861 to July 26, 1861) • 577

Appendix D: Collins on Indians
    "A Sermon for Sepoys." From Charles Dickens's
    Household Words: A Weekly Journal
    (February 27, 1858) • 587

Appendix E: Letters by Wilkie Collins Concerning *The Moonstone*
    (the Novel and the Play) • 594

Appendix F: *The Moonstone* (the Play) • 606

Appendix G: Reviews of the Olympic Theatre Performance of
        Wilkie Collins's *The Moonstone*
        1. *The Times* (September 21, 1877)   •   703
        2. *The Illustrated London News*
           (September 22, 1877)   •   707
        3. *The Athenaeum* (September 22, 1877)   •   708
        4. *The Spirit of the Times, New York*
           (October 6, 1877)   •   711

Select Bibliography   •   714

Acknowledgements

I am grateful to Faith Clarke, Andrew Gasson, Neil and Maria Nehring, Stephanie Farmer, Barbara Conolly, and the staff of the Harry Ransom Research Center at the University of Texas at Austin for their generous help during the preparation of this text.

Wilkie Collins (from the frontispiece of the first American edition of his novel *Man and Wife*, 1870)

Introduction

As Wilkie Collins's *The Moonstone* neared the end of its serial run in mid-summer 1868, public excitement about the mystery he had created built to a fever pitch. Each week in June and July, people lined Wellington Street outside the offices of Charles Dickens's weekly magazine *All the Year Round*, the publication in which the novel was then appearing, waiting to buy the new installment, hoping to be among the first to solve Collins's puzzles. William Tinsley, the London publisher who had purchased the rights to the three-volume first edition of the novel, described crowds "of anxious readers waiting for the new number" and remarked enthusiastically that these "were scenes ... that doubtless did the author's and publisher's hearts good."[1] And Collins, who had predicted a public success for his new novel, *was* pleased, but he was also anxious, as he always was, to see what the professional critics and reviewers – with whom he often sparred – would have to say about his latest literary experiment. Near the end of the novel, in a scene that seems to express this anxiety, Collins has Rachel Verinder – the novel's apprehensive heroine – ask Ezra Jennings for his reaction to several frustrating interruptions plaguing the remarkable experiment they both hope will solve the mystery surrounding the gem's disappearance: "They seem to be in a conspiracy to persecute you... . What does it mean?" Jennings, the story's recondite puzzle-solver, responds quietly but with a notable hint of fatigued cynicism: "Only the protest of the world, Miss Verinder – on a very small scale – against anything new" (*The Fourth Narrative – Extracted from the Journal of Ezra Jennings*).

Jennings's sentiments here echo Collins's, for by the time he wrote *The Moonstone*, his eighth novel, Collins had grown weary of curmudgeonly critics who seemed more often than not to frown on his literary experimentations, who frequently assailed his fiction as a cheap

---

1 This description appears in William Tinsley's memoirs, *Random Recollections of an Old Publisher* (2 volumes, London: Simpkin, Marshall, Hamilton, Kent, 1900). Tinsley also made the bold claim that "*The Moonstone* perhaps did more for [*All the Year Round*] than any other novel, not excepting *Great Expectations*."

nouveau sensationalism – "a plant of foreign growth" cried one critic[1] – or as nothing more than base demonstrations in new and often outlandish types of plot machinery.[2] Rather than buckle to what he perceived to be a constant barrage of criticism or to demands for subdued and to his mind rather dull fiction, though, Collins continued experimenting with his novels, attempting always to imbue them with that which he considered new and provocative.[3] *The Moonstone* was no exception; writing of the novel to his American publishers early in its serial run, he claimed boldly, "There are some effects to come, which – unless I am altogether mistaken – have never been tried in fiction before."[4]

As with Ezra Jennings's experiment in the novel, an unprecedented reenactment of the crime exactly one year after the fact, Collins had indeed tried something daring and new in *The Moonstone*, but at the time even he did not realize quite what it was or the far-reaching effect his experiment would have on the world of fiction.[5] In fact, it was not until some sixty years after the story's initial publication, with T.S. Eliot's often-quoted pronouncement that "*The Moonstone* is the

---

1   The critic was attacking the sensation school in general, Collins's *No Name* in particular in an unsigned review for the *Reader* (3 January 1863, 14).

2   In 1866 H.F. Chorley, a notoriously acerbic reviewer for the *Athenaeum*, had denounced *Armadale*, the novel preceding *The Moonstone*, as a "diseased invention," (2 June 1866, 732) and an anonymous critic for the *Westminster Review* had vilified the same work as part and parcel of the new "Sensational Mania ... its virus ... spreading in all directions" (October 1866, 269).

3   In a short preface to *Armadale* written in 1866, Collins remarked on what he perceived to be the reading public's unwillingness to consider something new: "Readers in particular will ... be here and there disturbed, perhaps even offended, by finding that *Armadale* oversteps, in more than one direction, the narrow limits with which they are disposed to restrict the development of modern fiction if they can."

4   See Appendix E for the full text of this and other of Collins's letters concerning *The Moonstone*.

5   Actually, what Collins claimed to be new in his fiction is an aspect of the book often overlooked today; he delineated his plan in the novel's preface, telling his readers that "In some of my former novels, the object proposed has been to trace the influence of circumstances upon character. In the present story I have reversed the process. The attempt made here is to trace the influence of character on circumstances." True enough, *The Moonstone* represents a first attempt by its author to allow the action of the story to be driven by the traits of its principal characters – Rachel Verinder's obdurate personality and Franklin Blake's weaknesses of habit serve to create a mystery where there would be none otherwise – but Collins and his readers failed at the time to notice the true watershed character of the novel.

first, the longest, and the best of modern English detective novels,"[1] that any notable critic, that any reader of the novel for that matter, identified exactly that aspect of the story that makes it one of the truly remarkable works of the mid-nineteenth century.

Eliot's frank statement, the first sentence of his landmark introduction to a 1928 edition of the novel, reveals to readers what even Collins did not realize as he wrote the book, that *The Moonstone* established precedents in fiction, detective fiction in particular, that have since been imitated by many but that have never been qualitatively surpassed. These several precedents have come to be expected features of many twentieth-century detective stories, so much so that *The Moonstone* often garners recognition as the novel that established what many perceive to be the "rules" of the genre.[2] Some of these precedents, common and immediately recognizable characteristics in a century's worth of detective fiction that has followed *The Moonstone*, go some way toward showing the reader the debt owed to Collins by countless writers, from Sir Arthur Conan Doyle, Anthony Trollope, and Thomas Hardy in the nineteenth century to G.K. Chesterton, John Dickson Carr, Agatha Christie, Dorothy Sayers, and P.D. James in the twentieth.[3]

Eliot, we should note, was careful to call *The Moonstone* the first English detective novel, for it was not the first work of fiction to contain elements of what has come to be considered the classic detective story. It was preceded, for instance, by Edgar Allen Poe's "The Murders in the Rue Morgue" (1841), "The Mystery of Marie Rogêt

---

1   This claim opens T.S. Eliot's introduction to the 1928 Oxford University Press edition of *The Moonstone*, an introduction based on an essay first published in the *Times Literary Supplement* in 1927 (1, 331, August 4, 1927).

2   In his *Stanford Companion to Victorian Fiction*, John Sutherland estimates that by the end of the nineteenth century, of the 800 weekly magazines in England, more than a quarter regularly ran detective stories of one sort or another (182). By the first quarter of the twentieth century, detective fiction societies had begun to spring up, and along with these came some semi-formal attempts at quality control in the form of suggested "rules" and "guidelines" for writers in the genre.

3   Though no one would consider Trollope and Hardy to have been writers of detective fiction, both owe a debt to Collins's fiction. Hardy's first novel, *Desperate Remedies* (1871) is a potboiler derived at least in part from *The Woman in White*. Trollope's *Eustace Diamonds* (1872) employs many of the notable detective fiction characteristics of *The Moonstone*.

(1842–43), and "The Purloined Letter" (1845),[1] as well as by French novelist Emile Gaboriau's *L'Affaire Lerouge* (1866). These early works, as well as some of England's so-called Newgate novels of the 1830s,[2] all contain rudimentary models of mysteries solved via some basic detection on the part of main characters. Each of Poe's stories, for example, offers readers Monsieur C. Auguste Dupin, a scholarly intellectual who demonstrates an ability to solve crimes by evaluating unobserved or misinterpreted clues. Gaboriau's novel introduces readers to Inspecteur Lecoq – he also appears in several of Gaboriau's later works – a master of disguises and deduction who out-duels criminals with skills of observation and scientific analysis.

Collins himself had experimented with basic models of mysteries of detection earlier in his career. In fact, according to early Collins biographer Robert Ashley, among others, Wilkie can be credited, in the decade before the publication of *The Moonstone*, with a number of landmarks in British detective fiction.[3] For instance, 1852's "A Terribly Strange Bed" – Collins's first contribution to Dickens's weekly magazine *Household Words* – may well be the first piece of British fiction to introduce police into the thick of mystery, though on this occasion the Parisian "Sub-prefect and several picked men among his subordinates" who appear near the end of the tale are not responsible for solving a crime. "A Stolen Letter," originally published as "The Fourth Poor Traveller" in the 1854 Christmas Extra Number of *Household Words*, can stake a claim, though it has been neglected by

---

1 Comparing Poe's "Purloined Letter" to Collins's similar and later "A Stolen Letter," Robert Ashley rather sardonically claims that though "The Purloined Letter" may have preceded some of Collins's work, may indeed have inspired Collins to write such fiction, Collins's "A Stolen Letter" is "at least as well told, is more credible, moves more swiftly, and is without the annoying pretentiousness of the earlier narrative" ("Wilkie Collins and the Detective Story," *Nineteenth-Century Fiction* 6, June 1951: 49.)

2 Linked most often with the novels of William Harrison Ainsworth and Edward Bulwer-Lytton, occasionally with the early novels of Charles Dickens, the Newgate novel – much to the dismay of those who would censor fiction, much to the delight of an eager and burgeoning reading public – flourished in the 1830s and 1840s and dealt rather sensationally with the lives of criminals chronicled in the *Newgate Calendar*, the name given to a collection of biographies of Newgate Prison's most notorious inmates.

3 Ashley's list of "firsts" appears in his article "Wilkie Collins and the Detective Story."

most historians, to being the first British work in which the main character, a lawyer named Boxsious, actually does solve a mystery – the whereabouts of a stolen letter – through basic detective work. The first woman detective in British fiction seems to have appeared in Collins's short story "The Diary of Anne Rodway," which first appeared in *Household Words* in the summer of 1856. The story's main figure, Anne, relentlessly follows the trail of the murderer, Noah Truscott, after discovering a single clue, a torn cravat that the victim is clutching when she dies. This story also shows Collins experimenting with epistolary narrative for the first time, the tale unfolding through several entries in Anne's diary.

"A Plot in Private Life," published in *Harper's Monthly Magazine* early in 1858 under the title "A Marriage Tragedy," is a noteworthy tale for a number of reasons. The reader of *The Moonstone* may recognize in the earlier tale's Mr. Dark – a lawyer's eccentric clerk and the story's sleuth – a model of the novel's esteemed Scotland Yard detective, Sergeant Cuff. The story's narrator, the congenial and faithful servant, William, who expresses a childlike awe of Dark's crime-solving skills, seems to be an early version of the Verinder family's devoted old steward, Gabriel Betteredge. And finally, at least part of this early story's mystery hinges on a blood-stained nightgown, which readers of *The Moonstone* will recognize as a precursor to the missing paint-stained nightgown that plays a central role in the novel's mystery.

Finally, later in 1858, Collins published "Who Is the Thief? – later re-titled "The Biter Bit" – in *The Atlantic Monthly*, a story notable as the first humorous detective story as well as for being another of Collins's early experiments with the epistolary narrative form.

It was not until *The Moonstone* appeared, however, that all the ingredients of this detective-fiction stew, ingredients Collins had been experimenting with for years, found their way, collectively, into an extended and substantial story that today defines the genre. Collins, for instance, may be said to have been the novelist who established detective fiction's "rules of fair play," rules not delineated until the first quarter of the twentieth century but whose roots are traceable directly to *The Moonstone*, rules that first and foremost, according to Dorothy Sayers, demand that "no vital clue should be concealed, that reader and detective should start from scratch and run neck and neck to the finish."[1] Though Collins knew nothing of this rule of fair play, he did realize that by distributing his tale among several narrators, he could plant all of his clues early in his story, keep his solution from his novel's several detectives, and sustain his mystery far longer than with a more conventional story-telling technique. His narrators knew only a portion of the story, and once they approached a critical point of discovery in the mystery, Collins simply replaced them with other figures, thus driving the narrative forward with a relentless and palpable tension. Collins also discovered that he could further sustain his drama by creating dual mysteries, one hinging on the thief's identity, the other pivoting on the location and recovery of the missing diamond. This masterful manipulation of character and action − counting the prologue and epilogue that frame the story, Collins manages eleven separate narrators, thirteen distinct narratives, and four separate thefts of the diamond − set a precedent for tight structure (Dorothy Sayers calls the novel "impeccable," Nuel Pharr Davis labels it "perfect," and Malcolm Elwin deems it "architecturally flawless"[2]) that every detective-fiction writer since has attempted to match.[3]

Any reader familiar with twentieth-century detective fiction will also recognize in *The Moonstone* many now-common features of the genre pioneered by Collins. A partial list of these features instantly reveals the extent of the debt owed to this single novel by anyone

---

1   In her famous 1944 "Introduction" to *The Moonstone*, Sayers points out that if readers will "examine carefully the first ten chapters of *The Moonstone* ... [they] will find that practically every clue necessary to the unraveling of the mystery is ... scrupulously set out in them" (Introduction to *The Moonstone*, London: J.M. Dent 1944: vi).

2   Sayers's comment comes from her 1944 "Introduction" to the novel (vi), Davis's comes from his 1956 biography *The Life of Wilkie Collins* (Urbana, Illinois: U of Illinois P: 284), and Elwin's comes from his article "Wilkie Collins: The Pioneer of the Thriller" (*London Mercury*, April 1931: 582).

3   One of the more interesting studies of *The Moonstone* and its place in the annals of detective fiction appears in D. A. Miller's "From 'roman policier' to 'roman-police': Wilkie Collins's *The Moonstone*" (*Novel*, Winter 1980, 153-170). Miller argues against the view of the novel as a tightly constructed masterpiece, maintaining that detective fiction by nature is paradoxically "parsimonious and squandering. On the one hand, the form is based on the hypothesis that *everything might count* ... yet if the criterion of total relevance is continually invoked by the text, it turns out to have a highly restricted applicability" (153).

who has written detective fiction since its publication.[1] For instance, in *The Moonstone*, for the first time in British fiction, the plot hinges on a single undetected crime committed on the grounds of a remote country-estate, undercutting the Victorian perception of crime as a distinctly urban phenomenon. On this country estate we see, also for the first time in such fiction, an embryonic "locked room" crime, and since the diamond disappears during the night after all the occupants of the house have been locked in, we see also an early example of the "inside job" crime that has become a staple of modern detective fiction. These features allowed Collins, as at least one early critic of the novel realized, to extend the mystery by gathering together in a single place a number of people "any one of whom may by possibility have stolen the jewel, and against each of whom the reader perceives strong circumstantial evidence."[2] Collins's ingenious handling of the crime itself gives way late in the novel to an equally ingenious and certainly original attempt at solution. Ezra Jennings's re-enactment of the crime, complete with an elaborate reconstruction of the scene and an uneasy reunion of the mystery's major players, is yet another feature that has found its way into more than a few modern detective stories.

The Moonstone also introduced to the genre the now-familiar image of the bungling local police force who are the first to appear at the scene of the crime but whose incompetencies muddy the story's waters with mis-information. Dull-witted and bombastic, the novel's Superintendent Seegrave and his men prolong the mystery by ignoring important clues, by alienating a household full of potential witnesses, and generally by pointing the reader – early in the story – in every direction but the right one, the several resulting "false clues" and "false suspects" becoming still more detective-fiction firsts. Seegrave had a real-life predecessor, but he may also rightly claim a place at the top of a long line of literary foils.

The character for whom he plays the foil – Scotland Yard's

---

1 In his recently published encyclopedic examination of all things Collinsian, *Wilkie Collins: An Illustrated Guide* (London: Oxford UP, 1998), Andrew Gasson enumerates the features discussed in this section of the introduction.

2 This passage appears in Geraldine Jewsbury's unsigned review from the *Spectator* (July 25, 1868, 882). For the full text of this and other early reviews of *The Moonstone*, see Appendix A.

Sergeant Cuff – is perhaps, at least in a discussion of *The Moonstone* as detective fiction, the most important figure in the novel. Though the appearance of a sleuthing professional is not among the novel's precedents,[1] Cuff is recognizably an archetypal figure, exhibiting many traits that subsequent writers have sought to imitate. With this in mind, his introduction into the novel – a pointed description from a rather sceptical Gabriel Betteredge – is worth noting:

> A fly from the railway drove up as I reached the lodge; and out got a grizzled, elderly man, so miserably lean that he looked as if he had not got an ounce of flesh on his bones in any part of him. He was dressed all in decent black, with a white cravat round his neck. His face was as sharp as a hatchet, and the skin of it was as yellow and dry and withered as an autumn leaf. His eyes, of a steely light grey, had a very disconcerting trick, when they encountered your eyes, of looking as if they expected something more from you than you were aware of yourself. His walk was soft; his voice was melancholy; his long lanky fingers were hooked like claws. He might have been a parson, or an undertaker – or anything else you like, except what he really was.[2] A more complete opposite to Superintendent Seegrave than Sergeant Cuff, and a less comforting officer to look at, for a family in distress, I defy you to discover, search where you may (*The Events Related by Gabriel Betteredge, House-Steward in the service of Julia, Lady Verinder*, Chapter XII).

Like many fictional detectives who have followed him, then, Cuff is a man whose appearance belies his choice of profession, and we may note also that his physique, his hatchet face, even his steely and expectant eyes remind a modern reader that Conan Doyle's famed detective Sherlock Holmes owes him quite a debt.[3]

---

1 Most point to Dickens's *Bleak House* (1852-53) as the first English novel to employ a professional detective, Inspector Bucket.
2 Collins biographer Catherine Peters comments on this description, suggesting that Cuff "is like many of Wilkie Collins' detectives, tinged with the clerical" (*The King of Inventors: A Life of Wilkie Collins*, London: Secker & Warburg, 1991: 306).
3 Malcom Elwin goes so far as to say, "It is fair to suppose that, but for *The Moonstone*, Conan Doyle would never have thought about little black men with poisoned

Collins humanizes Cuff with a wry sense of humour and with what Andrew Gasson calls an "amiable touch of eccentricity," (48) in this case a fierce and combative love for roses. Many of Cuff's detective descendants possess similarly memorable idiosyncrasies. More endearing, though, is that despite these characterizing brushstrokes, and despite his impressive observational skills and investigative abilities,[1] Cuff ultimately proves quite fallible; his initial conclusions and subsequent bold pronouncements about the missing diamond – at one point early in the story, he matter-of-factly and quite inaccurately tells Franklin Blake, "Nobody has stolen the Diamond" – fail to bring the case to a close. His attractive quality is diligence, not brilliance.

This fallibility, in addition to further humanizing the man, allowed Collins to toy with another device that soon became a common feature in the genre, for Cuff's failings go some way toward allowing the novel's amateur detectives Gabriel Betteredge, Franklin Blake, Rachel Verinder, and Ezra Jennings to enter the fray. They commandeer the story – Cuff disappears from the novel for hundreds of pages after his early failure – and accompany the readers, Collins's most significant amateur sleuths, toward the mystery's solution. The several amateur detectives, all with their own theories, also allowed Collins the luxury of so many potential thieves that he was able to introduce to fiction what has come to be known as the "least likely suspect" feature, insuring that the villain's identity remains hidden until the end of the novel.

All of these features remind us of how remarkable this novel is, not solely because its author manœuvres them into a tightly structured masterpiece of mystery, intrigue, and detection, but because this was the first time many of them had ever been employed. As Dorothy

---

darts. Possibly, even, the conception of Sherlock Holmes might never have occurred" ("Wilkie Collins: The Pioneer of the Thriller," *London Mercury*, April 1931: 584).

1   It is interesting to note that in a novel of firsts, the great Cuff seems even to possess a knowledge of the value of fingerprints long before the practice became standardized, even longer before it became a mainstay in detective fiction. Early in his investigation of the loss of the diamond, "he next sent for a magnifying-glass, and tried how the smear looked, seen that way. No skin-mark (as of a human hand) printed off on the paint."

Sayers claims, "It is not only a 'standard' work, the best of its class: it actually makes the class and sets the standard, so that what was the new and brilliant invention of its to-day becomes the commonplace of its to-morrow" (v).

Sayers augments the claim that we still marvel at *The Moonstone* because it broke detective-fiction ground by asserting that much of the novel's lure rests with Collins's "truthful and sympathetic" treatment of "life in a household of gentlefolk, both above and below stairs" (vii). It is a view quite contrary to early critics of the novel, one of whom argued that "In *The Moonstone* ... we have no person who can in any way be described as a character, no one who interests us, no one who is human enough to excite even a faint emotion of dull curiosity as to his or her fate," and who concluded, "Such an array of dummies was never got together in any book of Mr. Wilkie Collins's before, or, we venture to say, in any book written by a man with the same literary reputation."[1] Ignoring such declarations, Sayers quietly posits that "Collins's people do not exist simply and solely in order to make their moves on the chequer-board of intrigue; they have a full and lasting existence outside the story through which they pass; they are solid characters living in a real world." And she was, at least to an extent, right.

This is not to say that there are no stock characters in the novel, for there are many. There always are in Collins's fiction, which had its roots in the early comic fiction of Wilkie's friend and mentor, Charles Dickens. The hypocritical Godfrey Ablewhite, the sanctimonious Miss Drusilla Clack, the sceptical and stuffy family lawyer Mr. Bruff, Betteredge's flighty and headstrong daughter Penelope all exist on a single narrow plane throughout the work, either as apparent parts of the novel's machinery or as the easy and exaggerated embodiments of some social issue Collins felt the need to address. Both Ablewhite and Clack, for instance, play a large role in the novel, but in any discussion of the book, each initiates only very restricted single-track discussions of Collins's abhorrence of organized religious hypocrisy.

In many of the novel's other characters, though, we get some better indication of the foundations of Sayers's beliefs concerning the

---

1   For the full text of this nasty unsigned review from the *Spectator*, see Appendix A.

humanity of Collins's creations. In the novel's extended portrait of Gabriel Betteredge, for example, readers get a real sense that the Verinders' faithful old steward has made them privy to the inner workings of a country estate in the mid-nineteenth century. The details that Collins was so careful to have Betteredge provide[1] throughout the old man's narrative – the longest in the novel – offer a richer and far less sentimentalized view of such a world than any we get from Collins's contemporaries with the possible exception of Trollope.[2]

Several of the other characters, both main figures and bit players, also reveal Collins's astonishing ability to create human dimensions one would not ordinarily expect to find in a standard detective novel. Franklin Blake, for example, though at first glance a figure with the potential to remain a flat and caricaturistic rogue with his various continental personalities,[3] periodically shines as compellingly human. His painful interactions with the pathetic and suicidal Rosanna

---

1   To gain some insight into just how pernickety Collins could be with details of his novels, one need only read a portion of a letter he wrote to his American publishers gently chastising them for a flaw in one of their illustrations: "In the second number there is a mistake (as we should call it in England) of presenting Gabriel Betteredge in *livery*. As head-servant, he would wear plain black clothes and would look, with his white cravat and grey hair, like an old clergyman." For the full text of this letter, see Appendix E.

2   Trollope, who believed Collins to be a craftsman rather than an artist, would have objected to the claim that Collins's novels offered readers an accurate interpretation of the real world. In his 1882 *An Autobiography*, Trollope wrote of Collins's novels, "The construction is most minute and most wonderful. But I can never lose the taste of the construction. The author seems always to be warning me to remember that something happened at exactly half-past two o'clock on Tuesday morning; or that a woman disappeared from the road just fifteen yards beyond the fourth mile-stone. One is constrained by mysteries and hemmed in by difficulties, knowing, however, that the mysteries will be made clear and the difficulties overcome at the end of the third volume. Such work gives me no pleasure" (Trollope, Anthony. *An Autobiography*, ed. P.D. Edwards, Oxford: Oxford UP, 1980: 257).

3   *The Spectator*'s reviewer suggested bluntly, "The hero has no qualities at all." Much has been made of Blake's continental temperaments, as well as the "subjective" and "objective" sides to his personality. Perhaps the best of such studies is R. P. Laidlaw's "'Awful Images and Associations': A Study of Wilkie Collins's *The Moonstone*," in which Laidlaw argues that throughout the novel we see the "relationship between a totally secular and objective order and the subjective, or perhaps even supernatural, forces which continue to operate on mankind" (*Southern Review: An Australian Journal of Literary Studies* 9, November 1976: 211). Albert Hutter's Freudian reading of the book, "Dreams, Transformations, and Literature: The Implications of Detective

Spearman, his memorable encounter with an angry and viciously class-conscious Limping Lucy Yolland, his own painful self-loathing when he discovers sides of his character he had not known existed, all these touches comprise what readers must conclude is a striking and very human portraiture.

The novel's heroine, Rachel Verinder, is another figure treated unfairly by the seemingly short-sighted critics of her day. The *Spectator's* reviewer, for one, wrote that she is "a heroine who seems to have been borrowed from one of those old novels where everybody is miserable because nobody will talk common sense for five minutes" (882). Strong-willed, occasionally impertinent, and always assertive, Rachel is in many ways like other forceful women who populate Collins's novels. Her seaside duel with Drusilla Clack and the Ablewhites midway through the novel defines a keen intellect and an ability to rise to meet any challenge, traits that place her in the company of Collins's other strong female characters, Marian Halcombe of *The Woman in White*, Magdalen Vanstone of *No Name*, and Lydia Gwilt of *Armadale*, to name only a few. Rachel is much more than a portrait of a strong woman, though. Her character is rich and multi-sided, rounded by a broad sweep of human emotions one would expect to encounter in a young person besieged by adults she believes are undeserving of her affection. She shows an occasional naïve susceptibility, an occasional volatility; she occasionally chooses to be deliberately hurtful, occasionally repentant and annoyingly obsequious. She is, all told, a woman attempting to move her complicated life in several directions and once, and by the end of the novel, she has become part of what Sayers has called one of Collins's "finest and subtlest studies of women in love" (viii).

Some of the more fascinating studies of human nature that appear in *The Moonstone* can be found among the minor figures that people Collins's world. Mr. Murthwaite, Rosanna Spearman, Lucy Yolland,

---

Fiction" (*Victorian Studies* 19, December 1975: 181-209) also examines the novel's attempt to reconcile the opposing sides of Blake's character. And Jenny Bourne Taylor suggests that Franklin Blake's method of weighing matters reflects the way the novel "continually asserts and undermines the sources of its own coherence, most notably by breaking down the boundary between 'objective' and 'subjective' reality, so that it becomes a palimpsest of overt and covert meanings" (*In the Secret Theatre of Home: Wilkie Collins, Sensation Narrative, and Nineteenth-Century Psychology*, London: Routledge, 1988: 175).

Ezra Jennings all crowd Collins's canvas with peculiar but very real personalities, allowing the reader, as Sayers argues, "to escape from a narrow artificial stage to the crowded reality of the marketplace" (xi). Aside from offering intriguing touches of varied humanity, though, these figures reveal Collins's tendency in much of his fiction to create social outcasts whose unusual qualities are certainly unsettling but whose uniqueness and vitality demand a reader's sympathy.

The enigmatic and elegant world traveller Mr. Murthwaite, at one point unfairly labelled a "semi-savage" by an unenlightened and judgmental Gabriel Betteredge, is obviously a favourite of Collins, who spent a great deal of energy and time researching his character.[1] Murthwaite's patient explanations of the mysterious Brahmin priests who steal into England to retrieve their diamond, as well as his encyclopedic understanding of the cultures of the East, earn from the reader a deserved sympathy. His is an impressive character, one who goes some distance toward showing readers that Collins's social sympathies lay outside the narrow boundaries of English social propriety.

The dark Rosanna Spearman and her only friend, the angry Limping Lucy, are two more ultimately sympathetic outcasts. From the start Collins stacks the cards of convention against Rosanna, one of Lady Verinder's maidservants, by making her "the plainest woman in the house, with the additional misfortune of having one shoulder bigger than the other," and by giving her a mysterious criminal past and a quiet temperament that make her an object of suspicion to the other household servants, who immediately suspect her involvement when the diamond disappears. Rosanna's pitiful love for Franklin Blake – whose rather curt dismissal of the whole affair leaves him looking at best aloof, at worst partially responsible for her fate – serves as a painful reminder of Collins's apparent sympathy for those sufferers who, in the face of universal public scorn, maintain a personal integrity to the point that they are willing to die for it.

Rosanna's one true companion, Limping Lucy Yolland, substantiates the social commentary insinuated in the portrait of Rosanna Spearman. On a couple of occasions in the novel, Lucy calls attention, in general but very potent and provocative terms, to the abuse

---

1   As he researched his novel, Collins spent much time in 1867 consulting a renowned world traveller, John Wyllie, of the Indian Civil Service. Wyllie may very well be the model for Murthwaite.

that she and the Rosannas of the world have suffered at the hands of the Verinders and their kind. Speaking to Betteredge of her disgust with Franklin Blake, she shouts, "The day is not far off when the poor will rise against the rich. I pray Heaven they may begin with *him*." And later, when she confronts Blake himself, her powerful diatribe shows a remarkably sympathetic Collins willing to let his novel's previously vain and rather puffed-up hero be knocked down a peg or two by a crippled woman who under any other circumstances would be beneath his notice.

Perhaps the most carefully constructed of these sympathetic outsiders – Sue Lonoff calls him "the book's most extraordinary character"[1] – is Ezra Jennings, the misunderstood assistant to the Verinders' physician, Dr. Candy. Some have seen in Jennings clear touches of autobiography,[2] and indeed, the delicacy of the portrait suggests a special feeling on the part of its creator. As with Rosanna and Limping Lucy, Collins gave Ezra Jennings a number of physical irregularities – a dark, gipsy complexion, fleshless and sunken cheeks, freakish parti-coloured hair – that help set him apart from the conventional. He is defined, as well, by a dark past, a notably Collinsian addiction to laudanum, and an inability to escape the hounding persecution of the establishment. He is, alongside Rosanna and Lucy, a fellow sufferer and outcast. Ultimately, Franklin Blake, and through him Collins's audience, is compelled to admit that "it is not to be denied that Ezra Jennings made some inscrutable appeal to my sympathies, which I found it impossible to resist."

These minor characters, then, are noteworthy in a number of respects. They serve as mouthpieces for Collins's social scepticism, offering a view of a vibrant world counter to and critical of the staid world of Victorian propriety. They provide Collins's story breadth it could not have had without them. And finally, as Sayers would insist, they are genuinely real.

Sayers's argument goes only so far, though, for Collins's uniqueness

---

1 This passage appears in Lonoff's *Wilkie Collins and His Victorian Readers: A Study in the Rhetoric of Authorship* (New York: AMS, 1982: 202).

2 Peters, for one, writes, "Certainly the experiences of Ezra Jennings, his frightful dreams, the effect of being stunned after a larger than usual dose, the relief from intolerable pain, were based on Wilkie's own experiences at this time of severe pain and deep unhappiness" (303).

certainly does not stem entirely from his ability to create a realistic Victorian landscape. In fact, very few of Collins's readers would argue that his fiction succeeds solely because of its insightful or provocative examination of the ordinariness of his world. His uniqueness, on the contrary, derives from his willingness to manipulate his world to his own advantage, to work on the far outer edges of that world while somehow managing to maintain its basic integrity. Collins revealed this strategy early in his career, in an 1852 preface to *Basil*, his second published novel: "I have not thought it either politic or necessary, while adhering to realities, to adhere to every-day realities only. In other words ... those extraordinary accidents and events which happen to a few men, seemed to me to be as legitimate materials for fiction to work with – when there was a good object in using them – as the ordinary accidents and events which may, and do, happen to us all." He often took this theory to the extreme, priding himself on an ability to press the limits of verisimilitude, often practically daring critics to try to find that the extraordinary in his fiction was in fact impossible.[1] He routinely prefaced his novels with statements proclaiming that he had checked his facts with experts, that he had taken his material from verifiable sources, that he had researched his novels with the tenacity of a scientist, all with an eye toward provoking his critics and reviewers while at the same time stopping them in their tracks.[2]

The Moonstone is an instance of this theory put to practice, for into a story set in what Betteredge himself calls "our quiet English house" Collins injects numerous elements of the extraordinary that at times move the novel well beyond the realm of the believable. Even Dickens noticed this strange concoction of the real and the incredible and was, at least initially, very much intrigued by it. Writing to W. H. Wills, his friend and sub-editor on *All the Year Round*, he called *The Moonstone* "a very curious story – wild, yet domestic – with excellent character in it, great mystery, and nothing belonging to disguised women

---

1 A critic for the *Saturday Review* noted Collins's "strange capacity for weaving extraordinary plots" and deemed *Armadale* a "lurid labyrinth of improbabilities" (*Saturday Review*, 16 June 1866, 726).

2 A reviewer for the *Spectator* realized what Collins was doing, claiming "[He] is fond of challenging his critics, and we see no cause to shrink from accepting his challenge" (*Spectator*, 9 June 1866, 638).

or the like."[1] Having read only the first three numbers of the novel when he made this statement, Dickens was likely recalling the eerie and exotic atmosphere Collins establishes early on with memorable descriptions of mysterious Indian priests who seem so out of place on the Yorkshire coast, or with hints of deadly and impenetrably un-British curses that have followed the diamond from India. He was likely reacting to the mystery with much the same ambivalence as Gabriel Betteredge, who succumbs initially to the hypnotic power of the diamond and thereafter to "detective fever" while always John Bull-ishly cursing the "devilish Indian Diamond – bringing after it a conspiracy of living rogues, set loose on us by the vengeance of a dead man."

The element of foreign intrigue that is part of the fabric of the novel is something Collins had been exploring for upwards of ten years. A decade before he wrote the book, the Indian uprising of 1857[2] had generated in all of England a virulent and unwavering racial hatred. Dickens himself had suggested that if given the opportunity, "I should do my utmost to exterminate the Race upon whom the stain of the late cruelties rested ... to blot it out of mankind and

---

1   Dickens expressed this opinion in a letter to W. H. Wills, his partner and sub-editor at *All the Year Round*, on June 30th, 1867. By July 26, 1868, after what many claim had been a falling out between Dickens and Collins, Dickens again wrote to Wills of the novel, this time suggesting, "I quite agree with you about *The Moonstone*. The construction is wearisome beyond endurance, and there is a vein of obstinate conceit in it that makes enemies of the readers." Dickens was dead wrong in his concern about Collins's readers. The sales of *All the Year Round* skyrocketed during the last weeks of *The Moonstone*'s run.

2   Native Indian troops, sepoys, made up 96% of the nearly 300,000 British troops in India in the mid-nineteenth century. The General Service Enlistment Act of 1856 had upset a number of these sepoys by demanding that all enlistees swear an oath to cross the sea in ships if ordered to. To cross the sea was pollution to an orthodox Hindu. (Note that early in *The Moonstone* Mr. Murthwaite suggests that the Indian jugglers have sacrificed caste by crossing the sea.) In early 1857, matters worsened when the Ordnance department in India issued cartridges for the army's newly acquired Enfield rifles. The cartridges, which had to be bitten open to be used, were heavily greased with the fat of cows and pigs, causing tremendous problems for the Hindu and Muslim troops alike. Their complaints ignored, the sepoys rebelled, rampaging at certain military outposts, killing their British army superiors. In some instances, as at the massacre at Cawnpore on July 15, the sepoys killed hundreds of British women and children without mercy. British retaliation was swift and brutal, though order in India was not restored completely until March 1858. Thereafter, the British crown took rule of India away from the East India Company.

raze it off the face of the earth."[1] In late 1857, Dickens's idea was to collaborate with Collins on a story — to appear in the Christmas Extra Number of *Household Words* under the title "The Perils of Certain English Prisoners" — that would, at least indirectly, express his feelings about the uprising by casting British civilians as heroes in the face of savagery. Collins's portion of the tale, the second of three chapters, is noticeably more moderate than Dickens's tales.

Shortly after the appearance of this Christmas Extra, Dickens solicited from Collins an article more directly related to the recent sepoy uprising. It was probably Dickens's desire that Collins's article condemn the sepoys and their rebellion; instead, Collins, after researching his material with some care, wrote "A Sermon for Sepoys" (see Appendix D for the text of this article), which appeared in *Household Words* in late February 1858, and which speaks to both the English and the Indian rebels with a subdued and elegant equanimity. The understanding evident in this *Household Words* article foreshadows Collins's sensitive and sympathetic depiction of the mysterious Indians and their culture in *The Moonstone* ten years later.[2] More evidence of Collins's unusual empathy for things and people un-British appeared in 1869, a year after *The Moonstone*, when he wrote, with help from friend and playwright Charles Fechter, the drama *Black and White*. Set in Trinidad in 1830, the play has an evident anti-slavery theme and ends with the hero, a mixed-race slave named Count de Layrac, marrying the white heiress, Miss Milburn.

Collins did not, however, bank solely on foreign intrigue or the mysterious unworldly aura of his diamond as he applied *Basil*'s theory of the "power of the extraordinary" to *The Moonstone*'s plot. More than once over the course of the novel, he chose simply to borrow details from bizarre but well-known local crime stories of the day, realizing that most in his audience would readily recognize his literary manipulation of the prosaic.

Of these crimes, the most celebrated is the Road Murder of 1860.

---

1   Dickens expressed these surprising sentiments in an October 4, 1857 letter to his friend and occasional patroness Angela Burdett-Coutts (Osborne, Charles, ed. *The Letters of Charles Dickens to the Baroness Burdett-Coutts*. New York: E.P. Dutton, 1932, 188-89).
2   Note that Collins set the main action of *The Moonstone* in 1848 and 1849, well before the 1857 uprising. By doing so, he may have been attempting to disarm a still unabashedly anti-Indian reading public.

In late June of that year, sixteen-year old Constance Kent murdered her four year old half-brother, Francis, cutting his throat and stuffing his body down an outhouse on her family's property. She secreted and later destroyed a bloodied nightdress that she had worn during the crime. Local constabularies, led by a Mr. Superintendent Foley, bungled their investigation – at one point even discarding a bloody nightdress found at the murder scene as unimportant evidence and at another allowing themselves to be locked into the kitchen of the house they were supposed to be watching. Professional detectives from London, the well-known and respected Inspector Jonathan Whicher chief among them, took over the case, immediately focusing on the family linen-list and Constance's missing nightdress. Unable to find and produce the article of clothing, though, Whicher and his partner, Sergeant Frederick Williamson, watched helplessly as charges against Kent were dropped. Once free, Kent retreated to a convent in France for nearly five years before returning to England in the spring of 1865 to confess to the crime. She was tried, convicted on her own confession, and sentenced to death. Queen Victoria commuted the sentence to life in prison. Kent served twenty years in prison, was quietly released in 1885, and lived the rest of her life in anonymous obscurity. Inspector Whicher, whose reputation suffered because of his failure to solve the case, retired in disgrace in 1863, but was somewhat vindicated by Kent's admission of guilt.

The Moonstone's reader sees immediately that Collins borrowed extensively from the case as he devised the mystery surrounding the theft of the diamond. Of course there are noticeable differences between the Kent case and the novel's plotting, and some critics warn against making too much of the similarities, but the connections nevertheless are apparent.[1] Though Collins substituted theft for murder

---

1   Henry James Wye Milley, in his unpublished dissertation, "The Achievement of Wilkie Collins and His Influence on Dickens and Trollope" (Yale, 1941), is the first to warn readers against making too much of the case, suggesting that a bloodstained nightgown appears in Collins's "A Plot in Private Life" two years before the Road Murder of 1860. There is no question, though, that Collins followed the story as it unfolded in the local papers. An October 24, 1860 letter to Wilkie from Dickens, in which the writer spells out his belief (later proved incorrect) that Mr. Kent and the nursemaid killed young Francis after he discovered them in a compromising embrace, shows readers that the murder case was a topic of conversation for the two authors.

and smeared paint for blood, a family linen-list and a missing stained nightdress lie at the heart of his story. He also seems to have modelled the bungling Superintendent Seegrave of his novel after Mr. Foley, the very real local policeman whose ineptitudes caused innumerable problems for later professional investigators. And Collins's Detective Cuff is clearly modelled after Inspector Jonathan Whicher, a renowned detective whose sagacity and ingenuity were not immediately recognized or appreciated by others investigating the crime. (Many of *The Times* accounts of the crime and its aftermath appear in Appendix B.)

In addition to the Constance Kent Road Murder case, Collins borrowed details from another gruesome and equally weird crime that became a *cause célèbre* in London during the summer of 1861. In mid-July of that year, the city buzzed with the story of a puzzling and extremely violent attack committed by one Mr. William John Roberts on a Major William Murray. Apparently, near mid-day on July 12th, Mr. Roberts introduced himself to Murray, a director of the Grosvenor Hotel company,[1] as they both walked along the street in Hungerford Market. Roberts then lured Murray to some chambers in nearby Northumberland Street with the promise of some information concerning a business proposition. Once inside, Roberts accosted Murray, shooting him twice in the head from behind. Severely wounded, Murray nevertheless managed to fend off his attacker, beating him nearly to death before escaping. Murray recovered from his wounds; Roberts lingered for a week at the Charing Cross Hospital and then died of his injuries on the evening of July 18th. At the inquest that followed, the jury reached a unanimous verdict of justifiable homicide.

Collins spent the summer of 1861 in London, working on a new novel, No Name, securing a lucrative contract from George Smith for a novel to follow No Name, and doubtless reading daily accounts of the sensational Major Murray case. He used the case to his advantage while writing *The Moonstone* a few years later. Again, some critics warn against drawing too close a connection between the Murray case and the novel, for the former involved homicide while the latter

---

1 The Grosvenor Hotel, one of the earliest and one of the most splendid Railway Hotels, was opened in 1861 adjacent to Victoria Station.

does not. The similarities are too striking to be ignored, though. The reader of the novel will recall that Godfrey Ablewhite is lured, by a seemingly chance meeting with a perfect stranger, to an apartment of a house, also in Northumberland Street, where he is attacked from behind without warning and searched by three men he cannot identify. Later the same day, Mr. Septimus Luker is subjected to the same sort of ambush in Alfred Place, Tottenham Court Road, within a mile of the Northumberland Street address where Godfrey had been waylaid. With the exception of the brutality of the original, Collins has clearly used the Murray case as a model for an important and memorable scene in *The Moonstone*. (Several of *The Times* accounts of this attack and its aftermath appear in Appendix C.)

Of course, it is not entirely appropriate, nor is it wise, to limit a discussion of *The Moonstone* to its place in the front ranks of detective fiction, or to a consideration of long-running debate over Collins's skills as a creator of character, or to an exploration of his abilities to sensationalize the prosaic, for the novel offers its readers much more. John R. Reed suggests that "unlike its formulaic descendants, Collins' novel resists any simple pattern of interpretation,"[1] and recently scholars have begun to take their considerations of the story in altogether different directions, scrutinizing it in various lights, some intriguing and provocative, others merely amusing.

Among the most popular alternative readings are those studies that approach the novel from a social/historical slant, suggesting that *The Moonstone* appears to be Collins's thinly-veiled attack on British imperialism of the nineteenth century. Enough scholars have chosen to explore the novel in this light that Ashish Roy, in his own postcolonial reading of the book, was prompted to claim that as an antiimperialist text, "*The Moonstone* has recently begun a new career."[2] John Reed's 1973 article "English Imperialism and the Unacknowledged Crime of *The Moonstone*"[3] is the first and best of these readings. In it, Reed argues very convincingly that "Collins's detective

---

1 Reed makes this claim in his article "The Stories of *The Moonstone*," which appears in *Wilkie Collins to the Forefront: Some Reassessments* (Smith, Nelson, and R.C. Terry, eds. New York: AMS, 1995: 91).

2 From "The Fabulous Imperialist Semiotic of Wilkie Collins's *The Moonstone*," *New Literary History* 24 (Summer 1993): 657.

3 From *Clio* 2 (1973): 281–90.

novel, apparently concerned with little more than a love story and a theft, is actually a broad indictment of an entire way of life" (288). Suggesting that the individual greed represented by the Herncastle who first steals the diamond in 1799 is "emblematic of a far greater crime" (284) – England's conquest and commercial exploitation of India throughout the nineteenth century – Reed suggests that the diamond itself comes to represent the dark side of "England's gains from its Indian adventures" (287). He argues also that the novel's characters provide readers with a clear indication of the disdain Collins felt for what he saw as England's hollow social respectability, and that Collins's sympathies clearly lay with the mysterious Indians who are in England to retrieve the stolen gem.

Among subsequent similar readings of the novel, those that employ or further Reed's claims in one way or another, are Sue Lonoff's 1982 "*The Moonstone* and Its Audience," Patricia Miller Frick's 1984 "Wilkie Collins's 'Little Jewel': The Meaning of *The Moonstone*," Lillian Nayder's 1992 "Robinson Crusoe and Friday in Victorian Britain: 'Discipline,' 'Dialogue,' and Collins's Critique of Empire in *The Moonstone*," and Ian Duncan's 1994 "*The Moonstone*, the Victorian Novel, and Imperialist Panic."[1] Lonoff's views of the novel often agree with Reed's, but she claims finally that "he goes too far," that his views of what she sees to be an ultimately hopeful novel are too sombre, too dark, that "Collins was not so alienated as to indict all of English society" (225). Frick's interesting article also touches on some of the same social/political themes Reed explores; for instance, she asserts that "Collins was ... profoundly aware of the social, political, and moral ills of his own society and directly addressed many of them in *The Moonstone*" (317). Her claims, though, are only tangentially related to Reed's, for her article's main position is that Collins's

---

1 Lonoff's "*The Moonstone* and Its Audience" appeared as the seventh chapter of her 1982 *Wilkie Collins and His Victorian Readers* (New York: AMS: 170-227). Patricia Miller Frick's "Wilkie Collins's 'Little Jewel': The Meaning of *The Moonstone*" appeared in *Philological Quarterly* 63 (Summer 1984): 313-21. Lillian Nayder's "Robinson Crusoe and Friday in Victorian Britain: 'Discipline,' 'Dialogue,' and Collins's Critique of Empire in *The Moonstone*" appeared in *Dickens Studies Annual* 21 (1992): 213-31, and Ian Duncan's 1994 "*The Moonstone*, the Victorian Novel, and Imperialist Panic" may be found in *Modern Language Quarterly* 55 (September 1994): 297-319. Nayder extended her anti-imperialist reading of the novel in the full-length study *Wilkie Collins Revisited* (New York: Twayne, 1997).

primary source for *The Moonstone* was a novel that his grandfather had written in 1805. Nayder uses Defoe's *Robinson Crusoe*, "that idyll of empire building" (and the work admired so unabashedly by Gabriel Betteredge) to suggest that throughout the novel Collins was consciously and ironically advocating an anti-imperialist dogma by "subverting Defoe's distinction between the civilized Englishman and the uncivilized native"(220, 222). Duncan's is a Marxist reading that shows how Collins used the novel to depict India – to an anxious, even phobic England – "as a powerful alien origin that constitutes the limit or end of English national historical identity"(319).

In addition to these historical/political readings of the novel, several critics have offered Freudian psychoanalytical interpretations, which, more than any other reading, would have intrigued and amused Collins. Charles Rycroft's 1957 "A Detective Story: Psychoanalytic Observations"[1] is the first and most accessible of such readings. Rycroft concludes, "not only that the theme of *The Moonstone* is an unconscious representation of a sexual act, but also that its four leading characters, Franklin, Ablewhite, Rachel, and Rosanna represent different aspects of the sexual conflicts that arise in a society which sanctions the tendency of the man to deal with his oedipal conflicts by dissociated conceptions of woman, one idealized and asexual, the other degraded and sexual" (237-38).

Though he admits that "One of the pitfalls of psychoanalytical interpretations of literary works is the fallacy of attributing to fictional characters unconscious motivations and conflicts, which can in fact only legitimately be attributed to their creators" (238), he goes on to base his reading on "three assumptions about Wilkie Collins: 1, there were in his mind certain specific constellations which compelled him in his writing to give symbolic expression to an unconscious preoccupation with the primal scene; 2, dissociation between the ideal (incestuous) and the depreciated sexual objects and projection were among the defenses he used in his attempts to master anxiety; 3, he was obsessed with the idea of virginity" (238). Perhaps something *can* be wrestled out of Collins's rather unusual lifestyle – his living with one woman while occasionally fathering children by another who resided nearby – but Rycroft's psycho-sexual conclusions about *The*

---

1 From *Psychoanalytic Quarterly* 26 (1957): 229-45.

Moonstone, based in large part on a breezy interpretation of *Basil* (1852), Collins's second novel, seem strained at best.

Another psychoanalytical reading of the novel appears in Lewis Lawson's 1963 "Wilkie Collins and *The Moonstone*,"[1] in which Lawson concludes, after having spent a good deal of time discussing the several dream references that appear in the novel and after having called attention to Collins's addiction to laudanum, "The pattern of symbols in *The Moonstone* has shown that there is a residual sexual layer in the novel lying beneath the consciously censored literal layer" (71). Lawson's reading is full and interesting, but his is a conclusion hardly unique to *The Moonstone*; in fact, it could comfortably be applied to virtually every Victorian novel, beneath whose "censored literal layer[s]" often rested a seething sexuality suppressed only by the mores of the day.

Albert Hutter's Freudian reading of the novel in his 1975 "Dreams, Transformations, and Literature: The Implications of Detective Fiction"[2] treads on much of the same ground as the earlier considerations. Like Rycroft, Hutter employs rather elastic discussions of the novel's symbols – "[T]he title image, like all gems, may be linked with women and sexuality" (200) and "[w]hat is stolen from Rachel is both the actual gem and her symbolic virginity" (201) – to draw a number of psycho-sexual conclusions about the story. And like Lawson, he uses dream interpretation to assert an overriding and meaningful tension that exists everywhere in the novel between distrustful reader and untrustworthy narrators.

In her engaging study *Dead Secrets: Wilkie Collins and the Female Gothic*,[3] Tamar Heller successfully integrates these several historical and psychoanalytical interpretations of the novel. Her feminist reading argues convincingly that the novel is built around both "the private world of English families and the public dimension of imperialism" (144). She makes her case by enumerating and discussing the various dualities of character and plot Collins employs throughout the novel, dualities that allow her to conclude that "by juxtaposing the plots of courtship and colonialism, Collins suggests an analogy between sexual and imperial domination" (145).

---

1   From *American Imago* 20 (Spring 1963): 61-79.
2   From *Victorian Studies* 19 (December 1975): 181-209.
3   New Haven, CT: Yale UP, 1992.

Readings of *The Moonstone* are by no means limited to such social/political or psychoanalytical perspectives, though. Ira Nadel, for instance, offers a fascinating scientific reading of the novel in the 1983 study "Science and *The Moonstone*,"[1] one that argues that Collins's interest in making the gem the thematic and structural center of his novel manifested itself from "his deeply rooted attraction to things scientific" (240). Arguing that Collins's interest in the sciences and pseudo-sciences is evident in much of his fiction, Nadel lists several works in which forensic science, chemistry, biology, vivisection, psychology, phrenology, clairvoyance, mesmerism, hypnotism, and animal magnetism play a role. He reminds readers that Collins spent much of his time researching such matters so as to be able to work them effectively into his fiction, and he concludes that *The Moonstone* is the work that "best expresses [Collins's] absorption with science" (242) and that best "demonstrates his application of science to fiction" (242). Along the same lines, Mark M. Hennelly's "Detecting Collins' Diamond: From Serpentstone to Moonstone"[2] offers what one might call a gemological or mineralogical reading of the novel. Hennelly, after establishing that the gem is the symbolic center of the novel, explores its historical significance to Collins and its religious, scientific, and economic significance to the various characters in the story.

One of the most curious interpretations of the novel appears in William Burgan's 1995 article "Masonic Symbolism in *The Moonstone* and *The Mystery of Edwin Drood*."[3] Burgan meticulously searches the book for references to secret Masonic rituals, hidden patterns, zodiacal emblems, and Indian sexual symbolism in an effort to conclude that "whether or not Collins and Dickens were Freemasons in the strict sense, both seem to have written for two audiences at once – a group of insiders alerted to the Masonic context, and a group of outsiders completely unaware of its relevance" (101). Though the study is, indeed, intriguing, it seems intended primarily for Burgan's Masonic "insiders." Alluding to the study, Catherine Peters speaks bluntly for the novel's larger "group of outsiders" when she writes,

---

1   From *Dickens Studies Annual* 12 (1983): 239-59.
2   From *Nineteenth-Century Fiction* 39:1 (June 1984): 25-47.
3   Burgan's study is part of a collection of essays titled *Wilkie Collins to the Forefront: Some Reassessments*. Eds. Nelson Smith and R.C. Terry. New York: AMS, 1995: 101-148. It originally appeared in *Dickens Studies Annual* 16 (1987): 257-303.

"A more unlikely Freemason than Wilkie Collins can scarcely be imagined."[1]

Among the narrowest readings of the novel is Shepard Siegel's 1985 "Psychopharmacology and the Mystery of *The Moonstone*."[2] Siegel marvels at Collins's "exploitation of psychology principles ... before their discovery by psychologists"(580). He suggests that in *The Moonstone* Collins explored the phenomena of "drug dissociation" and "drug tolerance," and the role of "drug expectation" in "Pavlovian conditioning" (580) decades before they ever concerned psychopharmacologists. Along similar lines, Althea Hayter's 1968 *Opium and the Romantic Imagination*[3] examines the crucial role played by opium in the novel as manifested by Collins's own addiction to the drug, an addiction so severe that it occasionally threatened to interfere with the story's publication.

These are but some of the writers who have chosen to make Collins's masterpiece the object of their critical attention. Such a variety of views would no doubt have amused and pleased Collins, for he might conclude that his "leave no thread unravelled" approach to writing mystery and detective fiction had accomplished what he wanted; it has generated a huge crop of critical interpretations that attempt to consider every layer of the novel's rich fabric. Of all of these various interpretations, Collins biographer Catherine Peters states frankly, "Some ... can have nothing to do with the author's intentions – which does not, of course, invalidate them as fruitful ways of looking at the novel in its context."[4] Similarly, but with a greater expression of appreciation for the depth of the novel, E.R. Gregory writes: "Significantly, every detective-story critic with an axe to grind sharpens it sooner or later on *The Moonstone*. If he feels that detective stories are symbolic reenactments of the primal scene, he finds the evidence he needs in *The Moonstone*. If he feels that detective stories are pernicious purveyors of outmoded class values, he finds a perfect example in *The Moonstone*. Any one such approach is of

---

1   From Catherine Peters's "Introduction" to a recent Everyman's Library edition of *The Moonstone* (New York: Knopf, 1992: v-vi).

2   From *American Psychologist* 40 (May 1985): 580-81.

3   Berkeley and Los Angeles: U of California P, 1970: 255-270.

4   This passage appears in Catherine Peters's "Introduction" to a recent Everyman's Library edition of *The Moonstone*, (New York: Knopf, 1992: vi).

course misleading or inadequate, but it is a measure of *The Moonstone's* greatness that it accommodates itself to each."[1] Gregory is right; the book *is* accommodating, in almost every sense of the word. It indulges any reader, from the detective-fiction buff to the literary scholar; it rewards a comfortable and leisurely reading or a close critical scrutiny; it offers the light entertainment of mystery or romance at the same time it promotes a dark and stinging social commentary; unlike many novels of detection, it contains a large and detailed enough story to repay a second or third reading; and, finally, it charms and bewitches today just as it has every generation of readers since its first appearance in 1868.

---

1   From "Murder in Fact: Wilkie Collins," *The New Republic* July 22, 1978: 33-34.

William Wilkie Collins: A Brief Chronology

1824   William Wilkie Collins born (January 8) at 11 New
        Cavendish Street, St. Marylebone, London, to William
        Collins, RA (1788-1847) and Harriet Collins, née Geddes
        (1790-1868).

1826   Family moves to Pond Street, Hampstead.

1828   Brother, Charles Allston Collins, born.

1829   Family moves to Hampstead Square.

1830   Family moves to Porchester Terrace, Bayswater.

1835   Briefly attends school at the Maida Hill Academy.

1836   Family begins to travel in France and Italy.

1838   Family returns to England and settles at 20 Avenue Road,
        Regent's Park; begins to attend Mr. Cole's private school at
        Highbury Place.

1840   Family moves to 85 Oxford Terrace, Bayswater.

1841   Begins apprenticeship at Antrobus & Co., tea importers, the
        Strand.

1842   Travels with father to Scottish Highlands and Shetland
        Islands.

1843   "The Last Stage Coachman," Collins's first signed publica-
        tion, appears in *The Illuminated Magazine*; family moves to 1
        Devonport Street, Bayswater.

1844   Travels to Paris.

1845   First novel, with a Polynesian setting, rejected by Chapman
        & Hall, among other publishers.

1846   Enters Lincoln's Inn as law student.

1847   Father, William Collins, dies (February 17).

1848   Family moves to 38 Blandford Square, St. Marylebone; first
        book, *Memoirs of the Life of William Collins, Esq., RA*, pub-
        lished in two volumes by Longmans.

1850   First novel, *Antonina, or the Fall of Rome*, published in three
        volumes by Bentley; family moves to 17 Hanover Terrace,
        Regent's Park.

1851   *Rambles Beyond Railways* published by Bentley; meets Dick-
        ens; acts with Dickens in Bulwer Lytton's play *Not So Bad As
        We Seem*; called to Bar but never practises.

1852   *Mr. Wray's Cash Box* published by Bentley; first contribution
        to *Household Words*, the short story "A Terribly Strange Bed,"
        published; tours provinces with Dickens; second novel, *Basil*,
        published by Bentley.
1853   Tours Switzerland and Italy with Dickens and Augustus Egg.
1854   *Hide and Seek* published in three volumes by Bentley.
1855   First play, *The Lighthouse*, performed by Dickens's theatrical
        company at Tavistock House.
1856   *After Dark* published in two volumes by Smith, Elder; *A
        Rogue's Life* serialized in *Household Words*; travels to Paris with
        Dickens; joins staff of *Household Words*; "Wreck of the Gold-
        en Mary," a Christmas story written in collaboration with
        Dickens, published in *Household Words*.
1857   *The Dead Secret* published in two volumes by Bradbury &
        Evans following serialization in *Household Words*; the play
        The Frozen Deep performed by Dickens's company at Tavis-
        tock House. "The Lazy Tour of Two Idle Apprentices" and
        "The Perils of Certain English Prisoners," both written in
        collaboration with Dickens, published in *Household Words*.
1858   The play *The Red Vial* produced at The Olympic Theatre.
1859   Moves to 124 Albany Street, Regent's Park; moves to 2a
        New Cavendish Street, Marylebone; moves to 12 Harley
        Street, Marylebone; *The Queen of Hearts* published in three
        volumes by Hurst & Blackett; *The Woman in White* serialized
        in *All the Year Round* (November–August 1860); begins living
        with Caroline Graves.
1860   *The Woman in White* published in three volumes by Sampson
        Low. Brother, Charles Collins, marries Kate Dickens, Dick-
        ens's daughter.
1861   Resigns from staff of *All the Year Round*.
1862   *No Name* serialized in *All the Year Round* and published in
        three volumes by Sampson Low.
1863   *My Miscellanies* published in two volumes by Sampson Low;
        visits Germany and Italy with Caroline Graves.
1864   Moves to 9 Melcombe Place, Dorset Square; *Armadale* serial-
        ized in *The Cornhill* (November–June 1866).
1866   *Armadale* published in two volumes by Smith Elder.
1867   Moves to 90 Gloucester Place, Portman Square; *No Thor-*

oughfare, written in collaboration with Dickens, published in *All the Year Round*; dramatic version of *No Thoroughfare* produced at the Adelphi Theatre; begins writing *The Moonstone*.

1868   *The Moonstone* serialized in *All the Year Round* (January 4–August 8); published in three volumes by Tinsley Brothers on July 16; mother, Harriet Collins, dies (March 19); temporarily ends relationship with Caroline Graves; begins relationship with Martha Rudd (alias Mrs. Dawson); attends wedding of Caroline Graves and Joseph Charles Clow.

1869   The play *Black and White*, written in collaboration with Charles Fechter, produced at the Adelphi Theatre; daughter, Marian Dawson, by Martha Rudd, born (July 4).

1870   *Man and Wife* published in three volumes by F.S. Ellis, following serialization in *Cassell's Magazine*; Dickens dies (June 9).

1871   Second daughter, Harriet Constance Dawson, by Martha Rudd, born (May 14); resumes cohabitation with Caroline Graves; dramatic version of *No Name* produced in New York; dramatic version of *The Woman in White* performed at the Olympic Theatre; *Poor Miss Finch* serialized in *Cassell's Magazine* (October–March 1872).

1872   *Poor Miss Finch* published in three volumes by Bentley; *The New Magdalen* serialized in *Temple Bar*.

1873   Brother, Charles Allston Collins, dies (April 9); *The New Magdalen* published in two volumes by Bentley; dramatic version of *Man and Wife* produced at the Prince of Wales Theatre; dramatic version of *The New Magdalen* produced at the Olympic Theatre; *Miss or Mrs? and Other Stories in Outline* published by Bentley; begins six-month reading tour of United States and Canada.

1874   *The Law and the Lady* serialized in the *Graphic* (September–March 1875); *The Frozen Deep and Other Tales* published in two volumes by Bentley; son, William Charles Collins Dawson, born to Martha Rudd (December 25).

1875   Copyrights for most of Collins's works transferred to Chatto & Windus, who become his primary British publisher; *The Law and the Lady* published in three volumes by Chatto & Windus.

1876   *Miss Gwilt*, a dramatic version of *Armadale*, produced at the Globe Theatre; *The Two Destinies* published in two volumes by Chatto & Windus following serialization in *Temple Bar*.

1877   Dramatic version of *The Dead Secret* produced at the Lyceum Theatre; dramatic version of *The Moonstone* produced at the Olympic Theatre; *My Lady's Money* published in the *Illustrated London News*; travels in France, Germany, and Italy with Caroline Graves.

1878   *The Haunted Hotel* serialized in *Belgravia*; *My Lady's Money* and *The Haunted Hotel* published together in two volumes by Chatto & Windus; *The Fallen Leaves — First Series* serialized in both *The World* and *Canadian Monthly*.

1879   *The Fallen Leaves* published in three volumes by Chatto & Windus; *Jezebel's Daughter* syndicated by Tillotson & Son's newspaper chain and published in thirteen northern newspapers.

1880   *Jezebel's Daughter*, a novel based on the play *The Red Vial*, published in three volumes by Chatto & Windus.

1881   *The Black Robe* published in three volumes by Chatto & Windus following serialization in the *Sheffield Independent* and other provincial newspapers; A. P. Watt becomes Collins's literary agent.

1883   *Heart and Science* published in three volumes by Chatto & Windus following serial publication in *Belgravia*; the play *Rank and Riches* is produced at the Adelphi Theatre and proves to be an immediate disaster.

1884   *"I Say No"* published in three volumes by Chatto & Windus following serialization in the *London Society*.

1886   *The Evil Genius* published in three volumes by Chatto & Windus following serial syndication by Tillotson & Son in the *Leigh Journal & Times* and other provincial papers; "The Guilty River" published in *Arrowsmith's Christmas Annual*.

1887   *Little Novels*, fourteen reprinted short stories, published in three volumes by Chatto & Windus.

1888   *The Legacy of Cain* published in three volumes by Chatto & Windus following serial syndication by Tillotson & Son; moves to 82 Wimpole Street, Marylebone.

1889	Collins dies (September 23) at 82 Wimpole Street and is buried at Kensal Green Cemetery.
1890	*Blind Love*, completed by Walter Besant after Collins's death, published in three volumes by Chatto & Windus following serialization in the *Illustrated London News*.
1895	Caroline Graves dies and is buried in Collins's grave.
1913	Son, William Charles Collins Dawson, dies.
1919	Martha Rudd dies.
1955	Daughters, Marian and Constance Dawson, die.

A Note on the Text

Wilkie Collins serialized *The Moonstone* in Charles Dickens's weekly magazine *All the Year Round* during the first eight months of 1868 – between January 4 and August 8. In mid-1867 Dickens had paid Collins £850 for the serial rights to the novel, a work which Collins anticipated would run for 26-30 weeks. The novel, which approaches 200,000 words, appeared as the lead in thirty-two parts averaging 6,100 words, or about six of *All the Year Round*'s two-column pages per part. Two numbers, April 4 and April 11 (parts 14 and 15), are substantially shorter – 4,400 words and 4,200 words respectively – than the other parts, primarily because Collins's February battle with a severe attack of rheumatic gout and his concern over his mother's failing health (she would die in mid-March) kept him from writing as much as he would have liked. Four numbers – the first (January 4) and the last three (July 25, August 1, and August 8) – run considerably longer than the other parts, averaging 8,000 words. (Asterisks within the text of this edition mark the end of each original serial number.)

Tinsley Brothers, 18 Catherine Street, the Strand, at the time a little-known publishing firm headed by William Tinsley, published the three-volume edition of the novel on July 16, 1868, just before the final four serial numbers appeared in *All the Year Round*. (Harper and Brothers – who had paid Collins £750 for the serial rights to the novel and whose *Harper's Weekly* had run the novel in America at the same time that it was appearing in Britain – published the novel in one volume in the United States, also in July 1868.) Tinsley, who probably approached Collins through Dickens, struck a deal with Collins that gave the Tinsley Brothers firm, for £750 – relatively little money considering that Collins had been paid £5,000 by George Smith for *Armadale* a few years earlier – exclusive rights to publish volume editions of *The Moonstone* for one year. Anxious about sales figures, Tinsley printed only 1,500 copies of the first edition, which he sold out in two months. Based on these early sales, Collins requested a higher return for a second edition of 500 copies, but Tinsley, still claiming to be worried about sales, balked at paying Collins any more than £250. The two negotiated, quarrelled over the details of the contract, Collins relented – at the cost of a compensatory £50 pounds that Tinsley later claimed he had deducted from his client's payment – and Tinsley lost Collins's future business. Some scholars argue that a lengthy and favourable review of the novel that appeared in *The Times* on October 3, 1868 (see Appendix A, 4) went some distance toward helping Tinsley decide to produce another edition and thus played an important role in the novel's becoming one of Collins's best known and most respected works.

The complete 418-page holograph manuscript copy of the novel is held by the Pierpont Morgan Library. Though Collins claimed to have been compelled by a serious attack of rheumatic gout to dictate a good deal of the work's middle portions to various amanuenses, only small portions of the manuscript – seven pages in all – appear in different hands. Collins's biographer Catherine Peters suggests that the evidence provided by the extant manuscript, as well as by letters written during the novel's composition, reveals the later tale of the amanuenses to be "one of Wilkie's embroideries" (296).

The text of this edition is a reproduction of the revised one-volume Smith, Elder edition of 1871. Smith, Elder had in 1867 acquired the rights to all of Collins's previous fiction, but Collins had chosen to exclude them from initial involvement with *The Moonstone*, so the firm had to wait until Tinsley's rights had expired before publishing its edition of the novel in May 1871. Collins made only minor changes in the text between 1868 and 1871, the most noticeable being chapter shifts, noted below in footnotes to the serial division.

All the Year Round Serial Divisions

January 1868:

Part 1	January 4	"Prologue: The Storming of Seringapatam," Chapters I, II, III, IV; "First Period: The Loss of the Diamond, Events Related by Gabriel Betteredge," Chapters I, II, III (*All the Year Round,* Volume XIX, pages 73-80).
Part 2	January 11	Chapters IV, V (*AYR* pages 97-103).
Part 3	January 18	Chapters VI, VII (*AYR* pages 121-27).

Part 4   January 25   Chapters VIII, IX (*AYR* pages 145-52).

February 1868:

Part 5   February 1   Chapter X (*AYR* pages 169-74).
Part 6   February 8   Chapter XI[1] (*AYR* pages 193-99).
Part 7   February 15   Chapters XI (continued), XII (*AYR* pages
                         217-23).
Part 8   February 22   Chapters XIII, XIV (*AYR* pages 241-46).
Part 9   February 29   Chapter XV (*AYR* pages 265-70).

March 1868:

Part 10   March 7   Chapters XVI, XVII (*AYR* pages 289-95).
Part 11   March 14   Chapters XVIII, XIX[2], XX[3] (*AYR* pages
                         313-19).
Part 12   March 21   Chapters XX (continued), XXI[4] (*AYR* pages
                         337-43).
Part 13   March 28   Chapters XXI (continued), XXII (*AYR*
                         pages 361-67).

April 1868:

Part 14   April 4   "Second Period: The Discovery of the
                         Truth," First Narrative. Miss Clack,
                         Chapter I (*AYR*, pages 385-89).
Part 15   April 11   Chapter II (*AYR* pages 409-13).
Part 16   April 18   Chapters III, IV[5] (*AYR* pages 433-39).

---

1   Part 6 of the *AYR* serial (February 8) ends three-quarters of the way through chapter XI, in the paragraph that ends "... and out walked Rosanna Spearman!"

2   The end of chapter XIX marks the end of Volume I of Tinsley's 1868 three-volume edition.

3   Part 11 of the *AYR* serial (March 14) ends at what is now the conclusion of chapter XX but what was originally a break one quarter of the way through chapter XX. Collins originally split chapter XX into two parts but later divided it into two chapters.

4   Part 12 of the *AYR* serial (March 21) ends two thirds of the way through what is now chapter XXII but what was chapter XXI in the serial. The final sentence of the number reads, "Hot and angry as I was, the infernal confidence with which he gave me that answer closed my lips."

5   Part 16 of the *AYR* serial (April 18) ends halfway through chapter IV of Miss Clack's Narrative, in the paragraph that ends, "'... Lady Verinder's servant, to see Miss Clack.'"

Part 17   April 25   Chapters IV (continued),V (*AYR* pages 457-
                           62).

May 1868:

Part 18   May 2   Chapters VI, VII[1] (*AYR* pages 481-86).
Part 19   May 9   Chapter VII (continued) (*AYR* pages 505-
                           511).
Part 20   May 16   Second Narrative. Mathew Bruff, Chapters
                           I, II (*AYR* pages 529-35).
Part 21   May 23   Chapter III; Third Narrative. Franklin Blake,
                           Chapter I (*AYR* pages 553-59).
Part 22   May 30   Chapters II, III (*AYR* pages 577-83).

June 1868:

Part 23   June 6   Chapter IV[2] (*AYR* pages 601-06).
Part 24   June 13   Chapters V, VI (*AYR*, Volume XX, pages 1-8).
Part 25   June 20   Chapter VII (*AYR* pages 25-30).
Part 26   June 27   Chapter VIII (*AYR* pages 49-54).

July 1868:

Part 27   July 4   Chapter IX (*AYR* pages 73-79).
Part 28   July 11   Chapter X (*AYR* pages 97-103).
Part 29   July 18   Fourth Narrative. Journal of Ezra Jennings[3]
                          (*AYR* pages 121-27).
Part 30   July 25   Fourth Narrative. Journal of Ezra Jennings
                          (continued) (*AYR* pages 145-53).

August 1868:

Part 31   August 1   Fifth Narrative. Franklin Blake (*AYR* pages
                          169-76).

---

1   Part 18 of the *AYR* serial (May 2) ends at what is now the break between chapters
    VII and VIII of Miss Clack's Narrative but what was originally a split in the middle
    of chapter VII. Collins split chapter VII into two chapters when he revised in for
    volume publication.
2   The end of chapter IV of Franklin Blake's narrative also marks the end of Volume II
    of Tinsley's 1868 three-volume edition of the novel.
3   Part 29 of the *AYR* serial (July 18) ends with the third sentence – "We have just
    arrived at the house." – of Ezra Jennings's journal entry for June 25th, Monday.

Part 32 August 8   Sixth Narrative. Sergeant Cuff, Chapters I,
                       II, III, IV, V; Seventh Narrative. Mr.
                       Candy; Eighth Narrative. Gabriel Bet-
                       teredge; "Epilogue: The Finding of the
                       Diamond," Chapters I, II, III (*AYR*
                       pages 193-201).

THE MOONSTONE

PREFACE TO THE FIRST EDITION
(1868)[1]

IN some of my former novels, the object proposed has been to trace the influence of circumstances upon character. In the present story I have reversed the process. The attempt made, here, is to trace the influence of character on circumstances. The conduct pursued, under a sudden emergency, by a young girl, supplies the foundation on which I have built this book.

The same object has been kept in view, in the handling of the other characters which appear in these pages. Their course of thought and action under the circumstances which surround them, is shown to be (what it would most probably have been in real life) sometimes right, and sometimes wrong. Right, or wrong, their conduct, in either event, equally directs the course of those portions of the story in which they are concerned.

In the case of the physiological experiment which occupies a prominent place in the closing scenes of *The Moonstone*, the same principle has guided me once more. Having first ascertained, not only from books, but from living authorities as well,[2] what the result of that experiment would really have been, I have declined to avail myself of the novelist's privilege of supposing something which might have happened, and have so shaped the story as to make it grow out

---

1 An inveterate preface writer, Collins often attached to his novels brief statements explaining or defending his tactics as a writer of fiction. The two prefaces reprinted in this edition – from 1868 and 1871 – contain interesting information concerning both his literary methodology and the physical and familial difficulties he suffered through while writing *The Moonstone*.

2 Always sensitive to the critics who labelled his fiction sensational or unrealistic, Collins occasionally used his prefaces, as he does here, to document his research findings and legitimize them via usually unnamed authorities. In the preface to *The Woman in White*, he suggested that the novel's legal intricacies had been checked and approved by "a solicitor of great experience." In the preface to his anti-vivisection novel, *Heart and Science*, he claimed to have submitted his manuscript "for correction to an eminent London surgeon, whose experience extends over a period of forty years."

Collins's source materials for *The Moonstone*, when available, are noted over the course of the text. Sue Lonoff provides a thorough and valuable consideration of the novel's source material in her study *Wilkie Collins and His Victorian Readers* (New York: AMS, 1980: 174-88).

of what actually would have happened – which, I beg to inform my readers, is also what actually does happen, in these pages.

With reference to the story of the Diamond, as here set forth, I have to acknowledge that it is founded, in some important particulars, on the stories of two of the royal diamonds of Europe. The magnificent stone which adorns the top of the Russian Imperial Sceptre, was once the eye of an Indian idol. The famous Koh-i-Nor is also supposed to have been one of the sacred gems of India; and, more than this, to have been the subject of a prediction, which prophesied certain misfortune to the persons who should divert it from its ancient uses.[1]

GLOUCESTER PLACE, PORTMAN SQUARE, *June* 30th, 1868.[2]

In Memoriam Matris.[3]

★ ★ ★ ★ ★

PREFACE TO THE REVISED EDITION
(1871)

THE circumstances under which *The Moonstone* was originally written, have invested the book – in the author's mind – with an interest peculiarly its own.

While this work was still in course of periodical publication in England, and in the United States, and when not more than one third

---

1 Collins researched his diamond in at least a couple of sources, the eighth edition of *The Encyclopædia Britannica* and C.W. King's (1818-88) *The Natural History of Precious Stones* (1865, revised in 1867). He found information in both works about the actual diamonds – the Orloff and the Koh-i-Nor – he mentions in his preface. The Orloff was a large diamond that had been taken from the eye of an Indian idol and removed to Russia, where it found its way into the Emperor's sceptre. The Koh-i-Nor had been removed from India in 1849 and presented to Queen Victoria in 1850.

2 Collins penned this preface from his Portman Square home two weeks before the novel was published in three volumes by Tinsley Brothers, 18, Catherine-street, Strand on July 14, 1868.

3 Collins dedicated the first three-volume edition of the book to his mother, Harriet Collins (1790-1868), who died on March 19, 1868.

of it was completed, the bitterest affliction of my life and the severest illness from which I have ever suffered, fell on me together. At the time when my mother lay dying in her little cottage in the country, I was struck prostrate, in London; crippled in every limb by the torture of rheumatic gout.[1] Under the weight of this double calamity, I had my duty to the public still to bear in mind. My good readers in England and in America, whom I had never yet disappointed, were expecting their regular weekly instalments of the new story. I held to the story – for my own sake, as well as for theirs. In the intervals of grief, in the occasional remissions of pain, I dictated from my bed that portion of *The Moonstone* which has since proved most successful in amusing the public – the "Narrative of Miss Clack." Of the physical sacrifice which the effort cost me I shall say nothing. I only look back now at the blessed relief which my occupation (forced as it was) brought to my mind. The Art which had been always the pride and the pleasure of my life, became now more than ever "its own exceeding great reward." I doubt if I should have lived to write another book, if the responsibility of the weekly publication of this story had not forced me to rally my sinking energies of body and mind – to dry my useless tears, and to conquer my merciless pains.

The novel completed, I awaited its reception by the public with an eagerness of anxiety, which I have never felt before or since for the fate of any other writings of mine. If *The Moonstone* had failed, my mortification would have been bitter indeed. As it was, the welcome accorded to the story in England, in America, and on the Continent of Europe was instantly and universally favourable. Never have I had better reason than this work has given me to feel gratefully to novel-readers of all nations. Everywhere my characters made friends, and my story roused interest. Everywhere the public favour looked over my faults – and repaid me a hundred-fold for the hard toil which these pages cost me in the dark time of sickness and grief.

---

1   Collins suffered his first attack of the gout in 1862 while writing *No Name* for serialization in *All the Year Round*. To relieve his pain then, he started to take laudanum, a tincture of opium, to which he quickly became addicted. Thereafter, he lived with attacks of the ailment periodically – and with his addiction – until his death in 1889. A severe attack, which he mentions here, came in the early spring of 1868, when he was in the middle of writing *The Moonstone*. Late in the book, we learn that Mr. Bruff has suffered through an attack of the gout brought on by excitement.

I have only to add that the present edition has had the benefit of my careful revision. All that I can do towards making the book worthy of the readers' continued approval has now been done.

May, 1871.

CONTENTS

PROLOGUE

THE STORMING OF SERINGAPATAM (1799)
Extracted from a Family Paper

THE STORY

FIRST PERIOD: THE LOSS OF THE DIAMOND (1848)
*The Events Related by Gabriel Betteredge, House-Steward
in the Service of Julia, Lady Verinder*

SECOND PERIOD: THE DISCOVERY OF THE TRUTH (1848-1849)
The Events Related in Several Narratives
First Narrative
Contributed by Miss Clack, Niece of the Late Sir John Verinder
Second Narrative
Contributed by Mathew Bruff, Solicitor, of Gray's Inn Square
Third Narrative
Contributed by Franklin Blake
Fourth Narrative
Extracted from the Journal of Ezra Jennings
Fifth Narrative
The Story Resumed by Franklin Blake
Sixth Narrative
Contributed by Sergeant Cuff
Seventh Narrative
In a Letter from Mr. Candy
Eighth Narrative
Contributed by Gabriel Betteredge

EPILOGUE

THE FINDING OF THE DIAMOND
  I. The Statement of Sergeant Cuff's Man (1849)
 II. The Statement of the Captain (1849)
III. The Statement of Mr. Murthwaite (1850)
    In a Letter to Mr. Bruff

PROLOGUE

THE STORMING OF SERINGAPATAM (1799)[1]
Extracted from a Family Paper[2]

I

I ADDRESS these lines – written in India – to my relatives in England. My object is to explain the motive which has induced me to refuse the right hand of friendship to my cousin, John Herncastle.[3] The reserve which I have hitherto maintained in this matter has been misinterpreted by members of my family whose good opinion I cannot consent to forfeit. I request them to suspend their decision until they have read my narrative. And I declare, on my word of honour, that what I am now about to write is, strictly and literally, the truth.

The private difference between my cousin and me took its rise in a great public event in which we were both concerned – the storm-

---

1   Collins almost certainly got much of his information about Seringapatam from the recently published first volume of James Talboys Wheeler's (1824-97) *History of India* (1867). Wheeler's study would grow to four volumes by the time he completed it in 1881. Collins also read Theodore Hook's *The Life of General, The Right Honourable Sir David Baird, Bart.*, a two-volume biography published by Richard Bentley in 1832.

2   The multiple narrative – often aided by some rather unconventional epistolary forwarding of the action – was a formula for success that Collins had discovered while writing *The Woman in White* nearly ten years earlier. In addition to this "Family Paper," the action of *The Moonstone* is forwarded by diary entries, lengthy and informative letters, and some detailed journal material.

3   The Herncastle family tree, which helps to keep the players straight, is as follows:

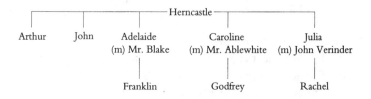

The fact that the love tangles of the novel involve the three cousins would not have bothered Collins's Victorian readers. Marriages between cousins were not uncommon in nineteenth-century England, and they appeared frequently in the pages of the fiction of the period.

ing of Seringapatam, under General Baird,[1] on the 4th of May, 1799.
In order that the circumstances may be clearly understood, I must
revert for a moment to the period before the assault, and to the stories current in our camp of the treasure in jewels and gold stored up
in the Palace of Seringapatam.

II

One of the wildest of these stories related to a Yellow Diamond – a
famous gem in the native annals of India.

The earliest known traditions describe the stone as having been set
in the forehead of the four-handed Indian god who typifies the
Moon. Partly from its peculiar colour, partly from a superstition
which represented it as feeling the influence of the deity whom it
adorned, and growing and lessening in lustre with the waxing and
waning of the moon, it first gained the name by which it continues to
be known in India to this day – the name of THE MOONSTONE.[2] A
similar superstition was once prevalent, as I have heard, in ancient
Greece and Rome; not applying, however (as in India), to a diamond
devoted to the service of a god, but to a semi-transparent stone of the
inferior order of gems, supposed to be affected by the lunar influences
– the moon, in this latter case also, giving the name by which the
stone is still known to collectors in our own time.

The adventures of the Yellow Diamond begin with the eleventh
century of the Christian era.

At that date, the Mohammedan conqueror, Mahmoud of Ghizni,
crossed India; seized on the holy city of Somnauth; and stripped of its
treasures the famous temple, which had stood for centuries – the
shrine of Hindoo pilgrimage, and the wonder of the eastern world.[3]

---

1 Sir David Baird (1757-1829) was the major-general who volunteered to lead the
storming of Seringapatam on May 4, 1799, in the last of the Mysore Wars. Despite
reports that Baird himself was responsible for some looting at Seringapatam, he was
knighted in 1805, after a quarter-century of service in India.

2 Some claim that Collins's diamond was inspired by a moonstone owned by friend
and fellow-novelist Charles Reade, whose brother had brought it to England from
India. Lady Constance Russell, in her memoir *Swallowfields and Its Owners* (1901),
claims that Collins's diamond was inspired by a moonstone in the Russell family,
the Pitt diamond.

3 Collins's primary source for this brief history was probably the eighth edition of
The Encyclopædia Britannica. "Mahmoud of Ghizni" was the conqueror of India in

Of all the deities worshipped in the temple, the moon-god alone escaped the rapacity of the conquering Mohammedans. Preserved by three Brahmins, the inviolate deity, bearing the Yellow Diamond in its forehead, was removed by night, and was transported to the second of the sacred cities of India – the city of Benares.[1]

Here, in a new shrine – in a hall inlaid with precious stones, under a roof supported by pillars of gold – the moon-god was set up and worshipped. Here, on the night when the shrine was completed, Vishnu the Preserver appeared to the three Brahmins in a dream.[2]

The deity breathed the breath of his divinity on the Diamond in the forehead of the god. And the Brahmins knelt and hid their faces in their robes. The deity commanded that the Moonstone should be watched, from that time forth, by three priests in turn, night and day, to the end of the generations of men. And the Brahmins heard, and bowed before his will. The deity predicted certain disaster to the presumptuous mortal who laid hands on the sacred gem, and to all of his house and name who received it after him. And the Brahmins caused the prophecy to be written over the gates of the shrine in letters of gold.

One age followed another – and still, generation after generation, the successors of the three Brahmins watched their priceless Moonstone, night and day. One age followed another, until the first years of the eighteenth Christian century saw the reign of Aurungzebe, Emperor of the Moguls.[3] At his command, havoc and rapine were let loose once more among the temples of the worship of Brahmah.

the 11th century. Legend claims that he kept four hundred greyhounds and blood-hounds, each of which wore a jewelled collar taken from the necks of captive sultanas. The holy city of Somnauth is located on the Kattiawar Peninsula – a part of the Gujarut State – which juts out into the Arabian Sea in northwestern India. Kattiawar is mentioned near the end of the novel.

1   Now Varanasi, Benares was a city in southeastern Uttar Pradesh, India. On the Ganges, Benares was a sacred city of the Hindus.

2   Vishnu the Preserver is the chief deity worshipped by the Hindu sect Vaishnava. Vishnu is one of the trinity that includes also Brahma the Creator and Shiva the Destroyer.

3   The Moguls were followers of Baber, who conquered India in 1526 and founded a Moslem empire. Aurungzebe, who reigned from 1658 until his death in 1707 expanded the empire but could never completely subdue the Hindus. His treasures included the Koh-i-Nor diamond. His three sons fought among themselves for succession, and the Mogol empire began to crumble.

The shrine of the four-handed god was polluted by the slaughter of sacred animals; the images of the deities were broken in pieces; and the Moonstone was seized by an officer of rank in the army of Aurungzebe.

Powerless to recover their lost treasure by open force, the three guardian priests followed and watched it in disguise. The generations succeeded each other; the warrior who had committed the sacrilege perished miserably; the Moonstone passed (carrying its curse with it) from one lawless Mohammedan hand to another; and still, through all chances and changes, the successors of the three guardian priests kept their watch, waiting the day when the will of Vishnu the Preserver should restore to them their sacred gem. Time rolled on from the first to the last years of the eighteenth Christian century. The Diamond fell into the possession of Tippoo, Sultan of Seringapatam,[1] who caused it to be placed as an ornament in the handle of a dagger, and who commanded it to be kept among the choicest treasures of his armoury. Even then – in the palace of the Sultan himself – the three guardian priests still kept their watch in secret. There were three officers of Tippoo's household, strangers to the rest, who had won their master's confidence by conforming, or appearing to conform, to the Mussulman faith; and to those three men report pointed as the three priests in disguise.

III

So, as told in our camp, ran the fanciful story of the Moonstone. It made no serious impression on any of us except my cousin – whose love of the marvellous induced him to believe it. On the night before the assault on Seringapatam, he was absurdly angry with me, and with others, for treating the whole thing as a fable. A foolish wrangle followed; and Herncastle's unlucky temper got the better of him. He declared, in his boastful way, that we should see the Diamond on his finger, if the English army took Seringapatam. The sally was saluted by a roar of laughter, and there, as we all thought that night, the thing ended.

---

1 Tippoo Sahib (1750?-99) was the Sultan of Mysore (1782-99). He long resisted British military influence in Mysore and was killed on May 4, 1799 during the storming of Seringapatam.

Let me now take you on to the day of the assault.

My cousin and I were separated at the outset. I never saw him when we forded the river; when we planted the English flag in the first breach; when we crossed the ditch beyond; and, fighting every inch of our way, entered the town. It was only at dusk, when the place was ours, and after General Baird himself had found the dead body of Tippoo under a heap of the slain, that Herncastle and I met.

We were each attached to a party sent out by the General's orders to prevent the plunder and confusion which followed our conquest. The camp-followers committed deplorable excesses; and, worse still, the soldiers found their way, by an unguarded door, into the treasury of the Palace, and loaded themselves with gold and jewels. It was in the court outside the treasury that my cousin and I met, to enforce the laws of discipline on our own soldiers. Herncastle's fiery temper had been, as I could plainly see, exasperated to a kind of frenzy by the terrible slaughter through which we had passed. He was very unfit, in my opinion, to perform the duty that had been entrusted to him.

There was riot and confusion enough in the treasury, but no violence that I saw. The men (if I may use such an expression) disgraced themselves good-humouredly. All sorts of rough jests and catchwords were bandied about among them; and the story of the Diamond turned up again unexpectedly, in the form of a mischievous joke. "Who's got the Moonstone?" was the rallying cry which perpetually caused the plundering, as soon as it was stopped in one place, to break out in another. While I was still vainly trying to establish order, I heard a frightful yelling on the other side of the courtyard, and at once ran towards the cries, in dread of finding some new outbreak of the pillage in that direction.

I got to an open door, and saw the bodies of two Indians (by their dress, as I guessed, officers of the Palace) lying across the entrance, dead.

A cry inside hurried me into a room, which appeared to serve as an armoury. A third Indian, mortally wounded, was sinking at the feet of a man whose back was towards me. The man turned at the instant when I came in, and I saw John Herncastle, with a torch in one hand, and a dagger dripping with blood in the other. A stone, set like a pommel, in the end of the dagger's handle, flashed in the torchlight, as he turned on me, like a gleam of fire. The dying Indian sank to his knees, pointed to the dagger in Herncastle's hand, and said, in his native language: – "The Moonstone will have its vengeance yet on you and yours!" He spoke those words, and fell dead on the floor.

Before I could stir in the matter, the men who had followed me across the courtyard crowded in. My cousin rushed to meet them, like a madman. "Clear the room!" he shouted to me, "and set a guard on the door!" The men fell back as he threw himself on them with his torch and his dagger. I put two sentinels of my own company, on whom I could rely, to keep the door. Through the remainder of the night, I saw no more of my cousin.

Early in the morning, the plunder still going on, General Baird announced publicly by beat of drum, that any thief detected in the fact, be he whom he might, should be hung. The provost-marshal[1] was in attendance, to prove that the General was in earnest; and in the throng that followed the proclamation, Herncastle and I met again.

He held out his hand, as usual, and said, "Good morning."

I waited before I gave him my hand in return.

"Tell me first," I said, "how the Indian in the armoury met his death, and what those last words meant, when he pointed to the dagger in your hand."

"The Indian met his death, as I suppose, by a mortal wound," said Herncastle. "What his last words meant I know no more than you do."

I looked at him narrowly. His frenzy of the previous day had all calmed down. I determined to give him another chance.

"Is that all you have to tell me?" I asked.

He answered, "That is all."

I turned my back on him; and we have not spoken since.

IV

I beg it to be understood that what I write here about my cousin (unless some necessity should arise for making it public) is for the information of the family only. Herncastle has said nothing that can

---

1   The provost-marshal was the head of military police.

justify me in speaking to our commanding officer. He has been taunted more than once about the Diamond, by those who recollect his angry outbreak before the assault; but, as may easily be imagined, his own remembrance of the circumstances under which I surprised him in the armoury has been enough to keep him silent. It is reported that he means to exchange into another regiment, avowedly for the purpose of separating himself from *me*.

Whether this be true or not, I cannot prevail upon myself to become his accuser – and I think with good reason. If I made the matter public, I have no evidence but moral evidence to bring forward. I have not only no proof that he killed the two men at the door; I cannot even declare that he killed the third man inside – for I cannot say that my own eyes saw the deed committed. It is true that I heard the dying Indian's words; but if those words were pronounced to be the ravings of delirium, how could I contradict the assertion from my own knowledge? Let our relatives, on either side, form their own opinion on what I have written, and decide for themselves whether the aversion I now feel towards this man is well or ill founded.

Although I attach no sort of credit to the fantastic Indian legend of the gem, I must acknowledge, before I conclude, that I am influenced by a certain superstition of my own in this matter. It is my conviction, or my delusion, no matter which, that crime brings its own fatality with it. I am not only persuaded of Herncastle's guilt; I am even fanciful enough to believe that he will live to regret it, if he keeps the Diamond; and that others will live to regret taking it from him, if he gives the Diamond away.

THE STORY

FIRST PERIOD

THE LOSS OF THE DIAMOND (1848)

The Events Related by GABRIEL BETTEREDGE, *House-Steward*[1] *in the Service of* JULIA, LADY VERINDER

CHAPTER I

IN the first part of *Robinson Crusoe*, at page one hundred and twenty-nine, you will find it thus written:

"Now I saw, though too late, the Folly of beginning a Work before we count the Cost, and before we judge rightly of our own Strength to go through with it."[2]

Only yesterday, I opened my *Robinson Crusoe* at that place. Only this morning (May twenty-first, eighteen hundred and fifty), came my lady's nephew, Mr. Franklin Blake, and held a short conversation with me, as follows: –

"Betteredge," says Mr. Franklin, "I have been to the lawyer's about some family matters; and, among other things, we have been talking of the loss of the Indian Diamond, in my aunt's house in Yorkshire,[3] two years since. Mr. Bruff thinks, as I think, that the whole story

---

1 As house-steward, Betteredge is head of the household's staff of servants.

2 Betteredge accurately quotes Daniel Defoe's (1660-1731) *Robinson Crusoe* (1719) on at least a half-dozen occasions in *The Moonstone*. Collins's biographer Catherine Peters, who argues that *The Moonstone* is in part an attack on organized Christianity, labels Betteredge's *Robinson Crusoe* his "secular bible" (306). Other studies have argued, with varying degrees of success, that Betteredge's dependence on Defoe's book, a paean to British imperialism, is one of the central ironies of Collins's anti-imperialist novel. Lillian Nayder's "Robinson Crusoe and Friday in Victorian Britain: 'Discipline,' 'Dialogue,' and Collins's Critique of Empire in *The Moonstone*" (*Dickens Studies Annual* 21, 1992: 213-31) is probably the best of these.

3 Collins is so detailed and precise in his descriptions of the Yorkshire coast that he must have visited locales that inspired the setting. Collins visited the north-Yorkshire coast in 1861, staying in Whitby. Nearby Mulgrave Castle may be a model for the Verinder estate. S.M. Ellis claims that Collins also visited the locality in August 1864 (*Wilkie Collins, Le Fanu, and Others*, London: Constable, 1931: 39). See note 1 on page 76 for more information on setting.

ought, in the interests of truth, to be placed on record in writing – and the sooner the better."

Not perceiving his drift yet, and thinking it always desirable for the sake of peace and quietness to be on the lawyer's side, I said I thought so too. Mr. Franklin went on.

"In this matter of the Diamond," he said, "the characters of innocent people have suffered under suspicion already – as you know. The memories of innocent people may suffer, hereafter, for want of a record of the facts to which those who come after us can appeal. There can be no doubt that this strange family story of ours ought to be told. And I think, Betteredge, Mr. Bruff and I together have hit on the right way of telling it."

Very satisfactory to both of them, no doubt. But I failed to see what I myself had to do with it, so far.

"We have certain events to relate," Mr. Franklin proceeded; "and we have certain persons concerned in those events who are capable of relating them. Starting from these plain facts, the idea is that we should all write the story of the Moonstone in turn – as far as our own personal experience extends, and no farther. We must begin by showing how the Diamond first fell into the hands of my uncle Herncastle, when he was serving in India fifty years since. This prefatory narrative I have already got by me in the form of an old family paper, which relates the necessary particulars on the authority of an eye-witness. The next thing to do is to tell how the Diamond found its way into my aunt's house in Yorkshire, two years ago, and how it came to be lost in little more than twelve hours afterwards. Nobody knows as much as you do, Betteredge, about what went on in the house at that time. So you must take the pen in hand, and start the story."

In those terms I was informed of what my personal concern was with the matter of the Diamond. If you are curious to know what course I took under the circumstances, I beg to inform you that I did what you would probably have done in my place. I modestly declared myself to be quite unequal to the task imposed upon me – and I privately felt, all the time, that I was quite clever enough to perform it, if I only gave my own abilities a fair chance. Mr. Franklin, I imagine, must have seen my private sentiments in my face. He declined to believe in my modesty; and he insisted on giving my abilities a fair chance.

Two hours have passed since Mr. Franklin left me. As soon as his back was turned, I went to my writing-desk to start the story. There I have sat helpless (in spite of my abilities) ever since; seeing what Robinson Crusoe saw, as quoted above – namely, the folly of beginning a work before we count the cost, and before we judge rightly of our own strength to go through with it. Please to remember, I opened the book by accident, at that bit, only the day before I rashly undertook the business now in hand; and, allow me to ask – if *that* isn't prophecy, what is?

I am not superstitious; I have read a heap of books in my time; I am a scholar in my own way. Though turned seventy, I possess an active memory, and legs to correspond. You are not to take it, if you please, as the saying of an ignorant man, when I express my opinion that such a book as *Robinson Crusoe* never was written, and never will be written again. I have tried that book for years – generally in combination with a pipe of tobacco – and I have found it my friend in need in all the necessities of this mortal life. When my spirits are bad – *Robinson Crusoe*. When I want advice – *Robinson Crusoe*. In past times, when my wife plagued me; in present times, when I have had a drop too much – *Robinson Crusoe*. I have worn out six stout *Robinson Crusoes* with hard work in my service. On my lady's last birthday she gave me a seventh. I took a drop too much on the strength of it; and *Robinson Crusoe* put me right again. Price four shillings and sixpence, bound in blue, with a picture into the bargain.

Still, this don't look much like starting the story of the Diamond – does it? I seem to be wandering off in search of Lord knows what, Lord knows where. We will take a new sheet of paper, if you please, and begin over again, with my best respects to you.

CHAPTER II

I SPOKE of my lady a line or two back. Now the Diamond could never have been in our house, where it was lost, if it had not been made a present of to my lady's daughter; and my lady's daughter would never have been in existence to have the present, if it had not been for my lady who (with pain and travail) produced her into the world. Consequently, if we begin with my lady, we are pretty sure of beginning far enough back. And that, let me tell you, when you have got such a job as mine in hand, is a real comfort at starting.

If you know anything of the fashionable world, you have heard tell of the three beautiful Miss Herncastles. Miss Adelaide; Miss Caroline; and Miss Julia — this last being the youngest and the best of the three sisters, in my opinion; and I had opportunities of judging, as you shall presently see. I went into the service of the old lord, their father (thank God, we have got nothing to do with *him*, in this business of the Diamond; he had the longest tongue and the shortest temper of any man, high or low, I ever met with) — I say, I went into the service of the old lord, as page-boy[1] in waiting on the three honourable young ladies, at the age of fifteen years. There I lived, till Miss Julia married the late Sir John Verinder. An excellent man, who only wanted somebody to manage him; and, between ourselves, he found somebody to do it; and what is more, he throve on it, and grew fat on it, and lived happy and died easy on it, dating from the day when my lady took him to church to be married, to the day when she relieved him of his last breath, and closed his eyes for ever.

I have omitted to state that I went with the bride to the bride's husband's house and lands down here. "Sir John," she says, "I can't do without Gabriel Betteredge." "My lady," says Sir John, "I can't do without him, either." That was his way with her — and that was how I went into his service. It was all one to me where I went, so long as my mistress and I were together.

Seeing that my lady took an interest in the out-of-door work, and the farms, and such like, I took an interest in them too — with all the more reason that I was a small farmer's seventh son myself. My lady got me put under the bailiff,[2] and I did my best, and gave satisfaction, and got promotion accordingly. Some years later, on the Monday as it might be, my lady says, "Sir John, your bailiff is a stupid old man. Pension him liberally, and let Gabriel Betteredge have his place." On the Tuesday as it might be, Sir John says, "My lady, the bailiff is pensioned liberally; and Gabriel Betteredge has got his place." You hear

---

1 A page-boy in a Victorian home was responsible for running general errands.
2 A farm-bailiff managed a farm for the master of the estate.

more than enough of married people living together miserably. Here is an example to the contrary. Let it be a warning to some of you, and an encouragement to others. In the meantime, I will go on with my story.

Well, there I was in clover, you will say. Placed in a position of trust and honour, with a little cottage of my own to live in, with my rounds on the estate to occupy me in the morning, and my accounts in the afternoon, and my pipe and my *Robinson Crusoe* in the evening – what more could I possibly want to make me happy? Remember what Adam wanted when he was alone in the Garden of Eden; and if you don't blame it in Adam, don't blame it in me.

The woman I fixed my eye on, was the woman who kept house for me at my cottage. Her name was Selina Goby. I agree with the late William Cobbett[1] about picking a wife. See that she chews her food well, and sets her foot down firmly on the ground when she walks, and you're all right. Selina Goby was all right in both these respects, which was one reason for marrying her. I had another reason, likewise, entirely of my own discovering. Selina, being a single woman, made me pay so much a week for her board and services. Selina, being my wife, couldn't charge for her board, and would have to give me her services for nothing. That was the point of view I looked at it from. Economy – with a dash of love. I put it to my mistress, as in duty bound, just as I had put it to myself.

"I have been turning Selina Goby over in my mind," I said, "and I think, my lady, it will be cheaper to marry her than to keep her."

My lady burst out laughing, and said she didn't know which to be most shocked at – my language or my principles. Some joke tickled her, I suppose, of the sort that you can't take unless you are a person of quality. Understanding nothing myself but that I was free to put it next to Selina, I went and put it accordingly. And what did Selina say? Lord! how little you must know of women, if you ask that. Of course she said, Yes.

---

1 Cobbett (1763-1835) was a self-educated and prolific writer whose *Advice to Young Men* (1829) is the work to which Betteredge here refers. Betteredge seems to be recalling two particular passages from Cobbett's work. The first: "Get to see her at work upon a mutton-chop, or a bit of bread and cheese; and if she deal quickly with these, you have a pretty good security for that activity. . . ." The second: "Another mark of industry is a quick step, and a somewhat heavy tread, showing that the foot comes down with a hearty good will."

As my time drew nearer, and there got to be talk of my having a new coat for the ceremony, my mind began to misgive me. I have compared notes with other men as to what they felt while they were in my interesting situation; and they have all acknowledged that, about a week before it happened, they privately wished themselves out of it. I went a trifle further than that myself; I actually rose up, as it were, and tried to get out of it. Not for nothing! I was too just a man to expect she would let me off for nothing. Compensation to the woman when the man gets out of it, is one of the laws of England. In obedience to the laws, and after turning it over carefully in my mind, I offered Selina Goby a feather-bed and fifty shillings to be off the bargain. You will hardly believe it, but it is nevertheless true – she was fool enough to refuse.

After that it was all over with me, of course. I got the new coat as cheap as I could, and I went through all the rest of it as cheap as I could. We were not a happy couple, and not a miserable couple. We were six of one and half a dozen of the other. How it was I don't understand, but we always seemed to be getting, with the best of motives, in one another's way. When I wanted to go upstairs, there was my wife coming down; or when my wife wanted to go down, there was I coming up. That is married life, according to my experience of it.

After five years of misunderstandings on the stairs, it pleased an all-wise Providence to relieve us of each other by taking my wife. I was left with my little girl Penelope, and with no other child. Shortly afterwards Sir John died, and my lady was left with her little girl, Miss Rachel, and no other child. I have written to very poor purpose of my lady, if you require to be told that my little Penelope was taken care of, under my good mistress's own eye, and was sent to school, and taught, and made a sharp girl, and promoted, when old enough, to be Miss Rachel's own maid.

As for me, I went on with my business as bailiff year after year up to Christmas 1847, when there came a change in my life. On that day, my lady invited herself to a cup of tea alone with me in my cottage. She remarked that, reckoning from the year when I started as page-boy in the time of the old lord, I had been more than fifty years in her service, and she put into my hands a beautiful waistcoat of wool that she had worked herself, to keep me warm in the bitter winter weather.

I received this magnificent present quite at a loss to find words to thank my mistress with for the honour she had done me. To my great astonishment, it turned out, however, that the waistcoat was not an honour, but a bribe. My lady had discovered that I was getting old before I had discovered it myself, and she had come to my cottage to wheedle me (if I may use such an expression) into giving up my hard out-of-door work as bailiff, and taking my ease for the rest of my days as steward in the house. I made as good a fight of it against the indignity of taking my ease as I could. But my mistress knew the weak side of me; she put it as a favour to herself. The dispute between us ended, after that, in my wiping my eyes, like an old fool, with my new woollen waistcoat, and saying I would think about it.

The perturbation in my mind, in regard to thinking about it, being truly dreadful after my lady had gone away, I applied the remedy which I have never yet found to fail me in cases of doubt and emergency. I smoked a pipe and took a turn at *Robinson Crusoe*. Before I had occupied myself with that extraordinary book five minutes, I came on a comforting bit (page one hundred and fifty-eight), as follows: "To-day we love, what to-morrow we hate." I saw my way clear directly. To-day I was all for continuing to be farm-bailiff; to-morrow, on the authority of *Robinson Crusoe*, I should be all the other way. Take myself to-morrow while in to-morrow's humour, and the thing was done. My mind being relieved in this manner, I went to sleep that night in the character of Lady Verinder's farm-bailiff, and I woke up the next morning in the character of Lady Verinder's house-steward. All quite comfortable, and all through *Robinson Crusoe!*

My daughter Penelope has just looked over my shoulder to see what I have done so far. She remarks that it is beautifully written and every word of it true. But she points out one objection. She says what I have done so far isn't in the least what I was wanted to do. I am asked to tell the story of the Diamond, and, instead of that, I have been telling the story of my own self. Curious, and quite beyond me to account for. I wonder whether the gentlemen who make a business and a living out of writing books, ever find their own selves getting in the way of their subjects, like me? If they do, I can feel for them. In the meantime, here is another false start, and more waste of good writing-paper. What's to be done now? Nothing that I know of, except for you to keep your temper, and for me to begin it all over again for the third time.

CHAPTER III

THE question of how I am to start the story properly I have tried to settle in two ways. First, by scratching my head, which led to nothing. Second, by consulting my daughter Penelope, which has resulted in an entirely new idea.

Penelope's notion is that I should set down what happened, regularly day by day, beginning with the day when we got the news that Mr. Franklin Blake was expected on a visit to the house. When you come to fix your memory with a date in this way, it is wonderful what your memory will pick up for you upon that compulsion. The only difficulty is to fetch out the dates, in the first place. This Penelope offers to do for me by looking into her own diary, which she was taught to keep when she was at school, and which she has gone on keeping ever since. In answer to an improvement on this notion, devised by myself, namely, that she should tell the story instead of me, out of her own diary, Penelope observes, with a fierce look and a red face, that her journal is for her own private eye, and that no living creature shall ever know what is in it but herself. When I inquire what this means, Penelope says, "Fiddlesticks!" I say, Sweethearts.

Beginning, then, on Penelope's plan, I beg to mention that I was specially called one Wednesday morning into my lady's own sitting-room, the date being the twenty-fourth of May, Eighteen hundred and forty-eight.

"Gabriel," says my lady, "here is news that will surprise you. Franklin Blake has come back from abroad. He has been staying with his father in London, and he is coming to us to-morrow to stop till next month, and keep Rachel's birthday."

If I had had a hat in my hand, nothing but respect would have prevented me from throwing that hat up to the ceiling. I had not seen Mr. Franklin since he was a boy, living along with us in this house. He was, out of all sight (as I remembered him), the nicest boy that ever spun a top or broke a window. Miss Rachel, who was present, and to whom I made that remark, observed, in return, that *she* remembered him as the most atrocious tyrant that ever tortured a doll, and the hardest driver of an exhausted little girl in string harness that England could produce. "I burn with indignation, and I ache with fatigue," was the way Miss Rachel summed it up, "when I think of Franklin Blake."

Hearing what I now tell you, you will naturally ask how it was that Mr. Franklin should have passed all the years, from the time when he was a boy to the time when he was a man, out of his own country. I answer, because his father had the misfortune to be next heir to a Dukedom, and not to be able to prove it.

In two words, this was how the thing happened:

My lady's eldest sister married the celebrated Mr. Blake – equally famous for his great riches, and his great suit at law. How many years he went on worrying the tribunals of his country to turn out the Duke in possession, and to put himself in the Duke's place – how many lawyers' purses he filled to bursting, and how many otherwise harmless people he set by the ears together disputing whether he was right or wrong – is more by a great deal than I can reckon up. His wife died, and two of his three children died, before the tribunals could make up their minds to show him the door and take no more of his money. When it was all over, and the Duke in possession was left in possession, Mr. Blake discovered that the only way of being even with his country for the manner in which it had treated him, was not to let his country have the honour of educating his son. "How can I trust my native institutions," was the form in which he put it, "after the way in which my native institutions have behaved to *me*?" Add to this, that Mr. Blake disliked all boys, his own included, and you will admit that it could only end in one way. Master Franklin was taken from us in England, and was sent to institutions which his father *could* trust, in that superior country, Germany; Mr. Blake himself, you will observe, remaining snug in England, to improve his fellow-countrymen in the Parliament House, and to publish a statement on the subject of the Duke in possession, which has remained an unfinished statement from that day to this.

There! thank God, that's told! Neither you nor I need trouble our heads any more about Mr. Blake, senior. Leave him to the Dukedom; and let you and I stick to the Diamond.

The Diamond takes us back to Mr. Franklin, who was the innocent means of bringing that unlucky jewel into the house.

Our nice boy didn't forget us after he went abroad. He wrote every now and then; sometimes to my lady, sometimes to Miss Rachel, and sometimes to me. We had a transaction together, before he left, which consisted in his borrowing of me a ball of string, a four-bladed knife, and seven-and-sixpence in money – the colour of which last I have not seen, and never expect to see again. His letters to me chiefly related to borrowing more. I heard, however, from my lady, how he got on abroad, as he grew in years and stature. After he had learnt what the institutions of Germany could teach him, he gave the French a turn next, and the Italians a turn after that.[1] They made him among them a sort of universal genius, as well as I could understand it. He wrote a little; he painted a little; he sang and played and composed a little – borrowing, as I suspect, in all these cases, just as he had borrowed from me. His mother's fortune (seven hundred a year) fell to him when he came of age, and ran through him, as it might be through a sieve. The more money he had, the more he wanted; there was a hole in Mr. Franklin's pocket that nothing would sew up. Wherever he went, the lively, easy way of him made him welcome. He lived here, there, and everywhere; his address (as he used to put it himself) being, "Post Office, Europe – to be left till called for." Twice over, he made up his mind to come back to England and see us; and twice over (saving your presence), some unmentionable woman stood in the way and stopped him. His third attempt succeeded, as you know already from what my lady told me. On Thursday, the twenty-fifth of May, we were to see for the first time what our nice boy had grown to be as a man. He came of good blood; he had a high courage; and he was five-and-twenty years of age, by our reckoning. Now you know as much of Mr. Franklin Blake as I did – before Mr. Franklin Blake came down to our house.

---

1   Though the several continental sides of Franklin Blake's character offer Betteredge an easy stage for humorous commentary, John R. Reed suggests more seriously that "it is because of his ability to recognize the multiplicity of personality in himself that Blake can function as well as he does. It is one of the great ironies of the novel that Blake, with such a varied character, should be ignorant of a critically important region of his personality, the unconscious" (*Victorian Conventions*, Athens: Ohio UP, 1975: 320-21).

The Thursday was as fine a summer's day as ever you saw: and my lady and Miss Rachel (not expecting Mr. Franklin till dinner-time) drove out to lunch with some friends in the neighbourhood. When they were gone, I went and had a look at the bedroom which had been got ready for our guest, and saw that all was straight. Then, being butler in my lady's establishment, as well as steward (at my own particular request, mind, and because it vexed me to see anybody but myself in possession of the key of the late Sir John's cellar) – then, I say, I fetched up some of our famous Latour claret,[1] and set it in the warm summer air to take off the chill before dinner. Concluding to set myself in the warm summer air next – seeing that what is good for old claret is equally good for old age – I took up my beehive chair[2] to go out into the back court, when I was stopped by hearing a sound like the soft beating of a drum, on the terrace in front of my lady's residence.

Going round to the terrace, I found three mahogany-coloured Indians, in white linen frocks and trousers looking up at the house.

The Indians, as I saw on looking closer, had small hand-drums slung in front of them. Behind them stood a little delicate-looking light-haired English boy carrying a bag. I judged the fellows to be strolling conjurers,[3] and the boy with the bag to be carrying the tools of their trade. One of the three, who spoke English, and who exhibited, I must own, the most elegant manners, presently informed me that my judgment was right. He requested permission to show his tricks in the presence of the lady of the house.

Now I am not a sour old man. I am generally all for amusement, and the last person in the world to distrust another person because he

1 Betteredge refers here to a dry red wine from the Châteaux Latour in the commune of Pauillac – thirty miles from Bordeaux – in the Médoc wine-growing region in southwestern France.
2 The beehive was so named because of its domed shape.
3 Hereafter, Betteredge refers to the Indians as jugglers, but apparently there is a distinction that he fails to draw. In Henry Mayhew's (1812-87) monumental 1851 study *London Labour and the London Poor*, a London street juggler – dressed as an Indian – explains the difference: "'I'm a juggler,' he said, 'but I don't know if that's the right term, for some people call conjurers jugglers; but it's wrong. When I was in Ireland they called me a 'manulist,' and it was a gentleman wrote the bill out for me. The difference I makes between conjuring and juggling is, one's deceiving to the eye and the other's pleasing to the eye – yes, that's it – it's dexterity'" (III, 104).

happens to be a few shades darker than myself. But the best of us have our weaknesses – and my weakness, when I know a family plate-basket to be out on a pantrytable, is to be instantly reminded of that basket by the sight of a strolling stranger whose manners are superior to my own. I accordingly informed the Indian that the lady of the house was out; and I warned him and his party off the premises. He made a beautiful bow in return; and he and his party went off the premises. On my side, I returned to my beehive chair, and set myself down on the sunny side of the court, and fell (if the truth must be owned), not exactly into a sleep, but into the next best thing to it.

I was roused up by my daughter Penelope running out at me as if the house was on fire. What do you think she wanted? She wanted to have the three Indian jugglers instantly taken up; for this reason, namely, that they knew who was coming from London to visit us, and that they meant some mischief to Mr. Franklin Blake.

Mr. Franklin's name roused me. I opened my eyes, and made my girl explain herself.

It appeared that Penelope had just come from our lodge, where she had been having a gossip with the lodge-keeper's daughter. The two girls had seen the Indians pass out, after I had warned them off, followed by their little boy. Taking it into their heads that the boy was ill-used by the foreigners – for no reason that I could discover, except that he was pretty and delicate-looking – the two girls had stolen along the inner side of the hedge between us and the road, and had watched the proceedings of the foreigners on the outer side. Those proceedings resulted in the performance of the following extra-ordinary tricks.

They first looked up the road, and down the road, and made sure that they were alone. Then they all three faced about, and stared hard in the direction of our house. Then they jabbered and disputed in their own language, and looked at each other like men in doubt. Then they all turned to their little English boy, as if they expected *him* to help them. And then the chief Indian, who spoke English, said to the boy, "Hold out your hand."

On hearing those dreadful words, my daughter Penelope said she didn't know what prevented her heart from flying straight out of her. I thought privately that it might have been her stays.[1] All I said, how-

---

1   Betteredge refers here to Penelope's corset.

ever, was, "You make my flesh creep." (*Nota bene:*[1] Women like these little compliments.)

Well, when the Indian said, "Hold out your hand," the boy shrunk back, and shook his head, and said he didn't like it. The Indian, thereupon, asked him (not at all unkindly), whether he would like to be sent back to London, and left where they had found him, sleeping in an empty basket in a market – a hungry, ragged, and forsaken little boy. This, it seems, ended the difficulty. The little chap unwillingly held out his hand. Upon that, the Indian took a bottle from his bosom, and poured out of it some black stuff, like ink, into the palm of the boy's hand. The Indian – first touching the boy's head, and making signs over it in the air – then said, "Look." The boy became quite stiff, and stood like a statue, looking into the ink in the hollow of his hand.

(So far, it seemed to me to be juggling, accompanied by a foolish waste of ink. I was beginning to feel sleepy again, when Penelope's next words stirred me up.)

The Indians looked up the road and down the road once more – and then the chief Indian said these words to the boy: "See the English gentleman from foreign parts."

The boy said, "I see him."

The Indian said, "Is it on the road to this house, and on no other, that the English gentleman will travel to-day?"

The boy said, "It is on the road to this house, and on no other, that the English gentleman will travel to-day."

The Indian put a second question – after waiting a little first. He said: "Has the English gentleman got It about him?"

The boy answered – also, after waiting a little first – "Yes." The Indian put a third and last question: "Will the English gentleman come here, as he has promised to come, at the close of day?"

The boy said, "I can't tell."

The Indian asked why.

The boy said, "I am tired. The mist rises in my head, and puzzles me. I can see no more to-day."

With that, the catechism ended. The chief Indian said something in his own language to the other two, pointing to the boy, and pointing towards the town, in which (as we afterwards discovered) they

---

1   *Nota bene* is a Latin phrase meaning "Note well."

were lodged. He then, after making more signs on the boy's head, blew on his forehead, and so woke him up with a start. After that, they all went on their way towards the town, and the girls saw them no more.[1]

Most things they say have a moral, if you only look for it. What was the moral of this?

The moral was, as I thought: First, that the chief juggler had heard Mr. Franklin's arrival talked of among the servants out-of-doors, and saw his way to making a little money by it. Second, that he and his men and boy (with a view to making the said money) meant to hang about till they saw my lady drive home, and then to come back, and foretell Mr. Franklin's arrival by magic. Third, that Penelope had heard them rehearsing their hocus-pocus, like actors rehearsing a play. Fourth, that I should do well to have an eye, that evening, on the plate-basket. Fifth, that Penelope would do well to cool down, and leave me, her father, to doze off again in the sun.

That appeared to me to be the sensible view. If you know anything of the ways of young women, you won't be surprised to hear that Penelope wouldn't take it. The moral of the thing was serious, according to my daughter. She particularly reminded me of the Indian's third question, Has the English gentleman got It about him? "Oh, father!" says Penelope, clasping her hands, "don't joke about this. What does 'It' mean?"

"We'll ask Mr. Franklin, my dear," I said, "if you can wait till Mr. Franklin comes." I winked to show I meant that in joke. Penelope took it quite seriously. My girl's earnestness tickled me. "What on earth should Mr. Franklin know about it?" I inquired. "Ask him," says Penelope. "And see whether *he* thinks it a laughing matter, too." With that parting shot, my daughter left me.

I settled it with myself, when she was gone, that I really would ask Mr. Franklin — mainly to set Penelope's mind at rest. What was said between us, when I did ask him, later on that same day, you will find set out fully in its proper place. But as I don't wish to raise your

---

1 Though sceptical of mesmerism by 1868, Collins was interested enough in it earlier in his life to research the subject and write six essays titled "Magnetic Evenings at Home" for George Henry Lewes's *Leader* between January 17 and March 13, 1852. Lewes followed the series with a response titled "The Fallacy of Clairvoyance" (March 27, 1852), which Collins answered with an article titled "The Incredible Not Always Impossible" (April 3, 1852).

expectations and then disappoint them, I will take leave to warn you here – before we go any further – that you won't find the ghost of a joke in our conversation on the subject of the jugglers. To my great surprise, Mr. Franklin, like Penelope, took the thing seriously. How seriously, you will understand, when I tell you that, in his opinion, "It" meant the Moonstone.

★1

CHAPTER IV

I AM truly sorry to detain you over me and my beehive chair. A sleepy old man, in a sunny back yard, is not an interesting object, I am well aware. But things must be put down in their places, as things actually happened – and you must please to jog on a little while longer with me, in expectation of Mr. Franklin Blake's arrival later in the day.

Before I had time to doze off again, after my daughter Penelope had left me, I was disturbed by a rattling of plates and dishes in the servants' hall, which meant that dinner was ready. Taking my own meals in my own sitting-room, I had nothing to do with the servants' dinner, except to wish them a good stomach to it all round, previous to composing myself once more in my chair. I was just stretching my legs, when out bounced another woman on me. Not my daughter again; only Nancy, the kitchen-maid,[2] this time. I was straight in her way out; and I observed, as she asked me to let her by, that she had a sulky face – a thing which, as head of the servants, I never allow, on principle, to pass me without inquiry.

"What are you turning your back on your dinner for?" I asked. "What's wrong now, Nancy?"

Nancy tried to push by, without answering; upon which I rose up, and took her by the ear. She is a nice plump young lass, and it is customary with me to adopt that manner of showing that I personally approve of a girl.

"What's wrong now?" I said once more.

1 This asterisk marks the end of the January 4, 1868 serial number of *The Moonstone*. Hereafter, an asterisk will mark the end of each original serial number. The divisions from the original three-volume edition are also marked in the text. See "A Note on the Text" pages 40-44, for specific information about serial installments of the novel.

2 The kitchen-maid in a Victorian home helped prepare and cook the meals.

"Rosanna's late again for dinner," says Nancy. "And I'm sent to fetch her in. All the hard work falls on my shoulders in this house. Let me alone, Mr. Betteredge!"

The person here mentioned as Rosanna was our second housemaid.[1] Having a kind of pity for our second housemaid (why, you shall presently know), and seeing in Nancy's face that she would fetch her fellow-servant in with more hard words than might be needful under the circumstances, it struck me that I had nothing particular to do, and that I might as well fetch Rosanna myself; giving her a hint to be punctual in future, which I knew she would take kindly from *me*.

"Where is Rosanna?" I inquired.

"At the sands, of course!" says Nancy, with a toss of her head. "She had another of her fainting fits this morning, and she asked to go out and get a breath of fresh air. I have no patience with her!"

"Go back to your dinner, my girl," I said. "I have patience with her, and I'll fetch her in."

Nancy (who has a fine appetite) looked pleased. When she looks pleased, she looks nice. When she looks nice, I chuck her under the chin. It isn't immorality – it's only habit.

Well, I took my stick, and set off for the sands.

No! it won't do to set off yet. I am sorry again to detain you; but you really must hear the story of the sands, and the story of Rosanna – for this reason, that the matter of the Diamond touches them both nearly. How hard I try to get on with my statement without stopping by the way, and how badly I succeed! But, there! – Persons and Things do turn up so vexatiously in this life, and will in a manner insist on being noticed. Let us take it easy, and let us take it short; we shall be in the thick of the mystery soon, I promise you!

Rosanna (to put the Person before the Thing, which is but common politeness) was the only new servant in our house. About four months before the time I am writing of, my lady had been in London, and had gone over a Reformatory,[2] intended to save forlorn women from drifting back into bad ways, after they had got released

---

1   A housemaid in a Victorian home did most of the bedroom work – cleaning, laundry, beds, and the like. As second housemaid, Rosanna Spearman was low on the domestic totem pole.

2   Private sponsors funded these half-way homes for the morally fallen or otherwise disadvantaged.

from prison. The matron, seeing my lady took an interest in the place, pointed out a girl to her, named Rosanna Spearman, and told her a most miserable story, which I haven't the heart to repeat here; for I don't like to be made wretched without any use, and no more do you. The upshot of it was, that Rosanna Spearman had been a thief, and not being of the sort that get up Companies in the City, and rob from thousands, instead of only robbing from one, the law laid hold of her, and the prison and the Reformatory followed the lead of the law. The matron's opinion of Rosanna was (in spite of what she had done) that the girl was one in a thousand, and that she only wanted a chance to prove herself worthy of any Christian woman's interest in her. My lady (being a Christian woman, if ever there was one yet) said to the matron, upon that, "Rosanna Spearman shall have her chance, in my service." In a week afterwards, Rosanna Spearman entered this establishment as our second housemaid.

Not a soul was told the girl's story, excepting Miss Rachel and me. My lady, doing me the honour to consult me about most things, consulted me about Rosanna. Having fallen a good deal latterly into the late Sir John's way of always agreeing with my lady, I agreed with her heartily about Rosanna Spearman.

A fairer chance no girl could have had than was given to this poor girl of ours. None of the servants could cast her past life in her teeth, for none of the servants knew what it had been. She had her wages and her privileges, like the rest of them; and every now and then a friendly word from my lady, in private, to encourage her. In return, she showed herself, I am bound to say, well worthy of the kind treatment bestowed upon her. Though far from strong, and troubled occasionally with those fainting-fits already mentioned, she went about her work modestly and uncomplainingly, doing it carefully, and doing it well. But, somehow, she failed to make friends among the other womenservants, excepting my daughter Penelope, who was always kind to Rosanna, though never intimate with her.

I hardly know what the girl did to offend them. There was certainly no beauty about her to make the others envious; she was the plainest woman in the house, with the additional misfortune of having one shoulder bigger than the other. What the servants chiefly resented, I think, was her silent tongue and her solitary ways. She read or worked in leisure hours when the rest gossiped. And when it came to her turn to go out, nine times out of ten she quietly put on her bonnet, and had her turn by herself. She never quarrelled, she never took offence; she only kept a certain distance, obstinately and civilly, between the rest of them and herself. Add to this that, plain as she was, there was just a dash of something that wasn't like a housemaid, and that *was* like a lady, about her. It might have been in her voice, or it might have been in her face. All I can say is, that the other women pounced on it like lightning the first day she came into the house, and said (which was most unjust) that Rosanna Spearman gave herself airs.

Having now told the story of Rosanna, I have only to notice one of the many queer ways of this strange girl to get on next to the story of the sands.

Our house is high up on the Yorkshire coast, and close by the sea. We have got beautiful walks all round us, in every direction but one. That one I acknowledge to be a horrid walk. It leads, for a quarter of a mile, through a melancholy plantation of firs, and brings you out between low cliffs on the loneliest and ugliest little bay on all our coast.

The sand-hills here run down to the sea, and end in two spits of rock jutting out opposite each other, till you lose sight of them in the water. One is called the North Spit, and one the South. Between the two, shifting backwards and forwards at certain seasons of the year, lies the most horrible quicksand on the shores of Yorkshire. At the turn of the tide, something goes on in the unknown deeps below, which sets the whole face of the quicksand shivering and trembling in a manner most remarkable to see, and which has given to it, among the people in our parts, the name of the Shivering Sand. A great bank, half a mile out, nigh the mouth of the bay, breaks the force of the main ocean coming in from the offing. Winter and summer, when the tide flows over the quicksand, the sea seems to leave the waves behind it on the bank, and rolls its waters in smoothly with a heave, and covers the sand in silence. A lonesome and a horrid retreat, I can tell you! No boat ever ventures into this bay. No children from our fishing-village, called Cobb's Hole,[1] ever come here to play. The very birds of the air,

---

1   Cobb's Hole is a fictional fishing village, perhaps modelled after a fishing hamlet named Hobb Holes. The neighbouring township, Frizinghall, is fictional as well, perhaps modelled after Runswick Bay, a town near Whitby, where Collins stayed in

as it seems to me, give the Shivering Sand a wide berth. That a young woman, with dozens of nice walks to choose from, and company to go with her, if she only said "Come!" should prefer this place, and should sit and work or read in it, all alone, when it's her turn out, I grant you, passes belief. It's true, nevertheless, account for it as you may, that this was Rosanna Spearman's favourite walk, except when she went once or twice to Cobb's Hole, to see the only friend she had in our neighbourhood, of whom more anon. It's also true that I was now setting out for this same place, to fetch the girl in to dinner, which brings us round happily to our former point, and starts us fair again on our way to the sands.

I saw no sign of the girl in the plantation. When I got out, through the sand-hills, on to the beach, there she was, in her little straw bonnet, and her plain grey cloak that she always wore to hide her deformed shoulder as much as might be – there she was, all alone, looking out on the quicksand and the sea.

She started when I came up with her, and turned her head away from me. Not looking me in the face being another of the proceedings which, as head of the servants, I never allow, on principle, to pass without inquiry – I turned her round my way, and saw that she was crying. My bandanna handkerchief – one of six beauties given to me by my lady – was handy in my pocket. I took it out, and I said to Rosanna, "Come and sit down, my dear, on the slope of the beach along with me. I'll dry your eyes for you first, and then I'll make so bold as to ask what you have been crying about."

When you come to my age, you will find sitting down on the slope of a beach a much longer job than you think it now. By the time I was settled, Rosanna had dried her own eyes with a very inferior handkerchief to mine – cheap cambric.[1] She looked very quiet, and very wretched; but she sat down by me like a good girl, when I told her. When you want to comfort a woman by the shortest way, take her on your knee. I thought of this golden rule. But there! Rosanna wasn't Nancy, and that's the truth of it!

"Now, tell me, my dear," I said, "what are you crying about?"

1861. Some of this information has been taken from Harry Mead's article "On the Trail of Yorkshire's Moonstone" (*Yorkshire Magazine*, Fall 1994: 26-31). See note 3 on page 59 for more information on setting.

1 Rosanna's handkerchief is made of a white linen or cotton fabric.

"About the years that are gone, Mr. Betteredge," says Rosanna quietly. "My past life still comes back to me sometimes." "Come, come, my girl," I said, "your past life is all sponged out. Why can't you forget it?"

She took me by one of the lappets[1] of my coat. I am a slovenly old man, and a good deal of my meat and drink gets splashed about on my clothes. Sometimes one of the women, and sometimes another, cleans me of my grease. The day before, Rosanna had taken out a spot for me on the lappet of my coat, with a new composition, warranted to remove anything. The grease was gone, but there was a little dull place left on the nap of the cloth where the grease had been. The girl pointed to that place, and shook her head.

"The stain is taken off," she said. "But the place shows, Mr. Betteredge – the place shows!"

A remark which takes a man unawares by means of his own coat is not an easy remark to answer. Something in the girl herself, too, made me particularly sorry for her just then. She had nice brown eyes, plain as she was in other ways – and she looked at me with a sort of respect for my happy old age and my good character, as things for ever out of her own reach, which made my heart heavy for our second housemaid. Not feeling myself able to comfort her, there was only one other thing to do. That thing was – to take her in to dinner.

"Help me up," I said. "You're late for dinner, Rosanna – and I have come to fetch you in."

"You, Mr. Betteredge!" says she.

"They told Nancy to fetch you," I said. "But I thought you might like your scolding better, my dear, if it came from me."

Instead of helping me up, the poor thing stole her hand into mine, and gave it a little squeeze. She tried hard to keep from crying again, and succeeded – for which I respected her. "You're very kind, Mr. Betteredge," she said. "I don't want any dinner to-day – let me bide a little longer here."

"What makes you like to be here?" I asked. "What is it that brings you everlastingly to this miserable place?"

"Something draws me to it," says the girl, making images with her finger in the sand. "I try to keep away from it, and I can't. Some-

---

1 A lappet is a decorative flap or fold on a garment.

times," says she in a low voice, as if she was frightened at her own fancy, "sometimes, Mr. Betteredge, I think that my grave is waiting for me here."

"There's roast mutton and suet-pudding[1] waiting for you!" says I. "Go in to dinner directly. This is what comes, Rosanna, of thinking on an empty stomach!" I spoke severely, being naturally indignant (at my time of life) to hear a young woman of five-and-twenty talking about her latter end!

She didn't seem to hear me: she put her hand on my shoulder, and kept me where I was, sitting by her side.

"I think the place has laid a spell on me," she said. "I dream of it night after night; I think of it when I sit stitching at my work. You know I am grateful, Mr. Betteredge – you know I try to deserve your kindness, and my lady's confidence in me. But I wonder sometimes whether the life here is too quiet and too good for such a woman as I am, after all I have gone through, Mr. Betteredge – after all I have gone through. It's more lonely to me to be among the other servants, knowing I am not what they are, than it is to be here. My lady doesn't know, the matron at the Reformatory doesn't know, what a dreadful reproach honest people are in themselves to a woman like me. Don't scold me, there's a dear good man. I do my work, don't I? Please not to tell my lady I am discontented – I am not. My mind's unquiet, sometimes, that's all." She snatched her hand off my shoulder, and suddenly pointed down to the quicksand. "Look!" she said. "Isn't it wonderful? Isn't it terrible? I have seen it dozens of times, and it's always as new to me as if I had never seen it before!"

I looked where she pointed. The tide was on the turn, and the horrid sand began to shiver. The broad brown face of it heaved slowly, and then dimpled and quivered all over. "Do you know what it looks like to *me*?" says Rosanna, catching me by the shoulder again. "It looks as if it had hundreds of suffocating people under it – all struggling to get to the surface, and all sinking lower and lower in the dreadful deeps! Throw a stone in, Mr. Betteredge! Throw a stone in, and let's see the sand suck it down!"

Here was unwholesome talk! Here was an empty stomach feeding on an unquiet mind! My answer – a pretty sharp one, in the poor

---

1 Suet-pudding consisted of flour and suet, the solid fat around the kidneys of cattle or sheep.

girl's own interests, I promise you! – was at my tongue's end, when it was snapped short off on a sudden by a voice among the sand-hills shouting for me by my name. "Betteredge!" cries the voice, "where are you?" "Here!" I shouted out in return, without a notion in my mind of who it was. Rosanna started to her feet, and stood looking towards the voice. I was just thinking of getting on my own legs next, when I was staggered by a sudden change in the girl's face.

Her complexion turned of a beautiful red, which I had never seen in it before; she brightened all over with a kind of speechless and breathless surprise. "Who is it?" I asked. Rosanna gave me back my own question. "Oh! who is it?" she said softly, more to herself than to me. I twisted round on the sand, and looked behind me. There, coming out on us from among the hills, was a bright-eyed young gentleman, dressed in a beautiful fawn-coloured suit, with gloves and hat to match, with a rose in his button-hole, and a smile on his face that might have set the Shivering Sand itself smiling at him in return. Before I could get on my legs, he plumped down on the sand by the side of me, put his arm round my neck, foreign fashion, and gave me a hug that fairly squeezed the breath out of my body. "Dear old Betteredge!" says he. "I owe you seven-and-sixpence. Now do you know who I am?"

Lord bless us and save us! Here – four good hours before we expected him – was Mr. Franklin Blake!

Before I could say a word, I saw Mr. Franklin, a little surprised to all appearance, look up from me to Rosanna. Following his lead, I looked at the girl too. She was blushing of a deeper red than ever, seemingly at having caught Mr. Franklin's eye; and she turned and left us suddenly, in a confusion quite unaccountable to my mind, without either making her curtsey to the gentleman or saying a word to me. Very unlike her usual self: a civiller and better-behaved servant, in general, you never met with.

"That's an odd girl," says Mr. Franklin. "I wonder what she sees in me to surprise her?"

"I suppose, sir," I answered, drolling on our young gentleman's Continental education, "it's the varnish from foreign parts."

I set down here Mr. Franklin's careless question, and my foolish answer, as a consolation and encouragement to all stupid people – it being, as I have remarked, a great satisfaction to our inferior fellow-creatures to find that their betters are, on occasions, no brighter than they are. Neither Mr. Franklin, with his wonderful foreign training, nor I, with my age, experience, and natural mother-wit, had the ghost of an idea of what Rosanna Spearman's unaccountable behaviour really meant. She was out of our thoughts, poor soul, before we had seen the last flutter of her little grey cloak among the sand-hills. And what of that? you will ask, naturally enough. Read on, good friend, as patiently as you can, and perhaps you will be as sorry for Rosanna Spearman as I was, when I found out the truth.

CHAPTER V

The first thing I did, after we were left together alone, was to make a third attempt to get up from my seat on the sand. Mr. Franklin stopped me.

"There is one advantage about this horrid place," he said; "we have got it all to ourselves. Stay where you are, Betteredge; I have something to say to you."

While he was speaking, I was looking at him, and trying to see something of the boy I remembered, in the man before me. The man put me out. Look as I might, I could see no more of his boy's rosy cheeks than of his boy's trim little jacket. His complexion had got pale: his face, at the lower part, was covered, to my great surprise and disappointment, with a curly brown beard and mustachios. He had a lively touch-and-go way with him, very pleasant and engaging, I admit; but nothing to compare with his free-and-easy manners of other times. To make matters worse, he had promised to be tall, and had not kept his promise. He was neat, and slim, and well made; but he wasn't by an inch or two up to the middle height. In short, he baffled me altogether. The years that had passed had left nothing of his old self, except the bright, straightforward look in his eyes. There I found our nice boy again, and there I concluded to stop in my investigation.

"Welcome back to the old place, Mr. Franklin," I said. "All the more welcome, sir, that you have come some hours before we expected you."

"I have a reason for coming before you expected me," answered Mr. Franklin. "I suspect, Betteredge, that I have been followed and watched in London, for the last three or four days; and I have travelled by the morning instead of the afternoon train, because I wanted to give a certain dark-looking stranger the slip."

Those words did more than surprise me. They brought back to my mind, in a flash, the three jugglers, and Penelope's notion that they meant some mischief to Mr. Franklin Blake.

"Who's watching you, sir, – and why?" I inquired.

"Tell me about the three Indians you have had at the house today," says Mr. Franklin, without noticing my question. "It's just possible, Betteredge, that my stranger and your three jugglers may turn out to be pieces of the same puzzle."

"How do you come to know about the jugglers, sir?" I asked, putting one question on the top of another, which was bad manners, I own. But you don't expect much from poor human nature – so don't expect much from me.

"I saw Penelope at the house," says Mr. Franklin; "and Penelope told me. Your daughter promised to be a pretty girl, Betteredge, and she has kept her promise. Penelope has got a small ear and a small foot. Did the late Mrs. Betteredge possess those inestimable advantages?"

"The late Mrs. Betteredge possessed a good many defects, sir," says I. "One of them (if you will pardon my mentioning it) was never keeping to the matter in hand. She was more like a fly than a woman: she couldn't settle on anything."

"She would just have suited me," says Mr. Franklin. "I never settle on anything either. Betteredge, your edge is better than ever. Your daughter said as much, when I asked for particulars about the jugglers. 'Father will tell you, sir. He's a wonderful man for his age; and he expresses himself beautifully.' Penelope's own words – blushing divinely. Not even my respect for you prevented me from – never mind; I knew her when she was a child, and she's none the worse for it. Let's be serious. What did the jugglers do?"

I was something dissatisfied with my daughter – not for letting Mr. Franklin kiss her; Mr. Franklin was welcome to *that* – but for forcing me to tell her foolish story at second hand. However, there was no help for it now but to mention the circumstances. Mr. Franklin's merriment all died away as I went on. He sat knitting his eyebrows, and twisting his beard. When I had done, he repeated after me two of the questions which the chief juggler had put to the boy – seemingly for the purpose of fixing them well in his mind.

"'Is it on the road to this house, and on no other, that the English gentleman will travel to-day?' 'Has the English gentleman got It about him?' I suspect," says Mr. Franklin, pulling a little sealed paper parcel out of his pocket, "that 'It' means *this*. And 'this,' Betteredge, means my uncle Herncastle's famous Diamond."

"Good Lord, sir!" I broke out, "how do you come to be in charge of the wicked Colonel's Diamond?"

"The wicked Colonel's will has left his Diamond as a birthday present to my cousin Rachel," says Mr. Franklin. "And my father, as the wicked Colonel's executor, has given it in charge to me to bring down here."

If the sea, then oozing in smoothly over the Shivering Sand, had been changed into dry land before my own eyes, I doubt if I could have been more surprised than I was when Mr. Franklin spoke those words.

"The Colonel's Diamond left to Miss Rachel!" says I. "And your father, sir, the Colonel's executor! Why, I would have laid any bet you like, Mr. Franklin, that your father wouldn't have touched the Colonel with a pair of tongs!"

"Strong language, Betteredge! What was there against the Colonel? He belonged to your time, not to mine. Tell me what you know about him, and I'll tell you how my father came to be his executor, and more besides. I have made some discoveries in London about my uncle Herncastle and his Diamond, which have rather an ugly look to my eyes; and I want you to confirm them. You called him the 'wicked Colonel' just now. Search you memory, my old friend, and tell me why."

I saw he was in earnest, and I told him.

Here follows the substance of what I said, written out entirely for your benefit. Pay attention to it, or you will be all abroad, when we get deeper into the story. Clear your mind of the children, or the dinner, or the new bonnet, or what not. Try if you can't forget politics, horses, prices in the City, and grievances at the club. I hope you won't take this freedom on my part amiss; it's only a way I have of appealing to the gentle reader. Lord! haven't I seen you with the greatest authors in your hands, and don't I know how ready your attention is to wander when it's a book that asks for it, instead of a person?

I spoke, a little way back, of my lady's father, the old lord with the short temper and the long tongue. He had five children in all. Two sons to begin with; then, after a long time, his wife broke out breeding again, and the three young ladies came briskly one after the other, as fast as the nature of things would permit; my mistress, as before mentioned, being the youngest and best of the three. Of the two sons, the eldest, Arthur, inherited the title and estates. The second, the Honourable John, got a fine fortune left him by a relative, and went into the army.

It's an ill bird, they say, that fouls its own nest.[1] I look on the noble family of the Herncastles as being my nest; and I shall take it as a favour if I am not expected to enter into particulars on the subject of the Honourable John. He was, I honestly believe, one of the greatest blackguards that ever lived. I can hardly say more or less for him than that. He went into the army, beginning in the Guards.[2] He had to leave the Guards before he was two-and-twenty – never mind why. They are very strict in the army, and they were too strict for the Honourable John. He went out to India to see whether they were equally strict there, and to try a little active service. In the matter of bravery (to give him his due), he was a mixture of bull-dog and game-cock, with a dash of the savage. He was at the taking of Seringapatam. Soon afterwards he changed into another regiment, and, in course of time, changed again into a third. In the third he got his last step as lieutenant-colonel, and, getting that, got also a sunstroke, and came home to England.

---

1 Another of Betteredge's colourful proverbs, this one dates from the eleventh century: "Nidos commaculans immundus habetitur ales" (Egbert Lüttich's *Fecunda Ratis*, line 148).

2 John Herncastle began army life with a brief stint in the Queen's "Household Troops," also known as the Guards. These were the army units – the Life Guards, the Royal Horse Guards, and the Foot Guards among them – assigned to protect the sovereign.

He came back with a character that closed the doors of all his family against him, my lady (then just married) taking the lead, and declaring (with Sir John's approval, of course) that her brother should never enter any house of hers. There was more than one slur on the Colonel that made people shy of him; but the blot of the Diamond is all I need mention here.

It was said he had got possession of his Indian jewel by means which, bold as he was, he didn't dare acknowledge. He never attempted to sell it – not being in need of money, and not (to give him his due again) making money an object. He never gave it away; he never even showed it to any living soul. Some said he was afraid of its getting him into a difficulty with the military authorities; others (very ignorant indeed of the real nature of the man) said he was afraid, if he showed it, of its costing him his life.

There was perhaps a grain of truth mixed up with this last report. It was false to say that he was afraid; but it was a fact that his life had been twice threatened in India; and it was firmly believed that the Moonstone was at the bottom of it. When he came back to England, and found himself avoided by everybody, the Moonstone was thought to be at the bottom of it again. The mystery of the Colonel's life got in the Colonel's way, and outlawed him, as you may say, among his own people. The men wouldn't let him into their clubs; the women – more than one – whom he wanted to marry, refused him; friends and relations got too near-sighted to see him in the street.

Some men in this mess would have tried to set themselves right with the world. But to give in, even when he was wrong, and had all society against him, was not the way of the Honourable John. He had kept the Diamond, in flat defiance of assassination, in India. He kept the Diamond, in flat defiance of public opinion, in England. There you have the portrait of the man before you, as in a picture: a character that braved everything; and a face, handsome as it was, that looked possessed by the devil.

We heard different rumours about him from time to time. Sometimes they said he was given up to smoking opium and collecting old books; sometimes he was reported to be trying strange things in chemistry; sometimes he was seen carousing and amusing himself among the lowest people in the lowest slums of London. Anyhow, a solitary, vicious, underground life was the life the Colonel led. Once, and once only, after his return to England, I myself saw him, face to face.

About two years before the time of which I am now writing, and about a year and a half before the time of his death, the Colonel came unexpectedly to my lady's house in London. It was the night of Miss Rachel's birthday, the twenty-first of June; and there was a party in honour of it, as usual. I received a message from the footman[1] to say that a gentleman wanted to see me. Going up into the hall, there I found the Colonel, wasted, and worn, and old, and shabby, and as wild and as wicked as ever."Go up to my sister," says he; "and say that I have called to wish my niece many happy returns of the day."

He had made attempts by letter, more than once already, to be reconciled with my lady, for no other purpose, I am firmly persuaded, than to annoy her. But this was the first time he had actually come to the house. I had it on the tip of my tongue to say that my mistress had a party that night. But the devilish look of him daunted me. I went upstairs with his message, and left him, by his own desire, waiting in the hall. The servants stood staring at him, at a distance, as if he was a walking engine of destruction, loaded with powder and shot, and likely to go off among them at a moment's notice.

My lady had a dash – no more – of the family temper. "Tell Colonel Herncastle," she said, when I gave her her brother's message, "that Miss Verinder is engaged, and that *I* decline to see him." I tried

---

1   The footman in a Victorian home was a male servant of a lower rank than butler or house-steward. He cleaned, answered doors, waited tables, announced visitors, and performed other similar household duties. The footman would dress in livery – knee breeches and powdered wigs. Collins was particular enough about the specific details of his work that he wrote to Harper Brothers, his American publishers, about inaccuracies in illustrations that accompanied his text: "In the second number, there is a mistake (as we should call it in England) of presenting Gabriel Betteredge in *livery*. As head-servant, he would wear plain black clothes and would look, with his white cravat and grey hair, like an old clergyman. I only mention this for future illustration – and because I see the dramatic effect of the story (in the first number) conveyed with such real intelligence by the artist that I want to see him taking the right direction, even in the smallest technical details." See Appendix E, 4 for the full text of this letter. Harper Brothers, claiming at the front of each weekly number that the text was "Richly Illustrated," provided its readers with nearly seventy illustrations during the novel's run. The artist, William Jewett, never corrected the mistake, presenting sketches of Betteredge in livery ten more times.

to plead for a civiller answer than that; knowing the Colonel's constitutional superiority to the restraints which govern gentlemen in general. Quite useless! The family temper flashed out at me directly. "When I want your advice," says my lady, "you know that I always ask for it. I don't ask for it now." I went downstairs with the message, of which I took the liberty of presenting a new and amended edition of my own contriving, as follows: "My lady and Miss Rachel regret that they are engaged, Colonel; and beg to be excused having the honour of seeing you."

I expected him to break out, even at that polite way of putting it. To my surprise he did nothing of the sort; he alarmed me by taking the thing with an unnatural quiet. His eyes, of a glittering bright grey, just settled on me for a moment; and he laughed, not *out* of himself, like other people, but *into* himself, in a soft, chuckling, horridly mischievous way. "Thank you, Betteredge," he said. "I shall remember my niece's birthday." With that, he turned on his heel, and walked out of the house.

The next birthday came round, and we heard he was ill in bed. Six months afterwards – that is to say, six months before the time I am now writing of – there came a letter from a highly respectable clergyman to my lady. It communicated two wonderful things in the way of family news. First, that the Colonel had forgiven his sister on his death-bed. Second, that he had forgiven everybody else, and had made a most edifying end. I have myself (in spite of the bishops and the clergy) an unfeigned respect for the Church; but I am firmly persuaded, at the same time, that the devil remained in undisturbed possession of the Honourable John, and that the last abominable act in the life of that abominable man was (saving your presence) to take the clergyman in!

This was the sum-total of what I had to tell Mr. Franklin. I remarked that he listened more and more eagerly the longer I went on. Also, that the story of the Colonel being sent away from his sister's door, on the occasion of his niece's birthday, seemed to strike Mr. Franklin like a shot that had hit the mark. Though he didn't acknowledge it, I saw that I had made him uneasy, plainly enough, in his face.

"You have said your say, Betteredge," he remarked. "It's my turn now. Before, however, I tell you what discoveries I have made in

London, and how I came to be mixed up in this matter of the Diamond, I want to know one thing. You look, my old friend, as if you didn't quite understand the object to be answered by this consultation of ours. Do your looks belie you?"

"No, sir," I said. "My looks, on this occasion at any rate, tell the truth."

"In that case," says Mr. Franklin, "suppose I put you up to my point of view, before we go any further. I see three very serious questions involved in the Colonel's birthday-gift to my cousin Rachel. Follow me carefully, Betteredge; and count me off on your fingers, if it will help you," says Mr. Franklin, with a certain pleasure in showing how clear-headed he could be, which reminded me wonderfully of old times when he was a boy. "Question the first: Was the Colonel's Diamond the object of a conspiracy in India? Question the second: Has the conspiracy followed the Colonel's Diamond to England? Question the third: Did the Colonel know the conspiracy followed the Diamond; and has he purposely left a legacy of trouble and danger to his sister, through the innocent medium of his sister's child? *That* is what I am driving at, Betteredge. Don't let me frighten you."

It was all very well to say that, but he *had* frightened me.

If he was right, here was our quiet English house suddenly invaded by a devilish Indian Diamond – bringing after it a conspiracy of living rogues, set loose on us by the vengeance of a dead man.[1] There was our situation as revealed to me in Mr. Franklin's last words! Who ever heard the like of it – in the nineteenth century, mind; in an age of progress, and in a country which rejoices in the blessings of the British constitution? Nobody ever heard the like of it, and, consequently, nobody can be expected to believe it. I shall go on with my story, however, in spite of that.

When you get a sudden alarm, of the sort that I had got now, nine times out of ten the place you feel it in is your stomach. When you feel it in your stomach, your attention wanders, and you begin to fidget. I fidgeted silently in my place on the sand. Mr. Franklin

---

1 Betteredge unwittingly lights upon one of the magical aspects of the story, the unsettling juxtaposition of the Moonstone's exotica and the "quiet English house." The juxtaposition brings to mind Dickens's pronouncement about the story, that "it is a very curious story – wild, and yet domestic" (*The Letters of Charles Dickens*, 3 volumes, ed. Walter Dexter. London: Constable, 1938: III, 534).

noticed me, contending with a perturbed stomach or mind – which you please; they mean the same thing – and, checking himself just as he was starting with his part of the story, said to me sharply, "What do you want?"

What did I want? I didn't tell *him*; but I'll tell *you*, in confidence. I wanted a whiff of my pipe, and a turn at *Robinson Crusoe*.

★

CHAPTER VI

KEEPING my private sentiments to myself, I respectfully requested Mr. Franklin to go on. Mr. Franklin replied, "Don't fidget, Betteredge," and went on.

Our young gentleman's first words informed me that his discoveries, concerning the wicked Colonel and the Diamond, had begun with a visit which he had paid (before he came to us) to the family lawyer, at Hampstead.[1] A chance word dropped by Mr. Franklin, when the two were alone, one day, after dinner, revealed that he had been charged by his father with a birthday present to be taken to Miss Rachel. One thing led to another; and it ended in the lawyer mentioning what the present really was, and how the friendly connexion between the late Colonel and Mr. Blake, Senior, had taken its rise. The facts here are really so extraordinary, that I doubt if I can trust my own language to do justice to them. I prefer trying to report Mr. Franklin's discoveries, as nearly as may be, in Mr. Franklin's own words.

"You remember the time, Betteredge," he said, "when my father was trying to prove his title to that unlucky Dukedom? Well! that was also the time when my uncle Herncastle returned from India. My father discovered that his brother-in-law was in possession of certain papers which were likely to be of service to him in his lawsuit. He called on the Colonel, on pretence of welcoming him back to England. The Colonel was not to be deluded in that way. 'You want something,' he said, 'or you would never have compromised your reputation by calling on *me*.' My father saw that the one chance for

---

1 Hampstead, now part of the borough of Camden, is northwest of the city centre. Collins lived in Hampstead for twelve years as a young boy.

him was to show his hand: he admitted, at once, that he wanted the papers. The Colonel asked for a day to consider his answer. His answer came in the shape of a most extraordinary letter, which my friend the lawyer showed me. The Colonel began by saying that he wanted something of my father, and that he begged to propose an exchange of friendly services between them. The fortune of war (that was the expression he used) had placed him in possession of one of the largest Diamonds in the world; and he had reason to believe that neither he nor his precious jewel was safe in any house, in any quarter of the globe, which they occupied together. Under these alarming circumstances, he had determined to place his Diamond in the keeping of another person. That person was not expected to run any risk. He might deposit the precious stone in any place especially guarded and set apart – like a banker's or jeweller's strong-room – for the safe custody of valuables of high price. His main personal responsibility in the matter was to be of the passive kind. He was to undertake – either by himself, or by a trustworthy representative – to receive at a pre-arranged address, on certain pre-arranged days in every year, a note from the Colonel, simply stating the fact that he was a living man at that date. In the event of the date passing over without the note being received, the Colonel's silence might be taken as a sure token of the Colonel's death by murder. In that case, and in no other, certain sealed instructions relating to the disposal of the Diamond, and deposited with it, were to be opened, and followed implicitly. If my father chose to accept this strange charge, the Colonel's papers were at his disposal in return. That was the letter."

"What did your father do, sir?" I asked.

"Do?" says Mr. Franklin. "I'll tell you what he did. He brought the invaluable faculty, called common sense, to bear on the Colonel's letter. The whole thing, he declared, was simply absurd. Somewhere in his Indian wanderings, the Colonel had picked up with some wretched crystal which he took for a diamond. As for the danger of his being murdered, and the precautions devised to preserve his life and his piece of crystal, this was the nineteenth century, and any man in his senses had only to apply to the police. The Colonel had been a notorious opium-eater for years past; and, if the only way of getting at the valuable papers he possessed was by accepting a matter of opium as a matter of fact, my father was quite willing to take the ridiculous responsibility imposed on him – all the more readily that it involved no trouble to himself. The Diamond and the sealed instructions went into his banker's strong-room, and the Colonel's letters, periodically reporting him a living man, were received and opened by our family lawyer, Mr. Bruff, as my father's representative. No sensible person, in a similar position, could have viewed the matter in any other way. Nothing in this world, Betteredge, is probable unless it appeals to our own trumpery experience; and we only believe in a romance when we see it in a newspaper."

It was plain to me from this, that Mr. Franklin thought his father's notion about the Colonel hasty and wrong.

"What is your own private opinion about the matter, sir?" I asked.

"Let's finish the story of the Colonel first," says Mr. Franklin. "There is a curious want of system, Betteredge, in the English mind; and your question, my old friend, is an instance of it. When we are not occupied in making machinery, we are (mentally speaking) the most slovenly people in the universe."

"So much," I thought to myself, "for a foreign education! He has learned that way of girding at us in France, I suppose."

Mr. Franklin took up the lost thread, and went on.

"My father," he said, "got the papers he wanted, and never saw his brother-in-law again from that time. Year after year, on the pre-arranged days, the prearranged letter came from the Colonel, and was opened by Mr. Bruff. I have seen the letters, in a heap, all of them written in the same brief, business-like form of words: 'Sir, – This is to certify that I am still a living man. Let the Diamond be. John Herncastle.' That was all he ever wrote, and that came regularly to the day; until some six or eight months since, when the form of the letter varied for the first time. It ran now: 'Sir, – They tell me I am dying. Come to me, and help me to make my Will.' Mr. Bruff went, and found him, in the little suburban villa, surrounded by its own grounds, in which he had lived alone, ever since he had left India. He had dogs, cats, and birds to keep him company; but no human being near him, except the person who came daily to do the house-work, and the doctor at the bedside. The Will was a very simple matter.[1] The

---

1   This Will may be a very simple matter, but generally speaking, wills, lawyers, and the perplexities of laws governing inheritance were a staple of Collins's fiction, driving several of his novels, including *The Woman in White*, *No Name*, *Armadale*, and *Heart*

Colonel had dissipated the greater part of his fortune in his chemical investigations. His Will began and ended in three clauses, which he dictated from his bed, in perfect possession of his faculties. The first clause provided for the safe keeping and support of his animals. The second founded a professorship of experimental chemistry[1] at a northern university. The third bequeathed the Moonstone as a birthday present to his niece, on condition that my father would act as executor. My father at first refused to act. On second thoughts, however, he gave way, partly because he was assured that the executorship would involve him in no trouble; partly because Mr. Bruff suggested, in Rachel's interest, that the Diamond might be worth something, after all."

"Did the Colonel give any reason, sir," I inquired, "why he left the Diamond to Miss Rachel?"

"He not only gave the reason – he had the reason written in his Will," said Mr. Franklin. "I have got an extract, which you shall see presently. Don't be slovenly-minded, Betteredge! One thing at a time. You have heard about the Colonel's Will; now you must hear what happened after the Colonel's death. It was formally necessary to have the Diamond valued, before the Will could be proved. All the jewellers consulted, at once confirmed the Colonel's assertion that he possessed one of the largest diamonds in the world. The question of accurately valuing it presented some serious difficulties. Its size made it a phenomenon in the diamond-market; its colour placed it in a category by itself; and, to add to these elements of uncertainty, there was a defect, in the shape of a flaw, in the very heart of the stone. Even with this last serious drawback, however, the lowest of the various estimates given was twenty thousand pounds. Conceive my father's astonishment! He had been within a hair's-breadth of refusing to act as executor, and of allowing this magnificent jewel to be lost to the family. The interest he took in the matter now, induced him to open

---

and *Science.* Collins entered Lincoln's Inn to study law in 1846 and was called to the Bar in 1851; he never practised law, but he remained intrigued by it and its practitioners throughout his life.

1   The reader may recall here another of Collins's novels, *The Woman in White,* in which the villain Count Fosco is said to be "one of the first experimental chemists living, and has discovered, among other wonderful inventions, a means of petrifying the body after death, so as to preserve it, as hard as marble, to the end of time" (Epoch II, Chapter ii).

the sealed instructions which had been deposited with the Diamond. Mr. Bruff showed this document to me, with the other papers; and it suggests (to my mind) a clue to the nature of the conspiracy which threatened the Colonel's life."

"Then you do believe, sir," I said, "that there was a conspiracy?"

"Not possessing my father's excellent common sense," answered Mr. Franklin, "I believe the Colonel's life was threatened, exactly as the Colonel said. The sealed instructions, as I think, explain how it was that he died, after all, quietly in his bed. In the event of his death by violence (that is to say, in the absence of the regular letter from him at the appointed date), my father was then directed to send the Moonstone secretly to Amsterdam. It was to be deposited in that city with a famous diamond-cutter, and it was to be cut up into from four to six separate stones.[1] The stones were then to be sold for what they would fetch, and the proceeds were to be applied to the founding of that professorship of experimental chemistry, which the Colonel has since endowed by his Will. Now, Betteredge, exert those sharp wits of yours, and observe the conclusion to which the Colonel's instructions point!"

I instantly exerted my wits. They were of the slovenly English sort; and they consequently muddled it all, until Mr. Franklin took them in hand, and pointed out what they ought to see.

"Remark," says Mr. Franklin, "that the integrity of the Diamond, as a whole stone, is here artfully made dependent on the preservation from violence of the Colonel's life. He is not satisfied with saying to the enemies he dreads, 'Kill me – and you will be no nearer to the Diamond than you are now; it is where you can't get at it – in the guarded strong-room of a bank.' He says instead, 'Kill me – and the Diamond will be the Diamond no longer; its identity will be destroyed.' What does that mean?"

Here I had (as I thought) a flash of the wonderful foreign brightness.

"I know," I said. "It means lowering the value of the stone and cheating the rogues in that way!"

"Nothing of the sort," says Mr. Franklin. "I have inquired about that. The flawed Diamond, cut up, would actually fetch more than the

---

1 The Koh-i-Nor diamond, one of the diamonds mentioned by Collins as having inspired his Moonstone, was actually sent to Amsterdam and cut into smaller stones.

Diamond as it now is; for this plain reason – that from four to six perfect brilliants might be cut from it, which would be, collectively, worth more money than the large – but imperfect – single stone. If robbery for the purpose of gain was at the bottom of the conspiracy, the Colonel's instructions absolutely made the Diamond better worth stealing. More money could have been got for it, and the disposal of it in the diamond-market would have been infinitely easier, if it had passed through the hands of the workmen of Amsterdam."

"Lord bless us, sir!" I burst out. "What was the plot, then?"

"A plot organised among the Indians who originally owned the jewel," says Mr. Franklin – "a plot with some old Hindoo superstition at the bottom of it. That is my opinion, confirmed by a family paper which I have about me at this moment."

I saw, now, why the appearance of the three Indian jugglers at our house had presented itself to Mr. Franklin in the light of a circumstance worth noting.

"I don't want to force my opinion on you," Mr. Franklin went on. "The idea of certain chosen servants of an old Hindoo superstition devoting themselves, through all difficulties and dangers, to watching the opportunity of recovering their sacred gem, appears to *me* to be perfectly consistent with everything that we know of the patience of Oriental races, and the influence of Oriental religions. But then I am an imaginative man; and the butcher, the baker, and the tax-gatherer, are not the only credible realities in existence to *my* mind. Let the guess I have made at the truth in this matter go for what it is worth, and let us get on to the only practical question that concerns us. Does the conspiracy against the Moonstone survive the Colonel's death? And did the Colonel know it, when he left the birthday gift to his niece?"

I began to see my lady and Miss Rachel at the end of it all, now. Not a word he said escaped me.

"I was not very willing, when I discovered the story of the Moonstone," said Mr. Franklin, "to be the means of bringing it here. But Mr. Bruff reminded me that somebody must put my cousin's legacy into my cousin's hands – and that I might as well do it as anybody else. After taking the Diamond out of the bank, I fancied I was followed in the streets by a shabby, dark-complexioned man. I went to my father's house to pick up my luggage, and found a letter there, which unexpectedly detained me in London. I went back to the bank with the Diamond, and thought I saw the shabby man again. Taking the Diamond once more out of the bank this morning, I saw the man for the third time, gave him the slip, and started (before he recovered the trace of me) by the morning instead of the afternoon train. Here I am, with the Diamond safe and sound – and what is the first news that meets me? I find that three strolling Indians have been at the house, and that my arrival from London, and something which I am expected to have about me, are two special objects of investigation to them when they believe themselves to be alone. I don't waste time and words on their pouring the ink into the boy's hand, and telling him to look in it for a man at a distance, and for something in that man's pocket. The thing (which I have often seen done in the East) is 'hocus-pocus' in my opinion, as it is in yours. The present question for us to decide is, whether I am wrongly attaching a meaning to a mere accident? or whether we really have evidence of the Indians being on the track of the Moonstone, the moment it is removed from the safe keeping of the bank?"

Neither he nor I seemed to fancy dealing with this part of the inquiry. We looked at each other, and then we looked at the tide, oozing in smoothly, higher and higher, over the Shivering Sand.

"What are you thinking of?" says Mr. Franklin, suddenly.

"I was thinking, sir," I answered, "that I should like to shy the Diamond into the quicksand, and settle the question in *that* way."

"If you have got the value of the stone in your pocket," answered Mr. Franklin, "say so, Betteredge, and in it goes!"

It's curious to note, when your mind's anxious, how very far in the way of relief a very small joke will go. We found a fund of merriment, at the time, in the notion of making away with Miss Rachel's lawful property, and getting Mr. Blake, as executor, into dreadful trouble – though where the merriment was, I am quite at a loss to discover now.

Mr. Franklin was the first to bring the talk back to the talk's proper purpose. He took an envelope out of his pocket, opened it, and handed to me the paper inside.

"Betteredge," he said, "we must face the question of the Colonel's motive in leaving this legacy to his niece, for my aunt's sake. Bear in mind how Lady Verinder treated her brother from the time when he returned to England, to the time when he told you he should remember his niece's birthday. And read that." He gave me the extract from the Colonel's Will. I have got it by me while I write these words; and I copy it, as follows, for your benefit:

"Thirdly, and lastly, I give and bequeath to my niece, Rachel Verinder, daughter and only child of my sister, Julia Verinder, widow – if her mother, the said Julia Verinder, shall be living on the said Rachel Verinder's next Birthday after my death – the yellow Diamond belonging to me, and known in the East by the name of the Moonstone: subject to this condition, that her mother, the said Julia Verinder, shall be living at the time. And I hereby desire my executor to give my Diamond, either by his own hands or by the hands of some trustworthy representative whom he shall appoint, into the personal possession of my said niece Rachel, on her next birthday after my death, and in the presence, if possible, of my sister, the said Julia Verinder. And I desire that my said sister may be informed, by means of a true copy of this, the third and last clause of my Will, that I give the Diamond to her daughter Rachel, in token of my free forgiveness of the injury which her conduct towards me has been the means of inflicting on my reputation in my lifetime; and especially in proof that I pardon, as becomes a dying man, the insult offered to me as an officer and a gentleman, when her servant, by her orders, closed the door of her house against me, on the occasion of her daughter's birthday."

More words followed these, providing, if my lady was dead, or if Miss Rachel was dead, at the time of the testator's decease, for the Diamond being sent to Holland, in accordance with the sealed instructions originally deposited with it. The proceeds of the sale were, in that case, to be added to the money already left by the Will for the professorship of chemistry at the university in the north.

I handed the paper back to Mr. Franklin, sorely troubled what to say to him. Up to that moment, my own opinion had been (as you know) that the Colonel had died as wickedly as he had lived. I don't say the copy from his Will actually converted me from that opinion: I only say it staggered me.

"Well," says Mr. Franklin, "now you have read the Colonel's own statement, what do you say? In bringing the Moonstone to my aunt's house, am I serving his vengeance blindfold, or am I vindicating him in the character of a penitent and Christian man?"

"It seems hard to say, sir," I answered, "that he died with a horrid revenge in his heart, and a horrid lie on his lips. God alone knows the truth. Don't ask *me*."

Mr. Franklin sat twisting and turning the extract from the Will in his fingers, as if he expected to squeeze the truth out of it in that manner. He altered quite remarkably, at the same time. From being brisk and bright, he now became, most unaccountably, a slow, solemn, and pondering young man.

"This question has two sides," he said. "An Objective side, and a Subjective side.[1] Which are we to take?"

He had had a German education as well as a French. One of the two had been in undisturbed possession of him (as I supposed) up to this time. And now (as well as I could make out) the other was taking its place. It is one of my rules in life, never to notice what I don't understand. I steered a middle course between the Objective side and the Subjective side. In plain English I stared hard, and said nothing.

"Let's extract the inner meaning of this," says Mr. Franklin. "Why did my uncle leave the Diamond to Rachel? Why didn't he leave it to my aunt?"

"That's not beyond guessing, sir, at any rate," I said. "Colonel Herncastle knew my lady well enough to know that she would have refused to accept any legacy that came to her from *him*."

"How did he know that Rachel might not refuse to accept it, too?"

"Is there any young lady in existence, sir, who could resist the temptation of accepting such a birthday present as the Moonstone?"

"That's the Subjective view," says Mr. Franklin. "It does you great credit, Betteredge, to be able to take the Subjective view. But there's another mystery about the Colonel's legacy which is not accounted for yet. How are we to explain his only giving Rachel her birthday present conditionally on her mother being alive?"

---

1   Jenny Bourne Taylor suggests that Franklin Blake's method of weighing matters reflects the way the novel "continually asserts and undermines the sources of its own coherence, most notably by breaking down the boundary between 'objective' and 'subjective' reality, so that it becomes a palimpsest of overt and covert meanings" (*In the Secret Theatre of the Home: Wilkie Collins, Sensation Narrative, and Nineteenth-Century Psychology*, London: Routledge, 1988: 175).

"I don't want to slander a dead man, sir," I answered. "But if he *has* purposely left a legacy of trouble and danger to his sister, by the means of her child, it must be a legacy made conditional on his sister's being alive to feel the vexation of it."

"Oh! That's your interpretation of his motive, is it? The Subjective interpretation again! Have you ever been in Germany, Betteredge?"

"No, sir. What's your interpretation; if you please?"

"I can see," says Mr. Franklin, "that the Colonel's object may, quite possibly, have been – not to benefit his niece, whom he had never even seen – but to prove to his sister that he had died forgiving her, and to prove it very prettily by means of a present made to her child. There is a totally different explanation from yours, Betteredge, taking its rise in a Subjective-Objective point of view. From all I can see, one interpretation is just as likely to be right as the other."

Having brought matters to this pleasant and comforting issue, Mr. Franklin appeared to think that he had completed all that was required of him. He laid down flat on his back on the sand, and asked what was to be done next.

He had been so clever, and clear-headed (before he began to talk the foreign gibberish), and had so completely taken the lead in the business up to the present time, that I was quite unprepared for such a sudden change as he now exhibited in this helpless leaning upon *me*. It was not till later that I learned – by assistance of Miss Rachel, who was the first to make the discovery – that these puzzling shifts and transformations in Mr. Franklin were due to the effect on him of his foreign training. At the age when we are all of us most apt to take our colouring, in the form of a reflection from the colouring of other people, he had been sent abroad, and had been passed on from one nation to another, before there was time for any one colouring more than another to settle itself on him firmly. As a consequence of this, he had come back with so may different sides to his character, all more or less jarring with each other, that he seemed to pass his life in a state of perpetual contradiction with himself. He could be a busy man, and a lazy man; cloudy in the head, and clear in the head; a model of determination, and a spectacle of helplessness, all together. He had his French side, and his German side, and his Italian side – the original English foundation showing through, every now and then, as much as to say, "Here I am, sorely transmogrified, as you see, but there's something of me left at the bottom of him still." Miss Rachel used to remark that the Italian side of him was uppermost, on those occasions when he unexpectedly gave in, and asked you in his nice sweet-tempered way to take his own responsibilities on your shoulders. You will do him no injustice, I think, if you conclude that the Italian side of him was uppermost now.

"Isn't it your business, sir," I asked, "to know what to do next? Surely it can't be mine?"

Mr. Franklin didn't appear to see the force of my question – not being in a position, at the time, to see anything but the sky over his head.

"I don't want to alarm my aunt without reason," he said. "And I don't want to leave her without what may be a needful warning. If you were in my place, Betteredge, tell me, in one word, what would you do?"

In one word, I told him: "Wait."

"With all my heart," says Mr. Franklin. "How long?"

I proceeded to explain myself.

"As I understand it, sir," I said, "somebody is bound to put this plaguy Diamond into Miss Rachel's hands on her birthday – and you may as well do it as another. Very good. This is the twenty-fifth of May, and the birthday is on the twenty-first of June. We have got close on four weeks before us. Let's wait and see what happens in that time; and let's warn my lady or not, as the circumstances direct us."

"Perfect, Betteredge, as far as it goes!" says Mr. Franklin. "But, between this and the birthday, what's to be done with the Diamond?"

"What your father did with it, to be sure, sir!" I answered. "Your father put it in the safe keeping of a bank in London. You put it in the safe keeping of the bank at Frizinghall." (Frizinghall was our nearest town, and the Bank of England[1] wasn't safer than the bank there.) "If I were you, sir," I added, "I would ride straight away with it to Frizinghall before the ladies come back."

The prospect of doing something – and, what is more, of doing that something on a horse – brought Mr. Franklin up like lightning from the flat of his back. He sprang to his feet, and pulled me up,

---

1 Established by the Bank of England Act in 1694, the Bank itself was built in 1734 on Threadneedle Street.

without ceremony, on to mine. "Betteredge, you are worth your weight in gold," he said. "Come along, and saddle the best horse in the stables directly!"

Here (God bless it!) was the original English foundation of him showing through all the foreign varnish at last! Here was the Master Franklin I remembered, coming out again in the good old way at the prospect of a ride, and reminding me of the good old times! Saddle a horse for him? I would have saddled a dozen horses, if he could only have ridden them all!

We went back to the house in a hurry; we had the fleetest horse in the stables saddled in a hurry; and Mr. Franklin rattled off in a hurry, to lodge the cursed Diamond once more in the strong-room of a bank. When I heard the last of his horse's hoofs on the drive, and when I turned about in the yard and found I was alone again, I felt half inclined to ask myself if I hadn't woke up from a dream.

CHAPTER VII

WHILE I was in this bewildered frame of mind, sorely needing a little quiet time by myself to put me right again, my daughter Penelope got in my way (just as her late mother used to get in my way on the stairs), and instantly summoned me to tell her all that had passed at the conference between Mr. Franklin and me. Under present circumstances, the one thing to be done was to clap the extinguisher upon Penelope's curiosity on the spot. I accordingly replied that Mr. Franklin and I had both talked of foreign politics, till we could talk no longer, and had then mutually fallen asleep in the heat of the sun. Try that sort of answer when your wife or your daughter next worries you with an awkward question at an awkward time, and depend on the natural sweetness of women for kissing and making it up again at the next opportunity.

The afternoon wore on, and my lady and Miss Rachel came back.

Needless to say how astonished they were, when they heard that Mr. Franklin Blake had arrived, and had gone off again on horseback. Needless also to say, that *they* asked awkward questions directly, and that the "foreign politics" and the "falling asleep in the sun" wouldn't serve a second time over with *them*. Being at the end of my invention,

I said Mr. Franklin's arrival by the early train was entirely attributable to one of Mr. Franklin's freaks. Being asked, upon that, whether his galloping off again on horseback was another of Mr. Franklin's freaks, I said, "Yes, it was"; and slipped out of it – I think very cleverly – in that way.

Having got over my difficulties with the ladies, I found more difficulties waiting for me when I went back to my own room. In came Penelope – with the natural sweetness of women – to kiss and make it up again; and – with the natural curiosity of women – to ask another question. This time she only wanted me to tell her what was the matter with our second housemaid, Rosanna Spearman.

After leaving Mr. Franklin and me at the Shivering Sand, Rosanna, it appeared, had returned to the house in a very unaccountable state of mind. She had turned (if Penelope was to be believed) all the colours of the rainbow. She had been merry without reason, and sad without reason. In one breath she asked hundreds of questions about Mr. Franklin Blake, and in another breath she had been angry with Penelope for presuming to suppose that a strange gentleman could possess any interest for her. She had been surprised, smiling, and scribbling Mr. Franklin's name inside her workbox. She had been surprised again, crying and looking at her deformed shoulder in the glass. Had she and Mr. Franklin known anything of each other before to-day? Quite impossible! Had they heard anything of each other? Impossible again! I could speak to Mr. Franklin's astonishment as genuine, when he saw how the girl stared at him. Penelope could speak to the girl's inquisitiveness as genuine, when she asked questions about Mr. Franklin. The conference between us, conducted in this way, was tiresome enough, until my daughter suddenly ended it by bursting out with what I thought the most monstrous supposition I had ever heard in my life.

"Father!" says Penelope, quite seriously, "there's only one explanation of it. Rosanna has fallen in love with Mr. Franklin Blake at first sight!"

You have heard of beautiful young ladies falling in love at first sight, and have thought it natural enough. But a housemaid out of a Reformatory, with a plain face and a deformed shoulder, falling in love, at first sight, with a gentleman who comes on a visit to her mistress's house, match me that, in the way of an absurdity, out of any story-book in Christendom, if you can! I laughed till the tears rolled down my cheeks. Penelope resented my merriment, in rather a strange way. "I never knew you cruel before, father," she said, very gently, and went out.

My girl's words fell upon me like a splash of cold water. I was savage with myself, for feeling uneasy in myself the moment she had spoken them – but so it was. We will change the subject, if you please. I am sorry I drifted into writing about it; and not without reason, as you will see when we have gone on together a little longer.

The evening came, and the dressing-bell for dinner rang, before Mr. Franklin returned from Frizinghall. I took his hot water up to his room myself, expecting to hear, after this extraordinary delay, that something had happened. To my great disappointment (and no doubt to yours also), nothing had happened. He had not met with the Indians, either going or returning. He had deposited the Moonstone in the bank – describing it merely as a valuable of great price – and he had got the receipt for it safe in his pocket. I went downstairs, feeling that this was rather a flat ending, after all our excitement about the Diamond earlier in the day.

How the meeting between Mr. Franklin and his aunt and cousin went off, is more than I can tell you.

I would have given something to have waited at table that day. But, in my position in the household, waiting at dinner (except on high family festivals) was letting down my dignity in the eyes of the other servants – a thing which my lady considered me quite prone enough to do already, without seeking occasions for it. The news brought to me from the upper regions, that evening, came from Penelope and the footman. Penelope mentioned that she had never known Miss Rachel so particular about the dressing of her hair, and had never seen her look so bright and pretty as she did when she went down to meet Mr. Franklin in the drawing-room. The footman's report was, that the preservation of a respectful composure in the presence of his betters, and the waiting on Mr. Franklin Blake at dinner, were two of the hardest things to reconcile with each other that had ever tried his training in service. Later in the evening, we heard them singing and playing duets, Mr. Franklin piping high, Miss Rachel piping higher, and my lady, on the piano, following them, as it were over hedge and ditch, and seeing them safe through it in a manner most wonderful and pleasant to hear through the open windows, on the terrace at night. Later still, I went to Mr. Franklin in the smoking-room, with the soda-water and brandy, and found that Miss Rachel had put the Diamond clean out of his head. "She's the most charming girl I have seen since I came back to England!" was all I could extract from him, when I endeavoured to lead the conversation to more serious things.

Towards midnight, I went round the house to lock up, accompanied by my second in command (Samuel, the footman), as usual. When all the doors were made fast, except the side door that opened on the terrace, I sent Samuel to bed, and stepped out for a breath of fresh air before I too went to bed in my turn.

The night was still and close, and the moon was at the full in the heavens. It was so silent out of doors, that I heard from time to time, very faint and low, the fall of the sea, as the ground-swell heaved it in on the sand-bank near the mouth of our little bay. As the house stood, the terrace side was the dark side; but the broad moonlight showed fair on the gravel walk that ran along the next side to the terrace. Looking this way, after looking up at the sky, I saw the shadow of a person in the moonlight thrown forward from behind the corner of the house.

Being old and sly, I forbore to call out; but being also, unfortunately, old and heavy, my feet betrayed me on the gravel. Before I could steal suddenly round the corner, as I had proposed, I heard lighter feet than mine – and more than one pair of them as I thought – retreating in a hurry. By the time I had got to the corner, the trespassers, whoever they were, had run into the shrubbery at the off side of the walk, and were hidden from sight among the thick trees and bushes in that part of the grounds. From the shrubbery, they could easily make their way, over our fence, into the road. If I had been forty years younger, I might have had a chance of catching them before they got clear of our premises. As it was, I went back to set a-going a younger pair of legs than mine. Without disturbing anybody, Samuel and I got a couple of guns, and went all round the house and through the shrubbery. Having made sure that no persons were lurking about anywhere in our grounds, we turned back. Passing over the walk where I had seen the shadow, I now noticed, for the first time, a little bright object, lying on the clean gravel, under the light of the moon. Picking the object up, I discovered it was a small bottle, containing a thick sweet-smelling liquor, as black as ink.

I said nothing to Samuel. But, remembering what Penelope had told me about the jugglers, and the pouring of the little pool of ink into the palm of the boy's hand, I instantly suspected that I had disturbed the three Indians, lurking about the house, and bent, in their heathenish way, on discovering the whereabouts of the Diamond that night.

★

CHAPTER VIII

HERE, for one moment, I find it necessary to call a halt.

On summoning up my own recollections – and on getting Penelope to help me, by consulting her journal – I find that we may pass pretty rapidly over the interval between Mr. Franklin Blake's arrival and Miss Rachel's birthday. For the greater part of that time the days passed, and brought nothing with them worth recording. With your good leave, then, and with Penelope's help, I shall notice certain dates only in this place; reserving to myself to tell the story day by day, once more, as soon as we get to the time when the business of the Moonstone became the chief business of everybody in our house.

This said, we may now go on again – beginning, of course, with the bottle of sweet-smelling ink which I found on the gravel walk at night.

On the next morning (the morning of the twenty-sixth) I showed Mr. Franklin this article of jugglery, and told him what I have already told you. His opinion was, not only that the Indians had been lurking about after the Diamond, but also that they were actually foolish enough to believe in their own magic – meaning thereby the making of signs on a boy's head, and the pouring of ink into a boy's hand, and then expecting him to see persons and things beyond the reach of human vision. In our country, as well as in the East, Mr. Franklin informed me, there are people who practise this curious hocus-pocus (without the ink, however); and who call it by a French name, signifying something like brightness of sight. "Depend upon it," says Mr. Franklin, "the Indians took it for granted that we should keep the Diamond here; and they brought their clairvoyant boy to show them the way to it, if they succeeded in getting into the house last night."

"Do you think they'll try again, sir?" I asked.

"It depends," says Mr. Franklin, "on what the boy can really do. If he can see the Diamond through the iron-safe of the bank at Frizinghall, we shall be troubled with no more visits from the Indians for the present. If he can't, we shall have another chance of catching them in the shrubbery, before many more nights are over our heads."

I waited pretty confidently for that latter chance; but, strange to relate, it never came.

Whether the jugglers heard, in the town, of Mr. Franklin having been seen at the bank, and drew their conclusions accordingly; or whether the boy really did see the Diamond where the Diamond was now lodged (which I, for one, flatly disbelieve); or whether, after all, it was a mere effect of chance, this at any rate is the plain truth – not the ghost of an Indian came near the house again, through the weeks that passed before Miss Rachel's birthday. The jugglers remained in and about the town plying their trade; and Mr. Franklin and I remained waiting to see what might happen, and resolute not to put the rogues on their guard by showing our suspicions of them too soon. With this report of the proceedings on either side, ends all that I have to say about the Indians for the present.

On the twenty-ninth of the month, Miss Rachel and Mr. Franklin hit on a new method of working their way together through the time which might otherwise have hung heavy on their hands. There are reasons for taking particular notice here of the occupation that amused them. You will find it has a bearing on something that is still to come.

Gentlefolks in general have a very awkward rock ahead in life – the rock ahead of their own idleness. Their lives being, for the most part, passed in looking about them for something to do, it is curious to see – especially when their tastes are of what is called the intellectual sort – how often they drift blindfold into some nasty pursuit. Nine times out of ten they take to torturing something, or to spoiling something – and they firmly believe they are improving their minds, when the plain truth is, they are only making a mess in the house. I have seen them (ladies, I am sorry to say, as well as gentlemen) go out, day after day, for example, with empty pill-boxes, and catch newts, and beetles, and spiders, and frogs, and come home and stick pins through the miserable wretches, or cut them up, without a pang of remorse, into little pieces. You see my young master, or my young mistress, poring over one of their spiders' insides with a magnifying-glass; or you meet one of their frogs walking downstairs without his head – and when you wonder what this cruel nastiness means, you are told that it means a taste in my young master or my young mistress for natural history.[1] Sometimes, again, you see them occupied for hours together in spoiling a pretty flower with pointed instruments, out of a stupid curiosity to know what the flower is made of. Is its colour any prettier, or its scent any sweeter, when you *do* know? But there! the poor souls must get through the time, you see – they must get through the time. You dabbled in nasty mud, and made pies, when you were a child; and you dabble in nasty science, and dissect spiders, and spoil flowers, when you grow up. In the one case and in the other, the secret of it is, that you have got nothing to think of in your poor empty head, and nothing to do with your poor idle hands. And so it ends in your spoiling canvas with paints, and making a smell in the house; or in keeping tadpoles in a glass box full of dirty water, and turning everybody's stomach in the house; or in chipping off bits of stone here, there, and everywhere, and dropping grit into all the victuals in the house; or in staining your fingers in the pursuit of photography, and doing justice without mercy on everybody's face in the house. It often falls heavy enough, no doubt, on people who are really obliged to get their living, to be forced to work for the clothes that cover them, the roof that shelters them, and the food that keeps them going. But compare the hardest day's work you ever did with the idleness that splits flowers and pokes its way into spiders'

---

1   Collins complains about the coldness of science, in much the same way he does here, in at least a couple of his other novels. In *No Name* the reptilian villainess Mrs. Lecount, the widow of "an eminent Swiss naturalist," keeps fish, eels, frogs, and toads, claiming at one point, "Properly understood, the reptile creation is beautiful. Properly dissected, the reptile creation is instructive in the last degree" (Scene III, Chapter ii). And Mrs. Gallilee, the cold-blooded devotee of modern science in *Heart and Science*, says at one point, "I sometimes dissect flowers, but I never trouble myself to arrange them" (Chapter xv).

stomachs, and thank your stars that your head has got something it *must* think of, and your hands something that they *must* do.

As for Mr. Franklin and Miss Rachel, they tortured nothing, I am glad to say. They simply confined themselves to making a mess; and all they spoilt, to do them justice, was the panelling of a door.

Mr. Franklin's universal genius, dabbling in everything, dabbled in what he called "decorative painting." He had invented, he informed us, a new mixture to moisten paint with, which he described as a "vehicle." What it was made of, I don't know. What it did, I can tell you in two words – it stank. Miss Rachel being wild to try her hand at the new process, Mr. Franklin sent to London for the materials; mixed them up, with accompaniment of a smell which made the very dogs sneeze when they came into the room; put an apron and a bib over Miss Rachel's gown, and set her to work decorating her own little sitting-room – called, for want of English to name it in, her "boudoir." They began with the inside of the door. Mr. Franklin scraped off all the nice varnish with pumice-stone, and made what he described as a surface to work on. Miss Rachel then covered the surface, under his directions and with his help, with patterns and devices – griffins, birds, flowers, cupids, and such like – copied from designs made by a famous Italian painter, whose name escapes me: the one, I mean, who stocked the world with Virgin Maries, and had a sweetheart at the baker's.[1] Viewed as work, this decoration was slow to do, and dirty to deal with. But our young lady and gentleman never seemed to tire of it. When they were not riding, or seeing company, or taking their meals, or piping their songs, there they were with their heads together, as busy as bees, spoiling the door. Who was the poet who said that Satan finds some mischief still for idle hands to do?[2] If he had occupied my place in the family, and had seen Miss Rachel with her brush, and Mr. Franklin with his vehicle, he could have written nothing truer of either of them than that.

The next date worthy of notice is Sunday the fourth of June.

---

1 Betteredge cannot quite remember Raphael (1483-1520), the Italian Renaissance painter and architect known for his glorious Madonnas. Raphael's mistress, La Fornarina, was noted in Giorgio Vasari's (1511-74) *Lives of the Painters* (1550), and a later tale described her as a baker's daughter from Trastevere.
2 The line comes from Isaac Watts's (1674-1748) "Against Idleness and Mischief," from *Divine Songs for Children* (1715).

On that evening we, in the servants' hall, debated a domestic question for the first time, which, like the decoration of the door, has its bearing on something that is still to come.

Seeing the pleasure which Mr. Franklin and Miss Rachel took in each other's society, and noting what a pretty match they were in all personal respects, we naturally speculated on the chance of their putting their heads together with other objects in view besides the ornamenting of a door. Some of us said there would be a wedding in the house before the summer was over. Others (led by me) admitted it was likely enough Miss Rachel might be married; but we doubted (for reasons which will presently appear) whether her bridegroom would be Mr. Franklin Blake.

That Mr. Franklin was in love, on his side, nobody who saw and heard him could doubt. The difficulty was to fathom Miss Rachel. Let me do myself the honour of making you acquainted with her; after which, I will leave you to fathom for yourself – if you can.

My young lady's eighteenth birthday was the birthday now coming, on the twenty-first of June. If you happen to like dark women (who, I am informed, have gone out of fashion latterly in the gay world), and if you have no particular prejudice in favour of size, I answer for Miss Rachel as one of the prettiest girls your eyes ever looked on. She was small and slim, but all in fine proportion from top to toe. To see her sit down, to see her get up, and specially to see her walk, was enough to satisfy any man in his senses that the graces of her figure (if you will pardon me the expression) were in her flesh and not in her clothes. Her hair was the blackest I ever saw. Her eyes matched her hair. Her nose was not quite large enough, I admit. Her mouth and chin were (to quote Mr. Franklin) morsels for the gods; and her complexion (on the same undeniable authority) was as warm as the sun itself, with this great advantage over the sun, that it was always in nice order to look at. Add to the foregoing that she carried her head as upright as a dart, in a dashing, spirited, thoroughbred way – that she had a clear voice, with a ring of the right metal in it, and a smile that began very prettily in her eyes before it got to her lips – and there behold the portrait of her, to the best of my painting, as large as life!

And what about her disposition next? Had this charming creature no faults? She had just as many faults as you have, ma'am – neither more nor less.

To put it seriously, my dear pretty Miss Rachel, possessing a host of graces and attractions, had one defect, which strict impartiality compels me to acknowledge. She was unlike most other girls of her age, in this – that she had ideas of her own, and was stiff-necked enough to set the fashions themselves at defiance, if the fashions didn't suit her views. In trifles, this independence of hers was all well enough; but in matters of importance, it carried her (as my lady thought, and as I thought) too far. She judged for herself, as few women of twice her age judge in general; never asked your advice; never told you beforehand what she was going to do; never came with secrets and confidences to anybody, from her mother downwards. In little things and great, with people she loved, and people she hated (and she did both with equal heartiness), Miss Rachel always went on a way of her own, sufficient for herself in the joys and sorrows of her life. Over and over again I have heard my lady say, "Rachel's best friend and Rachel's worst enemy are, one and the other – Rachel herself."

Add one thing more to this, and I have done.

With all her secrecy, and self-will, there was not so much as the shadow of anything false in her. I never remember her breaking her word; I never remember her saying No, and meaning Yes. I can call to mind, in her childhood, more than one occasion when the good little soul took the blame, and suffered the punishment, for some fault committed by a playfellow whom she loved. Nobody ever knew her to confess to it, when the thing was found out, and she was charged with it afterwards. But nobody ever knew her to lie about it, either. She looked you straight in the face, and shook her little saucy head, and said plainly, "I won't tell you!" Punished again for this, she would own to being sorry for saying "won't"; but, bread and water notwithstanding, she never told you. Self-willed – devilish self-willed sometimes – I grant; but the finest creature, nevertheless, that ever walked the ways of this lower world. Perhaps you think you see a certain contradiction here? In that case, a word in your ear. Study your wife closely, for the next four-and-twenty hours. If your good lady doesn't exhibit something in the shape of a contradiction in that time, Heaven help you! – you have married a monster.

I have now brought you acquainted with Miss Rachel, which you will find puts us face to face, next, with the question of that young lady's matrimonial views.

On June the twelfth, an invitation from my mistress was sent to a gentleman in London, to come and help to keep Miss Rachel's birthday. This was the fortunate individual on whom I believed her heart to be privately set! Like Mr. Franklin, he was a cousin of hers. His name was Mr. Godfrey Ablewhite.

My lady's second sister (don't be alarmed; we are not going very deep into family matters this time) – my lady's second sister, I say, had a disappointment in love; and taking a husband afterwards, on the neck-or-nothing principle, made what they call a misalliance. There was terrible work in the family when the Honourable Caroline insisted on marrying plain Mr. Ablewhite, the banker at Frizinghall. He was very rich and very respectable, and he begot a prodigious large family – all in his favour, so far. But he had presumed to raise himself from a low station in the world – and that was against him. However, Time and the progress of modern enlightenment put things right; and the misalliance passed muster very well. We are all getting liberal now; and (provided you can scratch me, if I scratch you) what do I care, in or out of Parliament, whether you are a Dustman or a Duke? That's the modern way of looking at it – and I keep up with the modern way. The Ablewhites lived in a fine house and grounds, a little out of Frizinghall. Very worthy people, and greatly respected in the neighbourhood. We shall not be much troubled with them in these pages – excepting Mr. Godfrey, who was Mr. Ablewhite's second son, and who must take his proper place here, if you please, for Miss Rachel's sake.

With all his brightness and cleverness and general good qualities, Mr. Franklin's chance of topping Mr. Godfrey in our young lady's estimation was, in my opinion, a very poor chance indeed.

In the first place, Mr. Godfrey was, in point of size, the finer man by far of the two. He stood over six feet high; he had a beautiful red and white colour; a smooth round face, shaved as bare as your hand; and a head of lovely long flaxen hair, falling negligently over the poll of his neck. But why do I try to give you this personal description of him? If you ever subscribed to a Ladies' Charity in London,[1] you

---

1   With the ridiculous "Mothers'-Small-Clothes-Conversion-Society," Collins intensifies his satire of organized religion. The reader is later introduced to the even

know Mr. Godfrey Ablewhite as well as I do. He was a barrister by profession;[1] a ladies' man by temperament; and a good Samaritan by choice. Female benevolence and female destitution could do nothing without him. Maternal societies for confining poor women; Magdalen societies for rescuing poor women; strong-minded societies for putting poor women into poor men's places, and leaving the men to shift for themselves; – he was vice-president, manager, referee to them all. Wherever there was a table with a committee of ladies sitting round it in council, there was Mr. Godfrey at the bottom of the board, keeping the temper of the committee, and leading the dear creatures along the thorny ways of business, hat in hand. I do suppose this was the most accomplished philanthropist (on a small independence) that England ever produced. As a speaker at charitable meetings the like of him for drawing your tears and your money was not easy to find. He was quite a public character. The last time I was in London, my mistress gave me two treats. She sent me to the theatre to see a dancing woman who was all the rage;[2] and she sent me to Exeter Hall[3] to hear Mr. Godfrey. The lady did it, with a band of music. The gentleman did it, with a handkerchief and a glass of water. Crowds at the performance with the legs. Ditto at the performance with the tongue. And with all this, the sweetest-tempered person (I allude to Mr. Godfrey) – the simplest and pleasantest and easiest to please – you ever met with. He loved everybody. And everybody loved *him*. What chance had Mr. Franklin – what chance had anybody of average reputation and capacities – against such a man as this?

---

more ridiculous "British-Ladies'-Servants'-Sunday-Sweetheart-Supervision Society." Collins and Dickens were often merciless in their attacks on pseudo-charitable organizations. Clack's earnest involvement with these organizations reminds the reader of *Bleak House*'s Mrs. Jellyby and her insistence that her children provide aid for the natives of Borrioboola-Gha, or of Mrs. Pardiggle's insistence – in the same novel – that *her* children give to the Tockahoopo Indians, the Great National Smithers Testimonial, the Superannuated Widows, or the Infant Bonds of Joy. Dickens called theirs a "rapacious benevolence."

1 Barristers were lawyers in the Court of Chancery, and as such they could argue in court.

2 Betteredge may be referring to Marie Taglioni (1804-84), the most famous dancer of the age. She danced in London often between 1829 and 1847, when she retired. A young Collins and an old Betteredge could have seen her perform.

3 A building in the Strand, Exeter Hall (built between 1829 and 1831 and demolished in 1907) was used for meetings of various religious and philanthropic organizations.

On the fourteenth, came Mr. Godfrey's answer.

He accepted my mistress's invitation, from the Wednesday of the birthday to the evening of Friday – when his duties to the Ladies' Charities would oblige him to return to town. He also enclosed a copy of verses on what he elegantly called his cousin's "natal day." Miss Rachel, I was informed, joined Mr. Franklin in making fun of the verses at dinner; and Penelope, who was all on Mr. Franklin's side, asked me, in great triumph, what I thought of that. "Miss Rachel has led *you* off on a false scent, my dear," I replied; "but *my* nose is not so easily mystified. Wait till Mr. Ablewhite's verses are followed by Mr. Ablewhite himself."

My daughter replied, that Mr. Franklin might strike in, and try his luck, before the verses were followed by the poet. In favour of this view, I must acknowledge that Mr. Franklin left no chance untried of winning Miss Rachel's good graces.

Though one of the most inveterate smokers I ever met with, he gave up his cigar, because she said, one day, she hated the stale smell of it in his clothes. He slept so badly, after this effort of self-denial, for want of the composing effect of the tobacco to which he was used, and came down morning after morning looking so haggard and worn, that Miss Rachel herself begged him to take to his cigars again. No! he would take to nothing again that could cause her a moment's annoyance; he would fight it out resolutely, and get back his sleep, sooner or later, by main force of patience in waiting for it. Such devotion as this, you may say (as some of them said downstairs), could never fail of producing the right effect on Miss Rachel – backed up, too, as it was, by the decorating work every day on the door. All very well – but she had a photograph of Mr. Godfrey in her bedroom; represented speaking at a public meeting, with all his hair blown out by the breath of his own eloquence, and his eyes, most lovely, charming the money out of your pockets. What do you say to that? Every morning – as Penelope herself owned to me – there was the man whom the women couldn't do without, looking on, in effigy, while Miss Rachel was having her hair combed. He would be looking on, in reality, before long – that was my opinion of it.

June the sixteenth brought an event which made Mr. Franklin's chance look, to my mind, a worse chance than ever.

A strange gentleman, speaking English with a foreign accent, came that morning to the house, and asked to see Mr. Franklin Blake on business. The business could not possibly have been connected with the Diamond, for these two reasons – first, that Mr. Franklin told me nothing about it; secondly, that he communicated it (when the gentleman had gone, as I suppose) to my lady. She probably hinted something about it next to her daughter. At any rate, Miss Rachel was reported to have said some severe things to Mr. Franklin, at the piano that evening, about the people he had lived among, and the principles he had adopted in foreign parts. The next day, for the first time, nothing was done towards the decoration of the door. I suspect some imprudence of Mr. Franklin's on the Continent – with a woman or a debt at the bottom of it – had followed him to England. But that is all guesswork. In this case, not only Mr. Franklin, but my lady too, for a wonder, left me in the dark.

On the seventeenth, to all appearance, the cloud passed away again. They returned to their decorating work on the door, and seemed to be as good friends as ever. If Penelope was to be believed, Mr. Franklin had seized the opportunity of the reconciliation to make an offer to Miss Rachel, and had neither been accepted nor refused. My girl was sure (from signs and tokens which I need not trouble you with) that her young mistress had fought Mr. Franklin off by declining to believe that he was in earnest, and had then secretly regretted treating him in that way afterwards. Though Penelope was admitted to more familiarity with her young mistress than maids generally are – for the two had been almost brought up together as children – still I knew Miss Rachel's reserved character too well to believe that she would show her mind to anybody in this way. What my daughter told me, on the present occasion, was, as I suspected, more what she wished than what she really knew.

On the nineteenth another event happened. We had the doctor in the house professionally. He was summoned to prescribe for a person whom I have had occasion to present to you in these pages – our second housemaid, Rosanna Spearman.

This poor girl – who had puzzled me, as you know already, at the Shivering Sand – puzzled me more than once again, in the interval time of which I am now writing. Penelope's notion that her fellow-servant was in love with Mr. Franklin (which my daughter, by my orders, kept strictly secret) seemed to be just as absurd as ever. But I must own that what I myself saw, and what my daughter saw also, of our second housemaid's conduct, began to look mysterious, to say the least of it.

For example, the girl constantly put herself in Mr. Franklin's way – very slyly and quietly, but she did it. He took about as much notice of her as he took of the cat: it never seemed to occur to him to waste a look on Rosanna's plain face. The poor thing's appetite, never much, fell away dreadfully; and her eyes in the morning showed plain signs of waking and crying at night. One day Penelope made an awkward discovery, which we hushed up on the spot. She caught Rosanna at Mr. Franklin's dressing-table, secretly removing a rose which Miss Rachel had given him to wear in his button-hole, and putting another rose like it, of her own picking, in its place. She was, after that, once or twice impudent to me, when I gave her a well-meant general hint to be careful in her conduct; and, worse still, she was not over-respectful now, on the few occasions when Miss Rachel accidentally spoke to her.

My lady noticed the change, and asked me what I thought about it. I tried to screen the girl by answering that I thought she was out of health; and it ended in the doctor being sent for, as already mentioned, on the nineteenth. He said it was her nerves, and doubted if she was fit for service. My lady offered to remove her for change of air to one of our farms, inland. She begged and prayed, with the tears in her eyes, to be let to stop; and, in an evil hour, I advised my lady to try her for a little longer. As the event proved, and as you will soon see, this was the worst advice I could have given. If I could only have looked a little way into the future, I would have taken Rosanna Spearman out of the house, then and there, with my own hand.

On the twentieth, there came a note from Mr. Godfrey. He had arranged to stop at Frizinghall that night, having occasion to consult his father on business. On the afternoon of the next day, he and his two eldest sisters would ride over to us on horseback, in good time before dinner. An elegant little casket in China accompanied the note, presented to Miss Rachel, with her cousin's love and best wishes. Mr. Franklin had only given her a plain locket not worth half the money.

My daughter Penelope, nevertheless – such is the obstinacy of women – still backed him to win. Thanks be to Heaven, we have arrived at the eve of the birthday at last! You will own, I think, that I have got you over the ground this time, without much loitering by the way. Cheer up! I'll ease you with another new chapter here – and, what is more, that chapter shall take you straight into the thick of the story.

CHAPTER IX

JUNE twenty-first, the day of the birthday, was cloudy and unsettled at sunrise, but towards noon it cleared up bravely.

We, in the servants' hall, began this happy anniversary, as usual, by offering our little presents to Miss Rachel, with the regular speech delivered annually by me as the chief. I follow the plan adopted by the Queen in opening Parliament[1] – namely, the plan of saying much the same thing regularly every year. Before it is delivered, my speech (like the Queen's) is looked for as eagerly as if nothing of the kind had ever been heard before. When it is delivered, and turns out not to be the novelty anticipated, though they grumble a little, they look forward hopefully to something newer next year. An easy people to govern, in the Parliament and in the Kitchen – that's the moral of it.

After breakfast, Mr. Franklin and I had a private conference on the subject of the Moonstone – the time having now come for removing it from the bank at Frizinghall, and placing it in Miss Rachel's own hands.

Whether he had been trying to make love to his cousin again, and had got a rebuff – or whether his broken rest, night after night, was aggravating the queer contradictions and uncertainties in his character – I don't know. But certain it is, that Mr. Franklin failed to show himself at his best on the morning of the birthday. He was in twenty different minds about the Diamond in as many minutes. For my part, I stuck fast to the plain facts as we knew them. Nothing had happened to justify us in alarming my lady on the subject of the jewel;

---

1 The ceremonial State Opening of Parliament, in which the reigning monarch rides to the Palace of Westminster to open a new session of Parliament by reading a summary of the Government's intentions in the House of Lords, dates to the sixteenth century.

and nothing could alter the legal obligation that now lay on Mr. Franklin to put it in his cousin's possession. That was my view of the matter; and, twist and turn it as he might, he was forced in the end to make it his view too. We arranged that he was to ride over, after lunch, to Frizinghall, and bring the Diamond back, with Mr. Godfrey and the two young ladies, in all probability, to keep him company on the way home again.

This settled, our young gentleman went back to Miss Rachel.

They consumed the whole morning, and part of the afternoon, in the everlasting business of decorating the door, Penelope standing by to mix the colours, as directed; and my lady, as luncheon time drew near, going in and out of the room, with her handkerchief to her nose (for they used a deal of Mr. Franklin's vehicle that day), and trying vainly to get the two artists away from their work. It was three o'clock before they took off their aprons, and released Penelope (much the worse for the vehicle), and cleaned themselves of their mess. But they had done what they wanted – they had finished the door on the birthday, and proud enough they were of it. The griffins, cupids, and so on, were, I must own, most beautiful to behold; though so many in number, so entangled in flowers and devices, and so topsy-turvy in their actions and attitudes, that you felt them unpleasantly in your head for hours after you had done with the pleasure of looking at them. If I add that Penelope ended her part of the morning's work by being sick in the back-kitchen, it is in no unfriendly spirit towards the vehicle. No! no! It left off stinking when it dried; and if Art requires these sort of sacrifices – though the girl is my own daughter – I say, let Art have them!

Mr. Franklin snatched a morsel from the luncheon-table, and rode off to Frizinghall – to escort his cousins, as he told my lady. To fetch the Moonstone, as was privately known to himself and to me.

This being one of the high festivals on which I took my place at the sideboard, in command of the attendance at table, I had plenty to occupy my mind while Mr. Franklin was away. Having seen to the wine, and reviewed my men and women who were to wait at dinner, I retired to collect myself before the company came. A whiff of – you know what, and a turn at a certain book which I have had occasion to mention in these pages, composed me, body and mind. I was aroused from what I am inclined to think must have been, not a nap, but a reverie, by the clatter of horses' hoofs outside; and, going to the door, received a cavalcade comprising Mr. Franklin and his three cousins, escorted by one of old Mr. Ablewhite's grooms.

Mr. Godfrey struck me, strangely enough, as being like Mr. Franklin in this respect – that he did not seem to be in his customary spirits. He kindly shook hands with me as usual, and was most politely glad to see his old friend Betteredge wearing so well. But there was a sort of cloud over him, which I couldn't at all account for; and when I asked how he had found his father in health, he answered rather shortly, "Much as usual." However, the two Miss Ablewhites were cheerful enough for twenty, which more than restored the balance. They were nearly as big as their brother; spanking, yellow-haired, rosy lasses, overflowing with superabundant flesh and blood; bursting from head to foot with health and spirits. The legs of the poor horses trembled with carrying them; and when they jumped from their saddles (without waiting to be helped), I declare they bounced on the ground as if they were made of india-rubber. Everything the Miss Ablewhites said began with a large O; everything they did was done with a bang; and they giggled and screamed, in season and out of season, on the smallest provocation. Bouncers – that's what I call them.

Under cover of the noise made by the young ladies, I had an opportunity of saying a private word to Mr. Franklin in the hall."Have you got the Diamond safe, sir?"

He nodded, and tapped the breast-pocket of his coat.

"Have you seen anything of the Indians?"

"Not a glimpse."With that answer, he asked for my lady, and, hearing she was in the small drawing-room, went there straight. The bell rang, before he had been a minute in the room, and Penelope was sent to tell Miss Rachel that Mr. Franklin Blake wanted to speak to her.

Crossing the hall, about half an hour afterwards, I was brought to a sudden standstill by an outbreak of screams from the small drawing-room. I can't say I was at all alarmed; for I recognised in the screams the favourite large O of the Miss Ablewhites. However, I went in (on pretence of asking for instructions about the dinner) to discover whether anything serious had really happened.

There stood Miss Rachel at the table, like a person fascinated, with the Colonel's unlucky Diamond in her hand. There, on either side of her, knelt the two Bouncers, devouring the jewel with their eyes, and screaming with ecstasy every time it flashed on them in a new light. There, at the opposite side of the table, stood Mr. Godfrey, clapping his hands like a large child, and singing out softly, "Exquisite! exquisite!" There sat Mr. Franklin, in a chair by the bookcase, tugging at his beard, and looking anxiously towards the window. And there, at the window, stood the object he was contemplating – my lady, having the extract from the Colonel's Will in her hand, and keeping her back turned on the whole of the company.

She faced me, when I asked for my instructions; and I saw the family frown gathering over her eyes, and the family temper twitching at the corners of her mouth.

"Come to my room in half an hour," she answered. "I shall have something to say to you then."

With those words, she went out. It was plain enough that she was posed by the same difficulty which had posed Mr. Franklin and me in our conference at the Shivering Sand. Was the legacy of the Moonstone a proof that she had treated her brother with cruel injustice? or was it a proof that he was worse than the worst she had ever thought of him? Serious questions those for my lady to determine, while her daughter, innocent of all knowledge of the Colonel's character, stood there with the Colonel's birthday gift in her hand.

Before I could leave the room, in my turn, Miss Rachel, always considerate to the old servant who had been in the house when she was born, stopped me. "Look, Gabriel!" she said, and flashed the jewel before my eyes in a ray of sunlight that poured through the window.

Lord bless us! it *was* a Diamond! As large, or nearly, as a plover's egg![1] The light that streamed from it was like the light of the harvest moon. When you looked down into the stone, you looked into a yellow deep that drew your eyes into it so that they saw nothing else. It seemed unfathomable; this jewel, that you could hold between your finger and thumb, seemed unfathomable as the heavens themselves. We set it in the sun, and then shut the light out of the room, and it shone awfully out of the depths of its own brightness, with a moony gleam, in the dark. No wonder Miss Rachel was fascinated: no won-

---

1 The Plover, known also as the "rain-piper" or the "rain-bird" is a wading bird whose eggs are slightly larger than a Robin's.

der her cousins screamed. The Diamond laid such a hold on *me* that I burst out with as large an "O" as the Bouncers themselves. The only one of us who kept his senses was Mr. Godfrey. He put an arm round each of his sisters' waists, and, looking compassionately backwards and forwards between the Diamond and me, said, "Carbon, Betteredge! mere carbon, my good friend, after all!"

His object, I suppose, was to instruct me. All he did, however, was to remind me of the dinner. I hobbled off to my army of waiters downstairs. As I went out, Mr. Godfrey said, "Dear old Betteredge, I have the truest regard for him!" He was embracing his sisters, and ogling Miss Rachel, while he honoured me with that testimony of affection. Something like a stock of love to draw on *there*! Mr. Franklin was a perfect savage by comparison with him.

At the end of half an hour, I presented myself, as directed, in my lady's room.

What passed between my mistress and me, on this occasion, was, in the main, a repetition of what had passed between Mr. Franklin and me at the Shivering Sand – with this difference, that I took care to keep my own counsel about the jugglers, seeing that nothing had happened to justify me in alarming my lady on this head. When I received my dismissal, I could see that she took the blackest view possible of the Colonel's motives, and that she was bent on getting the Moonstone out of her daughter's possession at the first opportunity.

On my way back to my own part of the house, I was encountered by Mr. Franklin. He wanted to know if I had seen anything of his cousin Rachel. I had seen nothing of her. Could I tell him where his cousin Godfrey was? I didn't know; but I began to suspect that cousin Godfrey might not be far away from cousin Rachel. Mr. Franklin's suspicions apparently took the same turn. He tugged hard at his beard, and went and shut himself up in the library, with a bang of the door that had a world of meaning in it.

I was interrupted no more in the business of preparing for the birthday dinner till it was time for me to smarten myself up for receiving the company. Just as I had got my white waistcoat on, Penelope presented herself at my toilet, on pretence of brushing what little hair I have got left, and improving the tie of my white cravat. My girl was in high spirits, and I saw she had something to say to me. She gave me a kiss on the top of my bald head, and whispered, "News for you, father! Miss Rachel has refused him."

"Who's '*him*'?" I asked.

"The ladies' committee-man, father," says Penelope. "A nasty sly fellow! I hate him for trying to supplant Mr. Franklin!"

If I had had breath enough, I should certainly have protested against this indecent way of speaking of an eminent philanthropic character. But my daughter happened to be improving the tie of my cravat at that moment, and the whole strength of her feelings found its way into her fingers. I never was more nearly strangled in my life.

"I saw him take her away alone into the rose-garden," says Penelope. "And I waited behind the holly to see how they came back. They had gone out arm-in-arm, both laughing. They came back, walking separate, as grave as grave could be, and looking straight away from each other in a manner which there was no mistaking. I never was more delighted, father, in my life! There's one woman in the world who can resist Mr. Godfrey Ablewhite, at any rate; and, if I was a lady, I should be another!"

Here I should have protested again. But my daughter had got the hair-brush by this time, and the whole strength of her feelings had passed into *that.* If you are bald, you will understand how she scarified me. If you are not, skip this bit, and thank God you have got something in the way of a defence between your hair-brush and your head.

"Just on the other side of the holly," Penelope went on, "Mr. Godfrey came to a standstill. 'You prefer,' says he, 'that I should stop here as if nothing had happened?' Miss Rachel turned on him like lightning. 'You have accepted my mother's invitation,' she said; 'and you are here to meet her guests. Unless you wish to make a scandal in the house, you will remain, of course!' She went on a few steps, and then seemed to relent a little. 'Let us forget what has passed, Godfrey,' she said, 'and let us remain cousins still.' She gave him her hand. He kissed it, which *I* should have considered taking a liberty, and then she left him. He waited a little by himself, with his head down, and his heel grinding a hole slowly in the gravel walk; you never saw a man look more put out in your life. 'Awkward!' he said between his teeth, when he looked up, and went on to the house – 'very awkward!' If that was his opinion of himself, he was quite right. Awkward enough, I'm sure. And the end of it is, father, what I told you all along," cries Penelope, finishing me off with a last scarification, the hottest of all. "Mr. Franklin's the man!"

I got possession of the hair-brush, and opened my lips to administer the reproof which, you will own, my daughter's language and conduct richly deserved.

Before I could say a word, the crash of carriage-wheels outside struck in, and stopped me. The first of the dinner-company had come. Penelope instantly ran off. I put on my coat, and looked in the glass. My head was as red as a lobster; but, in other respects, I was as nicely dressed for the ceremonies of the evening as a man need be. I got into the hall just in time to announce the two first of the guests. You needn't feel particularly interested about them. Only the philanthropist's father and mother – Mr. and Mrs. Ablewhite.

*

CHAPTER X

ONE on the top of the other, the rest of the company followed the Ablewhites, till we had the whole tale of them complete. Including the family, they were twenty-four in all. It was a noble sight to see, when they were settled in their places round the dinner-table, and the Rector[1] of Frizinghall (with beautiful elocution) rose and said grace.

There is no need to worry you with a list of the guests. You will meet none of them a second time – in my part of the story, at any rate – with the exception of two.

Those two sat on either side of Miss Rachel, who, as queen of the day, was naturally the great attraction of the party. On this occasion, she was more particularly the centre-point towards which everybody's eyes were directed; for (to my lady's secret annoyance) she wore her wonderful birthday present, which eclipsed all the rest – the Moonstone. It was without any setting when it had been placed in her hands; but that universal genius, Mr. Franklin, had contrived, with the help of his neat fingers and a little bit of silver wire, to fix it as a brooch in the bosom of her white dress. Everybody wondered at the prodigious size and beauty of the Diamond, as a matter of course. But the only two of the company who said anything out of the common

---

1   The rector is the parish clergyman.

way about it, were those two guests I have mentioned, who sat by Miss Rachel on her right hand and her left.

The guest on her left was Mr. Candy,[1] our doctor at Frizinghall. This was a pleasant, companionable little man, with the drawback, however, I must own, of being too fond, in season and out of season, of his joke, and of his plunging in rather a headlong manner into talk with strangers, without waiting to feel his way first. In society he was constantly making mistakes, and setting people unintentionally by the ears together. In his medical practice he was a more prudent man; picking up his discretion (as his enemies said) by a kind of instinct, and proving to be generally right where more carefully conducted doctors turned out to be wrong. What *he* said about the Diamond to Miss Rachel was said, as usual, by way of a mystification or joke. He gravely entreated her (in the interests of science) to let him take it home and burn it. "We will first heat it, Miss Rachel," says the doctor, "to such and such a degree; then we will expose it to a current of air; and, little by little – puff! – we evaporate the Diamond, and spare you a world of anxiety about the safe keeping of a valuable precious stone!" My lady, listening with rather a careworn expression on her face, seemed to wish that the doctor had been in earnest, and that he could have found Miss Rachel zealous enough in the cause of science to sacrifice her birthday gift.

The other guest, who sat on my young lady's right hand, was an eminent public character – being no other than the celebrated Indian traveller, Mr. Murthwaite,[2] who, at risk of his life, had penetrated in disguise where no European had ever set foot before.

This was a long, lean, wiry, brown, silent man. He had a weary look, and a very steady, attentive eye. It was rumoured that he was

---

1 Addressed as Mister, Candy was a surgeon, whose job it was to administer to external injuries such as cuts and bruises, or to deliver babies or set broken bones. As a surgeon, he did not need a licence to practise. Physicians, on the other hand, were addressed as Doctor and needed to be licensed by the Royal College of Physicians of London.

2 The mysterious world-traveller Mr. Murthwaite may have been modelled after Sir Austen Henry Layard (1817-94),who excavated the ruins of the Assyrian capital of Nineveh in the 1840s. Sue Lonoff points to a second model, John William Shaw Wyllie (1835-70), with whom Collins corresponded, who, "like Murthwaite in the novel, had travelled through 'a good deal of a very outlandish – and intensely Hindoo – part of India,' and who suggested Kattiawar, and especially its holy cities, Somnauth and Dwarka, as the locale that would best suit Collins's purposes" (177).

tired of the humdrum life among the people in our parts, and longing to go back and wander off on the tramp again in the wild places of the East. Except what he said to Miss Rachel about her jewel, I doubt if he spoke six words or drank so much as a single glass of wine, all through the dinner. The Moonstone was the only object that interested him in the smallest degree. The fame of it seemed to have reached him, in some of those perilous Indian places where his wanderings had lain. After looking at it silently for so long a time that Miss Rachel began to get confused, he said to her in his cool immovable way, "If you ever go to India, Miss Verinder, don't take your uncle's birthday gift with you. A Hindoo diamond is sometimes part of a Hindoo religion. I know a certain city, and a certain temple in that city, where, dressed as you are now, your life would not be worth five minutes' purchase." Miss Rachel, safe in England, was quite delighted to hear of her danger in India. The Bouncers were more delighted still; they dropped their knives and forks with a crash, and burst out together vehemently, "O! how interesting!" My lady fidgeted in her chair, and changed the subject.

As the dinner got on, I became aware, little by little, that this festival was not prospering as other like festivals had prospered before it.

Looking back at the birthday now, by the light of what happened afterwards, I am half inclined to think that the cursed Diamond must have cast a blight on the whole company. I plied them well with wine; and being a privileged character, followed the unpopular dishes round the table, and whispered to the company confidentially, "Please to change your mind and try it; for I know it will do you good." Nine times out of ten they changed their minds – out of regard for their old original Betteredge, they were pleased to say – but all to no purpose. There were gaps of silence in the talk, as the dinner got on, that made me feel personally uncomfortable. When they did use their tongues again, they used them innocently, in the most unfortunate manner and to the worst possible purpose. Mr. Candy, the doctor, for instance, said more unlucky things than I ever knew him to say before. Take one sample of the way in which he went on, and you will understand what I had to put up with at the sideboard, officiating as I was in the character of a man who had the prosperity of the festival at heart.

One of our ladies present at dinner was worthy Mrs. Threadgall, widow of the late Professor of that name. Talking of her deceased husband perpetually, this good lady never mentioned to strangers that he *was* deceased. She thought, I suppose, that every able-bodied adult in England ought to know as much as that. In one of the gaps of silence, somebody mentioned the dry and rather nasty subject of human anatomy; whereupon good Mrs. Threadgall straightway brought in her late husband as usual, without mentioning that he was dead. Anatomy she described as the Professor's favourite recreation in his leisure hours. As ill-luck would have it, Mr. Candy, sitting opposite (who knew nothing of the deceased gentleman), heard her. Being the most polite of men, he seized the opportunity of assisting the Professor's anatomical amusements on the spot.

"They have got some remarkably fine skeletons lately at the College of Surgeons,"[1] says Mr. Candy, across the table, in a loud cheerful voice. "I strongly recommend the Professor, ma'am, when he next has an hour to spare, to pay them a visit."

You might have heard a pin fall. The company (out of respect to the Professor's memory) all sat speechless. I was behind Mrs. Threadgall at the time, plying her confidentially with a glass of hock.[2] She dropped her head, and said in a very low voice, "My beloved husband is no more."

Unluckily Mr. Candy, hearing nothing, and miles away from suspecting the truth, went on across the table louder and politer than ever.

"The Professor may not be aware," says he, "that the card of a member of the College will admit him, on any day but Sunday, between the hours of ten and four."

Mrs. Threadgall dropped her head right into her tucker, and, in a lower voice still, repeated the solemn words, "My beloved husband is no more."

I winked hard at Mr. Candy across the table. Miss Rachel touched his arm. My lady looked unutterable things at him. Quite useless! On he went, with a cordiality that there was no stopping anyhow. "I shall

---

1   Located in Lincoln's Inn Fields, the College was given its first Royal Charter in 1800 and housed various laboratories and teaching facilities, as well as a museum and world famous collections of scientific specimens.
2   Hock is an Anglicized name for a white wine from Hochheim, Germany.

be delighted," says he, "to send the Professor my card, if you will oblige me by mentioning his present address."

"His present address, sir, is *the grave*," says Mrs. Threadgall, suddenly losing her temper, and speaking with an emphasis and fury that made the glasses ring again. "The Professor has been dead these ten years!"

"Oh, good heavens!" says Mr. Candy. Excepting the Bouncers, who burst out laughing, such a blank now fell on the company, that they might all have been going the way of the Professor, and hailing as he did from the direction of the grave.

So much for Mr. Candy. The rest of them were nearly as provoking in their different ways as the doctor himself. When they ought to have spoken, they didn't speak; or when they did speak they were perpetually at cross purposes. Mr. Godfrey, though so eloquent in public, declined to exert himself in private. Whether he was sulky, or whether he was bashful, after his discomfiture in the rose-garden, I can't say. He kept all his talk for the private ear of the lady (a member of our family) who sat next to him. She was one of his committee-women – a spiritually-minded person, with a fine show of collar-bone and a pretty taste in champagne; liked it dry, you understand, and plenty of it. Being close behind these two at the sideboard, I can testify, from what I heard pass between them, that the company lost a good deal of very improving conversation, which I caught up while drawing the corks, and carving the mutton, and so forth. What they said about their Charities I didn't hear. When I had time to listen to them, they had got a long way beyond their women to be confined, and their women to be rescued, and were disputing on serious subjects. Religion (I understand Mr. Godfrey to say, between the corks and the carving) meant love. And love meant religion. And earth was heaven a little the worse for wear. And heaven was earth, done up again to look like new. Earth had some very objectionable people in it; but, to make amends for that, all the women in heaven would be members of a prodigious committee that never quarrelled, with all the men in attendance on them as ministering angels. Beautiful! beautiful! But why the mischief did Mr. Godfrey keep it all to his lady and himself?

Mr. Franklin again – surely, you will say, Mr. Franklin stirred the company up into making a pleasant evening of it?

Nothing of the sort! He had quite recovered himself, and he was in wonderful force and spirits, Penelope having informed him, I suspect, of Mr. Godfrey's reception in the rose-garden. But, talk as he might, nine times out of ten he pitched on the wrong subject, or he addressed himself to the wrong person; the end of it being that he offended some, and puzzled all of them. That foreign training of his – those French and German and Italian sides of him, to which I have already alluded – came out, at my lady's hospitable board, in a most bewildering manner.

What do you think, for instance, of his discussing the lengths to which a married woman might let her admiration go for a man who was not her husband, and putting it in his clear-headed witty French way to the maiden aunt of the Vicar of Frizinghall? What do you think, when he shifted to the German side, of his telling the lord of the manor, while that great authority on cattle was quoting his experience in the breeding of bulls, that experience, properly understood, counted for nothing, and that the proper way to breed bulls was to look deep into your own mind, evolve out of it the idea of a perfect bull, and produce him? What do you say, when our county member, growing hot, at cheese and salad time, about the spread of democracy in England, burst out as follows: "If we once lose our ancient safe-guards, Mr. Blake, I beg to ask you, what have we got left?" – what do you say to Mr. Franklin answering, from the Italian point of view: "We have got three things left, sir – Love, Music, and Salad"? He not only terrified the company with such outbreaks as these, but, when the English side of him turned up in due course, he lost his foreign smoothness; and, getting on the subject of the medical profession, said such downright things in ridicule of doctors, that he actually put good-humoured little Mr. Candy in a rage.

The dispute between them began in Mr. Franklin being led – I forget how – to acknowledge that he had latterly slept very badly at night. Mr. Candy thereupon told him that his nerves were all out of order, and that he ought to go through a course of medicine immediately. Mr. Franklin replied that a course of medicine, and a course of groping in the dark, meant, in his estimation, one and the same thing. Mr. Candy, hitting back smartly, said that Mr. Franklin himself was, constitutionally speaking, groping in the dark after sleep, and that nothing but medicine could help him to find it. Mr. Franklin, keeping the ball up on his side, said he had often heard of the blind leading the blind, and now, for the first time, he knew what it meant. In this way, they kept it going briskly, cut and thrust, till they both of them got hot – Mr. Candy, in particular, so completely losing his self-control, in defence of his profession, that my lady was obliged to interfere, and forbid the dispute to go on. This necessary act of authority put the last extinguisher on the spirits of the company. The talk spurted up again here and there, for a minute or two at a time; but there was a miserable lack of life and sparkle in it. The devil (or the Diamond) possessed that dinner-party; and it was a relief to everybody when my mistress rose, and gave the ladies the signal to leave the gentlemen over their wine.

I had just ranged the decanters in a row before old Mr. Ablewhite (who represented the master of the house), when there came a sound from the terrace which startled me out of my company manners on the instant. Mr. Franklin and I looked at each other; it was the sound of the Indian drum. As I live by bread, here were the jugglers returning to us with the return of the Moonstone to the house!

As they rounded the corner of the terrace, and came in sight, I hobbled out to warn them off. But, as ill-luck would have it, the two Bouncers were beforehand with me. They whizzed out on to the terrace like a couple of skyrockets, wild to see the Indians exhibit their tricks. The other ladies followed; the gentlemen came out on their side. Before you could say, "Lord bless us!" the rogues were making their salaams; and the Bouncers were kissing the pretty little boy.

Mr. Franklin got on one side of Miss Rachel, and I put myself behind her. If our suspicions were right, there she stood, innocent of all knowledge of the truth, showing the Indians the Diamond in the bosom of her dress!

I can't tell you what tricks they performed, or how they did it. What with the vexation about the dinner, and what with the provocation of the rogues coming back just in the nick of time to see the jewel with their own eyes, I own I lost my head. The first thing that I remember noticing was the sudden appearance on the scene of the Indian traveller, Mr. Murthwaite. Skirting the half-circle in which the gentlefolks stood or sat, he came quietly behind the jugglers, and spoke to them on a sudden in the language of their own country.

If he had pricked them with a bayonet, I doubt if the Indians could have started and turned on him with a more tigerish quickness than they did, on hearing the first words that passed his lips. The next moment, they were bowing and salaaming to him in their most polite and snaky way. After a few words in the unknown tongue had passed on either side, Mr. Murthwaite withdrew as quietly as he had approached. The chief Indian, who acted as interpreter, thereupon wheeled about again towards the gentlefolks. I noticed that the fellow's coffee-coloured face had turned grey since Mr. Murthwaite had spoken to him. He bowed to my lady, and informed her that the exhibition was over. The Bouncers, indescribably disappointed, burst out with a loud "O!" directed against Mr. Murthwaite for stopping the performance. The chief Indian laid his hand humbly on his breast, and said a second time that the juggling was over. The little boy went round with the hat. The ladies withdrew to the drawing-room; and the gentlemen (excepting Mr. Franklin and Mr. Murthwaite) returned to their wine. I and the footman followed the Indians, and saw them safe off the premises.

Going back by way of the shrubbery, I smelt tobacco, and found Mr. Franklin and Mr. Murthwaite (the latter smoking a cheroot[1]) walking slowly up and down among the trees. Mr. Franklin beckoned to me to join them.

"This," says Mr. Franklin, presenting me to the great traveller, "is Gabriel Betteredge, the old servant and friend of our family of whom I spoke to you just now. Tell him, if you please, what you have just told me."

Mr. Murthwaite took his cheroot out of his mouth, and leaned, in his weary way, against the trunk of a tree.

"Mr. Betteredge," he began, "those three Indians are no more jugglers than you and I are."

Here was a new surprise! I naturally asked the traveller if he had ever met with the Indians before.

"Never," says Mr. Murthwaite; "but I know what Indian juggling really is. All you have seen to-night is a very bad and clumsy imitation of it. Unless, after long experience, I am utterly mistaken, those men are high-caste Brahmins.[2] I charged them with being disguised, and

---

1   The cheroot is a cigar with square-cut ends.
2   Brahmins *were* members of the highest Hindu caste. The caste, now occupationally diversified, was originally – and at the time the novel was written – composed entirely of priests.

you saw how it told on them, clever as the Hindoo people are in concealing their feelings. There is a mystery about their conduct that I can't explain. They have doubly sacrificed their caste – first, in crossing the sea; secondly, in disguising themselves as jugglers. In the land they live in, that is a tremendous sacrifice to make. There must be some very serious motive at the bottom of it, and some justification of no ordinary kind to plead for them, in recovery of their caste, when they return to their own country."

I was struck dumb. Mr. Murthwaite went on with his cheroot. Mr. Franklin, after what looked to me like a little private veering about between the different sides of his character, broke the silence as follows:

"I feel some hesitation, Mr. Murthwaite, in troubling you with family matters, in which you can have no interest and which I am not very willing to speak of out of our own circle. But, after what you have said, I feel bound, in the interests of Lady Verinder and her daughter, to tell you something which may possibly put the clue into your hands. I speak to you in confidence; you will oblige me, I am sure, by not forgetting that?"

With this preface, he told the Indian traveller all that he had told me at the Shivering Sand. Even the immovable Mr. Murthwaite was so interested in what he heard, that he let his cheroot go out.

"Now," says Mr. Franklin, when he had done, "what does your experience say?"

"My experience," answered the traveller, "says that you have had more narrow escapes of your life, Mr. Franklin Blake, than I have had of mine; and that is saying a great deal."

It was Mr. Franklin's turn to be astonished now.

"Is it really as serious as that?" he asked.

"In my opinion it is," answered Mr. Murthwaite. "I can't doubt, after what you have told me, that the restoration of the Moonstone to its place on the forehead of the Indian idol, is the motive and the justification of that sacrifice of caste which I alluded to just now. Those men will wait their opportunity with the patience of cats, and will use it with the ferocity of tigers. How you have escaped them I can't imagine," says the eminent traveller, lighting his cheroot again, and staring hard at Mr. Franklin. "You have been carrying the Diamond backwards and forwards, here and in London, and you are still a living man! Let us try and account for it. It was daylight, both times, I suppose, when you took the jewel out of the bank in London?"

"Broad daylight," says Mr. Franklin.

"And plenty of people in the streets?"

"Plenty."

"You settled, of course, to arrive at Lady Verinder's house at a certain time? It's a lonely country between this and the station. Did you keep your appointment?"

"No. I arrived four hours earlier than my appointment."

"I beg to congratulate you on that proceeding! When did you take the Diamond to the bank at the town here?"

"I took it an hour after I had brought it to this house – and three hours before anybody was prepared for seeing me in these parts."

"I beg to congratulate you again! Did you bring it back here alone?"

"No. I happened to ride back with my cousins and the groom."

"I beg to congratulate you for the third time! If you ever feel inclined to travel beyond the civilised limits, Mr. Blake, let me know, and I will go with you. You are a lucky man."

Here I struck in. This sort of thing didn't at all square with my English ideas.

"You don't really mean to say, sir," I asked, "that they would have taken Mr. Franklin's life, to get their Diamond, if he had given them the chance?"

"Do you smoke, Mr. Betteredge?" says the traveller.

"Yes, sir."

"Do you care much for the ashes left in your pipe, when you empty it?"

"No, sir."

"In the country those men came from, they care just as much about killing a man, as you care about emptying the ashes out of your pipe. If a thousand lives stood between them and the getting back of their Diamond – and if they thought they could destroy those lives without discovery – they would take them all. The sacrifice of caste is a serious thing in India, if you like. The sacrifice of life is nothing at all."

I expressed my opinion, upon this, that they were a set of murdering thieves. Mr. Murthwaite expressed *his* opinion that they were a wonderful people. Mr. Franklin, expressing no opinion at all, brought us back to the matter in hand.

"They have seen the Moonstone on Miss Verinder's dress," he said. "What is to be done?"

"What your uncle threatened to do," answered Mr. Murthwaite. "Colonel Herncastle understood the people he had to deal with. Send the Diamond to-morrow (under guard of more than one man) to be cut up at Amsterdam. Make half a dozen diamonds of it, instead of one. There is an end of its sacred identity as The Moonstone – and there is an end of the conspiracy."

Mr. Franklin turned to me.

"There is no help for it," he said. "We must speak to Lady Verinder to-morrow."

"What about to-night, sir?" I asked. "Suppose the Indians come back?"

Mr. Murthwaite answered me, before Mr. Franklin could speak. "The Indians won't risk coming back to-night," he said. "The direct way is hardly ever the way they take to anything – let alone a matter like this, in which the slightest mistake might be fatal to their reaching their end."

"But suppose the rogues are bolder than you think, sir?" I persisted.

"In that case," says Mr. Murthwaite, "let the dogs loose. Have you got any big dogs in the yard?"

"Two, sir. A mastiff and a bloodhound."

"They will do. In the present emergency, Mr. Betteredge, the mastiff and the bloodhound have one great merit – they are not likely to be troubled with your scruples about the sanctity of human life."

The strumming of the piano reached us from the drawing-room, as he fired that shot at me. He threw away his cheroot, and took Mr. Franklin's arm, to go back to the ladies. I noticed that the sky was clouding over fast, as I followed them to the house. Mr. Murthwaite noticed it too. He looked round at me, in his dry, drolling way, and said:

"The Indians will want their umbrellas, Mr. Betteredge, to-night!"

It was all very well for *him* to joke. But I was not an eminent traveller – and my way in this world had not led me into playing ducks and drakes[1] with my own life, among thieves and murderers in the outlandish places of the earth. I went into my own little room, and sat down in my chair in a perspiration, and wondered helplessly what was to be done next. In this anxious frame of mind, other men might have ended by working themselves up into a fever; I ended in a different way. I lit my pipe, and took a turn at *Robinson Crusoe*.

Before I had been at it five minutes, I came to this amazing bit – page one hundred and sixty-one – as follows:

"Fear of Danger is ten thousand times more terrifying than Danger itself, when apparent to the Eyes; and we find the Burthen of Anxiety greater, by much, than the Evil which we are anxious about."

The man who doesn't believe in *Robinson Crusoe*, after *that*, is a man with a screw loose in his understanding, or a man lost in the mist of his own self-conceit! Argument is thrown away upon him; and pity is better reserved for some person with a livelier faith.

I was far on with my second pipe, and still lost in admiration of that wonderful book, when Penelope (who had been handing round the tea) came in with her report from the drawing-room. She had left the Bouncers singing a duet – words beginning with a large "O," and music to correspond. She had observed that my lady made mistakes in her game of whist[2] for the first time in our experience of her. She had seen the great traveller asleep in a corner. She had overheard Mr. Franklin sharpening his wits on Mr. Godfrey, at the expense of Ladies' Charities in general; and she had noticed that Mr. Godfrey hit him back again rather more smartly than became a gentleman of his benevolent character. She had detected Miss Rachel, apparently engaged in appeasing Mrs. Threadgall by showing her some photographs, and really occupied in stealing looks at Mr. Franklin, which no intelligent lady's maid could misinterpret for a single instant. Finally, she had missed Mr. Candy, the doctor, who had mysteriously disappeared from the drawing-room, and had then mysteriously returned, and entered into conversation with Mr. Godfrey. Upon the whole,

---

1 Ducks and drakes is a game involving skipping flat stones along the surface of water. It has come to mean squandering or throwing away one's chances.

2 A favourite Victorian card game, Whist resembles Bridge. Played by two pairs of partners, it is a game in which each team gather tricks according to an established trump suit.

things were prospering better than the experience of the dinner gave us any right to expect. If we could only hold on for another hour, old Father Time would bring up their carriages, and relieve us of them altogether.

Everything wears off in this world; and even the comforting effect of *Robinson Crusoe* wore off, after Penelope left me. I got fidgety again, and resolved on making a survey of the grounds before the rain came. Instead of taking the footman, whose nose was human, and therefore useless in any emergency, I took the bloodhound with me. *His* nose for a stranger was to be depended on. We went all round the premises, and out into the road – and returned as wise as we went, having discovered no such thing as a lurking human creature anywhere.[1]

The arrival of the carriages was the signal for the arrival of the rain. It poured as if it meant to pour all night. With the exception of the doctor, whose gig[2] was waiting for him, the rest of the company went home snugly, under cover, in close carriages. I told Mr. Candy that I was afraid he would get wet through. He told me, in return, that he wondered I had arrived at my time of life, without knowing that a doctor's skin was waterproof. So he drove away in the rain, laughing over his own little joke; and so we got rid of our dinner company.

The next thing to tell is the story of the night.

★

---

1   One of the few major revisions between the first edition of 1868 and the 1871 version that has become the standard edition was the excision – from this spot in the text – of the following passage, which Collins must have believed gave the reader too much of a head start on the mystery's solution: "I chained up the dog again for the present; and returning once more by way of the shrubbery, met two of our gentlemen coming out towards me from the drawing-room. The two were Mr. Candy and Mr. Godfrey, still (as Penelope had reported them) in conversation together, and laughing softly over some pleasant conceit of their own. I thought it rather odd that those two should have run up a friendship together – but passed on, of course, without appearing to notice them."

2   A gig was a light, two-wheeled carriage drawn by one horse.

CHAPTER XI

WHEN the last of the guests had driven away, I went back into the inner hall and found Samuel at the side-table, presiding over the brandy and soda-water. My lady and Miss Rachel came out of the drawing-room, followed by the two gentlemen. Mr. Godfrey had some brandy and soda-water. Mr. Franklin took nothing. He sat down, looking dead tired; the talking on this birthday occasion had, I suppose, been too much for him.

My lady, turning round to wish them good-night, looked hard at the wicked Colonel's legacy shining in her daughter's dress.

"Rachel," she asked, "where are you going to put your Diamond to-night?"

Miss Rachel was in high good spirits, just in that humour for talking nonsense, and perversely persisting in it as if it was sense, which you may sometimes have observed in young girls, when they are highly wrought up, at the end of an exciting day. First, she declared she didn't know where to put the Diamond. Then she said, "On her dressing-table, of course, along with her other things." Then she remembered that the Diamond might take to shining of itself, with its awful moony light, in the dark – and that would terrify her in the dead of night. Then she bethought herself of an Indian cabinet which stood in her sitting-room; and instantly made up her mind to put the Indian diamond in the Indian cabinet, for the purpose of permitting two beautiful native productions to admire each other. Having let her little flow of nonsense run on as far as that point, her mother interposed and stopped her.

"My dear! your Indian cabinet has no lock to it," says my lady.

"Good Heavens, mamma!" cried Miss Rachel, "is this an hotel? Are there thieves in the house?"

Without taking notice of this fantastic way of talking, my lady wished the gentlemen good-night. She next turned to Miss Rachel, and kissed her. "Why not let *me* keep the Diamond for you to-night?" she asked.

Miss Rachel received that proposal as she might, ten years since, have received a proposal to part her from a new doll. My lady saw there was no reasoning with her that night. "Come into my room, Rachel, the first thing to-morrow morning," she said. "I shall have something to say to you." With those last words she left us slowly; thinking her own thoughts, and, to all appearance, not best pleased with the way by which they were leading her.

Miss Rachel was the next to say good-night. She shook hands first with Mr. Godfrey, who was standing at the other end of the hall, looking at a picture. Then she turned back to Mr. Franklin, still sitting weary and silent in a corner.

What words passed between them I can't say. But standing near the old oak frame which holds our large looking-glass, I saw her reflected in it, slyly slipping the locket which Mr. Franklin had given to her, out of the bosom of her dress, and showing it to him for a moment, with a smile which certainly meant something out of the common, before she tripped off to bed. This incident staggered me a little in the reliance I had previously felt on my own judgment. I began to think that Penelope might be right about the state of her young lady's affections, after all.

As soon as Miss Rachel left him eyes to see with, Mr. Franklin noticed me. His variable humour, shifting about everything, had shifted about the Indians already.

"Betteredge," he said, "I'm half inclined to think I took Mr. Murthwaite too seriously, when we had that talk in the shrubbery. I wonder whether he has been trying any of his traveller's tales on us? Do you really mean to let the dogs loose?"

"I'll relieve them of their collars, sir," I answered, "and leave them free to take a turn in the night, if they smell a reason for it."

"All right," says Mr. Franklin. "We'll see what is to be done to-morrow. I am not at all disposed to alarm my aunt, Betteredge, without a very pressing reason for it. Good-night."

He looked so worn and pale as he nodded to me, and took his candle to go upstairs, that I ventured to advise his having a drop of brandy-and-water, by way of nightcap. Mr. Godfrey, walking towards us from the other end of the hall, backed me. He pressed Mr. Franklin, in the friendliest manner, to take something, before he went to bed.

I only note these trifling circumstances, because, after all I had seen and heard, that day, it pleased me to observe that our two gentlemen were on just as good terms as ever. Their warfare of words (heard by Penelope in the drawing-room), and their rivalry for the best place in

Miss Rachel's good graces, seemed to have set no serious difference between them. But there! they were both good-tempered, and both men of the world. And there is certainly this merit in people of station, that they are not nearly so quarrelsome among each other as people of no station at all.

Mr. Franklin declined the brandy-and-water, and went upstairs with Mr. Godfrey, their rooms being next door to each other. On the landing, however, either his cousin persuaded him, or he veered about and changed his mind as usual. "Perhaps I may want it in the night," he called down to me. "Send up some brandy-and-water into my room."

I sent up Samuel with the brandy-and-water; and then went out, and unbuckled the dogs' collars. They both lost their heads with astonishment on being set loose at that time of night, and jumped upon me like a couple of puppies! However, the rain soon cooled them down again: they lapped a drop of water each, and crept back into their kennels. As I went into the house, I noticed signs in the sky which betokened a break in the weather for the better. For the present, it still poured heavily, and the ground was in a perfect sop.

Samuel and I went all over the house, and shut up as usual. I examined everything myself, and trusted nothing to my deputy on this occasion. All was safe and fast, when I rested my old bones in bed, between midnight and one in the morning.

The worries of the day had been a little too much for me, I suppose. At any rate, I had a touch of Mr. Franklin's malady that night. It was sunrise before I fell off at last into a sleep. All the time I lay awake, the house was as quiet as the grave. Not a sound stirred but the splash of the rain, and the sighing of the wind among the trees as a breeze sprang up with the morning.

About half-past seven I woke, and opened my window on a fine sunshiny day. The clock had struck eight, and I was just going out to chain up the dogs again, when I heard a sudden whisking of petticoats on the stairs behind me.

I turned about, and there was Penelope flying down after me like mad. "Father!" she screamed, "come upstairs, for God's sake! *The Diamond is gone!*"

"Are you out of your mind?" I asked her.

"Gone!" says Penelope. "Gone, nobody knows how! Come up and see."

She dragged me after her into our young lady's sitting-room, which opened into her bedroom. There, on the threshold of her bedroom door, stood Miss Rachel, almost as white in the face as the white dressing-gown that clothed her. There also stood the two doors of the Indian cabinet, wide open. One of the drawers inside was pulled out as far as it would go.

"Look!" says Penelope. "I myself saw Miss Rachel put the Diamond into that drawer last night."

I went to the cabinet. The drawer was empty.

"Is this true, miss?" I asked.

With a look that was not like herself, with a voice that was not like her own, Miss Rachel answered, as my daughter had answered:

"The Diamond is gone!"

Having said those words, she withdrew into her bedroom, and shut and locked the door.

Before we knew which way to turn next, my lady came in, hearing my voice in her daughter's sitting-room, and wondering what had happened. The news of the loss of the Diamond seemed to petrify her. She went straight to Miss Rachel's bedroom, and insisted on being admitted. Miss Rachel let her in.

The alarm, running through the house like fire, caught the two gentlemen next.

Mr. Godfrey was the first to come out of his room. All he did when he heard what had happened was to hold up his hands in a state of bewilderment, which didn't say much for his natural strength of mind. Mr. Franklin, whose clear head I had confidently counted on to advise us, seemed to be as helpless as his cousin when he heard the news in his turn. For a wonder, he had had a good night's rest at last; and the unaccustomed luxury of sleep had, as he said himself, apparently stupefied him. However, when he had swallowed his cup of coffee – which he always took, on the foreign plan, some hours before he ate any breakfast – his brains brightened; the clear-headed side of him turned up, and he took the matter in hand, resolutely and cleverly, much as follows:

He first sent for the servants, and told them to leave all the lower doors and windows (with the exception of the front door, which I had opened) exactly as they had been left when we locked up overnight. He next proposed to his cousin and to me to make quite sure, before we took any further steps, that the Diamond had not accidentally dropped somewhere out of sight – say at the back of the cabinet, or down behind the table on which the cabinet stood. Having searched in both places, and found nothing – having also questioned Penelope, and discovered from her no more than the little she had already told me – Mr. Franklin suggested next extending our inquiries to Miss Rachel, and sent Penelope to knock at her bedroom door.

My lady answered the knock, and closed the door behind her. The moment after, we heard it locked inside by Miss Rachel. My mistress came out among us, looking sorely puzzled and distressed. "The loss of the Diamond seems to have quite overwhelmed Rachel," she said, in reply to Mr. Franklin. "She shrinks, in the strangest manner, from speaking of it, even to *me*. It is impossible you can see her for the present."

Having added to our perplexities by this account of Miss Rachel, my lady, after a little effort, recovered her usual composure, and acted with her usual decision.

"I suppose there is no help for it?" she said, quietly. "I suppose I have no alternative but to send for the police?"

"And the first thing for the police to do," added Mr. Franklin, catching her up, "is to lay hands on the Indian jugglers who performed here last night."

My lady and Mr. Godfrey (not knowing what Mr. Franklin and I knew) both started, and both looked surprised.

"I can't stop to explain myself now," Mr. Franklin went on. "I can only tell you that the Indians have certainly stolen the Diamond. Give me a letter of introduction," says he, addressing my lady, "to one of the magistrates[1] at Frizinghall – merely telling him that I represent your interests and wishes, and let me ride off with it instantly. Our chance of catching the thieves may depend on our not wasting one unnecessary minute." (*Nota bene*: Whether it was the French side or the English, the right side of Mr. Franklin seemed to be uppermost now.

---

1 Magistrates were in essence "justices of the peace" doubling as the police in small towns like Frizinghall.

The only question was, How long would it last?)

He put pen, ink, and paper before his aunt, who (as it appeared to me) wrote the letter he wanted a little unwillingly. If it had been possible to overlook such an event as the loss of a jewel worth twenty thousand pounds, I believe – with my lady's opinion of her late brother, and her distrust of his birthday-gift – it would have been privately a relief to her to let the thieves get off with the Moonstone scot free.

I went out with Mr. Franklin to the stables, and took the opportunity of asking him how the Indians (whom I suspected, of course, as shrewdly as he did) could possibly have got into the house.

"One of them might have slipped into the hall, in the confusion, when the dinner company were going away," says Mr. Franklin. "The fellow may have been under the sofa while my aunt and Rachel were talking about where the Diamond was to be put for the night. He would only have to wait till the house was quiet, and there it would be in the cabinet, to be had for the taking." With those words, he called to the groom to open the gate, and galloped off.

This seemed certainly to be the only rational explanation. But how had the thief contrived to make his escape from the house? I had found the front door locked and bolted, as I had left it at night, when I went to open it, after getting up. As for the other doors and windows, there they were still, all safe and fast, to speak for themselves. The dogs, too? Suppose the thief had got away by dropping from one of the upper windows, how had he escaped the dogs? Had he come provided for them with drugged meat? As the doubt crossed my mind, the dogs themselves came galloping at me round a corner, rolling each other over on the wet grass, in such lively health and spirits that it was with no small difficulty I brought them to reason, and chained them up again. The more I turned it over in my mind, the less satisfactory Mr. Franklin's explanation appeared to be.

We had our breakfasts – whatever happens in a house, robbery or murder, it doesn't matter, you must have your breakfast. When we had done, my lady sent for me; and I found myself compelled to tell her all that I had hitherto concealed, relating to the Indians and their plot. Being a woman of a high courage, she soon got over the first startling effect of what I had to communicate. Her mind seemed to be far more perturbed about her daughter than about the heathen rogues and their conspiracy. "You know how odd Rachel is, and how differently she behaves sometimes from other girls," my lady said to me. "But I have never, in all my experience, seen her so strange and so reserved as she is now. The loss of her jewel seems almost to have turned her brain. Who would have thought that horrible Diamond could have laid such a hold on her in so short a time?"

It was certainly strange. Taking toys and trinkets in general, Miss Rachel was nothing like so mad after them as most young girls. Yet there she was, still locked up inconsolably in her bedroom. It is but fair to add that she was not the only one of us in the house who was thrown out of the regular groove. Mr. Godfrey, for instance – though professionally a sort of consoler-general – seemed to be at a loss where to look for his own resources. Having no company to amuse him, and getting no chance of trying what his experience of women in distress could do towards comforting Miss Rachel, he wandered hither and thither about the house and gardens in an aimless uneasy way. He was in two different minds about what it became him to do, after the misfortune that had happened to us. Ought he to relieve the family, in their present situation, of the responsibility of him as a guest, or ought he to stay on the chance that even his humble services might be of some use? He decided ultimately that the last course was perhaps the most customary and considerate course to take, in such a very peculiar case of family distress as this was. Circumstances try the metal a man is really made of. Mr. Godfrey, tried by circumstances, showed himself of weaker metal than I had thought him to be. As for the women-servants – excepting Rosanna Spearman, who kept by herself – they took to whispering together in corners, and staring at nothing suspiciously, as is the manner of that weaker half of the human family, when anything extraordinary happens in a house. I myself acknowledge to have been fidgety and ill-tempered. The cursed Moonstone had turned us all upside down.

A little before eleven Mr. Franklin came back. The resolute side of him had, to all appearance, given way, in the interval since his departure, under the stress that had been laid on it. He had left us at a gallop; he came back to us at a walk. When he went away, he was made of iron. When he returned, he was stuffed with cotton, as limp as limp could be.

"Well," says my lady, "are the police coming?"

"Yes," says Mr. Franklin; "they said they would follow me in a fly.[1] Superintendent Seegrave,[2] of your local police force, and two of his men. A mere form! The case is hopeless."

"What! have the Indians escaped, sir?" I asked.

"The poor ill-used Indians have been most unjustly put in prison," says Mr. Franklin. "They are as innocent as the babe unborn. My idea that one of them was hidden in the house, has ended, like all the rest of my ideas, in smoke. It's been proved," says Mr. Franklin, dwelling with great relish on his own incapacity, "to be simply impossible."

After astonishing us by announcing this totally new turn in the matter of the Moonstone, our young gentleman, at his aunt's request, took a seat, and explained himself.

It appeared that the resolute side of him had held out as far as Frizinghall. He had put the whole case plainly before the magistrate, and the magistrate had at once sent for the police. The first inquiries instituted about the Indians showed that they had not so much as attempted to leave the town. Further questions addressed to the police, proved that all three had been seen returning to Frizinghall with their boy, on the previous night between ten and eleven – which (regard being had to hours and distances) also proved that they had walked straight back, after performing on our terrace. Later still, at midnight, the police, having occasion to search the common lodging-house where they lived, had seen them all three again, and their little boy with them as usual. Soon after midnight I myself had safely shut up the house. Plainer evidence than this, in favour of the Indians, there could not well be. The magistrate said there was not even a case of suspicion against them so far. But, as it was just possible, when the

---

1   A fly was a one-horse carriage for hire.

2   Collins modelled some of his plot's intrigues after details of the sensational Constance Kent-Road-house murder case of 1860. In June of that year, a sixteen-year-old Constance Kent killed her half-brother, Francis, by cutting his throat. She then hid or destroyed her blood-stained nightdress, baffling police and gaining her freedom because of a lack of this vital evidence. She entered a convent in France, returned to England in 1863, and confessed her guilt early in 1865. Collins may also have modelled the bumbling Superintendent Seegrave after a Superintendent Foley, whose incompetence during the initial stages of the investigation of the Road-house murder muddied the waters for subsequent professional investigators. See Appendix B for newspaper accounts of the crime, the investigation, the confession, and the trial.

police came to investigate the matter, that discoveries affecting the jugglers might be made, he would contrive, by committing them as rogues and vagabonds, to keep them at our disposal, under lock and key, for a week. They had ignorantly done something (I forget what) in the town, which barely brought them within the operation of the law. Every human institution (Justice included) will stretch a little, if you only pull it the right way. The worthy magistrate was an old friend of my lady's – and the Indians were "committed" for a week, as soon as the court opened that morning.

Such was Mr. Franklin's narrative of events at Frizinghall. The Indian clue to the mystery of the lost jewel was now, to all appearance, a clue that had broken in our hands. If the jugglers were innocent, who, in the name of wonder, had taken the Moonstone out of Miss Rachel's drawer?

Ten minutes later, to our infinite relief, Superintendent Seegrave arrived at the house. He reported passing Mr. Franklin on the terrace, sitting in the sun (I suppose with the Italian side of him uppermost); and warning the police, as they went by, that the investigation was hopeless, before the investigation had begun.

For a family in our situation, the Superintendent of the Frizinghall police was the most comforting officer you could wish to see. Mr. Seegrave was tall and portly, and military in his manners. He had a fine commanding voice, and a mighty resolute eye, and a grand frock-coat which buttoned beautifully up to his leather stock. "I'm the man you want!" was written all over his face; and he ordered his two inferior policemen about with a severity which convinced us all that there was no trifling with *him*.

He began by going round the premises, outside and in; the result of that investigation proving to him that no thieves had broken in upon us from outside, and that the robbery, consequently, must have been committed by some person in the house. I leave you to imagine the state the servants were in when this official announcement first reached their ears. The Superintendent decided to begin by examining the boudoir; and, that done, to examine the servants next. At the same time, he posted one of his men on the staircase which led to the servants' bedrooms, with instructions to let nobody in the house pass him, till further orders.

At this latter proceeding, the weaker half of the human family went distracted on the spot. They bounced out of their corners; whisked upstairs in a body to Miss Rachel's room (Rosanna Spearman being carried away among them this time); burst in on Superintendent Seegrave; and, all looking equally guilty, summoned him to say which of them he suspected, at once.

Mr. Superintendent proved equal to the occasion – he looked at them with his resolute eye, and he cowed them with his military voice.

"Now, then, you women, go downstairs again, every one of you. I won't have you here. Look!" says Mr. Superintendent, suddenly pointing to a little smear of the decorative painting on Miss Rachel's door – at the outer edge, just under the lock. "Look what mischief the petticoats of some of you have done already. Clear out! clear out!" Rosanna Spearman, who was nearest to him, and nearest to the little smear on the door, set the example of obedience, and slipped off instantly to her work. The rest followed her out. The Superintendent finished his examination of the room; and, making nothing of it, asked me who had first discovered the robbery. My daughter had first discovered it. My daughter was sent for.

Mr. Superintendent proved to be a little too sharp with Penelope at starting. "Now, young woman, attend to me – and mind you speak the truth." Penelope fired up instantly. "I've never been taught to tell lies, Mr. Policeman! – and if father can stand there and hear me accused of falsehood and thieving, and my own bedroom shut against me, and my character taken away, which is all a poor girl has left, he's not the good father I take him for!" A timely word from me put Justice and Penelope on a pleasanter footing together. The questions and answers went swimmingly; and ended in nothing worth mentioning. My daughter had seen Miss Rachel put the Diamond in the drawer of the cabinet, the last thing at night. She had gone in with Miss Rachel's cup of tea, at eight the next morning, and had found the drawer open and empty. Upon that, she had alarmed the house – and there was an end of Penelope's evidence.

Mr. Superintendent next asked to see Miss Rachel herself. Penelope mentioned his request through the door. The answer reached us by the same road: – "I have nothing to tell the policeman – I can't see anybody." Our experienced officer looked equally surprised and offended when he heard that reply. I told him my young lady was ill, and begged him to wait a little and see her later. We thereupon went downstairs again, and were met by Mr. Godfrey and Mr. Franklin, crossing the hall.

The two gentlemen, being inmates of the house, were summoned to say if they could throw any light on the matter. Neither of them knew anything about it. Had they heard any suspicious noises during the previous night? They had heard nothing but the pattering of the rain. Had I, lying awake longer than either of them, heard nothing either? Nothing! Released from examination, Mr. Franklin (still sticking to the helpless view of our difficulty) whispered to me, – "That man will be of no earthly use to us. Superintendent Seegrave is an ass." Released in his turn, Mr. Godfrey whispered to me; – "Evidently a most competent person. Betteredge, I have the greatest faith in him!" Many men, many opinions, as one of the ancients said, before my time.[1]

Mr. Superintendent's next proceeding took him back to the "boudoir" again, with my daughter and me at his heels. His object was to discover whether any of the furniture had been moved, during the night, out of its customary place – his previous investigation in the room having, apparently, not gone quite far enough to satisfy his mind on this point.

While we were still poking about among the chairs and tables, the door of the bedroom was suddenly opened. After having denied herself to everybody, Miss Rachel, to our astonishment, walked into the midst of us of her own accord. She took up her garden hat from a chair, and then went straight to Penelope with this question: –

"Mr. Franklin Blake sent you with a message to me this morning?"

"Yes, miss."

"He wished to speak to me, didn't he?"

"Yes, miss."

"Where is he now?"

Hearing voices on the terrace below, I looked out of the window, and saw the two gentlemen walking up and down together.

---

1   Terence (185-159 B.C.), Roman author of comedies, is the ancient responsible for providing Betteredge with his "Many men, many opinions" bromide. The line comes from *Phormio* (161 B.C.): "Quot homines, tot sententiæ" (line 454).

Answering for my daughter, I said, "Mr. Franklin is on the terrace, miss."

Without another word, without heeding Mr. Superintendent, who tried to speak to her; pale as death, and wrapped up strangely in her own thoughts, she left the room, and went down to her cousins on the terrace.

It showed a want of due respect, it showed a breach of good manners, on my part; but, for the life of me, I couldn't help looking out of window when Miss Rachel met the gentlemen outside. She went up to Mr. Franklin without appearing to notice Mr. Godfrey, who thereupon drew back and left them by themselves. What she said to Mr. Franklin appeared to be spoken vehemently. It lasted but for a short time; and (judging by what I saw of his face from the window); seemed to astonish him beyond all power of expression. While they were still together, my lady appeared on the terrace. Miss Rachel saw her – said a few last words to Mr. Franklin – and suddenly went back into the house again, before her mother came up with her. My lady, surprised herself, and noticing Mr. Franklin's surprise, spoke to him. Mr. Godfrey joined them, and spoke also. Mr. Franklin walked away a little, between the two, telling them what had happened, I suppose; for they both stopped short, after taking a few steps, like persons struck with amazement. I had just seen as much as this, when the door of the sitting-room was opened violently. Miss Rachel walked swiftly through to her bedroom, wild and angry, with fierce eyes and flaming cheeks. Mr. Superintendent once more attempted to question her. She turned round on him at her bedroom door. "*I* have not sent for you!" she cried out vehemently. "*I* don't want you. My Diamond is lost. Neither you nor anybody else will ever find it!" With those words she went in, and locked the door in our faces. Penelope, standing nearest to it, heard her burst out crying the moment she was alone again.

In a rage, one moment; in tears, the next! What did it mean? I told the Superintendent it meant that Miss Rachel's temper was upset by the loss of her jewel. Being anxious for the honour of the family, it distressed me to see my young lady forget herself – even with a police-officer – and I made the best excuse I could, accordingly. In my own private mind, I was more puzzled by Miss Rachel's extraordinary language and conduct than words can tell. Taking what she had said at her bedroom door as a guide to guess by, I could only conclude that she was mortally offended by our sending for the police, and that Mr. Franklin's astonishment on the terrace was caused by her having expressed herself to him (as the person chiefly instrumental in fetching the police) to that effect. If this guess was right, why – having lost her Diamond – should she object to the presence in the house of the very people whose business it was to recover it for her? And how, in Heaven's name, could *she* know that the Moonstone would never be found again?

As things stood, at present, no answer to those questions was to be hoped for from anybody in the house. Mr. Franklin appeared to think it a point of honour to forbear repeating to a servant – even so old a servant as I was – what Miss Rachel had said to him on the terrace. Mr. Godfrey, who, as a gentleman and a relative, had been probably admitted into Mr. Franklin's confidence, respected that confidence as he was bound to do. My lady, who was also in the secret no doubt, and who alone had access to Miss Rachel, owned openly that she could make nothing of her. "You madden me when you talk of the Diamond!" All her mother's influence failed to extract from her a word more than that.

Here we were, then, at a deadlock about Miss Rachel – and at a deadlock about the Moonstone. In the first case, my lady was powerless to help us. In the second (as you shall presently judge), Mr. Seagrave was fast approaching the condition of a superintendent at his wits' end.

Having ferreted about all over the "boudoir," without making any discoveries among the furniture, our experienced officer applied to me to know, whether the servants in general were or were not acquainted with the place in which the Diamond had been put for the night.

"I knew where it was put, sir," I said, "to begin with. Samuel, the footman, knew also – for he was present in the hall, when they were talking about where the Diamond was to be kept that night. My daughter knew, as she has already told you. She or Samuel may have mentioned the thing to the other servants – or the other servants may have heard the talk for themselves, through the side-door of the hall, which might have been open to the back staircase. For all I can tell, everybody in the house may have known where the jewel was, last night."

My answer presenting rather a wide field for Mr. Superintendent's suspicions to range over, he tried to narrow it by asking about the servants' characters next.

I thought directly of Rosanna Spearman. But it was neither my place nor wish to direct suspicion against a poor girl, whose honesty had been above all doubt as long as I had known her. The matron at the reformatory had reported her to my lady as a sincerely penitent and thoroughly trustworthy girl. It was the Superintendent's business to discover reason for suspecting her first – and then, and not till then, it would be my duty to tell him how she came into my lady's service. "All our people have excellent characters," I said. "And all have deserved the trust their mistress has placed in them." After that, there was but one thing left for Mr. Seegrave to do – namely, to set to work, and tackle the servants' characters himself.

One after another, they were examined. One after another, they proved to have nothing to say – and said it (so far as the women were concerned) at great length, and with a very angry sense of the embargo laid on their bedrooms. The rest of them being sent back to their places downstairs, Penelope was then summoned, and examined separately a second time.

My daughter's little outbreak of temper in the "boudoir," and her readiness to think herself suspected, appeared to have produced an unfavourable impression on Superintendent Seegrave. It seemed also to dwell a little on his mind, that she had been the last person who saw the Diamond at night. When the second questioning was over, my girl came back to me in a frenzy. There was no doubt of it any longer – the police-officer had almost as good as told her she was the thief! I could scarcely believe him (taking Mr. Franklin's view) to be quite such an ass as that. But, though he said nothing, the eye with which he looked at my daughter was not a very pleasant eye to see. I laughed it off with poor Penelope, as something too ridiculous to be treated seriously – which it certainly was. Secretly, I am afraid I was foolish enough to be angry too. It was a little trying – it was, indeed. My girl sat down in a corner, with her apron over her head, quite broken-hearted. Foolish of her, you will say: she might have waited till he openly accused her. Well, being a man of just and equal temper, I admit that. Still, Mr. Superintendent might have remembered – never mind what he might have remembered. The devil take him!

The next and last step in the investigation brought matters, as they say, to a crisis. The officer had an interview (at which I was present) with my lady. After informing her that the Diamond *must* have been taken by somebody in the house, he requested permission for himself and his men to search the servants' rooms and boxes on the spot. My good mistress, like the generous high-bred woman she was, refused to let us be treated like thieves. "I will never consent to make such a return as that," she said, "for all I owe to the faithful servants who are employed in my house." Mr. Superintendent made his bow, with a look in my direction, which said plainly, "Why employ me, if you are to tie my hands in this way?" As head of the servants, I felt directly that we were bound, in justice to all parties, not to profit by our mistress's generosity. "We gratefully thank your ladyship," I said; "but we ask permission to do what is right in this matter, by giving up our keys. When Gabriel Betteredge sets the example," says I, stopping Superintendent Seegrave at the door, "the rest of the servants will follow, I promise you. There are my keys, to begin with!" My lady took me by the hand, and thanked me with the tears in her eyes. Lord! what would I not have given, at that moment, for the privilege of knocking Superintendent Seegrave down!

As I had promised for them, the other servants followed my lead, sorely against the grain, of course, but all taking the view that I took. The women were a sight to see, while the police-officers were rummaging among their things. The cook looked as if she could grill Mr. Superintendent alive on a furnace, and the other women looked as if they could eat him when he was done.

The search over, and no Diamond or sign of a Diamond being found, of course, anywhere, Superintendent Seegrave retired to my little room to consider with himself what he was to do next. He and his men had now been hours in the house, and had not advanced us one inch towards a discovery of how the Moonstone had been taken, or of whom we were to suspect as the thief.

While the police-officer was still pondering in solitude, I was sent for to see Mr. Franklin in the library. To my unutterable astonishment, just as my hand was on the door, it was suddenly opened from the inside, and out walked Rosanna Spearman!

★

After the library had been swept and cleaned in the morning, neither first nor second housemaid had any business in that room at any later period of the day. I stopped Rosanna Spearman, and charged her with a breach of domestic discipline on the spot.

"What might you want in the library at this time of day?" I inquired.

"Mr. Franklin Blake dropped one of his rings upstairs," says Rosanna; "and I have been into the library to give it to him." The girl's face was all in a flush as she made me that answer; and she walked away with a toss of her head and a look of self-importance which I was quite at a loss to account for. The proceedings in the house had doubtless upset all the women-servants more or less; but none of them had gone clean out of their natural characters, as Rosanna, to all appearance, had now gone out of hers.

I found Mr. Franklin writing at the library-table. He asked for a conveyance to the railway station the moment I entered the room. The first sound of his voice informed me that we now had the resolute side of him uppermost once more. The man made of cotton had disappeared; and the man made of iron sat before me again.

"Going to London, sir?" I asked.

"Going to telegraph to London," says Mr. Franklin. "I have convinced my aunt that we must have a cleverer head than Superintendent Seegrave's to help us; and I have got her permission to despatch a telegram to my father. He knows the Chief Commissioner of Police,[1] and the Commissioner can lay his hand on the right man to solve the mystery of the Diamond. Talking of mysteries, by-the-by," says Mr. Franklin, dropping his voice, "I have another word to say to

---

1   The Metropolitan Police Bill of 1829, drafted by Home Secretary Robert Peel, created the first metropolitan police force. Housed at 4 Whitehall, which backed onto Scotland Yard, the force soon became known as Scotland Yard. The first Chief Commissioner of Police was Colonel Charles Rowan, who ran the force from 1829 until his retirement in 1850. He was succeeded by Richard Mayne, who had been the junior Commissioner since 1829 and who remained in charge of the force until his death in 1868. The Detective Department, consisting of two Inspectors and six sergeants, was formed in 1842.

you before you go to the stables. Don't breathe a word of it to anybody as yet; but either Rosanna Spearman's head is not quite right, or I am afraid she knows more about the Moonstone than she ought to know."

I can hardly tell whether I was more startled or distressed at hearing him say that. If I had been younger, I might have confessed as much to Mr. Franklin. But when you are old, you acquire one excellent habit. In cases where you don't see your way clearly, you hold your tongue.

"She came in here with a ring I dropped in my bedroom," Mr. Franklin went on. "When I had thanked her, of course I expected her to go. Instead of that, she stood opposite to me at the table, looking at me in the oddest manner – half frightened, and half familiar – I couldn't make it out. 'This is a strange thing about the Diamond, sir,' she said, in a curiously sudden, headlong way. I said, 'Yes, it was,' and wondered what was coming next. Upon my honour, Betteredge, I think she must be wrong in the head! She said, 'They will never find the Diamond, sir, will they? No! nor the person who took it – I'll answer for that.' She actually nodded and smiled at me! Before I could ask her what she meant, we heard your step outside. I suppose she was afraid of your catching her here. At any rate, she changed colour, and left the room. What on earth does it mean?"

I could not bring myself to tell him the girl's story, even then. It would have been almost as good as telling him that she was the thief. Besides, even if I had made a clean breast of it, and even supposing she was the thief, the reason why she should let out her secret to Mr. Franklin, of all the people in the world, would have been still as far to seek as ever.

"I can't bear the idea of getting the poor girl into a scrape, merely because she has a flighty way with her, and talks very strangely," Mr. Franklin went on. "And yet if she had said to the Superintendent what she said to me, fool as he is, I'm afraid –" He stopped there, and left the rest unspoken.

"The best way, sir," I said, "will be for me to say two words privately to my mistress about it at the first opportunity. My lady has a very friendly interest in Rosanna; and the girl may only have been forward and foolish, after all. When there's a mess of any kind in a house, sir, the women-servants like to look at the gloomy side – it gives the poor wretches a kind of importance in their own eyes. If there's anybody ill, trust the women for prophesying that the person will die. If it's a jewel lost, trust them for prophesying that it will never be found again."

This view (which, I am bound to say, I thought a probable view myself, on reflection) seemed to relieve Mr. Franklin mightily: he folded up his telegram, and dismissed the subject. On my way to the stables, to order the pony-chaise,[1] I looked in at the servants' hall, where they were at dinner. Rosanna Spearman was not among them. On inquiry, I found that she had been suddenly taken ill, and had gone upstairs to her own room to lie down.

"Curious! She looked well enough when I saw her last," I remarked.

Penelope followed me out. "Don't talk in that way before the rest of them, father," she said. "You only make them harder on Rosanna than ever. The poor thing is breaking her heart about Mr. Franklin Blake."

Here was another view of the girl's conduct. If it was possible for Penelope to be right, the explanation of Rosanna's strange language and behaviour might have been all in this – that she didn't care what she said, so long as she could surprise Mr. Franklin into speaking to her. Granting that to be the right reading of the riddle, it accounted, perhaps, for her flighty self-conceited manner when she passed me in the hall. Though he had only said three words, still she had carried her point, and Mr. Franklin *had* spoken to her.

I saw the pony harnessed myself. In the infernal network of mysteries and uncertainties that now surrounded us, I declare it was a relief to observe how well the buckles and straps understood each other! When you had seen the pony backed into the shafts of the chaise, you had seen something there was no doubt about. And that, let me tell you, was becoming a treat of the rarest kind in our household.

Going round with the chaise to the front door, I found not only Mr. Franklin, but Mr. Godfrey and Superintendent Seegrave also waiting for me on the steps.

Mr. Superintendent's reflections (after failing to find the Diamond

---

1 In this case, the pony-chaise was probably a two-wheel carriage with room for four passengers.

in the servants' rooms or boxes) had led him, it appeared, to an entirely new conclusion. Still sticking to his first text, namely, that somebody in the house had stolen the jewel, our experienced officer was now of opinion that the thief (he was wise enough not to name poor Penelope, whatever he might privately think of her!) had been acting in concert with the Indians; and he accordingly proposed shifting his inquiries to the jugglers in the prison at Frizinghall. Hearing of this new move, Mr. Franklin had volunteered to take the Superintendent back to the town, from which he could telegraph to London as easily as from our station. Mr. Godfrey, still devoutly believing in Mr. Seegrave, and greatly interested in witnessing the examination of the Indians, had begged leave to accompany the officer to Frizinghall. One of the two inferior policemen was to be left at the house, in case anything happened. The other was to go back with the Superintendent to the town. So the four places in the pony-chaise were just filled.

Before he took the reins to drive off, Mr. Franklin walked me away a few steps out of hearing of the others.

"I will wait to telegraph to London," he said, "till I see what comes of our examination of the Indians. My own conviction is, that this muddle-headed local police-officer is as much in the dark as ever, and is simply trying to gain time. The idea of any of the servants being in league with the Indians is a preposterous absurdity, in my opinion. Keep about the house, Betteredge, till I come back, and try what you can make of Rosanna Spearman. I don't ask you to do anything degrading to your own self-respect, or anything cruel towards the girl. I only ask you to exercise your observation more carefully than usual. We will make as light of it as we can before my aunt – but this is a more important matter than you may suppose."

"It is a matter of twenty thousand pounds, sir," I said, thinking of the value of the Diamond.

"It's a matter of quieting Rachel's mind," answered Mr. Franklin gravely. "I am very uneasy about her."

He left me suddenly, as if he desired to cut short any further talk between us. I thought I understood why. Further talk might have let me into the secret of what Miss Rachel had said to him on the terrace.

So they drove away to Frizinghall. I was ready enough, in the girl's own interest, to have a little talk with Rosanna in private. But the needful opportunity failed to present itself. She only came downstairs again at tea-time. When she did appear, she was flighty and excited, had what they call an hysterical attack, took a dose of sal-volatile[1] by my lady's order, and was sent back to her bed.

The day wore on to its end drearily and miserably enough, I can tell you. Miss Rachel still kept her room, declaring that she was too ill to come down to dinner that day. My lady was in such low spirits about her daughter, that I could not bring myself to make her additionally anxious, by reporting what Rosanna Spearman had said to Mr. Franklin. Penelope persisted in believing that she was to be forthwith tried, sentenced, and transported for theft. The other women took to their Bibles and hymn-books, and looked as sour as verjuice[2] over their reading – a result, which I have observed, in my sphere of life, to follow generally on the performance of acts of piety at unaccustomed periods of the day. As for me, I hadn't even heart enough to open my *Robinson Crusoe*. I went out into the yard, and, being hard up for a little cheerful society, set my chair by the kennels, and talked to the dogs.

Half an hour before dinner-time, the two gentlemen came back from Frizinghall, having arranged with Superintendent Seegrave that he was to return to us the next day. They had called on Mr. Murthwaite, the Indian traveller, at his present residence, near the town. At Mr. Franklin's request, he had kindly given them the benefit of his knowledge of the language, in dealing with those two, out of the three Indians, who knew nothing of English. The examination, conducted carefully, and at great length, had ended in nothing; not the shadow of a reason being discovered for suspecting the jugglers of having tampered with any of our servants. On reaching that conclusion, Mr. Franklin had sent his telegraphic message to London, and there the matter now rested till to-morrow came.

So much for the history of the day that followed the birthday. Not a glimmer of light had broken in on us, so far. A day or two after, however, the darkness lifted a little. How, and with what result, you shall presently see.

---

1 Sal-volatile is a smelling salt, made with ammonium carbonate.
2 Verjuice is the acidic juice of such sour or unripe fruit as crab apples or grapes.

CHAPTER XII

THE Thursday night passed, and nothing happened. With the Friday morning came two pieces of news.

Item the first: the baker's man declared he had met Rosanna Spearman, on the previous afternoon, with a thick veil on, walking towards Frizinghall by the footpath way over the moor. It seemed strange that anybody should be mistaken about Rosanna, whose shoulder marked her out pretty plainly, poor thing – but mistaken the man must have been; for Rosanna, as you know, had been all the Thursday afternoon ill upstairs in her room.

Item the second came through the postman. Worthy Mr. Candy had said one more of his many unlucky things, when he drove off in the rain on the birthday night, and told me that a doctor's skin was waterproof. In spite of his skin, the wet had got through him. He had caught a chill that night, and was now down with a fever. The last accounts, brought by the postman, represented him to be light-headed – talking nonsense as glibly, poor man, in his delirium as he often talked it in his sober senses. We were all sorry for the little doctor; but Mr. Franklin appeared to regret his illness, chiefly on Miss Rachel's account. From what he said to my lady, while I was in the room at breakfast-time, he appeared to think that Miss Rachel – if the suspense about the Moonstone was not soon set at rest – might stand in urgent need of the best medical advice at our disposal.

Breakfast had not been over long, when a telegram from Mr. Blake, the elder, arrived, in answer to his son. It informed us that he had laid hands (by help of his friend, the Commissioner) on the right man to help us. The name of him was Sergeant Cuff;[1] and the arrival of him from London might be expected by the morning train.

---

1   Collins modelled Richard Cuff, among the first and most memorable detectives in English fiction, after the real-life Inspector Jonathan Whicher, who rightfully suspected Constance Kent of the murder of her half-brother in the Road-house murder investigation of 1860. See Appendix B for newspaper accounts of the crime, the investigation, the confession, and the trial. We should note, however, that private investigator Mr. Dark, of Collins's 1858 short story "A Marriage Tragedy" – later included in Collins's collection of short stories titled *The Queen of Hearts* (1859) as "A Plot in Private Life" – appears also to have been Cuff's *literary* predecessor. Dickens himself wrote two articles about Whicher – whom he re-named Witchem – for his magazine *Household Words* in 1850. The articles – "A Detective Police Party" (July 27, 1850, 409-14) and "Three 'Detective' Anecdotes" (September 14,

At reading the name of the new police-officer, Mr. Franklin gave a start. It seems that he had heard some curious anecdotes about Sergeant Cuff, from his father's lawyer, during his stay in London. "I begin to hope we are seeing the end of our anxieties already," he said. "If half the stories I have heard are true, when it comes to unravelling a mystery, there isn't the equal in England of Sergeant Cuff!"

We all got excited and impatient as the time drew near for the appearance of this renowned and capable character. Superintendent Seegrave, returning to us at his appointed time, and hearing that the Sergeant was expected, instantly shut himself up in a room, with pen, ink, and paper, to make notes of the Report which would be certainly expected from him. I should have liked to have gone to the station myself, to fetch the Sergeant. But my lady's carriage and horses were not to be thought of, even for the celebrated Cuff; and the pony-chaise was required later for Mr. Godfrey. He deeply regretted being obliged to leave his aunt at such an anxious time; and he kindly put off the hour of his departure till as late as the last train, for the purpose of hearing what the clever London police-officer thought of the case. But on Friday night he must be in town, having a Ladies' Charity, in difficulties, waiting to consult him on Saturday morning.

When the time came for the Sergeant's arrival, I went down to the gate to look out for him.

A fly from the railway drove up as I reached the lodge; and out got a grizzled, elderly man, so miserably lean that he looked as if he had not got an ounce of flesh on his bones in any part of him. He was dressed all in decent black, with a white cravat round his neck. His face was as sharp as a hatchet, and the skin of it was as yellow and dry and withered as an autumn leaf. His eyes, of a steely light grey, had a very disconcerting trick, when they encountered your eyes, of looking as if they expected something more from you than you were aware of yourself. His walk was soft; his voice was melancholy; his long lanky fingers were hooked like claws. He might have been a parson, or an undertaker – or anything else you like, except what he really was.[1] A more complete opposite to Superintendent Seegrave

---

1850, 577-80) capitalized on what Betteredge calls in *The Moonstone* a "Detective-Fever" that gripped England in the 1850s and 1860s.

1   Catherine Peters comments on this description of Cuff's appearance, suggesting the he "is like many of Wilkie Collins' detectives, tinged with the clerical" (306).

than Sergeant Cuff, and a less comforting officer to look at, for a family in distress, I defy you to discover, search where you may.

"Is this Lady Verinder's?" he asked.

"Yes, sir."

"I am Sergeant Cuff."

"This way, sir, if you please."

On our road to the house, I mentioned my name and position in the family, to satisfy him that he might speak to me about the business on which my lady was to employ him. Not a word did he say about the business, however, for all that. He admired the grounds, and remarked that he felt the sea air very brisk and refreshing. I privately wondered, on my side, how the celebrated Cuff had got his reputation. We reached the house, in the temper of two strange dogs, coupled up together for the first time in their lives by the same chain.

Asking for my lady, and hearing that she was in one of the conservatories, we went round to the gardens at the back, and sent a servant to seek her. While we were waiting, Sergeant Cuff looked through the evergreen arch on our left, spied out our rosery, and walked straight in, with the first appearance of anything like interest that he had shown yet. To the gardener's astonishment, and to my disgust, this celebrated policeman proved to be quite a mine of learning on the trumpery subject of rose-gardens.[1]

"Ah, you've got the right exposure here to the south and sou'-west," says the Sergeant, with a wag of his grizzled head, and a streak of pleasure in his melancholy voice. "This is the shape for a rosery —

---

1   Ian Ousby, in his article "Wilkie Collins's *The Moonstone* and the Constance Kent Case" (*Notes and Queries*, 21, 1 January 1974: 25), suggests that Cuff's attachment to roses originated in Sergeant Frederick Adolphus Williamson, who had aided Detective Whicher's investigation of the Constance Kent-Road-house murder case in 1860 and who became chief inspector of the Detective force by 1865. Williamson apparently had a passion for gardening. Collins seems also to have known his roses, several of which Cuff names and discusses over the next several pages. The musk rose, which Cuff calls an English rose, is a prickly shrub native to the Mediterranean region and named for its clustered, musk-scented white flowers. The damask is a rose native to Asia that has fragrant red or pink flowers used as a source of attar. The moss rose, another English rose, named for a moss-like growth on its stalk, is a variety of the cabbage rose. A dog rose is a common species of wild rose frequently found among hedges. It is pale red in colour. Cuff's ability to draw a sharp line between his profession and his passion recalls John Wemmick of Dickens's *Great Expectations*. Wemmick's character when on duty as Mr. Jaggers's clerk is dramatically different from the character he shows Pip when he is at home in Walworth with his "Aged Parent."

nothing like a circle set in a square. Yes, yes; with walks between all the beds. But they oughtn't to be gravel walks like these. Grass, Mr. Gardener – grass walks between your roses; gravel's too hard for them. That's a sweet pretty bed of white roses and blush roses. They always mix well together, don't they? Here's the white musk-rose, Mr. Betteredge – our old English rose holding up its head along with the best and the newest of them. Pretty dear!" says the Sergeant, fondling the Musk Rose with his lanky fingers, and speaking to it as if he was speaking to a child.

This was a nice sort of man to recover Miss Rachel's Diamond, and to find out the thief who stole it!

"You seem to be fond of roses, Sergeant?" I remarked.

"I haven't much time to be fond of anything," says Sergeant Cuff. "But when I *have* a moment's fondness to bestow, most times, Mr. Betteredge, the roses get it. I began my life among them in my father's nursery garden, and I shall end my life among them, if I can. Yes. One of these days (please God) I shall retire from catching thieves, and try my hand at growing roses. There will be grass walks, Mr. Gardener, between my beds," says the Sergeant, on whose mind the gravel paths of our rosery seemed to dwell unpleasantly.

"It seems an odd taste, sir," I ventured to say, "for a man in your line of life."

"If you will look about you (which most people won't do)," says Sergeant Cuff, "you will see that the nature of a man's tastes is, most times, as opposite as possible to the nature of a man's business. Show me any two things more opposite one from the other than a rose and a thief; and I'll correct my tastes accordingly – if it isn't too late at my time of life. You find the damask rose a goodish stock for most of the tender sorts, don't you, Mr. Gardener? Ah! I thought so. Here's a lady coming. Is it Lady Verinder?"

He had seen her before either I or the gardener had seen her – though we knew which way to look, and he didn't. I began to think him rather a quicker man than he appeared to be at first sight.

The Sergeant's appearance, or the Sergeant's errand – one or both – seemed to cause my lady some little embarrassment. She was, for the first time in all my experience of her, at a loss what to say at an interview with a stranger. Sergeant Cuff put her at ease directly. He asked if any other person had been employed about the robbery before we sent for him; and hearing that another person had been called in, and was now in the house, begged leave to speak to him before anything else was done.

My lady led the way back. Before he followed her, the Sergeant relieved his mind on the subject of the gravel walks by a parting word to the gardener. "Get her ladyship to try grass," he said, with a sour look at the paths. "No gravel! no gravel!"

Why Superintendent Seegrave should have appeared to be several sizes smaller than life, on being presented to Sergeant Cuff, I can't undertake to explain. I can only state the fact. They retired together; and remained a weary long time shut up from all mortal intrusion. When they came out, Mr. Superintendent was excited, and Mr. Sergeant was yawning.

"The Sergeant wishes to see Miss Verinder's sitting-room," says Mr. Seegrave, addressing me with great pomp and eagerness. "The Sergeant may have some questions to ask. Attend the Sergeant, if you please!"

While I was being ordered about in this way, I looked at the great Cuff. The great Cuff, on his side, looked at Superintendent Seegrave in that quietly expecting way which I have already noticed. I can't affirm that he was on the watch for his brother-officer's speedy appearance in the character of an Ass — I can only say that I strongly suspected it.

I led the way upstairs. The Sergeant went softly all over the Indian cabinet and all round the "boudoir"; asking questions (occasionally only of Mr. Superintendent, and continually of me), the drift of which I believe to have been equally unintelligible to both of us. In due time, his course brought him to the door, and put him face to face with the decorative painting that you know of. He laid one lean inquiring finger on the small smear, just under the lock, which Super-intendent Seegrave had already noticed, when he reproved the women-servants for all crowding together into the room.

"That's a pity," says Sergeant Cuff. "How did it happen?"

He put the question to me. I answered that the women-servants had crowded into the room on the previous morning, and that some of their petticoats had done the mischief. "Superintendent Seegrave ordered them out, sir," I added, "before they did any more harm."

"Right!" says Mr. Superintendent in his military way. "I ordered them out. The petticoats did it, Sergeant – the petticoats did it."

"Did you notice which petticoat did it?" asked Sergeant Cuff, still addressing himself, not to his brother-officer, but to me.

"No, sir."

He turned to Superintendent Seegrave upon that, and said, "*You* noticed, I suppose?"

Mr. Superintendent looked a little taken aback; but he made the best of it. "I can't charge my memory, Sergeant," he said, "a mere trifle – a mere trifle."

Sergeant Cuff looked at Mr. Seegrave as he had looked at the gravel walks in the rosery, and gave us, in his melancholy way, the first taste of his quality which we had had yet.

"I made a private inquiry last week, Mr. Superintendent," he said. "At one end of the inquiry there was a murder, and at the other end there was a spot of ink on a tablecloth that nobody could account for. In all my experience along the dirtiest ways of this dirty little world, I have never met with such a thing as a trifle yet. Before we go a step further in this business we must see the petticoat that made the smear, and we must know for certain when that paint was wet."

Mr. Superintendent – taking his set-down rather sulkily – asked if he should summon the women. Sergeant Cuff, after considering a minute, sighed, and shook his head.

"No," he said, "we'll take the matter of the paint first. It's a question of Yes or No with the paint – which is short. It's a question of petticoats with the women – which is long. What o'clock was it when the servants were in this room yesterday morning? Eleven o'clock – eh? Is there anybody in the house who knows whether that paint was wet or dry, at eleven yesterday morning?"

"Her ladyship's nephew, Mr. Franklin Blake, knows," I said.

"Is the gentleman in the house?"

Mr. Franklin was as close at hand as could be – waiting for his first chance of being introduced to the great Cuff. In half a minute he was in the room, and was giving his evidence as follows:

"That door, Sergeant," he said, "has been painted by Miss Verinder, under my inspection, with my help, and in a vehicle of my own composition. The vehicle dries whatever colours may be used with it, in twelve hours."

"Do you remember when the smeared bit was done, sir?" asked the Sergeant.

"Perfectly," answered Mr. Franklin. "That was the last morsel of the door to be finished. We wanted to get it done, on Wednesday last – and I myself completed it by three in the afternoon, or soon after."

"To-day is Friday," said Sergeant Cuff, addressing himself to Superintendent Seegrave. "Let us reckon back, sir. At three on the Wednesday afternoon, that bit of the painting was completed. The vehicle dried it in twelve hours – that is to say, dried it by three o'clock on Thursday morning. At eleven on Thursday morning you held your inquiry here. Take three from eleven, and eight remains. That paint had been *eight hours dry*, Mr. Superintendent, when you supposed that the women-servants' petticoats smeared it."

First knock-down blow for Mr. Seegrave! If he had not suspected poor Penelope, I should have pitied him.

Having settled the question of the paint, Sergeant Cuff, from that moment, gave his brother-officer up as a bad job – and addressed himself to Mr. Franklin, as the more promising assistant of the two.

"It's quite on the cards, sir," he said, "that you have put the clue into our hands."

As the words passed his lips, the bedroom door opened, and Miss Rachel came out among us suddenly.

She addressed herself to the Sergeant, without appearing to notice (or to heed) that he was a perfect stranger to her.

"Did you say," she asked, pointing to Mr. Franklin, "that *he* had put the clue into your hands?"

("This is Miss Verinder," I whispered, behind the Sergeant.) "That gentleman, miss," says the Sergeant – with his steely-grey eyes carefully studying my young lady's face – "has possibly put the clue into our hands."

She turned for one moment, and tried to look at Mr. Franklin. I say, tried, for she suddenly looked away again before their eyes met. There seemed to be some strange disturbance in her mind. She coloured up, and then she turned pale again. With the paleness, there came a new look into her face – a look which it startled me to see.

"Having answered your question, miss," says the Sergeant, "I beg leave to make an inquiry in my turn. There is a smear on the painting of your door, here. Do you happen to know when it was done? or who did it?"

Instead of making any reply, Miss Rachel went on with her questions, as if he had not spoken, or as if she had not heard him.

"Are you another police-officer?" she asked.

"I am Sergeant Cuff, miss, of the Detective Police."

"Do you think a young lady's advice worth having?"

"I shall be glad to hear it, miss."

"Do your duty by yourself – and don't allow Mr. Franklin Blake to help you!"

She said those words so spitefully, so savagely, with such an extraordinary outbreak of ill-will towards Mr. Franklin, in her voice and in her look, that – though I had known her from a baby, though I loved and honoured her next to my lady herself – I was ashamed of Miss Rachel for the first time in my life.

Sergeant Cuff's immovable eyes never stirred from off her face. "Thank you, miss," he said. "Do you happen to know anything about the smear? Might you have done it by accident yourself?"

"I know nothing about the smear."

With that answer, she turned away, and shut herself up again in her bedroom. This time, I heard her – as Penelope had heard her before – burst out crying as soon as she was alone again.

I couldn't bring myself to look at the Sergeant – I looked at Mr. Franklin, who stood nearest to me. He seemed to be even more sorely distressed at what had passed than I was.

"I told you I was uneasy about her," he said. "And now you see why."

"Miss Verinder appears to be a little out of temper about the loss of her Diamond," remarked the Sergeant. "It's a valuable jewel. Natural enough! natural enough!"

Here was the excuse that I had made for her (when she forgot herself before Superintendent Seegrave, on the previous day) being made for her over again, by a man who couldn't have had *my* interest in making it – for he was a perfect stranger! A kind of cold shudder ran through me, which I couldn't account for at the time. I know, now, that I must have got my first suspicion, at that moment, of a new light (and a horrid light) having suddenly fallen on the case, in the mind of Sergeant Cuff – purely and entirely in consequence of what he had seen in Miss Rachel, and heard from Miss Rachel, at that first interview between them.

"A young lady's tongue is a privileged member, sir," says the Sergeant to Mr. Franklin. "Let us forget what has passed, and go straight on with this business. Thanks to you, we know when the paint was dry. The next thing to discover is when the paint was last seen without that smear. You have got a head on your shoulders – and you understand what I mean."

Mr. Franklin composed himself, and came back with an effort from Miss Rachel to the matter in hand.

"I think I do understand," he said. "The more we narrow the question of time, the more we also narrow the field of inquiry."

"That's it, sir," said the Sergeant. "Did you notice your work here, on the Wednesday afternoon, after you had done it?"

Mr. Franklin shook his head, and answered, "I can't say I did."

"Did *you*?" inquired Sergeant Cuff, turning to me.

"I can't say I did either, sir."

"Who was the last person in the room, the last thing on Wednesday night?"

"Miss Rachel, I suppose, sir."

Mr. Franklin struck in there. "Or possibly your daughter, Betteredge." He turned to Sergeant Cuff, and explained that my daughter was Miss Verinder's maid.

"Mr. Betteredge, ask your daughter to step up. Stop!" says the Sergeant, taking me away to the window, out of earshot. "Your Superintendent here," he went on, in a whisper, "has made a pretty full report to me of the manner in which he has managed this case. Among other things, he has, by his own confession, set the servants' backs up. It's very important to smooth them down again. Tell your daughter, and tell the rest of them, these two things, with my compliments: First, that I have no evidence before me, yet, that the Diamond has been stolen; I only know that the Diamond has been lost. Second, that *my* business here with the servants is simply to ask them to lay their heads together and help me to find it."

My experience of the women-servants, when Superintendent Seegrave laid his embargo on their rooms, came in handy here.

"May I make so bold, Sergeant, as to tell the women a third thing?" I asked. "Are they free (with your compliments) to fidget up and downstairs, and whisk in and out of their bedrooms, if the fit takes them?"

"Perfectly free," said the Sergeant.

"*That* will smooth them down, sir," I remarked, "from the cook to the scullion."[1]

"Go, and do it at once, Mr. Betteredge."

I did it in less than five minutes. There was only one difficulty when I came to the bit about the bedrooms. It took a pretty stiff exertion of my authority, as chief, to prevent the whole of the female household from following me and Penelope upstairs, in the character of volunteer witnesses in a burning fever of anxiety to help Sergeant Cuff.

The Sergeant seemed to approve of Penelope. He became a trifle less dreary; and he looked much as he had looked when he noticed the white musk rose in the flower-garden. Here is my daughter's evidence, as drawn off from her by the Sergeant. She gave it, I think, very prettily — but, there! she is my child all over: nothing of her mother in her; Lord bless you, nothing of her mother in her!

Penelope examined: Took a lively interest in the painting on the door, having helped to mix the colours. Noticed the bit of work under the lock, because it was the last bit done. Had seen it, some hours afterwards, without a smear. Had left it, as late as twelve at night, without a smear. Had, at that hour, wished her young lady good-night in the bedroom; had heard the clock strike in the "boudoir"; had her hand at the time on the handle of the painted door; knew the paint was wet (having helped to mix the colours, as aforesaid); took particular pains not to touch it; could swear that she held up the skirts of her dress, and that there was no smear on the paint then; could *not* swear that her dress mightn't have touched it accidentally in going out; remembered the dress she had on, because it was new, a present from Miss Rachel; her father remembered, and could speak to it, too; could, and would, and did fetch it; dress recognised by her father as the dress she wore that night; skirts examined, a long job from the size of them; not the ghost of a paint-stain discovered anywhere. End of Penelope's evidence — and very pretty and convincing, too. Signed, Gabriel Betteredge.

---

1 A scullion was a servant employed to do menial chores in the kitchen.

The Sergeant's next proceeding was to question me about any large dogs in the house who might have got into the room, and done the mischief with a whisk of their tails. Hearing that this was impossible, he next sent for a magnifying-glass, and tried how the smear looked, seen that way. No skin-mark (as of a human hand) printed off on the paint. All the signs visible – signs which told that the paint had been smeared by some loose article of somebody's dress touching it in going by. That somebody (putting together Penelope's evidence and Mr. Franklin's evidence) must have been in the room, and done the mischief, between midnight and three o'clock on the Thursday morning.

Having brought his investigation to this point, Sergeant Cuff discovered that such a person as Superintendent Seegrave was still left in the room, upon which he summed up the proceedings for his brother-officer's benefit, as follows:

"This trifle of yours, Mr. Superintendent," says the Sergeant, pointing to the place on the door, "has grown a little in importance since you noticed it last. At the present stage of the inquiry there are, as I take it, three discoveries to make, starting from that smear. Find out (first) whether there is any article of dress in this house with the smear of the paint on it. Find out (second) who that dress belongs to. Find out (third) how the person can account for having been in this room, and smeared the paint, between midnight and three in the morning. If the person can't satisfy you, you haven't far to look for the hand that has got the Diamond.[1] I'll work this by myself, if you please, and detain you no longer from your regular business in the town. You have got one of your men here, I see. Leave him here at my disposal, in case I want him – and allow me to wish you good morning."

Superintendent Seegrave's respect for the Sergeant was great; but his respect for himself was greater still. Hit hard by the celebrated Cuff, he hit back smartly, to the best of his ability, on leaving the room.

"I have abstained from expressing any opinion, so far," says Mr.

---

1   The Constance Kent case suggests itself once again at this point of the story. Collins has substituted dried and smeared paint for bloodstains on a night-dress. Again, though, we should note that the paint-stained night-dress of *The Moonstone* may also be traceable to a literary predecessor, a blood-stained gown in Collins's 1858 short story "A Plot in Private Life."

Superintendent, with his military voice still in good working order. "I have now only one remark to offer, on leaving this case in your hands. There *is* such a thing, Sergeant, as making a mountain out of a molehill. Good morning."

"There is also such a thing as making nothing out of a molehill, in consequence of your head being too high to see it." Having returned his brother-officer's compliments in those terms, Sergeant Cuff wheeled about, and walked away to the window by himself.

Mr. Franklin and I waited to see what was coming next. The Sergeant stood at the window with his hands in his pockets, looking out, and whistling the tune of "The Last Rose of Summer"[1] softly to himself. Later in the proceedings, I discovered that he only forgot his manners so far as to whistle, when his mind was hard at work, seeing its way inch by inch to its own private ends, on which occasions "The Last Rose of Summer" evidently helped and encouraged him. I suppose it fitted in somehow with his character. It reminded him, you

---

1 Cuff's trademark "Last Rose of Summer" comes from Thomas Moore (1779-1852), an Irish-born poet and musician whose "'Tis the Last Rose of Summer" was among the most popular of a number of songs he published as his *Irish Melodies*. The text follows:

'Tis the last rose of summer
Left blooming alone;
All her lovely companions
Are faded and gone;
No flower of her kindred,
No rose-bud is nigh,
To reflect back her blushes,
Or give sigh for sigh.
I'll not leave thee, thou lone one!
To pine on the stem;
Since the lovely are sleeping,
Go, sleep thou with them.
Thus kindly I scatter
Thy leaves o'er the bed,
Where thy mates of the garden
Lie scentless and dead.
So soon may *I* follow,
When friendships decay,
And from Love's shining circle
The gems drop away.
When true hearts lie wither'd,
And fond ones are flown,
Oh! who would inhabit
This bleak world alone?

see, of his favourite roses, and, as *he* whistled it, it was the most melancholy tune going.

Turning from the window, after a minute or two, the Sergeant walked into the middle of the room, and stopped there, deep in thought, with his eyes on Miss Rachel's bedroom door. After a little he roused himself, nodded his head, as much as to say, "That will do!" and, addressing me, asked for ten minutes' conversation with my mistress, at her ladyship's earliest convenience.

Leaving the room with this message, I heard Mr. Franklin ask the Sergeant a question, and stopped to hear the answer also at the threshold of the door.

"Can you guess yet," inquired Mr. Franklin, "who has stolen the Diamond?"

"*Nobody has stolen the Diamond*," answered Sergeant Cuff.

We both started at that extraordinary view of the case, and both earnestly begged him to tell us what he meant.

"Wait a little," said the Sergeant. "The pieces of the puzzle are not all put together yet."

★

CHAPTER XIII

I FOUND my lady in her own sitting-room. She started and looked annoyed when I mentioned that Sergeant Cuff wished to speak to her.

"*Must* I see him?" she asked. "Can't you represent me, Gabriel?"

I felt at a loss to understand this, and showed it plainly, I suppose, in my face. My lady was so good as to explain herself. "I am afraid my nerves are a little shaken," she said. "There is something in that police-officer from London which I recoil from – I don't know why. I have a presentiment that he is bringing trouble and misery with him into the house. Very foolish, and very unlike *me* – but so it is."

I hardly knew what to say to this. The more *I* saw of Sergeant Cuff, the better I liked him. My lady rallied a little after having opened her heart to me – being, naturally, a woman of a high courage, as I have already told you.

"If I must see him, I must," she said. "But I can't prevail on myself to see him alone. Bring him in, Gabriel, and stay here as long as he stays."

This was the first attack of the megrims[1] that I remembered in my mistress since the time when she was a young girl. I went back to the "boudoir." Mr. Franklin strolled out into the garden, and joined Mr. Godfrey, whose time for departure was now drawing near. Sergeant Cuff and I went straight to my mistress's room.

I declare my lady turned a shade paler at the sight of him! She commanded herself, however, in other respects, and asked the Sergeant if he had any objection to my being present. She was so good as to add, that I was her trusted adviser, as well as her old servant, and that in anything which related to the household I was the person whom it might be most profitable to consult. The Sergeant politely answered that he would take my presence as a favour, having something to say about the servants in general, and having found my experience in that quarter already of some use to him. My lady pointed to two chairs, and we set in for our conference immediately.

"I have already formed an opinion on this case," says Sergeant Cuff, "which I beg your ladyship's permission to keep to myself for the present. My business now is to mention what I have discovered upstairs in Miss Verinder's sitting-room, and what I have decided (with your ladyship's leave) on doing next."

He then went into the matter of the smear on the paint, and stated the conclusions he drew from it – just as he had stated them (only with greater respect of language) to Superintendent Seegrave. "One thing," he said, in conclusion, "is certain. The Diamond is missing out of the drawer in the cabinet. Another thing is next to certain. The marks from the smear on the door must be on some article of dress belonging to somebody in this house. We must discover that article of dress before we go a step further."

"And that discovery," remarked my mistress, "implies, I presume, the discovery of the thief?"

"I beg your ladyship's pardon – I don't say the Diamond is stolen. I only say, at present, that the Diamond is missing. The discovery of the stained dress may lead the way to finding it."

Her ladyship looked at me. "Do you understand this?" she said.

"Sergeant Cuff understands it, my lady," I answered.

"How do you propose to discover the stained dress?" inquired my

---

1 Megrims are migraine headaches.

mistress, addressing herself once more to the Sergeant. "My good servants, who have been with me for years, have, I am ashamed to say, had their boxes and rooms searched already by the other officer. I can't and won't permit them to be insulted in that way a second time!"

(There was a mistress to serve! There was a woman in ten thousand, if you like!)

"That is the very point I was about to put to your ladyship," said the Sergeant. "The other officer has done a world of harm to this inquiry, by letting the servants see that he suspected them. If I give them cause to think themselves suspected a second time, there's no knowing what obstacles they may not throw in my way – the women especially. At the same time, their boxes *must* be searched again – for this plain reason, that the first investigation only looked for the Diamond, and that the second investigation must look for the stained dress. I quite agree with you, my lady, that the servants' feelings ought to be consulted. But I am equally clear that the servants' wardrobes ought to be searched."

This looked very like a deadlock. My lady said so, in choicer language than mine.

"I have got a plan to meet the difficulty," said Sergeant Cuff, "if your ladyship will consent to it. I propose explaining the case to the servants."

"The women will think themselves suspected directly," I said, interrupting him.

"The women won't, Mr. Betteredge," answered the Sergeant, "if I can tell them I am going to examine the wardrobes of *every* body – from her ladyship downwards – who slept in the house on Wednesday night. It's a mere formality," he added, with a side-look at my mistress; "but the servants will accept it as even dealing between them and their betters; and, instead of hindering the investigation, they will make a point of honour of assisting it."

I saw the truth of that. My lady, after her first surprise was over, saw the truth of it also.

"You are certain the investigation is necessary?" she said.

"It's the shortest way that I can see, my lady, to the end we have in view."

My mistress rose to ring the bell for her maid. "You shall speak to the servants," she said, "with the keys of my wardrobe in your hand."

Sergeant Cuff stopped her by a very unexpected question.

"Hadn't we better make sure first," he asked, "that the other ladies and gentlemen in the house will consent, too?"

"The only other lady in the house is Miss Verinder," answered my mistress, with a look of surprise. "The only gentlemen are my nephews, Mr. Blake and Mr. Ablewhite. There is not the least fear of a refusal from any of the three."

I reminded my lady here that Mr. Godfrey was going away. As I said the words, Mr. Godfrey himself knocked at the door to say good-bye, and was followed in by Mr. Franklin, who was going with him to the station. My lady explained the difficulty. Mr. Godfrey settled it directly. He called to Samuel, through the window, to take his portmanteau upstairs again, and he then put the key himself into Sergeant Cuff's hand. "My luggage can follow me to London," he said, "when the inquiry is over."

The Sergeant received the key with a becoming apology. "I am sorry to put you to any inconvenience, sir, for a mere formality; but the example of their betters will do wonders in reconciling the servants to this inquiry." Mr. Godfrey, after taking leave of my lady, in a most sympathizing manner, left a farewell message for Miss Rachel, the terms of which made it clear to my mind that he had not taken No for an answer, and that he meant to put the marriage question to her once more, at the next opportunity. Mr. Franklin, on following his cousin out, informed the Sergeant that all his clothes were open to examination, and that nothing he possessed was kept under lock and key. Sergeant Cuff made his best acknowledgments. His views, you will observe, had been met with the utmost readiness by my lady, by Mr. Godfrey, and by Mr. Franklin. There was only Miss Rachel now wanting to follow their lead, before we called the servants together, and began the search for the stained dress.

My lady's unaccountable objection to the Sergeant seemed to make our conference more distasteful to her than ever, as soon as we were left alone again. "If I send you down Miss Verinder's keys," she said to him, "I presume I shall have done all you want of me for the present?"

"I beg your ladyship's pardon," said Sergeant Cuff. "Before we begin, I should like, if convenient, to have the washing-book. The stained article of dress may be an article of linen. If the search leads to nothing, I want to be able to account next for all the linen in the house, and for all the linen sent to the wash. If there is an article missing, there will be at least a presumption that it has got the paint-stain on it, and that it has been purposely made away with, yesterday or to-day, by the person owning it. Superintendent Seegrave," added the Sergeant, turning to me, "pointed the attention of the women-servants to the smear, when they all crowded into the room on Thursday morning. That *may* turn out, Mr. Betteredge, to have been one more of Superintendent Seegrave's many mistakes."

My lady desired me to ring the bell, and order the washing-book. She remained with us until it was produced, in case Sergeant Cuff had any further request to make of her after looking at it.

The washing-book was brought in by Rosanna Spearman. The girl had come down to breakfast that morning miserably pale and haggard, but sufficiently recovered from her illness of the previous day to do her usual work. Sergeant Cuff looked attentively at our second housemaid – at her face, when she came in; at her crooked shoulder, when she went out.

"Have you anything more to say to me?" asked my lady, still as eager as ever to be out of the Sergeant's society.

The great Cuff opened the washing-book, understood it perfectly in half a minute, and shut it up again. "I venture to trouble your ladyship with one last question," he said. "Has the young woman who brought us this book been in your employment as long as the other servants?"

"Why do you ask?" said my lady.

"The last time I saw her," answered the Sergeant, "she was in prison for theft."

After that, there was no help for it, but to tell him the truth. My mistress dwelt strongly on Rosanna's good conduct in her service, and on the high opinion entertained of her by the matron at the Reformatory. "You don't suspect her, I hope," my lady added, in conclusion, very earnestly.

"I have already told your ladyship that I don't suspect any person in the house of thieving – up to the present time."

After that answer, my lady rose to go upstairs, and ask for Miss Rachel's keys. The Sergeant was beforehand with me in opening the door for her. He made a very low bow. My lady shuddered as she passed him.

We waited, and waited, and no keys appeared. Sergeant Cuff made no remark to me. He turned his melancholy face to the window; he put his lanky hands into his pockets; and he whistled "The Last Rose of Summer" softly to himself.

At last, Samuel came in, not with the keys, but with a morsel of paper for me. I got at my spectacles, with some fumbling and difficulty, feeling the Sergeant's dismal eyes fixed on me all the time. There were two or three lines on the paper, written in pencil by my lady. They informed me that Miss Rachel flatly refused to have her wardrobe examined. Asked for her reasons, she had burst out crying. Asked again, she had said: "I won't, because I won't. I must yield to force if you use it, but I will yield to nothing else." I understood my lady's disinclination to face Sergeant Cuff with such an answer from her daughter as that. If I had not been too old for the amiable weaknesses of youth, I believe I should have blushed at the notion of facing him myself.

"Any news of Miss Verinder's keys?" asked the Sergeant.

"My young lady refuses to have her wardrobe examined."

"Ah!" said the Sergeant.

His voice was not quite in such a perfect state of discipline as his face. When he said "Ah!" he said it in the tone of a man who had heard something which he expected to hear. He half angered and half frightened me – why, I couldn't tell, but he did it.

"Must the search be given up?" I asked.

"Yes," said the Sergeant, "the search must be given up, because your young lady refuses to submit to it like the rest. We must examine all the wardrobes in the house or none. Send Mr. Ablewhite's portmanteau to London by the next train, and return the washing-book, with my compliments and thanks, to the young woman who brought it in."

He laid the washing-book on the table, and, taking out his penknife, began to trim his nails.

"You don't seem to be much disappointed," I said.

"No," said Sergeant Cuff; "I am not much disappointed."

I tried to make him explain himself.

"Why should Miss Rachel put an obstacle in your way?" I

inquired. "Isn't it her interest to help you?"

"Wait a little, Mr. Betteredge – wait a little."

Cleverer heads than mine might have seen his drift. Or a person less fond of Miss Rachel than I was, might have seen his drift. My lady's horror of him might (as I have since thought) have meant that *she* saw his drift (as the scripture says) "in a glass darkly."[1] I didn't see it yet – that's all I know.

"What's to be done next?" I asked.

Sergeant Cuff finished the nail on which he was then at work, looked at it for a moment with a melancholy interest, and put up his penknife.

"Come out into the garden," he said, "and let's have a look at the roses."

CHAPTER XIV

THE nearest way to the garden, on going out of my lady's sitting-room, was by the shrubbery path, which you already know of. For the sake of your better understanding of what is now to come, I may add to this, that the shrubbery path was Mr. Franklin's favourite walk. When he was out in the grounds, and when we failed to find him anywhere else, we generally found him here.

I am afraid I must own that I am rather an obstinate old man. The more firmly Sergeant Cuff kept his thoughts shut up from me, the more firmly I persisted in trying to look in at them. As we turned into the shrubbery path, I attempted to circumvent him in another way.

"As things are now," I said, "if I was in your place, I should be at my wits' end."

"If you were in my place," answered the Sergeant, "you would have formed an opinion – and, as things are now, any doubt you might previously have felt about your own conclusions would be completely set at rest. Never mind for the present what those conclusions are, Mr. Betteredge. I haven't brought you out here to draw me like a badger; I have brought you out here to ask for some informa-

---

1   Betteredge here recalls I Corinthians: "For now we see through a glass, darkly; but then face to face: now I know in part; but then shall I know even as also I am known" (13:12).

tion. You might have given it to me, no doubt, in the house, instead of out of it. But doors and listeners have a knack of getting together; and, in my line of life, we cultivate a healthy taste for the open air."

Who was to circumvent *this* man? I gave in – and waited as patiently as I could to hear what was coming next.

"We won't enter into your young lady's motives," the Sergeant went on; "we will only say it's a pity she declines to assist me, because, by so doing, she makes this investigation more difficult than it might otherwise have been. We must now try to solve the mystery of the smear on the door – which, you may take my word for it, means the mystery of the Diamond also – in some other way. I have decided to see the servants, and to search their thoughts and actions, Mr. Betteredge, instead of searching their wardrobes. Before I begin, however, I want to ask you a question or two. You are an observant man – did you notice anything strange in any of the servants (making due allowance, of course, for fright and fluster), after the loss of the Diamond was found out? Any particular quarrel among them? Any one of them not in his or her usual spirits? Unexpectedly out of temper, for instance? or unexpectedly taken ill?"

I had just time to think of Rosanna Spearman's sudden illness at yesterday's dinner – but not time to make any answer – when I saw Sergeant Cuff's eyes suddenly turn aside towards the shrubbery; and I heard him say softly to himself, "Hullo!"

"What's the matter?" I asked.

"A touch of the rheumatics in my back," said the Sergeant, in a loud voice, as if he wanted some third person to hear us. "We shall have a change in the weather before long."

A few steps further brought us to the corner of the house. Turning off sharp to the right, we entered on the terrace, and went down, by the steps in the middle, into the garden below. Sergeant Cuff stopped there, in the open space, where we could see round us on every side.

"About that young person, Rosanna Spearman?" he said. "It isn't very likely, with her personal appearance, that she has got a lover. But, for the girl's own sake, I must ask you at once whether *she* has provided herself with a sweetheart, poor wretch, like the rest of them?"

What on earth did he mean, under present circumstances, by putting such a question to me as that? I stared at him, instead of answering him.

"I saw Rosanna Spearman hiding in the shrubbery as we went by," said the Sergeant.

"When you said 'Hullo'?"

"Yes – when I said 'Hullo!' If there's sweetheart in the case, the hiding doesn't much matter. If there isn't – as things are in this house – the hiding is a highly suspicious circumstance, and it will be my painful duty to act on it accordingly."

What, in God's name, was I to say to him? I knew the shrubbery was Mr. Franklin's favourite walk; I knew he would most likely turn that way when he came back from the station; I knew that Penelope had over and over again caught her fellow-servant hanging about there, and had always declared to me that Rosanna's object was to attract Mr. Franklin's attention. If my daughter was right, she might well have been lying in wait for Mr. Franklin's return when the Sergeant noticed her. I was put between the two difficulties of mentioning Penelope's fanciful notion as if it was mine, or of leaving an unfortunate creature to suffer the consequences, the very serious consequences, of exciting the suspicion of Sergeant Cuff. Out of pure pity for the girl – on my soul and my character, out of pure pity for the girl – I gave the Sergeant the necessary explanations, and told him that Rosanna had been mad enough to set her heart on Mr. Franklin Blake.

Sergeant Cuff never laughed. On the few occasions when anything amused him, he curled up a little at the corners of the lips, nothing more. He curled up now.

"Hadn't you better say she's mad enough to be an ugly girl and only a servant?" he asked. "The falling in love with a gentleman of Mr. Franklin Blake's manners and appearance doesn't seem to *me* to be the maddest part of her conduct by any means. However, I'm glad the thing is cleared up: it relieves one's mind to have things cleared up. Yes, I'll keep it a secret, Mr. Betteredge. I like to be tender to human infirmity – though I don't get many chances of exercising that virtue in my line of life. You think Mr. Franklin Blake hasn't got a suspicion of the girl's fancy for him? Ah! he would have found it out fast enough if she had been nice-looking. The ugly women have a bad time of it in this world; let's hope it will be made up to them in another. You have got a nice garden here, and a well-kept lawn. See for yourself how much better the flowers look with grass about them instead of gravel. No, thank you. I won't take a rose. It goes to my heart to break them off the stem. Just as it goes to your heart, you know, when there's something wrong in the servants' hall. Did you notice anything you couldn't account for in any of the servants when the loss of the Diamond was first found out?"

I had got on very fairly well with Sergeant Cuff so far. But the slyness with which he slipped in that last question put me on my guard. In plain English, I didn't at all relish the notion of helping his inquiries, when those inquiries took him (in the capacity of snake in the grass) among my fellow-servants.

"I noticed nothing," I said, "except that we all lost our heads together, myself included."

"Oh," says the Sergeant, "that's all you have to tell me, is it?"

I answered, with (as I flattered myself) an unmoved countenance, "That is all."

Sergeant Cuff's dismal eyes looked me hard in the face.

"Mr. Betteredge," he said, "have you any objection to oblige me by shaking hands? I have taken an extraordinary liking to you."

(Why he should have chosen the exact moment when I was deceiving him to give me that proof of his good opinion, is beyond all comprehension! I felt a little proud – I really did feel a little proud of having been one too many at last for the celebrated Cuff!)

We went back to the house; the Sergeant requesting that I would give him a room to himself, and then send in the servants (the indoor servants only), one after another, in the order of their rank, from first to last.

I showed Sergeant Cuff into my own room, and then called the servants together in the hall. Rosanna Spearman appeared among them, much as usual. She was as quick in her way as the Sergeant in his, and I suspect she had heard what he said to me about the servants in general, just before he discovered her. There she was, at any rate, looking as if she had never heard of such a place as the shrubbery in her life.

I sent them in, one by one, as desired. The cook was the first to enter the Court of Justice, otherwise my room. She remained but a short time. Report, on coming out: "Sergeant Cuff is depressed in his spirits; but Sergeant Cuff is a perfect gentleman." My lady's own maid followed. Remained much longer. Report, on coming out: "If

Sergeant Cuff doesn't believe a respectable woman, he might keep his opinion to himself, at any rate!" Penelope went next. Remained only a moment or two. Report, on coming out: "Sergeant Cuff is much to be pitied. He must have been crossed in love, father, when he was a young man." The first housemaid followed Penelope. Remained, like my lady's maid, a long time. Report, on coming out: "I didn't enter her ladyship's service, Mr. Betteredge, to be doubted to my face by a low police-officer!" Rosanna Spearman went next. Remained longer than any of them. No report on coming out – dead silence, and lips as pale as ashes. Samuel, the footman, followed Rosanna. Remained a minute or two. Report, on coming out: "Whoever blacks Sergeant Cuff's boots ought to be ashamed of himself." Nancy, the kitchen-maid, went last. Remained a minute or two. Report, on coming out: "Sergeant Cuff has a heart; *he* doesn't cut jokes, Mr. Betteredge, with a poor hard-working girl."

Going into the Court of Justice, when it was all over, to hear if there were any further commands for me, I found the Sergeant at his old trick – looking out of window, and whistling "The Last Rose of Summer" to himself.

"Any discoveries, sir?" I inquired.

"If Rosanna Spearman asks leave to go out," said the Sergeant, "let the poor thing go; but let me know first."

I might as well have held my tongue about Rosanna and Mr. Franklin! It was plain enough; the unfortunate girl had fallen under Sergeant Cuff's suspicions, in spite of all I could do to prevent it.

"I hope you don't think Rosanna is concerned in the loss of the Diamond?" I ventured to say.

The corners of the Sergeant's melancholy mouth curled up, and he looked hard in my face, just as he had looked in the garden.

"I think I had better not tell you, Mr. Betteredge," he said. "You might lose your head, you know, for the second time."

I began to doubt whether I had been one too many for the cele-brated Cuff, after all! It was rather a relief to me that we were inter-rupted here by a knock at the door, and a message from the cook. Rosanna Spearman *had* asked to go out, for the usual reason, that her head was bad, and she wanted a breath of fresh air. At a sign from the Sergeant, I said, Yes. "Which is the servants' way out?" he asked, when the messenger had gone. I showed him the servants' way out. "Lock the door of your room," says the Sergeant; "and if anybody asks for me, say I'm in there, composing my mind." He curled up again at the corners of the lips, and disappeared.

Left alone, under those circumstances, a devouring curiosity pushed me on to make some discoveries for myself.

It was plain that Sergeant Cuff's suspicions of Rosanna had been roused by something that he had found out at his examination of the servants in my room. Now, the only two servants (excepting Rosanna herself) who had remained under examination for any length of time, were my lady's own maid and the first housemaid, those two being also the women who had taken the lead in persecuting their unfortunate fellow-servant from the first. Reaching these conclusions, I looked in on them, casually as it might be, in the servants' hall, and, finding tea going forward, instantly invited myself to that meal. (For, *nota bene*, a drop of tea is to a woman's tongue what a drop of oil is to a wasting lamp.)

My reliance on the tea-pot, as an ally, did not go unrewarded. In less than half an hour I knew as much as the Sergeant himself.

My lady's maid and the housemaid had, it appeared, neither of them believed in Rosanna's illness of the previous day. These two devils – I ask your pardon; but how else *can* you describe a couple of spiteful women? – had stolen upstairs, at intervals during the Thursday afternoon; had tried Rosanna's door, and found it locked; had knocked, and not been answered; had listened, and not heard a sound inside. When the girl had come down to tea, and had been sent up, still out of sorts, to bed again, the two devils aforesaid had tried her door once more, and found it locked; had looked at the keyhole, and found it stopped up; had seen a light under the door at midnight, and had heard the crackling of a fire (a fire in a servant's bedroom in the month of June!) at four in the morning. All this they had told Sergeant Cuff, who, in return for their anxiety to enlighten him, had eyed them with sour and suspicious looks, and had shown them plainly that he didn't believe either one or the other. Hence, the unfavourable reports of him which these two women had brought out with them from the examination. Hence, also (without reckoning the influence of the tea-pot), their readiness to let their tongues run to any length on the subject of the Sergeant's ungracious behaviour to them.

Having had some experience of the great Cuff's roundabout ways, and having last seen him evidently bent on following Rosanna privately when she went out for her walk, it seemed clear to me that he had thought it unadvisable to let the lady's maid and the housemaid know how materially they had helped him. They were just the sort of women, if he had treated their evidence as trustworthy, to have been puffed up by it, and to have said or done something which would have put Rosanna Spearman on her guard.

I walked out in the fine summer afternoon, very sorry for the poor girl, and very uneasy in my mind at the turn things had taken. Drifting towards the shrubbery, some time later, there I met Mr. Franklin. After returning from seeing his cousin off at the station, he had been with my lady, holding a long conversation with her. She had told him of Miss Rachel's unaccountable refusal to let her wardrobe be examined; and had put him in such low spirits about my young lady, that he seemed to shrink from speaking on the subject. The family temper appeared in his face that evening, for the first time in my experience of him.

"Well, Betteredge," he said, "how does the atmosphere of mystery and suspicion in which we are all living now, agree with you? Do you remember that morning when I first came here with the Moonstone? I wish to God we had thrown it into the quicksand!"

After breaking out in that way, he abstained from speaking again until he had composed himself. We walked silently, side by side, for a minute or two, and then he asked me what had become of Sergeant Cuff. It was impossible to put Mr. Franklin off with the excuse of the Sergeant being in my room, composing his mind. I told him exactly what had happened, mentioning particularly what my lady's maid and the housemaid had said about Rosanna Spearman.

Mr. Franklin's clear head saw the turn the Sergeant's suspicions had taken, in the twinkling of an eye.

"Didn't you tell me this morning," he said, "that one of the tradespeople declared he had met Rosanna yesterday, on the footway to Frizinghall, when we supposed her to be ill in her room?"

"Yes, sir."

"If my aunt's maid and the other woman have spoken the truth, you may depend upon it the tradesman *did* meet her. The girl's attack of illness was a blind to deceive us. She had some guilty reason for going to the town secretly. The paint-stained dress is a dress of hers; and the fire heard crackling in her room at four in the morning was a fire lit to destroy it. Rosanna Spearman has stolen the Diamond. I'll go in directly, and tell my aunt the turn things have taken."

"Not just yet, if you please, sir," said a melancholy voice behind us. We both turned about, and found ourselves face to face with Sergeant Cuff.

"Why not just yet?" asked Mr. Franklin.

"Because, sir, if you tell her ladyship, her ladyship will tell Miss Verinder."

"Suppose she does. What then?" Mr. Franklin said those words with a sudden heat and vehemence, as if the Sergeant had mortally offended him.

"Do you think it's wise, sir," said Sergeant Cuff, quietly, "to put such a question as that to me – at such a time as this?"

There was a moment's silence between them: Mr. Franklin walked close up to the Sergeant. The two looked each other straight in the face. Mr. Franklin spoke first, dropping his voice as suddenly as he had raised it.

"I suppose you know, Mr. Cuff," he said, "that you are treading on delicate ground?"

"It isn't the first time, by a good many hundreds, that I find myself treading on delicate ground," answered the other, as immovable as ever.

"I am to understand that you forbid me to tell my aunt what has happened?"

"You are to understand, if you please, sir, that I throw up the case, if you tell Lady Verinder, or tell anybody, what has happened, until I give you leave."

That settled it. Mr. Franklin had no choice but to submit. He turned away in anger – and left us.

I had stood there listening to them, all in a tremble; not knowing whom to suspect, or what to think next. In the midst of my confusion, two things, however, were plain to me. First, that my young lady was, in some unaccountable manner, at the bottom of the sharp speeches that had passed between them. Second, that they thoroughly understood each other, without having previously exchanged a word of explanation on either side.

"Mr. Betteredge," says the Sergeant, "you have done a very foolish thing in my absence. You have done a little detective business on your own account. For the future, perhaps you will be so obliging as to do your detective business along with me."

He took me by the arm, and walked me away with him along the road by which he had come. I dare say I had deserved his reproof – but I was not going to help him to set traps for Rosanna Spearman, for all that. Thief or no thief, legal or not legal, I don't care – I pitied her.

"What do you want of me?" I asked, shaking him off, and stopping short.

"Only a little information about the country round here," said the Sergeant.

I couldn't well object to improve Sergeant Cuff in his geography.

"Is there any path, in that direction, leading to the sea-beach from this house?" asked the Sergeant. He pointed, as he spoke, to the fir-plantation which led to the Shivering Sand.

"Yes," I said, "there is a path."

"Show it to me."

Side by side, in the grey of the summer evening, Sergeant Cuff and I set forth for the Shivering Sand.

★

CHAPTER XV

THE Sergeant remained silent, thinking his own thoughts, till we entered the plantation of firs which led to the quicksand. There he roused himself, like a man whose mind was made up, and spoke to me again.

"Mr. Betteredge," he said, "as you have honoured me by taking an oar in my boat, and as you may, I think, be of some assistance to me before the evening is out, I see no use in our mystifying one another any longer, and I propose to set you an example of plain speaking on my side. You are determined to give me no information to the prejudice of Rosanna Spearman, because she has been a good girl to *you*, and because you pity her heartily. Those humane considerations do you a world of credit, but they happen in this instance to be humane considerations clean thrown away. Rosanna Spearman is not in the slightest danger of getting into trouble – no, not if I fix her with being concerned in the disappearance of the Diamond, on evidence which is as plain as the nose on your face!"

"Do you mean that my lady won't prosecute?" I asked.

"I mean that your lady *can't* prosecute," said the Sergeant.

"Rosanna Spearman is simply an instrument in the hands of another person, and Rosanna Spearman will be held harmless for that other person's sake."

He spoke like a man in earnest – there was no denying that. Still, I felt something stirring uneasily against him in my mind. "Can't you give that other person a name?" I said.

"Can't *you*, Mr. Betteredge?"

"No."

Sergeant Cuff stood stock-still, and surveyed me with a look of melancholy interest.

"It's always a pleasure to me to be tender towards human infirmity," he said. "I feel particularly tender at the present moment, Mr. Betteredge, towards you. And you, with the same excellent motive, feel particularly tender towards Rosanna Spearman, don't you? Do you happen to know whether she has had a new outfit of linen lately?"

What he meant by slipping in this extraordinary question unawares, I was at a total loss to imagine. Seeing no possible injury to Rosanna if I owned the truth, I answered that the girl had come to us rather sparely provided with linen, and that my lady, in recompense for her good conduct (I laid a stress on her good conduct), had given her a new outfit not a fortnight since.

"This is a miserable world," says the Sergeant. "Human life, Mr. Betteredge, is a sort of target – misfortune is always firing at it, and always hitting the mark. But for that outfit, we should have discovered a new nightgown or petticoat among Rosanna's things, and have nailed her in that way. You're not at a loss to follow me, are you? You have examined the servants yourself, and you know what discoveries two of them made outside Rosanna's door. Surely you know what the girl was about yesterday, after she was taken ill? You can't guess? Oh dear me, it's as plain as that strip of light there, at the end of the trees. At eleven, on Thursday morning, Superintendent Seegrave (who is a mass of human infirmity) points out to all the women-servants the smear on the door. Rosanna has her own reasons for suspecting her own things; she takes the first opportunity of getting to her room, finds the paint-stain on her nightgown, or petticoat, or what not, shams ill and slips away to the town, gets the materials for making a new petticoat or nightgown, makes it alone in her room on the Thursday night, lights a fire (not to destroy it; two of her fellow-servants are prying outside her door, and she knows better than to make a smell of burning, and to have a lot of tinder to get rid of) – lights a fire, I say, to dry and iron the substitute dress after wringing it out, keeps the stained dress hidden (probably *on* her), and is at this moment occupied in making away with it, in some convenient place, on that lonely bit of beach ahead of us. I have traced her this evening to your fishing village, and to one particular cottage, which we may possibly have to visit, before we go back. She stopped in the cottage for some time, and she came out with (as I believe) something hidden under her cloak. A cloak (on a woman's back) is an emblem of chari-ty – it covers a multitude of sins. I saw her set off northwards along the coast, after leaving the cottage. Is your sea-shore here considered a fine specimen of marine landscape, Mr. Betteredge?"

I answered, "Yes," as shortly as might be.

"Tastes differ," says Sergeant Cuff. "Looking at it from my point of view, I never saw a marine landscape that I admired less. If you hap-pen to be following another person along your sea-coast, and if that person happens to look round, there isn't scrap of cover to hide you anywhere. I had to choose between taking Rosanna in custody on suspicion, or leaving her, for the time being, with her little game in her own hands. For reasons which I won't trouble you with, I decided on making any sacrifice rather than give the alarm as soon as to-night to a certain person who shall be nameless between us. I came back to the house to ask you to take me to the north-end of the beach by another way. Sand – in respect of its printing off people's footsteps – is one of the best detective officers I know. If we don't meet with Rosanna Spearman by coming round on her in this way, the sand may tell us what she has been at, if the light only lasts long enough. Here *is* the sand. If you will excuse my suggesting it – suppose you hold your tongue, and let me go first?"

If there is such a thing known at the doctor's shop as a *detective-fever*, that disease had now got fast hold of your humble servant. Sergeant Cuff went on between the hillocks of sand, down to the beach. I followed him (with my heart in my mouth); and waited at a little distance for what was to happen next.

As it turned out, I found myself standing nearly in the same place where Rosanna Spearman and I had been talking together when Mr. Franklin suddenly appeared before us, on arriving at our house from London. While my eyes were watching the Sergeant, my mind wandered away in spite of me to what had passed, on that former occasion, between Rosanna and me. I declare I almost felt the poor thing slip her hand again into mine, and give it a little grateful squeeze to thank me for speaking kindly to her. I declare I almost heard her voice telling me again that the Shivering Sand seemed to draw her to it against her own will, whenever she went out – almost saw her face brighten again, as it brightened when she first set eyes upon Mr. Franklin coming briskly out on us from among the hillocks. My spirits fell lower and lower as I thought of these things – and the view of the lonesome little bay, when I looked about to rouse myself, only served to make me feel more uneasy still.

The last of the evening light was fading away; and over all the desolate place there hung a still and awful calm. The heave of the main ocean on the great sandbank out in the bay, was a heave that made no sound. The inner sea lay lost and dim, without a breath of wind to stir it. Patches of nasty ooze floated, yellow-white, on the dead surface of the water. Scum and slime shone faintly in certain places, where the last of the light still caught them on the two great spits of rock jutting out, north and south, into the sea. It was now the time of the turn of the tide: and even as I stood there waiting, the broad brown face of the quicksand began to dimple and quiver – the only moving thing in all the horrid place.

I saw the Sergeant start as the shiver of the sand caught his eye. After looking at it for a minute or so, he turned and came back to me.

"A treacherous place, Mr. Betteredge," he said; "and no signs of Rosanna Spearman anywhere on the beach, look where you may."

He took me down lower on the shore, and I saw for myself that his footsteps and mine were the only footsteps printed off on the sand.

"How does the fishing village bear, standing where we are now?" asked Sergeant Cuff.

"Cobb's Hole," I answered (that being the name of the place), "bears as near as may be, due south."

"I saw the girl this evening, walking northward along the shore, from Cobb's Hole," said the Sergeant. "Consequently, she must have been walking towards this place. Is Cobb's Hole on the other side of that point of land there? And can we get to it — now it's low water — by the beach?"

I answered, "Yes," to both those questions.

"If you'll excuse my suggesting it, we'll step out briskly," said the Sergeant. "I want to find the place where she left the shore, before it gets dark."

We had walked, I should say, a couple of hundred yards towards Cobb's Hole, when Sergeant Cuff suddenly went down on his knees on the beach, to all appearance seized with a sudden frenzy for saying his prayers.

"There's something to be said for your marine landscape here, after all," remarked the Sergeant. "Here are a woman's footsteps, Mr. Betteredge! Let us call them Rosanna's footsteps, until we find evidence to the contrary that we can't resist. Very confused footsteps, you will please to observe — purposely confused, I should say. Ah, poor soul, she understands the detective virtues of sand as well as I do! But hasn't she been in rather too great a hurry to tread out the marks thoroughly? I think she has. Here's one footstep going *from* Cobb's Hole; and here is another going back to it. Isn't that the toe of her shoe pointing straight to the water's edge? And don't I see two heel-marks farther down the beach, close at the water's edge also? I don't want to hurt your feelings, but I'm afraid Rosanna is sly. It looks as if she had determined to get to that place you and I have just come from, without leaving any marks on the sand to trace her by. Shall we say that she walked through the water from this point till she got to that ledge of rocks behind us, and came back the same way, and then took to the beach again where those two heel-marks are still left? Yes, we'll say that. It seems to fit in with my notion that she had something under her cloak, when she left the cottage. No! not something to destroy — for, in that case, where would have been the need of all these precautions to prevent my tracing the place at which her walk ended? Something to hide is, I think, the better guess of the two. Perhaps, if we go on to the cottage, we may find out what that something is."

At this proposal, my detective-fever suddenly cooled. "You don't want me," I said. "What good can I do?"

"The longer I know you, Mr. Betteredge," said the Sergeant, "the more virtues I discover. Modesty – oh dear me, how rare modesty is in this world! and how much of that rarity you possess! If I go alone to the cottage, the people's tongues will be tied at the first question I put to them. If I go with you, I go introduced by a justly respected neighbour, and a flow of conversation is the necessary result. It strikes me in that light; how does it strike you?"

Not having an answer of the needful smartness as ready as I could have wished, I tried to gain time by asking him what cottage he wanted to go to.

On the Sergeant describing the place, I recognised it as a cottage inhabited by a fisherman named Yolland, with his wife and two grown-up children, a son and a daughter. If you will look back, you will find that, in first presenting Rosanna Spearman to your notice, I have described her as occasionally varying her walk to the Shivering Sand, by a visit to some friends of hers at Cobb's Hole. Those friends were the Yollands – respectable, worthy people, a credit to the neighbourhood. Rosanna's acquaintance with them had begun by means of the daughter, who was afflicted with a misshapen foot, and who was known in our parts by the name of Limping Lucy. The two deformed girls had, I suppose, a kind of fellow-feeling for each other. Any way, the Yollands and Rosanna always appeared to get on together, at the few chances they had of meeting, in a pleasant and friendly manner. The fact of Sergeant Cuff having traced the girl to *their* cottage, set the matter of my helping his inquiries in quite a new light. Rosanna had merely gone where she was in the habit of going; and to show that she had been in company with the fisherman and his family was as good as to prove that she had been innocently occupied, so far, at any rate. It would be doing the girl a service, therefore, instead of an injury, if I allowed myself to be convinced by Sergeant Cuff's logic. I professed myself convinced by it accordingly.

We went on to Cobb's Hole, seeing the footsteps on the sand, as long as the light lasted.

On reaching the cottage, the fisherman and his son proved to be out in the boat; and Limping Lucy, always weak and weary, was resting on her bed upstairs. Good Mrs. Yolland received us alone in her kitchen. When she heard that Sergeant Cuff was a celebrated character in London, she clapped a bottle of Dutch gin and a couple of clean pipes on the table, and stared as if she could never see enough of him.

I sat quiet in a corner, waiting to hear how the Sergeant would find his way to the subject of Rosanna Spearman. His usual roundabout manner of going to work proved, on this occasion, to be more roundabout than ever. How he managed it is more than I could tell at the time, and more than I can tell now. But this is certain, he began with the Royal Family, the Primitive Methodists,[1] and the price of fish; and he got from that (in his dismal, underground way) to the loss of the Moonstone, the spitefulness of our first housemaid, and the hard behaviour of the women-servants generally towards Rosanna Spearman. Having reached his subject in this fashion, he described himself as making his inquiries about the lost Diamond, partly with a view to find it, and partly for the purpose of clearing Rosanna from the unjust suspicions of her enemies in the house. In about a quarter of an hour from the time when we entered the kitchen, good Mrs. Yolland was persuaded that she was talking to Rosanna's best friend, and was pressing Sergeant Cuff to comfort his stomach and revive his spirits out of the Dutch bottle.

Being firmly persuaded that the Sergeant was wasting his breath to no purpose on Mrs. Yolland, I sat enjoying the talk between them, much as I have sat, in my time, enjoying a stage play. The great Cuff showed a wonderful patience; trying his luck drearily this way and that way, and firing shot after shot, as it were, at random, on the chance of hitting the mark. Everything to Rosanna's credit, nothing to Rosanna's prejudice – that was how it ended, try as he might; with Mrs. Yolland talking nineteen to the dozen,[2] and placing the most entire confidence in him. His last effort was made, when we had

---

1 William Clowes (1780-1851) co-founded – with Hugh Bourne (1772-1852) – Primitive Methodism in 1810. Given to large and boisterous open-air congregations, the group became known to many as the Ranters. Clowes lived, worked, and retired in Hull on the eastern coast of Yorkshire, near where much of the action of the novel takes place. In Thomas Hardy's (1840-1928) *Tess of the d'Urbervilles* (1891), Alec d'Urberville has become a "ranter . . . an excellent, fiery, Christian man, they say" when Tess meets him on the road near the village of Evershead at the end of novel's "Phase the Fifth, The Woman Pays."

2 Betteredge's colloquialism suggests that Mrs. Yolland talks without pause at a great rate.

looked at our watches, and had got on our legs previous to taking leave.

"I shall now wish you good-night, ma'am," says the Sergeant. "And I shall only say, at parting, that Rosanna Spearman has a sincere well-wisher in myself, your obedient servant. But, oh dear me! she will never get on in her present place; and my advice to her is – leave it."

"Bless your heart alive! she is *going* to leave it!" cries Mrs. Yolland. (*Nota bene* – I translate Mrs. Yolland out of the Yorkshire language into the English language. When I tell you that the all-accomplished Cuff was every now and then puzzled to understand her until I helped him, you will draw your own conclusions as to what *your* state of mind would be if I reported her in her native tongue.)

Rosanna Spearman going to leave us! I pricked up my ears at that. It seemed strange, to say the least of it, that she should have given no warning, in the first place, to my lady or to me. A certain doubt came up in my mind whether Sergeant Cuff's last random shot might not have hit the mark. I began to question whether my share in the proceedings was quite as harmless a one as I had thought it. It might be all in the way of the Sergeant's business to mystify an honest woman by wrapping her round in a network of lies; but it was my duty to have remembered, as a good Protestant, that the father of lies is the Devil – and that mischief and the Devil are never far apart. Beginning to smell mischief in the air, I tried to take Sergeant Cuff out. He sat down again instantly, and asked for a little drop of comfort out of the Dutch bottle. Mrs. Yolland sat down opposite to him, and gave him his nip. I went to the door, excessively uncomfortable, and said I thought I must bid them good-night – and yet I didn't go.

"So she means to leave?" says the Sergeant. "What is she to do when she does leave? Sad, sad! The poor creature has got no friends in the world, except you and me."

"Ah, but she has though!" says Mrs. Yolland. "She came in here, as I told you, this evening; and, after sitting and talking a little with my girl Lucy and me, she asked to go upstairs by herself, into Lucy's room. It's the only room in our place where there's pen and ink. 'I want to write a letter to a friend,' she says, 'and I can't do it for the prying and peeping of the servants up at the house.' Who the letter was written to I can't tell you: it must have been a mortal long one, judging by the time she stopped upstairs over it. I offered her a postage-stamp when she came down. She hadn't got the letter in her hand, and she didn't accept the stamp. A little close, poor soul (as you know), about herself and her doings. But a friend she has got somewhere, I can tell you; and to that friend, you may depend upon it, she will go."

"Soon?" asked the Sergeant.

"As soon as she can," says Mrs. Yolland.

Here I stepped in again from the door. As chief of my lady's establishment, I couldn't allow this sort of loose talk about a servant of ours going, or not going, to proceed any longer in my presence, without noticing it.

"You must be mistaken about Rosanna Spearman," I said. "If she had been going to leave her present situation, she would have mentioned it, in the first place, to *me*."

"Mistaken?" cries Mrs. Yolland. "Why, only an hour ago she bought some things she wanted for travelling – of my own self, Mr. Betteredge, in this very room. And that reminds me," says the wearisome woman, suddenly beginning to feel in her pocket, "of something I have got it on my mind to say about Rosanna and her money. Are you either of you likely to see her when you go back to the house?"

"I'll take a message to the poor thing, with the greatest pleasure," answered Sergeant Cuff, before I could put in a word edgewise.

Mrs. Yolland produced out of her pocket, a few shillings and sixpences, and counted them out with a most particular and exasperating carefulness in the palm of her hand. She offered the money to the Sergeant, looking mighty loth to part with it all the while.

"Might I ask you to give this back to Rosanna, with my love and respects?" says Mrs. Yolland. "She insisted on paying me for the one or two things she took a fancy to this evening – and money's welcome enough in our house, I don't deny it. Still, I'm not easy in my mind about taking the poor thing's little savings. And to tell you the truth, I don't think my man would like to hear that I had taken Rosanna Spearman's money, when he comes back to-morrow morning from his work. Please say she's heartily welcome to the things she bought of me – as a gift. And don't leave the money on the table," says Mrs. Yolland, putting it down suddenly before the Sergeant, as if it burnt her fingers – "don't, there's a good man! For times are hard, and flesh is weak; and I *might* feel tempted to put it back in my pocket again."

"Come along!" I said, "I can't wait any longer: I must go back to the house."

"I'll follow you directly," says Sergeant Cuff.

For the second time, I went to the door; and, for the second time, try as I might, I couldn't cross the threshold.

"It's delicate matter, ma'am," I heard the Sergeant say, "giving money back. You charged her cheap for the things, I'm sure?"

"Cheap!" says Mrs. Yolland. "Come and judge for yourself."

She took up the candle and led the Sergeant to a corner of the kitchen. For the life of me, I couldn't help following them. Shaken down in the corner was a heap of odds and ends (mostly old metal), which the fisherman had picked up at different times from wrecked ships, and which he hadn't found a market for yet, to his own mind. Mrs. Yolland dived into this rubbish, and brought up an old japanned tin case, with a cover to it, and a hasp to hang it up by – the sort of thing they use, on board ship, for keeping their maps and charts, and such-like, from the wet.

"There!" says she. "When Rosanna came in this evening, she bought the fellow to that. 'It will just do,' she says, 'to put my cuffs and collars in, and keep them from being crumpled in my box.' One and ninepence, Mr. Cuff. As I live by bread, not a halfpenny more!"

"Dirt cheap!" says the Sergeant, with a heavy sigh.

He weighed the case in his hand. I thought I heard a note or two of "The Last Rose of Summer" as he looked at it. There was no doubt now! He had made another discovery to the prejudice of Rosanna Spearman, in the place of all others where I thought her character was safest, and all through me! I leave you to imagine what I felt, and how sincerely I repented having been the medium of introduction between Mrs. Yolland and Sergeant Cuff.

"That will do," I said. "We really must go."

Without paying the least attention to me, Mrs. Yolland took another dive into the rubbish, and came up out of it, this time, with a dog-chain.

"Weigh it in your hand, sir," she said to the Sergeant. "We had three of these; and Rosanna has taken two of them. 'What can you want, my dear, with a couple of dog-chains?' says I. 'If I join them together they'll go round my box nicely,' says she. 'Rope's cheapest,' says I. 'Chain's surest,' says she. 'Who ever heard of a box corded with chain!' says I. 'Oh, Mrs. Yolland, don't make objections!' says she; 'let me have my chains!' A strange girl, Mr. Cuff – good as gold, and kinder than a sister to my Lucy – but always a little strange. There! I humoured her. Three and sixpence. On the word of an honest woman, three and sixpence, Mr. Cuff!"

"Each?" says the Sergeant.

"Both together!" says Mrs. Yolland. "Three and sixpence for the two."

"Given away, ma'am," says the Sergeant, shaking his head. "Clean given away!"

"There's the money," says Mrs. Yolland, getting back sideways to the little heap of silver on the table, as if it drew her in spite of herself. "The tin case and the dog-chains were all she bought, and all she took away. One and ninepence and three and sixpence – total, five and three. With my love and respects – and I can't find it in my conscience to take a poor girl's savings, when she may want them herself."

"I can't find it in *my* conscience, ma'am, to give the money back," says Sergeant Cuff. "You have as good as made her a present of the things – you have indeed."

"Is that your sincere opinion, sir?" says Mrs. Yolland brightening up wonderfully.

"There can't be a doubt about it," answered the Sergeant. "Ask Mr. Betteredge."

It was no use asking *me*. All they got out of *me* was, "Good-night."

"Bother the money!" says Mrs. Yolland. With these words, she appeared to lose all command over herself; and, making a sudden snatch at the heap of silver, put it back, holus-bolus,[1] in her pocket. "It upsets one's temper, it does, to see it lying there, and nobody taking it," cries this unreasonable woman, sitting down with a thump, and looking at Sergeant Cuff, as much as to say, "It's in my pocket again now – get it out if you can!"

This time, I not only went to the door, but went fairly out on the road back. Explain it how you may, I felt as if one or both of them

---

1   A mock Latinization of "whole bolus," holus-bolus means "all at once."

had mortally offended me. Before I had taken three steps down the village, I heard the Sergeant behind me.

"Thank you for your introduction, Mr. Betteredge," he said. "I am indebted to the fisherman's wife for an entirely new sensation. Mrs. Yolland has puzzled me."

It was on the tip of my tongue to have given him a sharp answer, for no better reason than this – that I was out of temper with him, because I was out of temper with myself. But when he owned to being puzzled, a comforting doubt crossed my mind whether any great harm had been done after all. I waited in discreet silence to hear more.

"Yes," says the Sergeant, as if he was actually reading my thoughts in the dark. "Instead of putting me on the scent, it may console you to know, Mr. Betteredge (with your interest in Rosanna), that you have been the means of throwing me off. What the girl has done, to-night, is clear enough, of course. She has joined the two chains, and has fastened them to the hasp in the tin case. She has sunk the case, in the water or in the quicksand. She has made the loose end of the chain fast to some place under the rocks, known only to herself. And she will leave the case secure at its anchorage till the present proceedings have come to an end; after which she can privately pull it up again out of its hiding-place, at her own leisure and convenience. All perfectly plain, so far. But," says the Sergeant, with the first tone of impatience in his voice that I had heard yet, "the mystery is – what the devil has she hidden in the tin case?"

I thought to myself, "The Moonstone!" But I only said to Sergeant Cuff, "Can't you guess?"

"It's not the Diamond," says the Sergeant. "The whole experience of my life is at fault, if Rosanna Spearman has got the Diamond."

On hearing those words, the infernal detective-fever began, I suppose, to burn in me again. At any rate, I forgot myself in the interest of guessing this new riddle. I said rashly, "The stained dress!"

Sergeant Cuff stopped short in the dark, and laid his hand on my arm.

"Is anything thrown into that quicksand of yours, ever thrown up on the surface again?" he asked.

"Never," I answered. "Light or heavy, whatever goes into the Shivering Sand is sucked down, and seen no more."

"Does Rosanna Spearman know that?"

"She knows it as well as I do."

"Then," says the Sergeant, "what on earth has she got to do but to tie up a bit of stone in the stained dress, and throw it into the quicksand? There isn't the shadow of a reason why she should have hidden it – and yet she *must* have hidden it. Query," says the Sergeant, walking on again, "is the paint-stained dress a petticoat or a nightgown? or is it something else which there is a reason for preserving at any risk? Mr. Betteredge, if nothing occurs to prevent it, I must go to Frizinghall to-morrow, and discover what she bought in the town, when she privately got the materials for making the substitute dress. It's a risk to leave the house, as things are now – but it's a worse risk still to stir another step in this matter in the dark. Excuse my being a little out of temper; I'm degraded in my own estimation – I have let Rosanna Spearman puzzle me."

When we got back, the servants were at supper. The first person we saw in the outer yard was the policeman whom Superintendent Seegrave had left at the Sergeant's disposal. The Sergeant asked if Rosanna Spearman had returned. Yes. When? Nearly an hour since. What had she done? She had gone upstairs to take off her bonnet and cloak – and she was now at supper quietly with the rest.

Without making any remark, Sergeant Cuff walked on, sinking lower and lower in his own estimation, to the back of the house. Missing the entrance in the dark, he went on (in spite of my calling to him) till he was stopped by a wicket-gate which led into the garden. When I joined him to bring him back by the right way, I found that he was looking up attentively at one particular window, on the bedroom floor, at the back of the house.

Looking up, in my turn, I discovered that the object of his contemplation was the window of Miss Rachel's room, and that lights were passing backwards and forwards there as if something unusual was going on.

"Isn't that Miss Verinder's room?" asked Sergeant Cuff.

I replied that it was, and invited him to go in with me to supper. The Sergeant remained in his place, and said something about enjoying the smell of the garden at night. I left him to his enjoyment. Just as I was turning in at the door, I heard "The Last Rose of Summer" at the wicket-gate. Sergeant Cuff had made another discovery! And my young lady's window was at the bottom of it this time!

The latter reflection took me back again to the Sergeant, with a polite intimation that I could not find it in my heart to leave him by himself. "Is there anything you don't understand up there?" I added, pointing to Miss Rachel's window.

Judging by his voice, Sergeant Cuff had suddenly risen again to the right place in his own estimation. "You are great people for betting in Yorkshire, are you not?" he asked.

"Well?" I said. "Suppose we are?"

"If I was a Yorkshireman," proceeded the Sergeant, taking my arm, "I would lay you an even sovereign,[1] Mr. Betteredge, that your young lady has suddenly resolved to leave the house. If I won on that event, I should offer to lay another sovereign, that the idea has occurred to her within the last hour."

The first of the Sergeant's guesses startled me. The second mixed itself up somehow in my head with the report we had heard from the policeman, that Rosanna Spearman had returned from the sands within the last hour. The two together had a curious effect on me as we went in to supper. I shook off Sergeant Cuff's arm, and, forgetting my manners, pushed by him through the door to make my own inquiries for myself.

Samuel, the footman, was the first person I met in the passage.

"Her ladyship is waiting to see you and Sergeant Cuff," he said, before I could put any questions to him.

"How long has she been waiting?" asked the Sergeant's voice behind me.

"For the last hour, sir."

There it was again! Rosanna had come back; Miss Rachel had taken some resolution out of the common; and my lady had been waiting to see the Sergeant – all within the last hour! It was not pleasant to find these very different persons and things linking themselves together in this way. I went on upstairs, without looking at Sergeant Cuff, or speaking to him. My hand took a sudden fit of trembling as I lifted it to knock at my mistress's door.

---

1   Sergeant Cuff is willing to wager a gold coin worth £1. Sovereigns were first minted in 1819.

"I shouldn't be surprised," whispered the Sergeant over my shoulder, "if a scandal was to burst up in the house to-night. Don't be alarmed! I have put the muzzle on worse family difficulties than this, in my time." As he said the words, I heard my mistress's voice calling to us to come in.

★

CHAPTER XVI

WE found my lady with no light in the room but the reading-lamp. The shade was screwed down so as to overshadow her face. Instead of looking up at us in her usual straightforward way, she sat close at the table, and kept her eyes fixed obstinately on an open book.

"Officer," she said, "is it important to the inquiry you are conducting, to know beforehand if any person now in this house wishes to leave it?"

"Most important, my lady."

"I have to tell you, then, that Miss Verinder proposes going to stay with her aunt, Mrs. Ablewhite, of Frizinghall. She has arranged to leave us the first thing to-morrow morning."

Sergeant Cuff looked at me. I made a step forward to speak to my mistress – and, feeling my heart fail me (if I must own it), took a step back again, and said nothing.

"May I ask your ladyship *when* Miss Verinder informed you that she was going to her aunt's?" inquired the Sergeant.

"About an hour since," answered my mistress.

Sergeant Cuff looked at me once more. They say old people's hearts are not very easily moved. *My* heart couldn't have thumped much harder than it did now, if I had been five-and-twenty again!"I have no claim, my lady," says the Sergeant, "to control Miss Verinder's actions. All I can ask you to do is to put off her departure, if possible, till later in the day. I must go to Frizinghall myself to-morrow morning – and I shall be back by two o'clock, if not before. If Miss Verinder can be kept here till that time, I should wish to say two words to her – unexpectedly – before she goes."

My lady directed me to give the coachman her orders, that the carriage was not to come for Miss Rachel until two o'clock. "Have you more to say?" she asked of the Sergeant, when this had been done.

"Only one thing, your ladyship. If Miss Verinder is surprised at this change in the arrangements, please not to mention Me as being the cause of putting off her journey."

My mistress lifted her head suddenly from her book as if she was going to say something – checked herself by a great effort – and, looking back again at the open page, dismissed us with a sign of her hand.

"That's a wonderful woman," said Sergeant Cuff, when we were out in the hall again. "But for her self-control, the mystery that puzzles you, Mr. Betteredge, would have been at an end to-night."

At those words, the truth rushed at last into my stupid old head. For the moment, I suppose I must have gone clean out of my senses. I seized the Sergeant by the collar of his coat, and pinned him against the wall.

"Damn you!" I cried out, "there's something wrong about Miss Rachel – and you have been hiding it from me all this time!"

Sergeant Cuff looked up at me – flat against the wall – without stirring a hand, or moving a muscle of his melancholy face.

"Ah," he said, "you've guessed it at last."

My hand dropped from his collar, and my head sunk on my breast. Please to remember, as some excuse for my breaking out as I did, that I had served the family for fifty years. Miss Rachel had climbed upon my knees, and pulled my whiskers, many and many a time when she was a child. Miss Rachel, with all her faults, had been, to my mind, the dearest and prettiest and best young mistress that ever an old servant waited on, and loved. I begged Sergeant Cuff's pardon, but I am afraid I did it with watery eyes, and not in a very becoming way.

"Don't distress yourself, Mr. Betteredge," says the Sergeant, with more kindness than I had any right to expect from him. "In my line of life, if we were quick at taking offence, we shouldn't be worth salt to our porridge. If it's any comfort to you, collar me again. You don't in the least know how to do it; but I'll overlook your awkwardness in consideration of your feelings."

He curled up at the corners of his lips, and, in his own dreary way, seemed to think he had delivered himself of a very good joke.

I led him into my own little sitting-room, and closed the door.

"Tell me the truth, Sergeant," I said. "What do you suspect? It's no kindness to hide it from me now."

"I don't suspect," said Sergeant Cuff. "I know."

My unlucky temper began to get the better of me again.

"Do you mean to tell me, in plain English," I said, "that Miss Rachel has stolen her own Diamond?"

"Yes," says the Sergeant; "that is what I mean to tell you, in so many words. Miss Verinder has been in secret possession of the Moonstone from first to last; and she has taken Rosanna Spearman into her confidence, because she has calculated on our suspecting Rosanna Spearman of the theft. There is the whole case in a nutshell. Collar me again, Mr. Betteredge. If it's any vent to your feelings, collar me again."

God help me! my feelings were not to be relieved in that way. "Give me your reasons!" That was all I could say to him.

"You shall hear my reasons to-morrow," said the Sergeant. "If Miss Verinder refuses to put off her visit to her aunt (which you will find Miss Verinder will do), I shall be obliged to lay the whole case before your mistress to-morrow. And, as I don't know what may come of it, I shall request you to be present, and to hear what passes on both sides. Let the matter rest for to-night. No, Mr. Betteredge, you don't get a word more on the subject of the Moonstone out of me. There is your table spread for supper. That's one of the many human infirmities which I always treat tenderly. If you will ring the bell, I'll say grace. 'For what we are going to receive – '"

"I wish you a good appetite to it, Sergeant," I said. "My appetite is gone. I'll wait and see you served, and then I'll ask you to excuse me, if I go away, and try to get the better of this by myself."

I saw him served with the best of everything – and I shouldn't have been sorry if the best of everything had choked him. The head gardener (Mr. Begbie) came in at the same time, with his weekly account. The Sergeant got on the subject of roses and the merits of grass walks and gravel walks immediately. I left the two together, and went out with a heavy heart. This was the first trouble I remember for many a long year which wasn't to be blown off by a whiff of tobacco, and which was even beyond the reach of *Robinson Crusoe*.

Being restless and miserable, and having no particular room to go to, I took a turn on the terrace, and thought it over in peace and quietness by myself. It doesn't much matter what my thoughts were. I felt wretchedly old, and worn out, and unfit for my place – and began to wonder, for the first time in my life, when it would please God to take me. With all this, I held firm, notwithstanding, to my belief in Miss Rachel. If Sergeant Cuff had been Solomon in all his glory, and had told me that my young lady had mixed herself up in a mean and guilty plot, I should have had but one answer for Solomon, wise as he was, "You don't know her; and I do."

My meditations were interrupted by Samuel. He brought me a written message from my mistress.

Going into the house to get a light to read it by, Samuel remarked that there seemed a change coming in the weather. My troubled mind had prevented me from noticing it before. But, now my attention was roused, I heard the dogs uneasy, and the wind moaning low. Looking up at the sky, I saw the rack of clouds getting blacker and blacker, and hurrying faster and faster over a watery moon. Wild weather coming – Samuel was right, wild weather coming.

The message from my lady informed me, that the magistrate at Frizinghall had written to remind her about the three Indians. Early in the coming week, the rogues must needs be released, and left free to follow their own devices. If we had any more questions to ask them, there was no time to lose. Having forgotten to mention this, when she had last seen Sergeant Cuff, my mistress now desired me to supply the omission. The Indians had gone clean out of my head (as they have, no doubt, gone clean out of yours). I didn't see much use in stirring that subject again. However, I obeyed my orders on the spot, as a matter of course.

I found Sergeant Cuff and the gardener, with a bottle of Scotch whisky between them, head over ears in an argument on the growing of roses. The Sergeant was so deeply interested that he held up his hand, and signed to me not to interrupt the discussion, when I came in. As far as I could understand it, the question between them was, whether the white moss-rose did, or did not, require to be budded on the dog-rose to make it grow well. Mr. Begbie said, Yes; and Sergeant Cuff said, No. They appealed to me, as hotly as a couple of boys. Knowing nothing whatever about the growing of roses, I steered a middle course – just as her Majesty's judges do, when the scales of justice bother them by hanging even to a hair. "Gentlemen," I remarked, "there is much to be said on both sides." In the temporary lull produced by that impartial sentence, I laid my lady's written message on the table, under the eyes of Sergeant Cuff.

I had got by this time, as nearly as might be, to hate the Sergeant. But truth compels me to acknowledge that, in respect of readiness of mind, he was a wonderful man.

In half a minute after he had read the message, he had looked back into his memory for Superintendent Seegrave's report; had picked out that part of it in which the Indians were concerned; and was ready with his answer. A certain great traveller, who understood the Indians and their language, had figured in Mr. Seegrave's report, hadn't he? Very well. Did I know the gentleman's name and address? Very well again. Would I write them on the back of my lady's message? Much obliged to me. Sergeant Cuff would look that gentleman up, when he went to Frizinghall in the morning.

"Do you expect anything to come of it?" I asked. "Superintendent Seegrave found the Indians as innocent as the babe unborn."

"Superintendent Seegrave has been proved wrong, up to this time, in all his conclusions," answered the Sergeant. "It may be worth while to find out to-morrow whether Superintendent Seegrave was wrong about the Indians as well." With that he turned to Mr. Begbie, and took up the argument again exactly at the place where it had left off. "This question between us is a question of soils and seasons, and patience and pains, Mr. Gardener. Now let me put it to you from another point of view. You take your white moss-rose — "

By that time, I had closed the door on them, and was out of hearing of the rest of the dispute.

In the passage, I met Penelope hanging about, and asked what she was waiting for.

She was waiting for her young lady's bell, when her young lady chose to call her back to go on with the packing for the next day's journey. Further inquiry revealed to me, that Miss Rachel had given it as a reason for wanting to go to her aunt at Frizinghall, that the house was unendurable to her, and that she could bear the odious presence of a policeman under the same roof with herself no longer. On being informed, half an hour since, that her departure would be delayed till two in the afternoon, she had flown into a violent passion. My lady, present at the time, had severely rebuked her, and then (having apparently something to say, which was reserved for her daughter's private ear) had sent Penelope out of the room. My girl was in wretchedly low spirits about the changed state of things in the house. "Nothing goes right, father; nothing is like what it used to be. I feel as if some dreadful misfortune was hanging over us all."

That was my feeling too. But I put a good face on it, before my daughter. Miss Rachel's bell rang while we were talking. Penelope ran up the back stairs to go on with the packing. I went by the other way to the hall, to see what the glass said about the change in the weather.

Just as I approached the swing-door leading into the hall from the servants' offices, it was violently opened from the other side; and Rosanna Spearman ran by me, with a miserable look of pain in her face, and one of her hands pressed hard over her heart, as if the pang was in that quarter. "What's the matter, my girl?" I asked, stopping her. "Are you ill?" "For God's sake, don't speak to me," she answered, and twisted herself out of my hands, and ran on towards the servants' staircase. I called to the cook (who was within hearing) to look after the poor girl. Two other persons proved to be within hearing, as well as the cook. Sergeant Cuff darted softly out of my room, and asked what was the matter. I answered "Nothing." Mr. Franklin, on the other side, pulled open the swing-door, and beckoning me into the hall, inquired if I had seen anything of Rosanna Spearman.

"She has just passed me, sir, with a very disturbed face, and in a very odd manner."

"I am afraid I am innocently the cause of that disturbance, Betteredge."

"You, sir!"

"I can't explain it," says Mr. Franklin; "but, if the girl *is* concerned in the loss of the Diamond, I do really believe she was on the point of confessing everything – to me, of all the people in the world – not two minutes since."

Looking towards the swing-door, as he said those last words, I fancied I saw it opened a little way from the inner side.

Was there anybody listening? The door fell to, before I could get to it. Looking through, the moment after, I thought I saw the tails of Sergeant Cuff's respectable black coat disappearing round the corner of the passage. He knew, as well as I did, that he could expect no more help from me, now that I had discovered the turn which his investigations were really taking. Under those circumstances, it was quite in his character to help himself, and to do it by the underground way.

Not feeling sure that I had really seen the Sergeant – and not desiring to make needless mischief, where, Heaven knows, there was mischief enough going on already – I told Mr. Franklin that I thought one of the dogs had got into the house – and then begged him to describe what had happened between Rosanna and himself.

"Were you passing through the hall, sir?" I asked. "Did you meet her accidentally, when she spoke to you?"

Mr. Franklin pointed to the billiard-table.

"I was knocking the balls about," he said, "and trying to get this miserable business of the Diamond out of my mind. I happened to look up – and there stood Rosanna Spearman at the side of me, like a ghost! Her stealing on me in that way was so strange, that I hardly knew what to do at first. Seeing a very anxious expression in her face, I asked her if she wished to speak to me. She answered, 'Yes, if I dare.' Knowing what suspicion attached to her, I could only put one construction on such language as that. I confess it made me uncomfortable. I had no wish to invite the girl's confidence. At the same time, in the difficulties that now beset us, I could hardly feel justified in refusing to listen to her, if she was really bent on speaking to me. It was an awkward position; and I dare say I got out of it awkwardly enough. I said to her, 'I don't quite understand you. Is there anything you want me to do?' Mind, Betteredge, I didn't speak unkindly! The poor girl can't help being ugly – I felt that, at the time. The cue was still in my hand, and I went on knocking the balls about, to take off the awkwardness of the thing. As it turned out, I only made matters worse still. I'm afraid I mortified her without meaning it! She suddenly turned away. 'He looks at the billiard balls,' I heard her say. 'Anything rather than look at *me*!' Before I could stop her, she had left the hall. I am not quite easy about it, Betteredge. Would you mind telling Rosanna that I meant no unkindness? I have been a little hard on her, perhaps, in my own thoughts – I have almost hoped that the loss of the Diamond might be traced to *her*. Not from any ill-will to the poor girl: but – " He stopped there, and going back to the billiard-table, began to knock the balls about once more.

After what had passed between the Sergeant and me, I knew what it was that he had left unspoken as well as he knew it himself.

Nothing but the tracing of the Moonstone to our second house-maid could now raise Miss Rachel above the infamous suspicion that rested on her in the mind of Sergeant Cuff. It was no longer a question of quieting my young lady's nervous excitement; it was a question of proving her innocence. If Rosanna had done nothing to compromise herself, the hope which Mr. Franklin confessed to having felt would have been hard enough on her in all conscience. But this was not the case. She had pretended to be ill, and had gone secretly to Frizinghall. She had been up all night, making something or destroying something, in private. And she had been at the Shivering Sand, that evening, under circumstances which were highly suspicious, to say the least of them. For all these reasons (sorry as I was for Rosanna) I could not but think that Mr. Franklin's way of looking at the matter was neither unnatural nor unreasonable, in Mr. Franklin's position. I said a word to him to that effect.

"Yes, yes!" he said in return. "But there is just a chance – a very poor one, certainly – that Rosanna's conduct may admit of some explanation which we don't see at present. I hate hurting a woman's feelings, Betteredge! Tell the poor creature what I told you to tell her. And if she wants to speak to me – I don't care whether I get into a scrape or not – send her to me in the library." With those kind words he laid down the cue and left me.

Inquiry at the servants' offices informed me that Rosanna had retired to her own room. She had declined all offers of assistance with thanks, and had only asked to be left to rest in quiet. Here, therefore, was an end of any confession on her part (supposing she really had a confession to make) for that night. I reported the result to Mr. Franklin, who, thereupon, left the library, and went up to bed.

I was putting the lights out, and making the windows fast, when Samuel came in with news of the two guests whom I had left in my room.

The argument about the white moss-rose had apparently come to an end at last. The gardener had gone home, and Sergeant Cuff was nowhere to be found in the lower regions of the house.

I looked into my room. Quite true – nothing was to be discovered there but a couple of empty tumblers and a strong smell of hot grog.[1] Had the Sergeant gone of his own accord to the bed-chamber that was prepared for him? I went upstairs to see.

After reaching the second landing, I thought I heard a sound of quiet and regular breathing on my left-hand side. My left-hand side led to the corridor which communicated with Miss Rachel's room. I looked in, and there, coiled up on three chairs placed right across the passage – there, with a red handkerchief tied round his grizzled head, and his respectable black coat rolled up for a pillow, lay and slept Sergeant Cuff!

He woke, instantly and quietly, like a dog, the moment I approached him.

"Good-night, Mr. Betteredge," he said. "And mind, if you ever take to growing roses, the white moss-rose is all the better for not being budded on the dog-rose, whatever the gardener may say to the contrary!"

"What are you doing here?" I asked. "Why are you not in your proper bed?"

"I am not in my proper bed," answered the Sergeant, "because I am one of the many people in this miserable world who can't earn their money honestly and easily at the same time. There was a coincidence, this evening, between the period of Rosanna Spearman's return from the Sands and the period when Miss Verinder stated her resolution to leave the house. Whatever Rosanna may have hidden, it's clear to my mind that your young lady couldn't go away until she knew that it was hidden. The two must have communicated privately once already to-night. If they try to communicate again, when the house is quiet, I want to be in the way, and stop it. Don't blame me for upsetting your sleeping arrangements, Mr. Betteredge – blame the Diamond."

"I wish to God the Diamond had never found its way into this house!" I broke out.

Sergeant Cuff looked with a rueful face at the three chairs on which he had condemned himself to pass the night.

"So do I," he said gravely.

---

1   Grog consists of warmed rum diluted with water.

CHAPTER XVII

NOTHING happened in the night; and (I am happy to add) no attempt at communication between Miss Rachel and Rosanna rewarded the vigilance of Sergeant Cuff.

I had expected the Sergeant to set off for Frizinghall the first thing in the morning. He waited about, however, as if he had something else to do first. I left him to his own devices; and going into the grounds shortly after, met Mr. Franklin on his favourite walk by the shrubbery side.

Before we had exchanged two words, the Sergeant unexpectedly joined us. He made up to Mr. Franklin, who received him, I must own, haughtily enough. "Have you anything to say to me?" was all the return he got for politely wishing Mr. Franklin good morning."I have something to say to you, sir," answered the Sergeant, "on the subject of the inquiry I am conducting here. You detected the turn that inquiry was really taking, yesterday. Naturally enough, in your position, you are shocked and distressed. Naturally enough, also, you visit your own angry sense of your own family scandal upon Me."

"What do you want?" Mr. Franklin broke in, sharply enough.

I want to remind you, sir, that I have at any rate, thus far, not been *proved* to be wrong. Bearing that in mind, be pleased to remember, at the same time, that I am an officer of the law acting here under the sanction of the mistress of the house. Under these circumstances, is it, or is it not, your duty as a good citizen, to assist me with any special information which you may happen to possess?"

"I possess no special information," says Mr. Franklin.

Sergeant Cuff put that answer by him, as if no answer had been made.

"You may save my time, sir, from being wasted on an inquiry at a distance," he went on, "if you choose to understand me and speak out."

"I don't understand you," answered Mr. Franklin; "and I have nothing to say."

"One of the female servants (I won't mention names) spoke to you privately, sir, last night."

Once more Mr. Franklin cut him short; once more Mr. Franklin answered, "I have nothing to say."

Standing by in silence, I thought of the movement in the swing-door on the previous evening, and of the coat-tails which I had seen disappearing down the passage. Sergeant Cuff had, no doubt, just heard enough, before I interrupted him, to make him suspect that Rosanna had relieved her mind by confessing something to Mr. Franklin Blake.

This notion had barely struck me – when who should appear at the end of the shrubbery walk but Rosanna Spearman in her own proper person! She was followed by Penelope, who was evidently trying to make her retrace her steps to the house. Seeing that Mr. Franklin was not alone, Rosanna came to a standstill, evidently in great perplexity what to do next. Penelope waited behind her. Mr. Franklin saw the girls as soon as I saw them. The Sergeant, with his devilish cunning, took on not to have noticed them at all. All this happened in an instant. Before either Mr. Franklin or I could say a word, Sergeant Cuff struck in smoothly, with an appearance of continuing the previous conversation.

"You needn't be afraid of harming the girl, sir," he said to Mr. Franklin, speaking in a loud voice, so that Rosanna might hear him. "On the contrary, I recommend you to honour me with your confidence, if you feel any interest in Rosanna Spearman."

Mr. Franklin instantly took on not to have noticed the girls either. He answered, speaking loudly on his side:

"I take no interest whatever in Rosanna Spearman."

I looked towards the end of the walk. All I saw at the distance was that Rosanna suddenly turned round, the moment Mr. Franklin had spoken. Instead of resisting Penelope, as she had done the moment before, she now let my daughter take her by the arm and lead her back to the house.

The breakfast-bell rang as the two girls disappeared – and even Sergeant Cuff was now obliged to give it up as a bad job! He said to me quietly, "I shall go to Frizinghall, Mr. Betteredge; and I shall be back before two." He went his way without a word more – and for some few hours we were well rid of him.

"You must make it right with Rosanna," Mr. Franklin said to me, when we were alone. "I seem to be fated to say or do something awkward, before that unlucky girl. You must have seen yourself that Sergeant Cuff laid a trap for both of us. If he could confuse *me*, or irritate *her* into breaking out, either she or I might have said something which would answer his purpose. On the spur of the moment, I saw no better way out of it than the way I took. It stopped the girl from saying anything, and it showed the Sergeant that I saw through him. He was evidently listening, Betteredge, when I was speaking to you last night."

He had done worse than listen, as I privately thought to myself. He had remembered my telling him that the girl was in love with Mr. Franklin; and he had calculated on *that*, when he appealed to Mr. Franklin's interest in Rosanna – in Rosanna's hearing.

"As to listening, sir," I remarked (keeping the other point to myself), "we shall all be rowing in the same boat, if this sort of thing goes on much longer. Prying, and peeping, and listening are the natural occupations of people situated as we are. In another day or two, Mr. Franklin, we shall all be struck dumb together – for this reason, that we shall all be listening to surprise each other's secrets, and all know it. Excuse my breaking out, sir. The horrid mystery hanging over us in this house gets into my head like liquor, and makes me wild. I won't forget what you have told me. I'll take the first opportunity of making it right with Rosanna Spearman."

"You haven't said anything to her yet about last night, have you?" Mr. Franklin asked.

"No, sir."

"Then say nothing now. I had better not invite the girl's confidence, with the Sergeant on the look-out to surprise us together. My conduct is not very consistent, Betteredge – is it? I see no way out of this business, which isn't dreadful to think of, unless the Diamond is traced to Rosanna. And yet I can't, and won't, help Sergeant Cuff to find the girl out."

Unreasonable enough, no doubt. But it was my state of mind as well. I thoroughly understood him. If you will, for once in your life, remember that you are mortal, perhaps you will thoroughly understand him too.

The state of things, indoors and out, while Sergeant Cuff was on his way to Frizinghall, was briefly this:

Miss Rachel waited for the time when the carriage was to take her to her aunt's, still obstinately shut up in her own room. My lady and Mr. Franklin breakfasted together. After breakfast, Mr. Franklin took one of his sudden resolutions, and went out precipitately to quiet his mind by a long walk. I was the only person who saw him go; and he told me he should be back before the Sergeant returned. The change in the weather, foreshadowed overnight, had come. Heavy rain had been followed, soon after dawn, by high wind. It was blowing fresh as the day got on. But though the clouds threatened more than once, the rain still held off. It was not a bad day for a walk, if you were young and strong, and could breast the great gusts of wind which came sweeping in from the sea.

I attended my lady after breakfast, and assisted her in the settlement of our household accounts. She only once alluded to the matter of the Moonstone, and that was in the way of forbidding any present mention of it between us. "Wait till that man comes back," she said, meaning the Sergeant. "We *must* speak of it then: we are not obliged to speak of it now."

After leaving my mistress, I found Penelope waiting for me in my room.

"I wish, father, you would come and speak to Rosanna," she said. "I am very uneasy about her."

I suspected what was the matter readily enough. But it is a maxim of mine that men (being superior creatures) are bound to improve women – if they can. When a woman wants me to do anything (my daughter, or not, it doesn't matter), I always insist on knowing why. The oftener you make them rummage their own minds for a reason, the more manageable you will find them in all the relations of life. It isn't their fault (poor wretches!) that they act first, and think afterwards; it's the fault of the fools who humour them.

Penelope's reason why, on this occasion, may be given in her own words. "I am afraid, father," she said, "Mr. Franklin has hurt Rosanna cruelly, without intending it."

"What took Rosanna into the shrubbery walk?" I asked.

"Her own madness," says Penelope; "I can call it nothing else. She was bent on speaking to Mr. Franklin, this morning, come what might of it. I did my best to stop her; you saw that. If I could only have got her away before she heard those dreadful words –"

"There! there!" I said, "don't lose your head. I can't call to mind that anything happened to alarm Rosanna."

"Nothing to alarm her, father. But Mr. Franklin said he took no interest whatever in her – and, oh, he said it in such a cruel voice!"

"He said it to stop the Sergeant's mouth," I answered.

"I told her that," says Penelope. "But you see, father (though Mr. Franklin isn't to blame), he's been mortifying and disappointing her for weeks and weeks past; and now this comes on the top of it all! She has no right, of course, to expect him to take any interest in her. It's quite monstrous that she should forget herself and her station in that way. But she seems to have lost pride, and proper feeling, and everything. She frightened me, father, when Mr. Franklin said those words. They seemed to turn her into stone. A sudden quiet came over her, and she has gone about her work, ever since, like a woman in a dream."

I began to feel a little uneasy. There was something in the way Penelope put it which silenced my superior sense. I called to mind, now my thoughts were directed that way, what had passed between Mr. Franklin and Rosanna overnight. She looked cut to the heart on that occasion; and now, as ill-luck would have it, she had been unavoidably stung again, poor soul, on the tender place. Sad! sad! – all the more sad because the girl had no reason to justify her, and no right to feel it.

I had promised Mr. Franklin to speak to Rosanna, and this seemed the fittest time for keeping my word.

We found the girl sweeping the corridor outside the bedrooms, pale and composed, and neat as ever in her modest print dress. I noticed a curious dimness and dullness in her eyes – not as if she had been crying, but as if she had been looking at something too long. Possibly, it was a misty something raised by her own thoughts. There was certainly no object about her to look at which she had not seen already hundreds on hundreds of times.

"Cheer up, Rosanna!" I said. "You mustn't fret over your own fancies. I have got something to say to you from Mr. Franklin."

I thereupon put the matter in the right view before her, in the friendliest and most comforting words I could find. My principles, in regard to the other sex, are, as you may have noticed, very severe. But somehow or other, when I come face to face with the women, my practice (I own) is not conformable.

"Mr. Franklin is very kind and considerate. Please to thank him." That was all the answer she made me.

My daughter had already noticed that Rosanna went about her work like a woman in a dream. I now added to this observation, that she also listened and spoke like a woman in a dream. I doubted if her mind was in a fit condition to take in what I had said to her.

"Are you quite sure, Rosanna, that you understand me?" I asked.

"Quite sure."

She echoed me, not like a living woman, but like a creature moved by machinery. She went on sweeping all the time. I took away the broom as gently and as kindly as I could.

"Come, come, my girl!" I said, "this is not like yourself. You have got something on your mind. I'm your friend – and I'll stand your friend, even if you have done wrong. Make a clean breast of it, Rosanna – make a clean breast of it!"

The time had been, when my speaking to her in that way would have brought the tears into her eyes. I could see no change in them now.

"Yes," she said, "I'll make a clean breast of it."

"To my lady?" I asked.

"No."

"To Mr. Franklin?"

"Yes; to Mr. Franklin."

I hardly knew what to say to that. She was in no condition to understand the caution against speaking to him in private, which Mr. Franklin had directed me to give her. Feeling my way, little by little, I only told her Mr. Franklin had gone out for a walk.

"It doesn't matter," she answered. "I shan't trouble Mr. Franklin, to-day."

"Why not speak to my lady?" I said. "The way to relieve your mind is to speak to the merciful and Christian mistress who has always been kind to you."

She looked at me for a moment with a grave and steady attention, as if she was fixing what I said in her mind. Then she took the broom out of my hands; and moved off with it slowly, a little way down the corridor.

"No," she said, going on with her sweeping, and speaking to herself; "I know a better way of relieving my mind than that."

"What is it?"

"Please to let me go on with my work."

Penelope followed her, and offered to help her.

She answered, "No. I want to do my work. Thank you, Penelope."

She looked round at me. "Thank you, Mr. Betteredge."

There was no moving her – there was nothing more to be said. I signed to Penelope to come away with me. We left her, as we had found her, sweeping the corridor, like a woman in a dream.

"This is a matter for the doctor to look into," I said. "It's beyond me."

My daughter reminded me of Mr. Candy's illness, owing (as you may remember) to the chill he had caught on the night of the dinner-party. His assistant – a certain Mr. Ezra Jennings – was at our disposal, to be sure. But nobody knew much about him in our parts. He had been engaged by Mr. Candy, under rather peculiar circumstances; and, right or wrong, we none of us liked him or trusted him. There were other doctors at Frizinghall. But they were strangers to our house; and Penelope doubted, in Rosanna's present state, whether strangers might not do her more harm than good.

I thought of speaking to my lady. But, remembering the heavy weight of anxiety which she already had on her mind, I hesitated to add to all the other vexations this new trouble. Still, there was a necessity for doing something. The girl's state was, to my thinking, downright alarming – and my mistress ought to be informed of it. Unwilling enough, I went to her sitting-room. No one was there. My lady was shut up with Miss Rachel. It was impossible for me to see her till she came out again.

I waited in vain till the clock on the front staircase struck the quarter to two. Five minutes afterwards, I heard my name called, from the drive outside the house. I knew the voice directly. Sergeant Cuff had returned from Frizinghall.

★

CHAPTER XVIII

GOING down to the front door, I met the Sergeant on the steps.

It went against the grain with me, after what had passed between us, to show him that I felt any sort of interest in his proceedings. In spite of myself, however, I felt an interest that there was no resisting. My sense of dignity sank from under me, and out came the words: "What news from Frizinghall?"

"I have seen the Indians," answered Sergeant Cuff. "And I have found out what Rosanna bought privately in the town, on Thursday last. The Indians will be set free on Wednesday in next week. There isn't a doubt on my mind, and there isn't a doubt on Mr. Murthwaite's mind, that they came to this place to steal the Moonstone. Their calculations were all thrown out, of course, by what happened in the house on Wednesday night; and they have no more to do with the actual loss of the jewel than you have. But I can tell you one thing, Mr. Betteredge – if *we* don't find the Moonstone, *they* will. You have not heard the last of the three jugglers yet."

Mr. Franklin came back from his walk as the Sergeant said those startling words. Governing his curiosity better than I had governed mine, he passed us without a word, and went on into the house.

As for me, having already dropped my dignity, I determined to have the whole benefit of the sacrifice. "So much for the Indians," I said. "What about Rosanna next?"

Sergeant Cuff shook his head.

"The mystery in that quarter is thicker than ever," he said. "I have traced her to a shop at Frizinghall, kept by a linen-draper named Maltby. She bought nothing whatever at any of the other drapers' shops, or at any milliners' or tailors' shops; and she bought nothing at Maltby's but a piece of long cloth. She was very particular in choosing a certain quality. As to quantity, she bought enough to make a nightgown."

"Whose nightgown?" I asked.

"Her own, to be sure. Between twelve and three, on the Thursday morning, she must have slipped down to your young lady's room, to settle the hiding of the Moonstone while all the rest of you were in bed. In going back to her own room, her nightgown must have brushed the wet paint on the door. She couldn't wash out the stain; and she couldn't safely destroy the nightgown without first providing another like it, to make the inventory of her linen complete."

"What proves that it was Rosanna's nightgown?" I objected.

"The material she bought for making the substitute dress," answered the Sergeant. "If it had been Miss Verinder's nightgown, she would have had to buy lace, and frilling, and Lord knows what besides; and she wouldn't have had time to make it in one night. Plain long cloth means a plain servant's nightgown. No, no, Mr. Betteredge

– all that is clear enough. The pinch of the question is – why, after having provided the substitute dress, does she hide the smeared night-gown, instead of destroying it? If the girl won't speak out, there is only one way of settling the difficulty. The hiding-place at the Shivering Sand must be searched – and the true state of the case will be discovered there."

"How are you to find the place?" I inquired.

"I am sorry to disappoint you," said the Sergeant – "but that's a secret which I mean to keep to myself."

(Not to irritate your curiosity, as he irritated mine, I may here inform you that he had come back from Frizinghall provided with a search-warrant. His experience in such matters told him that Rosanna was in all probability carrying about her a memorandum of the hiding-place, to guide her, in case she returned to it, under changed circumstances and after a lapse of time. Possessed of this memorandum, the Sergeant would be furnished with all that he could desire.)

"Now, Mr. Betteredge," he went on, "suppose we drop speculation, and get to business. I told Joyce to have an eye on Rosanna. Where is Joyce?"

Joyce was the Frizinghall policeman, who had been left by Superintendent Seegrave at Sergeant Cuff's disposal. The clock struck two, as he put the question; and, punctual to the moment, the carriage came round to take Miss Rachel to her aunt's.

"One thing at a time," said the Sergeant, stopping me as I was about to send in search of Joyce. "I must attend to Miss Verinder first."

As the rain was still threatening, it was the close carriage that had been appointed to take Miss Rachel to Frizinghall. Sergeant Cuff beckoned Samuel to come down to him from the rumble behind.

"You will see a friend of mine waiting among the trees, on this side of the lodge gate," he said. "My friend, without stopping the carriage, will get up into the rumble with you. You have nothing to do but to hold your tongue, and shut your eyes. Otherwise, you will get into trouble."

With that advice, he sent the footman back to his place. What Samuel thought I don't know. It was plain, to my mind, that Miss Rachel was to be privately kept in view from the time when she left our house – if she did leave it. A watch set on my young lady! A spy behind her in the rumble of her mother's carriage! I could have cut my own tongue out for having forgotten myself so far as to speak to Sergeant Cuff.

The first person to come out of the house was my lady. She stood aside, on the top step, posting herself there to see what happened. Not a word did she say, either to the Sergeant or to me. With her lips closed, and her arms folded in the light garden cloak which she had wrapped round her on coming into the air, there she stood, as still as a statue, waiting for her daughter to appear.

In a minute more, Miss Rachel came downstairs – very nicely dressed in some soft yellow stuff, that set off her dark complexion, and clipped her tight (in the form of a jacket) round the waist. She had a smart little straw hat on her head, with a white veil twisted round it. She had primrose-coloured gloves that fitted her hands like a second skin. Her beautiful black hair looked as smooth as satin under her hat. Her little ears were like rosy shells – they had a pearl dangling from each of them. She came swiftly out to us, as straight as a lily on its stem, and as lithe and supple in every movement she made as a young cat. Nothing that I could discover was altered in her pretty face, but her eyes and her lips. Her eyes were brighter and fiercer than I liked to see; and her lips had so completely lost their colour and their smile that I hardly knew them again. She kissed her mother in a hasty and sudden manner on the cheek. She said, "Try to forgive me, mamma" – and then pulled down her veil over her face so vehemently that she tore it. In another moment she had run down the steps, and had rushed into the carriage as if it was a hiding-place.

Sergeant Cuff was just as quick on his side. He put Samuel back, and stood before Miss Rachel, with the open carriage-door in his hand, at the instant when she settled herself in her place.

"What do you want?" says Miss Rachel, from behind her veil.

"I want to say one word to you, miss," answered the Sergeant, "before you go. I can't presume to stop your paying a visit to your aunt. I can only venture to say that your leaving us, as things are now, puts an obstacle in the way of my recovering your Diamond. Please to understand that; and now decide for yourself whether you go or stay."

Miss Rachel never even answered him. "Drive on, James!" she called out to the coachman.

Without another word, the Sergeant shut the carriage-door. Just as he closed it, Mr. Franklin came running down the steps. "Good-bye,

Rachel," he said, holding out his hand.

"Drive on!" cried Miss Rachel, louder than ever, and taking no more notice of Mr. Franklin than she had taken of Sergeant Cuff.

Mr. Franklin stepped back thunderstruck, as well he might be. The coachman, not knowing what to do, looked towards my lady, still standing immovable on the top step. My lady, with anger and sorrow and shame all struggling together in her face, made him a sign to start the horses, and then turned back hastily into the house. Mr. Franklin, recovering the use of his speech, called after her, as the carriage drove off, "Aunt! you were quite right. Accept my thanks for all your kindness – and let me go."

My lady turned as though to speak to him. Then, as if distrusting herself, waved her hand kindly. "Let me see you, before you leave us, Franklin," she said, in a broken voice – and went on to her own room.

"Do me a last favour, Betteredge," says Mr. Franklin, turning to me, with the tears in his eyes. "Get me away to the train as soon as you can!"

He too went his way into the house. For the moment, Miss Rachel had completely unmanned him. Judge from that, how fond he must have been of her!

Sergeant Cuff and I were left face to face, at the bottom of the steps. The Sergeant stood with his face set towards a gap in the trees, commanding a view of one of the windings of the drive which led from the house. He had his hands in his pockets, and he was softly whistling "The Last Rose of Summer" to himself.

"There's a time for everything," I said, savagely enough. "This isn't a time for whistling."

At that moment, the carriage appeared in the distance, through the gap, on its way to the lodge-gate. There was another man, besides Samuel, plainly visible in the rumble behind.

"All right!" said the Sergeant to himself. He turned round to me. "It's no time for whistling, Mr. Betteredge, as you say. It's time to take this business in hand, now, without sparing anybody. We'll begin with Rosanna Spearman. Where is Joyce?"

We both called for Joyce, and received no answer. I sent one of the stable-boys to look for him.

"You heard what I said to Miss Verinder?" remarked the Sergeant, while we were waiting. "And you saw how she received it? I tell her plainly that her leaving us will be an obstacle in the way of my recovering her Diamond – and she leaves, in the face of that statement! Your young lady has got a travelling companion in her mother's carriage, Mr. Betteredge – and the name of it is, the Moonstone."

I said nothing. I only held on like death to my belief in Miss Rachel.

The stable-boy came back, followed – very unwillingly, as it appeared to me – by Joyce.

"Where is Rosanna Spearman?" asked Sergeant Cuff.

"I can't account for it, sir," Joyce began; "and I am very sorry. But somehow or other – "

"Before I went to Frizinghall," said the Sergeant, cutting him short, "I told you to keep your eyes on Rosanna Spearman, without allowing her to discover that she was being watched. Do you mean to tell me that you have let her give you the slip?"

"I am afraid, sir," says Joyce, beginning to tremble, "that I was perhaps a little *too* careful not to let her discover me. There are such a many passages in the lower parts of this house – "

"How long is it since you missed her?"

"Nigh on an hour since, sir."

"You can go back to your regular business at Frizinghall," said the Sergeant, speaking just as composedly as ever, in his usual quiet and dreary way. "I don't think your talents are at all in our line, Mr. Joyce. Your present form of employment is a trifle beyond you. Good morning."

The man slunk off. I find it very difficult to describe how I was affected by the discovery that Rosanna Spearman was missing. I seemed to be in fifty different minds about it, all at the same time. In that state, I stood staring at Sergeant Cuff – and my powers of language quite failed me.

"No, Mr. Betteredge," said the Sergeant, as if he had discovered the uppermost thought in me, and was picking it out to be answered, before all the rest. "Your young friend, Rosanna, won't slip through my fingers so easy as you think. As long as I know where Miss Verinder is, I have the means at my disposal of tracing Miss Verinder's accomplice. I prevented them from communicating last night. Very good. They will get together at Frizinghall, instead of getting together here. The present inquiry must be simply shifted (rather sooner than I had anticipated) from this house, to the house at which Miss Verinder is visiting. In the meantime, I'm afraid I must trouble you to call the servants together again."

I went round with him to the servants' hall. It is very disgraceful, but it is not the less true, that I had another attack of the detective-fever, when he said those last words. I forgot that I hated Sergeant Cuff. I seized him confidentially by the arm. I said, "For goodness' sake, tell us what you are going to do with the servants now?"

The great Cuff stood stockstill, and addressed himself in a kind of melancholy rapture to the empty air.

"If this man," said the Sergeant (apparently meaning me), "only understood the growing of roses, he would be the most completely perfect character on the face of creation!" After that strong expression of feeling, he sighed, and put his arm through mine. "This is how it stands," he said, dropping down again to business. "Rosanna has done one of two things. She has either gone direct to Frizinghall (before I can get there), or she has gone first to visit her hiding-place at the Shivering Sand. The first thing to find out is, which of the servants saw the last of her before she left the house."

On instituting this inquiry, it turned out that the last person who had set eyes on Rosanna was Nancy, the kitchenmaid.

Nancy had seen her slip out with a letter in her hand, and stop the butcher's man who had just been delivering some meat at the back door. Nancy had heard her ask the man to post the letter when he got back to Frizinghall. The man had looked at the address, and had said it was a round-about way of delivering a letter, directed to Cobb's Hole, to post it at Frizinghall – and that, moreover, on a Saturday, which would prevent the letter from getting to its destination until Monday morning. Rosanna had answered that the delivery of the let-ter being delayed till Monday was of no importance. The only thing she wished to be sure of was that the man would do what she told him. The man had promised to do it, and had driven away. Nancy had been called back to her work in the kitchen. And no other person had seen anything afterwards of Rosanna Spearman.

"Well?" I asked, when we were alone again.

"Well," says the Sergeant. "I must go to Frizinghall."

"About the letter, sir?"

"Yes. The memorandum of the hiding-place is in that letter. I must see the address at the post-office. If it is the address I suspect, I shall pay our friend, Mrs. Yolland, another visit on Monday next."

I went with the Sergeant to order the pony-chaise. In the stable-yard we got a new light thrown on the missing girl.

CHAPTER XIX

THE news of Rosanna's disappearance had, as it appeared, spread among the out-of-door servants. They too had made their inquiries; and they had just laid hands on a quick little imp, nick-named "Duffy" – who was occasionally employed in weeding the garden, and who had seen Rosanna Spearman as lately as half an hour since. Duffy was certain that the girl had passed him in the fir-plantation, not walking, but *running*, in the direction of the sea-shore.

"Does this boy know the coast hereabouts?" asked Sergeant Cuff.

"He has been born and bred on the coast," I answered.

"Duffy!" says the Sergeant, "do you want to earn a shilling? If you do, come along with me. Keep the pony-chaise ready, Mr. Betteredge, till I come back."

He started for the Shivering Sand, at a rate that my legs (though well enough preserved for my time of life) had no hope of matching. Little Duffy, as the way is with the young savages in our parts when they are in high spirits, gave a howl, and trotted off at the Sergeant's heels.

Here again, I find it impossible to give anything like a clear account of the state of my mind in the interval after Sergeant Cuff had left us. A curious and stupefying restlessness got possession of me. I did a dozen different needless things in and out of the house, not one of which I can now remember. I don't even know how long it was after the Sergeant had gone to the sands, when Duffy came running back with a message for me. Sergeant Cuff had given the boy a leaf torn out of his pocket-book, on which was written in pencil, "Send me one of Rosanna Spearman's boots, and be quick about it."

I despatched the first woman-servant I could find to Rosanna's room; and I sent the boy back to say that I myself would follow him with the boot.

This, I am well aware, was not the quickest way to take of obeying the directions which I had received. But I was resolved to see for myself what new mystification was going on, before I trusted Rosanna's boot in the Sergeant's hands. My old notion of screening the girl, if I could, seemed to have come back on me again, at the eleventh hour.[1] This state of feeling (to say nothing of the detective-fever) hurried me off, as soon as I had got the boot, at the nearest approach to a run which a man turned seventy can reasonably hope to make.

As I got near the shore, the clouds gathered black, and the rain came down, drifting in great white sheets of water before the wind. I heard the thunder of the sea on the sand-bank at the mouth of the bay. A little further on, I passed the boy crouching for shelter under the lee of the sand-hills. Then I saw the raging sea, and the rollers tumbling in on the sand-bank, and the driven rain sweeping over the waters like a flying garment, and the yellow wilderness of the beach with one solitary black figure standing on it – the figure of Sergeant Cuff.

He waved his hand towards the north, when he first saw me. "Keep on that side!" he shouted. "And come on down here to me!"

I went down to him, choking for breath, with my heart leaping as if it was like to leap out of me. I was past speaking. I had a hundred questions to put to him; and not one of them would pass my lips. His face frightened me. I saw a look in his eyes which was a look of horror. He snatched the boot out of my hand, and set it in a footmark on the sand, bearing south from us as we stood, and pointing straight towards the rocky ledge called the South Spit. The mark was not yet blurred out by the rain – and the girl's boot fitted it to a hair.

The Sergeant pointed to the boot in the footmark, without saying a word.

I caught at his arm, and tried to speak to him, and failed as I had failed when I tried before. He went on, following the footsteps down and down to where the rocks and the sand joined. The South Spit was just awash with the flowing tide; the waters heaved over the hidden

---

1   Having come to mean "the latest possible time," the phrase "the eleventh hour" comes from the New Testament, Matthew 20: 6: "And about the eleventh hour he went out, and found others standing idle, and saith unto them, 'Why stand ye here all the day idle?'" In the parable, those labourers hired at the eleventh hour were paid the same hourly wage as those hired earlier in the day.

face of the Shivering Sand. Now this way and now that, with an obstinate patience that was dreadful to see, Sergeant Cuff tried the boot in the footsteps, and always found it pointing the same way – straight *to* the rocks. Hunt as he might, no sign could he find anywhere of the footsteps walking *from* them.

He gave it up at last. Still keeping silence, he looked again at me; and then he looked out at the waters before us, heaving in deeper and deeper over the quicksand. I looked where he looked – and I saw his thought in his face. A dreadful dumb trembling crawled all over me on a sudden. I fell upon my knees on the beach.

"She has been back at the hiding-place," I heard the Sergeant say to himself. "Some fatal accident has happened to her on those rocks."

The girl's altered looks, and words, and actions – the numbed, deadened way in which she listened to me, and spoke to me – when I had found her sweeping the corridor but a few hours since, rose up in my mind, and warned me, even as the Sergeant spoke, that his guess was wide of the dreadful truth. I tried to tell him of the fear that had frozen me up. I tried to say, "The death she has died, Sergeant, was a death of her own seeking." No! the words wouldn't come. The dumb trembling held me in its grip. I couldn't feel the driving rain. I couldn't see the rising tide. As in the vision of a dream, the poor lost creature came back before me. I saw her again as I had seen her in the past time – on the morning when I went to fetch her into the house. I heard her again, telling me that the Shivering Sand seemed to draw her to it against her will, and wondering whether her grave was waiting for her *there*. The horror of it struck at me, in some unfathomable way, through my own child. My girl was just her age. My girl, tried as Rosanna was tried, might have lived that miserable life, and died this dreadful death.

The Sergeant kindly lifted me up, and turned me away from the sight of the place where she had perished.

With that relief, I began to fetch my breath again, and to see things about me, as things really were. Looking towards the sand-hills, I saw the men-servants from out-of-doors, and the fisherman, named Yolland, all running down to us together; and all, having taken the alarm, calling out to know if the girl had been found. In the fewest words, the Sergeant showed them the evidence of the footmarks, and told them that a fatal accident must have happened to her. He then picked out the fisherman from the rest, and put a question to him, turning about again towards the sea: "Tell me," he said. "Could a boat have taken her off, in such weather as this, from those rocks where her footmarks stop?" The fisherman pointed to the rollers tumbling in on the sand-bank, and to the great waves leaping up in clouds of foam against the headlands on either side of us.

"No boat that ever was built," he answered, "could have got to her through *that*."

Sergeant Cuff looked for the last time at the footmarks on the sand, which the rain was now fast blurring out.

"There," he said, "is the evidence that she can't have left this place by land. And here," he went on, looking at the fisherman, "is the evidence that she can't have got away by sea." He stopped, and considered for a minute. "She was seen running towards this place, half an hour before I got here from the house," he said to Yolland. "Some time has passed since then. Call it, altogether, an hour ago. How high would the water be, at that time, on this side of the rocks?" He pointed to the south side – otherwise, the side which was not filled up by the quicksand.

"As the tide makes to-day," said the fisherman, "there wouldn't have been water enough to drown a kitten on that side of the Spit, an hour since."

Sergeant Cuff turned about northward, towards the quicksand. "How much on this side?" he asked.

"Less still," answered Yolland. "The Shivering Sand would have been just awash, and no more."

The Sergeant turned to me, and said that the accident must have happened on the side of the quicksand. My tongue was loosened at that. "No accident!" I told him. "When she came to this place, she came, weary of her life, to end it here."

He started back from me. "How do you know?" he asked. The rest of them crowded round. The Sergeant recovered himself instantly. He put them back from me; he said I was an old man; he said the discovery had shaken me; he said, "Let him alone a little." Then he turned to Yolland, and asked, "Is there any chance of finding her, when the tide ebbs again?" And Yolland answered, "None. What the Sand gets, the Sand keeps for ever." Having said that, the fisherman came a step nearer, and addressed himself to me.

"Mr. Betteredge," he said, "I have a word to say to you about the young woman's death. Four foot out, broadwise, along the side of the Spit, there's a shelf of rock, about half fathom down under the sand. My question is – why didn't she strike that? If she slipped, by accident, from off the Spit, she fell in where there's foothold at the bottom, at a depth that would barely cover her to the waist. She must have waded out, or jumped out, into the Deeps beyond – or she wouldn't be missing now. No accident, sir! The Deeps of the Quicksand have got her. And they have got her by her own act."

After that testimony from a man whose knowledge was to be relied on, the Sergeant was silent. The rest of us, like him, held our peace. With one accord, we all turned back up the slope of the beach.

At the sand-hillocks we were met by the under-groom, running to us from the house. The lad is a good lad, and has an honest respect for me. He handed me a little note, with a decent sorrow in his face. "Penelope sent me with this, Mr. Betteredge," he said. "She found it in Rosanna's room."

It was her last farewell word to the old man who had done his best – thank God, always done his best – to befriend her.

"You have often forgiven me, Mr. Betteredge, in past times. When you next see the Shivering Sand, try to forgive me once more. I have found my grave where my grave was waiting for me. I have lived, and died, sir, grateful for your kindness."

There was no more than that. Little as it was, I hadn't manhood enough to hold up against it. Your tears come easy, when you're young, and beginning the world. Your tears come easy, when you're old, and leaving it. I burst out crying.

Sergeant Cuff took a step nearer to me – meaning kindly, I don't doubt. I shrank back from him. "Don't touch me," I said. "It's the dread of you, that has driven her to it."

"You are wrong, Mr. Betteredge," he answered, quietly. "But there will be time enough to speak of it when we are indoors again."

I followed the rest of them, with the help of the groom's arm. Through the driving rain we went back – to meet the trouble and the terror that were waiting for us at the house.

End of Volume I of First Three-Volume Edition (1868)

CHAPTER XX

Those in front had spread the news before us. We found the servants in a state of panic. As we passed my lady's door, it was thrown open violently from the inner side. My mistress came out among us (with Mr. Franklin following, and trying vainly to compose her), quite beside herself with the horror of the thing.

"You are answerable for this!" she cried out, threatening the Sergeant wildly with her hand. "Gabriel! give that wretch his money – and release me from the sight of him!"

The Sergeant was the only one among us who was fit to cope with her – being the only one among us who was in possession of himself.

"I am no more answerable for this distressing calamity, my lady, than you are," he said. "If, in half an hour from this, you still insist on my leaving the house, I will accept your ladyship's dismissal, but not your ladyship's money."

It was spoken very respectfully, but very firmly at the same time – and it had its effect on my mistress as well as on me. She suffered Mr. Franklin to lead her back into the room. As the door closed on the two, the Sergeant, looking about among the women-servants in his observant way, noticed that while all the rest were merely frightened, Penelope was in tears. "When your father has changed his wet clothes," he said to her, "come and speak to us, in your father's room."

Before the half-hour was out, I had got my dry clothes on, and had lent Sergeant Cuff such change of dress as he required. Penelope came in to us to hear what the Sergeant wanted with her. I don't think I ever felt what a good dutiful daughter I had, so strongly as I felt it at that moment. I took her and sat her on my knee – and I prayed God bless her. She hid her head on my bosom, and put her arms round my neck – and we waited a little while in silence. The poor dead girl must have been at the bottom of it, I think, with my daughter and with me. The Sergeant went to the window, and stood there looking out. I thought it right to thank him for considering us both in this way – and I did.

People in high life have all the luxuries to themselves – among others, the luxury of indulging their feelings. People in low life have no such privilege. Necessity, which spares our betters, has no pity on *us.* We learn to put our feelings back into ourselves, and to jog on with our duties as patiently as may be. I don't complain of this – I only notice it. Penelope and I were ready for the Sergeant, as soon as the Sergeant was ready on his side. Asked if she knew what had led her fellow-servant to destroy herself, my daughter answered (as you will foresee) that it was for love of Mr. Franklin Blake. Asked next, if she had mentioned this notion of hers to any other person, Penelope answered, "I have not mentioned it, for Rosanna's sake." I felt it necessary to add a word to this. I said, "And for Mr. Franklin's sake, my dear, as well. If Rosanna *has* died for love of him, it is not with his knowledge or by his fault. Let him leave the house to-day, if he does leave it, without the useless pain of knowing the truth." Sergeant Cuff said, "Quite right," and fell silent again; comparing Penelope's notion (as it seemed to me) with some other notion of his own which he kept to himself.

At the end of the half-hour, my mistress's bell rang.

On my way to answer it, I met Mr. Franklin coming out of his aunt's sitting-room. He mentioned that her ladyship was ready to see Sergeant Cuff – in my presence as before – and he added that he himself wanted to say two words to the Sergeant first. On our way back to my room, he stopped, and looked at the railway time-table[1] in the hall.

"Are you really going to leave us, sir?" I asked. "Miss Rachel will surely come right again, if you only give her time?"

"She will come right again," answered Mr. Franklin, "when she hears that I have gone away, and that she will see me no more."

I thought he spoke in resentment of my young lady's treatment of him. But it was not so. My mistress had noticed, from the time when the police first came into the house, that the bare mention of him was enough to set Miss Rachel's temper in a flame. He had been too fond of his cousin to like to confess this to himself, until the truth had been forced on him, when she drove off to her aunt's. His eyes once opened in that cruel way which you know of, Mr. Franklin had taken his resolution – the one resolution which a man of any spirit *could* take – to leave the house.

---

1   The time-table was probably *Bradshaw's Railway Guide*, the standard time-table for all passenger trains of the day.

What he had to say to the Sergeant was spoken in my presence. He described her ladyship as willing to acknowledge that she had spoken over-hastily. And he asked if Sergeant Cuff would consent – in that case – to accept his fee, and to leave the matter of the Diamond where the matter stood now. The Sergeant answered, "No, sir. My fee is paid me for doing my duty. I decline to take it, until my duty is done."

"I don't understand you," says Mr. Franklin.

"I'll explain myself, sir," says the Sergeant. "When I came here, I undertook to throw the necessary light on the matter of the missing Diamond. I am now ready, and waiting, to redeem my pledge. When I have stated the case to Lady Verinder as the case now stands, and when I have told her plainly what course of action to take for the recovery of the Moonstone, the responsibility will be off my shoulders. Let her ladyship decide, after that, whether she does, or does not, allow me to go on. I shall then have done what I undertook to do – and I'll take my fee."

In those words Sergeant Cuff reminded us that, even in the Detective Police, a man may have a reputation to lose.

The view he took was so plainly the right one, that there was no more to be said. As I rose to conduct him to my lady's room, he asked if Mr. Franklin wished to be present. Mr. Franklin answered, "Not unless Lady Verinder desires it." He added, in a whisper to me, as I was following the Sergeant out, "I know what that man is going to say about Rachel; and I am too fond of her to hear it, and keep my temper. Leave me by myself."

I left him, miserable enough, leaning on the sill of my window, with his face hidden in his hands – and Penelope peeping through the door, longing to comfort him. In Mr. Franklin's place, I should have called her in. When you are ill-used by one woman, there is great comfort in telling it to another – because, nine times out of ten, the other always takes your side. Perhaps, when my back was turned, he did call her in? In that case, it is only doing my daughter justice to declare that she would stick at nothing, in the way of comforting Mr. Franklin Blake.

In the meantime, Sergeant Cuff and I proceeded to my lady's room.

At the last conference we had held with her, we had found her not over willing to lift her eyes from the book which she had on the table. On this occasion there was a change for the better. She met the Sergeant's eye with an eye that was as steady as his own. The family spirit showed itself in every line of her face; and I knew that Sergeant Cuff would meet his match, when a woman like my mistress was strung up to hear the worst he could say to her.

★

CHAPTER XXI

THE first words, when we had taken our seats, were spoken by my lady.

"Sergeant Cuff," she said, "there was perhaps some excuse for the inconsiderate manner in which I spoke to you half an hour since. I have no wish, however, to claim that excuse. I say, with perfect sincerity, that I regret it, if I wronged you."

The grace of voice and manner with which she made him that atonement had its due effect on the Sergeant. He requested permission to justify himself – putting his justification as an act of respect to my mistress. It was impossible, he said, that he could be in any way responsible for the calamity which had shocked us all, for this sufficient reason, that his success in bringing his inquiry to its proper end depended on his neither saying nor doing anything that could alarm Rosanna Spearman. He appealed to me to testify whether he had, or had not, carried that object out. I could, and did, bear witness that he had. And there, as I thought, the matter might have been judiciously left to come to an end.

Sergeant Cuff, however, took it a step further, evidently (as you shall now judge) with the purpose of forcing the most painful of all possible explanations to take place between her ladyship and himself.

"I have heard a motive assigned for the young woman's suicide," said the Sergeant, "which may possibly be the right one. It is a motive quite unconnected with the case which I am conducting here. I am bound to add, however, that my own opinion points the other way. Some unbearable anxiety in connexion with the missing Diamond, has, I believe, driven the poor creature to her destruction. I don't pretend to know what that unbearable anxiety may have been. But

I think (with your ladyship's permission) I can lay my hand on a person who is capable of deciding whether I am right or wrong."

"Is the person now in the house?" my mistress asked, after waiting a little.

"The person has left the house, my lady."

That answer pointed as straight to Miss Rachel as straight could be. A silence dropped on us which I thought would never come to an end. Lord! how the wind howled, and how the rain drove at the window, as I sat there waiting for one or other of them to speak again!

"Be so good as to express yourself plainly," said my lady. "Do you refer to my daughter?"

"I do," said Sergeant Cuff, in so many words.

My mistress had her cheque-book on the table when we entered the room – no doubt to pay the Sergeant his fee. She now put it back in the drawer. It went to my heart to see how her poor hand trembled – the hand that had loaded her old servant with benefits; the hand that, I pray God, may take mine, when my time comes, and I leave my place for ever![1]

"I had hoped," said my lady, very slowly and quietly, "to have recompensed your services, and to have parted with you without Miss Verinder's name having been openly mentioned between us as it has been mentioned now. My nephew has probably said something of this, before you came into my room?"

"Mr. Blake gave his message, my lady. And I gave Mr. Blake a reason –"

"It is needless to tell me your reason. After what you have just said, you know as well as I do that you have gone too far to go back. I owe it to myself, and I owe it to my child, to insist on your remaining here, and to insist on your speaking out."

The Sergeant looked at his watch.

"If there had been time, my lady," he answered, "I should have preferred writing my report, instead of communicating it by word of mouth. But, if this inquiry is to go on, time is of too much importance to be wasted in writing. I am ready to go into the matter at

---

1   Betteredge writes this in 1850, *after* Julia Verinder's death! Collins overlooked this
    anachronism, which he slips into again in the last paragraph of Betteredge's first
    narrative.

once. It is a very painful matter for me to speak of, and for you to hear —"

There my mistress stopped him once more.

"I may possibly make it less painful to you, and to my good servant and friend here," she said, "if I set the example of speaking boldly, on my side. You suspect Miss Verinder of deceiving us all, by secreting the Diamond for some purpose of her own? Is that true?"

"Quite true, my lady."

"Very well. Now, before you begin, I have to tell you, as Miss Verinder's mother, that she is *absolutely incapable* of doing what you suppose her to have done. Your knowledge of her character dates from a day or two since. My knowledge of her character dates from the beginning of her life. State your suspicion of her as strongly as you please — it is impossible that you can offend me by doing so. I am sure, beforehand, that (with all your experience) the circumstances have fatally misled you in this case. Mind! I am in possession of no private information. I am as absolutely shut out of my daughter's confidence as you are. My one reason for speaking positively, is the reason you have heard already. I know my child."

She turned to me, and gave me her hand. I kissed it in silence. "You may go on," she said, facing the Sergeant again as steadily as ever.

Sergeant Cuff bowed. My mistress had produced but one effect on him. His hatchet-face softened for a moment, as if he was sorry for her. As to shaking him in his own conviction, it was plain to see that she had not moved him by a single inch. He settled himself in his chair; and he began his vile attack on Miss Rachel's character in these words:

"I must ask your ladyship," he said, "to look this matter in the face, from my point of view as well as from yours. Will you please to suppose yourself coming down here, in my place, and with my experience? and will you allow me to mention very briefly what that experience has been?"

My mistress signed to him that she would do this. The Sergeant went on:

"For the last twenty years," he said, "I have been largely employed in cases of family scandal, acting in the capacity of confidential man. The one result of my domestic practice which has any bearing on the matter now in hand, is a result which I may state in two words. It is well within my experience, that young ladies of rank and position do occasionally have private debts which they dare not acknowledge to their nearest relatives and friends. Sometimes, the milliner and the jeweller are at the bottom of it. Sometimes, the money is wanted for purposes which I don't suspect in this case, and which I won't shock you by mentioning. Bear in mind what I have said, my lady – and now let us see how events in this house have forced me back on my own experience, whether I liked it or not!"

He considered with himself for a moment, and went on – with a horrid clearness that obliged you to understand him; with an abominable justice that favoured nobody.

"My first information relating to the loss of the Moonstone," said the Sergeant, "came to me from Superintendent Seegrave. He proved to my complete satisfaction that he was perfectly incapable of managing the case. The one thing he said which struck me as worth listening to, was this – that Miss Verinder had declined to be questioned by him, and had spoken to him with a perfectly incomprehensible rudeness and contempt. I thought this curious – but I attributed it mainly to some clumsiness on the Superintendent's part which might have offended the young lady. After that, I put it by in my mind, and applied myself, single-handed, to the case. It ended, as you are aware, in the discovery of the smear on the door, and in Mr. Franklin Blake's evidence satisfying me, that this same smear, and the loss of the Diamond, were pieces of the same puzzle. So far, if I suspected anything, I suspected that the Moonstone had been stolen, and that one of the servants might prove to be the thief. Very good. In this state of things, what happens? Miss Verinder suddenly comes out of her room, and speaks to me. I observe three suspicious appearances in that young lady. She is still violently agitated, though more than four-and-twenty hours have passed since the Diamond was lost. She treats me, as she has already treated Superintendent Seegrave. And she is mortally offended with Mr. Franklin Blake. Very good again. Here (I say to myself) is a young lady who has lost a valuable jewel – a young lady, also, as my own eyes and ears inform me, who is of an impetuous temperament. Under these circumstances, and with that character, what does she do? She betrays an incomprehensible resentment against Mr. Blake, Mr. Superintendent, and myself – otherwise, the very three people who have all, in their different ways, been trying to help her to recover her lost jewel. Having brought my inquiry to that point – *then*, my lady, and not till then, I begin to look back into my own mind for my own experience. My own experience explains Miss Verinder's otherwise incomprehensible conduct. It associates her with those other young ladies that I know of. It tells me she has debts she daren't acknowledge, that must be paid. And it sets me asking myself, whether the loss of the Diamond may not mean – that the Diamond must be secretly pledged to pay them. That is the conclusion which my experience draws from plain facts. What does your ladyship's experience say against it?"

"What I have said already," answered my mistress. "The circumstances have misled you."

I said nothing on my side. *Robinson Crusoe* – God knows how – had got into my muddled old head. If Sergeant Cuff had found himself, at that moment, transported to a desert island, without a man Friday to keep him company, or a ship to take him off – he would have found himself exactly where I wished him to be! (*Nota bene*: – I am an average good Christian, when you don't push my Christianity too far. And all the rest of you – which is a great comfort – are, in this respect, much the same as I am.)

Sergeant Cuff went on:

"Right or wrong, my lady," he said, "having drawn my conclusion, the next thing to do was to put it to the test. I suggested to your ladyship the examination of all the wardrobes in the house. It was a means of finding the article of dress which had, in all probability, made the smear; and it was a means of putting my conclusion to the test. How did it turn out? Your ladyship consented; Mr. Blake consented; Mr. Ablewhite consented. Miss Verinder alone stopped the whole proceeding by refusing point-blank. That result satisfied me that my view was the right one. If your ladyship and Mr. Betteredge persist in not agreeing with me, you must be blind to what happened before you this very day. In your hearing, I told the young lady that her leaving the house (as things were then) would put an obstacle in the way of my recovering her jewel. You saw yourselves that she drove off in the face of that statement. You saw yourselves that, so far from forgiving Mr. Blake for having done more than all the rest of you to put the clue into my hands, she publicly insulted Mr. Blake, on the steps of her mother's house. What do these things mean? If Miss Verinder is not privy to the suppression of the Diamond, what do these things mean?"

This time he looked my way. It was downright frightful to hear him piling up proof after proof against Miss Rachel, and to know, while one was longing to defend her, that there was no disputing the truth of what he said. I am (thank God!) constitutionally superior to reason. This enabled me to hold firm to my lady's view, which was my view also. This roused my spirit, and made me put a bold face on it before Sergeant Cuff. Profit, good friends, I beseech you, by my example. It will save you from many troubles of the vexing sort. Cultivate a superiority to reason, and see how you pare the claws of all the sensible people when they try to scratch you for your own good!

Finding that I made no remark, and that my mistress made no remark, Sergeant Cuff proceeded. Lord! how it did enrage me to notice that he was not in the least put out by our silence!

"There is the case, my lady, as it stands against Miss Verinder alone," he said. "The next thing is to put the case as it stands against Miss Verinder and the deceased Rosanna Spearman, taken together. We will go back for a moment, if you please, to your daughter's refusal to let her wardrobe be examined. My mind being made up, after that circumstance, I had two questions to consider next. First, as to the right method of conducting my inquiry. Second, as to whether Miss Verinder had an accomplice among the female servants in the house. After carefully thinking it over, I determined to conduct the inquiry in, what we should call at our office, a highly irregular manner. For this reason: I had a family scandal to deal with, which it was my business to keep within the family limits. The less noise made, and the fewer strangers employed to help me, the better. As to the usual course of taking people in custody on suspicion, going before the magistrate, and all the rest of it – nothing of the sort was to be thought of, when your ladyship's daughter was (as I believed) at the bottom of the whole business. In this case, I felt that a person of Mr. Betteredge's character and position in the house – knowing the servants as he did, and having the honour of the family at heart – would be safer to take as an assistant than any other person whom I could lay my hand on. I should have tried Mr. Blake as well – but for one obstacle in the way. *He* saw the drift of my proceedings at a very early date; and, with his interest in Miss Verinder, any mutual understanding was impossible between him and me. I trouble your ladyship with these particulars to show you that I have kept the family secret within the family circle. I am the only outsider who knows it – and my professional existence depends on holding my tongue."

Here I felt that *my* professional existence depended on not holding *my* tongue. To be held up before my mistress, in my old age, as a sort of deputy-policeman, was, once again, more than my Christianity was strong enough to bear.

"I beg to inform your ladyship," I said, "that I never, to my knowledge, helped this abominable detective business, in any way, from first to last; and I summon Sergeant Cuff to contradict me, if he dares!"

Having given vent in those words, I felt greatly relieved. Her ladyship honoured me by a little friendly pat on the shoulder. I looked with righteous indignation at the Sergeant to see what he thought of such a testimony as *that*. The Sergeant looked back like a lamb, and seemed to like me better than ever.

My lady informed him that he might continue his statement. "I understand," she said, "that you have honestly done your best, in what you believe to be my interest. I am ready to hear what you have to say next."

"What I have to say next," answered Sergeant Cuff, "relates to Rosanna Spearman. I recognised the young woman, as your ladyship may remember, when she brought the washing-book into this room. Up to that time I was inclined to doubt whether Miss Verinder had trusted her secret to any one. When I saw Rosanna, I altered my mind. I suspected her at once of being privy to the suppression of the Diamond. The poor creature has met her death by a dreadful end, and I don't want your ladyship to think, now she's gone, that I was unduly hard on her. If this had been a common case of thieving, I should have given Rosanna the benefit of the doubt just as freely as I should have given it to any of the other servants in the house. Our experience of the reformatory women is, that when tried in service – and when kindly and judiciously treated – they prove themselves in the majority of cases to be honestly penitent, and honestly worthy of the pains taken with them. But this was not a common case of thieving. It was a case – in my mind – of a deeply planned fraud, with the owner of the Diamond at the bottom of it. Holding this view, the first consideration which naturally presented itself to me, in connexion with Rosanna, was this. Would Miss Verinder be satisfied (begging your ladyship's pardon) with leading us all to think that the Moonstone was merely lost? Or would she go a step further, and delude us into believing that the Moonstone was stolen? In the latter event there was Rosanna Spearman – with the character of a thief – ready to her hand; the person of all others to lead your ladyship off, and to lead me off, on a false scent."

Was it possible (I asked myself) that he could put his case against Miss Rachel and Rosanna in a more horrid point of view than this? It *was* possible, as you shall now see.

"I had another reason for suspecting the deceased woman," he said, "which appears to me to have been stronger still. Who would be the very person to help Miss Verinder in raising money privately on the Diamond? Rosanna Spearman. No young lady in Miss Verinder's position could manage such a risky matter as that by herself. A go-between she must have, and who so fit, I ask again, as Rosanna Spearman? Your ladyship's deceased housemaid was at the top of her profession when she was a thief. She had relations, to my certain knowledge, with one of the few men in London (in the money-lending line) who would advance a large sum on such a notable jewel as the Moonstone, without asking awkward questions, or insisting on awkward conditions. Bear this in mind, my lady; and now let me show you how my suspicions have been justified by Rosanna's own acts, and by the plain inferences to be drawn from them."

He thereupon passed the whole of Rosanna's proceedings under review. You are already as well acquainted with those proceedings as I am; and you will understand how unanswerably this part of his report fixed the guilt of being concerned in the disappearance of the Moonstone on the memory of the poor dead girl. Even my mistress was daunted by what he said now. She made him no answer when he had done. It didn't seem to matter to the Sergeant whether he was answered or not. On he went (devil take him!), just as steady as ever.

"Having stated the whole case as I understand it," he said, "I have only to tell your ladyship, now, what I propose to do next. I see two ways of bringing this inquiry successfully to an end. One of those ways I look upon as a certainty. The other, I admit, is a bold experiment, and nothing more. Your ladyship shall decide. Shall we take the certainty first?"

My mistress made him a sign to take his own way, and choose for himself.

"Thank you," said the Sergeant. "We'll begin with the certainty, as your ladyship is so good as to leave it to me. Whether Miss Verinder remains at Frizinghall, or whether she returns here, I propose, in either case, to keep a careful watch on all her proceedings – on the people she sees, on the rides and walks she may take, and on the letters she may write and receive."

"What next?" asked my mistress.

"I shall next," answered the Sergeant, "request your ladyship's leave to introduce into the house, as a servant in the place of Rosanna Spearman, a woman accustomed to private inquiries of this sort, for whose discretion I can answer."

"What next?" repeated my mistress.

"Next," proceeded the Sergeant, "and last, I propose to send one of my brother-officers to make an arrangement with that money-lender in London, whom I mentioned just now as formerly acquainted with Rosanna Spearman – and whose name and address, your ladyship may rely on it, have been communicated by Rosanna to Miss Verinder. I don't deny that the course of action I am now suggesting will cost money, and consume time. But the result is certain. We run a line round the Moonstone, and we draw that line closer and closer till we find it in Miss Verinder's possession, supposing she decides to keep it. If her debts press, and she decides on sending it away, then we have our man ready, and we meet the Moonstone on its arrival in London."

To hear her own daughter made the subject of such a proposal as this, stung my mistress into speaking angrily for the first time.

"Consider your proposal declined, in every particular," she said. "And go on to your other way of bringing the inquiry to an end."

"My other way," said the Sergeant, going on as easy as ever, "is to try that bold experiment to which I have alluded. I think I have formed a pretty correct estimate of Miss Verinder's temperament. She is quite capable (according to my belief) of committing a daring fraud. But she is too hot and impetuous in temper, and too little accustomed to deceit as a habit, to act the hypocrite in small things, and to restrain herself under all provocations. Her feelings, in this case, have repeatedly got beyond her control, at the very time when it was plainly her interest to conceal them. It is on this peculiarity in her character that I now propose to act. I want to give her a great shock suddenly, under circumstances that will touch her to the quick. In plain English, I want to tell Miss Verinder, without a word of warning, of Rosanna's death – on the chance that her own better feelings will hurry her into making a clean breast of it. Does your ladyship accept *that* alternative?"

My mistress astonished me beyond all power of expression. She answered him on the instant:

"Yes; I do."

"The pony-chaise is ready," said the Sergeant. "I wish your ladyship good morning."

My lady held up her hand, and stopped him at the door.

"My daughter's better feelings shall be appealed to, as you propose," she said. "But I claim the right, as her mother, of putting her to the test myself. You will remain here, if you please; and I will go to Frizinghall."

For once in his life, the great Cuff stood speechless with amazement, like an ordinary man.

My mistress rang the bell, and ordered her waterproof things. It was still pouring with rain; and the close carriage had gone, as you know, with Miss Rachel to Frizinghall. I tried to dissuade her ladyship from facing the severity of the weather. Quite useless! I asked leave to go with her, and hold the umbrella. She wouldn't hear of it. The pony-chaise came round, with the groom in charge. "You may rely on two things," she said to Sergeant Cuff, in the hall. "I will try the experiment on Miss Verinder as boldly as you could try it yourself. And I will inform you of the result, either personally or by letter, before the last train leaves for London to-night."

With that, she stepped into the chaise, and, taking the reins herself, drove off to Frizinghall.

CHAPTER XXII

My mistress having left us, I had leisure to think of Sergeant Cuff. I found him sitting in a snug corner of the hall, consulting his memorandum book, and curling up viciously at the corners of the lips.

"Making notes of the case?" I asked.

"No," said the Sergeant. "Looking to see what my next professional engagement is."

"Oh!" I said. "You think it's all over then, here?"

"I think," answered Sergeant Cuff, "that Lady Verinder is one of the cleverest women in England. I also think a rose much better worth looking at than a diamond. Where is the gardener, Mr. Betteredge?"

There was no getting a word more out of him on the matter of the Moonstone. He had lost all interest in his own inquiry; and he would persist in looking for the gardener. An hour afterwards, I heard them at high words in the conservatory, with the dog-rose once more at the bottom of the dispute.

In the meantime, it was my business to find out whether Mr. Franklin persisted in his resolution to leave us by the afternoon train. After having been informed of the conference in my lady's room, and of how it had ended, he immediately decided on waiting to hear the news from Frizinghall. This very natural alteration in his plans – which, with ordinary people, would have led to nothing in particular – proved, in Mr. Franklin's case, to have one objectionable result. It left him unsettled, with a legacy of idle time on his hands, and in so doing, it let out all the foreign sides of his character, one on the top of another, like rats out of a bag.

Now as an Italian-Englishman, now as a German-Englishman, and now as a French-Englishman, he drifted in and out of all the sitting-rooms in the house, with nothing to talk of but Miss Rachel's treatment of him; and with nobody to address himself to but me. I found him (for example) in the library, sitting under the map of Modern Italy, and quite unaware of any other method of meeting his troubles, except the method of talking about them. "I have several worthy aspirations, Betteredge; but what am I to do with them now? I am full of dormant good qualities, if Rachel would only have helped me to bring them out!" He was so eloquent in drawing the picture of his own neglected merits, and so pathetic in lamenting over it when it was done, that I felt quite at my wits' end how to console him, when it suddenly occurred to me that here was a case for the wholesome application of a bit of *Robinson Crusoe*. I hobbled out to my own room, and hobbled back with that immortal book. Nobody in the library! The map of Modern Italy stared at *me*; and *I* stared at the map of Modern Italy.

I tried the drawing-room. There was his handkerchief on the floor, to prove that he had drifted in. And there was the empty room to prove that he had drifted out again.

I tried the dining-room, and discovered Samuel with a biscuit and a glass of sherry, silently investigating the empty air. A minute since, Mr. Franklin had rung furiously for a little light refreshment. On its production, in a violent hurry, by Samuel, Mr. Franklin had vanished before the bell downstairs had quite done ringing with the pull he had given to it.

I tried the morning-room, and found him at last. There he was at the window, drawing hieroglyphics with his finger in the damp on the glass.

"Your sherry is waiting for you, sir," I said to him. I might as well have addressed myself to one of the four walls of the room; he was down in the bottomless deep of his own meditations, past all pulling up. "How do *you* explain Rachel's conduct, Betteredge?" was the only answer I received. Not being ready with the needful reply, I produced *Robinson Crusoe*, in which I am firmly persuaded some explanation might have been found, if we had only searched long enough for it. Mr. Franklin shut up *Robinson Crusoe*, and floundered into his German-English gibberish on the spot. "Why not look into it?" he said, as if I had personally objected to looking into it. "Why the devil lose your patience, Betteredge, when patience is all that's wanted to arrive at the truth? Don't interrupt me. Rachel's conduct is perfectly intelligible, if you will only do her the common justice to take the Objective view first, and the Subjective view next, and the Objective-Subjective view to wind up with. What do we know? We know that the loss of the Moonstone, on Thursday morning last, threw her into a state of nervous excitement, from which she has not recovered yet. Do you mean to deny the Objective view, so far? Very well, then – don't interrupt me. Now, being in a state of nervous excitement, how are we to expect that she should behave as she might otherwise have behaved to any of the people about her? Arguing in this way, from within-outwards, what do we reach? We reach the Subjective view. I defy you to controvert the Subjective view. Very well then – what follows? Good Heavens! the Objective-Subjective explanation follows, of course! Rachel, properly speaking, is *not* Rachel, but Somebody Else. Do I mind being cruelly treated by Somebody Else? You are unreasonable enough, Betteredge; but you can hardly accuse me of that. Then how does it end? It ends, in spite of your confounded English narrowness and prejudice, in my being perfectly happy and comfortable. Where's the sherry?"

My head was by this time in such a condition, that I was not quite sure whether it was my own head, or Mr. Franklin's. In this deplorable state, I contrived to do, what I take to have been, three Objective things. I got Mr. Franklin his sherry; I retired to my own room; and I solaced myself with the most composing pipe of tobacco I ever remember to have smoked in my life.

Don't suppose, however, that I was quit of Mr. Franklin on such easy terms as these. Drifting again, out of the morning-room into the hall, he found his way to the offices next, smelt my pipe, and was instantly reminded that he had been simple enough to give up smoking for Miss Rachel's sake. In the twinkling of an eye, he burst in on me with his cigar-case, and came out strong on the one everlasting subject, in his neat, witty, unbelieving, French way. "Give me a light, Betteredge. Is it conceivable that a man can have smoked as long as I have without discovering that there is a complete system for the treatment of women at the bottom of his cigar-case? Follow me carefully, and I will prove it in two words. You choose a cigar, you try it, and it disappoints you. What do you do upon that? You throw it away and try another. Now observe the application! You choose a woman, you try her, and she breaks your heart. Fool! take a lesson from your cigar-case. Throw her away, and try another!"

I shook my head at that. Wonderfully clever, I dare say, but my own experience was dead against it. "In the time of the late Mrs. Betteredge," I said, "I felt pretty often inclined to try your philosophy, Mr. Franklin. But the law insists on your smoking your cigar, sir, when you have once chosen it." I pointed that observation with a wink. Mr. Franklin burst out laughing – and we were as merry as crickets, until the next new side of his character turned up in due course. So things went on with my young master and me; and so (while the Sergeant and the gardener were wrangling over the roses), we two spent the interval before the news came back from Frizinghall.

The pony-chaise returned a good half-hour before I had ventured to expect it. My lady had decided to remain for the present, at her sister's house. The groom brought two letters from his mistress; one addressed to Mr. Franklin, and the other to me.

Mr. Franklin's letter I sent to him in the library – into which refuge his driftings had now taken him for the second time. My own letter, I read in my own room. A cheque, which dropped out when I opened it, informed me (before I had mastered the contents) that Sergeant Cuff's dismissal from the inquiry after the Moonstone was now a settled thing.

I sent to the conservatory to say that I wished to speak to the Sergeant directly. He appeared, with his mind full of the gardener and the dog-rose, declaring that the equal of Mr. Begbie for obstinacy never had existed yet, and never would exist again. I requested him to dismiss such wretched trifling as this from our conversation, and to give his best attention to a really serious matter. Upon that he exerted himself sufficiently to notice the letter in my hand. "Ah!" he said in a weary way, "you have heard from her ladyship. Have I anything to do with it, Mr. Betteredge?"

"You shall judge for yourself, Sergeant." I thereupon read him the letter (with my best emphasis and discretion), in the following words:

"MY GOOD GABRIEL, – I request that you will inform Sergeant Cuff, that I have performed the promise I made to him; with this result, so far as Rosanna Spearman is concerned. Miss Verinder solemnly declares, that she has never spoken a word in private to Rosanna, since that unhappy woman first entered my house. They never met, even accidentally, on the night when the Diamond was lost; and no communication of any sort whatever took place between them, from the Thursday morning when the alarm was first raised in the house, to this present Saturday afternoon, when Miss Verinder left us. After telling my daughter suddenly, and in so many words, of Rosanna Spearman's suicide – this is what has come of it."

Having reached that point, I looked up, and asked Sergeant Cuff what he thought of the letter, so far?

"I should only offend you if I expressed *my* opinion," answered the Sergeant. "Go on, Mr. Betteredge," he said, with the most exasperating resignation, "go on."

When I remembered that this man had had the audacity to complain of our gardener's obstinacy, my tongue itched to "go on" in other words than my mistress's. This time, however, my Christianity held firm. I proceeded steadily with her ladyship's letter:

"Having appealed to Miss Verinder in the manner which the officer thought most desirable, I spoke to her next in the manner which I myself thought most likely to impress her. On two different occasions, before my daughter left my roof, I privately warned her that she was exposing herself to suspicion of the most unendurable and most degrading kind. I have now told her, in the plainest terms, that my apprehensions have been realized.

"Her answer to this, on her own solemn affirmation, is as plain as words can be. In the first place, she owes no money privately to any living creature. In the second place, the Diamond is not now, and never has been, in her possession, since she put it into her cabinet on Wednesday night.

"The confidence which my daughter has placed in me goes no further than this. She maintains an obstinate silence, when I ask her if she can explain the disappearance of the Diamond. She refuses, with tears, when I appeal to her to speak out for my sake. 'The day will come when you will know why I am careless about being suspected, and why I am silent even to *you*. I have done much to make my mother pity me – nothing to make my mother blush for me.' Those are my daughter's own words.

"After what has passed between the officer and me, I think – stranger as he is – that he should be made acquainted with what Miss Verinder has said, as well as you. Read my letter to him, and then place in his hands the cheque which I enclose. In resigning all further claim on his services, I have only to say that I am convinced of his honesty and his intelligence; but I am more firmly persuaded than ever, that the circumstances, in this case, have fatally misled him."

There the letter ended. Before presenting the cheque, I asked Sergeant Cuff if he had any remark to make.

"It's no part of my duty, Mr. Betteredge," he answered, "to make remarks on a case, when I have done with it."

I tossed the cheque across the table to him. "Do you believe in *that* part of her ladyship's letter?" I said indignantly.

The Sergeant looked at the cheque, and lifted up his dismal eyebrows in acknowledgment of her ladyship's liberality.

"This is such a generous estimate of the value of my time," he said, "that I feel bound to make some return for it. I'll bear in mind the amount in this cheque, Mr. Betteredge, when the occasion comes round for remembering it."

"What do you mean?" I asked.

"Her ladyship has smoothed matters over for the present very cleverly," said the Sergeant. "But *this* family scandal is of the sort that bursts up again when you least expect it. We shall have more detective-business on our hands, sir, before the Moonstone is many months older."

If those words meant anything, and if the manner in which he spoke them meant anything – it came to this. My mistress's letter had proved, to his mind, that Miss Rachel was hardened enough to resist the strongest appeal that could be addressed to her, and that she had deceived her own mother (good God, under what circumstances!) by a series of abominable lies. How other people, in my place, might have replied to the Sergeant, I don't know. I answered what he said in these plain terms:

"Sergeant Cuff, I consider your last observation as an insult to my lady and her daughter!"

"Mr. Betteredge, consider it as a warning to yourself, and you will be nearer the mark."

Hot and angry as I was, the infernal confidence with which he gave me that answer closed my lips.

★

I walked to the window to compose myself. The rain had given over; and, who should I see in the courtyard, but Mr. Begbie, the gardener, waiting outside to continue the dog-rose controversy with Sergeant Cuff.

"My compliments to the Sairgent," said Mr. Begbie, the moment he set eyes on me. "If he's minded to walk to the station, I'm agreeable to go with him."

"What!" cries the Sergeant, behind me, "are you not convinced yet?"

"The de'il a bit I'm convinced!" answered Mr. Begbie.

"Then I'll walk to the station!" says the Sergeant.

"Then I'll meet you at the gate!" says Mr. Begbie.

I was angry enough, as you know – but how was any man's anger to hold out against such an interruption as this? Sergeant Cuff noticed the change in me, and encouraged it by a word in season. "Come! come!" he said, "why not treat my view of the case as her ladyship treats it? Why not say, the circumstances have fatally misled me?"

To take anything as her ladyship took it, was a privilege worth enjoying – even with the disadvantage of its having been offered to me by Sergeant Cuff. I cooled slowly down to my customary level. I regarded any other opinion of Miss Rachel, than my lady's opinion or mine, with a lofty contempt. The only thing I could *not* do, was to keep off the subject of the Moonstone! My own good sense ought to have warned me, I know, to let the matter rest – but, there! the virtues which distinguish the present generation were not invented in my time. Sergeant Cuff had hit me on the raw, and, though I did look down upon him with contempt, the tender place still tingled for all that. The end of it was that I perversely led him back to the subject of her ladyship's letter. "I am quite satisfied myself," I said. "But never mind that! Go on, as if I was still open to conviction. You think Miss Rachel is not to be believed on her word; and you say we shall hear of the Moonstone again. Back your opinion, Sergeant," I concluded, in an airy way. "Back your opinion."

Instead of taking offence, Sergeant Cuff seized my hand, and shook it till my fingers ached again.

"I declare to heaven," says this strange officer solemnly, "I would take to domestic service to-morrow, Mr. Betteredge, if I had a chance of being employed along with You! To say you are as transparent as a child, sir, is to pay the children a compliment which nine out of ten of them don't deserve. There! there! we won't begin to dispute again. You shall have it out of me on easier terms than that. I won't say a word more about her ladyship, or about Miss Verinder – I'll only turn prophet, for once in a way, and for your sake. I have warned you already that you haven't done with the Moonstone yet. Very well. Now I'll tell you, at parting, of three things which will happen in the future, and which, I believe, will force themselves on your attention, whether you like it or not."

"Go on!" I said, quite unabashed, and just as airy as ever.

"First," said the Sergeant, "you will hear something from the Yollands – when the postman delivers Rosanna's letter at Cobb's Hole, on Monday next."

If he had thrown a bucket of cold water over me, I doubt if I could have felt it much more unpleasantly than I felt those words. Miss Rachel's assertion of her innocence had left Rosanna's conduct – the making the new nightgown, the hiding the smeared nightgown, and all the rest of it – entirely without explanation. And this had never occurred to me, till Sergeant Cuff forced it on my mind all in a moment!

"In the second place," proceeded the Sergeant, "you will hear of the three Indians again. You will hear of them in the neighbourhood, if Miss Rachel remains in the neighbourhood. You will hear of them in London, if Miss Rachel goes to London."

Having lost all interest in the three jugglers, and having thoroughly convinced myself of my young lady's innocence, I took this second prophecy easily enough. "So much for two of the three things that are going to happen," I said. "Now for the third!"

"Third, and last," said Sergeant Cuff, "you will, sooner or later, hear something of that money-lender in London, whom I have twice taken the liberty of mentioning already. Give me your pocket-book, and I'll make a note for you of his name and address – so that there may be no mistake about it if the thing really happens."

He wrote accordingly on a blank leaf: – "Mr. Septimus Luker, Middlesex-place, Lambeth,[1] London."

---

1 Just south of the Thames and Waterloo Station, Lambeth was at the time Septimus Luker claimed it as his address beginning to become an industrial slum. The moneylender's surname is, of course, Collins's play on "lucre."

"There," he said, pointing to the address, "are the last words, on the subject of the Moonstone, which I shall trouble you with for the present. Time will show whether I am right or wrong. In the meanwhile, sir, I carry away with me a sincere personal liking for you, which I think does honour to both of us. If we don't meet again before my professional retirement takes place, I hope you will come and see me in a little house near London, which I have got my eye on. There will be grass walks, Mr. Betteredge, I promise you, in *my* garden. And as for the white moss-rose —"

"The de'il a bit ye'll get the white moss-rose to grow, unless ye bud him on the dogue-rose first," cried a voice at the window.

We both turned round. There was the everlasting Mr. Begbie, too eager for the controversy to wait any longer at the gate. The Sergeant wrung my hand, and darted out into the courtyard, hotter still on his side. "Ask him about the moss-rose, when he comes back, and see if I have left him a leg to stand on!" cried the great Cuff, hailing me through the window in his turn. "Gentlemen, both!" I answered, moderating them again as I had moderated them once already. "In the matter of the moss-rose there is a great deal to be said on both sides!" I might as well (as the Irish say) have whistled jigs to a milestone. Away they went together, fighting the battle of the roses without asking or giving quarter on either side. The last I saw of them, Mr. Begbie was shaking his obstinate head, and Sergeant Cuff had got him by the arm like a prisoner in charge. Ah, well! well! I own I couldn't help liking the Sergeant — though I hated him all the time.

Explain that state of mind, if you can. You will soon be rid, now, of me and my contradictions. When I have reported Mr. Franklin's departure, the history of the Saturday's events will be finished at last. And when I have next described certain strange things that happened in the course of the new week, I shall have done my part of the Story, and shall hand over the pen to the person who is appointed to follow my lead. If you are as tired of reading this narrative as I am of writing it — Lord, how we shall enjoy ourselves on both sides a few pages further on!

CHAPTER XXIII

I HAD kept the pony-chaise ready, in case Mr. Franklin persisted in leaving us by the train that night. The appearance of the luggage, followed downstairs by Mr. Franklin himself, informed me plainly enough that he had held firm to a resolution for once in his life.

"So you have really made up your mind, sir?" I said, as we met in the hall. "Why not wait a day or two longer, and give Miss Rachel another chance?"

The foreign varnish appeared to have all worn off Mr. Franklin, now that the time had come for saying good-bye. Instead of replying to me in words, he put the letter which her ladyship had addressed to him into my hand. The greater part of it said over again what had been said already in the other communication received by me. But there was a bit about Miss Rachel added at the end, which will account for the steadiness of Mr. Franklin's determination, if it accounts for nothing else.

"You will wonder, I dare say" (her ladyship wrote), "at my allowing my own daughter to keep me perfectly in the dark. A Diamond worth twenty thousand pounds has been lost – and I am left to infer that the mystery of its disappearance is no mystery to Rachel, and that some incomprehensible obligation of silence has been laid on her, by some person or persons utterly unknown to me, with some object in view at which I cannot even guess. Is it conceivable that I should allow myself to be trifled with in this way? It is quite conceivable, in Rachel's present state. She is in a condition of nervous agitation pitiable to see. I dare not approach the subject of the Moonstone again until time has done something to quiet her. To help this end, I have not hesitated to dismiss the police-officer. The mystery which baffles us, baffles him too. This is not a matter in which any stranger can help us. He adds to what I have to suffer; and he maddens Rachel if she only hears his name.

"My plans for the future are as well settled as they can be. My present idea is to take Rachel to London – partly to relieve her mind by a complete change, partly to try what may be done by consulting the best medical advice. Can I ask you to meet us in town? My dear Franklin, you, in your way, must imitate my patience, and wait, as I do, for a fitter time. The valuable assistance which you rendered to the inquiry after the lost jewel is still an unpardoned offence, in the present dreadful state of Rachel's mind. Moving blindfold in this matter, you have added to the burden of anxiety which she has had to bear, by innocently threatening her secret with discovery, through your exertions. It is impossible for me to excuse the perversity that holds you responsible for consequences which neither you nor I could imagine or foresee. She is not to be reasoned with – she can only be pitied. I am grieved to have to say it, but, for the present, you and Rachel are better apart. The only advice I can offer you is, to give her time."

I handed the letter back, sincerely sorry for Mr. Franklin, for I knew how fond he was of my young lady; and I saw that her mother's account of her had cut him to the heart. "You know the proverb, sir," was all I said to him. "When things are at the worst, they're sure to mend. Things can't be much worse, Mr. Franklin, than they are now."

Mr. Franklin folded up his aunt's letter, without appearing to be much comforted by the remark which I had ventured on addressing to him.

"When I came here from London with that horrible Diamond," he said, "I don't believe there was a happier household in England than this. Look at the household now! Scattered, disunited – the very air of the place poisoned with mystery and suspicion! Do you remember that morning at the Shivering Sand, when we talked about my uncle Herncastle, and his birthday gift? The Moonstone has served the Colonel's vengeance, Betteredge, by means which the Colonel himself never dreamt of!"

With that he shook me by the hand, and went out to the pony-chaise.

I followed him down the steps. It was very miserable to see him leaving the old place, where he had spent the happiest years of his life, in this way. Penelope (sadly upset by all that had happened in the house) came round crying, to bid him good-bye. Mr. Franklin kissed her. I waved my hand as much as to say, "You're heartily welcome, sir." Some of the other female servants appeared, peeping after him round the corner. He was one of those men whom the women all like. At the last moment, I stopped the pony-chaise, and begged as a favour that he would let us hear from him by letter. He didn't seem to heed what I said – he was looking round from one thing to another, taking a sort of farewell of the old house and grounds. "Tell us where you are going to, sir!" I said, holding on by the chaise, and trying to get at his future plans in that way. Mr. Franklin pulled his hat down suddenly over his eyes. "Going?" says he, echoing the word after me. "I am going to the devil!" The pony started at the word, as if he had felt a Christian horror of it. "God bless you, sir, go where you may!" was all I had time to say, before he was out of sight and hearing. A sweet and pleasant gentleman! With all his faults and follies, a sweet and pleasant gentleman! He left a sad gap behind him, when he left my lady's house.

It was dull and dreary enough, when the long summer evening closed in, on that Saturday night.

I kept my spirits from sinking by sticking fast to my pipe and my *Robinson Crusoe*. The women (excepting Penelope) beguiled the time by talking of Rosanna's suicide. They were all obstinately of opinion that the poor girl had stolen the Moonstone, and that she had destroyed herself in terror of being found out. My daughter, of course, privately held fast to what she had said all along. Her notion of the motive which was really at the bottom of the suicide failed, oddly enough, just where my young lady's assertion of her innocence failed also. It left Rosanna's secret journey to Frizinghall, and Rosanna's proceedings in the matter of the nightgown entirely unaccounted for. There was no use in pointing this out to Penelope; the objection made about as much impression on her as a shower of rain on a waterproof coat. The truth is, my daughter inherits my superiority to reason – and, in respect to that accomplishment, has got a long way ahead of her own father.

On the next day (Sunday), the close carriage, which had been kept at Mr. Ablewhite's, came back to us empty. The coachman brought a message for me, and written instructions for my lady's own maid and for Penelope.

The message informed me that my mistress had determined to take Miss Rachel to her house in London, on the Monday. The written instructions informed the two maids of the clothing that was wanted, and directed them to meet their mistresses in town at a given hour. Most of the other servants were to follow. My lady had found

Miss Rachel so unwilling to return to the house, after what had happened in it, that she had decided on going to London direct from Frizinghall. I was to remain in the country, until further orders, to look after things indoors and out. The servants left with me were to be put on board wages.[1]

Being reminded, by all this, of what Mr. Franklin had said about our being a scattered and disunited household, my mind was led naturally to Mr. Franklin himself. The more I thought of him, the more uneasy I felt about his future proceedings. It ended in my writing, by the Sunday's post, to his father's valet,[2] Mr. Jeffco (whom I had known in former years) to beg he would let me know what Mr. Franklin had settled to do, on arriving in London.

The Sunday evening was, if possible, duller even than the Saturday evening. We ended the day of rest, as hundreds of thousands of people end it regularly, once a week, in these islands – that is to say, we all anticipated bedtime, and fell asleep in our chairs.

How the Monday affected the rest of the household I don't know. The Monday gave *me* a good shake up. The first of Sergeant Cuff's prophecies of what was to happen – namely, that I should hear from the Yollands – came true on that day.

I had seen Penelope and my lady's maid off in the railway with the luggage for London, and was pottering about the grounds, when I heard my name called. Turning round, I found myself face to face with the fisherman's daughter, Limping Lucy. Bating her lame foot and her leanness (this last a horrid drawback to a woman, in my opinion), the girl had some pleasing qualities in the eye of a man. A dark, keen, clever face, and a nice clear voice, and a beautiful brown head of hair counted among her merits. A crutch appeared in the list of her misfortunes. And a temper reckoned high in the sum-total of her defects.

"Well, my dear," I said, "what do you want with me?"

"Where's the man you call Franklin Blake?" says the girl, fixing me with a fierce look, as she rested herself on her crutch.

---

1 Reduced wages paid to servants during those periods of time when the home was unoccupied, board wages were often just enough to keep them fed.

2 A valet's job was to assist his gentleman master when needed. High-ranking among household servant, his primary duties were to see to it that his master was well dressed, at home or out and about.

"That's not a respectful way to speak of any gentleman," I answered. "If you wish to inquire for my lady's nephew, you will please to mention him as Mr. Franklin Blake."

She limped a step nearer to me, and looked as if she could have eaten me alive. "*Mr.* Franklin Blake?" she repeated after me. "Murderer Franklin Blake would be a fitter name for him."

My practice with the late Mrs. Betteredge came in handy here. Whenever a woman tries to put *you* out of temper, turn the tables, and put *her* out of temper instead. They are generally prepared for every effort you can make in your own defence, but that. One word does it as well as a hundred; and one word did it with Limping Lucy. I looked her pleasantly in the face; and I said – "Pooh!"

The girl's temper flamed out directly. She poised herself on her sound foot, and she took her crutch, and beat it furiously three times on the ground. "He's a murderer! he's a murderer! he's a murderer! He has been the death of Rosanna Spearman!" She screamed that answer out at the top of her voice. One or two of the people at work in the grounds near us looked up – saw it was Limping Lucy – knew what to expect from that quarter – and looked away again.

"He has been the death of Rosanna Spearman?" I repeated. "What makes you say that, Lucy?"

"What do you care? What does any man care? Oh! if she had only thought of the men as I think, she might have been living now!"

"She always thought kindly of *me*, poor soul!" I said; "and, to the best of my ability, I always tried to act kindly by *her*."

I spoke those words in as comforting a manner as I could. The truth is, I hadn't the heart to irritate the girl by another of my smart replies. I had only noticed her temper at first. I noticed her wretchedness now – and wretchedness is not uncommonly insolent, you will find, in humble life. My answer melted Limping Lucy. She bent her head down, and laid it on the top of her crutch.

"I loved her," the girl said softly. "She had lived a miserable life, Mr. Betteredge – vile people had ill-treated her and led her wrong – and it hadn't spoiled her sweet temper. She was an angel. She might have been happy with me. I had a plan for our going to London together like sisters, and living by our needles. That man came here, and spoilt it all. He bewitched her. Don't tell me he didn't mean it, and didn't know it. He ought to have known it. He ought to have taken pity on her. 'I can't live without him – and, oh, Lucy, he never even looks at me.' That's what she said. Cruel, cruel, cruel. I said, 'No man is worth fretting for in that way.' And she said, 'There are men worth dying for, Lucy, and he is one of them.' I had saved up a little money. I had settled things with father and mother. I meant to take her away from the mortification she was suffering here. We should have had a little lodging in London, and lived together like sisters. She had a good education, sir, as you know, and she wrote a good hand. She was quick at her needle. I have a good education, and I write a good hand. I am not as quick at my needle as she was – but I could have done. We might have got our living nicely. And, oh! what happens this morning? what happens this morning? Her letter comes and tells me that she has done with the burden of her life. Her letter comes, and bids me good-bye for ever. Where is he?" cries the girl, lifting her head from the crutch, and flaming out again through her tears. "Where's this gentleman that I mustn't speak of, except with respect? Ha, Mr. Betteredge, the day is not far off when the poor will rise against the rich. I pray Heaven they may begin with *him*. I pray Heaven they may begin with *him*."

Here was another of your average good Christians, and here was the usual break-down, consequent on that same average Christianity being pushed too far! The parson himself (though I own this is saying a great deal) could hardly have lectured the girl in the state she was in now. All I ventured to do was to keep her to the point – in the hope of something turning up which might be worth hearing.

"What do you want with Mr. Franklin Blake?" I asked.

"I want to see him."

"For anything particular?"

"I have got a letter to give him."

"From Rosanna Spearman?"

"Yes."

"Sent to you in your own letter?"

"Yes."

Was the darkness going to lift? Were all the discoveries that I was dying to make, coming and offering themselves to me of their own accord? I was obliged to wait a moment. Sergeant Cuff had left his infection behind him. Certain signs and tokens, personal to myself, warned me that the detective-fever was beginning to set in again.

"You can't see Mr. Franklin," I said.

"I must, and will, see him."

"He went to London last night."

Limping Lucy looked me hard in the face, and saw that I was speaking the truth. Without a word more, she turned about again instantly towards Cobb's Hole.

"Stop!" I said. "I expect news of Mr. Franklin Blake to-morrow. Give me your letter, and I'll send it on to him by the post."

Limping Lucy steadied herself on her crutch and looked back at me over her shoulder.

"I am to give it from my hands into his hands," she said. "And I am to give it to him in no other way."

"Shall I write, and tell him what you have said?"

"Tell him I hate him. And you will tell him the truth."

"Yes, yes. But about the letter – ?"

"If he wants the letter, he must come back here, and get it from Me."

With those words she limped off on the way to Cobb's Hole. The detective-fever burnt up all my dignity on the spot. I followed her, and tried to make her talk. All in vain. It was my misfortune to be a man – and Limping Lucy enjoyed disappointing me. Later in the day, I tried my luck with her mother. Good Mrs. Yolland could only cry, and recommend a drop of comfort out of the Dutch bottle. I found the fisherman on the beach. He said it was "a bad job," and went on mending his net. Neither father nor mother knew more than I knew. Then one way left to try was the chance, which might come with the morning, of writing to Mr. Franklin Blake.

I leave you to imagine how I watched for the postman on Tuesday morning. He brought me two letters. One, from Penelope (which I had hardly patience enough to read), announced that my lady and Miss Rachel were safely established in London. The other, from Mr. Jeffco, informed me that his master's son had left England already.

On reaching the metropolis, Mr. Franklin had, it appeared, gone straight to his father's residence. He arrived at an awkward time. Mr. Blake, the elder, was up to his eyes in the business of the House of Commons, and was amusing himself at home that night with the favourite parliamentary plaything which they call "a private bill."[1] Mr. Jeffco himself showed Mr. Franklin into his father's study. "My dear Franklin! why do you surprise me in this way? Anything wrong?" "Yes; something wrong with Rachel; I am dreadfully distressed about it." "Grieved to hear it. But I can't listen to you now." "When *can* you listen?" "My dear boy! I won't deceive you. I can listen at the end of the session, not a moment before.[2] Good-night." "Thank you, sir. Good-night."

Such was the conversation, inside the study, as reported to me by Mr. Jeffco. The conversation outside the study, was shorter still. "Jeffco, see what time the tidal train[3] starts to-morrow morning?" "At six-forty, Mr. Franklin." "Have me called at five." "Going abroad, sir?" "Going, Jeffco, wherever the railway chooses to take me." "Shall I tell your father, sir?" "Yes; tell him at the end of the session."

The next morning Mr. Franklin had started for foreign parts.[4] To what particular place he was bound, nobody (himself included) could presume to guess. We might hear of him next in Europe, Asia, Africa, or America. The chances were as equally divided as possible, in Mr. Jeffco's opinion, among the four quarters of the globe.

This news – by closing up all prospect of my bringing Limping Lucy and Mr. Franklin together – at once stopped any further progress of mine on the way to discovery. Penelope's belief that her fellow-servant had destroyed herself through unrequited love for Mr. Franklin Blake, was confirmed – and that was all. Whether the letter which Rosanna had left to be given to him after her death did,

---

1   This was a parliamentary bill sponsored by an individual rather than by the government, a bill that affected only the interests of an individual. We may assume, then, that the elder Blake's bill has something to do with the disputed Dukedom Betteredge mentions in third chapter of his narrative.

2   Blake's father may not be able to hear him out until the middle of August, then, when the annual sessions of Parliament – which convened in January or February – ended.

3   A tidal train ran in connection with a tidal steamer, whose departure times were dependent on the time of the high tides.

4   Sending an ineffectual hero to foreign parts while the conflicts of the novel begin to resolve themselves was a technique Collins employed more than once in his fiction. In *The Woman in White* Walter Hartright retreats to the wilds of Central America while Marian Halcombe and Laura Fairlie battle Count Fosco and Sir Percival Glyde at Blackwater Park. Similarly, Captain Kirke is overseas for most of *No Name* while Magdalen Vanstone wars with Mrs. Lecount. And in *Heart and Science* Ovid Vere ventures to Canada while his sweetheart, Carmina, duels with Mrs. Gallilee and Dr. Benjulia.

or did not, contain the confession which Mr. Franklin had suspected her of trying to make to him in her life-time, it was impossible to say. It might be only a farewell word, telling nothing but the secret of her unhappy fancy for a person beyond her reach. Or it might own the whole truth about the strange proceedings in which Sergeant Cuff had detected her, from the time when the Moonstone was lost, to the time when she rushed to her own destruction at the Shivering Sand. A sealed letter it had been placed in Limping Lucy's hands, and a sealed letter it remained to me and to every one about the girl, her own parents included. We all suspected her of having been in the dead woman's confidence; we all tried to make her speak; we all failed. Now one, and now another, of the servants – still holding to the belief that Rosanna had stolen the Diamond and had hidden it – peered and poked about the rocks to which she had been traced, and peered and poked in vain. The tide ebbed, and the tide flowed; the summer went on, and the autumn came. And the Quicksand, which hid her body, hid her secret too.

The news of Mr. Franklin's departure from England on the Sunday morning, and the news of my lady's arrival in London with Miss Rachel on the Monday afternoon, had reached me, as you are aware, by the Tuesday's post. The Wednesday came, and brought nothing. The Thursday produced a second budget of news from Penelope.

My girl's letter informed me that some great London doctor had been consulted about her young lady, and had earned a guinea[1] by remarking that she had better be amused. Flower-shows, operas, balls – there was a whole round of gaieties in prospect; and Miss Rachel, to her mother's astonishment, eagerly took it all. Mr. Godfrey had called; evidently as sweet as ever on his cousin, in spite of the reception he had met with, when he tried his luck on the occasion of the birthday. To Penelope's great regret, he had been most graciously received, and had added Miss Rachel's name to one of his Ladies' Charities on the spot. My mistress was reported to be out of spirits, and to have held two long interviews with her lawyer. Certain speculations followed, referring to a poor relation of the family – one Miss Clack,[2] whom I

---

1   A gold coin worth one pound and one shilling.
2   Betteredge identifies Miss Clack as a "poor relation of the family," and Collins portrays her as Sir John Verinder's niece, but given the family history related by Betteredge earlier in his narrative, Clack simply cannot be a relative.

have mentioned in my account of the birthday dinner, as sitting next to Mr. Godfrey, and having a pretty taste in champagne. Penelope was astonished to find that Miss Clack had not called yet. She would surely not be long before she fastened herself on my lady as usual – and so forth, and so forth, in the way women have of girding at each other, on and off paper. This would not have been worth mentioning, I admit, but for one reason. I hear you are likely to be turned over to Miss Clack, after parting with me. In that case, just do me the favour of not believing a word she says, if she speaks of your humble servant.

On Friday, nothing happened – except that one of the dogs showed signs of a breaking-out behind the ears. I gave him a dose of syrup of buckthorn, and put him on a diet of pot-liquor and vegetables till further orders. Excuse my mentioning this. It has slipped in somehow. Pass it over please. I am fast coming to the end of my offences against your cultivated modern taste. Besides, the dog was a good creature, and deserved a good physicking; he did indeed.

Saturday, the last day of the week, is also the last day in my narrative.

The morning's post brought me a surprise in the shape of a London newspaper. The handwriting on the direction puzzled me. I compared it with the money-lender's name and address as recorded in my pocket-book, and identified it at once as the writing of Sergeant Cuff.

Looking through the paper eagerly enough, after this discovery, I found an ink-mark drawn round one of the police reports. Here it is, at your service. Read it as I read it, and you will set the right value on the Sergeant's polite attention in sending me the news of the day:

"LAMBETH – Shortly before the closing of the court, Mr. Septimus Luker, the well-known dealer in ancient gems, carvings, intagli, &c., &c., applied to the sitting magistrate for advice. The applicant stated that he had been annoyed, at intervals throughout the day, by the proceedings of some of those strolling Indians who infest the streets. The persons complained of were three in number. After having been sent away by the police, they had returned again and again, and had attempted to enter the house on pretence of asking for charity. Warned off in the front, they had been discovered again at the back of the premises. Besides the annoyance complained of, Mr. Luker expressed himself as being under some apprehension that robbery might be contemplated. His collection contained many unique gems, both classical and Oriental, of the highest value. He had only the day before been compelled to dismiss a skilled workman in ivory carving from his employment (a native of India, as we understood), on suspicion of attempted theft; and he felt by no means sure that this man and the street jugglers of whom he complained, might not be acting in concert. It might be their object to collect a crowd, and create a disturbance in the street, and, in the confusion thus caused, to obtain access to the house. In reply to the magistrate, Mr. Luker admitted that he had no evidence to produce of any attempt at robbery being in contemplation. He could speak positively to the annoyance and interruption caused by the Indians, but not to anything else. The magistrate remarked that, if the annoyance were repeated, the applicant could summon the Indians to that court, where they might easily be dealt with under the Act. As to the valuables in Mr. Luker's possession, Mr. Luker himself must take the best measures for their safe custody. He would do well perhaps to communicate with the police, and to adopt such additional precautions as their experience might suggest. The applicant thanked his worship, and withdrew."

One of the wise ancients is reported (I forget on what occasion) as having recommended his fellow-creatures to "look to the end."[1] Looking to the end of these pages of mine, and wondering for some days past how I should manage to write it, I find my plain statement of facts coming to a conclusion, most appropriately, of its own self. We have gone on, in this matter of the Moonstone, from one marvel to another; and here we end with the greatest marvel of all – namely, the accomplishment of Sergeant Cuff's three predictions in less than a week from the time when he had made them.

After hearing from the Yollands on the Monday, I had now heard of the Indians, and heard of the money-lender, in the news from London – Miss Rachel herself, remember, being also in London at the time. You see, I put things at their worst, even when they tell dead

---

1 Betteredge's ancient here is Aristotle, who quotes Solon speaking to Croesus in his *Nicomachean Ethics*: τέλος Ἰύᾶν (1,10, 1).

against my own view. If you desert me, and side with the Sergeant, on the evidence before you – if the only rational explanation you can see is, that Miss Rachel and Mr. Luker must have got together, and that the Moonstone must be now in pledge in the money-lender's house – I own I can't blame you for arriving at that conclusion. In the dark, I have brought you thus far. In the dark I am compelled to leave you, with my best respects.

Why compelled? it may be asked. Why not take the persons who have gone along with me, so far, up into those regions of superior enlightenment in which I sit myself?

In answer to this, I can only state that I am acting under orders, and that those orders have been given to me (as I understand) in the interests of truth. I am forbidden to tell more in this narrative than I knew myself at the time. Or, to put it plainer, I am to keep strictly within the limits of my own experience, and am not to inform you of what other persons told me – for the very sufficient reason that you are to have the information from those other persons themselves, at first hand. In this matter of the Moonstone the plan is, not to present reports, but to produce witnesses. I picture to myself a member of the family reading these pages fifty years hence. Lord! what a compliment he will feel it, to be asked to take nothing on hearsay, and to be treated in all respects like a Judge on the bench.

At this place, then, we part – for the present, at least – after long journeying together, with a companionable feeling, I hope, on both sides. The devil's dance of the Indian Diamond has threaded its way to London; and to London you must go after it, leaving me at the country-house. Please to excuse the faults of this composition – my talking so much of myself, and being too familiar, I am afraid, with you. I mean no harm; and I drink most respectfully (having just done dinner) to your health and prosperity, in a tankard of her ladyship's ale. May you find in these leaves of my writing, what Robinson Crusoe found in his experience on the desert island – namely, "something to comfort yourselves from, and to set in the Description of Good and Evil, on the Credit Side of the Account." – Farewell.

THE END OF THE FIRST PERIOD

★

SECOND PERIOD

THE DISCOVERY OF THE TRUTH (1848 - 1849)

The Events Related in several Narratives

FIRST NARRATIVE

Contributed by MISS CLACK;
Niece of the Late SIR JOHN VERINDER

CHAPTER I

I AM indebted to my dear parents (both now in heaven) for having
had habits of order and regularity instilled into me at a very early age.

In that happy bygone time, I was taught to keep my hair tidy at all
hours of the day and night, and to fold up every article of my clothing carefully, in the same order, on the same chair, in the same place at
the foot of the bed, before retiring to rest. An entry of the day's events
in my little diary invariably preceded the folding up. The "Evening
Hymn"[1] (repeated in bed) invariably followed the folding up. And the
sweet sleep of childhood invariably followed the "Evening Hymn."

In later life (alas!) the Hymn has been succeeded by sad and bitter
meditations; and the sweet sleep has been but ill exchanged for the
broken slumbers which haunt the uneasy pillow of care. On the other
hand, I have continued to fold my clothes, and to keep my little diary.
The former habit links me to my happy childhood – before papa was
ruined. The latter habit – hitherto mainly useful in helping me to discipline the fallen nature which we all inherit from Adam – has unexpectedly proved important to my humble interests in quite another
way. It has enabled poor Me to serve the caprice of a wealthy member
of the family into which my late uncle married. I am fortunate
enough to be useful to Mr. Franklin Blake.

I have been cut off from all news of my relatives by marriage
for some time past. When we are isolated and poor, we are not

---

1 This hymn is Bishop Thomas Ken's (1637-1711) "Glory to thee, my God, this
night," which was sung daily – to Thomas Tallis's (1505-85) *Canon* – in many homes
across England in the nineteenth century.

infrequently forgotten. I am now living, for economy's sake, in a little town in Brittany,[1] inhabited by a select circle of serious English friends, and possessed of the inestimable advantages of a Protestant clergyman and a cheap market.

In this retirement – a Patmos[2] amid the howling ocean of popery that surrounds us – a letter from England has reached me at last. I find my insignificant existence suddenly remembered by Mr. Franklin Blake. My wealthy relative – would that I could add my spiritually-wealthy relative! – writes, without even an attempt at disguising that he wants something of me. The whim has seized him to stir up the deplorable scandal of the Moonstone: and I am to help him by writing the account of what I myself witnessed while visiting at Aunt Verinder's house in London. Pecuniary remuneration is offered me – with the want of feeling peculiar to the rich. I am to re-open wounds that Time has barely closed; I am to recall the most intensely painful remembrances – and this done, I am to feel myself compensated by a new laceration, in the shape of Mr. Blake's cheque. My nature is weak. It cost me a hard struggle, before Christian humility conquered sinful pride, and self-denial accepted the cheque.

Without my diary, I doubt – pray let me express it in the grossest terms! – if I could have honestly earned my money. With my diary, the poor labourer (who forgives Mr. Blake for insulting her) is worthy of her hire. Nothing escaped me at the time I was visiting dear Aunt Verinder. Everything was entered (thanks to my early training) day by day as it happened; and everything, down to the smallest particular, shall be told here. My sacred regard for truth is (thank God) far above my respect for persons. It will be easy for Mr. Blake to suppress what may not prove to be sufficiently flattering in these pages to the person

---

1 Miss Clack removed herself from London to a region of France on a peninsula extending into the Atlantic between the English Channel and the Bay of Biscay.
2 Patmos sits in the Aegean Sea, one of the Dodecanese Islands of southeast Greece. Tradition suggests that Saint John wrote the Book of Revelation while exiled on Patmos. Of Patmos, John writes in Revelation 1:9: "I John, who also am your brother, and companion in tribulation, and in the kingdom and patience of Jesus Christ, was in the isle that is called Patmos, for the word of God, and for the testimony of Jesus Christ." Thus, to Miss Clack, Patmos represents a sanctuary. An evangelical Christian and a conservative Briton, Clack does not miss an opportunity to denounce Catholicism and France.

chiefly concerned in them. He has purchased my time; but not even *his* wealth can purchase my conscience too.*

My diary informs me, that I was accidentally passing Aunt Verinder's house in Montagu Square,[1] on Monday, 3rd July, 1848.

Seeing the shutters opened, and the blinds drawn up, I felt that it would be an act of polite attention to knock, and make inquiries. The person who answered the door, informed me that my aunt and her daughter (I really cannot call her my cousin!) had arrived from the country a week since, and meditated making some stay in London. I sent up a message at once, declining to disturb them, and only begging to know whether I could be of any use.

The person who answered the door, took my message in insolent silence, and left me standing in the hall. She is the daughter of a heathen old man named Betteredge – long, too long, tolerated in my aunt's family. I sat down in the hall to wait for my answer – and, having always a few tracts in my bag, I selected one which proved to be quite providentially applicable to the person who answered the door. The hall was dirty, and the chair was hard; but the blessed consciousness of returning good for evil raised me quite above any trifling considerations of that kind. The tract was one of a series addressed to young women on the sinfulness of dress. In style it was devoutly familiar. Its title was, "A Word With You On Your Cap-Ribbons."[2]

---

* NOTE: *Added by Franklin Blake.* – Miss Clack may make her mind quite easy on this point. Nothing will be added, altered, or removed, in her manuscript, or in any of the other manuscripts which pass through my hands. Whatever opinions any of the writers may express, whatever peculiarities of treatment may mark, and perhaps in a literary sense, disfigure, the narratives which I am now collecting, not a line will be tampered with anywhere, from first to last. As genuine documents they are sent to me – and as genuine documents I shall preserve them; endorsed by the attestations of witnesses who can speak to the facts. It only remains to be added, that "the person chiefly concerned" in Miss Clack's narrative, is happy enough at the present moment, not only to brave the smartest exercise of Miss Clack's pen, but even to recognize its unquestionable value as an instrument for the exhibition of Miss Clack's character.

---

1 Montagu Square, located a block from the Portman Square home in which Collins lived while he wrote *The Moonstone*, was a row of terraced houses built by David Porter in 1811. Novelist Anthony Trollope lived at 39 Montagu Square for eight years late in his life.

2 Miss Clack's religious tracts obviously provide humour, but their titles are, according to Catherine Peters, "only slightly parodied" (305).

"My lady is much obliged, and begs you will come and lunch to-morrow at two."

I passed over the manner in which she gave her message, and the dreadful boldness of her look. I thanked this young castaway; and I said, in a tone of Christian interest, "Will you favour me by accepting a tract?"

She looked at the title. "Is it written by a man or a woman, Miss? If it's written by a woman, I had rather not read it on that account. If it's written by a man, I beg to inform him that he knows nothing about it." She handed me back the tract, and opened the door. We must sow the good seed somehow. I waited till the door was shut on me, and slipped the tract into the letter-box. When I had dropped another tract through the area railings, I felt relieved, in some small degree, of a heavy responsibility towards others.

We had a meeting that evening of the Select Committee of the Mothers'-Small-Clothes-Conversion-Society. The object of this excellent Charity is – as all serious people know – to rescue unredeemed fathers' trousers from the pawnbroker, and to prevent their resumption, on the part of the irreclaimable parent, by abridging them immediately to suit the proportions of the innocent son. I was a member, at that time, of the Select Committee; and I mention the Society here, because my precious and admirable friend, Mr. Godfrey Ablewhite, was associated with our work of moral and material usefulness. I had expected to see him in the board-room, on the Monday evening of which I am now writing, and had proposed to tell him, when we met, of dear Aunt Verinder's arrival in London. To my great disappointment he never appeared. On my expressing a feeling of surprise at his absence, my sisters of the Committee all looked up together from their trousers (we had a great pressure of business that night), and asked in amazement, if I had not heard the news. I acknowledged my ignorance, and was then told, for the first time, of an event which forms, so to speak, the starting-point of this narrative. On the previous Friday, two gentlemen – occupying widely-different positions in society – had been the victims of an outrage which had startled all London. One of the gentlemen was Mr. Septimus Luker, of Lambeth. The other was Mr. Godfrey Ablewhite.[1]

---

1 The attacks on Ablewhite and Luker had their source in an actual and quite notorious criminal case of the period, the Murray case of July 1861. A Major William

Living in my present isolation, I have no means of introducing the newspaper-account of the outrage into my narrative. I was also deprived, at the time, of the inestimable advantage of hearing the events related by the fervid eloquence of Mr. Godfrey Ablewhite. All I can do is to state the facts as they were stated, on that Monday evening, to me; proceeding on the plan which I have been taught from infancy to adopt in folding up my clothes. Everything shall be put neatly, and everything shall be put in its place. These lines are written by a poor weak woman. From a poor weak woman who will be cruel enough to expect more?

The date – thanks to my dear parents, no dictionary that ever was written can be more particular than I am about dates – was Friday, June 30th, 1848.

Early on that memorable day, our gifted Mr. Godfrey happened to be cashing a cheque at a banking-house in Lombard Street.[1] The name of the firm is accidentally blotted in my diary, and my sacred regard for truth forbids me to hazard a guess in a matter of this kind. Fortunately, the name of the firm doesn't matter. What does matter is a circumstance that occurred when Mr. Godfrey had transacted his business. On gaining the door, he encountered a gentleman – a perfect stranger to him – who was accidentally leaving the office exactly at the same time as himself. A momentary contest of politeness ensued between them as to who should be the first to pass through the door of the bank. The stranger insisted on making Mr. Godfrey precede him; Mr. Godfrey said a few civil words; they bowed, and parted in the street.

Thoughtless and superficial people may say, Here is surely a very trumpery little incident related in an absurdly circumstantial manner. Oh, my young friends and fellow-sinners! beware of presuming to exercise your poor carnal reason. Oh, be morally tidy! Let your faith

---

Murray was lured to a Northumberland-street, the Strand address, attacked from behind, and shot by a Mr. William Roberts, a man he had never seen before in his life. The wounded Murray struggled with and overcame his assailant, and *The Times* thereafter rather cryptically proclaimed, "There is, apparently, some inexplicable mystery enveloping the circumstances connected with this fearful affray" (July 16, 1861, 9). See Appendix C for *The Times* accounts of this bizarre crime and its aftermath. Richard Altick offers a fascinating and thorough account of this case in his study *Deadly Encounters* (Philadelphia: U of Pennsylvania P, 1986).

1   Lombard Street, a block north of London Bridge, has been the banking centre of London since the twelfth century.

be as your stockings, and your stockings as your faith. Both ever spotless, and both ready to put on at a moment's notice!

I beg a thousand pardons. I have fallen insensibly into my Sunday-school style. Most inappropriate in such a record as this. Let me try to be worldly – let me say that trifles, in this case as in many others, led to terrible results. Merely premising that the polite stranger was Mr. Luker, of Lambeth, we will now follow Mr. Godfrey home to his residence at Kilburn.[1]

He found waiting for him, in the hall, a poorly clad but delicate and interesting-looking little boy. The boy handed him a letter, merely mentioning that he had been entrusted with it by an old lady whom he did not know, and who had given him no instructions to wait for an answer. Such incidents as these were not uncommon in Mr. Godfrey's large experience as a promoter of public charities. He let the boy go, and opened the letter.

The handwriting was entirely unfamiliar to him. It requested his attendance, within an hour's time, at a house in Northumberland-street, Strand,[2] which he had never had occasion to enter before. The object sought was to obtain from the worthy manager certain details on the subject of the Mothers'-Small-Clothes-Conversion-Society, and the information was wanted by an elderly lady who proposed adding largely to the resources of the charity, if her questions were met by satisfactory replies. She mentioned her name, and she added that the shortness of her stay in London prevented her from giving any longer notice to the eminent philanthropist whom she addressed.

Ordinary people might have hesitated before setting aside their own engagements to suit the convenience of a stranger. The Christian Hero never hesitates where good is to be done. Mr. Godfrey instantly turned back, and proceeded to the house in Northumberland-street. A most respectable though somewhat corpulent man answered the door, and, on hearing Mr. Godfrey's name, immediately conducted

---

1 At the time Godfrey Ablewhite lived in Kilburn, located a mile or so west of Regent's Park along the Edgware Road, it was just beginning to become a bustling commercial centre.

2 Charing Cross, Northumberland-street, Strand – where Godfrey is attacked – is an address within a mile of Alfred Place, Tottenham Court Road, where Mr. Luker is similarly waylaid.

him into an empty apartment at the back, on the drawing-room floor. He noticed two unusual things on entering the room. One of them was a faint odour of musk and camphor. The other was an ancient Oriental manuscript, richly illuminated with Indian figures and devices, that lay open to inspection on a table.

He was looking at the book, the position of which caused him to stand with his back turned towards the closed folding doors communicating with the front room, when, without the slightest previous noise to warn him, he felt himself suddenly seized round the neck from behind. He had just time to notice that the arm round his neck was naked and of a tawny-brown colour, before his eyes were bandaged, his mouth was gagged, and he was thrown helpless on the floor by (as he judged) two men. A third rifled his pockets, and – if, as a lady, I may venture to use such an expression – searched him, without ceremony, through and through to his skin.

Here I should greatly enjoy saying a few cheering words on the devout confidence which could alone have sustained Mr. Godfrey in an emergency so terrible as this. Perhaps, however, the position and appearance of my admirable friend at the culminating period of the outrage (as above described) are hardly within the proper limits of female discussion. Let me pass over the next few moments, and return to Mr. Godfrey at the time when the odious search of his person had been completed. The outrage had been perpetrated throughout in dead silence. At the end of it some words were exchanged, among the invisible wretches, in a language which he did not understand, but in tones which were plainly expressive (to his cultivated ear) of disappointment and rage. He was suddenly lifted from the ground, placed in a chair, and bound there hand and foot. The next moment he felt the air flowing in from the open door, listened, and concluded that he was alone again in the room.

An interval elapsed, and he heard a sound below like the rustling sound of a woman's dress. It advanced up the stairs, and stopped. A female scream rent the atmosphere of guilt. A man's voice below exclaimed "Hullo!" A man's feet ascended the stairs. Mr. Godfrey felt Christian fingers unfastening his bandage, and extracting his gag. He looked in amazement at two respectable strangers, and faintly articulated, "What does it mean?" The two respectable strangers looked back, and said, "Exactly the question we were going to ask *you*."

The inevitable explanation followed. No! Let me be scrupulously particular. Salvolatile and water followed, to compose dear Mr. Godfrey's nerves. The explanation came next.

It appeared, from the statement of the landlord and landlady of the house (persons of good repute in the neighbourhood), that their first- and second-floor apartments had been engaged, on the previous day, for a week certain, by a most respectable-looking gentleman – the same who has been already described as answering the door to Mr. Godfrey's knock. The gentleman had paid the week's rent and all the week's extras in advance, stating that the apartments were wanted for three Oriental noblemen, friends of his, who were visiting England for the first time. Early on the morning of the outrage, two of the Oriental strangers, accompanied by their respectable English friend, took possession of the apartments. The third was expected to join them shortly; and the luggage (reported as very bulky) was announced to follow when it had passed through the Custom-house,[1] late in the afternoon. Not more than ten minutes previous to Mr. Godfrey's visit, the third foreigner had arrived. Nothing out of the common had happened, to the knowledge of the landlord and landlady downstairs, until within the last five minutes – when they had seen the three foreigners, accompanied by their respectable English friend, all leave the house together, walking quietly in the direction of the Strand. Remembering that a visitor had called, and not having seen the visitor also leave the house, the landlady had thought it rather strange that the gentleman should be left by himself upstairs. After a short discussion with her husband, she had considered it advisable to ascertain whether anything was wrong. The result had followed, as I have already attempted to describe it; and there the explanation of the landlord and the landlady came to an end.

An investigation was next made in the room. Dear Mr. Godfrey's property was found scattered in all directions. When the articles were collected, however, nothing was missing; his watch, chain, purse, keys, pocket-handkerchief, note-book, and all his loose papers had been closely examined, and had then been left unharmed to be resumed by the owner. In the same way, not the smallest morsel of property belonging to the proprietors of the house had been abstracted. The

---

1 The Custom-house, built between 1814 and 1817, stands east of London Bridge on the north bank of the Thames. It was at the time the official entrance point of the port of London.

Oriental noblemen had removed their own illuminated manuscript, and had removed nothing else.

What did it mean? Taking the worldly point of view, it appeared to mean that Mr. Godfrey had been the victim of some incomprehensible error, committed by certain unknown men. A dark conspiracy was on foot in the midst of us; and our beloved and innocent friend had been entangled in its meshes. When the Christian hero of a hundred charitable victories plunges into a pitfall that has been dug for him by mistake, oh, what a warning it is to the rest of us to be unceasingly on our guard! How soon may our own evil passions prove to be Oriental noblemen who pounce on us unawares!

I could write pages of affectionate warning on this one theme, but (alas!) I am not permitted to improve – I am condemned to narrate. My wealthy relative's cheque – henceforth, the incubus of my existence – warns me that I have not done with this record of violence yet. We must leave Mr. Godfrey to recover in Northumberland-street, and must follow the proceedings of Mr. Luker at a later period of the day.

After leaving the bank, Mr. Luker had visited various parts of London on business errands. Returning to his own residence, he found a letter waiting for him, which was described as having been left a short time previously by a boy. In this case, as in Mr. Godfrey's case, the handwriting was strange; but the name mentioned was the name of one of Mr. Luker's customers. His correspondent announced (writing in the third person – apparently by the hand of a deputy) that he had been unexpectedly summoned to London. He had just established himself in lodgings in Alfred Place, Tottenham Court Road;[1] and he desired to see Mr. Luker immediately, on the subject of a purchase which he contemplated making. The gentleman was an enthusiastic collector of oriental antiquities, and had been for many years a liberal patron of the establishment in Lambeth. Oh, when shall we wean ourselves from the worship of Mammon![2] Mr. Luker called a cab, and drove off instantly to his liberal patron.

Exactly what had happened to Mr. Godfrey in Northumberland-street now happened to Mr. Luker in Alfred Place. Once more the respectable man answered the door, and showed the visitor upstairs

---

1   Alfred Place, a half-block from the British Museum, is a mile from Northumberland Street, where Godfrey Ablewhite is attacked.

2   In the New Testament, Mammon, a false god, personifies avarice and worldly gain.

into the back drawing-room. There, again, lay the illuminated manuscript on a table. Mr. Luker's attention was absorbed, as Mr. Godfrey's attention had been absorbed, by this beautiful work of Indian art. He too was aroused from his studies by a tawny naked arm round his throat, by a bandage over his eyes, and by a gag in his mouth. He too was thrown prostrate, and searched to the skin. A longer interval had then elapsed than had passed in the experience of Mr. Godfrey; but it had ended as before, in the persons of the house suspecting something wrong, and going upstairs to see what had happened. Precisely the same explanation which the landlord in Northumberland-street had given to Mr. Godfrey, the landlord in Alfred Place now gave to Mr. Luker. Both had been imposed on in the same way by the plausible address and well-filled purse of the respectable stranger, who introduced himself as acting for his foreign friends. The one point of difference between the two cases occurred when the scattered contents of Mr. Luker's pockets were being collected from the floor. His watch and purse were safe, but (less fortunate than Mr. Godfrey) one of the loose papers that he carried about him had been taken away. The paper in question acknowledged the receipt of a valuable of great price which Mr. Luker had that day left in the care of his bankers. This document would be useless for purposes of fraud, inasmuch as it provided that the valuable should only be given up on the personal application of the owner. As soon as he recovered himself, Mr. Luker hurried to the bank, on the chance that the thieves who had robbed him might ignorantly present themselves with the receipt. Nothing had been seen of them when he arrived at the establishment, and nothing was seen of them afterwards. Their respectable English friend had (in the opinion of the bankers) looked the receipt over before they attempted to make use of it, and had given them the necessary warning in good time.

Information of both outrages was communicated to the police, and the needful investigations were pursued, I believe, with great energy. The authorities held that a robbery had been planned, on insufficient information received by the thieves. They had been plainly not sure whether Mr. Luker had, or had not, trusted the transmission of his precious gem to another person; and poor polite Mr. Godfrey had paid the penalty of having been seen accidentally speaking to him. Add to this, that Mr. Godfrey's absence from our Monday evening meeting had been occasioned by a consultation of the authorities, at which he was requested to assist – and all the explanations required being now given, I may proceed with the simpler story of my own little personal experiences in Montagu Square.

I was punctual to the luncheon hour on Tuesday. Reference to my diary shows this to have been a chequered day – much in it to be devoutly regretted, much in it to be devoutly thankful for.

Dear Aunt Verinder received me with her usual grace and kindness. But I noticed, after a little while, that something was wrong. Certain anxious looks escaped my aunt, all of which took the direction of her daughter. I never see Rachel myself without wondering how it can be that so insignificant-looking a person should be the child of such distinguished parents as Sir John and Lady Verinder. On this occasion, however, she not only disappointed – she really shocked me. There was an absence of all lady-like restraint in her language and manner most painful to see. She was possessed by some feverish excitement which made her distressingly loud when she laughed, and sinfully wasteful and capricious in what she ate and drank at lunch. I felt deeply for her poor mother, even before the true state of the case had been confidentially made known to me.

Luncheon over, my aunt said: "Remember what the doctor told you, Rachel, about quieting yourself with a book after taking your meals."

"I'll go into the library, mamma," she answered. "But if Godfrey calls, mind I am told of it. I am dying for more news of him, after his adventure in Northumberland-street." She kissed her mother on the forehead, and looked my way. "Good-bye, Clack," she said, carelessly. Her insolence roused no angry feeling in me. I only made a private memorandum to pray for her.

When we were left by ourselves, my aunt told me the whole horrible story of the Indian Diamond, which, I am happy to know, it is not necessary to repeat here. She did not conceal from me that she would have preferred keeping silence on the subject. But when her own servants all knew of the loss of the Moonstone, and when some of the circumstances had actually found their way into the newspapers – when strangers were speculating whether there was any connexion between what had happened at Lady Verinder's country-house, and what had happened in Northumberland-street and Alfred Place — concealment was not to be thought of; and perfect frankness became a necessity as well as a virtue.

Some persons, hearing what I now heard, would have been probably overwhelmed with astonishment. For my own part, knowing Rachel's spirit to have been essentially unregenerate from her childhood upwards, I was prepared for whatever my aunt could tell me on the subject of her daughter. It might have gone on from bad to worse till it ended in Murder; and I should still have said to myself, The natural result! oh, dear, dear, the natural result! The one thing that *did* shock me was the course my aunt had taken under the circumstances. Here surely was a case for a clergyman, if ever there was one yet! Lady Verinder had thought it a case for a physician. All my poor aunt's early life had been passed in her father's godless household. The natural result again! Oh, dear, dear, the natural result again!

"The doctors recommend plenty of exercise and amusement for Rachel, and strongly urge me to keep her mind as much as possible from dwelling on the past," said Lady Verinder.

"Oh, what heathen advice!" I thought to myself. "In this Christian country, what heathen advice!"

My aunt went on, "I do my best to carry out my instructions. But this strange adventure of Godfrey's happens at a most unfortunate time. Rachel has been incessantly restless and excited since she first heard of it. She left me no peace till I had written and asked my nephew Ablewhite to come here. She even feels an interest in the other person who was roughly used — Mr. Luker, or some such name — though the man is, of course, a total stranger to her."

"Your knowledge of the world, dear aunt, is superior to mine," I suggested diffidently. "But there must be a reason surely for this extraordinary conduct on Rachel's part. She is keeping a sinful secret from you and from everybody. May there not be something in these recent events which threatens her secret with discovery?"

"Discovery?" repeated my aunt. "What can you possibly mean? Discovery through Mr. Luker? Discovery through my nephew?"

As the word passed her lips, a special providence occurred. The servant opened the door, and announced Mr. Godfrey Ablewhite.

★

CHAPTER II

MR. GODFREY followed the announcement of his name – as Mr. Godfrey does everything else – exactly at the right time. He was not so close on the servant's heels as to startle us. He was not so far behind as to cause us the double inconvenience of a pause and an open door. It is in the completeness of his daily life that the true Christian appears. This dear man was very complete.

"Go to Miss Verinder," said my aunt, addressing the servant, "and tell her Mr. Ablewhite is here."

We both inquired after his health. We both asked him together whether he felt like himself again, after his terrible adventure of the past week. With perfect tact, he contrived to answer us at the same moment. Lady Verinder had his reply in words. I had his charming smile.

"What," he cried, with infinite tenderness, "have I done to deserve all this sympathy? My dear aunt! my dear Miss Clack! I have merely been mistaken for somebody else. I have only been blindfolded; I have only been strangled; I have only been thrown flat on my back, on a very thin carpet, covering a particularly hard floor. Just think how much worse it might have been! I might have been murdered; I might have been robbed. What have I lost? Nothing but Nervous Force – which the law doesn't recognise as property; so that, strictly speaking, I have lost nothing at all. If I could have had my own way, I would have kept my adventure to myself – I shrink from all this fuss and publicity. But Mr. Luker made *his* injuries public, and *my* injuries, as the necessary consequence, have been proclaimed in their turn. I have become the property of the newspapers, until the gentle reader gets sick of the subject. I am very sick indeed of it myself. May the gentle reader soon be like me! And how is dear Rachel? Still enjoying the gaieties of London? So glad to hear it! Miss Clack, I need all your indulgence. I am sadly behind-hand with my Committee Work and my dear Ladies. But I really do hope to look in at the Mothers'-Small-Clothes next week. Did you make cheering progress at Monday's Committee? Was the Board hopeful about future prospects? And are we nicely off for Trousers?"

The heavenly gentleness of his smile made his apologies irresistible. The richness of his deep voice added its own indescribable charm to the interesting business question which he had just addressed to me. In truth, we were almost *too* nicely off for Trousers; we were quite overwhelmed by them. I was just about to say so, when the door opened again, and an element of worldly disturbance entered the room, in the person of Miss Verinder.

She approached dear Mr. Godfrey at a most unlady-like rate of speed, with her hair shockingly untidy, and her face, what *I* should call, unbecomingly flushed.

"I am charmed to see you, Godfrey," she said, addressing him, I grieve to add, in the off-hand manner of one young man talking to another. "I wish you had brought Mr. Luker with you. You and he (as long as our present excitement lasts) are the two most interesting men in all London. It's morbid to say this; it's unhealthy; it's all that a well-regulated mind like Miss Clack's most instinctively shudders at. Never mind that. Tell me the whole of the Northumberland-street story directly. I know the newspapers have left some of it out."

Even dear Mr. Godfrey partakes of the fallen nature which we all inherit from Adam — it is a very small share of our human legacy, but, alas! he has it. I confess it grieved me to see him take Rachel's hand in both of his own hands, and lay it softly on the left side of his waist-coat. It was a direct encouragement to her reckless way of talking, and her insolent reference to me.

"Dearest Rachel," he said, in the same voice which had thrilled me when he spoke of our prospects and our trousers, "the newspapers have told you everything — and they have told it much better than I can."

"Godfrey thinks we all make too much of the matter," my aunt remarked. "He has just been saying that he doesn't care to speak of it."

"Why?"

She put the question with a sudden flash in her eyes, and a sudden look up into Mr. Godfrey's face. On his side, he looked down at her with an indulgence so injudicious and so ill-deserved, that I really felt called on to interfere.

"Rachel, darling!" I remonstrated, gently, "true greatness and true courage are ever modest."

"You are a very good fellow in your way, Godfrey," she said — not taking the smallest notice, observe, of me, and still speaking to her cousin as if she was one young man addressing another. "But I am quite sure you are not great; I don't believe you possess any extraordinary courage; and I am firmly persuaded – if you ever had any modesty – that your lady-worshippers relieved you of that virtue a good many years since. You have some private reason for not talking of your adventure in Northumberland-street; and I mean to know it."

"My reason is the simplest imaginable, and the most easily acknowledged," he answered, still bearing with her. "I am tired of the subject."

"You are tired of the subject? My dear Godfrey, I am going to make a remark."

"What is it?"

"You live a great deal too much in the society of women. And you have contracted two very bad habits in consequence. You have learnt to talk nonsense seriously, and you have got into a way of telling fibs for the pleasure of telling them. You can't go straight with your lady-worshippers. I mean to make you go straight with *me*. Come, and sit down. I am brimful of downright questions; and I expect you to be brimful of downright answers."

She actually dragged him across the room to a chair by the window, where the light would fall on his face. I deeply feel being obliged to report such language, and to describe such conduct. But, hemmed in as I am, between Mr. Franklin Blake's cheque on one side and my own sacred regard for truth on the other, what am I to do? I looked at my aunt. She sat unmoved; apparently in no way disposed to interfere. I had never noticed this kind of torpor in her before. It was, perhaps, the reaction after the trying time she had had in the country. Not a pleasant symptom to remark, be it what it might, at dear Lady Verinder's age, and with dear Lady Verinder's autumnal exuberance of figure.

In the meantime, Rachel had settled herself at the window with our amiable and forbearing – our too forbearing – Mr. Godfrey. She began the string of questions with which she had threatened him, taking no more notice of her mother, or of myself, than if we had not been in the room.

"Have the police done anything, Godfrey?"

"Nothing whatever."

"It is certain, I suppose, that the three men who laid the trap for you were the same three men who afterwards laid the trap for Mr. Luker?"

"Humanly speaking, my dear Rachel, there can be no doubt of it."

"And not a trace of them has been discovered?"

"Not a trace."

"It is thought – is it not? – that these three men are the three Indians who came to our house in the country."

"Some people think so."

"Do you think so?"

"My dear Rachel, they blindfolded me before I could see their faces. I know nothing whatever of the matter. How can I offer an opinion on it?"

Even the angelic gentleness of Mr. Godfrey was, you see, beginning to give way at last under the persecution inflicted on him. Whether unbridled curiosity, or ungovernable dread, dictated Miss Verinder's questions I do not presume to inquire. I only report that, on Mr. Godfrey's attempting to rise, after giving her the answer just described, she actually took him by the two shoulders, and pushed him back into his chair – Oh, don't say this was immodest! Don't even hint that the recklessness of guilty terror could alone account for such conduct as I have described! We must not judge others. My Christian friends, indeed, indeed, indeed, we must not judge others!

She went on with her questions, unabashed. Earnest Biblical students will perhaps be reminded – as I was reminded – of the blinded children of the devil, who went on with their orgies, unabashed, in the time before the Flood.

"I want to know something about Mr. Luker, Godfrey."

"I am again unfortunate, Rachel. No man knows less of Mr. Luker than I do."

"You never saw him before you and he met accidentally at the bank?"

"Never."

"You have seen him since?"

"Yes. We have been examined together, as well as separately, to assist the police."

"Mr. Luker was robbed of a receipt which he had got from his banker's – was he not? What was the receipt for?"

"For a valuable gem which he had placed in the safe keeping of the bank."

"That's what the newspapers say. It may be enough for the general reader; but it is not enough for me. The banker's receipt must have mentioned what the gem was?"

"The banker's receipt, Rachel – as I have heard it described – mentioned nothing of the kind. A valuable gem, belonging to Mr. Luker; deposited by Mr. Luker; sealed with Mr. Luker's seal; and only to be given up on Mr. Luker's personal application. That was the form, and that is all I know about it."

She waited a moment, after he had said that. She looked at her mother, and sighed. She looked back again at Mr. Godfrey, and went on.

"Some of our private affairs, at home," she said, "seem to have got into the newspapers?"

"I grieve to say, it is so."

"And some idle people, perfect strangers to us, are trying to trace a connexion between what happened at our house in Yorkshire and what has happened since, here in London?"

"The public curiosity, in certain quarters, is, I fear, taking that turn."

"The people who say that the three unknown men who ill-used you and Mr. Luker are the three Indians, also say that the valuable gem –"

There she stopped. She had become gradually, within the last few moments, whiter and whiter in the face. The extraordinary blackness of her hair made this paleness, by contrast, so ghastly to look at, that we all thought she would faint, at the moment when she checked herself in the middle of her question. Dear Mr. Godfrey made a second attempt to leave his chair. My aunt entreated her to say no more. I followed my aunt with a modest medicinal peace-offering, in the shape of a bottle of salts. We none of us produced the slightest effect on her. "Godfrey, stay where you are. Mamma, there is not the least reason to be alarmed about me. Clack, you're dying to hear the end of it – I won't faint, expressly to oblige *you*."

Those were the exact words she used – taken down in my diary the moment I got home. But, oh, don't let us judge! My Christian friends, don't let us judge!

She turned once more to Mr. Godfrey. With an obstinacy dreadful to see, she went back again to the place where she had checked herself, and completed her question in these words:

"I spoke to you, a minute since, about what people were saying in certain quarters. Tell me plainly, Godfrey, do they any of them say that Mr. Luker's valuable gem is – The Moonstone?"

As the name of the Indian Diamond passed her lips, I saw a change come over my admirable friend. His complexion deepened. He lost the genial suavity of manner which is one of his greatest charms. A noble indignation inspired his reply.

"They *do* say it," he answered. "There are people who don't hesitate to accuse Mr. Luker of telling a falsehood to serve some private interests of his own. He has over and over again solemnly declared that, until this scandal assailed him, he had never even heard of the Moonstone. And these vile people reply, without a shadow of proof to justify them, He has his reasons for concealment; we decline to believe him on his oath. Shameful! shameful!"

Rachel looked at him very strangely – I can't well describe how – while he was speaking. When he had done, she said,

"Considering that Mr. Luker is only a chance acquaintance of yours, you take up his cause, Godfrey, rather warmly."

My gifted friend made her one of the most truly evangelical answers I ever heard in my life.

"I hope, Rachel, I take up the cause of all oppressed people rather warmly," he said.

The tone in which those words were spoken might have melted a stone. But, oh dear, what is the hardness of stone? Nothing, compared to the hardness of the unregenerate human heart! She sneered. I blush to record it – she sneered at him to his face.

"Keep your noble sentiments for your Ladies' Committees, Godfrey. I am certain that the scandal which has assailed Mr. Luker, has not spared You."

Even my aunt's torpor was roused by those words.

"My dear Rachel," she remonstrated, "you have really no right to say that!"

"I mean no harm, mamma – I mean good. Have a moment's patience with me, and you will see."

She looked back at Mr. Godfrey, with what appeared to be a

sudden pity for him. She went the length – the very unladylike length – of taking him by the hand.

"I am certain," she said, "that I have found out the true reason of your unwillingness to speak of this matter before my mother and before me. An unlucky accident has associated you in people's minds with Mr. Luker. You have told me what scandal says of *him*. What does scandal say of *you*?"

Even at the eleventh hour, dear Mr. Godfrey – always ready to return good for evil – tried to spare her.

"Don't ask me!" he said. "It's better forgotten, Rachel – it is, indeed."

"I *will* hear it!" she cried out, fiercely, at the top of her voice.

"Tell her, Godfrey!" entreated my aunt. "Nothing can do her such harm as your silence is doing now!"

Mr. Godfrey's fine eyes filled with tears. He cast one last appealing look at her – and then he spoke the fatal words:

"If you will have it, Rachel – scandal says that the Moonstone is in pledge to Mr. Luker, and that I am the man who has pawned it."

She started to her feet with a scream. She looked backwards and forwards from Mr. Godfrey to my aunt, and from my aunt to Mr. Godfrey, in such a frantic manner that I really thought she had gone mad.

"Don't speak to me! Don't touch me!" she exclaimed, shrinking back from all of us (I declare like some hunted animal!) into a corner of the room. "This is my fault! I must set it right. I have sacrificed myself – I had a right to do that, if I liked. But to let an innocent man be ruined; to keep a secret which destroys his character for life – Oh, good God, it's too horrible! I can't bear it!"

My aunt half rose from her chair, then suddenly sat down again. She called to me faintly, and pointed to a little phial in her work-box.

"Quick!" she whispered. "Six drops, in water. Don't let Rachel see."

Under other circumstances, I should have thought this strange. There was no time now to think – there was only time to give the medicine. Dear Mr. Godfrey unconsciously assisted me in concealing what I was about from Rachel, by speaking composing words to her at the other end of the room.

"Indeed, indeed, you exaggerate," I heard him say. "My reputation stands too high to be destroyed by a miserable passing scandal like this. It will be all forgotten in another week. Let us never speak of it again." She was perfectly inaccessible, even to such generosity as this. She went on from bad to worse.

"I must, and will, stop it," she said. "Mamma! hear what I say. Miss Clack! hear what I say. I know the hand that took the Moonstone. I know – " she laid a strong emphasis on the words; she stamped her foot in the rage that possessed her – "*I know that Godfrey Ablewhite is innocent*. Take me to the magistrate, Godfrey! Take me to the magistrate, and I will swear it!"

My aunt caught me by the hand, and whispered. "Stand between us for a minute or two. Don't let Rachel see me." I noticed a bluish tinge in her face which alarmed me. She saw I was startled. "The drops will put me right in a minute or two," she said, and so closed her eyes, and waited a little.

While this was going on, I heard dear Mr. Godfrey still gently remonstrating.

"You must not appear publicly in such a thing as this," he said. "*Your* reputation, dearest Rachel, is something too pure and too sacred to be trifled with."

"*My* reputation!" She burst out laughing. "Why, I am accused, Godfrey, as well as you. The best detective-officer in England declares that I have stolen my own Diamond. Ask him what he thinks – and he will tell you that I have pledged the Moonstone to pay my private debts!" She stopped, ran across the room – and fell on her knees at her mother's feet. "Oh, mamma! mamma! mamma! I must be mad – mustn't I? – not to own the truth *now*." She was too vehement to notice her mother's condition – she was on her feet again, and back with Mr. Godfrey, in an instant. "I won't let you – I won't let any innocent man – be accused and disgraced through my fault. If you won't take me before the magistrate, draw out a declaration of your innocence on paper, and I will sign it. Do as I tell you, Godfrey, or I'll write it to the newspapers – I'll go out, and cry it in the streets!"

We will not say this was the language of remorse – we will say it was the language of hysterics. Indulgent Mr. Godfrey pacified her by taking a sheet of paper, and drawing out the declaration. She signed it in a feverish hurry. "Show it everywhere – don't think of *me*," she said, as she gave it to him. "I am afraid, Godfrey, I have not done you justice, hitherto, in my thoughts. You are more unselfish – you are a better man than I believed you to be. Come here when you can, and I will try and repair the wrong I have done you."

She gave him her hand. Alas, for our fallen nature! Alas, for Mr. Godfrey! He not only forgot himself so far as to kiss her hand – he adopted a gentleness of tone in answering her which, in such a case, was little better than a compromise with sin. "I will come, dearest," he said, "on condition that we don't speak of this hateful subject again." Never had I seen and heard our Christian Hero to less advantage than on this occasion.

Before another word could be said by anybody, a thundering knock at the street door startled us all. I looked through the window, and saw the World, the Flesh, and the Devil waiting before the house – as typified in a carriage and horses, a powdered footman, and three of the most audaciously dressed women I ever beheld in my life.

Rachel started, and composed herself. She crossed the room to her mother.

"They have come to take me to the flower-show," she said. "One word, mamma, before I go. I have not distressed you, have I?"

(Is the bluntness of moral feeling which could ask such a question as that, after what had just happened, to be pitied or condemned? I like to lean towards mercy. Let us pity it.)

The drops had produced their effect. My poor aunt's complexion was like itself again. "No, no, my dear," she said. "Go with our friends, and enjoy yourself."

Her daughter stooped, and kissed her. I had left the window, and was near the door, when Rachel approached it to go out. Another change had come over her – she was in tears. I looked with interest at the momentary softening of that obdurate heart. I felt inclined to say a few earnest words. Alas! my well-meant sympathy only gave offence. "What do you mean by pitying me?" she asked, in a bitter whisper, as she passed to the door. "Don't you see how happy I am? I'm going to the flower-show, Clack; and I've got the prettiest bonnet in London." She completed the hollow mockery of that address by blowing me a kiss – and so left the room.

I wish I could describe in words the compassion I felt for this miserable and misguided girl. But I am almost as poorly provided with words as with money. Permit me to say – my heart bled for her.

Returning to my aunt's chair, I observed dear Mr. Godfrey searching for something softly, here and there, in different parts of the room. Before I could offer to assist him, he had found what he wanted. He came back to my aunt and me, with his declaration of innocence in one hand, and with a box of matches in the other.

"Dear aunt, a little conspiracy!" he said. "Dear Miss Clack, a pious fraud which even your high moral rectitude will excuse! Will you leave Rachel to suppose that I accept the generous self-sacrifice which has signed this paper? And will you kindly bear witness that I destroy it in your presence, before I leave the house?" He kindled a match, and, lighting the paper, laid it to burn in a plate on the table. "Any trifling inconvenience that I may suffer is as nothing," he remarked, "compared with the importance of preserving that pure name from the contaminating contact of the world. There! We have reduced it to a little harmless heap of ashes; and our dear impulsive Rachel will never know what we have done! How do you feel? My precious friends, how do you feel? For my poor part, I am as light-hearted as a boy!"

He beamed on us with his beautiful smile; he held out a hand to my aunt, and a hand to me. I was too deeply affected by his noble conduct to speak. I closed my eyes; I put his hand, in a kind of spiritual self-forgetfulness, to my lips. He murmured a soft remonstrance. Oh the ecstasy, the pure, unearthly ecstasy of that moment! I sat – I hardly know on what – quite lost in my own exalted feelings. When I opened my eyes again, it was like descending from heaven to earth. There was nobody but my aunt in the room. He had gone.

I should like to stop here – I should like to close my narrative with the record of Mr. Godfrey's noble conduct. Unhappily, there is more, much more, which the unrelenting pecuniary pressure of Mr. Blake's cheque obliges me to tell. The painful disclosures which were to reveal themselves in my presence, during that Tuesday's visit to Montagu Square, were not at an end yet.

Finding myself alone with Lady Verinder, I turned naturally to the subject of her health; touching delicately on the strange anxiety which she had shown to conceal her indisposition, and the remedy applied to it, from the observation of her daughter.

My aunt's reply greatly surprised me.

"Drusilla," she said (if I have not already mentioned that my Christian name is Drusilla, permit me to mention it now), "you are touching – quite innocently, I know – on a very distressing subject."

I rose immediately. Delicacy left me but one alternative – the alternative, after first making my apologies, of taking my leave. Lady Verinder stopped me, and insisted on my sitting down again.

"You have surprised a secret," she said, "which I had confided to my sister Mrs. Ablewhite, and to my lawyer Mr. Bruff, and to no one else. I can trust in their discretion; and I am sure, when I tell you the circumstances, I can trust in yours. Have you any pressing engagement, Drusilla? or is your time your own this afternoon?"

It is needless to say that my time was entirely at my aunt's disposal.

"Keep me company then," she said, "for another hour. I have something to tell you which I believe you will be sorry to hear. And I shall have a service to ask of you afterwards, if you don't object to assist me."

It is again needless to say that, so far from objecting, I was all eagerness to assist her.

"You can wait here," she went on, "till Mr. Bruff comes at five. And you can be one of the witnesses, Drusilla, when I sign my Will."

Her Will! I thought of the drops which I had seen in her work-box. I thought of the bluish tinge which I had noticed in her complexion. A light which was not of this world – a light shining prophetically from an unmade grave – dawned on my mind. My aunt's secret was a secret no longer.

*

CHAPTER III

CONSIDERATION for poor Lady Verinder forbade me even to hint that I had guessed the melancholy truth, before she opened her lips. I waited her pleasure in silence; and, having privately arranged to say a few sustaining words at the first convenient opportunity, felt prepared for any duty that could claim me, no matter how painful it might be.

"I have been seriously ill, Drusilla, for some time past," my aunt began. "And, strange to say, without knowing it myself."

I thought of the thousands and thousands of perishing human

creatures who were all at that moment spiritually ill, without knowing it themselves. And I greatly feared that my poor aunt might be one of the number. "Yes, dear," I said, sadly. "Yes."

"I brought Rachel to London, as you know, for medical advice," she went on. "I thought it right to consult two doctors."

Two doctors! And, oh me (in Rachel's state), not one clergyman! "Yes, dear?" I said once more. "Yes?"

"One of the two medical men," proceeded my aunt, "was a stranger to me. The other had been an old friend of my husband's, and had always felt a sincere interest in me for my husband's sake. After prescribing for Rachel, he said he wished to speak to me privately in another room. I expected, of course, to receive some special directions for the management of my daughter's health. To my surprise, he took me gravely by the hand, and said, 'I have been looking at you, Lady Verinder, with a professional as well as a personal interest. You are, I am afraid, far more urgently in need of medical advice than your daughter.' He put some questions to me, which I was at first inclined to treat lightly enough, until I observed that my answers distressed him. It ended in his making an appointment to come and see me, accompanied by a medical friend, on the next day, at an hour when Rachel would not be at home. The result of that visit − most kindly and gently conveyed to me − satisfied both the physicians that there had been precious time lost, which could never be regained, and that my case had now passed beyond the reach of their art. For more than two years I have been suffering under an insidious form of heart disease, which, without any symptoms to alarm me, has, by little and little, fatally broken me down. I may live for some months, or I may die before another day has passed over my head − the doctors cannot, and dare not, speak more positively than this. It would be vain to say, my dear, that I have not had some miserable moments since my real situation has been made known to me. But I am more resigned than I was, and I am doing my best to set my worldly affairs in order. My one great anxiety is that Rachel should be kept in ignorance of the truth. If she knew it, she would at once attribute my broken health to anxiety about the Diamond, and would reproach herself bitterly, poor child, for what is in no sense her fault. Both the doctors agree that the mischief began two, if not three years since. I am sure you will keep my secret, Drusilla – for I am sure I see sincere sorrow and sympathy for me in your face."

Sorrow and sympathy! Oh, what Pagan emotions to expect from a Christian Englishwoman anchored firmly on her faith!

Little did my poor aunt imagine what a gush of devout thankfulness thrilled through me as she approached the close of her melancholy story. Here was a career of usefulness opened before me! Here was a beloved relative and perishing fellow-creature, on the eve of the great change, utterly unprepared; and led, providentially led, to reveal her situation to Me! How can I describe the joy with which I now remembered that the precious clerical friends on whom I could rely, were to be counted, not by ones or twos, but by tens and twenties! I took my aunt in my arms – my overflowing tenderness was not to be satisfied, *now*, with anything less than an embrace. "Oh!" I said to her, fervently, "the indescribable interest with which you inspire me! Oh! the good I mean to do you, dear, before we part!" After another word or two of earnest prefatory warning, I gave her her choice of three precious friends, all plying the work of mercy from morning to night in her own neighbourhood; all equally inexhaustible in exhortation; all affectionately ready to exercise their gifts at a word from *me*. Alas! the result was far from encouraging. Poor Lady Verinder looked puzzled and frightened, and met everything I could say to her with the purely wordly objection that she was not strong enough to face strangers. I yielded – for the moment only, of course. My large experience (as Reader and Visitor, under not less, first and last, than fourteen beloved clerical friends) informed me that this was another case for preparation by books. I possessed a little library of works, all suitable to the present emergency, all calculated to arouse, convince, prepare, enlighten, and fortify my aunt. "You will read, dear, won't you?" I said, in my most winning way. "You will read, if I bring you my own precious books? Turned down at all the right places, aunt. And marked in pencil where you are to stop and ask yourself, 'Does this apply to me?'" Even that simple appeal – so absolutely heathenizing is the influence of the world – appeared to startle my aunt. She said, "I will do what I can, Drusilla, to please you," with a look of surprise, which was at once instructive and terrible to see. Not a moment was to be lost. The clock on the mantel-piece informed me that I had just time to hurry home; to provide myself with a first series of selected readings (say a dozen only); and to return in time to meet the lawyer, and witness Lady Verinder's Will. Promising faithfully to be back by five o'clock, I left the house on my errand of mercy.

When no interests but my own are involved, I am humbly content to get from place to place by the omnibus. Permit me to give an idea of my devotion to my aunt's interests by recording that, on this occasion, I committed the prodigality of taking a cab.[1]

I drove home, selected and marked my first series of readings, and drove back to Montagu Square, with a dozen works in a carpet-bag, the like of which, I firmly believe, are not to be found in the literature of any other country in Europe. I paid the cabman exactly his fare. He received it with an oath; upon which I instantly gave him a tract. If I had presented a pistol at his head, this abandoned wretch could hardly have exhibited greater consternation. He jumped up on his box, and, with profane exclamations of dismay, drove off furiously. Quite useless, I am happy to say! I sowed the good seed, in spite of him, by throwing a second tract in at the window of the cab.

The servant who answered the door – not the person with the cap-ribbons, to my great relief, but the footman – informed me that the doctor had called, and was still shut up with Lady Verinder. Mr. Bruff, the lawyer, had arrived a minute since and was waiting in the library. I was shown into the library to wait too.

Mr. Bruff looked surprised to see me. He is the family solicitor,[2] and we had met more than once, on previous occasions, under Lady Verinder's roof. A man, I grieve to say, grown old and grizzled in the service of the world. A man who, in his hours of business, was the chosen prophet of Law and Mammon; and who, in his hours of leisure, was equally capable of reading a novel and of tearing up a tract.

"Have you come to stay here, Miss Clack?" he asked, with a look at my carpet-bag.

---

1 The London omnibus that Clack avoids taking was the horse-drawn forerunner of the bus; it was cramped, dirty, crowded – seating upwards of twenty-five people – but inexpensive. The more expensive cab to which Clack treats herself, to the dismay of her driver, was probably a hansom, a two-wheeled covered carriage with the driver's seat above and behind the passengers.

2 Mr. Bruff is the Verinder family solicitor, a lawyer who managed such family matters as wills and estates.

To reveal the contents of my precious bag to such a person as this would have been simply to invite an outburst of profanity. I lowered myself to his own level, and mentioned my business in the house.

"My aunt has informed me that she is about to sign her Will," I answered. "She has been so good as to ask me to be one of the witnesses."

"Aye? aye? Well, Miss Clack, you will do. You are over twenty-one, and you have not the slightest pecuniary interest in Lady Verinder's Will."

Not the slightest pecuniary interest in Lady Verinder's Will. Oh, how thankful I felt when I heard that! If my aunt, possessed of thousands, had remembered poor Me, to whom five pounds is an object – if my name had appeared in the Will, with a little comforting legacy attached to it – my enemies might have doubted the motive which had loaded me with the choicest treasures of my library, and had drawn upon my failing resources for the prodigal expenses of a cab. Not the cruellest scoffer of them all could doubt now. Much better as it was! Oh, surely, surely, much better as it was!

I was aroused from these consoling reflections by the voice of Mr. Bruff. My meditative silence appeared to weigh upon the spirits of this worldling, and to force him, as it were, into talking to me against his own will.

"Well, Miss Clack, what's the last news in the charitable circles? How is your friend Mr. Godfrey Ablewhite, after the mauling he got from the rogues in Northumberland-street? Egad! they're telling a pretty story about that charitable gentleman at my club!"

I had passed over the manner in which this person had remarked that I was more than twenty-one, and that I had no pecuniary interest in my aunt's Will. But the tone in which he alluded to dear Mr. Godfrey was too much for my forbearance. Feeling bound, after what had passed in my presence that afternoon, to assert the innocence of my admirable friend, whenever I found it called in question – I own to having also felt bound to include in the accomplishment of this righteous purpose, a stinging castigation in the case of Mr. Bruff.

"I live very much out of the world," I said; "and I don't possess the advantage, sir, of belonging to a club. But I happen to know the story to which you allude; and I also know that a viler falsehood than that story never was told."

"Yes, yes, Miss Clack – you believe in your friend. Natural enough. Mr. Godfrey Ablewhite won't find the world in general quite so easy to convince as a committee of charitable ladies. Appearances are dead against him. He was in the house when the Diamond was lost. And he was the first person in the house to go to London afterwards. Those are ugly circumstances, ma'am, viewed by the light of later events."

I ought, I know, to have set him right before he went any further. I ought to have told him that he was speaking in ignorance of a testimony to Mr. Godfrey's innocence, offered by the only person who was undeniably competent to speak from a positive knowledge of the subject. Alas! the temptation to lead the lawyer artfully on to his own discomfiture was too much for me. I asked what he meant by "later events" – with an appearance of the utmost innocence.

"By later events, Miss Clack, I mean events in which the Indians are concerned," proceeded Mr. Bruff, getting more and more superior to poor Me, the longer he went on. "What do the Indians do, the moment they are let out of the prison at Frizinghall? They go straight to London, and fix on Mr. Luker. What follows? Mr. Luker feels alarmed for the safety of 'a valuable of great price,' which he has got in the house. He lodges it privately (under a general description) in his bankers' strong-room. Wonderfully clever of him: but the Indians are just as clever on their side. They have their suspicions that the 'valuable of great price' is being shifted from one place to another; and they hit on a singularly bold and complete way of clearing those suspicions up. Whom do they seize and search? Not Mr. Luker only – which would be intelligible enough – but Mr. Godfrey Ablewhite as well. Why? Mr. Ablewhite's explanation is, that they acted on blind suspicion, after seeing him accidentally speaking to Mr. Luker. Absurd! Half a dozen other people spoke to Mr. Luker that morning. Why were they not followed home too, and decoyed into the trap? No! no! The plain inference is, that Mr. Ablewhite had his private interest in the 'valuable' as well as Mr. Luker, and that the Indians were so uncertain as to which of the two had the disposal of it, that there was no alternative but to search them both. Public opinion says that, Miss Clack. And public opinion, on this occasion, is not easily refuted."

He said those last words, looking so wonderfully wise in his own worldly conceit, that I really (to my shame be it spoken) could not resist leading him a little further still, before I overwhelmed him with the truth.

"I don't presume to argue with a clever lawyer like you," I said. "But is it quite fair, sir, to Mr. Ablewhite to pass over the opinion of the famous London police-officer who investigated this case? Not the shadow of a suspicion rested upon anybody but Miss Verinder, in the mind of Sergeant Cuff."

"Do you mean to tell me, Miss Clack, that you agree with the Sergeant?"

"I judge nobody, sir, and I offer no opinion."

"And I commit both those enormities, ma'am. I judge the Sergeant to have been utterly wrong; and I offer the opinion that, if he had known Rachel's character as I know it, he would have suspected everybody in the house but *her*. I admit that she has her faults − she is secret, and self-willed; odd and wild, and unlike other girls of her age. But true as steel, and high-minded and generous to a fault. If the plainest evidence in the world pointed one way, and if nothing but Rachel's word of honour pointed the other, I would take her word before the evidence, lawyer as I am! Strong language, Miss Clack; but I mean it."

"Would you object to illustrate your meaning, Mr. Bruff, so that I may be sure I understand it? Suppose you found Miss Verinder quite unaccountably interested in what has happened to Mr. Ablewhite and Mr. Luker? Suppose she asked the strangest questions about this dreadful scandal, and displayed the most ungovernable agitation when she found out the turn it was taking?"

"Suppose anything you please, Miss Clack, it wouldn't shake my belief in Rachel Verinder by a hair's-breadth."

"She is so absolutely to be relied on as that?"

"So absolutely to be relied on as that."

"Then permit me to inform you, Mr. Bruff, that Mr. Godfrey Ablewhite was in this house not two hours since, and that his entire innocence of all concern in the disappearance of the Moonstone was proclaimed by Miss Verinder herself, in the strongest language I ever heard used by a young lady in my life."

I enjoyed the triumph – the unholy triumph, I fear, I must admit – of seeing Mr. Bruff utterly confounded and overthrown by a few plain words from Me. He started to his feet, and stared at me in silence. I kept my seat, undisturbed, and related the whole scene as it had occurred. "And what do you say about Mr. Ablewhite *now*?" I asked, with the utmost possible gentleness, as soon as I had done.

"If Rachel has testified to his innocence, Miss Clack, I don't scruple to say that I believe in his innocence as firmly as you do. I have been misled by appearances, like the rest of the world; and I will make the best atonement I can, by publicly contradicting the scandal which has assailed your friend wherever I meet with it. In the meantime, allow me to congratulate you on the masterly manner in which you have opened the full fire of your batteries on me at the moment when I least expected it. You would have done great things in my profession, ma'am, if you had happened to be a man."

With those words he turned away from me, and began walking irritably up and down the room.

I could see plainly that the new light I had thrown on the subject had greatly surprised and disturbed him. Certain expressions dropped from his lips, as he became more and more absorbed in his own thoughts, which suggested to my mind the abominable view that he had hitherto taken of the mystery of the lost Moonstone. He had not scrupled to suspect dear Mr. Godfrey of the infamy of stealing the Diamond, and to attribute Rachel's conduct to a generous resolution to conceal the crime. On Miss Verinder's own authority – a perfectly unassailable authority, as you are aware, in the estimation of Mr. Bruff – that explanation of the circumstances was now shown to be utterly wrong. The perplexity into which I had plunged this high legal authority was so overwhelming that he was quite unable to conceal it from notice. "What a case!" I heard him say to himself, stopping at the window in his walk, and drumming on the glass with his fingers. "It not only defies explanation, it's even beyond conjecture."

There was nothing in these words which made any reply at all needful, on my part – and yet, I answered them! It seems hardly credible that I should not have been able to let Mr. Bruff alone, even now. It seems almost beyond mere mortal perversity that I should have discovered, in what he had just said, a new opportunity of making myself personally disagreeable to him. But – ah, my friends! nothing is beyond mortal perversity; and anything is credible when our fallen natures get the better of us!

"Pardon me for intruding on your reflections," I said to the unsuspecting Mr. Bruff. "But surely there is a conjecture to make which has not occurred to us yet."

"Maybe, Miss Clack. I own I don't know what it is."

"Before I was so fortunate, sir, as to convince you of Mr. Ablewhite's innocence, you mentioned it as one of the reasons for suspecting him, that he was in the house at the time when the Diamond was lost. Permit me to remind you that Mr. Franklin Blake was also in the house at the time when the Diamond was lost."

The old worldling left the window, took a chair exactly opposite to mine, and looked at me steadily, with a hard and vicious smile.

"You are not so good a lawyer, Miss Clack," he remarked in a meditative manner, "as I supposed. You don't know how to let well alone."

"I am afraid I fail to follow you, Mr. Bruff," I said, modestly.

"It won't do, Miss Clack – it really won't do a second time. Franklin Blake is a prime favourite of mine, as you are well aware. But that doesn't matter. I'll adopt your view, on this occasion, before you have time to turn round on me. You're quite right, ma'am. I have suspected Mr. Ablewhite, on grounds which abstractedly justify suspecting Mr. Blake too. Very good – let's suspect them together. It's quite in his character, we will say, to be capable of stealing the Moonstone. The only question is, whether it was his interest to do so."

"Mr. Franklin Blake's debts," I remarked, "are matters of family notoriety."

"And Mr. Godfrey Ablewhite's debts have not arrived at that stage of development yet. Quite true. But there happen to be two difficulties in the way of your theory, Miss Clack. I manage Franklin Blake's affairs, and I beg to inform you that the vast majority of his creditors (knowing his father to be a rich man) are quite content to charge interest on their debts, and to wait for their money. There is the first difficulty – which is tough enough. You will find the second tougher still. I have it on the authority of Lady Verinder herself, that her daughter was ready to marry Franklin Blake, before that infernal Indian Diamond disappeared from the house. She had drawn him on and put him off again, with the coquetry of a young girl. But she had confessed to her mother that she loved cousin Franklin, and her mother had trusted cousin Franklin with the secret. So there he was, Miss Clack, with his creditors content to wait, and with the certain prospect before him of marrying an heiress. By all means consider him a scoundrel; but tell me, if you please, why he should steal the Moonstone?"

"The human heart is unsearchable," I said gently. "Who is to fathom it?"

"In other words, ma'am – though he hadn't the shadow of a reason for taking the Diamond – he might have taken it, nevertheless, through natural depravity. Very well. Say he did. Why the devil – "

"I beg your pardon, Mr. Bruff. If I hear the devil referred to in that manner, I must leave the room."

"I beg *your* pardon, Miss Clack – I'll be more careful in my choice of language for the future. All I meant to ask was this. Why – even supposing he did take the Diamond – should Franklin Blake make himself the most prominent person in the house in trying to recover it? You may tell me he cunningly did that to divert suspicion from himself. I answer that he had no need to divert suspicion – because nobody suspected him. He first steals the Moonstone (without the slightest reason) through natural depravity; and he then acts a part, in relation to the loss of the jewel, which there is not the slightest necessity to act, and which leads to his mortally offending the young lady who would otherwise have married him. That is the monstrous proposition which you are driven to assert, if you attempt to associate the disappearance of the Moonstone with Franklin Blake. No, no, Miss Clack! After what has passed here to-day, between us two, the deadlock, in this case, is complete. Rachel's own innocence is (as her mother knows, and as I know) beyond a doubt. Mr. Ablewhite's innocence is equally certain – or Rachel would never have testified to it. And Franklin Blake's innocence, as you have just seen, unanswerably asserts itself. On the one hand, we are morally certain of all these things. And, on the other hand, we are equally sure that somebody has brought the Moonstone to London, and that Mr. Luker, or his banker, is in private possession of it at this moment. What is the use of my experience, what is the use of any person's experience, in such a case as that? It baffles me; it baffles you; it baffles everybody."

No – not everybody. It had not baffled Sergeant Cuff. I was about to mention this, with all possible mildness, and with every necessary protest against being supposed to cast a slur upon Rachel – when the servant came in to say that the doctor had gone, and that my aunt was waiting to receive us.

This stopped the discussion. Mr. Bruff collected his papers, looking a little exhausted by the demands which our conversation had made on him. I took up my bagfull of precious publications, feeling as if I could have gone on talking for hours. We proceeded in silence to Lady Verinder's room.

Permit me to add here, before my narrative advances to other events, that I have not described what passed between the lawyer and me, without having a definite object in view. I am ordered to include in my contribution to the shocking story of the Moonstone a plain disclosure, not only of the turn which suspicion took, but even of the names of the persons on whom suspicion rested, at the time when the Indian Diamond was believed to be in London. A report of my conversation in the library with Mr. Bruff appeared to me to be exactly what was wanted to answer this purpose – while, at the same time, it possessed the great moral advantage of rendering a sacrifice of sinful self-esteem essentially necessary on my part. I have been obliged to acknowledge that my fallen nature got the better of me. In making that humiliating confession, *I* get the better of my fallen nature. The moral balance is restored; the spiritual atmosphere feels clear once more. Dear friends, we may go on again.

CHAPTER IV

THE signing of the Will was a much shorter matter than I had antici-pated. It was hurried over, to my thinking, in indecent haste. Samuel, the footman, was sent for to act as second witness – and the pen was put at once into my aunt's hand. I felt strongly urged to say a few appropriate words on this solemn occasion. But Mr. Bruff's manner convinced me that it was wisest to check the impulse while he was in the room. In less than two minutes it was all over – and Samuel (unbenefited by what I might have said) had gone downstairs again.

Mr. Bruff folded up the Will, and then looked my way; apparently wondering whether I did or did not mean to leave him alone with my aunt. I had my mission of mercy to fulfil, and my bag of precious publications ready on my lap. He might as well have expected to move St. Paul's Cathedral by looking at it, as to move Me. There was one merit about him (due no doubt to his worldly training) which I have no wish to deny. He was quick at seeing things. I appeared to produce almost the same impression on him which I had produced on the cabman. *He* too uttered a profane expression, and withdrew in a violent hurry, and left me mistress of the field.

As soon as we were alone, my aunt reclined on the sofa, and then alluded, with some appearance of confusion, to the subject of her Will.

"I hope you won't think yourself neglected, Drusilla," she said. "I mean to *give* you your little legacy, my dear, with my own hand."

Here was a golden opportunity! I seized it on the spot. In other words, I instantly opened my bag, and took out the top publication. It proved to be an early edition – only the twenty-fifth – of the famous anonymous work (believed to be by precious Miss Bellows), entitled *The Serpent at Home.* The design of the book – with which the world-ly reader may not be acquainted – is to show how the Evil One lies in wait for us in all the most apparently innocent actions of our daily lives. The chapters best adapted to female perusal are "Satan in the Hair Brush"; "Satan behind the Looking Glass"; "Satan under the Tea Table"; "Satan out of the Window" – and many others.

"Give your attention, dear aunt, to this precious book – and you will give me all I ask." With those words, I handed it to her open, at a marked passage – one continuous burst of burning eloquence! Sub-ject: Satan among the Sofa Cushions.

Poor Lady Verinder (reclining thoughtlessly on her own sofa cush-ions) glanced at the book, and handed it back to me looking more confused than ever.

"I'm afraid, Drusilla," she said, "I must wait till I am a little better, before I can read that. The doctor –"

The moment she mentioned the doctor's name, I knew what was coming. Over and over again in my past experience among my perishing fellow-creatures, the members of the notoriously infidel profession of Medicine had stepped between me and my mission of mercy – on the miserable pretence that the patient wanted quiet, and that the disturbing influence of all others which they most dreaded, was the influence of Miss Clack and her Books. Precisely the same blinded materialism (working treacherously behind my back) now sought to rob me of the only right of property that my poverty could claim – my right of spiritual property in my perishing aunt.

"The doctor tells me," my poor misguided relative went on, "that I am not so well to-day. He forbids me to see any strangers; and he orders me, if I read at all, only to read the lightest and the most amusing books. 'Do nothing, Lady Verinder, to weary your head, or to quicken your pulse' – those were his last words, Drusilla, when he left me to-day."

There was no help for it but to yield again – for the moment only, as before. Any open assertion of the infinitely superior importance of such a ministry as mine, compared with the ministry of the medical man, would only have provoked the doctor to practise on the human weakness of his patient, and to threaten to throw up the case. Happily, there are more ways than one of sowing the good seed, and few persons are better versed in those ways than myself.

"You might feel stronger, dear, in an hour or two," I said. "Or you might wake, to-morrow morning, with a sense of something wanting, and even this unpretending volume might be able to supply it. You will let me leave the book, aunt? The doctor can hardly object to that!"

I slipped it under the sofa cushions, half in, and half out, close by her handkerchief, and her smelling-bottle. Every time her hand searched for either of these, it would touch the book; and, sooner or later (who knows?) the book might touch *her*. After making this arrangement, I thought it wise to withdraw. "Let me leave you to repose, dear aunt; I will call again to-morrow." I looked accidentally towards the window as I said that. It was full of flowers, in boxes and pots. Lady Verinder was extravagantly fond of these perishable treasures, and had a habit of rising every now and then, and going to look at them and smell them. A new idea flashed across my mind. "Oh! may I take a flower?" I said – and got to the window unsuspected, in that way. Instead of taking away a flower, I added one, in the shape of another book from my bag, which I left, to surprise my aunt, among the geraniums and roses. The happy thought followed, "Why not do the same for her, poor dear, in every other room that she enters?"

I immediately said good-bye; and, crossing the hall, slipped into the library. Samuel, coming up to let me out, and supposing I had gone, went downstairs again. On the library table I noticed two of the "amusing books" which the infidel doctor had recommended. I instantly covered them from sight with two of my own precious publications. In the breakfast-room I found my aunt's favourite canary singing in his cage. She was always in the habit of feeding the bird herself. Some groundsel was strewed on a table which stood immediately under the cage. I put a book among the groundsel. In the drawing-room I found more cheering opportunities of emptying my bag. My aunt's favourite musical pieces were on the piano. I slipped in two more books among the music. I disposed of another in the back drawing-room, under some unfinished embroidery, which I knew to be of Lady Verinder's working. A third little room opened out of the back drawing-room, from which it was shut off by curtains instead of a door. My aunt's plain old-fashioned fan was on the chimney-piece. I opened my ninth book at a very special passage, and put the fan in as a marker, to keep the place. The question then came, whether I should go higher still, and try the bedroom floor − at the risk, undoubtedly, of being insulted, if the person with the cap-ribbons happened to be in the upper regions of the house, and to find me out. But oh, what of that? It is a poor Christian that is afraid of being insulted. I went upstairs, prepared to bear anything. All was silent and solitary − it was the servants' tea-time, I suppose. My aunt's room was in front. The miniature of my late dear uncle, Sir John, hung on the wall opposite the bed. It seemed to smile at me; it seemed to say, "Drusilla! deposit a book." There were tables on either side of my aunt's bed. She was a bad sleeper, and wanted, or thought she wanted, many things at night. I put a book near the matches on one side, and a book under the box of chocolate drops on the other. Whether she wanted a light, or whether she wanted a drop, there was a precious publication to meet her eye, or to meet her hand, and to say with silent eloquence, in either case, "Come, try me! try me!" But one book was now left at the bottom of my bag, and but one apartment was still unexplored − the bathroom, which opened out of the bedroom. I peeped in; and the holy inner voice that never deceives, whispered to me, "You have met her, Drusilla, everywhere else; meet her at the bath, and the work is done." I observed a dressing-gown thrown across a chair. It had a pocket in it, and in that pocket I put my last book. Can words express my exquisite sense of duty done, when I had slipped out of the house, unsuspected by any of them, and when I found myself in the street with my empty bag under my arm? Oh, my worldly friends, pursuing the phantom, Pleasure, through the guilty mazes of Dissipation, how easy it is to be happy, if you will only be good!

When I folded up my things that night – when I reflected on the *true* riches which I had scattered with such a lavish hand, from top to bottom of the house of my wealthy aunt – I declare I felt as free from all anxiety as if I had been a child again. I was so light-hearted that I sang a verse of the Evening Hymn. I was so light-hearted that I fell asleep before I could sing another. Quite like a child again! quite like a child again!

So I passed that blissful night. On rising the next morning, how young I felt! I might add, how young I looked, if I were capable of dwelling on the concerns of my own perishable body. But I am not capable – and I add nothing.

Towards luncheon-time – not for the sake of the creature-comforts, but for the certainty of finding dear aunt – I put on my bonnet to go to Montagu Square. Just as I was ready, the maid at the lodgings in which I then lived looked in at the door, and said, "Lady Verinder's servant, to see Miss Clack."

★

I occupied the parlour-floor, at that period of my residence in London. The front parlour was my sitting-room.[1] Very small, very low in the ceiling, very poorly furnished – but, oh, so neat! I looked into the passage to see which of Lady Verinder's servants had asked for me. It was the young footman, Samuel – a civil fresh-coloured person, with a teachable look and a very obliging manner. I had always felt a spiritual interest in Samuel, and a wish to try him with a few serious

---

1 Clack's proclamation that she resides on the parlour-floor, that her front parlour was her sitting-room, suggests that her abode is quite modest, that she has no formal room set apart for the entertainment of visitors. Homes of the wealthy, the Verinders for instance, had grander drawing-rooms – apart from sitting-rooms – for entertainment. The drawing-room – short for "withdrawing-room" – was originally a room to which one retired for rest.

words. On this occasion, I invited him into my sitting-room.

He came in, with a large parcel under his arm. When he put the parcel down, it appeared to frighten him. "My lady's love, Miss; and I was to say that you would find a letter inside." Having given that message, the fresh-coloured young footman surprised me by looking as if he would have liked to run away.

I detained him to make a few kind inquiries. Could I see my aunt, if I called in Montagu Square? No; she had gone out for a drive. Miss Rachel had gone with her, and Mr. Ablewhite had taken a seat in the carriage, too. Knowing how sadly dear Mr. Godfrey's charitable work was in arrear, I thought it odd that he should be going out driving, like an idle man. I stopped Samuel at the door, and made a few more kind inquiries. Miss Rachel was going to a ball that night, and Mr. Ablewhite had arranged to come to coffee, and go with her. There was a morning concert advertised for to-morrow, and Samuel was ordered to take places for a large party, including a place for Mr. Ablewhite. "All the tickets may be gone, Miss," said this innocent youth, "if I don't run and get them at once!" He ran as he said the words – and I found myself alone again, with some anxious thoughts to occupy me.

We had a special meeting of the Mothers'-Small-Clothes-Conversion Society, that night, summoned expressly with a view to obtaining Mr. Godfrey's advice and assistance. Instead of sustaining our sisterhood, under an overwhelming flow of Trousers which quite prostrated our little community, he had arranged to take coffee in Montagu Square, and to go to a ball afterwards! The afternoon of the next day had been selected for the Festival of the British-Ladies'-Servants'-Sunday-Sweetheart-Supervision Society. Instead of being present, the life and soul of that struggling Institution, he had engaged to make one of a party of worldlings at a morning concert! I asked myself what did it mean? Alas! it meant that our Christian Hero was to reveal himself to me in a new character, and to become associated in my mind with one of the most awful back-slidings of modern times.

To return, however, to the history of the passing day. On finding myself alone in my room, I naturally turned my attention to the parcel which appeared to have so strangely intimidated the fresh-coloured young footman. Had my aunt sent me my promised legacy? and had it taken the form of cast-off clothes, or worn-out silver spoons, or unfashionable jewellery, or anything of that sort? Prepared to accept all, and to resent nothing, I opened the parcel – and what met my view? The twelve precious publications which I had scattered through the house, on the previous day; all returned to me by the doctor's orders! Well might the youthful Samuel shrink when he brought his parcel into my room! Well might he run when he had performed his miserable errand! As to my aunt's letter, it simply amounted, poor soul, to this – that she dare not disobey her medical man.

What was to be done now? With my training and my principles, I never had a moment's doubt.

Once self-supported by conscience, once embarked on a career of manifest usefulness, the true Christian never yields. Neither public nor private influences produce the slightest effect on us, when we have once got our mission. Taxation may be the consequence of a mission; riots may be the consequence of a mission; wars may be the consequence of a mission: we go on with our work, irrespective of every human consideration which moves the world outside us. We are above reason; we are beyond ridicule; we see with nobody's eyes, we hear with nobody's ears, we feel with nobody's hearts, but our own. Glorious, glorious privilege! And how is it earned? Ah, my friends, you may spare yourselves the useless inquiry! We are the only people who can earn it – for we are the only people who are always right.

In the case of my misguided aunt, the form which pious persever-ance was next to take revealed itself to me plainly enough.

Preparation by clerical friends had failed, owing to Lady Verinder's own reluctance. Preparation by books had failed, owing to the doc-tor's infidel obstinacy. So be it! What was the next thing to try? The next thing to try was – Preparation by Little Notes. In other words, the books themselves having been sent back, select extracts from the books, copied by different hands, and all addressed as letters to my aunt, were, some to be sent by post, and some to be distributed about the house on the plan I had adopted on the previous day. As letters they would excite no suspicion; as letters they would be opened – and, once opened, might be read. Some of them I wrote myself. "Dear aunt, may I ask your attention to a few lines?" &c. "Dear aunt, I was reading last night, and I chanced on the following passage," &c. Other letters were written for me by my valued fellow-workers, the sisterhood at the Mothers'-Small-Clothes. "Dear madam, pardon the interest taken in you by a true, though humble, friend." "Dear madam, may a serious person surprise you by saying a few cheering words?" Using these and other similar forms of courteous appeal, we reintroduced all my precious passages under a form which not even the doctor's watchful materialism could suspect. Before the shades of evening had closed around us, I had a dozen awakening letters for my aunt, instead of a dozen awakening books. Six I made immediate arrangements for sending through the post, and six I kept in my pocket for personal distribution in the house the next day.

Soon after two o'clock I was again on the field of pious conflict, addressing more kind inquiries to Samuel at Lady Verinder's door.

My aunt had had a bad night. She was again in the room in which I had witnessed her Will, resting on the sofa, and trying to get a little sleep.

I said I would wait in the library, on the chance of seeing her. In the fervour of my zeal to distribute the letters, it never occurred to me to inquire about Rachel. The house was quiet, and it was past the hour at which the musical performance began. I took it for granted that she and her party of pleasure-seekers (Mr. Godfrey, alas! included) were all at the concert, and eagerly devoted myself to my good work, while time and opportunity were still at my own disposal.

My aunt's correspondence of the morning – including the six awakening letters which I had posted overnight – was lying unopened on the library table. She had evidently not felt herself equal to dealing with a large mass of letters – and she might be daunted by the number of them, if she entered the library later in the day. I put one of my second set of six letters on the chimney-piece by itself; leaving it to attract her curiosity, by means of its solitary position, apart from the rest. A second letter I put purposely on the floor in the breakfast-room. The first servant who went in after me would conclude that my aunt had dropped it, and would be specially careful to restore it to her. The field thus sown on the basement story, I ran lightly upstairs to scatter my mercies next over the drawing-room floor.

Just as I entered the front room, I heard a double-knock at the street-door – a soft, fluttering, considerate little knock. Before I could think of slipping back to the library (in which I was supposed to be waiting), the active young footman was in the hall, answering the door. It mattered little, as I thought. In my aunt's state of health, visitors in general were not admitted. To my horror and amazement, the performer of the soft little knock proved to be an exception to general rules. Samuel's voice below me (after apparently answering some questions which I did not hear) said, unmistakably, "Upstairs, if you please, sir." The next moment I heard footsteps – a man's footsteps – approaching the drawing-room floor. Who could this favoured male visitor possibly be? Almost as soon as I asked myself the question, the answer occurred to me. Who *could* it be but the doctor?

In the case of any other visitor, I should have allowed myself to be discovered in the drawing-room. There would have been nothing out of the common in my having got tired of the library, and having gone upstairs for a change. But my own self-respect stood in the way of my meeting the person who had insulted me by sending me back my books. I slipped into the little third room, which I have mentioned as communicating with the back drawing-room, and dropped the curtains which closed the open doorway. If I only waited there for a minute or two, the usual result in such cases would take place. That is to say, the doctor would be conducted to his patient's room.

I waited a minute or two, and more than a minute or two. I heard the visitor walking restlessly backwards and forwards. I also heard him talking to himself. I even thought I recognised the voice. Had I made a mistake? Was it not the doctor, but somebody else? Mr. Bruff, for instance? No! an unerring instinct told me it was not Mr. Bruff. Whoever he was, he was still talking to himself. I parted the heavy curtains the least little morsel in the world, and listened.

The words I heard were, "I'll do it to-day!" And the voice that spoke them was Mr. Godfrey Ablewhite's.

CHAPTER V

MY hand dropped from the curtain. But don't suppose – oh, don't suppose – that the dreadful embarrassment of my situation was the uppermost idea in my mind! So fervent still was the sisterly interest I felt in Mr. Godfrey, that I never stopped to ask myself why he was not at the concert. No! I thought only of the words – the startling words

– which had just fallen from his lips. He would do it to-day. He had said, in a tone of terrible resolution, he would do it to-day. What, oh what, would he do? Something even more deplorably unworthy of him than what he had done already? Would he apostatize from the faith? Would he abandon us at the Mothers'-Small-Clothes? Had we seen the last of his angelic smile in the committee-room? Had we heard the last of his unrivalled eloquence at Exeter Hall? I was so wrought up by the bare idea of such awful eventualities as these in connexion with such a man, that I believe I should have rushed from my place of concealment, and implored him in the name of all the Ladies' Committees in London to explain himself – when I suddenly heard another voice in the room. It penetrated through the curtains; it was loud, it was bold, it was wanting in every female charm. The voice of Rachel Verinder!

"Why have you come up here, Godfrey?" she asked. "Why didn't you go into the library?"

He laughed softly, and answered, "Miss Clack is in the library."

"Clack in the library!" She instantly seated herself on the ottoman in the back drawing-room. "You are quite right, Godfrey. We had much better stop here."

I had been in a burning fever, a moment since, and in some doubt what to do next. I became extremely cold now, and felt no doubt whatever. To show myself, after what I had heard, was impossible. To retreat – except into the fireplace – was equally out of the question. A martyrdom was before me. In justice to myself, I noiselessly arranged the curtains so that I could both see and hear. And then I met my martyrdom, with the spirit of a primitive Christian.[1]

"Don't sit on the ottoman," the young lady proceeded. "Bring a chair, Godfrey. I like people to be opposite to me when I talk to them."

---

1 Characters in several of Collins's novels discover important information by eaves-dropping. In *Basil*, Basil hears his wife betraying him by listening through a bed-room wall. Magdalen Vanstone, of *No Name*, learns she has been left penniless by listening at an open window as Mr. Pendril and Miss Garth discuss her inheritance. Most memorable, of course, is *The Woman in White*'s Marian Halcombe, who takes the notion of eavesdropping to a literal level, practically dangling from the roof of the verandah at Blackwater Park in an attempt to overhear Fosco and Glyde plan their treachery.

He took the nearest seat. It was a low chair. He was very tall, and many sizes too large for it. I never saw his legs to such disadvantage before.

"Well?" she went on. "What did you say to them?"

"Just what you said, dear Rachel, to me."

"That mamma was not at all well to-day? And that I didn't quite like leaving her to go to the concert?"

"Those were the words. They were grieved to lose you at the concert, but they quite understood. All sent their love; and all expressed a cheering belief that Lady Verinder's indisposition would soon pass away."

"*You* don't think it's serious, do you, Godfrey?"

"Far from it! In a few days, I feel quite sure, all will be well again."

"I think so, too. I was a little frightened at first, but I think so too. It was very kind to go and make my excuses for me to people who are almost strangers to you. But why not have gone with them to the concert? It seems very hard that you should miss the music too."

"Don't say that, Rachel! If you only knew how much happier I am – here, with you!"

He clasped his hands, and looked at her. In the position which he occupied, when he did that, he turned my way. Can words describe how I sickened when I noticed exactly the same pathetic expression on his face, which had charmed me when he was pleading for destitute millions of his fellow-creatures on the platform at Exeter Hall!

"It's hard to get over one's bad habits, Godfrey. But do try to get over the habit of paying compliments – do, to please me."

"I never paid *you* a compliment, Rachel, in my life. Successful love may sometimes use the language of flattery, I admit. But hopeless love, dearest, always speaks the truth."

He drew his chair close, and took her hand, when he said "hopeless love." There was a momentary silence. He, who thrilled everybody, had doubtless thrilled *her*. I thought I now understood the words which had dropped from him when he was alone in the drawing-room, "I'll do it to-day." Alas! the most rigid propriety could hardly have failed to discover that he was doing it now.

"Have you forgotten what we agreed on, Godfrey, when you spoke to me in the country? We agreed that we were to be cousins, and nothing more."

"I break the agreement, Rachel, every time I see you."

"Then don't see me."

"Quite useless! I break the agreement every time I think of you. Oh, Rachel! how kindly you told me, only the other day, that my place in your estimation was a higher place than it had ever been yet! Am I mad to build the hopes I do on those dear words? Am I mad to dream of some future day when your heart may soften to me? Don't tell me so, if I am! Leave me my delusion, dearest! I must have *that* to cherish, and to comfort me, if I have nothing else!"

His voice trembled, and he put his white handkerchief to his eyes. Exeter Hall again! Nothing wanting to complete the parallel but the audience, the cheers, and the glass of water.

Even *her* obdurate nature was touched. I saw her lean a little nearer to him. I heard a new tone of interest in her next words.

"Are you really sure, Godfrey, that you are so fond of me as that?"

"Sure! You know what I was, Rachel. Let me tell you what I am. I have lost every interest in life, but my interest in you. A transformation has come over me which I can't account for, myself. Would you believe it? My charitable business is an unendurable nuisance to me; and when I see a Ladies' Committee now, I wish myself at the uttermost ends of the earth!"

If the annals of apostasy offer anything comparable to such a declaration as that, I can only say that the case in point is not producible from the stores of *my* reading. I thought of the Mothers'-Small-Clothes. I thought of the Sunday-Sweetheart-Supervision. I thought of the other Societies, too numerous to mention, all built up on this man as on a tower of strength. I thought of the struggling Female Boards, who, so to speak, drew the breath of their business-life through the nostrils of Mr. Godfrey – of that same Mr. Godfrey who had just reviled our good work as a "nuisance" – and just declared that he wished he was at the uttermost ends of the earth when he found himself in our company! My young female friends will feel encouraged to persevere, when I mention that it tried even My discipline before I could devour my own righteous indignation in silence. At the same time, it is only justice to myself to add, that I didn't lose a syllable of the conversation. Rachel was the next to speak.

"You have made your confession," she said. "I wonder whether it would cure you of your unhappy attachment to me, if I made mine?"

He started. I confess I started too. He thought, and I thought, that she was about to divulge the mystery of the Moonstone.

"Would you think, to look at me," she went on, "that I am the wretchedest girl living? It's true, Godfrey. What greater wretchedness can there be than to live degraded in your own estimation? That is my life now."

"My dear Rachel! it's impossible you can have any reason to speak of yourself in that way!"

"How do you know I have no reason?"

"Can you ask me the question! I know it, because I know *you*. Your silence, dearest, has never lowered you in the estimation of your true friends. The disappearance of your precious birthday gift may seem strange; your unexplained connexion with that event may seem stranger still – "

"Are you speaking of the Moonstone, Godfrey?"

"I certainly thought that you referred –"

"I referred to nothing of the sort. I can hear of the loss of the Moonstone, let who will speak of it, without feeling degraded in my own estimation. If the story of the Diamond ever comes to light, it will be known that I accepted a dreadful responsibility; it will be known that I involved myself in the keeping of a miserable secret – but it will be as clear as the sun at noonday that I did nothing mean! You have misunderstood me, Godfrey. It's my fault for not speaking more plainly. Cost me what it may, I will be plainer now. Suppose you were not in love with me? Suppose you were in love with some other woman?"

"Yes?"

"Suppose you discovered that woman to be utterly unworthy of you? Suppose you were quite convinced that it was a disgrace to you to waste another thought on her? Suppose the bare idea of ever marrying such a person made your face burn, only with thinking of it?"

"Yes?"

"And, suppose, in spite of all that – you couldn't tear her from your heart? Suppose the feeling she had roused in you (in the time when you believed in her) was not a feeling to be hidden? Suppose the love this wretch had inspired in you – ? Oh, how can I find words to say it in! How can I make a *man* understand that a feeling which horrifies me at myself, can be a feeling that fascinates me at the same time? It's the breath of my life, Godfrey, and it's the poison that kills me – both in one! Go away! I must be out of my mind to talk as I am talking now. No! you mustn't leave me – you mustn't carry away a wrong impression. I must say, what is to be said in my own defence. Mind this! *He* doesn't know – he never will know, what I have told *you*. I will never see him – I don't care what happens – I will never, never, never see him again! Don't ask me his name! Don't ask me any more! Let's change the subject. Are you doctor enough, Godfrey, to tell me why I feel as if I was stifling for want of breath? Is there a form of hysterics that bursts into words instead of tears? I dare say! What does it matter? You will get over any trouble I have caused you, easily enough now. I have dropped to my right place in your estimation, haven't I? Don't notice me! Don't pity me! For God's sake, go away!"

She turned round on a sudden, and beat her hands wildly on the back of the ottoman. Her head dropped on the cushions; and she burst out crying. Before I had time to feel shocked at this, I was hor-ror-struck by an entirely unexpected proceeding on the part of Mr. Godfrey. Will it be credited that he fell on his knees at her feet? – on *both* knees, I solemnly declare! May modesty mention that he put his arms round her next? And may reluctant admiration acknowledge that he electrified her with two words?

"Noble creature!"

No more than that! But he did it with one of the bursts which have made his fame as a public speaker. She sat, either quite thunder-struck, or quite fascinated – I don't know which – without even making an effort to put his arms back where his arms ought to have been. As for me, my sense of propriety was completely bewildered. I was so painfully uncertain whether it was my first duty to close my eyes, or to stop my ears, that I did neither. I attribute my being still able to hold the curtain in the right position for looking and listen-ing, entirely to suppressed hysterics. In suppressed hysterics, it is admitted, even by the doctors, that one must hold something.

"Yes," he said, with all the fascination of his evangelical voice and manner, "you are a noble creature! A woman who can speak the truth, for the truth's own sake – a woman who will sacrifice her pride, rather than sacrifice an honest man who loves her – is the most priceless of all treasures. When such a woman marries, if her husband only wins her esteem and regard, he wins enough to ennoble his whole life. You have spoken, dearest, of your place in my estimation. Judge what that place is – when I implore you on my knees, to let the cure of your poor wounded heart be my care. Rachel! will you honour me, will you bless me, by being my wife?"

By this time I should certainly have decided on stopping my ears, if Rachel had not encouraged me to keep them open, by answering him in the first sensible words I had ever heard fall from her lips.

"Godfrey!" she said, "you must be mad!"

"I never spoke more reasonably, dearest – in your interests, as well as in mine. Look for a moment to the future. Is your happiness to be sacrificed to a man who has never known how you feel towards him, and whom you are resolved never to see again? Is it not your duty to yourself to forget this ill-fated attachment? and is forgetfulness to be found in the life you are leading now? You have tried that life, and you are wearying of it already. Surround yourself with nobler interests than the wretched interests of the world. A heart that loves and honours you; a home whose peaceful claims and happy duties win gently on you day by day – try the consolation, Rachel, which is to be found *there!* I don't ask for your love – I will be content with your affection and regard. Let the rest be left, confidently left, to your husband's devotion, and to Time that heals even wounds as deep as yours."

She began to yield already. Oh, what a bringing-up she must have had! Oh, how differently I should have acted in her place!

"Don't tempt me, Godfrey," she said; "I am wretched enough and reckless enough as it is. Don't tempt me to be more wretched and more reckless still!"

"One question, Rachel. Have you any personal objection to me?"

"I! I always liked you. After what you have just said to me, I should be insensible indeed if I didn't respect and admire you as well."

"Do you know many wives, my dear Rachel, who respect and admire their husbands? And yet they and their husbands get on very well. How many brides go to the altar with hearts that would bear inspection by the men who take them there? And yet it doesn't end unhappily – somehow or other the nuptial establishment jogs on. The truth is, that women try marriage as a Refuge, far more numerously than they are willing to admit; and, what is more, they find that marriage has justified their confidence in it. Look at your own case once again. At your age, and with your attractions, is it possible for you to sentence yourself to a single life? Trust my knowledge of the world – nothing is less possible. It is merely a question of time. You may marry some other man, some years hence. Or you may marry the man, dearest, who is now at your feet, and who prizes your respect and admiration above the love of any other woman on the face of the earth."

"Gently, Godfrey! you are putting something into my head which I never thought of before. You are tempting me with a new prospect, when all my other prospects are closed before me. I tell you again, I am miserable enough and desperate enough, if you say another word, to marry you on your own terms. Take the warning, and go!"

"I won't even rise from my knees, till you have said yes!"

"If I say yes you will repent, and shall repent, when it is too late!"

"We shall both bless the day, darling, when I pressed, and when you yielded."

"Do you feel as confidently as you speak?"

"You shall judge for yourself. I speak from what I have seen in my own family. Tell me what you think of our household at Frizinghall. Do my father and mother live unhappily together?"

"Far from it – so far as I can see."

"When my mother was a girl, Rachel (it is no secret in the family), she had loved as you love – she had given her heart to a man who was unworthy of her. She married my father, respecting him, admiring him, but nothing more. Your own eyes have seen the result. Is there no encouragement in it for you and for me?"*

"You won't hurry me, Godfrey?"

"My time shall be yours."

"You won't ask me for more than I can give?"

"My angel! I only ask you to give me yourself."

"Take me!"

In those two words she accepted him!

He had another burst – a burst of unholy rapture this time. He drew her nearer and nearer to him till her face touched his; and then – No! I really cannot prevail upon myself to carry this shocking disclosure any farther. Let me only say, that I tried to close my eyes before it happened, and that I was just one moment too late. I had calculated, you see, on her resisting. She submitted. To every right-

---

* See Betteredge's Narrative, chapter viii.

feeling person of my own sex, volumes could say no more.

Even my innocence in such matters began to see its way to the end of the interview now. They understood each other so thoroughly by this time, that I fully expected to see them walk off together, arm in arm, to be married. There appeared, however, judging by Mr. Godfrey's next words, to be one more trifling formality which it was necessary to observe. He seated himself – unforbidden this time – on the ottoman by her side. "Shall I speak to your dear mother?" he asked. "Or will you?"

She declined both alternatives.

"Let my mother hear nothing from either of us, until she is better. I wish it to be kept a secret for the present, Godfrey. Go now, and come back this evening. We have been here alone together quite long enough."

She rose, and, in rising, looked for the first time towards the little room in which my martyrdom was going on.

"Who has drawn those curtains?" she exclaimed. "The room is close enough, as it is, without keeping the air out of it in that way."

She advanced to the curtains. At the moment when she laid her hand on them – at the moment when the discovery of me appeared to be quite inevitable – the voice of the fresh-coloured young footman, on the stairs, suddenly suspended any further proceedings on her side or on mine. It was unmistakably the voice of a man in great alarm.

"Miss Rachel!" he called out, "where are you, Miss Rachel?"

She sprang back from the curtains, and ran to the door.

The footman came just inside the room. His ruddy colour was all gone. He said, "Please to come downstairs, Miss! My lady has fainted, and we can't bring her to again."

In a moment more I was alone, and free to go downstairs in my turn, quite unobserved.

Mr. Godfrey passed me in the hall, hurrying out, to fetch the doctor. "Go in, and help them!" he said, pointing to the room. I found Rachel on her knees by the sofa, with her mother's head on her bosom. One look at my aunt's face (knowing what I knew) was enough to warn me of the dreadful truth. I kept my thoughts to myself till the doctor came in. It was not long before he arrived. He began by sending Rachel out of the room – and then he told the rest of us that Lady Verinder was no more. Serious persons, in search of proofs of hardened scepticism, may be interested in hearing that he showed no signs of remorse when he looked at Me.

At a later hour I peeped into the breakfast-room, and the library. My aunt had died without opening one of the letters which I had addressed to her. I was so shocked at this, that it never occurred to me, until some days afterwards, that she had also died without giving me my little legacy.

★

CHAPTER VI

(1) "Miss Clack presents here compliments to Mr. Franklin Blake; and, in sending him the fifth chapter of her humble narrative, begs to say that she feels quite unequal to enlarge as she could wish on an event so awful, under the circumstances, as Lady Verinder's death. She has, therefore, attached to her own manuscript, copious Extracts from precious publications in her possession, all bearing on this terrible subject. And may those Extracts (Miss Clack fervently hopes) sound as the blast of a trumpet in the ears of her respected kinsman, Mr. Franklin Blake."

(2) "Mr. Franklin Blake presents his compliments to Miss Clack, and begs to thank her for the fifth chapter of her narrative. In returning the extracts sent with it, he will refrain from mentioning any personal objection which he may entertain to this species of literature, and will merely say that the proposed additions to the manuscript are not necessary to the fulfilment of the purpose that he has in view."

(3) "Miss Clack begs to acknowledge the return of her Extracts. She affectionately reminds Mr. Franklin Blake that she is a Christian, and that it is, therefore, quite impossible for him to offend her. Miss C. persists in feeling the deepest interest in Mr. Blake, and pledges herself, on the first occasion when sickness may lay him low, to offer him the use of her Extracts for the second time. In the meanwhile she would be glad to know, before beginning the final chapters of her narrative, whether she may be permitted to make her humble contribution complete, by availing herself of the light which later discoveries have thrown on the mystery of the Moonstone."

(4) "Mr. Franklin Blake is sorry to disappoint Miss Clack. He can only repeat the instructions which he had the honour of giving her when she began her narrative. She is requested to limit herself to her own individual experience of persons and events, as recorded in her diary. Later discoveries she will be good enough to leave to the pens of those persons who can write in the capacity of actual witnesses."

(5) "Miss Clack is extremely sorry to trouble Mr. Franklin Blake with another letter. Her Extracts have been returned, and the expression of her matured views on the subject of the Moonstone has been forbidden. Miss Clack is painfully conscious that she ought (in the worldly phrase) to feel herself put down. But, no – Miss C. has learnt Perseverance in the School of Adversity. Her object in writing is to know whether Mr. Blake (who prohibits everything else) prohibits the appearance of the present correspondence in Miss Clack's narrative? Some explanation of the position in which Mr. Blake's interference has placed her as an authoress, seems due on the ground of common justice. And Miss Clack, on her side, is most anxious that her letters should be produced to speak for themselves."

(6) "Mr. Franklin Blake agrees to Miss Clack's proposal, on the understanding that she will kindly consider this intimation of his consent as closing the correspondence between them."

(7) "Miss Clack feels it an act of Christian duty (before the correspondence closes) to inform Mr. Franklin Blake that his last letter – evidently intended to offend her – has not succeeded in accomplishing the object of the writer. She affectionately requests Mr. Blake to retire to the privacy of his own room, and to consider with himself whether the training which can thus elevate a poor weak woman above the reach of insult, be not worthy of greater admiration than he is now disposed to feel for it. On being favoured with an intimation to that effect, Miss C. solemnly pledges herself to send back the complete series of her Extracts to Mr. Franklin Blake."

[To this letter no answer was received. Comment is needless.

(Signed)   DRUSILLA CLACK.]

CHAPTER VII

THE foregoing correspondence will sufficiently explain why no choice is left to me but to pass over Lady Verinder's death with the simple announcement of the fact which ends my fifth chapter.

Keeping myself for the future strictly within the limits of my own personal experience, I have next to relate that a month elapsed from the time of my aunt's decease before Rachel Verinder and I met again. That meeting was the occasion of my spending a few days under the same roof with her. In the course of my visit, something happened, relating to her marriage engagement with Mr. Godfrey Ablewhite, which is important enough to require special notice in these pages. When this last of many painful family circumstances has been disclosed, my task will be completed; for I shall then have told all that I know, as an actual (and most unwilling) witness of events.

My aunt's remains were removed from London, and were buried in the little cemetery attached to the church in her own park. I was invited to the funeral with the rest of the family. But it was impossible (with my religious views) to rouse myself in a few days only from the shock which this death had caused me. I was informed, moreover, that the rector of Frizinghall was to read the service. Having myself in past times seen this clerical castaway making one of the players at Lady Verinder's whist-table, I doubt, even if I had been fit to travel, whether I should have felt justified in attending the ceremony.

Lady Verinder's death left her daughter under the care of her brother-in-law, Mr. Ablewhite the elder. He was appointed guardian by the will, until his niece married, or came of age. Under these circumstances, Mr. Godfrey informed his father, I suppose, of the new relation in which he stood towards Rachel. At any rate, in ten days from my aunt's death, the secret of the marriage engagement was no secret at all within the circle of the family, and the grand question for Mr. Ablewhite senior – another confirmed castaway! – was how to make himself and his authority most agreeable to the wealthy young lady who was going to marry his son.

Rachel gave him some trouble at the outset, about the choice of a place in which she could be prevailed upon to reside. The house in Montagu Square was associated with the calamity of her mother's death. The house in Yorkshire was associated with the scandalous affair of the lost Moonstone. Her guardian's own residence at Frizinghall was open to neither of these objections. But Rachel's presence in it, after her recent bereavement, operated as a check on the gaieties of her cousins, the Miss Ablewhites – and she herself requested that her visit might be deferred to a more favourable opportunity. It ended in a proposal, emanating from old Mr. Ablewhite, to try a furnished house at Brighton.[1] His wife, an invalid daughter, and Rachel were to inhabit it together, and were to expect him to join them later in the season. They would see no society but a few old friends, and they would have his son Godfrey, travelling backwards and forwards by the London train, always at their disposal.

I describe this aimless flitting about from one place of residence to another – this insatiate restlessness of body and appalling stagnation of soul – merely with the view to arriving at results. The event which (under Providence) proved to be the means of bringing Rachel Verinder and myself together again, was no other than the hiring of the house at Brighton.

My Aunt Ablewhite is a large, silent, fair-complexioned woman, with one noteworthy point in her character. From the hour of her birth she has never been known to do anything for herself. She has gone through life, accepting everybody's help, and adopting everybody's opinions. A more hopeless person, in a spiritual point of view, I have never met with – there is absolutely, in this perplexing case, no obstructive material to work upon. Aunt Ablewhite would listen to the Grand Lama of Thibet exactly as she listens to Me, and would reflect his views quite as readily as she reflects mine. She found the furnished house at Brighton by stopping at an hotel in London, composing herself on a sofa, and sending for her son. She discovered the necessary servants by breakfasting in bed one morning (still at the hotel), and giving her maid a holiday on condition that the girl "would begin enjoying herself by fetching Miss Clack." I found her placidly fanning herself in her dressing-gown at eleven o'clock. "Drusilla, dear, I want some servants. You are so clever – please get them for me." I looked round the untidy room. The church-bells were going for a week-day service; they suggested a word of

---

1 Brighton was and remains a popular seaside resort on the English Channel about fifty miles southwest of London.

affectionate remonstrance on my part. "Oh, aunt!" I said sadly. "Is *this* worthy of a Christian Englishwoman? Is the passage from time to eternity to be made in *this* manner?" My aunt answered, "I'll put on my gown, Drusilla, if you will be kind enough to help me." What was to be said after that? I have done wonders with murderesses – I have never advanced an inch with Aunt Ablewhite. "Where is the list," I asked, "of the servants whom you require?" My aunt shook her head; she hadn't even energy enough to keep the list. "Rachel has got it, dear," she said, "in the next room." I went into the next room, and so saw Rachel again, for the first time since we had parted in Montagu Square.

She looked pitiably small and thin in her deep mourning. If I attached any serious importance to such a perishable trifle as personal appearance, I might be inclined to add that hers was one of those unfortunate complexions which always suffer when not relieved by a border of white next the skin. But what are our complexions and our looks? Hindrances and pitfalls, dear girls, which beset us on our way to higher things! Greatly to my surprise, Rachel rose when I entered the room, and came forward to meet me with outstretched hand.

"I am glad to see you," she said. "Drusilla, I have been in the habit of speaking very foolishly and very rudely to you, on former occasions. I beg your pardon. I hope you will forgive me."

My face, I suppose, betrayed the astonishment I felt at this. She coloured up for a moment, and then proceeded to explain herself.

"In my poor mother's lifetime," she went on, "her friends were not always my friends, too. Now I have lost her, my heart turns for comfort to the people she liked. She liked you. Try to be friends with me, Drusilla, if you can."

To any rightly-constituted mind, the motive thus acknowledged was simply shocking. Here in Christian England was a young woman in a state of bereavement, with so little idea of where to look for true comfort, that she actually expected to find it among her mother's friends! Here was a relative of mine, awakened to a sense of her shortcomings towards others, under the influence, not of conviction and duty, but of sentiment and impulse! Most deplorable to think of – but, still, suggestive of something hopeful, to a person of my experience in plying the good work. There could be no harm, I thought, in ascertaining the extent of the change which the loss of her mother had wrought in Rachel's character. I decided, as a useful test, to probe her on the subject of her marriage engagement to Mr. Godfrey Able-white.

Having first met her advances with all possible cordiality, I sat by her on the sofa, at her own request. We discussed family affairs and future plans – always excepting that one future plan which was to end in her marriage. Try as I might to turn the conversation that way, she resolutely declined to take the hint. Any open reference to the question, on my part, would have been premature at this early stage of our reconciliation. Besides, I had discovered all I wanted to know. She was no longer the reckless, defiant creature whom I had heard and seen, on the occasion of my martyrdom in Montagu Square. This was, of itself, enough to encourage me to take her future conversion in hand – beginning with a few words of earnest warning directed against the hasty formation of the marriage tie, and so getting on to higher things. Looking at her, now, with this new interest – and calling to mind the headlong suddenness with which she had met Mr. Godfrey's matrimonial views – I felt the solemn duty of interfering, with a fervour which assured me that I should achieve no common results. Rapidity of proceeding was, as I believed, of importance in this case. I went back at once to the question of the servants wanted for the furnished house.

"Where is the list, dear?"

Rachel produced it.

"Cook, kitchen-maid, housemaid, and footman," I read. "My dear Rachel, these servants are only wanted for a term – the term during which your guardian has taken the house. We shall have great difficulty in finding persons of character and capacity to accept a temporary engagement of that sort, if we try in London. Has the house in Brighton been found yet?"

"Yes. Godfrey has taken it; and persons in the house wanted him to hire them as servants. He thought they would hardly do for us, and came back having settled nothing."

"And you have no experience yourself in these matters, Rachel?"

"None whatever."

"And Aunt Ablewhite won't exert herself?"

"No, poor dear. Don't blame her, Drusilla. I think she is the only really happy woman I have ever met with."

"There are degrees in happiness, darling. We must have a little talk, some day, on that subject. In the meantime I will undertake to meet the difficulty about the servants. Your aunt will write a letter to the people of the house –"

"She will sign a letter, if I write if for her, which comes to the same thing."

"Quite the same thing. I shall get the letter, and I will go to Brighton to-morrow."

"How extremely kind of you! We will join you as soon as you are ready for us. And you will stay, I hope, as *my* guest. Brighton is so lively; you are sure to enjoy it."

In those words the invitation was given, and the glorious prospect of interference was opened before me.

It was then the middle of the week. By Saturday afternoon the house was ready for them. In that short interval I had sifted, not the characters only, but the religious views as well, of all the disengaged servants who applied to me, and had succeeded in making a selection which my conscience approved. I also discovered, and called on, two serious friends of mine, residents in the town, to whom I knew I could confide the pious object which had brought me to Brighton. One of them – a clerical friend – kindly helped me to take sittings for our little party in the church in which he himself ministered. The other – a single lady, like myself – placed the resources of her library (composed throughout of precious publications) entirely at my disposal. I borrowed half-a-dozen works, all carefully chosen with a view to Rachel. When these had been judiciously distributed in the various rooms she would be likely to occupy, I considered that my preparations were complete. Sound doctrine in the servants who waited on her; sound doctrine in the minister who preached to her; sound doctrine in the books that lay on her table – such was the treble welcome which my zeal had prepared for the motherless girl! A heavenly composure filled my mind, on that Saturday afternoon, as I sat at the window waiting the arrival of my relatives. The giddy throng passed and repassed before my eyes. Alas! how many of them felt my exquisite sense of duty done? An awful question. Let us not pursue it.

Between six and seven the travellers arrived. To my indescribable surprise, they were escorted, not by Mr. Godfrey (as I had anticipated), but by the lawyer, Mr. Bruff.

"How do you do, Miss Clack?" he said. "I mean to stay this time."

That reference to the occasion on which I had obliged him to postpone his business to mine, when we were both visiting in Montagu Square, satisfied me that the old worldling had come to Brighton with some object of his own in view. I had prepared quite a little Paradise for my beloved Rachel – and here was the Serpent already!

"Godfrey was very much vexed, Drusilla, not to be able to come with us," said my Aunt Ablewhite. "There was something in the way which kept him in town. Mr. Bruff volunteered to take his place, and make a holiday of it till Monday morning. By-the-bye, Mr. Bruff, I'm ordered to take exercise, and I don't like it. That," added Aunt Ablewhite, pointing out of window to an invalid going by in a chair on wheels, drawn by a man, "is my idea of exercise. If it's air you want, you get it in your chair. And if it's fatigue you want, I am sure it's fatiguing enough to look at the man."

Rachel stood silent, at a window by herself, with her eyes fixed on the sea.

"Tired, love?" I inquired.

"No. Only a little out of spirits," she answered. "I have often seen the sea, on our Yorkshire coast, with that light on it. And I was thinking, Drusilla, of the days that can never come again."

Mr. Bruff remained to dinner, and stayed through the evening. The more I saw of him, the more certain I felt that he had some private end to service in coming to Brighton. I watched him carefully. He maintained the same appearance of ease, and talked the same godless gossip, hour after hour, until it was time to take leave. As he shook hands with Rachel, I caught his hard and cunning eye resting on her for a moment with a peculiar interest and attention. She was plainly concerned in the object that he had in view. He said nothing out of the common to her or to anyone on leaving. He invited himself to luncheon the next day, and then he went away to his hotel.

It was impossible the next morning to get my Aunt Ablewhite out of her dressing-gown in time for church. Her invalid daughter (suffering from nothing, in my opinion, but incurable laziness, inherited from her mother) announced that she meant to remain in bed for the day. Rachel and I went alone together to church. A magnificent sermon was preached by my gifted friend on the heathen indifference of the world to the sinfulness of little sins. For more than an hour his eloquence (assisted by his glorious voice) thundered through the sacred edifice. I said to Rachel, when we came out, "Has it found its way to your heart, dear?" And she answered, "No; it has only made my head ache." This might have been discouraging to some people; but, once embarked on a career of manifest usefulness, nothing discourages Me.

We found Aunt Ablewhite, and Mr. Bruff at luncheon. When Rachel declined eating anything, and gave as a reason for it that she was suffering from a headache, the lawyer's cunning instantly saw, and seized, the chance that she had given him.

"There is only one remedy for a headache," said this horrible old man. "A walk, Miss Rachel, is the thing to cure you. I am entirely at your service, if you will honour me by accepting my arm."

"With the greatest pleasure. A walk is the very thing I was longing for."

"It's past two," I gently suggested. "And the afternoon service, Rachel, begins at three."

"How can you expect me to go to church again," she asked, petulantly, "with such a headache as mine?"

Mr. Bruff officiously opened the door for her. In another minute more they were both out of the house. I don't know when I have felt the solemn duty of interfering so strongly as I felt it at that moment. But what was to be done? Nothing was to be done but to interfere at the first opportunity, later in the day.

On my return from the afternoon service I found that they had just got back. One look at them told me that the lawyer had said what he wanted to say. I had never before seen Rachel so silent, and so thoughtful. I had never before seen Mr. Bruff pay her such devoted attention, and look at her with such marked respect. He had (or pretended that he had) an engagement to dinner that day – and he took an early leave of us all; intending to go back to London by the first train the next morning.

"Are you sure of your own resolution?" he said to Rachel at the door.

"Quite sure," she answered – and so they parted.

The moment his back was turned, Rachel withdrew to her own

room. She never appeared at dinner. Her maid (the person with the cap-ribbons) was sent downstairs to announce that her headache had returned. I ran up to her and made all sorts of sisterly offers through the door. It was locked, and she kept it locked. Plenty of obstructive material to work on here! I felt greatly cheered and stimulated by her locking the door.

When her cup of tea went up to her the next morning, I followed it in. I sat by her bedside and said a few earnest words. She listened with languid civility. I noticed my serious friend's precious publications huddled together on a table in a corner. Had she chanced to look into them? – I asked. Yes – and they had not interested her. Would she allow me to read a few passages of the deepest interest, which had probably escaped her eye? No, not now – she had other things to think of. She gave these answers, with her attention apparently absorbed in folding and refolding the frilling of her nightgown. It was plainly necessary to rouse her by some reference to those worldly interests which she still had at heart.

"Do you know, love," I said, "I had an odd fancy, yesterday, about Mr. Bruff? I thought, when I saw you after your walk with him, that he had been telling you some bad news."

Her fingers dropped from the frilling of her nightgown, and her fierce black eyes flashed at me.

"Quite the contrary!" she said. "It was news I was interested in hearing – and I am deeply indebted to Mr. Bruff for telling me of it."

"Yes?" I said, in a tone of gentle interest.

Her fingers went back to the frilling, and she turned her head sullenly away from me. I had been met in this manner, in the course of plying the good work, hundreds of times. She merely stimulated me to try again. In my dauntless zeal for her welfare, I ran the great risk, and openly alluded to her marriage engagement.

"News you were interested in hearing?" I repeated. "I suppose, my dear Rachel, that must be news of Mr. Godfrey Ablewhite?"

She started up in the bed, and turned deadly pale. It was evidently on the tip of her tongue to retort on me with the unbridled insolence of former times. She checked herself – laid her head back on the pillow – considered a minute – and then answered in these remarkable words:

"*I shall never marry Mr. Godfrey Ablewhite.*"

It was my turn to start at that.

"What can you possibly mean?" I exclaimed. "The marriage is considered by the whole family as a settled thing!"

"Mr. Godfrey Ablewhite is expected here to-day," she said doggedly. "Wait till he comes – and you will see."

"But, my dear Rachel –"

She rang the bell at the head of her bed. The person with the cap-ribbons appeared.

"Penelope! my bath."

Let me give her her due. In the state of my feelings at that moment, I do sincerely believe that she had hit on the only possible way of forcing me to leave the room.

By the mere worldly mind my position towards Rachel might have been viewed as presenting difficulties of no ordinary kind. I had reckoned on leading her to higher things by means of a little earnest exhortation on the subject of her marriage. And now, if she was to be believed, no such event as her marriage was to take place at all. But ah, my friends! a working Christian of my experience (with an evangelising prospect before her) takes broader views than these. Supposing Rachel really broke off the marriage, on which the Ablewhites, father and son, counted as a settled thing, what would be the result? It could only end, if she held firm, in an exchanging of hard words and bitter accusations on both sides. And what would be the effect on Rachel when the stormy interview was over? A salutary moral depression would be the effect. Here pride would be exhausted, her stubbornness would be exhausted, by the resolute resistance which it was in her character to make under the circumstances. She would turn for sympathy to the nearest person who had sympathy to offer. And I was that nearest person – brimful of comfort, charged to overflowing with seasonable and reviving words. Never had the evangelising prospect looked brighter, to *my* eyes, than it looked now.

She came down to breakfast, but she ate nothing, and hardly uttered a word.

After breakfast she wandered listlessly from room to room – then suddenly roused herself, and opened the piano. The music she selected to play was of the most scandalously profane sort, associated with performances on the stage which it curdles one's blood to think of. It would have been premature to interfere with her at such a time as this. I privately ascertained the hour at which Mr. Godfrey Ablewhite was expected, and then I escaped the music by leaving the house.

Being out alone, I took the opportunity of calling upon my two resident friends. It was an indescribable luxury to find myself indulging in earnest conversation with serious persons. Infinitely encouraged and refreshed, I turned my steps back again to the house, in excellent time to await the arrival of our expected visitor. I entered the dining-room, always empty at that hour of the day, and found myself face to face with Mr. Godfrey Ablewhite!

He made no attempt to fly the place. Quite the contrary. He advanced to meet me with the utmost eagerness.

"Dear Miss Clack, I have been only waiting to see *you*! Chance set me free of my London engagements to-day sooner than I had expected, and I have got here, in consequence, earlier than my appointed time."

Not the slightest embarrassment encumbered his explanation, though this was his first meeting with me after the scene in Montagu Square. He was not aware, it is true, of my having been a witness of that scene. But he knew, on the other hand, that my attendances at the Mothers'-Small-Clothes, and my relations with friends attached to other charities, must have informed me of his shameless neglect of his Ladies and of his Poor. And yet there he was before me, in full possession of his charming voice and his irresistible smile!

"Have you seen Rachel yet?" I asked.

He sighed gently, and took me by the hand. I should certainly have snatched my hand away, if the manner in which he gave his answer had not paralysed me with astonishment.

"I have seen Rachel," he said with perfect tranquillity. "You are aware, dear friend, that she was engaged to me? Well, she has taken a sudden resolution to break the engagement. Reflection has convinced her that she will best consult her welfare and mine by retracting a rash promise, and leaving me free to make some happier choice elsewhere. That is the only reason she will give, and the only answer she will make to every question that I can ask of her."

"What have you done on your side?" I inquired. "Have you submitted."

"Yes," he said with the most unruffled composure, "I have submitted."

His conduct, under the circumstances, was so utterly inconceivable, that I stood bewildered with my hand in his. It is a piece of rudeness to stare at anybody, and it is an act of indelicacy to stare at a gentleman. I committed both those improprieties. And I said, as if in a dream, "What does it mean?"

"Permit me to tell you," he replied. "And suppose we sit down?"

He led me to a chair. I have an indistinct remembrance that he was very affectionate. I don't think he put his arm round my waist to support me – but I am not sure. I was quite helpless, and his ways with ladies were very endearing. At any rate, we sat down. I can answer for that, if I can answer for nothing more.

★

CHAPTER VIII

"I have lost a beautiful girl, an excellent social position, and a handsome income," Mr. Godfrey began; "and I have submitted to it without a struggle. What can be the motive for such extraordinary conduct as that? My precious friend, there is no motive."

"No motive?" I repeated.

"Let me appeal, my dear Miss Clack, to your experience of children," he went on. "A child pursues a certain course of conduct. You are greatly struck by it, and you attempt to get at the motive. The dear little thing is incapable of telling you its motive. You might as well ask the grass why it grows, or the birds why they sing. Well! in this matter, I am like the dear little thing – like the grass – like the birds. I don't know why I made a proposal of marriage to Miss Verinder. I don't know why I have shamefully neglected my dear Ladies. I don't know why I have apostatized from the Mothers'-Small-Clothes. You say to the child, Why have you been naughty? And the little angel puts its finger into its mouth, and doesn't know. My case exactly, Miss Clack! I couldn't confess it to anybody else. I feel impelled to confess it to *you*!"

I began to recover myself. A mental problem was involved here. I am deeply interested in mental problems – and I am not, it is thought, without some skill in solving them.

"Best of friends, exert your intellect, and help me," he proceeded. "Tell me – why does a time come when these matrimonial proceedings of mine begin to look like something done in a dream? Why does it suddenly occur to me that my true happiness is in helping my dear Ladies, in going my modest round of useful work, in saying my few earnest words when called on by my Chairman? What do I want with a position? I have got a position. What do I want with an income? I can pay for my bread and cheese, and my nice little lodging, and my two coats a year. What do I want with Miss Verinder? She has told me with her own lips (this, dear lady, is between ourselves) that she loves another man, and that her only idea in marrying me is to try and put that other man out of her head. What a horrid union is this! Oh, dear me, what a horrid union is this! Such are my reflections, Miss Clack, on my way to Brighton. I approach Rachel with the feeling of a criminal who is going to receive his sentence. When I find that she has changed her mind too – when I hear her propose to break the engagement – I experience (there is no sort of doubt about it) a most overpowering sense of relief. A month ago I was pressing her rapturously to my bosom. An hour ago, the happiness of knowing that I shall never press her again, intoxicates me like strong liquor. The thing seems impossible – the thing can't be. And yet there are the facts, as I had the honour of stating them when we first sat down together in these two chairs. I have lost a beautiful girl, an excellent social position, and a handsome income; and I have submitted to it without a struggle. Can *you* account for it, dear friend? It's quite beyond *me*."

His magnificent head sank on his breast, and he gave up his own mental problem in despair.

I was deeply touched. The case (if I may speak as a spiritual physician) was now quite plain to me. It is no uncommon event, in the experience of us all, to see the possessors of exalted ability occasionally humbled to the level of the most poorly gifted people about them. The object, no doubt, in the wise economy of Providence, is to remind greatness that it is mortal, and that the power which has conferred it can also take it away. It was now – to my mind – easy to discern one of these salutary humiliations in the deplorable proceedings on dear Mr. Godfrey's part, of which I had been the unseen witness.

And it was equally easy to recognise the welcome reappearance of his own finer nature in the horror with which he recoiled from the idea of a marriage with Rachel, and in the charming eagerness which he showed to return to his Ladies and his Poor.

I put this view before him in a few simple and sisterly words. His joy was beautiful to see. He compared himself, as I went on, to a lost man emerging from the darkness into the light. When I answered for a loving reception of him at the Mothers'-Small-Clothes, the grateful heart of our Christian Hero overflowed. He pressed my hands alternately to his lips. Overwhelmed by the exquisite triumph of having got him back among us, I let him do what he liked with my hands. I closed my eyes. I felt my head, in an ecstasy of spiritual self-forgetfulness, sinking on his shoulder. In a moment more I should certainly have swooned away in his arms, but for an interruption from the outer world, which brought me to myself again. A horrid rattling of knives and forks sounded outside the door, and the footman came in to lay the table for luncheon.

Mr. Godfrey started up, and looked at the clock on the mantel-piece.

"How time flies with *you!*" he exclaimed. "I shall barely catch the train."

I ventured on asking why he was in such a hurry to get back to town. His answer reminded me of family difficulties that were still to be reconciled, and of family disagreements that were yet to come.

"I have heard from my father," he said. "Business obliges him to leave Frizinghall for London to-day, and he proposes coming on here, either this evening or to-morrow. I must tell him what has happened between Rachel and me. His heart is set on our marriage – there will be great difficulty, I fear, in reconciling him to the breaking-off of the engagement. I must stop him, for all our sakes, from coming here till he *is* reconciled. Best and dearest of friends, we shall meet again!"

With those words he hurried out. In equal haste on my side, I ran upstairs to compose myself in my own room before meeting Aunt Ablewhite and Rachel at the luncheon-table.

I am well aware – to dwell for a moment yet on the subject of Mr. Godfrey – that the all-profaning opinion of the world has charged him with having his own private reasons for releasing Rachel from her engagement, at the first opportunity she gave him. It has also reached my ears, that his anxiety to recover his place in my estimation has been attributed, in certain quarters, to a mercenary eagerness to make his peace (through me) with a venerable committee-woman at the Mothers'-Small-Clothes, abundantly blessed with the goods of this world, and a beloved and intimate friend of my own. I only notice these odious slanders for the sake of declaring that they never had a moment's influence on my mind. In obedience to my instructions, I have exhibited the fluctuations in my opinion of our Christian Hero, exactly as I find them recorded in my diary. In justice to myself, let me here add that, once reinstated in his place in my estimation, my gifted friend never lost that place again. I write with the tears in my eyes, burning to say more. But no – I am cruelly limited to my actual experience of persons and things. In less than a month from the time of which I am now writing, events in the money-market (which diminished even *my* miserable little income) forced me into foreign exile, and left me with nothing but a loving remembrance of Mr. Godfrey which the slander of the world has assailed, and assailed in vain.

Let me dry my eyes, and return to my narrative.

I went downstairs to luncheon, naturally anxious to see how Rachel was affected by her release from her marriage engagement.

It appeared to me – but I own I am a poor authority in such matters – that the recovery of her freedom had set her thinking again of that other man whom she loved, and that she was furious with herself for not being able to control a revulsion of feeling of which she was secretly ashamed. Who was the man? I had my suspicions – but it was needless to waste time in idle speculation. When I had converted her, she would, as a matter of course, have no concealments from Me. I should hear all about the man; I should hear all about the Moonstone. If I had had no higher object in stirring her up to a sense of spiritual things, the motive of relieving her mind of its guilty secrets would have been enough of itself to encourage me to go on.

Aunt Ablewhite took her exercise in the afternoon in an invalid chair. Rachel accompanied her. "I wish I could drag the chair," she broke out, recklessly. "I wish I could fatigue myself till I was ready to drop."

She was in the same humour in the evening. I discovered in one of my friend's precious publications – the *Life, Letters, and Labours of Miss*

Jane Ann Stamper, forty-fourth edition – passages which bore with a marvellous appropriateness on Rachel's present position. Upon my proposing to read them, she went to the piano. Conceive how little she must have known of serious people, if she supposed that my patience was to be exhausted in that way! I kept Miss Jane Ann Stamper by me, and waited for events with the most unfaltering trust in the future.

Old Mr. Ablewhite never made his appearance that night. But I knew the importance which his worldly greed attached to his son's marriage with Miss Verinder – and I felt a positive conviction (do what Mr. Godfrey might to prevent it) that we should see him the next day. With his interference in the matter, the storm on which I had counted would certainly come, and the salutary exhaustion of Rachel's resisting powers would as certainly follow. I am not ignorant that old Mr. Ablewhite has the reputation generally (especially among his inferiors) of being a remarkably good-natured man. According to my observation of him, he deserves his reputation as long as he has his own way, and not a moment longer.

The next day, exactly as I had foreseen, Aunt Ablewhite was as near to being astonished as her nature would permit, by the sudden appearance of her husband. He had barely been a minute in the house, before he was followed, to *my* astonishment this time, by an unexpected complication, in the shape of Mr. Bruff.

I never remember feeling the presence of the lawyer to be more unwelcome than I felt it at that moment. He looked ready for anything in the way of an obstructive proceeding – capable even of keeping the peace, with Rachel for one of the combatants!

"This is a pleasant surprise, sir," said Mr. Ablewhite, addressing himself with his deceptive cordiality to Mr. Bruff. "When I left your office yesterday, I didn't expect to have the honour of seeing you at Brighton to-day."

"I turned over our conversation in my mind, after you had gone," replied Mr. Bruff. "And it occurred to me that I might perhaps be of some use on this occasion. I was just in time to catch the train, and I had no opportunity of discovering the carriage in which you were travelling."

Having given that explanation he seated himself by Rachel. I retired modestly to a corner – with Miss Jane Ann Stamper on my lap, in case of emergency. My aunt sat at the window, placidly fanning herself as usual. Mr. Ablewhite stood up in the middle of the room, with his bald head much pinker than I had ever seen it yet, and addressed himself in the most affectionate manner to his niece.

"Rachel, my dear," he said, "I have heard some very extraordinary news from Godfrey. And I am here to inquire about it. You have a sitting-room of your own in this house. Will you honour me by showing me the way to it?"

Rachel never moved. Whether she was determined to bring matters to a crisis, or whether she was prompted by some private sign from Mr. Bruff, is more than I can tell. She declined doing old Mr. Ablewhite the honour of conducting him into her sitting-room.

"Whatever you wish to say to me," she answered, "can be said here – in the presence of my relatives, and in the presence" (she looked at Mr. Bruff) "of my mother's trusted old friend."

"Just as you please, my dear," said the amiable Mr. Ablewhite. He took a chair. The rest of them looked at his face – as if they expected it, after seventy years of worldly training, to speak the truth. *I* looked at the top of his bald head; having noticed on other occasions that the temper which was really in him had a habit of registering itself *there*.

"Some weeks ago," pursued the old gentleman, "my son informed me that Miss Verinder had done him the honour to engage herself to marry him. Is it possible, Rachel, that he can have misinterpreted – or presumed upon – what you really said to him?"

"Certainly not," she replied. "I did engage myself to marry him."

"Very frankly answered!" said Mr. Ablewhite. "And most satisfactory, my dear, so far. In respect to what happened some weeks since, Godfrey has made no mistake. The error is evidently in what he told me yesterday. I begin to see it now. You and he have had a lovers' quarrel – and my foolish son has interpreted it seriously. Ah! I should have known better than that at his age."

The fallen nature in Rachel – the mother Eve, so to speak – began to chafe at this.

"Pray let us understand each other, Mr. Ablewhite," she said. "Nothing in the least like a quarrel took place yesterday between your son and me. If he told you that I proposed breaking off our marriage engagement, and that he agreed on his side – he told you the truth."

The self-registering thermometer at the top of Mr. Ablewhite's bald head began to indicate a rise of temper. His face was more amiable than ever – but *there* was the pink at the top of his face, a shade deeper already!

"Come, come, my dear!" he said, in his most soothing manner, "now don't be angry, and don't be hard on poor Godfrey! He has evidently said some unfortunate thing. He was always clumsy from a child – but he means well, Rachel, he means well!"

"Mr. Ablewhite, I have either expressed myself very badly, or you are purposely mistaking me. Once for all, it is a settled thing between your son and myself that we remain, for the rest of our lives, cousins and nothing more. Is that plain enough?"

The tone in which she said those words made it impossible, even for old Mr. Ablewhite, to mistake her any longer. His thermometer went up another degree, and his voice when he next spoke ceased to be the voice which is appropriate to a notoriously good-natured man.

"I am to understand, then," he said, "that your marriage engagement is broken off?"

"You are to understand that, Mr. Ablewhite, if you please."

"I am also to take it as a matter of fact that the proposal to withdraw from the engagement came, in the first instance, from *you*?"

"It came, in the first instance, from me. And it met, as I have told you, with your son's consent and approval."

The thermometer went up to the top of the register. I mean, the pink changed suddenly to scarlet.

"My son is a mean-spirited hound!" cried this furious old worldling. "In justice to myself as his father – not in justice to *him* – I beg to ask you, Miss Verinder, what complaint you have to make of Mr. Godfrey Ablewhite?"

Here Mr. Bruff interfered for the first time.

"You are not bound to answer that question," he said to Rachel.

Old Mr. Ablewhite fastened on him instantly.

"Don't forget, sir," he said, "that you are a self-invited guest here. Your interference would have come with a better grace if you had waited until it was asked for."

Mr. Bruff took no notice. The smooth varnish on *his* wicked old face never cracked. Rachel thanked him for the advice he had given to her, and then turned to old Mr. Ablewhite – preserving her composure in a manner which (having regard to her age and her sex) was simply awful to see.

"Your son put the same question to me which you have just asked," she said. "I had only one answer for him, and I have only one answer for you. I proposed that we should release each other, because reflection had convinced me that I should best consult his welfare and mine by retracting a rash promise, and leaving him free to make his choice elsewhere."

"What has my son done?" persisted Mr. Ablewhite. "I have a right to know that. What has my son done?"

She persisted just as obstinately on her side.

"You have had the only explanation which I think it necessary to give to you, or to him," she answered.

"In plain English, it's your sovereign will and pleasure, Miss Verinder, to jilt my son?"

Rachel was silent for a moment. Sitting close behind her, I heard her sigh. Mr. Bruff took her hand, and gave it a little squeeze. She recovered herself, and answered Mr. Ablewhite as boldly as ever.

"I have exposed myself to worse misconstruction than that," she said. "And I have borne it patiently. The time has gone by, when you could mortify me by calling me a jilt."

She spoke with a bitterness of tone which satisfied me that the scandal of the Moonstone had been in some way recalled to her mind. "I have no more to say," she added, wearily, not addressing the words to anyone in particular, and looking away from us all, out of the window that was nearest to her.

Mr. Ablewhite got upon his feet, and pushed away his chair so violently that it toppled over and fell on the floor.

"I have something more to say on my side," he announced, bringing down the flat of his hand on the table with a bang. "I have to say that if my son doesn't feel this insult, I do!"

Rachel started, and looked at him in sudden surprise.

"Insult?" she repeated. "What do you mean?"

"Insult!" reiterated Mr. Ablewhite. "I know your motive, Miss Verinder, for breaking your promise to my son! I know it as certainly as if you had confessed it in so many words. Your cursed family pride is insulting Godfrey, as it insulted *me* when I married your aunt. Her family – her beggarly family – turned their backs on her for marrying an honest man, who had made his own place and won his own fortune. I had no ancestors. I wasn't descended from a set of cut-throat scoundrels who lived by robbery and murder. I couldn't point to the time when the Ablewhites hadn't a shirt to their backs, and couldn't sign their own names. Ha! ha! I wasn't good enough for the Herncastles, when *I* married. And, now it comes to the pinch, my son isn't good enough for *you*. I suspected it all along. You have got the Herncastle blood in you, my young lady! I suspected it all along."

"A very unworthy suspicion," remarked Mr. Bruff. "I am astonished that you have the courage to acknowledge it."

Before Mr. Ablewhite could find words to answer in, Rachel spoke in a tone of the most exasperating contempt.

"Surely," she said to the lawyer, "this is beneath notice. If he can think in *that* way, let us leave him to think as he pleases."

From scarlet, Mr. Ablewhite was now becoming purple. He gasped for breath; he looked backwards and forwards from Rachel to Mr. Bruff in such a frenzy of rage with both of them that he didn't know which to attack first. His wife, who had sat impenetrably fanning herself up to this time, began to be alarmed, and attempted, quite uselessly, to quiet him. I had, throughout this distressing interview, felt more than one inward call to interfere with a few earnest words, and had controlled myself under a dread of the possible results, very unworthy of a Christian Englishwoman who looks, not to what is merely prudent, but to what is morally right. At the point at which matters had now arrived, I rose superior to all considerations of mere expediency. If I had contemplated interposing any remonstrance of my own humble devising, I might possibly have still hesitated. But the distressing domestic emergency which now confronted me was most marvellously and beautifully provided for in the Correspondence of Miss Jane Ann Stamper – Letter one thousand and one, on "Peace in Families." I rose in my modest corner, and I opened my precious book.

"Dear Mr. Ablewhite," I said, "one word!"

When I first attracted the attention of the company by rising, I could see that he was on the point of saying something rude to me. My sisterly form of address checked him. He stared at me in heathen astonishment.

"As an affectionate well-wisher and friend," I proceeded, "and as one long accustomed to arouse, convince, prepare, enlighten, and fortify others, permit me to take the most pardonable of all liberties – the liberty of composing your mind."

He began to recover himself; he was on the point of breaking out – he *would* have broken out, with anybody else. But my voice (habitually gentle) possesses a high note or so, in emergencies. In this emergency, I felt imperatively called upon to have the highest voice of the two.

I held up my precious book before him; I rapped the open page impressively with my forefinger. "Not my words!" I exclaimed, in a burst of fervent interruption. "Oh, don't suppose that I claim attention for My humble words! Manna in the wilderness, Mr. Ablewhite! Dew on the parched earth! Words of comfort, words of wisdom, words of love – the blessed, blessed, blessed words of Miss Jane Ann Stamper!"

I was stopped there by a momentary impediment of the breath. Before I could recover myself, this monster in human form shouted out furiously:

"Miss Jane Ann Stamper be – !"

It is impossible for me to write the awful word, which is here represented by a blank. I shrieked as it passed his lips; I flew to my little bag on the side table; I shook out all my tracts; I seized the one particular tract on profane swearing, entitled, "Hush, for Heaven's Sake!"; I handed it to him with an expression of agonized entreaty. He tore it in two, and threw it back at me across the table. The rest of them rose in alarm, not knowing what might happen next. I instantly sat down again in my corner. There had once been an occasion, under somewhat similar circumstances, when Miss Jane Ann Stamper had been taken by the two shoulders and turned out of a room. I waited, inspired by *her* spirit, for a repetition of *her* martyrdom.

But no – it was not to be. His wife was the next person whom he addressed. "Who – who – who," he said, stammering with rage, "asked this impudent fanatic into the house? Did you?"

Before Aunt Ablewhite could say a word, Rachel answered for her. "Miss Clack is here," she said, "as my guest."

Those words had a singular effect on Mr. Ablewhite. They suddenly changed him from a man in a state of red-hot anger to a man in a state of icy-cold contempt. It was plain to everybody that Rachel had said something – short and plain as her answer had been – which gave him the upper hand of her at last.

"Oh?" he said. "Miss Clack is here as *your* guest – in *my* house?"

It was Rachel's turn to lose her temper at that. Her colour rose, and her eyes brightened fiercely. She turned to the lawyer, and, pointing to Mr. Ablewhite, asked haughtily, "What does he mean?"

Mr. Bruff interfered for the third time.

"You appear to forget," he said, addressing Mr. Ablewhite, "that you took this house as Miss Verinder's guardian, for Miss Verinder's use."

"Not quite so fast," interposed Mr. Ablewhite. "I have a last word to say, which I should have said some time since, if this" – he looked my way, pondering what abominable name he should call me – "if this Rampant Spinster had not interrupted us. I beg to inform you, sir, that, if my son is not good enough to be Miss Verinder's husband, I cannot presume to consider his father good enough to be Miss Verinder's guardian. Understand, if you please, that I refuse to accept the position which is offered to me by Lady Verinder's Will. In your legal phrase, I decline to act. This house has necessarily been hired in my name. I take the entire responsibility of it on my shoulders. It is my house. I can keep it, or let it, just as I please. I have no wish to hurry Miss Verinder. On the contrary, I beg her to remove her guest and her luggage, at her own entire convenience." He made a low bow, and walked out of the room.

That was Mr. Ablewhite's revenge on Rachel, for refusing to marry his son!

The instant the door closed, Aunt Ablewhite exhibited a phenomenon which silenced us all. She became endowed with energy enough to cross the room!

"My dear," she said, taking Rachel by the hand, "I should be ashamed of my husband, if I didn't know that it is his temper which has spoken to you, and not himself. You," continued Aunt Ablewhite, turning on me in my corner with another endowment of energy, in her looks this time instead of her limbs – "you are the mischievous person who irritated him. I hope I shall never see you or your tracts again." She went back to Rachel and kissed her. "I beg your pardon, my dear," she said, "in my husband's name. What can I do for you?"

Consistently perverse in everything – capricious and unreasonable in all the actions of her life – Rachel melted into tears at those commonplace words, and returned her aunt's kiss in silence.

"If I may be permitted to answer for Miss Verinder," said Mr. Bruff, "might I ask you, Mrs. Ablewhite, to send Penelope down with her mistress's bonnet and shawl. Leave us ten minutes together," he added, in a lower tone, "and you may rely on my setting matters right, to your satisfaction as well as to Rachel's."

The trust of the family in this man was something wonderful to see. Without a word more, on her side, Aunt Ablewhite left the room.

"Ah!" said Mr. Bruff, looking after her. "The Herncastle blood has its drawbacks, I admit. But there *is* something in good breeding after all!"

Having made that purely worldly remark, he looked hard at my corner, as if he expected me to go. My interest in Rachel – an infinitely higher interest than his – riveted me to my chair.

Mr. Bruff gave it up, exactly as he had given it up at Aunt Verinder's, in Montagu Square. He led Rachel to a chair by the window, and spoke to her there.

"My dear young lady," he said, "Mr. Ablewhite's conduct has naturally shocked you, and taken you by surprise. If it was worth while to contest the question with such a man, we might soon show him that he is not to have things all his own way. But it isn't worth while. You were quite right in what you said just now; he is beneath our notice."

He stopped, and looked round at my corner. I sat there quite immovable, with my tracts at my elbow, and with Miss Jane Ann Stamper on my lap.

"You know," he resumed, turning back again to Rachel, "that it was part of your poor mother's fine nature always to see the best of the people about her, and never the worst. She named her brother-in-law your guardian because she believed in him, and because she thought it would please her sister. I had never liked Mr. Ablewhite myself, and I induced your mother to let me insert a clause in the Will, empowering her executors, in certain events, to consult with me about the appointment of a new guardian. One of those events has happened to-day; and I find myself in a position to end all these dry business details, I hope agreeably, with a message from my wife. Will you honour Mrs. Bruff by becoming her guest? And will you remain under my roof, and be one of my family, until we wise people have laid our heads together, and have settled what is to be done next?"

At those words, I rose to interfere. Mr. Bruff had done exactly what I had dreaded he would do, when he asked Mrs. Ablewhite for Rachel's bonnet and shawl.

Before I could interpose a word, Rachel had accepted his invitation in the warmest terms. If I suffered the arrangement thus made between them to be carried out – if she once passed the threshold of Mr. Bruff's door – farewell to the fondest hope of my life, the hope of bringing my lost sheep back to the fold! The bare idea of such a calamity as this quite overwhelmed me. I cast the miserable trammels of worldly discretion to the winds, and spoke with the fervour that filled me, in the words that came first.

"Stop!" I said – "stop! I must be heard. Mr. Bruff! you are not related to her, and I am. *I* invite her – I summon the executors to appoint *me* guardian. Rachel, dearest Rachel, I offer you my modest home; come to London by the next train, love, and share it with me!"

Mr. Bruff said nothing. Rachel looked at me with a cruel astonishment which she made no effort to conceal.

"You are very kind, Drusilla," she said. "I shall hope to visit you whenever I happen to be in London. But I have accepted Mr. Bruff's invitation, and I think it will be best, for the present, if I remain under Mr. Bruff's care."

"Oh, don't say so!" I pleaded. "I can't part with you, Rachel, – I can't part with you!"

I tried to fold her in my arms. But she drew back. My fervour did not communicate itself; it only alarmed her.

"Surely," she said, "this is a very unnecessary display of agitation? I don't understand it."

"No more do I," said Mr. Bruff.

Their hardness – their hideous, worldly hardness – revolted me.

"Oh, Rachel! Rachel!" I burst out. "Haven't you seen *yet*, that my heart yearns to make a Christian of you? Has no inner voice told you that I am trying to do for *you*, what I was trying to do for your dear mother when death snatched her out of my hands?"

Rachel advanced a step nearer, and looked at me very strangely.

"I don't understand your reference to my mother," she said. "Miss Clack, will you have the goodness to explain yourself?"

Before I could answer, Mr. Bruff came forward, and offering his arm to Rachel, tried to lead her out of the room.

"You had better not pursue the subject, my dear," he said. "And Miss Clack had better not explain herself."

If I had been a stock or a stone, such an interference as this must have roused me into testifying to the truth. I put Mr. Bruff aside indignantly with my own hand, and, in solemn and suitable language, I stated the view with which sound doctrine does not scruple to regard the awful calamity of dying unprepared.

Rachel started back from me – I blush to write it – with a scream of horror.

"Come away!" she said to Mr. Bruff. "Come away, for God's sake, before that woman can say any more! Oh, think of my poor mother's harmless, useful, beautiful life! You were at the funeral, Mr. Bruff; you saw how everybody loved her; you saw the poor helpless people crying at her grave over the loss of their best friend. And that wretch stands there, and tries to make me doubt that my mother, who was an angel on earth, is an angel in heaven now! Don't stop to talk about it! Come away! It stifles me to breathe the same air with her! It frightens me to feel that we are in the same room together!"

Deaf to all remonstrance, she ran to the door.

At the same moment, her maid entered with her bonnet and shawl. She huddled them on anyhow. "Pack my things," she said, "and bring them to Mr. Bruff's." I attempted to approach her – I was shocked and grieved, but, it is needless to say, not offended. I only wished to say to her, "May your hard heart be softened! I freely forgive you!" She pulled down her veil, and tore her shawl away from my hand, and, hurrying out, shut the door in my face. I bore the insult with my customary fortitude. I remember it now with my customary superiority to all feeling of offence.

Mr. Bruff had his parting word of mockery for me, before he too hurried out, in his turn.

"You had better not have explained yourself, Miss Clack," he said, and bowed, and left the room.

The person with the cap-ribbons followed.

"It's easy to see who has set them all by the ears together," she said. "I'm only a poor servant – but I declare I'm ashamed of you!" She too went out, and banged the door after her.I was left alone in the room. Reviled by them all, deserted by them all, I was left alone in the room.

Is there more to be added to this plain statement of facts – to this touching picture of a Christian persecuted by the world? No! My diary reminds me that one more of the many chequered chapters in my life ends here. From that day forth, I never saw Rachel Verinder again. She had my forgiveness at the time when she insulted me. She has had my prayerful good wishes ever since. And when I die – to complete the return on my part of good for evil – she will have the *Life, Letters, and Labours of Miss Jane Ann Stamper* left her as a legacy by my Will.

★

SECOND NARRATIVE

Contributed by MATTHEW BRUFF, *Solicitor, of Gray's Inn Square*[1]

CHAPTER I

My fair friend, Miss Clack, having laid down the pen, there are two reasons for my taking it up next, in my turn.

In the first place, I am in a position to throw the necessary light on certain points of interest which have thus far been left in the dark. Miss Verinder had her own private reason for breaking her marriage engagement – and I was at the bottom of it. Mr. Godfrey Ablewhite had his own private reason for withdrawing all claim to the hand of his charming cousin – and I discovered what it was.

In the second place, it was my good or ill fortune, I hardly know which, to find myself personally involved – at the period of which I am now writing – in the mystery of the Indian Diamond. I had the honour of an interview, at my own office, with an Oriental stranger of distinguished manners, who was no other, unquestionably, than the chief of the three Indians. Add to this, that I met with the celebrated traveller, Mr. Murthwaite, the day afterwards, and that I held a conversation with him on the subject of the Moonstone, which has a very important bearing on later events. And there you have the statement of my claims to fill the position which I occupy in these pages.

The true story of the broken marriage engagement comes first in point of time, and must therefore take the first place in the present narrative. Tracing my way back along the chain of events, from one end to the other, I find it necessary to open the scene, oddly enough as you will think, at the bedside of my excellent client and friend, the late Sir John Verinder.

Sir John had his share – perhaps rather a large share – of the more harmless and amiable of the weaknesses incidental to humanity. Among these, I may mention as applicable to the matter in hand, an invincible reluctance – so long as he enjoyed his usual good health – to face the responsibility of making his Will. Lady Verinder exerted

---

1   One of the four Inns of Court, Gray's Inn was located near the western boundaries of the City. For the most part, the Inns housed law offices.

her influence to rouse him to a sense of duty in this matter; and I exerted my influence. He admitted the justice of our views – but he went no further than that, until he found himself afflicted with the illness which ultimately brought him to his grave. Then I was sent for at last, to take my client's instructions on the subject of his Will. They proved to be the simplest instructions I had ever received in the whole of my professional career.

Sir John was dozing, when I entered the room. He roused himself at the sight of me.

"How do you do, Mr. Bruff?" he said. "I shan't be very long about this. And then I'll go to sleep again." He looked on with great interest while I collected pens, ink, and paper. "Are you ready?" he asked. I bowed, and took a dip of ink, and waited for my instructions.

"I leave everything to my wife," said Sir John. "That's all." He turned round on his pillow, and composed himself to sleep again.

I was obliged to disturb him.

"Am I to understand," I asked, "that you leave the whole of the property, of every sort and description, of which you die possessed, absolutely to Lady Verinder?"

"Yes," said Sir John. "Only, *I* put it shorter. Why can't *you* put it shorter, and let me go to sleep again? Everything to my wife. That's my Will."

His property was entirely at his own disposal, and was of two kinds. Property in land (I purposely abstain from using technical language), and property in money. In the majority of cases, I am afraid I should have felt it my duty to my client to ask him to reconsider his Will. In the case of Sir John, I knew Lady Verinder to be, not only worthy of the unreserved trust which her husband had placed in her (all good wives are worthy of that) – but to be also capable of properly administering a trust (which, in my experience of the fair sex, not one in a thousand of them is competent to do). In ten minutes, Sir John's Will was drawn, and executed, and Sir John himself, good man, was finishing his interrupted nap.

Lady Verinder amply justified the confidence which her husband had placed in her. In the first days of her widowhood, she sent for me, and made her Will. The view she took of her position was so thoroughly sound and sensible, that I was relieved of all necessity for advising her. My responsibility began and ended with shaping her instructions into the proper legal form. Before Sir John had been a fortnight in his grave, the future of his daughter had been most wisely and most affectionately provided for.

The Will remained in its fireproof box at my office, through more years than I like to reckon up. It was not till the summer of eighteen hundred and forty-eight that I found occasion to look at it again under very melancholy circumstances.

At the date I have mentioned, the doctors pronounced the sentence on poor Lady Verinder, which was literally a sentence of death. I was the first person whom she informed of her situation; and I found her anxious to go over her Will again with me.

It was impossible to improve the provisions relating to her daughter. But, in the lapse of time, her wishes in regard to certain minor legacies, left to different relatives, had undergone some modification; and it became necessary to add three or four Codicils to the original document. Having done this at once, for fear of accident, I obtained her ladyship's permission to embody her recent instructions in a second Will. My object was to avoid certain inevitable confusions and repetitions which now disfigured the original document, and which, to own the truth, grated sadly on my professional sense of the fitness of things.

The execution of this second Will has been described by Miss Clack, who was so obliging as to witness it. So far as regarded Rachel Verinder's pecuniary interests, it was, word for word, the exact counterpart of the first Will. The only changes introduced related to the appointment of a guardian, and to certain provisions concerning that appointment which were made under my advice. On Lady Verinder's death, the Will was placed in the hands of my proctor to be "proved" (as the phrase is) in the usual way.[1]

In about three weeks from that time – as well as I can remember – the first warning reached me of something unusual going on under the surface. I happened to be looking in at my friend the proctor's office, and I observed that he received me with an appearance of greater interest than usual.

---

[1] Proving a Will meant obtaining a probate, or opening, publishing, and establishing its authenticity.

"I have some news for you," he said. "What do you think I heard at Doctors' Commons[1] this morning? Lady Verinder's Will has been asked for, and examined, already!"

This was news indeed! There was absolutely nothing which could be contested in the Will; and there was nobody I could think of who had the slightest interest in examining it. (I shall perhaps do well if I explain in this place, for the benefit of the few people who don't know it already, that the law allows all Wills to be examined at Doctors' Commons by anybody who applies, on the payment of a shilling fee.)

"Did your hear who asked for the Will?" I asked.

"Yes; the clerk had no hesitation in telling *me*. Mr. Smalley, of the firm of Skipp and Smalley, asked for it. The Will has not been copied yet into the great Folio Registers. So there was no alternative but to depart from the usual course, and to let him see the original document. He looked it over carefully, and made a note in his pocket-book. Have you any idea of what he wanted with it?"

I shook my head. "I shall find out," I answered, "before I am a day older." With that I went back at once to my own office.

If any other firm of solicitors had been concerned in this unaccountable examination of my deceased client's Will, I might have found some difficulty in making the necessary discovery. But I had a hold over Skipp and Smalley which made my course in this matter a comparatively easy one. My common-law clerk (a most competent and excellent man) was a brother of Mr. Smalley's; and, owing to this sort of indirect connexion with me, Skipp and Smalley had, for some years past, picked up the crumbs that fell from my table, in the shape of cases brought to my office, which, for various reasons, I did not think it worth while to undertake. My professional patronage was, in this way, of some importance to the firm. I intended, if necessary, to remind them of that patronage, on the present occasion.

The moment I got back I spoke to my clerk; and, after telling him what had happened, I sent him to his brother's office, "with Mr. Bruff's compliments, and he would be glad to know why Messrs. Skipp and Smalley had found it necessary to examine Lady Verinder's

---

1 The Doctors' Commons is the colloquial name for the College of Advocates and Doctors of Law located near St. Paul's Cathedral. Wills and marriage licences were stored here for scrutiny by the public. The Society broke up in 1858, and the building was razed in 1867.

Will."

This message brought Mr. Smalley back to my office, in company with his brother. He acknowledged that he had acted under instructions received from a client. And then he put it to me, whether it would not be a breach of professional confidence on his part to say more.

We had a smart discussion upon that. He was right, no doubt; and I was wrong. The truth is, I was angry and suspicious – and I insisted on knowing more. Worse still, I declined to consider any additional information offered me, as a secret placed in my keeping: I claimed perfect freedom to use my own discretion. Worse even than that, I took an unwarrantable advantage of my position. "Choose, sir," I said to Mr. Smalley, "between the risk of losing your client's business and the risk of losing Mine." Quite indefensible, I admit – an act of tyranny, and nothing else. Like other tyrants, I carried my point. Mr. Smalley chose his alternative, without a moment's hesitation. He smiled resignedly, and gave up the name of his client:

Mr. Godfrey Ablewhite.

That was good enough for me – I wanted to know no more.

Having reached this point in my narrative, it now becomes necessary to place the reader of these lines – so far as Lady Verinder's Will is concerned – on a footing of perfect equality, in respect of information, with myself.

Let me state, then, in the fewest possible words, that Rachel Verinder had nothing but a life-interest in the property. Her mother's excellent sense, and my long experience, had combined to relieve her of all responsibility, and to guard her from all danger of becoming the victim in the future of some needy and unscrupulous man. Neither she, nor her husband (if she married), could raise sixpence, either on the property in land, or on the property in money. They would have the houses in London and in Yorkshire to live in, and they would have the handsome income – and that was all.

When I came to think over what I had discovered, I was sorely perplexed what to do next.

Hardly a week had passed since I had heard (to my surprise and distress) of Miss Verinder's proposed marriage. I had the sincerest admiration and affection for her; and I had been inexpressibly grieved when I heard that she was about to throw herself away on Mr. Godfrey Ablewhite. And now, here was the man – whom I had always believed to be a smooth-tongued impostor – justifying the very worst that I had thought of him, and plainly revealing the mercenary object of the marriage, on his side! And what of that? – you may reply – the thing is done every day. Granted, my dear sir. But would you think of it quite as lightly as you do, if the thing was done (let us say) with your own sister?

The first consideration which now naturally occurred to me was this. Would Mr. Godfrey Ablewhite hold to his engagement, after what his lawyer had discovered for him?

It depended entirely on his pecuniary position, of which I knew nothing. If that position was not a desperate one, it would be well worth his while to marry Miss Verinder for her income alone. If, on the other hand, he stood in urgent need of realising a large sum by a given time, then Lady Verinder's Will would exactly meet the case, and would preserve her daughter from falling into a scoundrel's hands.

In the latter event, there would be no need for me to distress Miss Rachel, in the first days of her mourning for her mother, by an immediate revelation of the truth. In the former event, if I remained silent, I should be conniving at a marriage which would make her miserable for life.

My doubts ended in my calling at the hotel in London, at which I knew Mrs. Ablewhite and Miss Verinder to be staying. They informed me that they were going to Brighton the next day, and that an unexpected obstacle prevented Mr. Godfrey Ablewhite from accompanying them. I at once proposed to take his place. While I was only thinking of Rachel Verinder, it was possible to hesitate. When I actually saw her, my mind was made up directly, come what might of it, to tell her the truth.

I found my opportunity, when I was out walking with her, on the day after my arrival.

"May I speak to you," I asked, "about your marriage engagement?"

"Yes," she said, indifferently, "if you have nothing more interesting to talk about."

"Will you forgive an old friend and servant of your family, Miss

Rachel, if I venture on asking whether your heart is set on this marriage?"

"I am marrying in despair, Mr. Bruff – on the chance of dropping into some sort of stagnant happiness which may reconcile me to my life."

Strong language! and suggestive of something below the surface, in the shape of a romance. But I had my own object in view, and I declined (as we lawyers say) to pursue the question into its side issues.

"Mr. Godfrey Ablewhite can hardly be of your way of thinking," I said. "*His* heart must be set on the marriage at any rate?"

"He says so, and I suppose I ought to believe him. He would hardly marry me, after what I have owned to him, unless he was fond of me."

Poor thing! The bare idea of a man marrying her for his own selfish and mercenary ends had never entered her head. The task I had set myself began to look like a harder task than I had bargained for.

"It sounds strangely," I went on, "in my old-fashioned ears –"

"What sounds strangely?" she asked.

"To hear you speak of your future husband as if you were not quite sure of the sincerity of his attachment. Are you conscious of any reason in your own mind for doubting him?"

Her astonishing quickness of perception detected a change in my voice, or my manner, when I put that question, which warned her that I had been speaking all along with some ulterior object in view. She stopped, and taking her arm out of mine, looked me searchingly in the face.

"Mr. Bruff," she said, "you have something to tell me about Godfrey Ablewhite. Tell it."

I knew her well enough to take her at her word. I told it.

She put her arm again into mine, and walked on with me slowly. I felt her hand tightening its grasp mechanically on my arm, and I saw her getting paler and paler as I went on – but, not a word passed her lips while I was speaking. When I had done, she still kept silence. Her head drooped a little, and she walked by my side, unconscious of my presence, unconscious of everything about her; lost – buried, I might almost say – in her own thoughts.

I made no attempt to disturb her. My experience of her disposition warned me, on this, as on former occasions, to give her time.

The first instinct of girls in general, on being told of anything which interests them, is to ask a multitude of questions, and then to run off, and talk it all over with some favourite friend. Rachel Verinder's first instinct, under similar circumstances, was to shut herself up in her own mind, and to think it over by herself. This absolute self-dependence is a great virtue in a man. In a woman it has the serious drawback of morally separating her from the mass of her sex, and so exposing her to misconstruction by the general opinion. I strongly suspect myself of thinking as the rest of the world think in this matter – except in the case of Rachel Verinder. The self-dependence in *her* character was one of its virtues in my estimation; partly, no doubt, because I sincerely admired and liked her; partly because the view I took of her connexion with the loss of the Moonstone was based on my own special knowledge of her disposition. Badly as appearances might look, in the matter of the Diamond – shocking as it undoubtedly was to know that she was associated in any way with the mystery of an undiscovered theft – I was satisfied nevertheless that she had done nothing unworthy of her, because I was also satisfied that she had not stirred a step in the business, without shutting herself up in her own mind, and thinking it over first.

We had walked on, for nearly a mile I should say, before Rachel roused herself. She suddenly looked up at me with a faint reflection of her smile of happier times – the most irresistible smile I have ever seen on a woman's face.

"I owe much already to your kindness," she said. "And I feel more deeply indebted to it now than ever. If you hear any rumours of my marriage when you get back to London, contradict them at once, on my authority."

"Have you resolved to break your engagement?" I asked.

"Can you doubt it?" she returned proudly, "after what you have told me!"

"My dear Miss Rachel, you are very young – and you may find more difficulty in withdrawing from your present position than you anticipate. Have you no one – I mean a lady, of course – whom you could consult?"

"No one," she answered.

It distressed me, it did indeed distress me, to hear her say that. She was so young and so lonely – and she bore it so well! The impulse to help her got the better of any sense of my own unfitness which I might have felt under the circumstances; and I stated such ideas on the subject as occurred to me on the spur of the moment, to the best of my ability. I have advised a prodigious number of clients, and have dealt with some exceedingly awkward difficulties, in my time. But this was the first occasion on which I had ever found myself advising a young lady how to obtain her release from a marriage engagement. The suggestion I offered amounted briefly to this. I recommended her to tell Mr. Godfrey Ablewhite – at a private interview, of course – that he had, to her certain knowledge, betrayed the mercenary nature of the motive on his side. She was then to add that their marriage, after what she had discovered, was a simple impossibility – and she was to put it to him, whether he thought it wisest to secure her silence by falling in with her views, or to force her, by opposing them, to make the motive under which she was acting generally known. If he attempted to defend himself, or to deny the facts, she was, in that event, to refer him to *me*.

Miss Verinder listened attentively till I had done. She then thanked me very prettily for my advice, but informed me at the same time that it was impossible for her to follow it.

"May I ask," I said, "what objection you see to following it?"

She hesitated – and then met me with a question on her side.

"Suppose you were asked to express your opinion of Mr. Godfrey Ablewhite's conduct?" she began.

"Yes?"

"What would you call it?"

"I should call it the conduct of a meanly deceitful man."

"Mr. Bruff! I have believed in that man. I have promised to marry that man. How can I tell him he is mean, how can I tell him he has deceived me, how can I disgrace him in the eyes of the world after that? I have degraded myself by ever thinking of him as my husband. If I say what you tell me to say to him – I am owning that I have degraded myself to his face. I can't do that. After what has passed between us, I can't do that! The shame of it would be nothing to *him*. But the shame of it would be unendurable to *me*."

Here was another of the marked peculiarities in her character disclosing itself to me without reserve. Here was her sensitive horror of the bare contact with anything mean, blinding her to every consideration of what she owed to herself, hurrying her into a false position which might compromise her in the estimation of all her friends! Up to this time, I had been a little diffident about the propriety of the advice I had given to her. But, after what she had just said, I had no sort of doubt that it was the best advice that could have been offered; and I felt no sort of hesitation in pressing it on her again.

She only shook her head, and repeated her objection in other words.

"He has been intimate enough with me to ask me to be his wife. He has stood high enough in my estimation to obtain my consent. I can't tell him to his face that he is the most contemptible of living creatures, after that!"

"But, my dear Miss Rachel," I remonstrated, "it's equally impossible for you to tell him that you withdraw from your engagement without giving some reason for it."

"I shall say that I have thought it over, and that I am satisfied it will be best for both of us if we part."

"No more than that?"

"No more."

"Have you thought of what he may say, on his side?"

"He may say what he pleases."

It was impossible not to admire her delicacy and her resolution, and it was equally impossible not to feel that she was putting herself in the wrong. I entreated her to consider her own position. I reminded her that she would be exposing herself to the most odious misconstruction of her motives. "You can't brave public opinion," I said, "at the command of private feeling."

"I can," she answered. "I have done it already."

"What do you mean?"

"You have forgotten the Moonstone, Mr. Bruff. Have I not braved public opinion, *there*, with my own private reasons for it?"

Her answer silenced me for the moment. It set me trying to trace the explanation of her conduct, at the time of the loss of the Moonstone, out of the strange avowal which had just escaped her. I might perhaps have done it when I was younger. I certainly couldn't do it now.

I tried a last remonstrance before we returned to the house. She was just as immovable as ever. My mind was in a strange conflict of feelings about her when I left her that day. She was obstinate; she was wrong. She was interesting; she was admirable; she was deeply to be pitied. I made her promise to write to me the moment she had any news to send. And I went back to my business in London, with a mind exceedingly ill at ease.

On the evening of my return, before it was possible for me to receive my promised letter, I was surprised by a visit from Mr. Ablewhite the elder, and was informed that Mr. Godfrey had got his dismissal – *and had accepted it* – that very day.

With the view I already took of the case, the bare fact, stated in the words that I have underlined, revealed Mr. Godfrey Ablewhite's motive for submission as plainly as if he had acknowledged it himself. He needed a large sum of money; and he needed it by a given time. Rachel's income, which would have helped him to anything else, would not help him here; and Rachel had accordingly released herself, without encountering a moment's serious opposition on his part. If I am told that this is a mere speculation, I ask, in my turn, What other theory will account for his giving up a marriage which would have maintained him in splendour for the rest of his life?

Any exultation I might otherwise have felt at the lucky turn which things had now taken, was effectually checked by what passed at my interview with old Mr. Ablewhite.

He came, of course, to know whether I could give him any explanation of Miss Verinder's extraordinary conduct. It is needless to say that I was quite unable to afford him the information he wanted. The annoyance which I thus inflicted, following on the irritation produced by a recent interview with his son, threw Mr. Ablewhite off his guard. Both his looks and his language convinced me that Miss Verinder would find him a merciless man to deal with, when he joined the ladies at Brighton the next day.

I had a restless night, considering what I ought to do next. How my reflections ended, and how thoroughly well founded my distrust of Mr. Ablewhite proved to be, are items of information which (as I am told) have already been put tidily in their proper places, by that exemplary person, Miss Clack. I have only to add – in completion of her narrative – that Miss Verinder found the quiet and repose which she sadly needed, poor thing, in my house at Hampstead. She honoured us by making a long stay. My wife and daughters were charmed with her; and, when the executors decided on the appointment of a new guardian, I feel sincere pride and pleasure in recording that my guest and my family parted like old friends, on either side.

CHAPTER II

THE next thing I have to do, is to present such additional information as I possess on the subject of the Moonstone, or, to speak more correctly, on the subject of the Indian plot to steal the Diamond. The little that I have to tell is (as I think I have already said) of some importance, nevertheless, in respect of its bearing very remarkably on events which are still to come.

About a week or ten days after Miss Verinder had left us, one of my clerks entered the private room at my office, with a card in his hand, and informed me that a gentleman was below, who wanted to speak to me.

I looked at the card. There was a foreign name written on it, which has escaped my memory. It was followed by a line written in English at the bottom of the card, which I remember perfectly well:

"Recommended by Mr. Septimus Luker."

The audacity of a person in Mr. Luker's position presuming to recommend anybody to *me*, took me so completely by surprise, that I sat silent for the moment, wondering whether my own eyes had not deceived me. The clerk, observing my bewilderment, favoured me with the result of his own observation of the stranger who was waiting downstairs.

"He is rather a remarkable-looking man, sir. So dark in the complexion that we all set him down in the office for an Indian, or something of that sort."

Associating the clerk's idea with the line inscribed on the card in my hand, I thought it possible that the Moonstone might be at the bottom of Mr. Luker's recommendation, and of the stranger's visit at my office. To the astonishment of my clerk, I at once decided on granting an interview to the gentleman below.

In justification of the highly unprofessional sacrifice to mere curiosity which I thus made, permit me to remind anybody who may read these lines, that no living person (in England, at any rate) can claim to have had such an intimate connexion with the romance of the Indian Diamond as mine has been. I was trusted with the secret of Colonel Herncastle's plan for escaping assassination. I received the Colonel's letters, periodically reporting himself a living man. I drew his Will, leaving the Moonstone to Miss Verinder. I persuaded his executor to act, on the chance that the jewel might prove to be a valuable acquisition to the family. And, lastly, I combated Mr. Franklin Blake's scruples, and induced him to be the means of transporting the Diamond to Lady Verinder's house. If anyone can claim a prescriptive right of interest in the Moonstone, and in everything connected with it, I think it is hardly to be denied that I am the man.

The moment my mysterious client was shown in, I felt an inner conviction that I was in the presence of one of the three Indians – probably of the chief. He was carefully dressed in European costume. But his swarthy complexion, his long lithe figure, and his grave and graceful politeness of manner, were enough to betray his Oriental origin to any intelligent eyes that looked at him.

I pointed to a chair, and begged to be informed of the nature of his business with me.

After first apologising – in an excellent selection of English words – for the liberty which he had taken in disturbing me, the Indian produced a small parcel the outer covering of which was of cloth of gold. Removing this and a second wrapping of some silken fabric, he placed a little box, or casket, on my table, most beautifully and richly inlaid in jewels, on an ebony ground.

"I have come, sir," he said, "to ask you to lend me some money. And I leave this as an assurance to you that my debt will be paid back."

I pointed to his card. "And you apply to me," I rejoined, "at Mr. Luker's recommendation?"

The Indian bowed.

"May I ask how it is that Mr. Luker himself did not advance the money that you require?"

"Mr. Luker informed me, sir, that he had no money to lend."

"And so he recommended you to come to me?"

The Indian, in his turn, pointed to the card. "It is written there," he said.

Briefly answered, and thoroughly to the purpose! If the Moonstone had been in my possession, this Oriental gentleman would have murdered me, I am well aware, without a moment's hesitation. At the same time, and barring that slight drawback, I am bound to testify that he was the perfect model of a client. He might not have respected my life. But he did what none of my own countrymen had ever done, in all my experience of them – he respected my time.

"I am sorry," I said, "that you should have had the trouble of coming to me. Mr. Luker is quite mistaken in sending you here. I am trusted, like other men in my profession, with money to lend. But I never lend it to strangers, and I never lend it on such a security as you have produced."

Far from attempting, as other people would have done, to induce me to relax my own rules, the Indian only made me another bow, and wrapped up his box in its two coverings without a word of protest. He rose – this admirable assassin rose to go, the moment I had answered him!

"Will your condescension towards a stranger, excuse my asking one question," he said, "before I take my leave?"

I bowed on my side. Only one question at parting! The average in my experience was fifty.

"Supposing, sir, it had been possible (and customary) for *you* to lend me the money," he said, "in what space of time would it have been possible (and customary) for *me* to pay it back?"

"According to the usual course pursued in this country," I answered, "you would have been entitled to pay the money back (if you liked) in one year's time from the date at which it was first advanced to you."

The Indian made me a last bow, the lowest of all – and suddenly and softly walked out of the room.

It was done in a moment, in a noiseless, supple, cat-like way, which a little startled me, I own. As soon as I was composed enough to think, I arrived at one distinct conclusion in reference to the otherwise incomprehensible visitor who had favoured me with a call.

His face, voice, and manner – while I was in his company – were under such perfect control that they set all scrutiny at defiance. But he had given me one chance of looking under the smooth outer surface of him, for all that. He had not shown the slightest sign of attempting to fix anything that I had said to him in his mind, until I mentioned the time at which it was customary to permit the earliest repayment, on the part of a debtor, of money that had been advanced as a loan. When I gave him that piece of information, he looked me straight in the face, while I was speaking, for the first time. The inference I drew from this was – that he had a special purpose in asking me his last question, and a special interest in hearing my answer to it. The more carefully I reflected on what had passed between us, the more shrewdly I suspected the production of the casket, and the application for the loan, of having been mere formalities, designed to pave the way for the parting inquiry addressed to me.

I had satisfied myself of the correctness of this conclusion – and was trying to get on a step further, and penetrate the Indian's motives next – when a letter was brought to me, which proved to be from no less a person than Mr. Septimus Luker himself. He asked my pardon in terms of sickening servility, and assured me that he could explain matters to my satisfaction, if I would honour him by consenting to a personal interview.

I made another unprofessional sacrifice to mere curiosity. I honoured him by making an appointment at my office, for the next day.

Mr. Luker was, in every respect, such an inferior creature to the Indian – he was so vulgar, so ugly, so cringing, and so prosy – that he is quite unworthy of being reported, at any length, in these pages. The substance of what he had to tell me may be fairly stated as follows:

The day before I had received the visit of the Indian, Mr. Luker had been favoured with a call from that accomplished gentleman. In spite of his European disguise, Mr. Luker had instantly identified his visitor with the chief of the three Indians, who had formerly annoyed him by loitering about his house, and who had left him no alternative but to consult a magistrate. From this startling discovery he had rushed to the conclusion (naturally enough, I own) that he must certainly be in the company of one of the three men who had blindfolded him, gagged him, and robbed him of his banker's receipt. The result was that he became quite paralysed with terror, and that he firmly believed his last hour had come.

On his side, the Indian preserved the character of a perfect stranger. He produced the little casket, and made exactly the same application which he had afterwards made to me. As the speediest way of getting rid of him, Mr. Luker had at once declared that he had no money. The Indian had thereupon asked to be informed of the best and safest person to apply to for the loan he wanted. Mr. Luker had answered that the best and safest person, in such cases, was usually a respectable solicitor. Asked to name some individual of that character and profession, Mr. Luker had mentioned me – for the one simple reason that, in the extremity of his terror, mine was the first name which occurred to him. "The perspiration was pouring off me like rain, sir," the wretched creature concluded. "I didn't know what I was talking about. And I hope you'll look over it, Mr. Bruff, sir, in consideration of my having been really and truly frightened out of my wits."

I excused the fellow graciously enough. It was the readiest way of releasing myself from the sight of him. Before he left me, I detained him to make one inquiry. Had the Indian said anything noticeable, at the moment of quitting Mr. Luker's house?

Yes! The Indian had put precisely the same question to Mr. Luker, at parting, which he had put to me; receiving, of course, the same answer as the answer which I had given him.

What did it mean? Mr. Luker's explanation gave me no assistance towards solving the problem. My own unaided ingenuity, consulted next, proved quite unequal to grapple with the difficulty. I had a dinner engagement that evening; and I went upstairs, in no very genial frame of mind, little suspecting that the way to my dressing-room and the way to discovery, meant, on this particular occasion, one and the same thing.

★

CHAPTER III

THE prominent personage among the guests at the dinner-party I found to be Mr. Murthwaite.

On his appearance in England, after his wanderings, society had been greatly interested in the traveller, as a man who had passed through many dangerous adventures, and who had escaped to tell the tale. He had now announced his intention of returning to the scene of his exploits, and of penetrating into regions left still unexplored. This magnificent indifference to placing his safety in peril for the second time, revived the flagging interest of the worshippers in the hero. The law of chances was clearly against his escaping on this occasion. It is not every day that we can meet an eminent person at dinner, and feel that there is a reasonable prospect of the news of his murder being the news that we hear of him next.

When the gentlemen were left by themselves in the dining-room, I found myself sitting next to Mr. Murthwaite. The guests present being all English, it is needless to say that, as soon as the wholesome check exercised by the presence of the ladies was removed, the conversation turned on politics as a necessary result.

In respect to this all-absorbing national topic, I happen to be one of the most un-English Englishmen living. As a general rule, political talk appears to me to be of all talk the most dreary and the most profitless. Glancing at Mr. Murthwaite, when the bottles had made their first round of the table, I found that he was apparently of my way of thinking. He was doing it very dexterously – with all possible consideration for the feelings of his host – but it is not the less certain that he was composing himself for a nap. It struck me as an experiment worth attempting, to try whether a judicious allusion to the subject of the Moonstone would keep him awake, and, if it did, to see what *he* thought of the last new complication in the Indian conspiracy, as revealed in the prosaic precincts of my office.

"If I am not mistaken, Mr. Murthwaite," I began, "you were acquainted with the late Lady Verinder, and you took some interest in the strange succession of events which ended in the loss of the Moonstone?"

The eminent traveller did me the honour of waking up in an instant, and asking me who I was.

I informed him of my professional connexion with the Herncastle family, not forgetting the curious position which I had occupied towards the Colonel and his Diamond in the bygone time.

Mr. Murthwaite shifted round in his chair, so as to put the rest of the company behind him (Conservatives and Liberals alike), and concentrated his whole attention on plain Mr. Bruff, of Gray's Inn Square.

"Have you heard anything, lately, of the Indians?" he asked.

"I have every reason to believe," I answered, "that one of them had an interview with me, in my office, yesterday."

Mr. Murthwaite was not an easy man to astonish; but that last answer of mine completely staggered him. I described what had happened to Mr. Luker, and what had happened to myself, exactly as I have described it here. "It is clear that the Indian's parting inquiry had an object," I added. "Why should he be so anxious to know the time at which a borrower of money is usually privileged to pay the money back?"

"Is it possible that you don't see his motive, Mr. Bruff?"

"I am ashamed of my stupidity, Mr. Murthwaite – but I certainly don't see it."

The great traveller became quite interested in sounding the immense vacuity of my dullness to its lowest depths.

"Let me ask you one question," he said. "In what position does the conspiracy to seize the Moonstone now stand?"

"I can't say," I answered. "The Indian plot is a mystery to me."

"The Indian plot, Mr. Bruff, can only be a mystery to you, because you have never seriously examined it. Shall we run it over together, from the time when you drew Colonel Herncastle's Will, to the time when the Indian called at your office? In your position, it may be of very serious importance to the interests of Miss Verinder, that you should be able to take a clear view of this matter in case of need. Tell me, bearing that in mind, whether you will penetrate the Indian's motive for yourself? or whether you wish me to save you the trouble of making any inquiry into it?"

It is needless to say that I thoroughly appreciated the practical purpose which I now saw that he had in view, and that the first of the two alternatives was the alternative I chose.

"Very good," said Mr. Murthwaite. "We will take the question of the ages of the three Indians first. I can testify that they all look much about the same age – and you can decide for yourself, whether the man whom you saw was, or was not, in the prime of life.

Not forty, you think? My idea too. We will say not forty. Now look back to the time when Colonel Herncastle came to England, and when you were concerned in the plan he adopted to preserve his life. I don't want you to count the years. I will only say, it is clear that these present Indians, at their age, must be the successors of three other Indians (high-caste Brahmins all of them, Mr. Bruff, when they left their native country!) who followed the Colonel to these shores. Very well. These present men of ours have succeeded to the men who were here before them. If they had only done that, the matter would not have been worth inquiring into. But they have done more. They have succeeded to the organisation which their predecessors established in this country. Don't start! The organisation is a very trumpery affair, according to our ideas, I have no doubt. I should reckon it up as including the command of money; the services, when needed, of that shady sort of Englishman, who lives in the byways of foreign life in London; and, lastly, the secret sympathy of such few men of their own country, and (formerly, at least) of their own religion, as happen to be employed in ministering to some of the multitudinous wants of this great city. Nothing very formidable, as you see! But worth notice at starting, because we *may* find occasion to refer to this modest little Indian organisation as we go on. Having now cleared the ground, I am going to ask you a question; and I expect your experience to answer it. What was the event which gave the Indians their first chance of seizing the Diamond?"

I understood the allusion to my experience.

"The first chance they got," I replied, "was clearly offered to them by Colonel Herncastle's death. They would be aware of his death, I suppose, as a matter of course?"

"As a matter of course. And his death, as you say, gave them their first chance. Up to that time the Moonstone was safe in the strong-room of the bank. You drew the Colonel's Will leaving his jewel to his niece; and the Will was proved in the usual way. As a lawyer, you can be at no loss to know what course the Indians would take (under English advice) after *that*."

"They would provide themselves with a copy of the Will from Doctors' Commons," I said.

"Exactly. One or other of those shady Englishmen to whom I have alluded, would get them the copy you have described. That copy would inform them that the Moonstone was bequeathed to the daughter of Lady Verinder, and that Mr. Blake the elder, or some person appointed by him, was to place it in her hands. You will agree with me that the necessary information about persons in the position of Lady Verinder and Mr. Blake, would be perfectly easy information to obtain. The one difficulty for the Indians would be to decide, whether they should make their attempt on the Diamond when it was in course of removal from the keeping of the bank, or whether they should wait until it was taken down to Yorkshire to Lady Verinder's house. The second way would be manifestly the safest way – and there you have the explanation of the appearance of the Indians at Frizinghall, disguised as jugglers, and waiting their time. In London, it is needless to say, they had their organisation at their disposal to keep them informed of events. Two men would do it. One to follow anybody who went from Mr. Blake's house to the bank. And one to treat the lower men servants with beer, and to hear the news of the house. These commonplace precautions would readily inform them that Mr. Franklin Blake had been to the bank, and that Mr. Franklin Blake was the only person in the house who was going to visit Lady Verinder. What actually followed upon that discovery, you remember, no doubt, quite as correctly as I do."

I remembered that Franklin Blake had detected one of the spies, in the street – that he had, in consequence, advanced the time of his arrival in Yorkshire by some hours – and that (thanks to old Betteredge's excellent advice) he had lodged the Diamond in the bank at Frizinghall, before the Indians were so much as prepared to see him in the neighbourhood. All perfectly clear so far. But, the Indians being ignorant of the precaution thus taken, how was it that they had made no attempt on Lady Verinder's house (in which they must have supposed the Diamond to be) through the whole of the interval that elapsed before Rachel's birthday?

In putting this difficulty to Mr. Murthwaite, I thought it right to add that I had heard of the little boy, and the drop of ink, and the rest of it, and that any explanation based on the theory of clairvoyance was an explanation which would carry no conviction whatever with it, to *my* mind.

"Nor to mine either," said Mr. Murthwaite. "The clairvoyance in this case is simply a development of the romantic side of the Indian character. It would be a refreshment and an encouragement to those men – quite inconceivable, I grant you, to the English mind – to surround their wearisome and perilous errand in this country with a certain halo of the marvellous and the supernatural. Their boy is unquestionably a sensitive subject to the mesmeric influence – and, under that influence, he has no doubt reflected what was already in the mind of the person mesmerising him. I have tested the theory of clairvoyance – and I have never found the manifestations get beyond that point. The Indians don't investigate the matter in this way; the Indians look upon their boy as a Seer of things invisible to their eyes – and, I repeat, in that marvel they find the source of a new interest in the purpose that unites them. I only notice this as offering a curious view of human character, which must be quite new to you. We have nothing whatever to do with clairvoyance, or with mesmerism, or with anything else that is hard of belief to a practical man, in the inquiry that we are now pursuing. My object in following the Indian plot, step by step, is to trace results back, by rational means, to natural causes. Have I succeeded to your satisfaction so far?"[1]

"Not a doubt of it, Mr. Murthwaite! I am waiting, however, with some anxiety, to hear the rational explanation of the difficulty which I have just had the honour of submitting to you."

Mr. Murthwaite smiled. "It's the easiest difficulty to deal with of all," he said. "Permit me to begin by admitting your statement of the case as a perfectly correct one. The Indians were undoubtedly not aware of what Mr. Franklin Blake had done with the Diamond – for we find them making their first mistake, on the first night of Mr. Blake's arrival at his aunt's house."

"Their first mistake?" I repeated.

"Certainly! The mistake of allowing themselves to be surprised, lurking about the terrace at night, by Gabriel Betteredge. However, they had the merit of seeing for themselves that they had taken a false step – for, as you say, again, with plenty of time at their disposal, they never came near the house for weeks afterwards."

"Why, Mr. Murthwaite? That's what I want to know! Why?"

---

1 According to Sue Lonoff, Murthwaite's reassurances here represent Collins's attempt to "avoid any trace of the supernatural. The book has its share of exotic elements, but all can be logically accounted for" (187).

"Because no Indian, Mr. Bruff, ever runs an unnecessary risk. The clause you drew in Colonel Herncastle's Will, informed them (didn't it?) that the Moonstone was to pass absolutely into Miss Verinder's possession on her birthday. Very well. Tell me which was the safest course for men in their position? To make their attempt on the Diamond while it was under the control of Mr. Franklin Blake, who had shown already that he could suspect and outwit them? Or to wait till the Diamond was at the disposal of a young girl, who would innocently delight in wearing the magnificent jewel at every possible opportunity? Perhaps you want a proof that my theory is correct? Take the conduct of the Indians themselves as the proof. They appeared at the house, after waiting all these weeks, on Miss Verinder's birthday; and they were rewarded for the patient accuracy of their calculations by seeing the Moonstone in the bosom of her dress! When I heard the story of the Colonel and the Diamond, later in the evening, I felt so sure about the risk Mr. Franklin Blake had run (they would have certainly attacked him, if he had not happened to ride back to Lady Verinder's in the company of other people); and I was so strongly convinced of the worse risks still, in store for Miss Verinder, that I recommended following the Colonel's plan, and destroying the identity of the gem by having it cut into separate stones. How its extraordinary disappearance that night made my advice useless, and utterly defeated the Hindoo plot – and how all further action on the part of the Indians was paralysed the next day by their confinement in prison as rogues and vagabonds – you know as well as I do. The first act in the conspiracy closes there. Before we go on to the second, may I ask whether I have met your difficulty, with an explanation which is satisfactory to the mind of a practical man?"

It was impossible to deny that he had met my difficulty fairly; thanks to his superior knowledge of the Indian character – and thanks to his not having had hundreds of other Wills to think of since Colonel Herncastle's time!

"So far, so good," resumed Mr. Murthwaite. "The first chance the Indians had of seizing the Diamond was a chance lost, on the day when they were committed to the prison at Frizinghall. When did the second chance offer itself? The second chance offered itself – as I am in a condition to prove – while they were still in confinement."

He took out his pocket-book, and opened it at a particular leaf, before he went on.

"I was staying," he resumed, "with some friends at Frizinghall, at the time. A day or two before the Indians were set free (on a Monday, I think), the governor of the prison came to me with a letter. It had been left for the Indians by one Mrs. Macann, of whom they had hired the lodging in which they lived; and it had been delivered at Mrs. Macann's door, in ordinary course of post, on the previous morning. The prison authorities had noticed that the postmark was 'Lambeth,' and that the address on the outside, though expressed in correct English, was, in form, oddly at variance with the customary method of directing a letter. On opening it, they had found the contents to be written in a foreign language, which they rightly guessed at as Hindustani. Their object in coming to me was, of course, to have the letter translated to them. I took a copy in my pocket-book of the original, and of my translation – and there they are at your service."

He handed me the open pocket-book. The address on the letter was the first thing copied. It was all written in one paragraph, without any attempt at punctuation, thus: "To the three Indian men living with the lady called Macann at Frizinghall in Yorkshire." The Hindoo characters followed; and the English translation appeared at the end, expressed in these mysterious words:

"In the name of the Regent of the Night, whose seat is on the Antelope, whose arms embrace the four corners of the earth.

"Brothers, turn your faces to the south, and come to me in the street of many noises, which leads down to the muddy river.

"The reason is this.

"My own eyes have seen it."

There the letter ended, without either date or signature. I handed it back to Mr. Murthwaite, and owned that this curious specimen of Hindoo correspondence rather puzzled me.

"I can explain the first sentence to you," he said; "and the conduct of the Indians themselves will explain the rest. The god of the moon is represented, in the Hindoo mythology, as a four-armed deity, seated on an antelope; and one of his titles is the regent of the night. Here, then, to begin with, is something which looks suspiciously like an indirect reference to the Moonstone. Now, let us see what the Indians did, after the prison authorities had allowed them to receive their letter. On the very day when they were set free they went at once to the railway station, and took their places in the first train that started for London. We all thought it a pity at Frizinghall that their proceedings were not privately watched. But, after Lady Verinder had dismissed the police-officer, and had stopped all further inquiry into the loss of the Diamond, no one else could presume to stir in the matter. The Indians were free to go to London, and to London they went. What was the next news we heard of them, Mr. Bruff?"

"They were annoying Mr. Luker," I answered, "by loitering about the house at Lambeth."

"Did you read the report of Mr. Luker's application to the magistrate?"

"Yes."

"In the course of his statement he referred, if you remember, to a foreign workman in his employment, whom he had just dismissed on suspicion of attempted theft, and whom he also distrusted as possibly acting in collusion with the Indians who had annoyed him. The inference is pretty plain, Mr. Bruff, as to who wrote that letter which puzzled you just now, and as to which of Mr. Luker's Oriental treasures the workman had attempted to steal."

The inference (as I hastened to acknowledge) was too plain to need being pointed out. I had never doubted that the Moonstone had found its way into Mr. Luker's hands, at the time Mr. Murthwaite alluded to. My only question had been, How had the Indians discovered the circumstance? This question (the most difficult to deal with of all, as I had thought) had now received its answer, like the rest. Lawyer as I was, I began to feel that I might trust Mr. Murthwaite to lead me blindfold through the last windings of the labyrinth, along which he had guided me thus far. I paid him the compliment of telling him this, and found my little concession very graciously received.

"You shall give me a piece of information in your turn before we go on," he said. "Somebody must have taken the Moonstone from Yorkshire to London. And somebody must have raised money on it, or it would never have been in Mr. Luker's possession. Has there been any discovery made of who that person was?"

"None that I know of."

"There was a story (was there not?) about Mr. Godfrey Ablewhite. I am told he is an eminent philanthropist – which is decidedly against him, to begin with."

I heartily agreed in this with Mr. Murthwaite. At the same time, I felt bound to inform him (without, it is needless to say, mentioning Miss Verinder's name) that Mr. Godfrey Ablewhite had been cleared of all suspicion, on evidence which I could answer for as entirely beyond dispute.

"Very well," said Mr. Murthwaite quietly, "let us leave it to time to clear the matter up. In the meanwhile, Mr. Bruff, we must get back again to the Indians, on your account. Their journey to London simply ended in their becoming the victims of another defeat. The loss of their second chance of seizing the Diamond is mainly attributable, as I think, to the cunning and foresight of Mr. Luker – who doesn't stand at the top of the prosperous and ancient profession of usury for nothing! By the prompt dismissal of the man in his employment, he deprived the Indians of the assistance which their confederate would have rendered them in getting into the house. By the prompt transport of the Moonstone to his banker's, he took the conspirators by surprise before they were prepared with a new plan for robbing him. How the Indians, in this latter case, suspected what he had done, and how they contrived to possess themselves of his banker's receipt, are events too recent to need dwelling on. Let it be enough to say that they know the Moonstone to be once more out of their reach; deposited (under the general description of 'a valuable of great price') in a banker's strong-room. Now, Mr. Bruff, what is their third chance of seizing the Diamond? and when will it come?"

As the question passed his lips, I penetrated the motive of the Indian's visit to my office at last!

"I see it!" I exclaimed. "The Indians take it for granted, as we do, that the Moonstone has been pledged; and they want to be certainly informed of the earliest period at which the pledge can be redeemed – because that will be the earliest period at which the Diamond can be removed from the safe keeping of the bank!"

"I told you you would find it out for yourself, Mr. Bruff, if I only gave you a fair chance. In a year from the time when the Moonstone was pledged, the Indians will be on the watch for their third chance.

Mr. Luker's own lips have told them how long they will have to wait, and your respectable authority has satisfied them that Mr. Luker has spoken the truth. When do we suppose, at a rough guess, that the Diamond found its way into the money-lender's hands?"

"Towards the end of last June," I answered, "as well as I can reckon it."

"And we are now in the year 'forty-eight. Very good. If the unknown person who has pledged the Moonstone can redeem it in a year, the jewel will be in that person's possession again at the end of June, 'forty-nine. I shall be thousands of miles away from England and English news at that date. But it may be worth *your* while to take a note of it, and to arrange to be in London at the time."

"You think something serious will happen?" I said.

"I think I shall be safer," he answered, "among the fiercest fanatics of Central Asia than I should be if I crossed the door of the bank with the Moonstone in my pocket. The Indians have been defeated twice running, Mr. Bruff. It's my firm belief that they won't be defeated a third time."

Those were the last words he said on the subject. The coffee came in; the guests rose, and dispersed themselves about the room; and we joined the ladies of the dinner-party upstairs.

I made a note of the date, and it may not be amiss if I close my narrative by repeating that note here:

June, 'forty-nine. Expect news of the Indians, towards the end of the month.

And that done, I hand the pen, which I have now no further claim to use, to the writer who follows me next.

THIRD NARRATIVE

Contributed by FRANKLIN BLAKE

CHAPTER I

IN the spring of the year eighteen hundred and forty-nine I was wandering in the East, and had then recently altered the travelling plans which I had laid out some months before, and which I had communicated to my lawyer and my banker in London.

This change made it necessary for me to send one of my servants to obtain my letters and remittances from the English consul in a certain city, which was no longer included as one of my resting-places in my new travelling scheme. The man was to join me again at an appointed place and time. An accident, for which he was not responsible, delayed him on his errand. For a week I and my people waited, encamped on the borders of a desert. At the end of that time the missing man made his appearance, with the money and the letters, at the entrance of my tent.

"I am afraid I bring you bad news, sir," he said, and pointed to one of the letters, which had a mourning border round it, and the address on which was in the handwriting of Mr. Bruff.

I know nothing, in a case of this kind, so unendurable as suspense. The letter with the mourning border was the letter that I opened first.

It informed me that my father was dead, and that I was heir to his great fortune. The wealth which had thus fallen into my hands brought its responsibilities with it, and Mr. Bruff entreated me to lose no time in returning to England.

By daybreak the next morning I was on my way back to my own country.

The picture presented of me, by my old friend Betteredge, at the time of my departure from England, is (as I think) a little overdrawn. He has, in his own quaint way, interpreted seriously one of his young mistress's many satirical references to my foreign education; and has persuaded himself that he actually saw those French, German, and Italian sides to my character, which my lively cousin only professed to discover in jest, and which never had any real existence, except in our good Betteredge's own brain. But, barring this drawback, I am bound to own that he has stated no more than the truth in representing me as wounded to the heart by Rachel's treatment, and as leaving England in the first keenness of suffering caused by the bitterest disappointment of my life.

I went abroad, resolved – if change and absence could help me – to forget her. It is, I am persuaded, no true view of human nature which denies that change and absence *do* help a man under these circumstances: they force his attention away from the exclusive contemplation of his own sorrow. I never forgot her; but the pang of remembrance lost its worst bitterness, little by little, as time, distance, and novelty interposed themselves more and more effectually between Rachel and me.

On the other hand, it is no less certain that, with the act of turning homeward, the remedy which had gained its ground so steadily, began now, just as steadily, to drop back. The nearer I drew to the country which she inhabited, and to the prospect of seeing her again, the more irresistibly her influence began to recover its hold on me. On leaving England she was the last person in the world whose name I would have suffered to pass my lips. On returning to England, she was the first person I inquired after, when Mr. Bruff and I met again.

I was informed, of course, of all that had happened in my absence: in other words, of all that has been related here in continuation of Betteredge's narrative – one circumstance only being excepted. Mr. Bruff did not, at that time, feel himself at liberty to inform me of the motives which had privately influenced Rachel and Godfrey Ablewhite in recalling the marriage promise, on either side. I troubled him with no embarrassing questions on this delicate subject. It was relief enough to me, after the jealous disappointment caused by hearing that she had ever contemplated being Godfrey's wife, to know that reflection had convinced her of acting rashly, and that she had effected her own release from her marriage engagement.

Having heard the story of the past, my next inquiries (still inquiries after Rachel!) advanced naturally to the present time. Under whose care had she been placed after leaving Mr. Bruff's house? and where was she living now?

She was living under the care of a widowed sister of the late Sir

John Verinder – one Mrs. Merridew – whom her mother's executors had requested to act as guardian, and who had accepted the proposal. They were reported to me as getting on together admirably well, and as being now established, for the season, in Mrs. Merridew's house in Portland Place.[1]

Half an hour after receiving this information, I was on my way to Portland Place – without having had the courage to own it to Mr. Bruff!

The man who answered the door was not sure whether Miss Verinder was at home or not. I sent him upstairs with my card, as the speediest way of setting the question at rest. The man came down again with an impenetrable face, and informed me that Miss Verinder was out.

I might have suspected other people of purposely denying themselves to me. But it was impossible to suspect Rachel. I left word that I would call again at six o'clock that evening.

At six o'clock I was informed for the second time that Miss Verinder was not at home. Had any message been left for me? No message had been left for me. Had Miss Verinder not received my card? The servant begged my pardon – Miss Verinder *had* received it.

The inference was too plain to be resisted. Rachel declined to see me.

On my side, I declined to be treated in this way, without making an attempt, at least, to discover a reason for it. I sent up my name to Mrs. Merridew, and requested her to favour me with a personal interview at any hour which it might be most convenient to her to name.

Mrs. Merridew made no difficulty about receiving me at once. I was shown into a comfortable little sitting-room, and found myself in the presence of a comfortable little elderly lady. She was so good as to feel great regret and much surprise, entirely on my account. She was at the same time, however, not in a position to offer me any explanation, or to press Rachel on a matter which appeared to relate to a question of private feeling alone. This was said over and over again, with a polite patience that nothing could tire; and this was all I gained by applying to Mrs. Merridew.

---

1 Mrs. Merridew's home at Portland Place, a block from where Collins was born and very near a half-dozen of the homes he lived in at one time or another, was among the grandest streets of London in the eighteenth and nineteenth centuries.

My last chance was to write to Rachel. My servant took a letter to her the next day, with strict instructions to wait for an answer.

The answer came back, literally in one sentence.

"Miss Verinder begs to decline entering into any correspondence with Mr. Franklin Blake."

Fond as I was of her, I felt indignantly the insult offered to me in that reply. Mr. Bruff came in to speak to me on business, before I had recovered possession of myself. I dismissed the business on the spot, and laid the whole case before him. He proved to be as incapable of enlightening me as Mrs. Merridew herself. I asked him if any slander had been spoken of me in Rachel's hearing. Mr. Bruff was not aware of any slander of which I was the object. Had she referred to me in any way, while she was staying under Mr. Bruff's roof? Never. Had she not so much as asked, during all my long absence, whether I was living or dead? No such question had ever passed her lips. I took out of my pocket-book the letter which poor Lady Verinder had written to me from Frizinghall, on the day when I left her house in Yorkshire. And I pointed Mr. Bruff's attention to these two sentences in it:

"The valuable assistance which you rendered to the inquiry after the lost jewel is still an unpardoned offence, in the present dreadful state of Rachel's mind. Moving blindfold in this matter, you have added to the burden of anxiety which she has had to bear, by innocently threatening her secret with discovery through your exertions."

"Is it possible," I asked, "that the feeling towards me which is there described, is as bitter as ever against me now?"

Mr. Bruff looked unaffectedly distressed.

"If you insist on an answer," he said, "I own I can place no other interpretation on her conduct than that."

I rang the bell, and directed my servant to pack my portmanteau, and to send out for a railway guide. Mr. Bruff asked, in astonishment, what I was going to do.

"I am going to Yorkshire," I answered, "by the next train."

"May I ask for what purpose?"

"Mr. Bruff, the assistance I innocently rendered to the inquiry after the Diamond was an unpardoned offence, in Rachel's mind, nearly a year since; and it remains an unpardoned offence still. I won't accept that position! I am determined to find out the secret of her silence towards her mother, and her enmity towards *me*. If time, pains, and money can do it, I will lay my hand on the thief who took the Moonstone!"

The worthy old gentleman attempted to remonstrate – to induce me to listen to reason – to do his duty towards me, in short. I was deaf to everything that he could urge. No earthly consideration would, at that moment, have shaken the resolution that was in me.

"I shall take up the inquiry again," I went on, "at the point where I dropped it; and I shall follow it onwards, step by step, till I come to the present time. There are missing links in the evidence, as *I* left it, which Gabriel Betteredge can supply, and to Gabriel Betteredge I go!"

Towards sunset that evening I stood again on the well-remembered terrace, and looked once more at the peaceful old country house. The gardener was the first person whom I saw in the deserted grounds. He had left Betteredge, an hour since, sunning himself in the customary corner of the back yard. I knew it well; and I said I would go and seek him myself.

I walked round by the familiar paths and passages, and looked in at the open gate of the yard.

There he was – the dear old friend of the happy days that were never to come again – there he was in the old corner, on the old bee-hive chair, with his pipe in his mouth, and his *Robinson Crusoe* on his lap, and his two friends, the dogs, dozing on either side of him! In the position in which I stood, my shadow was projected in front of me by the last slanting rays of the sun. Either the dogs saw it, or their keen scent informed them of my approach: they started up with a growl. Starting in his turn, the old man quieted them by a word, and then shaded his failing eyes with his hand, and looked inquiringly at the figure at the gate.

My own eyes were full of tears. I was obliged to wait for a moment before I could trust myself to speak to him.

★

CHAPTER II

"BETTEREDGE!" I said, pointing to the well-remembered book on his knee, "has *Robinson Crusoe* informed you, this evening, that you might expect to see Franklin Blake?"

"By the lord Harry, Mr. Franklin!" cried the old man, "that's exactly what *Robinson Crusoe* has done!"

He struggled to his feet with my assistance, and stood for a moment, looking backwards and forwards between *Robinson Crusoe* and me, apparently at a loss to discover which of us had surprised him most. The verdict ended in favour of the book. Holding it open before him in both hands, he surveyed the wonderful volume with a stare of unutterable anticipation – as if he expected to see Robinson Crusoe himself walk out of the pages, and favour us with a personal interview.

"Here's the bit, Mr. Franklin!" he said, as soon as he had recovered the use of his speech. "As I live by bread, sir, here's the bit I was reading, the moment before you came in! Page one hundred and fifty-six as follows: – 'I stood like one Thunderstruck, or as if I had seen an Apparition.' If that isn't as much as to say: 'Expect the sudden appearance of Mr. Franklin Blake' – there's no meaning in the English language!" said Betteredge, closing the book with a bang, and getting one of his hands free at last to take the hand which I offered him.

I had expected him, naturally enough under the circumstances, to overwhelm me with questions. But no – the hospitable impulse was the uppermost impulse in the old servant's mind, when a member of the family appeared (no matter how!) as a visitor at the house.

"Walk in, Mr. Franklin," he said, opening the door behind him, with his quaint old-fashioned bow. "I'll ask what brings you here afterwards – I must make you comfortable first. There have been sad changes, since you went away. The house is shut up, and the servants are gone. Never mind that! I'll cook your dinner; and the gardener's wife will make your bed – and if there's a bottle of our famous Latour claret left in the cellar, down your throat, Mr. Franklin, that bottle shall go. I bid you welcome, sir! I bid you heartily welcome!" said the poor old fellow, fighting manfully against the gloom of the deserted house, and receiving me with the sociable and courteous attention of the bygone time.

It vexed me to disappoint him. But the house was Rachel's house, now. Could I eat in it, or sleep in it, after what had happened in London? The commonest sense of self-respect forbade me – properly forbade me – to cross the threshold.

I took Betteredge by the arm, and led him out into the garden. There was no help for it. I was obliged to tell him the truth. Between his attachment to Rachel, and his attachment to me, he was sorely puzzled and distressed at the turn things had taken. His opinion, when he expressed it, was given in his usual downright manner, and was agreeably redolent of the most positive philosophy I know – the philosophy of the Betteredge school.

"Miss Rachel has her faults – I've never denied it," he began. "And riding the high horse, now and then, is one of them. She has been trying to ride over *you* – and you have put up with it. Lord, Mr. Franklin, don't you know women by this time better than that? You have heard me talk of the late Mrs. Betteredge?"

I had heard him talk of the late Mrs. Betteredge pretty often – invariably producing her as his one undeniable example of the inbred frailty and perversity of the other sex. In that capacity he exhibited her now.

"Very well, Mr. Franklin. Now listen to me. Different women have different ways of riding the high horse. The late Mrs. Betteredge took her exercise on that favourite female animal whenever I happened to deny her anything that she had set her heart on. So sure as I came home from my work on these occasions, so sure was my wife to call to me up the kitchen stairs, and to say that, after my brutal treatment of her, she hadn't the heart to cook me my dinner. I put up with it for some time – just as you are putting up with it now from Miss Rachel. At last my patience wore out. I went downstairs, and I took Mrs. Betteredge – affectionately, you understand – up in my arms, and carried her, holus-bolus, into the best parlour, where she received her company. I said, 'That's the right place for you, my dear,' and so went back to the kitchen. I locked myself in, and took off my coat, and turned up my shirt-sleeves, and cooked my own dinner. When it was done, I served it up in my best manner, and enjoyed it most heartily. I had my pipe and my drop of grog afterwards; and then I cleared the table, and washed the crockery, and cleaned the knives and forks, and put the things away, and swept up the hearth. When things were as bright and clean again, as bright and clean could be, I opened the door and let Mrs. Betteredge in. 'I've had my dinner, my dear,' I said; 'and I hope you will find that I have left the kitchen all that your fondest wishes can desire.' For the rest of that woman's life, Mr. Franklin, I never had to cook my dinner again! Moral: You have put up with Miss Rachel in London; don't put up with her in Yorkshire. Come back to the house."

Quite unanswerable! I could only assure my good friend that even *his* powers of persuasion were, in this case, thrown away on me.

"It's a lovely evening," I said. "I shall walk to Frizinghall, and stay at the hotel, and you must come to-morrow morning and breakfast with me. I have something to say to you."

Betteredge shook his head gravely.

"I am heartily sorry for this," he said. "I had hoped, Mr. Franklin, to hear that things were all smooth and pleasant again between you and Miss Rachel. If you must have your own way, sir," he continued, after a moment's reflection, "there is no need to go to Frizinghall to-night for a bed. It's to be had nearer than that. There's Hotherstone's Farm, barely two miles from here. You can hardly object to *that* on Miss Rachel's account," the old man added slyly. "Hotherstone lives, Mr. Franklin, on his own freehold."[1]

I remembered the place the moment Betteredge mentioned it. The farm-house stood in a sheltered inland valley, on the banks of the prettiest stream in that part of Yorkshire: and the farmer had a spare bedroom and parlour, which he was accustomed to let to artists, anglers, and tourists in general. A more agreeable place of abode, during my stay in the neighbourhood, I could not have wished to find.

"Are the rooms to let?" I inquired.

"Mrs. Hotherstone herself, sir, asked for my good word to recommend the rooms, yesterday."

"I'll take them, Betteredge, with the greatest pleasure."

We went back to the yard, in which I had left my travelling-bag. After putting a stick through the handle, and swinging the bag over his shoulder, Betteredge appeared to relapse into the bewilderment which my sudden appearance had caused, when I surprised him in the beehive chair. He looked incredulously at the house, and then he wheeled about, and looked more incredulously still at me.

"I've lived a goodish long time in the world," said this best and dearest of all old servants – "but the like of this, I never did expect to

---

1 Freeholders were landowners – as opposed to renters or lessees – in a community.

see. There stands the house, and here stands Mr. Franklin Blake – and, Damme, if one of them isn't turning his back on the other, and going to sleep in a lodging!"

He led the way out, wagging his head and growling ominously. "There's only one more miracle that *can* happen," he said to me, over his shoulder. "The next thing you'll do, Mr. Franklin, will be to pay me back that seven and sixpence you borrowed of me when you were a boy."

This stroke of sarcasm put him in a better humour with himself and with me. We left the house, and passed through the lodge gates. Once clear of the grounds, the duties of hospitality (in Betteredge's code of morals) ceased, and the privileges of curiosity began.

He dropped back, so as to let me get on a level with him. "Fine evening for a walk, Mr. Franklin," he said, as if we had just accidentally encountered each other at that moment. "Supposing you had gone to the hotel at Frizinghall, sir?"

"Yes?"

"I should have had the honour of breakfasting with you, tomorrow morning."

"Come and breakfast with me at Hotherstone's Farm, instead."

"Much obliged to you for your kindness, Mr. Franklin. But it wasn't exactly breakfast that I was driving at. I think you mentioned that you had something to say to me? If it's no secret, sir," said Betteredge, suddenly abandoning the crooked way, and taking the straight one, "I'm burning to know what's brought you down here, if you please, in this sudden way."

"What brought me here before?" I asked.

"The Moonstone, Mr. Franklin. But what brings you now, sir?"

"The Moonstone again, Betteredge."

The old man suddenly stood still, and looked at me in the grey twilight as if he suspected his own ears of deceiving him.

"If that's a joke, sir," he said, "I am afraid I'm getting a little dull in my old age. I don't take it."

"It's no joke," I answered. "I have come here to take up the inquiry which was dropped when I left England. I have come here to do what nobody has done yet – to find out who took the Diamond."

"Let the Diamond be, Mr. Franklin! Take my advice, and let the Diamond be! That cursed Indian jewel has misguided everybody who has come near it. Don't waste your money and your temper – in the fine springtime of your life, sir – by meddling with the Moonstone. How can *you* hope to succeed (saving your presence), when Sergeant Cuff himself made a mess of it? Sergeant Cuff!" repeated Betteredge, shaking his forefinger at me sternly. "The greatest policeman in England!"

"My mind is made up, my old friend. Even Sergeant Cuff doesn't daunt me. – By-the-bye, I may want to speak to him, sooner or later. Have you heard anything of him lately?"

"The Sergeant won't help you, Mr. Franklin."

"Why not?"

"There has been an event, sir, in the police-circles, since you went away. The great Cuff has retired from business. He has got a little cottage at Dorking;[1] and he's up to his eyes in the growing of roses. I have it in his own handwriting, Mr. Franklin. He has grown the white moss-rose, without budding it on the dog-rose first. And Mr. Begbie the gardener is to go to Dorking, and own that the Sergeant has beaten him at last."

"It doesn't much matter," I said. "I must do without Sergeant Cuff's help. And I must trust to you, at starting."

It is likely enough that I spoke rather carelessly. At any rate, Betteredge seemed to be piqued by something in the reply which I had just made to him. "You might trust to worse than me, Mr. Franklin – I can tell you that," he said, a little sharply.

The tone in which he retorted, and a certain disturbance, after he had spoken, which I detected in his manner, suggested to me that he was possessed of some information which he hesitated to communicate.

"I expect you to help me," I said, "in picking up the fragments of evidence which Sergeant Cuff has left behind him. I know you can do that. Can you do no more?"

"What more can you expect from me, sir?" asked Betteredge, with an appearance of the utmost humility.

"I expect more – from what you said just now."

"Mere boasting, Mr. Franklin," returned the old man obstinately.

---

1 Cuff has retired to a town in Surrey, a county in southern England.

"Some people are born boasters, and they never get over it to their dying day. I'm one of them."

There was only one way to take with him. I appealed to his interest in Rachel, and his interest in me.

"Betteredge, would you be glad to hear that Rachel and I were good friends again?"

"I have served your family, sir, to mighty little purpose, if you doubt it!"

"Do you remember how Rachel treated me, before I left England?"

"As well as if it was yesterday! My lady herself wrote you a letter about it; and you were so good as to show the letter to me. It said that Miss Rachel was mortally offended with you, for the part you had taken in trying to recover her jewel. And neither my lady, nor you, nor anybody else could guess why."

"Quite true, Betteredge! And I come back from my travels, and find her mortally offended with me still. I knew that the Diamond was at the bottom of it, last year, and I know that the Diamond is at the bottom of it now. I have tried to speak to her, and she won't see me. I have tried to write to her, and she won't answer me. How, in Heaven's name, am I to clear the matter up? The chance of searching into the loss of the Moonstone, is the one chance of inquiry that Rachel herself has left me."

Those words evidently put the case before him, as he had not seen it yet. He asked a question which satisfied me that I had shaken him.

"There is no ill-feeling in this, Mr. Franklin, on your side – is there?"

"There was some anger," I answered, "when I left London. But that is all worn out now. I want to make Rachel come to an understanding with me – and I want nothing more."

"You don't feel any fear, sir – supposing you make any discoveries – in regard to what you may find out about Miss Rachel?"

I understood the jealous belief in his young mistress which prompted those words.

"I am as certain of her as you are," I answered. "The fullest disclosure of her secret will reveal nothing that can alter her place in your estimation, or in mine."

Betteredge's last-left scruples vanished at that.

"If I am doing wrong to help you, Mr. Franklin," he exclaimed, "all I can say is – I am as innocent of seeing it as the babe unborn! I can put you on the road to discovery, if you can only go on by yourself. You remember that poor girl of ours – Rosanna Spearman?"

"Of course!"

"You always thought she had some sort of confession, in regard to this matter of the Moonstone, which she wanted to make to you?"

"I certainly couldn't account for her strange conduct in any other way."

"You may set that doubt at rest, Mr. Franklin, whenever you please."

It was my turn to come to a standstill now. I tried vainly, in the gathering darkness, to see his face. In the surprise of the moment, I asked a little impatiently what he meant.

"Steady, sir!" proceeded Betteredge. "I mean what I say. Rosanna Spearman left a sealed letter behind her – a letter addressed to *you.*"

"Where is it?"

"In the possession of a friend of hers, at Cobb's Hole. You must have heard tell, when you were here last, sir, of Limping Lucy – a lame girl with a crutch."

"The fisherman's daughter?"

"The same, Mr. Franklin."

"Why wasn't the letter forwarded to me?"

"Limping Lucy has a will of her own, sir. She wouldn't give it into any hands but yours. And you had left England before I could write to you."

"Let's go back, Betteredge, and get it at once!"

"Too late, sir, to-night. They're great savers of candles along our coast; and they go to bed early at Cobb's Hole."

"Nonsense! We might get there in half an hour."

"*You* might, sir. And when you did get there, you would find the door locked." He pointed to a light, glimmering below us; and, at the same moment, I heard through the stillness of the evening the bubbling of a stream. "There's the Farm, Mr. Franklin! Make yourself comfortable for to-night, and come to me to-morrow morning – if you'll be so kind?"

"You will go with me to the fisherman's cottage?"

"Yes, sir."

"Early?"

"As early, Mr. Franklin, as you like."

We descended the path that led to the Farm.

CHAPTER III

I HAVE only the most indistinct recollection of what happened at Hotherstone's Farm.

I remember a hearty welcome; a prodigious supper, which would have fed a whole village in the East; a delightfully clean bedroom, with nothing in it to regret but that detestable product of the folly of our forefathers – a feather-bed; a restless night, with much kindling of matches, and many lightings of one little candle; and an immense sensation of relief when the sun rose, and there was a prospect of getting up.

It had been arranged over-night with Betteredge, that I was to call for him, on our way to Cobb's Hole, as early as I liked – which, interpreted by my impatience to get possession of the letter, meant as early as I could. Without waiting for breakfast at the Farm, I took a crust of bread in my hand, and set forth, in some doubt whether I should not surprise the excellent Betteredge in his bed. To my great relief he proved to be quite as excited about the coming event as I was. I found him ready, and waiting for me, with his stick in his hand.

"How are you this morning, Betteredge?"

"Very poorly, sir."

"Sorry to hear it. What do you complain of?"

"I complain of a new disease, Mr. Franklin, of my own inventing. I don't want to alarm you, but you're certain to catch it before the morning is out."

"The devil I am!"

"Do you feel an uncomfortable heat at the pit of your stomach, sir? and a nasty thumping at the top of your head? Ah! not yet? It will lay hold of you at Cobb's Hole, Mr. Franklin. I call it the detective-fever; and *I* first caught it in the company of Sergeant Cuff."

"Aye! aye! and the cure in this instance is to open Rosanna Spearman's letter, I suppose? Come along, and let's get it."

Early as it was, we found the fisherman's wife astir in her kitchen.

On my presentation by Betteredge, good Mrs. Yolland performed a social ceremony, strictly reserved (as I afterwards learnt) for strangers of distinction. She put a bottle of Dutch gin and a couple of clean pipes on the table, and opened the conversation by saying, "What news from London, sir?"

Before I could find an answer to this immensely comprehensive question, an apparition advanced towards me, out of a dark corner of the kitchen. A wan, wild, haggard girl, with remarkably beautiful hair, and with a fierce keenness in her eyes, came limping up on a crutch to the table at which I was sitting, and looked at me as if I was an object of mingled interest and horror, which it quite fascinated her to see.

"Mr. Betteredge," she said, without taking her eyes off me, "mention his name again, if you please."

"This gentleman's name," answered Betteredge (with a strong emphasis on *gentleman*), "is Mr. Franklin Blake."

The girl turned her back on me, and suddenly left the room. Good Mrs. Yolland – as I believe – made some apologies for her daughter's odd behaviour, and Betteredge (probably) translated them into polite English. I speak of this in complete uncertainty. My attention was absorbed in following the sound of the girl's crutch. Thump-thump, up the wooden stairs; thump-thump across the room above our heads; thump-thump down the stairs again – and there stood the apparition at the open door, with a letter in its hand, beckoning me out!

I left more apologies in course of delivery behind me, and followed this strange creature – limping on before me, faster and faster – down the slope of the beach. She led me behind some boats, out of sight and hearing of the few people in the fishing-village, and then stopped, and faced me for the first time.

"Stand there," she said, "I want to look at you."

There was no mistaking the expression on her face. I inspired her with the strongest emotions of abhorrence and disgust. Let me not be vain enough to say that no woman had ever looked at me in this manner before. I will only venture on the more modest assertion that no woman had ever let me perceive it yet. There is a limit to the length of the inspection which a man can endure, under certain circumstances. I attempted to direct Limping Lucy's attention to some less revolting object than my face.

"I think you have got a letter to give me," I began. "Is it the letter there, in your hand?"

"Say that again," was the only answer I received.

I repeated the words, like a good child learning its lesson.

"No," said the girl, speaking to herself, but keeping her eyes still mercilessly fixed on me. "I can't find out what she saw in his face. I can't guess what she heard in his voice." She suddenly looked away from me, and rested her head wearily on the top of her crutch. "Oh, my poor dear!" she said, in the first soft tones which had fallen from her, in my hearing. "Oh, my lost darling! what could you see in this man?" She lifted her head again fiercely, and looked at me once more. "Can you eat and drink?" she asked.

I did my best to preserve my gravity, and answered, "Yes."

"Can you sleep?"

"Yes."

"When you see a poor girl in service, do you feel no remorse?"

"Certainly not. Why should I?"

She abruptly thrust the letter (as the phrase is) into my face.

"Take it!" she exclaimed furiously. "I never set eyes on you before. God Almighty forbid I should ever set eyes on you again."

With those parting words she limped away from me at the top of her speed. The one interpretation that I could put on her conduct has, no doubt, been anticipated by everybody. I could only suppose that she was mad.

Having reached that inevitable conclusion, I turned to the more interesting object of investigation which was presented to me by Rosanna Spearman's letter. The address was written as follows: – "For Franklin Blake, Esq. To be given into his own hands (and not to be trusted to anyone else), by Lucy Yolland."

I broke the seal. The envelope contained a letter: and this, in its turn, contained a slip of paper. I read the letter first: –

"Sir, – If you are curious to know the meaning of my behaviour to you, whilst you were staying in the house of my mistress, Lady Verinder, do what you are told to do in the memorandum enclosed with this – and do it without any person being present to overlook you. Your humble servant,

"Rosanna Spearman."

I turned to the slip of paper next. Here is the literal copy of it, word for word:

"*Memorandum*: – To go to the Shivering Sand at the turn of the tide. To walk out on the South Spit, until I get the South Spit. Beacon, and the flagstaff at the Coast-guard station[1] above Cobb's Hole in a line together. To lay down on the rocks, a stick, or any straight thing to guide my hand, exactly in the line of the beacon and the flagstaff. To take care, in doing this, that one end of the stick shall be at the edge of the rocks, on the side of them which overlooks the quicksand. To feel along the stick, among the sea-weed (beginning from the end of the stick which points towards the beacon), for the Chain. To run my hand along the Chain, when found, until I come to the part of it which stretches over the edge of the rocks, down into the quicksand. *And then, to pull the chain.*"

Just as I had read the last words – underlined in the original – I heard the voice of Betteredge behind me. The inventor of the detective-fever had completely succumbed to that irresistible malady. "I can't stand it any longer, Mr. Franklin. What does her letter say? For mercy's sake, sir, tell us, what does her letter say?"

I handed him the letter, and the memorandum. He read the first without appearing to be much interested in it. But the second – the memorandum – produced a strong impression on him.

"The Sergeant said it!" cried Betteredge. "From first to last, sir, the Sergeant said she had got a memorandum of the hiding-place. And here it is! Lord save us, Mr. Franklin, here is the secret that puzzled everybody, from the great Cuff downwards, ready and waiting, as one may say, to show itself to *you*! It's the ebb now, sir, as anybody may see for themselves. How long will it be till the turn of the tide?" He

---

1 According to the *OED*, "the Coast Guard was originally employed under the Customs department to prevent smuggling (hence called the *Preventive Service*); the force was in 1856 transferred to the Admiralty, to be used as a general police force for the coast, available also as a defensive force." There is a real coast guard station at Kettleness, very close to Hobb Holes, the probable model for Cobb's Hole.

looked up, and observed a lad at work, at some little distance from us, mending a net. "Tammie Bright!" he shouted at the top of his voice.

"I hear you!" Tammie shouted back.

"When's the turn of the tide?"

"In an hour's time."

We both looked at our watches.

"We can go round by the coast, Mr. Franklin," said Betteredge; "and get to the quicksand in that way, with plenty of time to spare. What do you say, sir?"

"Come along."

On our way to the Shivering Sand, I applied to Betteredge to revive my memory of events (as affecting Rosanna Spearman) at the period of Sergeant Cuff's inquiry. With my old friend's help, I soon had the succession of circumstances clearly registered in my mind. Rosanna's journey to Frizinghall, when the whole household believed her to be ill in her own room – Rosanna's mysterious employment of the night-time, with her door locked, and her candle burning till the morning – Rosanna's suspicious purchase of the japanned tin case, and the two dog-chains from Mrs. Yolland – the Sergeant's positive conviction that Rosanna had hidden something at the Shivering Sand, and the Sergeant's absolute ignorance as to what that something might be – all these strange results of the abortive inquiry into the loss of the Moonstone were clearly present to me again, when we reached the quicksand, and walked out together on the low ledge of rocks called the South Spit.

With Betteredge's help, I soon stood in the right position to see the Beacon and the Coast-guard flagstaff in a line together. Following the memorandum as our guide, we next laid my stick in the necessary direction, as neatly as we could, on the uneven surface of the rocks. And then we looked at our watches once more.

It wanted nearly twenty minutes yet of the turn of the tide. I suggested waiting through this interval on the beach, instead of on the wet and slippery surface of the rocks. Having reached the dry sand, I prepared to sit down; and, greatly to my surprise, Betteredge prepared to leave me.

"What are you going away for?" I asked.

"Look at the letter again, sir, and you will see."

A glance at the letter reminded me that I was charged, when I made my discovery, to make it alone.

"It's hard enough for me to leave you, at such a time as this," said Betteredge. "But she died a dreadful death, poor soul – and I feel a kind of call on me, Mr. Franklin, to humour that fancy of hers. Besides," he added confidentially, "there's nothing in the letter against your letting out the secret afterwards. I'll hang about in the fir plantation, and wait till you pick me up. Don't be longer than you can help, sir. The detective-fever isn't an easy disease to deal with, under *these* circumstances."

With that parting caution, he left me.

The interval of expectation, short as it was when reckoned by the measure of time, assumed formidable proportions when reckoned by the measure of suspense. This was one of the occasions on which the invaluable habit of smoking becomes especially precious and consolatory. I lit a cigar, and sat down on the slope of the beach.

The sunlight poured its unclouded beauty on every object that I could see. The exquisite freshness of the air made the mere act of living and breathing a luxury. Even the lonely little bay welcomed the morning with a show of cheerfulness; and the bared wet surface of the quicksand itself, glittering with a golden brightness, hid the horror of its false brown face under a passing smile. It was the finest day I had seen since my return to England.

The turn of the tide came, before my cigar was finished. I saw the preliminary heaving of the Sand, and then the awful shiver that crept over its surface – as if some spirit of terror lived and moved and shuddered in the fathomless deeps beneath. I threw away my cigar, and went back again to the rocks.

My directions in the memorandum instructed me to feel along the line traced by the stick, beginning with the end which was nearest to the beacon.

I advanced, in this manner, more than half-way along the stick, without encountering anything but the edges of the rocks. An inch or two further on, however, my patience was rewarded. In a narrow little fissure, just within reach of my forefinger, I felt the chain. Attempting, next, to follow it, by touch, in the direction of the quicksand, I found my progress stopped by a thick growth of seaweed – which had fastened itself into the fissure, no doubt, in the time that had elapsed since Rosanna Spearman had chosen her hiding-place.

It was equally impossible to pull up the seaweed, or to force my hand through it. After marking the spot indicated by the end of the stick which was placed nearest to the quicksand, I determined to pursue the search for the chain on a plan of my own. My idea was to "sound" immediately under the rocks, on the chance of recovering the lost trace of the chain at the point at which it entered the sand. I took up the stick, and knelt down on the brink of the South Spit.

In this position, my face was within a few feet of the surface of the quicksand. The sight of it so near me, still disturbed at intervals by its hideous shivering fit, shook my nerves for the moment. A horrible fancy that the dead woman might appear on the scene of her suicide, to assist my search – an unutterable dread of seeing her rise through the heaving surface of the sand, and point to the place – forced itself into my mind, and turned me cold in the warm sunlight. I own I closed my eyes at the moment when the point of the stick first entered the quicksand.

The instant afterwards, before the stick could have been submerged more than a few inches, I was free from the hold of my own superstitious terror, and was throbbing with excitement from head to foot. Sounding blindfold, at my first attempt – at that first attempt I had sounded right! The stick struck the chain.

Taking a firm hold of the roots of the seaweed with my left hand, I laid myself down over the brink, and felt with my right hand under the overhanging edges of the rock. My right hand found the chain.

I drew it up without the slightest difficulty. And there was the japanned tin case fastened to the end of it.

The action of the water had so rusted the chain, that it was impossible for me to unfasten it from the hasp which attached it to the case. Putting the case between my knees and exerting my utmost strength, I contrived to draw off the cover. Some white substance filled the whole interior when I looked in. I put in my hand, and found it to be linen.

In drawing out the linen, I also drew out a letter crumpled up with it. After looking at the direction, and discovering that it bore my name, I put the letter in my pocket, and completely removed the linen. It came out in a thick roll, moulded, of course, to the shape of the case in which it had been so long confined, and perfectly preserved from any injury by the sea.

I carried the linen to the dry sand of the beach, and there unrolled and smoothed it out. There was no mistaking it as an article of dress. It was a nightgown.

The uppermost side, when I spread it out, presented to view innumerable folds and creases, and nothing more. I tried the undermost side, next – and instantly discovered the smear of the paint from the door of Rachel's boudoir!

My eyes remained riveted on the stain, and my mind took me back at a leap from present to past. The very words of Sergeant Cuff recurred to me, as if the man himself was at my side again, pointing to the unanswerable inference which he drew from the smear on the door.

"Find out whether there is any article of dress in this house with the stain of paint on it. Find out who that dress belongs to. Find out how the person can account for having been in the room, and smeared the paint, between midnight and three in the morning. If the person can't satisfy you, you haven't far to look for the hand that took the Diamond."

One after another those words travelled over my memory, repeating themselves again and again with a wearisome, mechanical reiteration. I was roused from what felt like a trance of many hours – from what was really, no doubt, the pause of a few moments only – by a voice calling to me. I looked up, and saw that Betteredge's patience had failed him at last. He was just visible between the sand-hills, returning to the beach.

The old man's appearance recalled me, the moment I perceived it, to my sense of present things, and reminded me that the inquiry which I had pursued thus far still remained incomplete. I had discovered the smear on the nightgown. To whom did the nightgown belong?

My first impulse was to consult the letter in my pocket – the letter which I had found in the case.

As I raised my hand to take it out, I remembered that there was a shorter way to discovery than this. The nightgown itself would reveal the truth; for, in all probability, the nightgown was marked with its owner's name.

I took it from the sand, and looked for the mark.

I found the mark, and read –

MY OWN NAME.

There were the familiar letters which told me that the nightgown was mine. I looked up from them. There was the sun; there were the glittering waters of the bay; there was old Betteredge, advancing nearer and nearer to me. I looked back again at the letters. My own name. Plainly confronting me – my own name.

"If time, pains, and money can do it, I will lay my hand on the thief who took the Moonstone." – I had left London, with those words on my lips. I had penetrated the secret which the quicksand had kept from every other living creature. And, on the unanswerable evidence of the paint-stain, I had discovered Myself as the Thief.

★

End of Volume II of First Three-Volume Edition (1868)

CHAPTER IV

I HAVE not a word to say about my own sensations.

My impression is, that the shock inflicted on me completely suspended my thinking and feeling power. I certainly could not have known what I was about when Betteredge joined me – for I have it on his authority that I laughed, when he asked what was the matter, and putting the nightgown into his hands, told him to read the riddle for himself.

Of what was said between us on the beach, I have not the faintest recollection. The first place in which I can now see myself again plainly is the plantation of firs. Betteredge and I are walking back together to the house; and Betteredge is telling me that I shall be able to face it, and he will be able to face it, when we have had a glass of grog.

The scene shifts from the plantation to Betteredge's little sitting-room. My resolution not to enter Rachel's house is forgotten. I feel gratefully the coolness and shadiness and quiet of the room. I drink the grog (a perfectly new luxury to me, at that time of day), which my good old friend mixes with icy-cold water from the well. Under any other circumstances, the drink would simply stupefy me. As things are, it strings up my nerves. I begin to "face it," as Betteredge has predicted. And Betteredge, on his side, begins to "face it," too.

The picture which I am now presenting of myself, will, I suspect, be thought a very strange one, to say the least of it. Placed in a situation which may, I think, be described as entirely without parallel, what is the first proceeding to which I resort? Do I seclude myself from all human society? Do I set my mind to analyse the abominable impossibility which, nevertheless, confronts me as an undeniable fact? Do I hurry back to London by the first train to consult the highest authorities, and to set a searching inquiry on foot immediately? No. I accept the shelter of a house which I had resolved never to degrade myself by entering again; and I sit, tippling spirits and water in the company of an old servant, at ten o'clock in the morning. Is this the conduct that might have been expected from a man placed in my horrible position? I can only answer that the sight of old Betteredge's familiar face was an inexpressible comfort to me, and that the drinking of old Betteredge's grog helped me, as I believe nothing else would have helped me, in the state of complete bodily and mental prostration into which I had fallen. I can only offer this excuse for myself; and I can only admire that invariable preservation of dignity, and that strictly logical consistency of conduct which distinguish every man and woman who may read these lines, in every emergency of their lives from the cradle to the grave.

"Now, Mr. Franklin, there's one thing certain, at any rate," said Betteredge, throwing the nightgown down on the table between us, and pointing to it as if it was a living creature that could hear him. "*He's* a liar, to begin with."

This comforting view of the matter was not the view that presented itself to my mind.

"I am as innocent of all knowledge of having taken the Diamond as you are," I said. "But there is the witness against me! The paint on the nightgown, and the name on the nightgown are facts."

Betteredge lifted my glass, and put it persuasively into my hand.

"Facts?" he repeated. "Take a drop more grog, Mr. Franklin, and you'll get over the weakness of believing in facts! Foul play, sir!" he continued, dropping his voice confidentially. "That is how I read the riddle. Foul play somewhere – and you and I must find it out. Was there nothing else in the tin case, when you put your hand into it?"

The question instantly reminded me of the letter in my pocket. I took it out, and opened it. It was a letter of many pages, closely written. I looked impatiently for the signature at the end. "Rosanna Spearman."

As I read the name, a sudden remembrance illuminated my mind, and a sudden suspicion rose out of the new light.

"Stop!" I exclaimed. "Rosanna Spearman came to my aunt out of a reformatory? Rosanna Spearman had once been a thief?"

"There's no denying that, Mr. Franklin. What of it now, if you please?"

"What of it now? How do we know she may not have stolen the Diamond after all? How do we know she may not have smeared my nightgown purposely with the paint – ?"

Betteredge laid his hand on my arm, and stopped me before I could say any more.

"You will be cleared of this, Mr. Franklin, beyond all doubt. But I hope you won't be cleared in *that* way. See what the letter says, sir. In justice to the girl's memory, see what it says."

I felt the earnestness with which he spoke – felt it as a friendly rebuke to me. "You shall form your own judgment on her letter," I said. "I will read it out."

I began – and read these lines:

"Sir, – I have something to own to you. A confession which means much misery, may sometimes be made in very few words. This confession can be made in three words. I love you."

The letter dropped from my hand. I looked at Betteredge. "In the name of Heaven," I said, "what does it mean?"

He seemed to shrink from answering the question.

"You and Limping Lucy were alone together this morning, sir," he said. "Did she say nothing about Rosanna Spearman?"

"She never even mentioned Rosanna Spearman's name."

"Please to go back to the letter, Mr. Franklin. I tell you plainly, I can't find it in my heart to distress you, after what you have had to bear already. Let her speak for herself, sir. And get on with your grog. For your own sake, get on with your grog."

I resumed the reading of the letter.

"It would be very disgraceful to me to tell you this, if I was a living woman when you read it. I shall be dead and gone, sir, when you find my letter. It is that which makes me bold. Not even my grave will be left to tell of me. I may own the truth – with the quicksand waiting to hide me when the words are written.[1]

"Besides, you will find your nightgown in my hiding-place, with the smear of the paint on it; and you will want to know how it came to be hidden by me? and why I said nothing to you about it in my life-time? I have only one reason to give. I did these strange things

---

1   Rosanna's drowning in quicksand has its predecessors in nineteenth-century literature, scenes Collins probably knew, created by writers Collins admired. Edgar
Ravenswood, of Sir Walter Scott's (1771-1832) *The Bride of Lammermoor* (1818), is
swallowed up in a quicksand while on his way to his duels with Lucy Ashton's
brother and husband. In Thomas De Quincey's 1849 essay "The English Mail
Coach," De Quincey relates a dream of a girl swallowed by quicksand.

because I loved you.

"I won't trouble you with much about myself, or my life, before you came to my lady's house. Lady Verinder took me out of a reformatory. I had gone to the reformatory from the prison. I was put in the prison, because I was a thief. I was a thief, because my mother went on the streets when I was quite a little girl. My mother went on the streets, because the gentleman who was my father deserted her. There is no need to tell such a common story as this, at any length. It is told quite often enough in the newspapers.

"Lady Verinder was very kind to me, and Mr. Betteredge was very kind to me. Those two, and the matron at the reformatory are the only good people I have ever met with in all my life. I might have got on in my place – not happily – but I might have got on, if you had not come visiting. I don't blame *you*, sir. It's my fault – all my fault.

"Do you remember when you came out on us from among the sandhills, that morning, looking for Mr. Betteredge? You were like a prince in a fairy-story. You were like a lover in a dream. You were the most adorable human creature I had ever seen. Something that felt like the happy life I had never led yet, leapt up in me at the instant I set eyes on you.[1] Don't laugh at this if you can help it. Oh, if I could only make you feel how serious it is to *me*!

"I went back to the house, and wrote your name and mine in my work-box, and drew a true lovers' knot under them. Then, some devil – no, I ought to say some good angel – whispered to me, 'Go and look in the glass.' The glass told me – never mind what. I was too foolish to take the warning. I went on getting fonder and fonder of you, just as if I was a lady in your own rank of life, and the most beautiful creature your eyes ever rested on. I tried – oh, dear, how I tried – to get you to look at me. If you had known how I used to cry at night with the misery and the mortification of your never taking any notice of me, you would have pitied me perhaps, and have given me a look now and then to live on.

"It would have been no very kind look, perhaps, if you had known how I hated Miss Rachel. I believe I found out you were in love with her, before you knew it yourself. She used to give you roses to wear in your button-hole. Ah, Mr. Franklin, you wore *my* roses oftener than

---

1   Collins employed the notion of love at first sight in other novels, including *Basil*, *The Woman in White*, and *Heart and Science*.

either you or she thought! The only comfort I had at that time, was putting my rose secretly in your glass of water, in place of hers – and then throwing her rose away.

"If she had been really as pretty as you thought her, I might have borne it better. No; I believe I should have been more spiteful against her still. Suppose you put Miss Rachel into a servant's dress, and took her ornaments off – ? I don't know what is the use of my writing in this way. It can't be denied that she had a bad figure; she was too thin. But who can tell what the men like? And young ladies may behave in a manner which would cost a servant her place. It's no business of mine. I can't expect you to read my letter, if I write it in this way. But it does stir one up to hear Miss Rachel called pretty, when one knows all the time that it's her dress does it, and her confidence in herself.

"Try not to lose patience with me, sir. I will get on as fast as I can to the time which is sure to interest you – the time when the Diamond was lost.

"But there is one thing which I have got it on my mind to tell you first.

"My life was not a very hard life to bear, while I was a thief. It was only when they had taught me at the reformatory to feel my own degradation, and to try for better things, that the days grew long and weary. Thoughts of the future forced themselves on me now. I felt the dreadful reproach that honest people – even the kindest of honest people – were to me in themselves. A heart-breaking sensation of loneliness kept with me, go where I might, and do what I might, and see what persons I might. It was my duty, I know, to try and get on with my fellow-servants in my new place. Somehow, I couldn't make friends with them. They looked (or I thought they looked) as if they suspected what I had been. I don't regret, far from it, having been roused to make the effort to be a reformed woman – but, indeed, indeed it was a weary life. You had come across it like a beam of sunshine at first – and then you too failed me. I was mad enough to love you; and I couldn't even attract your notice. There was great misery – there really was great misery in that.

"Now I am coming to what I wanted to tell you. In those days of bitterness, I went two or three times, when it was my turn to go out, to my favourite place – the beach above the Shivering Sand. And I said to myself, 'I think it will end here. When I can bear it no longer, I think it will end here.'You will understand, sir, that the place had laid a kind of spell on me before you came. I had always had a notion that something would happen to me at the quicksand. But I had never looked at it, with the thought of its being the means of my making away with myself, till the time came of which I am now writing. Then I did think that here was a place which would end all my troubles for me in a moment or two – and hide me for ever afterwards.

"This is all I have to say about myself, reckoning from the morning when I first saw you, to the morning when the alarm was raised in the house that the Diamond was lost.

"I was so aggravated by the foolish talk among the womenservants, all wondering who was to be suspected first; and I was so angry with you (knowing no better at that time) for the pains you took in hunting for the jewel, and sending for the police, that I kept as much as possible away by myself, until later in the day, when the officer from Frizinghall came to the house.

"Mr. Seegrave began, as you may remember, by setting a guard on the women's bedrooms; and the women all followed him upstairs in a rage, to know what he meant by the insult he had put on them. I went with the rest, because if I had done anything different from the rest, Mr. Seegrave was the sort of man who would have suspected me directly. We found him in Miss Rachel's room. He told us he wouldn't have a lot of women there; and he pointed to the smear on the painted door, and said some of our petticoats had done the mischief, and sent us all downstairs again.

"After leaving Miss Rachel's room, I stopped a moment on one of the landings, by myself, to see if I had got the paint-stain by any chance on *my* gown. Penelope Betteredge (the only one of the women with whom I was on friendly terms) passed, and noticed what I was about.

"'You needn't trouble yourself, Rosanna,' she said. 'The paint on Miss Rachel's door has been dry for hours. If Mr. Seegrave hadn't set a watch on our bedrooms, I might have told him as much. I don't know what *you* think – *I* was never so insulted before in my life!'

"Penelope was a hot-tempered girl. I quieted her, and brought her back to what she had said about the paint on the door having been dry for hours.

"'How do you know that?' I asked.

"'I was with Miss Rachel, and Mr. Franklin, all yesterday morning,' Penelope said, 'mixing the colours, while they finished the door. I heard Miss Rachel ask whether the door would be dry that evening, in time for the birthday company to see it. And Mr. Franklin shook his head, and said it wouldn't be dry in less than twelve hours. It was long past luncheon-time – it was three o'clock before they had done. What does your arithmetic say, Rosanna? Mine says the door was dry by three this morning.'

"'Did some of the ladies go upstairs yesterday evening to see it?' I asked. 'I thought I heard Miss Rachel warning them to keep clear of the door.'

"'None of the ladies made the smear,' Penelope answered. 'I left Miss Rachel in bed at twelve last night. And I noticed the door, and there was nothing wrong with it then.'

"'Oughtn't you to mention this to Mr. Seegrave, Penelope?'

"'I wouldn't say a word to help Mr. Seegrave for anything that could be offered to me!'

"She went to her work, and I went to mine.

"My work, sir, was to make your bed, and to put your room tidy. It was the happiest hour I had in the whole day. I used to kiss the pillow on which your head had rested all night. No matter who has done it since, you have never had your clothes folded as nicely as I folded them for you. Of all the little knick-knacks in your dressing-case, there wasn't one that had so much as a speck on it. You never noticed it, any more than you noticed me. I beg your pardon; I am forgetting myself. I will make haste, and go on again.

"Well, I went in that morning to do my work in your room. There was your nightgown tossed across the bed, just as you had thrown it off. I took it up to fold it – and I saw the stain of the paint from Miss Rachel's door!

"I was so startled by the discovery that I ran out, with the night-gown in my hand, and made for the back stairs, and locked myself into my own room, to look at it in a place where nobody could intrude and interrupt me.

"As soon as I got my breath again, I called to mind my talk with Penelope, and I said to myself, 'Here's the proof that he was in Miss Rachel's sitting-room between twelve last night, and three this morning!'

"I shall not tell you in plain words what was the first suspicion that crossed my mind, when I had made that discovery. You would only be angry – and, if you were angry, you might tear my letter up and read no more of it.

"Let it be enough, if you please, to say only this. After thinking it over to the best of my ability, I made it out that the thing wasn't likely, for a reason that I will tell you. If you had been in Miss Rachel's sitting-room, at that time of night, with Miss Rachel's knowledge (and if you had been foolish enough to forget to take care of the wet door) *she* would have reminded you – *she* would never have let you carry away such a witness against her, as the witness I was looking at now! At the same time, I own I was not completely certain in my own mind that I had proved my own suspicion to be wrong. You will not have forgotten that I have owned to hating Miss Rachel. Try to think, if you can, that there was a little of that hatred in all this. It ended in my determining to keep the nightgown, and to wait, and watch, and see what use I might make of it. At that time, please to remember, not the ghost of an idea entered my head that *you* had stolen the Diamond."

There, I broke off in the reading of the letter for the second time.

I had read those portions of the miserable woman's confession which related to myself, with unaffected surprise, and, I can honestly add, with sincere distress. I had regretted, truly regretted, the aspersion which I had thoughtlessly cast on her memory, before I had seen a line of her letter. But when I had advanced as far as the passage which is quoted above, I own I felt my mind growing bitterer and bitterer against Rosanna Spearman as I went on. "Read the rest for yourself," I said, handing the letter to Betteredge across the table. "If there is anything in it that I *must* look at, you can tell me as you go on."

"I understand you, Mr. Franklin," he answered. "It's natural, sir, in *you*. And, God help us all!" he added in a lower tone, "it's no less natural in *her*."

I proceed to copy the continuation of the letter from the original, in my own possession:

"Having determined to keep the nightgown, and to see what use my love, or my revenge (I hardly know which) could turn it to in the future, the next thing to discover was how to keep it without the risk of being found out.

"There was only one way – to make another nightgown exactly like it, before Saturday came, and brought the laundry-woman and her inventory to the house.

"I was afraid to put it off till next day (the Friday); being in doubt lest some accident might happen in the interval. I determined to make the new nightgown on that same day (the Thursday), while I could count, if I played my cards properly, on having my time to myself. The first thing to do (after locking up your nightgown in my drawer) was to go back to your bedroom – not so much to put it to rights (Penelope would have done that for me, if I had asked her) as to find out whether you had smeared off any of the paint-stain from your nightgown, on the bed, or on any piece of furniture in the room.

"I examined everything narrowly, and at last, I found a few streaks of the paint on the inside of your dressing-gown – not the linen dressing-gown you usually wore in that summer season, but a flannel dressing-gown which you had with you also. I suppose you felt chilly after walking to and fro in nothing but your night-dress, and put on the warmest thing you could find. At any rate, there were the stains, just visible, on the inside of the dressing-gown. I easily got rid of these by scraping away the stuff of the flannel. This done, the only proof left against you was the proof locked up in my drawer.

"I had just finished your room when I was sent for to be questioned by Mr. Seegrave, along with the rest of the servants. Next came the examination of all our boxes. And then followed the most extraordinary event of the day – to *me* – since I had found the paint on your nightgown. This event came out of the second questioning of Penelope Betteredge by Superintendent Seegrave.

"Penelope returned to us quite beside herself with rage at the manner in which Mr. Seegrave had treated her. He had hinted, beyond the possibility of mistaking him, that he suspected her of being the thief. We were all equally astonished at hearing this, and we all asked, Why?

"'Because the Diamond was in Miss Rachel's sitting-room,' Penelope answered. 'And because I was the last person in the sitting-room at night!'

"Almost before the words had left her lips, I remembered that another person had been in the sitting-room later than Penelope. That person was yourself. My head whirled round, and my thoughts were in dreadful confusion. In the midst of it all, something in my mind whispered to me that the smear on your nightgown might have a meaning entirely different to the meaning which I had given to it up to that time. 'If the last person who was in the room is the person to be suspected,' I thought to myself, 'the thief is not Penelope, but Mr. Franklin Blake!'

"In the case of any other gentleman, I believe I should have been ashamed of suspecting him of theft, almost as soon as the suspicion had passed through my mind.

"But the bare thought that YOU had let yourself down to my level, and that I, in possessing myself of your nightgown, had also possessed myself of the means of shielding you from being discovered, and disgraced for life – I say sir, the bare thought of this seemed to open such a chance before me of winning your good will, that I passed blindfold, as one may say, from suspecting to believing. I made up my mind, on the spot, that you had shown yourself the busiest of anybody in fetching the police, as a blind to deceive us all; and that the hand which had taken Miss Rachel's jewel could by no possibility be any other hand than yours.

"The excitement of this new discovery of mine must, I think, have turned my head for a while. I felt such a devouring eagerness to see you – to try you with a word or two about the Diamond, and to *make* you look at me, and speak to me, in that way – that I put my hair tidy, and made myself as nice as I could, and went to you boldly in the library where I knew you were writing.

"You had left one of your rings upstairs, which made as good an excuse for my intrusion as I could have desired. But, oh, sir! if you have ever loved, you will understand how it was that all my courage cooled, when I walked into the room, and found myself in your presence. And then, you looked up at me so coldly, and you thanked me for finding your ring in such an indifferent manner, that my knees trembled under me, and I felt as if I should drop on the floor at your feet. When you had thanked me, you looked back, if you remember, at your writing. I was so mortified at being treated in this way, that I plucked up spirit enough to speak. I said, 'This is a strange thing about the Diamond, sir.' And you looked up again, and said, 'Yes, it is!' You spoke civilly (I can't deny that); but still you kept a distance – a cruel distance between us. Believing, as I did, that you had got the lost Diamond hidden about you, while you were speaking, your coolness so provoked me that I got bold enough, in the heat of the moment, to give you a hint. I said, 'They will never find the Diamond, sir, will they? No! nor the person who took it. I'll answer for that.' I nodded, and smiled at you, as much as to say, 'I know!' *This* time, you looked up at me with something like interest in your eyes; and I felt that a few more words on your side and mine might bring out the truth. Just at that moment, Mr. Betteredge spoilt it all by coming to the door. I knew his footstep, and I also knew that it was against his rules for me to be in the library at that time of day – let alone being there along with you. I had only just time to get out of my own accord, before he could come in and tell me to go. I was angry and disappointed; but I was not entirely without hope for all that. The ice, you see, was broken between us – and I thought I would take care, on the next occasion, that Mr. Betteredge was out of the way.

"When I got back to the servants' hall, the bell was going for our dinner. Afternoon already! and the materials for making the new nightgown were still to be got! There was but one chance of getting them. I shammed ill at dinner; and so secured the whole of the interval from then till tea-time to my own use.

"What I was about, while the household believed me to be lying down in my own room; and how I spent the night, after shamming ill again at tea-time, and having been sent up to bed, there is no need to tell you. Sergeant Cuff discovered that much, if he discovered nothing more. And I can guess how. I was detected (though I kept my veil down) in the draper's shop at Frizinghall. There was a glass in front of me, at the counter where I was buying the longcloth; and – in that glass – I saw one of the shopmen point to my shoulder and whisper to another. At night again, when I was secretly at work, locked into my room, I heard the breathing of the women-servants who suspected me, outside my door.

"It didn't matter then; it doesn't matter now. On the Friday morning, hours before Sergeant Cuff entered the house, there was the new nightgown – to make up your number in place of the nightgown that

I had got – made, wrung out, dried, ironed, marked, and folded as the laundry woman folded all the others, safe in your drawer. There was no fear (if the linen in the house was examined) of the newness of the nightgown betraying me. All your under-clothing had been renewed, when you came to our house – I suppose on your return home from foreign parts.

"The next thing was the arrival of Sergeant Cuff; and the next great surprise was the announcement of what *he* thought about the smear on the door.

"I had believed you to be guilty (as I have owned) more because I wanted you to be guilty than for any other reason. And now, the Sergeant had come round by a totally different way to the same conclusion (respecting the nightgown) as mine! And I had got the dress that was the only proof against you! And not a living creature knew it – yourself included! I am afraid to tell you how I felt when I called these things to mind – you would hate my memory for ever afterwards."

At that place, Betteredge looked up from the letter.

"Not a glimmer of light so far, Mr. Franklin," said the old man, taking off his heavy tortoiseshell spectacles, and pushing Rosanna Spearman's confession a little away from him. "Have you come to any conclusion, sir, in your own mind, while I have been reading?"

"Finish the letter first, Betteredge; there may be something to enlighten us at the end of it. I shall have a word or two to say to you after that."

"Very good, sir. I'll just rest my eyes, and then I'll go on again. In the meantime, Mr. Franklin – I don't want to hurry you – but would you mind telling me, in one word, whether you see your way out of this dreadful mess yet?"

"I see my way back to London," I said, "to consult Mr. Bruff. If he can't help me –"

"Yes, sir?"

"And if the Sergeant won't leave his retirement at Dorking –"

"He won't, Mr. Franklin!"

"Then, Betteredge – as far as I can see now – I am at the end of my resources. After Mr. Bruff and the Sergeant, I don't know of a living creature who can be of the slightest use to me."

As the words passed my lips, some person outside knocked at the door of the room.

Betteredge looked surprised as well as annoyed by the interruption.

"Come in," he called out irritably, "whoever you are!"

The door opened, and there entered to us, quietly, the most remarkable-looking man that I had ever seen. Judging him by his figure and his movements, he was still young. Judging him by his face, and comparing him with Betteredge, he looked the elder of the two. His complexion was of a gipsy darkness; his fleshless cheeks had fallen into deep hollows, over which the bone projected like a pent-house. His nose presented the fine shape and modelling so often found among the ancient people of the East, so seldom visible among the newer races of the West. His forehead rose high and straight from the brow. His marks and wrinkles were innumerable. From this strange face, eyes, stranger still, of the softest brown – eyes dreamy and mournful, and deeply sunk in their orbits – looked out at you, and (in my case, at least) took your attention captive at their will. Add to this a quantity of thick closely-curling hair, which, by some freak of Nature, had lost its colour in the most startlingly partial and capricious manner. Over the top of his head it was still of the deep black which was its natural colour. Round the sides of his head – without the slightest gradation of grey to break the force of the extraordinary contrast – it had turned completely white. The line between the two colours preserved no sort of regularity. At one place, the white hair ran up into the black; at another, the black hair ran down into the white. I looked at the man with a curiosity which, I am ashamed to say, I found it quite impossible to control. His soft brown eyes looked back at me gently; and he met my involuntary rudeness in staring at him, with an apology which I was conscious that I had not deserved.

"I beg your pardon," he said. "I had no idea that Mr. Betteredge was engaged." He took a slip of paper from his pocket, and handed it to Betteredge. "The list for next week," he said. His eyes just rested on me again – and he left the room as quietly as he had entered it.

"Who is that?" I asked.

"Mr. Candy's assistant," said Betteredge. "By-the-by, Mr. Franklin, you will be sorry to hear that the little doctor has never recovered that illness he caught, going home from the birthday dinner. He's pretty well in health; but he lost his memory in the fever, and he has never recovered more than the wreck of it since. The work all falls on his assistant. Not much of it now, except among the poor. *They* can't help themselves, you know. *They* must put up with the man with the piebald hair, and the gipsy complexion – or they would get no doctoring at all."

"You don't seem to like him, Betteredge?"

"Nobody likes him, sir."

"Why is he so unpopular?"

"Well, Mr. Franklin, his appearance is against him, to begin with. And then there's a story that Mr. Candy took him with a very doubtful character. Nobody knows who he is – and he hasn't a friend in the place. How can you expect one to like him, after that?"

"Quite impossible, of course! May I ask what he wanted with you, when he gave you that bit of paper?"

"Only to bring me the weekly list of the sick people about here, sir, who stand in need of a little wine. My lady always had a regular distribution of good sound port and sherry among the infirm poor; and Miss Rachel wishes the custom to be kept up. Times have changed! times have changed! I remember when Mr. Candy himself brought the list to my mistress. Now it's Mr. Candy's assistant who brings the list to me. I'll go on with the letter, if you will allow me, sir," said Betteredge, drawing Rosanna Spearman's confession back to him. "It isn't lively reading, I grant you. But, there! it keeps me from getting sour with thinking of the past." He put on his spectacles, and wagged his head gloomily. "There's a bottom of good sense, Mr. Franklin, in our conduct to our mothers, when they first start us on the journey of life. We are all of us more or less unwilling to be brought into the world. And we are all of us right."

Mr. Candy's assistant had produced too strong an impression on me to be immediately dismissed from my thoughts. I passed over the last unanswerable utterance of the Betteredge philosophy; and returned to the subject of the man with the piebald hair.

"What is his name?" I asked.

"As ugly a name as need be," Betteredge answered gruffly. "Ezra Jennings."

★

CHAPTER V

HAVING told me the name of Mr. Candy's assistant, Betteredge appeared to think that we had wasted enough of our time on an insignificant subject. He resumed the perusal of Rosanna Spearman's letter.

On my side, I sat at the window, waiting until he had done. Little by little, the impression produced on me by Ezra Jennings – it seemed perfectly unaccountable, in such a situation as mine, that any human being should have produced an impression on me at all! – faded from my mind. My thoughts flowed back into their former channel. Once more, I forced myself to look my own incredible position resolutely in the face. Once more, I reviewed in my own mind the course which I had at last summoned composure enough to plan out for the future.

To go back to London that day; to put the whole case before Mr. Bruff; and, last and most important, to obtain (no matter by what means or at what sacrifice) a personal interview with Rachel – this was my plan of action, so far as I was capable of forming it at the time. There was more than an hour still to spare before the train started. And there was the bare chance that Betteredge might discover something in the unread portion of Rosanna Spearman's letter, which it might be useful for me to know before I left the house in which the Diamond had been lost. For that chance I was now waiting.

The letter ended in these terms:

"You have no need to be angry, Mr. Franklin, even if I did feel some little triumph at knowing that I held all your prospects in life in my own hands. Anxieties and fears soon came back to me. With the view Sergeant Cuff took of the loss of the Diamond, he would be sure to end in examining our linen and our dresses. There was no place in my room – there was no place in the house – which I could feel satisfied would be safe from him. How to hide the nightgown so that not even the Sergeant could find it? and how to do that without losing one moment of precious time? – these were not easy questions to answer. My uncertainties ended in my taking a way that may make you laugh. I undressed, and put the nightgown on me. You had worn it – and I had another little moment of pleasure in wearing it after you.

"The next news that reached us in the servants' hall showed that I had not made sure of the nightgown a moment too soon. Sergeant Cuff wanted to see the washing-book.

"I found it, and took it to him in my lady's sitting-room. The Sergeant and I had come across each other more than once in former days. I was certain he would know me again – and I was *not* certain of what he might do when he found me employed as servant in a house in which a valuable jewel had been lost. In this suspense, I felt it would be a relief to me to get the meeting between us over, and to know the worst of it at once.

"He looked at me as if I was a stranger, when I handed him the washing-book; and he was very specially polite in thanking me for bringing it. I thought those were both bad signs. There was no knowing what he might say of me behind my back; there was no knowing how soon I might not find myself taken in custody on suspicion, and searched. It was then time for your return from seeing Mr. Godfrey Ablewhite off by the railway; and I went to your favourite walk in the shrubbery, to try for another chance of speaking to you – the last chance, for all I knew to the contrary, that I might have.

"You never appeared; and, what was worse still, Mr. Betteredge and Sergeant Cuff passed by the place where I was hiding – and the Sergeant saw me.

"I had no choice, after that, but to return to my proper place and my proper work, before more disasters happened to me. Just as I was going to step across the path, you came back from the railway. You were making straight for the shrubbery, when you saw me – I am certain, sir, you saw me – and you turned away as if I had got the plague, and went into the house.*

"I made the best of my way indoors again, returning by the servants' entrance. There was nobody in the laundry-room at that time; and I sat down there alone. I have told you already of the thoughts which the Shivering Sand put into my head. Those thoughts came back to me now. I wondered in myself which it would be hardest to do, if things went on in this manner – to bear Mr. Franklin Blake's

---

* Note; by Franklin Blake. – The writer is entirely mistaken, poor creature. I never noticed her. My intention was certainly to have taken a turn in the shrubbery. But, remembering at the same moment that my aunt might wish to see me, after my return from the railway, I altered my mind, and went into the house.

indifference to me, or to jump into the quicksand and end it for ever in that way?

"It's useless to ask me to account for my own conduct, at this time. I try – and I can't understand it myself.

"Why didn't I stop you, when you avoided me in that cruel manner? Why didn't I call out, 'Mr. Franklin, I have got something to say to you; it concerns yourself, and you must, and shall, hear it?' You were at my mercy – I had got the whip-hand of you, as they say. And better than that, I had the means (if I could only make you trust me) of being useful to you in the future. Of course, I never supposed that you – a gentleman – had stolen the Diamond for the mere pleasure of stealing it. No. Penelope had heard Miss Rachel, and I had heard Mr. Betteredge, talk about your extravagance and your debts. It was plain enough to me that you had taken the Diamond to sell it, or pledge it, and so to get the money of which you stood in need. Well! I could have told you of a man in London who would have advanced a good large sum on the jewel, and who would have asked no awkward questions about it either.

"Why didn't I speak to you! why didn't I speak to you!

"I wondered whether the risks and difficulties of keeping the nightgown were as much as I could manage, without having other risks and difficulties added to them? This might have been the case with some women – but how could it be the case with me? In the days when I was a thief, I had run fifty times greater risks, and found my way out of difficulties to which *this* difficulty was mere child's play. I had been apprenticed, as you may say, to frauds and deceptions – some of them on such a grand scale, and managed so cleverly, that they became famous, and appeared in the newspapers. Was such a little thing as the keeping of the nightgown likely to weigh on my spirits, and to set my heart sinking within me, at the time when I ought to have spoken to you? What nonsense to ask the question! The thing couldn't be.

"Where is the use of my dwelling in this way on my own folly? The plain truth is plain enough, surely? Behind your back, I loved you with all my heart and soul. Before your face – there's no denying it – I was frightened of you; frightened of making you angry with me; frightened of what you might say to me (though you *had* taken the Diamond) if I presumed to tell you that I had found it out. I had gone as near to it as I dared when I spoke to you in the library. You had not turned your back on me then. You had not started away from me as if I had got the plague. I tried to provoke myself into feeling angry with you, and to rouse up my courage in that way. No! I couldn't feel anything but the misery and the mortification of it. 'You're a plain girl; you have got a crooked shoulder; you're only a housemaid – what do you mean by attempting to speak to Me?' You never uttered a word of that, Mr. Franklin; but you said it all to me, nevertheless! Is such madness as this to be accounted for? No. There is nothing to be done but to confess it, and let it be.

"I ask your pardon, once more, for this wandering of my pen. There is no fear of its happening again. I am close at the end now.

"The first person who disturbed me by coming into the empty room was Penelope. She had found out my secret long since, and she had done her best to bring me to my senses – and done it kindly too.

"'Ah!' she said, 'I know why you're sitting here, and fretting, all by yourself. The best thing that can happen for your advantage, Rosanna, will be for Mr. Franklin's visit here to come to an end. It's my belief that he won't be long now before he leaves the house.'

"In all my thoughts of you I had never thought of your going away. I couldn't speak to Penelope. I could only look at her.

"'I've just left Miss Rachel,' Penelope went on. 'And a hard matter I have had of it to put up with her temper. She says the house is unbearable to her with the police in it; and she's determined to speak to my lady this evening, and to go to her Aunt Ablewhite to-morrow. If she does that, Mr. Franklin will be the next to find a reason for going away, you may depend on it!'

"I recovered the use of my tongue at that. 'Do you mean to say Mr. Franklin will go with her?' I asked.

"'Only too gladly, if she would let him; but she won't. *He* has been made to feel her temper; *he* is in her black books too – and that after having done all he can to help her, poor fellow! No! no! If they don't make it up before to-morrow, you will see Miss Rachel go one way, and Mr. Franklin another. Where he may betake himself to I can't say. But he will never stay here, Rosanna, after Miss Rachel has left us.'

"I managed to master the despair I felt at the prospect of your going away. To own the truth, I saw a little glimpse of hope for myself if there was really a serious disagreement between Miss Rachel and you. 'Do you know,' I asked, 'what the quarrel is between them?'

"'It is all on Miss Rachel's side,' Penelope said. 'And for anything I know to the contrary, it's all Miss Rachel's temper, and nothing else. I am loth to distress you, Rosanna; but don't run away with the notion that Mr. Franklin is ever likely to quarrel with *her*. He's a great deal too fond of her for that!'

"She had only just spoken those cruel words when there came a call to us from Mr. Betteredge. All the indoor servants were to assemble in the hall. And then we were to go in, one by one, and be questioned in Mr. Betteredge's room by Sergeant Cuff.

"It came to my turn to go in, after her ladyship's maid and the upper housemaid had been questioned first. Sergeant Cuff's inquiries – though he wrapped them up very cunningly – soon showed me that those two women (the bitterest enemies I had in the house) had made their discoveries outside my door, on the Tuesday afternoon, and again on the Thursday night. They had told the Sergeant enough to open his eyes to some part of the truth. He rightly believed me to have made a new nightgown secretly, but he wrongly believed the paint-stained nightgown to be mine. I felt satisfied of another thing, from what he said, which it puzzled me to understand. He suspected me, of course, of being concerned in the disappearance of the Diamond. But, at the same time, he let me see – purposely, as I thought – that he did not consider me as the person chiefly answerable for the loss of the jewel. He appeared to think that I had been acting under the direction of somebody else. Who that person might be, I couldn't guess then, and can't guess now.

"In this uncertainty, one thing was plain – that Sergeant Cuff was miles away from knowing the whole truth. You were safe as long as the nightgown was safe – and not a moment longer.

"I quite despair of making you understand the distress and terror which pressed upon me now. It was impossible for me to risk wearing your nightgown any longer. I might find myself taken off, at a moment's notice, to the police court at Frizinghall, to be charged on suspicion, and searched accordingly. While Sergeant Cuff still left me free, I had to choose – and at once – between destroying the nightgown, or hiding it in some safe place, at some safe distance from the house.

"If I had only been a little less fond of you, I think I should have destroyed it. But oh! how could I destroy the only thing I had which proved that I had saved you from discovery? If we did come to an explanation together, and if you suspected me of having some bad motive, and denied it all, how could I win upon you to trust me, unless I had the nightgown to produce? Was it wronging you to believe, as I did, and do still, that you might hesitate to let a poor girl like me be the sharer of your secret, and your accomplice in the theft which your money-troubles had tempted you to commit? Think of your cold behaviour to me, sir, and you will hardly wonder at my unwillingness to destroy the only claim on your confidence and your gratitude which it was my fortune to possess.

"I determined to hide it; and the place I fixed on was the place I knew best – the Shivering Sand.

"As soon as the questioning was over, I made the first excuse that came into my head and got leave to go out for a breath of fresh air. I went straight to Cobb's Hole, to Mr. Yolland's cottage. His wife and daughter were the best friends I had. Don't suppose I trusted them with your secret – I have trusted nobody. All I wanted was to write this letter to you, and to have a safe opportunity of taking the night-gown off me. Suspected as I was, I could do neither of those things, with any sort of security, up at the house.

"And now I have nearly got through with my long letter, writing it alone in Lucy Yolland's bedroom. When it is done, I shall go down-stairs with the nightgown rolled up, and hidden under my cloak. I shall find the means I want for keeping it safe and dry in its hiding-place, among the litter of old things in Mrs. Yolland's kitchen. And then I shall go to the Shivering Sand – don't be afraid of my letting my footmarks betray me! – and hide the nightgown down in the sand, where no living creature can find it without being first let into the secret by myself.

"And when that's done, what then?

"Then, Mr. Franklin, I shall have two reasons for making another attempt to say the words to you which I have not said yet. If you leave the house, as Penelope believes you will leave it, and if I haven't spo-ken to you before that, I shall lose my opportunity for ever. That is one reason. Then, again, there is the comforting knowledge – if my speaking does make you angry – that I have got the nightgown ready to plead my cause for me as nothing else can. That is my other reason. If these two together don't harden my heart against the coldness which has hitherto frozen it up (I mean the coldness of your treatment of me), there will be the end of my efforts – and the end of my life.

"Yes. If I miss my next opportunity – if you are as cruel as ever, and if I feel it again as I have felt it already – good-bye to the world which has grudged me the happiness that it gives to others. Good-bye to life, which nothing but a little kindness from *you* can ever make pleasurable to me again. Don't blame yourself, sir, if it ends in this way. But try – do try – to feel some forgiving sorrow for me! I shall take care that you find out what I have done for you, when I am past telling you of it myself. Will you say something kind of me then – in the same gentle way that you have when you speak to Miss Rachel? If you do that, and if there are such things as ghosts, I believe my ghost will hear it, and tremble with the pleasure of it.

"It's time I left off. I am making myself cry. How am I to see my way to the hiding-place if I let these useless tears come and blind me?

"Besides, why should I look at the gloomy side? Why not believe, while I can, that it will end well after all? I may find you in a good humour to-night – or, if not, I may succeed better tomorrow morning. I shan't improve my plain face by fretting – shall I? Who knows but I may have filled all these weary long pages of paper for nothing? They will go, for safety's sake (never mind now for what other reason) into the hiding-place along with the nightgown. It has been hard, hard work writing my letter. Oh! if we only end in understanding each other, how I shall enjoy tearing it up.

"I beg to remain, sir, your true lover and humble servant,
"ROSANNA SPEARMAN."

The reading of the letter was completed by Betteredge in silence. After carefully putting it back in the envelope, he sat thinking, with his head bowed down, and his eyes on the ground.

"Betteredge," I said, "is there any hint to guide me at the end of the letter?"

He looked up slowly, with a heavy sigh.

"There is nothing to guide you, Mr. Franklin," he answered. "If you take my advice you will keep the letter in the cover till these present anxieties of yours have come to an end. It will sorely distress you, whenever you read it. Don't read it now."

I put the letter away in my pocket-book.

A glance back at the sixteenth and seventeenth chapters of Betteredge's Narrative will show that there really was a reason for my thus sparing myself, at a time when my fortitude had been already cruelly tried. Twice over, the unhappy woman had made her last attempt to speak to me. And twice over, it had been my misfortune (God knows how innocently!) to repel the advances she had made to me. On the Friday night, as Betteredge truly describes it, she had found me alone at the billiard-table. Her manner and language suggested to me – and would have suggested to any man, under the circumstances – that she was about to confess a guilty knowledge of the disappearance of the Diamond. For her own sake, I had purposely shown no special interest in what was coming; for her own sake, I had purposely looked at the billiardballs, instead of looking at *her* – and what had been the result? I had sent her away from me, wounded to the heart! On the Saturday again – on the day when she must have foreseen – after what Penelope had told her, that my departure was close at hand – the same fatality still pursued us. She had once more attempted to meet me in the shrubbery walk, and she had found me there in company with Betteredge and Sergeant Cuff. In her hearing, the Sergeant, with his own underhand object in view, had appealed to my interest in Rosanna Spearman. Again for the poor creature's own sake, I had met the police-officer with a flat denial, and had declared – loudly declared, so that she might hear me too – that I felt "no interest whatever in Rosanna Spearman." At those words, solely designed to warn her against attempting to gain my private ear, she had turned away and left the place: cautioned of her danger, as I then believed; self-doomed to destruction, as I know now. From that point, I have already traced the succession of events which led me to the astounding discovery at the quicksand. The retrospect is now complete. I may leave the miserable story of Rosanna Spearman – to which, even at this distance of time, I cannot revert without a pang of distress – to suggest for itself all that is here purposely left unsaid. I may pass from the suicide at the Shivering Sand, with its strange and terrible influence on my present position and future prospects, to interests which concern the living people of this narrative, and to events which were already paving my way for the slow and toilsome journey from the darkness to the light.

CHAPTER VI

I WALKED to the railway-station accompanied, it is needless to say, by Gabriel Betteredge. I had the letter in my pocket, and the nightgown safely packed in a little bag – both to be submitted, before I slept that night, to the investigation of Mr. Bruff.

We left the house in silence. For the first time in my experience of him, I found old Betteredge in my company without a word to say to me. Having something to say on my side, I opened the conversation as soon as we were clear of the lodge gates.

"Before I go to London," I began, "I have two questions to ask you. They relate to myself, and I believe they will rather surprise you."

"If they will put that poor creature's letter out of my head," Mr. Franklin, "they may do anything else they like with me. Please to begin surprising me, sir, as soon as you can."

"My first question, Betteredge, is this. Was I drunk on the night of Rachel's Birthday?"

"You drunk!" exclaimed the old man. "Why, it's the great defect of your character, Mr. Franklin, that you only drink with your dinner, and never touch a drop of liquor afterwards!"

"But the birthday was a special occasion. I might have abandoned my regular habits, on that night of all others."

Betteredge considered for a moment.

"You did go out of your habits, sir," he said. "And I'll tell you how. You looked wretchedly ill – and we persuaded you to have a drop of brandy-and-water to cheer you up a little."

"I am not used to brandy-and-water. It is quite possible –"

"Wait a bit, Mr. Franklin. I knew you were not used, too. I poured you out half a wineglass-full of our fifty-year-old Cognac; and (more shame for me!) I drowned that noble liquor in nigh on a tumbler-full of cold water. A child couldn't have got drunk on it – let alone a grown man!"

I knew I could depend on his memory, in a matter of this kind. It was plainly impossible that I could have been intoxicated. I passed on to the second question.

"Before I was sent abroad, Betteredge, you saw a great deal of me when I was a boy? Now tell me plainly, do you remember anything strange of me, after I had gone to bed at night? Did you ever discover me walking in my sleep?"

Betteredge stopped, looked at me for a moment, nodded his head, and walked on again.

"I see your drift now, Mr. Franklin! You're trying to account for how you got the paint on your nightgown, without knowing it yourself. It won't do, sir. You're miles away still from getting at the truth. Walk in your sleep? You never did such a thing in your life!"

Here again, I felt that Betteredge must be right. Neither at home nor abroad had my life ever been of the solitary sort. If I had been a sleep-walker, there were hundreds on hundreds of people who must have discovered me, and who, in the interest of my own safety, would have warned me of the habit, and have taken precautions to restrain it.

Still, admitting all this, I clung – with an obstinacy which was surely natural and excusable, under the circumstances – to one or other of the only two explanations that I could see which accounted for the unendurable position in which I then stood. Observing that I was not yet satisfied, Betteredge shrewdly adverted to certain later events in the history of the Moonstone; and scattered both my theories to the wind at once and for ever.

"Let's try it another way, sir," he said. "Keep your own opinion, and see how far it will take you towards finding out the truth. If we are to believe the nightgown – which I don't for one – you not only smeared off the paint from the door, without knowing it, but you also took the Diamond without knowing it. Is that right, so far?"

"Quite right. Go on."

"Very good, sir. We'll say you were drunk, or walking in your sleep, when you took the jewel. That accounts for the night and morning, after the birthday. But how does it account for what has happened since that time? The Diamond has been taken to London, since that time. The Diamond has been pledged to Mr. Luker, since that time. Did you do those two things, without knowing it, too? Were you drunk when I saw you off in the pony-chaise on that Saturday evening? And did you walk in your sleep to Mr. Luker's, when the train had brought you to your journey's end? Excuse me for saying it, Mr. Franklin, but this business has so upset you, that you're not fit yet to judge for yourself. The sooner you lay your head alongside of Mr. Bruff's head, the sooner you will see your way out of the deadlock that has got you now."

We reached the station, with only a minute or two to spare.

I hurriedly gave Betteredge my address in London, so that he might write to me, if necessary; promising, on my side, to inform him of any news which I might have to communicate. This done, and just as I was bidding him farewell, I happened to glance towards the book-and-newspaper stall. There was Mr. Candy's remarkable-looking assistant again, speaking to the keeper of the stall! Our eyes met at the same moment. Ezra Jennings took off his hat to me. I returned the salute, and got into a carriage just as the train started. It was a relief to my mind, I suppose, to dwell on any subject which appeared to be, personally, of no sort of importance to me. At all events, I began the momentous journey back which was to take me to Mr. Bruff, wondering – absurdly enough, I admit – that I should have seen the man with the piebald hair twice in one day!

The hour at which I arrived in London precluded all hope of my finding Mr. Bruff at his place of business. I drove from the railway to his private residence at Hampstead, and disturbed the old lawyer dozing alone in his dining-room, with his favourite pug-dog on his lap, and his bottle of wine at his elbow.

I shall best describe the effect which my story produced on the mind of Mr. Bruff by relating his proceedings when he had heard it to the end. He ordered lights, and strong tea, to be taken into his study; and he sent a message to the ladies of his family, forbidding them to disturb us on any pretence whatever. These preliminaries disposed of, he first examined the nightgown, and then devoted himself to the reading of Rosanna Spearman's letter.

The reading completed, Mr. Bruff addressed me for the first time since we had been shut up together in the seclusion of his own room.

"Franklin Blake," said the old gentleman, "this is a very serious matter, in more respects than one. In my opinion, it concerns Rachel quite as nearly as it concerns you. Her extraordinary conduct is no mystery *now*. She believes you have stolen the Diamond."

I had shrunk from reasoning my own way fairly to that revolting conclusion. But it had forced itself on me, nevertheless. My resolution to obtain a personal interview with Rachel, rested really and truly on the ground just stated by Mr. Bruff.

"The first step to take in this investigation," the lawyer proceeded, "is to appeal to Rachel. She has been silent all this time, from motives which I (who know her character) can readily understand. It is impossible, after what has happened, to submit to that silence any longer. She must be persuaded to tell us, or she must be forced to tell us, on what grounds she bases her belief that you took the Moonstone. The chances are, that the whole of this case, serious as it seems now, will tumble to pieces, if we can only break through Rachel's inveterate reserve, and prevail upon her to speak out."

"That is a very comforting opinion for *me*," I said. "I own I should like to know –"

"You would like to know how I can justify it," interposed Mr. Bruff. "I can tell you in two minutes. Understand, in the first place, that I look at this matter from a lawyer's point of view. It's a question of evidence, with me. Very well. The evidence breaks down, at the outset, on one important point."

"On what point?"

"You shall hear. I admit that the mark of the name proves the nightgown to be yours. I admit that the mark of the paint proves the nightgown to have made the smear on Rachel's door. But what evidence is there to prove that your are the person who wore it, on the night when the Diamond was lost?"

The objection struck me, all the more forcibly that it reflected an objection which I had felt myself.

"As to this," pursued the lawyer, taking up Rosanna Spearman's confession, "I can understand that the letter is a distressing one to *you*. I can understand that you may hesitate to analyse it from a purely impartial point of view. But I am not in your position. I can bring my professional experience to bear on this document, just as I should bring it to bear on any other. Without alluding to the woman's career as a thief, I will merely remark that her letter proves her to have been an adept at deception, on her own showing; and I argue from that, that I am justified in suspecting her of not having told the whole truth. I won't start any theory, at present, as to what she may or may not have done. I will only say that, if Rachel has suspected you *on the evidence of the nightgown only*, the chances are ninety-nine to a hundred that Rosanna Spearman was the person who showed it to her. In that case, there is the woman's letter, confessing that she was jealous of Rachel, confessing that she changed the roses, confessing that she saw a glimpse of hope for herself, in the prospect of a quarrel between Rachel and you. I don't stop to ask who took the Moonstone (as a means to her end, Rosanna Spearman would have taken fifty Moonstones) – I only say that the disappearance of the jewel gave this reclaimed thief who was in love with you, an opportunity of setting you and Rachel at variance for the rest of your lives. She had not decided on destroying herself, *then*, remember; and, having the opportunity, I distinctly assert that it was in her character, and in her position at the time, to take it. What do you say to that?"

"Some such suspicion," I answered, "crossed my own mind, as soon as I opened the letter."

"Exactly! And when you had read the letter, you pitied the poor creature, and couldn't find it in your heart to suspect her. Does you credit, my dear sir – does you credit!"

"But suppose it turns out that I did wear the nightgown? What then?"

"I don't see how the fact is to be proved," said Mr. Bruff. "But assuming the proof to be possible, the vindication of your innocence would be no easy matter. We won't go into that, now. Let us wait and see whether Rachel hasn't suspected you on the evidence of the nightgown only."

"Good God, how coolly you talk of Rachel suspecting me!" I broke out. "What right has she to suspect Me, on any evidence, of being a thief?"

"A very sensible question, my dear sir. Rather hotly put – but well worth considering for all that. What puzzles you, puzzles me too. Search your memory, and tell me this. Did anything happen while you were staying at the house – not, of course, to shake Rachel's belief in your honour – but, let us say, to shake her belief (no matter with how little reason) in your principles generally?"

I started, in ungovernable agitation, to my feet. The lawyer's question reminded me, for the first time since I had left England, that something *had* happened.

In the eighth chapter of Betteredge's Narrative, an allusion will be found to the arrival of a foreigner and a stranger at my aunt's house, who came to see me on business. The nature of his business was this.

I had been foolish enough (being, as usual, straitened for money at the time) to accept a loan from the keeper of a small restaurant in Paris, to whom I was well known as a customer. A time was settled between us for paying the money back; and when the time came, I found it (as thousands of other honest men have found it) impossible to keep my engagement. I sent the man a bill. My name was unfortunately too well known on such documents: he failed to negotiate it. His affairs had fallen into disorder, in the interval since I had borrowed of him; bankruptcy stared him in the face; and a relative of his, a French lawyer, came to England to find me, and to insist upon the payment of my debt. He was a man of violent temper; and he took the wrong way with me. High words passed on both sides; and my aunt and Rachel were unfortunately in the next room, and heard us. Lady Verinder came in, and insisted on knowing what was the matter. The Frenchman produced his credentials, and declared me to be responsible for the ruin of a poor man, who had trusted in my honour. My aunt instantly paid him the money, and sent him off. She knew me better, of course, than to take the Frenchman's view of the transaction. But she was shocked at my carelessness, and justly angry with me for placing myself in a position, which, but for her interference, might have become a very disgraceful one. Either her mother told her, or Rachel heard what passed – I can't say which. She took her own romantic, high-flown view of the matter. I was "heartless"; I was "dishonourable"; I had "no principle"; there was "no knowing what I might do next" – in short, she said some of the severest things to me which I had ever heard from a young lady's lips. The breach between us lasted for the whole of the next day. The day after, I succeeded in making my peace, and thought no more of it. Had Rachel reverted to this unlucky accident, at the critical moment when my place in her estimation was again, and far more seriously, assailed? Mr. Bruff, when I had mentioned the circumstances to him, answered the question at once in the affirmative.

"It would have its effect on her mind," he said gravely. "And I wish, for your sake, the thing had not happened. However, we have discovered that there *was* a predisposing influence against you – and there is one uncertainty cleared out of our way, at any rate. I see nothing more that we can do now. Our next step in this inquiry must be the step that takes us to Rachel."

He rose, and began walking thoughtfully up and down the room. Twice, I was on the point of telling him that I had determined on seeing Rachel personally; and twice, having regard to his age and his character, I hesitated to take him by surprise at an unfavourable moment.

"The grand difficulty is," he resumed, "how to make her show her whole mind in this matter, without reserve. Have you any suggestions to offer?"

"I have made up my mind, Mr. Bruff, to speak to Rachel myself."

"You!" He suddenly stopped in his walk, and looked at me as if he thought I had taken leave of my senses. "You, of all the people in the world!" He abruptly checked himself, and took another turn in the room. "Wait a little," he said. "In cases of this extraordinary kind, the rash way is sometimes the best way." He considered the question for a moment or two, under that new light, and ended boldly by a decision in my favour. "Nothing venture, nothing have," the old gentleman resumed. "You have a chance in your favour which I don't possess – and you shall be the first to try the experiment."

"A chance in my favour?" I repeated, in the greatest surprise.

Mr. Bruff's face softened, for the first time, into a smile.

"This is how it stands," he said. "I tell you fairly, I don't trust your discretion, and I don't trust your temper. But I do trust in Rachel's still preserving, in some remote little corner of her heart, a certain perverse weakness for *you*. Touch that – and trust to the consequences for the fullest disclosures that can flow from a woman's lips! The question is – how are you to see her?"

"She has been a guest of yours at this house," I answered. "May I venture to suggest – if nothing was said about me beforehand – that I might see her here?"

"Cool!" said Mr. Bruff. With that one word of comment on the reply that I had made to him, he took another turn up and down the room.

"In plain English," he said, "my house is to be turned into a trap to catch Rachel; with a bait to tempt her, in the shape of an invitation from my wife and daughters. If you were anybody else but

Mr. Franklin Blake, and if this matter was one atom less serious than it really is, I should refuse point-blank. As things are, I firmly believe Rachel will live to thank me for turning traitor to her in my old age. Consider me your accomplice. Rachel shall be asked to spend the day here; and you shall receive due notice of it."

"When? To-morrow?"

"To-morrow won't give us time enough to get her answer. Say the day after."

"How shall I hear from you?"

"Stay at home all the morning and expect me to call on you."

I thanked him for the inestimable assistance which he was rendering to me, with the gratitude that I really felt; and, declining a hospitable invitation to sleep that night at Hampstead, returned to my lodgings in London.

Of the day that followed, I have only to say that it was the longest day of my life. Innocent as I knew myself to be, certain as I was that the abominable imputation which rested on me must sooner or later be cleared off, there was nevertheless a sense of self-abasement in my mind which instinctively disinclined me to see any of my friends. We often hear (almost invariably, however, from superficial observers) that guilt can look like innocence. I believe it to be infinitely the truer axiom of the two that innocence can look like guilt. I caused myself to be denied all day, to every visitor who called; and I only ventured out under cover of the night.

The next morning, Mr. Bruff surprised me at the breakfast-table. He handed me a large key, and announced that he felt ashamed of himself for the first time in his life.

"Is she coming?"

"She is coming to-day, to lunch and spend the afternoon with my wife and my girls."

"Are Mrs. Bruff, and your daughters, in the secret?"

"Inevitably. But women, as you may have observed, have no principles. My family don't feel my pangs of conscience. The end being to bring you and Rachel together again, my wife and daughters pass over the means employed to gain it, as composedly as if they were Jesuits."

"I am infinitely obliged to them. What is this key?"

"The key of the gate in my back-garden wall. Be there at three this afternoon. Let yourself into the garden, and make your way in by the conservatory door. Cross the small drawing-room, and open the door in front of you which leads into the music-room. There, you will find Rachel – and find her alone."

"How can I thank you!"

"I will tell you how. Don't blame *me* for what happens afterwards." With those words, he went out.

I had many weary hours still to wait through. To while away the time, I looked at my letters. Among them was a letter from Betteredge.

I opened it eagerly. To my surprise and disappointment, it began with an apology warning me to expect no news of any importance. In the next sentence the everlasting Ezra Jennings appeared again! He had stopped Betteredge on the way out of the station, and had asked who I was. Informed on this point, he had mentioned having seen me to his master Mr. Candy. Mr. Candy hearing of this, had himself driven over to Betteredge, to express his regret at our having missed each other. He had a reason for wishing particularly to speak to me; and when I was next in the neighbourhood of Frizinghall, he begged I would let him know. Apart from a few characteristic utterances of the Betteredge philosophy, this was the sum and substance of my correspondent's letter. The warm-hearted, faithful old man acknowledged that he had written "mainly for the pleasure of writing to me."

I crumpled up the letter in my pocket, and forgot it the moment after, in the all-absorbing interest of my coming interview with Rachel.

As the clock of Hampstead church struck three, I put Mr. Bruff's key into the lock of the door in the wall. When I first stepped into the garden, and while I was securing the door again on the inner side, I own to having felt a certain guilty doubtfulness about what might happen next. I looked furtively on either side of me, suspicious of the presence of some unexpected witness in some unknown corner of the garden. Nothing appeared to justify my apprehensions. The walks were, one and all, solitudes; and the birds and the bees were the only witnesses.

I passed through the garden; entered the conservatory; and crossed the small drawing-room. As I laid my hand on the door opposite, I heard a few plaintive chords struck on the piano in the room within.

She had often idled over the instrument in this way, when I was staying at her mother's house. I was obliged to wait a little, to steady myself. The past and present rose side by side, at that supreme moment – and the contrast shook me. After the lapse of a minute, I roused my manhood, and opened the door.

★

CHAPTER VII

AT the moment when I showed myself in the doorway, Rachel rose from the piano.

I closed the door behind me. We confronted each other in silence, with the full length of the room between us. The movement she had made in rising appeared to be the one exertion of which she was capable. All use of every other faculty, bodily or mental, seemed to be merged in the mere act of looking at me.

A fear crossed my mind that I had shown myself too suddenly. I advanced a few steps towards her. I said gently, "Rachel!"

The sound of my voice brought the life back to her limbs, and the colour to her face. She advanced, on her side, still without speaking. Slowly, as if acting under some influence independent of her own will, she came nearer and nearer to me; the warm dusky colour flushing her cheeks, the light of reviving intelligence brightening every instant in her eyes. I forgot the object that had brought me into her presence; I forgot the vile suspicion that rested on my good name; I forgot every consideration, past, present, and future, which I was bound to remember. I saw nothing but the woman I loved coming nearer and nearer to me. She trembled; she stood irresolute. I could resist it no longer – I caught her in my arms, and covered her face with kisses.

There was a moment when I thought the kisses were returned; a moment when it seemed as if she, too, might have forgotten. Almost before the idea could shape itself in my mind, her first voluntary action made me feel that she remembered. With a cry which was like a cry of horror – with a strength which I doubt if I could have resisted if I had tried – she thrust me back from her. I saw merciless anger in her eyes; I saw merciless contempt on her lips. She looked me over, from head to foot, as she might have looked at a stranger who had insulted her.

"You coward!" she said. "You mean, miserable, heartless coward!"

Those were her first words! The most unendurable reproach that a woman can address to a man, was the reproach that she picked out to address to Me.

"I remember the time, Rachel," I said, "when you could have told me that I had offended you, in a worthier way than that. I beg your pardon."

Something of the bitterness that I felt may have communicated itself to my voice. At the first words of my reply, her eyes, which had been turned away the moment before, looked back at me unwillingly. She answered in a low tone, with a sullen submission of manner which was quite new in my experience of her.

"Perhaps there is some excuse for me," she said. "After what you have done, is it a manly action, on your part, to find your way to me as you have found it to-day? It seems a cowardly experiment, to try an experiment on my weakness for you. It seems a cowardly surprise, to surprise me into letting you kiss me. But that is only a woman's view. I ought to have known it couldn't be your view. I should have done better if I had controlled myself, and said nothing."

The apology was more unendurable than the insult. The most degraded man living would have felt humiliated by it.

"If my honour was not in your hands," I said, "I would leave you this instant, and never see you again. You have spoken of what I have done. What have I done?"

"What have you done! *You* ask that question of *me*?"

"I ask it."

"I have kept your infamy a secret," she answered. "And I have suffered the consequences of concealing it. Have I no claim to be spared the insult of your asking me what you have done? Is *all* sense of gratitude dead in you? You were once a gentleman. You were once dear to my mother, and dearer still to me –"

Her voice failed her. She dropped into a chair, and turned her back on me, and covered her face with her hands.

I waited a little before I trusted myself to say any more. In that moment of silence, I hardly know which I felt most keenly – the sting which her contempt had planted in me, or the proud resolution which shut me out from all community with her distress.

"If you will not speak first," I said, "I must. I have come here with something serious to say to you. Will you do me the common justice of listening while I say it?"

She neither moved, nor answered. I made no second appeal to her; I never advanced an inch nearer to her chair. With a pride which was as obstinate as her pride, I told her of my discovery at the Shivering Sand, and of all that had led to it. The narrative, of necessity, occupied some little time. From beginning to end, she never looked round at me, and she never uttered a word.

I kept my temper. My whole future depended, in all probability, on my not losing possession of myself at that moment. The time had come to put Mr. Bruff's theory to the test. In the breathless interest of trying that experiment, I moved round so as to place myself in front of her.

"I have a question to ask you," I said. "It obliges me to refer again to a painful subject. Did Rosanna Spearman show you the night-gown? Yes, or No?"

She started to her feet; and walked close up to me of her own accord. Her eyes looked me searchingly in the face, as if to read something there which they had never read yet.

"Are you mad?" she asked.

I still restrained myself. I said quietly, "Rachel, will you answer my question?"

She went on, without heeding me.

"Have you some object to gain which I don't understand? Some mean fear about the future, in which I am concerned? They say your father's death has made you a rich man. Have you come here to compensate me for the loss of my Diamond? And have you heart enough left to feel ashamed of your errand? Is *that* the secret of your pretence of innocence, and your story about Rosanna Spearman? Is there a motive of shame at the bottom of all the falsehood, this time?"

I stopped her there. I could control myself no longer.

"You have done me an infamous wrong!" I broke out hotly. "You suspect me of stealing your Diamond. I have a right to know, and I *will* know, the reason why!"

"Suspect you!" she exclaimed, her anger rising with mine. *"You villain, I saw you take the Diamond with my own eyes!"*

The revelation which burst upon me in those words, the overthrow which they instantly accomplished of the whole view of the case on which Mr. Bruff had relied, struck me helpless. Innocent as I was, I stood before her in silence. To her eyes, to any eyes, I must have looked like a man overwhelmed by the discovery of his own guilt.

She drew back from the spectacle of my humiliation, and of her triumph. The sudden silence that had fallen upon me seemed to frighten her. "I spared you, at the time," she said. "I would have spared you now, if you had not forced me to speak." She moved away as if to leave the room – and hesitated before she got to the door. "Why did you come here to humiliate yourself?" she asked. "Why did you come here to humiliate me?" She went on a few steps, and paused once more. "For God's sake, say something!" she exclaimed, passionately. "If you have any mercy left, don't let me degrade myself in this way! Say something – and drive me out of the room!"

I advanced towards her, hardly conscious of what I was doing. I had possibly some confused idea of detaining her until she had told me more. From the moment when I knew that the evidence on which I stood condemned in Rachel's mind, was the evidence of her own eyes, nothing – not even my conviction of my own innocence – was clear to my mind. I took her by the hand; I tried to speak firmly and to the purpose. All I could say was, "Rachel, you once loved me."

She shuddered, and looked away from me. Her hand lay powerless and trembling in mine. "Let go of it," she said faintly.

My touch seemed to have the same effect on her which the sound of my voice had produced when I first entered the room. After she had said the word which called me a coward, after she had made the avowal which branded me as a thief – while her hand lay in mine I was her master still!

I drew her gently back into the middle of the room. I seated her by the side of me. "Rachel," I said, "I can't explain the contradiction in what I am going to tell you. I can only speak the truth as you have spoken it. You saw me – with your own eyes, you saw me take the Diamond. Before God who hears us, I declare that I now know I took it for the first time! Do you doubt me still?"

She had neither heeded nor heard me. "Let go of my hand," she repeated faintly. That was her only answer. Her head sank on my shoulder; and her hand unconsciously closed on mine, at the moment when she asked me to release it.

I refrained from pressing the question. But there my forbearance stopped. My chance of ever holding up my head again among honest men depended on my chance of inducing her to make her disclosure complete. The one hope left for me was the hope that she might have overlooked something in the chain of evidence – some mere trifle, perhaps, which might nevertheless, under careful investigation, be made the means of vindicating my innocence in the end. I own I kept possession of her hand. I own I spoke to her with all that I could summon back of the sympathy and confidence of the bygone time.

"I want to ask you something," I said. "I want you to tell me everything that happened, from the time when we wished each other good-night, to the time when you saw me take the Diamond."

She lifted her head from my shoulder, and made an effort to release her hand. "Oh, why go back to it!" she said. "Why go back to it!"

"I will tell you why, Rachel. You are the victim, and I am the victim, of some monstrous delusion which has worn the mask of truth. If we look at what happened on the night of your birthday together, we may end in understanding each other yet."

Her head dropped back on my shoulder. The tears gathered in her eyes, and fell slowly over her cheeks. "Oh!" she said, "have *I* never had that hope? Have *I* not tried to see it, as you are trying now?"

"You have tried by yourself," I answered. "You have not tried with me to help you."

Those words seemed to awaken in her something of the hope which I felt myself when I uttered them. She replied to my questions with more than docility – she exerted her intelligence; she willingly opened her whole mind to me.

"Let us begin," I said, "with what happened after we had wished each other good-night. Did you go to bed? or did you sit up?"

"I went to bed."

"Did you notice the time? Was it late?"

"Not very. About twelve o'clock, I think."

"Did you fall asleep?"

"No. I couldn't sleep that night."

"You were restless?"

"I was thinking of you."

The answer almost unmanned me. Something in the tone, even more than in the words, went straight to my heart. It was only after pausing a little first that I was able to go on.

"Had you any light in your room?" I asked.

"None – until I got up again, and lit my candle."

"How long was that, after you had gone to bed?"

"About an hour after, I think. About one o'clock."

"Did you leave your bedroom?"

"I was going to leave it. I had put on my dressing-gown; and I was going into my sitting-room to get a book –"

"Had you opened your bedroom door?"

"I had just opened it."

"But you had not gone into the sitting-room?"

"No – I was stopped from going into it."

"What stopped you?"

"I saw a light, under the door; and I heard footsteps approaching it."

"Were you frightened?"

"Not then. I knew my poor mother was a bad sleeper; and I remembered that she had tried hard, that evening, to persuade me to let her take charge of my Diamond. She was unreasonably anxious about it, as I thought; and I fancied she was coming to me to see if I was in bed, and to speak to me about the Diamond again, if she found that I was up."

"What did you do?"

"I blew out my candle, so that she might think I was in bed. I was unreasonable, on my side – I was determined to keep my Diamond in the place of my own choosing."

"After blowing the candle out, did you go back to bed?"

"I had no time to go back. At the moment when I blew the candle out, the sitting-room door opened, and I saw –"

"You saw?"

"You."

"Dressed as usual?"

"No."

"In my nightgown?"

"In your nightgown – with your bedroom candle in your hand."

"Alone?"

"Alone."

"Could you see my face?"

"Yes."

"Plainly?"

"Quite plainly. The candle in your hand showed it to me."

"Were my eyes open?"

"Yes."

"Did you notice anything strange in them? Anything like a fixed, vacant expression?"

"Nothing of the sort. Your eyes were bright – brighter than usual. You looked about in the room, as if you knew you were where you ought not to be, and as if you were afraid of being found out."

"Did you observe one thing when I came into the room – did you observe how I walked?"

"You walked as you always do. You came in as far as the middle of the room – and then you stopped and looked about you."

"What did you do, on first seeing me?"

"I could do nothing. I was petrified. I couldn't speak, I couldn't call out, I couldn't even move to shut my door."

"Could I see you, where you stood?"

"You might certainly have seen me. But you never looked towards me. It's useless to ask the question. I am sure you never saw me."

"How are you sure?"

"Would you have taken the Diamond? would you have acted as you did afterwards? would you be here now – if you had seen that I was awake and looking at you? Don't make me talk of that part of it! I want to answer you quietly. Help me to keep as calm as I can. Go on to something else."

She was right – in every way, right. I went on to other things.

"What did I do, after I had got to the middle of the room, and had stopped there?"

"You turned away, and went straight to the corner near the window – where my Indian cabinet stands."

"When I was at the cabinet, my back must have been turned towards you. How did you see what I was doing?"

"When you moved, I moved."

"So as to see what I was about with my hands?"

"There are three glasses in my sitting-room. As you stood there, I saw all that you did, reflected in one of them."

"What did you see?"

"You put your candle on the top of the cabinet. You opened, and shut, one drawer after another, until you came to the drawer in which I had put my Diamond. You looked at the open drawer for a moment. And then you put your hand in, and took the Diamond out."

"How do you know I took the Diamond out?"

"I saw your hand go into the drawer. And I saw the gleam of the stone between your finger and thumb, when you took your hand out."

"Did my hand approach the drawer again – to close it, for instance?"

"No. You had the Diamond in your right hand; and you took the candle from the top of the cabinet with your left hand."

"Did I look about me again, after that?"

"No."

"Did I leave the room immediately?"

"No. You stood quite still, for what seemed a long time. I saw your face sideways in the glass. You looked like a man thinking, and dissatisfied with his own thoughts."

"What happened next?"

"You roused yourself on a sudden, and you went straight out of the room."

"Did I close the door after me?"

"No. You passed out quickly into the passage, and left the door open."

"And then?"

"Then, your light disappeared, and the sound of your steps died away, and I was left alone in the dark."

"Did nothing happen – from that time, to the time when the whole house knew that the Diamond was lost?"

"Nothing."

"Are you sure of that? Might you not have been asleep a part of the time?"

"I never slept. I never went back to my bed. Nothing happened until Penelope came in, at the usual time in the morning."

I dropped her hand, and rose, and took a turn in the room. Every question that I could put had been answered. Every detail that I could desire to know had been placed before me. I had even reverted to the idea of sleep-walking, and the idea of intoxication; and, again, the worthlessness of the one theory and the other had been proved – on the authority, this time, of the witness who had seen me. What was to be said next? what was to be done next? There rose the horrible fact of the Theft – the one visible, tangible object that confronted me, in the midst of the impenetrable darkness which enveloped all besides! Not a glimpse of light to guide me, when I had possessed myself of Rosanna Spearman's secret at the Shivering Sand. And not a glimpse of light now, when I had appealed to Rachel herself, and had heard the hateful story of the night from her own lips.

She was the first, this time, to break the silence.

"Well?" she said, "you have asked, and I have answered. You have made me hope something from all this, because *you* hoped something from it. What have you to say now?"

The tone in which she spoke warned me that my influence over her was a lost influence once more.

"We were to look at what happened on my birthday night, together," she went on; "and we were then to understand each other. Have we done that?"

She waited pitilessly for my reply. In answering her I committed a fatal error – I let the exasperating helplessness of my situation get the better of my self-control. Rashly and uselessly, I reproached her for the silence which had kept me until that moment in ignorance of the truth.

"If you had spoken when you ought to have spoken," I began: "if you had done me the common justice to explain yourself –"

She broke in on me with a cry of fury. The few words I had said seemed to have lashed her on the instant into a frenzy of rage.

"Explain myself!" she repeated. "Oh! is there another man like this in the world? I spare him, when my heart is breaking; I screen him when my own character is at stake; and he – of all human beings, he – turns on me now, and tells me that I ought to have explained myself! After believing in him as I did, after loving him as I did, after thinking of him by day, and dreaming of him by night – he wonders I didn't charge him with his disgrace the first time we met: 'My heart's darling, you are a Thief! My hero whom I love and honour, you have crept into my room under cover of the night, and stolen my Diamond!' That is what I ought to have said. You villain, you mean, mean, mean villain, I would have lost fifty diamonds, rather than see your face lying to me, as I see it lying now!"

I took up my hat. In mercy to *her* – yes! I can honestly say it – in mercy to *her*, I turned away without a word, and opened the door by which I had entered the room.

She followed, and snatched the door out of my hand; she closed it, and pointed back to the place that I had left.

"No!" she said. "Not yet! It seems that *I* owe a justification of my conduct to *you*. You shall stay and hear it. Or you shall stoop to the lowest infamy of all, and force your way out."

It wrung my heart to see her; it wrung my heart to hear her. I answered by a sign – it was all that I could do – that I submitted myself to her will.

The crimson flush of anger began to fade out of her face, as I went back, and took my chair in silence. She waited a little, and steadied herself. When she went on, but one sign of feeling was discernible in her. She spoke without looking at me. Her hands were fast clasped in her lap, and her eyes were fixed on the ground.

"I ought to have done you the common justice to explain myself," she said, repeating my own words. "You shall see whether I did try to do you justice, or not. I told you just now that I never slept, and never returned to my bed, after you had left my sitting-room. It's useless to trouble you by dwelling on what I thought – you would not understand my thoughts – I will only tell you what I did, when time enough had passed to help me to recover myself. I refrained from alarming the house, and telling everybody what had happened – as I ought to have done. In spite of what I had seen, I was fond enough of you to believe – no matter what! – any impossibility, rather than admit it to my own mind that you were deliberately a thief. I thought and thought – and I ended in writing to you."

"I never received the letter."

"I know you never received it. Wait a little, and you shall hear why. My letter would have told you nothing openly. It would not have ruined you for life, if it had fallen into some other person's hands. It would only have said – in a manner which you yourself could not possibly have mistaken – that I had reason to know you were in debt, and that it was in my experience and in my mother's experience of you, that you were not very discreet, or very scrupulous about how you got money when you wanted it. You would have remembered the visit of the French lawyer, and you would have known what I referred to. If you had read on with some interest after that, you would have come to an offer I had to make to you – the offer, privately (not a word, mind, to be said openly about it between us!), of the loan of as large a sum of money as I could get. – And I would have got it!" she exclaimed, her colour beginning to rise again, and her eyes looking up at me once more. "I would have pledged the Diamond myself, if I could have got the money in no other way! In those words I wrote to you. Wait! I did more than that. I arranged with Penelope to give you the letter when nobody was near. I planned to shut myself into my bedroom, and to have the sitting-room left open and empty all the morning. And I hoped – with all my heart and soul I hoped! – that you would take the opportunity, and put the Diamond back secretly in the drawer."

I attempted to speak. She lifted her hand impatiently, and stopped me. In the rapid alternations of her temper, her anger was beginning to rise again. She got up from her chair, and approached me.

"I know what you are going to say," she went on. "You are going to remind me again that you never received my letter. I can tell you why. I tore it up."

"For what reason?" I asked.

"For the best of reasons. I preferred tearing it up to throwing it away upon such a man as you! What was the first news that reached me in the morning? Just as my little plan was complete, what did I hear? I heard that you – you!!! – were the foremost person in the house in fetching the police. You were the active man; you were the leader; you were working harder than any of them to recover the jewel! You even carried your audacity far enough to ask to speak to *me* about the loss of the Diamond – the Diamond which you yourself had stolen; the Diamond which was all the time in your own hands! After that proof of your horrible falseness and cunning, I tore up my letter. But even then – even when I was maddened by the searching and questioning of the policeman, whom *you* had sent in – even then, there was some infatuation in my mind which wouldn't let me give you up. I said to myself, 'He has played his vile farce before everybody else in the house. Let him try if he can play it before me.' Somebody told me you were on the terrace. I went down to the terrace. I forced myself to look at you; I forced myself to speak to you. Have you forgotten what I said?"

I might have answered that I remembered every word of it. But what purpose, at that moment, would the answer have served?

How could I tell her that what she had said had astonished me, had distressed me, had suggested to me that she was in a state of dangerous nervous excitement, had even roused a moment's doubt in my mind whether the loss of the jewel was as much a mystery to her as to the rest of us – but had never once given me so much as a glimpse at the truth? Without the shadow of a proof to produce in vindication of my innocence, how could I persuade her that I knew no more than the veriest stranger could have known of what was really in her thoughts when she spoke to me on the terrace?

"It may suit your convenience to forget; it suits my convenience to remember," she went on. "I know what I said – for I considered it with myself, before I said it. I gave you one opportunity after another of owning the truth. I left nothing unsaid that I *could* say – short of actually telling you that I knew you had committed the theft. And all the return you made, was to look at me with your vile pretence of astonishment, and your false face of innocence – just as you have looked at me to-day; just as you are looking at me now! I left you, that morning, knowing you at last for what you were – for what you are – as base a wretch as ever walked the earth!"

"If you had spoken out at the time, you might have left me, Rachel, knowing that you had cruelly wronged an innocent man."

"If I had spoken out before other people," she retorted, with another burst of indignation, "you would have been disgraced for life! If I had spoken out to no ears but yours, you would have denied it, as you are denying it now! Do you think I should have believed you? Would a man hesitate at a lie, who had done what I saw *you* do – who had behaved about it afterwards, as I saw *you* behave? I tell you again, I shrank from the horror of hearing you lie, after the horror of seeing you thieve. You talk as if this was a misunderstanding which a few words might have set right! Well! the misunderstanding is at an end. Is the thing set right? No! the thing is just where it was. I don't believe you *now*! I don't believe you found the nightgown, I don't believe in Rosanna Spearman's letter, I don't believe a word you have said. You stole it – I saw you! You affected to help the police – I saw you! You pledged the Diamond to the money-lender in London – I am sure of it! You cast the suspicion of your disgrace (thanks to my base silence)! on an innocent man! You fled to the Continent with your plunder the next morning! After all that vileness, there was but one thing more you *could* do. You could come here with a last falsehood on your lips – you could come here, and tell me that I have wronged you!"

If I had stayed a moment more, I know not what words might have escaped me which I should have remembered with vain repentance and regret. I passed by her, and opened the door for the second time. For the second time – with the frantic perversity of a roused woman – she caught me by the arm, and barred my way out.

"Let me go, Rachel," I said. "It will be better for both of us. Let me go."

The hysterical passion swelled in her bosom – her quickened convulsive breathing almost beat on my face, as she held me back at the door.

"Why did you come here?" she persisted, desperately. "I ask you again – why did you come here? Are you afraid I shall expose you? Now you are a rich man, now you have got a place in the world, now you may marry the best lady in the land – are you afraid I shall say the words which I have never said yet to anybody but you? I can't say the words! I can't expose you! I am worse, if worse can be, than you are yourself." Sobs and tears burst from her. She struggled with them fiercely; she held me more and more firmly. "I can't tear you out of my heart," she said, "even now! You may trust in the shameful, shameful weakness which can only struggle against you in this way!" She suddenly let go of me – she threw up her hands, and wrung them frantically in the air. "Any other woman living would shrink from the disgrace of touching him!" she exclaimed. "Oh, God! I despise myself even more heartily than I despise *him*!"

The tears were forcing their way into my eyes in spite of me – the horror of it was to be endured no longer.

"You shall know that you have wronged me, yet," I said. "Or you shall never see me again!"

With those words, I left her. She started up from the chair on which she had dropped the moment before: she started up – the noble creature! – and followed me across the outer room, with a last merciful word at parting.

"Franklin!" she said, "I forgive you! Oh, Franklin, Franklin! we shall never meet again. Say you forgive *me!*"

I turned, so as to let my face show her that I was past speaking – I turned, and waved my hand, and saw her dimly, as in a vision, through the tears that had conquered me at last.

The next moment, the worst bitterness of it was over. I was out in the garden again. I saw her, and heard her, no more.

★

CHAPTER VIII

LATE that evening, I was surprised at my lodgings by a visit from Mr. Bruff.

There was a noticeable change in the lawyer's manner. It had lost its usual confidence and spirit. He shook hands with me, for the first time in his life, in silence.

"Are you going back to Hampstead?" I asked, by way of saying something.

"I have just left Hampstead," he answered. "I know, Mr. Franklin, that you have got at the truth at last. But, I tell you plainly, if I could have foreseen the price that was to be paid for it, I should have preferred leaving you in the dark."

"You have seen Rachel?"

"I have come here after taking her back to Portland Place; it was impossible to let her return in the carriage by herself. I can hardly hold you responsible – considering that you saw her in my house and by my permission – for the shock that this unlucky interview has inflicted on her. All I can do is to provide against a repetition of the mischief. She is young – she has a resolute spirit – she will get over this, with time and rest to help her. I want to be assured that you will do nothing to hinder her recovery. May I depend on your making no second attempt to see her – except with my sanction and approval?"

"After what she has suffered, and after what I have suffered," I said, "you may rely on me."

"I have your promise?"

"You have my promise."

Mr. Bruff looked relieved. He put down his hat, and drew his chair nearer to mine.

"That's settled!" he said. "Now, about the future – *your* future, I mean. To my mind, the result of the extraordinary turn which the matter has now taken is briefly this. In the first place, we are sure that Rachel has told you the whole truth, as plainly as words can tell it. In the second place – though we know that there must be some dreadful mistake somewhere – we can hardly blame her for believing you to be guilty, on the evidence of her own senses; backed, as that evidence has been, by circumstances which appear, on the face of them, to tell dead against you."

There I interposed. "I don't blame Rachel," I said. "I only regret that she could not prevail on herself to speak more plainly to me at the time."

"You might as well regret that Rachel is not somebody else," rejoined Mr. Bruff. "And even then, I doubt if a girl of any delicacy, whose heart had been set on marrying you, could have brought herself to charge you to your face with being a thief. Anyhow, it was not in Rachel's nature to do it. In a very different matter to this matter of yours – which placed her, however, in a position not altogether unlike her position towards you – I happen to know that she was influenced by a similar motive to the motive which actuated her conduct in your case. Besides, as she told me herself, on our way to town this evening, if she *had* spoken plainly, she would no more have believed your denial then than she believes it now. What answer can you make to that? There is no answer to be made to it. Come, come, Mr. Franklin! my view of the case has been proved to be all wrong, I admit – but, as things are now, my advice may be worth having for all that. I tell you plainly, we shall be wasting our time, and cudgelling our brains to no purpose, if we attempt to try back, and unravel this frightful complication from the beginning. Let us close our minds resolutely to all that happened last year at Lady Verinder's country house; and let us look to what we *can* discover in the future, instead of to what we can *not* discover in the past."

"Surely you forget," I said, "that the whole thing is essentially a matter of the past – so far as I am concerned?"

"Answer me this," retorted Mr. Bruff. "Is the Moonstone at the bottom of all the mischief – or is it not?"

"It is – of course."

"Very good. What do we believe was done with the Moonstone, when it was taken to London?"

"It was pledged to Mr. Luker."

"We know that you are not the person who pledged it. Do we know who did?"

"No."

"Where do we believe the Moonstone to be now?"

"Deposited in the keeping of Mr. Luker's bankers."

"Exactly. Now observe. We are already in the month of June. Towards the end of the month (I can't be particular to a day) a year will have elapsed from the time when we believe the jewel to have been pledged. There is a chance – to say the least – that the person who pawned it, may be prepared to redeem it when the year's time has expired. If he redeems it, Mr. Luker must himself – according to the terms of his own arrangement – take the Diamond out of his banker's hands. Under these circumstances, I propose setting a watch at the bank, as the present month draws to an end, and discovering who the person is to whom Mr. Luker restores the Moonstone. Do you see it now?"

I admitted (a little unwillingly) that the idea was a new one, at any rate.

"It's Mr. Murthwaite's idea quite as much as mine," said Mr. Bruff. "It might have never entered my head, but for a conversation we had together some time since. If Mr. Murthwaite is right, the Indians are likely to be on the look-out at the bank, towards the end of the month too – and something serious may come of it. What comes of it doesn't matter to you and me – except as it may help us to lay our hands on the mysterious Somebody who pawned the Diamond. That person, you may rely on it, is responsible (I don't pretend to know how) for the position in which you stand at this moment; and that person alone can set you right in Rachel's estimation."

"I can't deny," I said, "that the plan you propose meets the difficulty in a way that is very daring, and very ingenious, and very new. But –"

"But you have an objection to make?"

"Yes. My objection is, that your proposal obliges us to wait."

"Granted. As I reckon the time, it requires you to wait about a fortnight – more or less. Is that so very long?"

"It's a lifetime, Mr. Bruff, in such a situation as mine. My existence will be simply unendurable to me, unless I do something towards clearing my character at once."

"Well, well, I understand that. Have you thought yet of what you can do?"

"I have thought of consulting Sergeant Cuff."

"He has retired from the police. It's useless to expect the Sergeant to help you."

"I know where to find him; and I can but try."

"Try," said Mr. Bruff, after a moment's consideration. "The case has assumed such an extraordinary aspect since Sergeant Cuff's time, that you *may* revive his interest in the inquiry. Try, and let me hear the result. In the meanwhile," he continued, rising, "if you make no discoveries between this, and the end of the month, am I free to try, on my side, what can be done by keeping a look-out at the bank?"

"Certainly," I answered – "unless I relieve you of all necessity for trying the experiment in the interval."

Mr. Bruff smiled, and took up his hat.

"Tell Sergeant Cuff," he rejoined, "that *I* say the discovery of the truth depends on the discovery of the person who pawned the Diamond. And let me hear what the Sergeant's experience says to that."

So we parted.

Early the next morning, I set forth for the little town of Dorking – the place of Sergeant Cuff's retirement, as indicated to me by Betteredge.

Inquiring at the hotel, I received the necessary directions for finding the Sergeant's cottage. It was approached by a quiet by-road, a little way out of the town, and it stood snugly in the middle of its own plot of garden ground, protected by a good brick wall at the back and the sides, and by a high quickset hedge[1] in front. The gate, ornamented at the upper part by smartly-painted trellis-work, was locked. After ringing at the bell, I peered through the trellis-work, and saw

---

1 A quickset hedge is a hedge made from the cuttings of hawthorn shrubs.

the great Cuff's favourite flower everywhere; blooming in his garden, clustering over his door, looking in at his windows. Far from the crimes and the mysteries of the great city, the illustrious thief-taker was placidly living out the last Sybarite[1] years of his life, smothered in roses!

A decent elderly woman opened the gate to me, and at once annihilated all the hopes I had built on securing the assistance of Sergeant Cuff. He had started, only the day before, on a journey to Ireland.

"Has he gone there on business?" I asked.

The woman smiled. "He has only one business now, sir," she said; "and that's roses. Some great man's gardener in Ireland has found out something new in the growing of roses – and Mr. Cuff's away to inquire into it."

"Do you know when he will be back?"

"It's quite uncertain, sir. Mr. Cuff said he should come back directly, or be away some time, just according as he found the new discovery worth nothing, or worth looking into. If you have any message to leave for him, I'll take care, sir, that he gets it."

I gave her my card, having first written on it in pencil: "I have something to say about the Moonstone. Let me hear from you as soon as you get back." That done, there was nothing left but to submit to circumstances, and return to London.

In the irritable condition of my mind, at the time of which I am now writing, the abortive result of my journey to the Sergeant's cottage simply aggravated the restless impulse in me to be doing something. On the day of my return from Dorking, I determined that the next morning should find me bent on a new effort at forcing my way, through all obstacles, from the darkness to the light.

What form was my next experiment to take?

If the excellent Betteredge had been present while I was considering that question, and if he had been let into the secret of my thoughts, he would, no doubt, have declared that the German side of me was, on this occasion, my uppermost side. To speak seriously, it is perhaps possible that my German training was in some degree responsible for the labyrinth of useless speculations in which I now

---

1 Derived from Sybaris, an ancient Greek city in southern Italy that came to be known as a centre of luxurious living, a Sybarite is a person devoted to pleasure.

involved myself. For the greater part of the night, I sat smoking, and building up theories, one more profoundly improbable than another. When I did get to sleep, my waking fancies pursued me in dreams. I rose the next morning, with Objective-Subjective and Subjective-Objective inextricably entangled together in my mind; and I began the day which was to witness my next effort at practical action of some kind by doubting whether I had any sort of right (on purely philosophical grounds) to consider any sort of thing (the Diamond included) as existing at all.

How long I might have remained lost in the mist of my own metaphysics, if I had been left to extricate myself, it is impossible for me to say. As the event proved, accident came to my rescue, and happily delivered me. I happened to wear, that morning, the same coat which I had worn on the day of my interview with Rachel. Searching for something else in one of the pockets, I came upon a crumpled piece of paper, and, taking it out, found Betteredge's forgotten letter in my hand.

It seemed hard on my good old friend to leave him without a reply. I went to my writing-table, and read his letter again.

A letter which has nothing of the slightest importance in it, is not always an easy letter to answer. Betteredge's present effort at corresponding with me came within this category. Mr. Candy's assistant, otherwise Ezra Jennings, had told his master that he had seen me; and Mr. Candy, in his turn, wanted to see me and say something to me, when I was next in the neighbourhood of Frizinghall. What was to be said in answer to that, which would be worth the paper it was written on? I sat idly drawing likenesses from memory of Mr. Candy's remarkable-looking assistant on the sheet of paper which I had vowed to dedicate to Betteredge – until it suddenly occurred to me that here was the irrepressible Ezra Jennings getting in my way again! I threw a dozen portraits, at least, of the man with the piebald hair (the hair in every case, remarkably like), into the waste-paper basket – and then and there, wrote my answer to Betteredge. It was a perfectly commonplace letter – but it had one excellent effect on me. The effort of writing a few sentences, in plain English, completely cleared my mind of the cloudy nonsense which had filled it since the previous day.

Devoting myself once more to the elucidation of the impenetrable puzzle which my own position presented to me, I now tried to meet the difficulty by investigating it from a plainly practical point of view. The events of the memorable night being still unintelligible to me, I looked a little farther back, and searched my memory of the earlier hours of the birthday for any incident which might prove of some assistance to me in finding the clue.

Had anything happened while Rachel and I were finishing the painted door? or, later, when I rode over to Frizinghall? or afterwards, when I went back with Godfrey Ablewhite and his sisters? or, later again, when I put the Moonstone into Rachel's hands? or, later still, when the company came, and we all assembled round the dinner-table? My memory disposed of that string of questions readily enough, until I came to the last. Looking back at the social events of the birthday dinner, I found myself brought to a standstill at the out-set of the inquiry. I was not even capable of accurately remembering the number of the guests who had sat at the same table with me.

To feel myself completely at fault here, and to conclude, there-upon, that the incidents of the dinner might especially repay the trouble of investigating them, formed parts of the same mental process, in my case. I believe other people, in a similar situation, would have reasoned as I did. When the pursuit of our own interests causes us to become objects of inquiry to ourselves, we are naturally suspicious of what we don't know. Once in possession of the names of the persons who had been present at the dinner, I resolved – as a means of enriching the deficient resources of my own memory – to appeal to the memory of the rest of the guests; to write down all that they could recollect of the social events of the birthday; and to test the result, thus obtained, by the light of what had happened after-wards, when the company had left the house.

This last and newest of my many contemplated experiments in the art of inquiry – which Betteredge would probably have attributed to the clear-headed, or French, side of me being uppermost for the moment – may fairly claim record here, on its own merits. Unlikely as it may seem, I had now actually groped my way to the root of the matter at last. All I wanted was a hint to guide me in the right direction at starting. Before another day had passed over my head, that hint was given me by one of the company who had been present at the birthday feast!

With the plan of proceeding which I now had in view, it was first necessary to possess the complete list of the guests. This I could easily obtain from Gabriel Betteredge. I determined to go back to Yorkshire on that day, and to begin my contemplated investigation the next morning.

It was just too late to start by the train which left London before noon. There was no alternative but to wait, nearly three hours, for the departure of the next train. Was there anything I could do in London, which might usefully occupy this interval of time?

My thoughts went back again obstinately to the birthday dinner.

Though I had forgotten the numbers, and, in many cases, the names of the guests, I remembered readily enough that by far the larger proportion of them came from Frizinghall, or from its neighbourhood. But the larger proportion was not all. Some few of us were not regular residents in the country. I myself was one of the few. Mr. Murthwaite was another. Godfrey Ablewhite was a third. Mr. Bruff – no: I called to mind that business had prevented Mr. Bruff from making one of the party. Had any ladies been present, whose usual residence was in London? I could only remember Miss Clack as coming within this latter category. However, here were three of the guests, at any rate, whom it was clearly advisable for me to see before I left town. I drove off at once to Mr. Bruff's office; not knowing the addresses of the persons of whom I was in search, and thinking it probable that he might put me in the way of finding them.

Mr. Bruff proved to be too busy to give me more than a minute of his valuable time. In that minute, however, he contrived to dispose – in the most discouraging manner – of all the questions I had to put to him.

In the first place, he considered my newly discovered method of finding a clue to the mystery as something too purely fanciful to be seriously discussed. In the second, third, and fourth places, Mr. Murthwaite was now on his way back to the scene of his past adventures; Miss Clack had suffered losses, and had settled, from motives of economy, in France; Mr. Godfrey Ablewhite might, or might not, be discoverable somewhere in London. Suppose I inquired at his club? And suppose I excused Mr. Bruff, if he went back to his business and wished me good morning?

The field of inquiry in London, being now so narrowed as only to include the one necessity of discovering Godfrey's address, I took the lawyer's hint, and drove to his club.

In the hall, I met with one of the members, who was an old friend of my cousin's, and who was also an acquaintance of my own. This gentleman, after enlightening me on the subject of Godfrey's address, told me of two recent events in his life, which were of some importance in themselves, and which had not previously reached my ears.

It appeared that Godfrey, far from being discouraged by Rachel's withdrawal from her engagement to him, had made matrimonial advances soon afterwards to another young lady, reputed to be a great heiress. His suit had prospered, and his marriage had been considered as a settled and certain thing. But, here again, the engagement had been suddenly and unexpectedly broken off – owing, it was said, on this occasion, to a serious difference of opinion between the bridegroom and the lady's father, on the question of settlements.

As some compensation for this second matrimonial disaster, Godfrey had soon afterwards found himself the object of fond pecuniary remembrance, on the part of one of his many admirers. A rich old lady – highly respected at the Mothers'-Small-Clothes-Conversion Society, and a great friend of Miss Clack's (to whom she had left nothing but a mourning ring)[1] – had bequeathed to the admirable and meritorious Godfrey a legacy of five thousand pounds. After receiving this handsome addition to his own modest pecuniary resources, he had been heard to say that he felt the necessity of getting a little respite from his charitable labours, and that his doctor prescribed "a run on the Continent, as likely to be productive of much future benefit to his health."[2] If I wanted to see him, it would be advisable to lose no time in paying my contemplated visit.

I went, then and there, to pay my visit.

The same fatality which had made me just one day too late in calling on Sergeant Cuff, made me again one day too late in calling on

---

1 The Victorians took their mourning seriously, and ceremoniously. The ring given to Miss Clack, which she was to wear for a prescribed period of time, probably held a polished black stone.

2 Victorian doctors often prescribed a "run on the continent" for patients suffering rheumatic ailments. In 1863 Collins himself visited the German resorts of Aix-la-Chapelle and Wildbad for the climate and for the famous sulphurous hot baths.

Godfrey. He had left London, on the previous morning, by the tidal train, for Dover. He was to cross to Ostend; and his servant believed he was going on to Brussels. The time of his return was rather uncertain; but I might be sure he would be away at least three months.

I went back to my lodgings a little depressed in spirits. Three of the guests at the birthday dinner – and those three all exceptionally intelligent people – were out of my reach, at the very time when it was most important to be able to communicate with them. My last hopes now rested on Betteredge, and on the friends of the late Lady Verinder whom I might still find living in the neighbourhood of Rachel's country house.

On this occasion, I travelled straight to Frizinghall – the town being now the central point in my field of inquiry. I arrived too late in the evening to be able to communicate with Betteredge. The next morning, I sent a messenger with a letter, requesting him to join me at the hotel, at his earliest convenience.

Having taken the precaution – partly to save time, partly to accommodate Betteredge – of sending my messenger in a fly, I had a reasonable prospect, if no delays occurred, of seeing the old man within less than two hours from the time when I had sent for him. During this interval, I arranged to employ myself in opening my contemplated inquiry, among the guests present at the birthday dinner who were personally known to me, and who were easily within my reach. These were my relatives, the Ablewhites, and Mr. Candy. The doctor had expressed a special wish to see me, and the doctor lived in the next street. So to Mr. Candy I went first.

After what Betteredge had told me, I naturally anticipated finding traces in the doctor's face of the severe illness from which he had suffered. But I was utterly unprepared for such a change as I saw in him when he entered the room and shook hands with me. His eyes were dim; his hair had turned completely grey; his face was wizen; his figure had shrunk. I looked at the once lively, rattlepated, humorous little doctor – associated in my remembrance with the perpetration of incorrigible social indiscretions and innumerable boyish jokes – and I saw nothing left of his former self, but the old tendency to vulgar smartness in his dress. The man was a wreck; but his clothes and his jewellery – in cruel mockery of the change in him – were as gay and as gaudy as ever.

"I have often thought of you, Mr. Blake," he said; "and I am heartily glad to see you again at last. If there is anything I can do for you, pray command my services, sir – pray command my services!"

He said those few commonplace words with needless hurry and eagerness, and with a curiosity to know what had brought me to Yorkshire, which he was perfectly – I might say childishly – incapable of concealing from notice.

With the object that I had in view, I had of course foreseen the necessity of entering into some sort of personal explanation, before I could hope to interest people, mostly strangers to me, in doing their best to assist my inquiry. On the journey to Frizinghall I had arranged what my explanation was to be – and I seized the opportunity now offered to me of trying the effect of it on Mr. Candy.

"I was in Yorkshire, the other day, and I am in Yorkshire again now, on rather a romantic errand," I said. "It is a matter, Mr. Candy, in which the late Lady Verinder's friends all took some interest. You remember the mysterious loss of the Indian Diamond, now nearly a year since? Circumstances have lately happened which lead to the hope that it may yet be found – and I am interesting myself, as one of the family, in recovering it. Among the obstacles in my way, there is the necessity of collecting again all the evidence which was discovered at the time, and more if possible. There are peculiarities in this case which make it desirable to revive my recollection of everything that happened in the house, on the evening of Miss Verinder's birthday. And I venture to appeal to her late mother's friends who were present on that occasion, to lend me the assistance of their memories –"

I had got as far as that in rehearsing my explanatory phrases, when I was suddenly checked by seeing plainly in Mr. Candy's face that my experiment on him was a total failure.

The little doctor sat restlessly picking at the points of his fingers all the time I was speaking. His dim watery eyes were fixed on my face with an expression of vacant and wistful inquiry very painful to see. What he was thinking of, it was impossible to divine. The one thing clearly visible was that I had failed, after the first two or three words, in fixing his attention. The only chance of recalling him to himself appeared to lie in changing the subject. I tried a new topic immediately.

"So much," I said, gaily, "for what brings me to Frizinghall! Now, Mr. Candy, it's your turn. You sent me a message by Gabriel Betteredge —"

He left off picking at his fingers, and suddenly brightened up.

"Yes! yes! yes!" he exclaimed eagerly. "That's it! I sent you a message!"

"And Betteredge duly communicated it by letter," I went on. "You had something to say to me, the next time I was in your neighbourhood. Well, Mr. Candy, here I am!"

"Here you are!" echoed the doctor. "And Betteredge was quite right. I had something to say to you. That was my message. Betteredge is a wonderful man. What a memory! At his age, what a memory!"

He dropped back into silence, and began picking at his fingers again. Recollecting what I had heard from Betteredge about the effect of the fever on his memory, I went on with the conversation, in the hope that I might help him at starting.

"It's a long time since we met," I said. "We last saw each other at the last birthday dinner my poor aunt was ever to give."

"That's it!" cried Mr. Candy. "The birthday dinner!" He started impulsively to his feet, and looked at me. A deep flush suddenly overspread his faded face, and he abruptly sat down again, as if conscious of having betrayed a weakness which he would fain have concealed. It was plain, pitiably plain, that he was aware of his own defect of memory, and that he was bent on hiding it from the observation of his friends.

Thus far he had appealed to my compassion only. But the words he had just said — few as they were — roused my curiosity instantly to the highest pitch. The birthday dinner had already become the one event in the past, at which I looked back with strangely mixed feelings of hope and distrust. And here was the birthday dinner unmistakably proclaiming itself as the subject on which Mr. Candy had something important to say to me!

I attempted to help him out once more. But, this time, my own interests were at the bottom of my compassionate motive, and they hurried me on a little too abruptly, to the end I had in view.

"It's nearly a year now," I said, "since we sat at that pleasant table. Have you made any memorandum – in your diary, or otherwise – of what you wanted to say to me?"

Mr. Candy understood the suggestion, and showed me that he understood it, as an insult.

"I require no memorandums, Mr. Blake," he said, stiffly enough. "I am not such a very old man, yet – and my memory (thank God) is to be thoroughly depended on!"

It is needless to say that I declined to understand that he was offended with me.

"I wish I could say the same of *my* memory," I answered. "When *I* try to think of matters that are a year old, I seldom find my remembrance as vivid as I could wish it to be. Take the dinner at Lady Verinder's, for instance –"

Mr. Candy brightened up again, the moment the allusion passed my lips.

"Ah, the dinner, the dinner at Lady Verinder's!" he exclaimed, more eagerly than ever. "I have got something to say to you about that."

His eyes looked at me again with the painful expression of inquiry, so wistful, so vacant, so miserably helpless to see. He was evidently trying hard, and trying in vain, to recover the lost recollection. "It was a very pleasant dinner," he burst out suddenly, with an air of saying exactly what he wanted to say. "A very pleasant dinner, Mr. Blake, wasn't it?" He nodded and smiled, and appeared to think, poor fellow, that he had succeeded in concealing the total failure of his memory, by a well-timed exertion of his own presence of mind.

It was so distressing that I at once shifted the talk – deeply as I was interested in his recovering the lost remembrance – to topics of local interest.

Here, he got on glibly enough. Trumpery little scandals and quarrels in the town, some of them as much as a month old, appeared to recur to his memory readily. He chattered on, with something of the smooth gossiping fluency of former times. But there were moments, even in the full flow of his talkativeness, when he suddenly hesitated – looked at me for a moment with the vacant inquiry once more in his eyes – controlled himself – and went on again. I submitted patiently to my martyrdom (it is surely nothing less than martyrdom to a man of cosmopolitan sympathies, to absorb in silent resignation the news of a country town?) until the clock on the chimney-piece told me that my visit had been prolonged beyond half an hour. Having now some right to consider the sacrifice as complete, I rose to take leave. As we shook hands, Mr. Candy reverted to the birthday festival of his own accord.

"I am so glad we have met again," he said. "I had it on my mind – I really had it on my mind, Mr. Blake, to speak to you. About the dinner at Lady Verinder's, you know? A pleasant dinner – really a pleasant dinner now, wasn't it?"

On repeating the phrase, he seemed to feel hardly as certain of having prevented me from suspecting his lapse of memory, as he had felt on the first occasion. The wistful look clouded his face again: and, after apparently designing to accompany me to the street door, he suddenly changed his mind, rang the bell for the servant, and remained in the drawing-room.

I went slowly down the doctor's stairs, feeling the disheartening conviction that he really had something to say which it was vitally important to me to hear, and that he was morally incapable of saying it. The effort of remembering that he wanted to speak to me was, but too evidently, the only effort that his enfeebled memory was now able to achieve.

Just as I reached the bottom of the stairs and had turned a corner on my way to the outer hall, a door opened softly somewhere on the ground floor of the house, and a gentle voice said behind me:

"I am afraid, sir, you find Mr. Candy sadly changed?"

I turned round, and found myself face to face with Ezra Jennings.

★

CHAPTER IX

THE doctor's pretty housemaid stood waiting for me, with the street door open in her hand. Pouring brightly into the hall, the morning light fell full on the face of Mr. Candy's assistant when I turned, and looked at him.

It was impossible to dispute Betteredge's assertion that the appearance of Ezra Jennings, speaking from a popular point of view, was against him. His gipsy complexion, his fleshless cheeks, his gaunt facial bones, his dreamy eyes, his extraordinary parti-coloured hair, the puzzling contradiction between his face and figure which made him look old and young both together – were all more or less calculated to produce an unfavourable impression of him on a stranger's mind.[1] And yet – feeling this as I certainly did – it is not to be denied that Ezra Jennings made some inscrutable appeal to my sympathies, which I found it impossible to resist. While my knowledge of the world warned me to answer the question which he had put, acknowledging that I did indeed find Mr. Candy sadly changed, and then to proceed on my way out of the house – my interest in Ezra Jennings held me rooted to the place, and gave him the opportunity of speaking to me in private about his employer, for which he had been evidently on the watch.

"Are you walking my way, Mr. Jennings?" I said, observing that he held his hat in his hand. "I am going to call on my aunt, Mrs. Ablewhite."

Ezra Jennings replied that he had a patient to see, and that he was walking my way.

We left the house together. I observed that the pretty servant girl – who was all smiles and amiability, when I wished her good-morning on my way out – received a modest little message from Ezra Jennings, relating to the time at which he might be expected to return, with

---

1   The bohemian outcast Ezra Jennings has his roots in one of Collins's early short stories, "The Double-Bedded Room," a piece that formed part of his and Dickens's collaborative *The Lazy Tour or Two Idle Apprentices* in 1857. Mr. Lorn, the medical student and physician's assistant with his "colourless face, his sunken cheeks, his wild black eyes, and his long black hair," is without question an early version of Ezra Jennings, whose description here is strikingly similar. Jennings may also remind the reader of *Armadale's* Ozias Midwinter, another character of similar appearance.

pursed-up lips, and with eyes which ostentatiously looked anywhere rather than look in his face. The poor wretch was evidently no favourite in the house. Out of the house, I had Betteredge's word for it that he was unpopular everywhere. "What a life!" I thought to myself, as we descended the doctor's doorsteps.

Having already referred to Mr. Candy's illness on his side, Ezra Jennings now appeared determined to leave it to me to resume the subject. His silence said significantly, "It's your turn now." I, too, had my reasons for referring to the doctor's illness; and I readily accepted the responsibility of speaking first.

"Judging by the change I see in him," I began, "Mr. Candy's illness must have been far more serious than I had supposed."

"It is almost a miracle," said Ezra Jennings, "that he lived through it."

"Is his memory never any better than I have found it to-day? He has been trying to speak to me –"

"Of something which happened before he was taken ill?" asked the assistant, observing that I hesitated.

"Yes."

"His memory of events, at that past time, is hopelessly enfeebled," said Ezra Jennings. "It is almost to be deplored, poor fellow, that even the wreck of it remains. While he remembers dimly plans that he formed – things, here and there, that he had to say or do before his illness – he is perfectly incapable of recalling what the plans were, or what the thing was that he had to say or do. He is painfully conscious of his own deficiency, and painfully anxious, as you must have seen, to hide it from observation. If he could only have recovered in a complete state of oblivion as to the past, he would have been a happier man. Perhaps we should all be happier," he added, with a sad smile, "if we could but completely forget!"

"There are some events surely in all men's lives," I replied, "the memory of which they would be unwilling entirely to lose?"

"That is, I hope, to be said of most men, Mr. Blake. I am afraid it cannot truly be said of all. Have you any reason to suppose that the lost remembrance which Mr. Candy tried to recover – while you were speaking to him just now – was a remembrance which it was important to *you* that he should recall?"

In saying those words, he had touched, of his own accord, on the very point upon which I was anxious to consult him. The interest I felt in this strange man had impelled me, in the first instance, to give him the opportunity of speaking to me; reserving what I might have to say, on my side, in relation to his employer, until I was first satisfied that he was a person in whose delicacy and discretion I could trust. The little that he had said, thus far, had been sufficient to convince me that I was speaking to a gentleman. He had what I may venture to describe as the *unsought self-possession*, which is a sure sign of good breeding, not in England only, but everywhere else in the civilized world. Whatever the object which he had in view, in putting the question that he had just addressed to me, I felt no doubt that I was justified – so far – in answering him without reserve.

"I believe I have a strong interest," I said, "in tracing the lost remembrance which Mr. Candy was unable to recall. May I ask whether you can suggest to me any method by which I might assist his memory?"

Ezra Jennings looked at me, with a sudden flash of interest in his dreamy brown eyes.

"Mr. Candy's memory is beyond the reach of assistance," he said. "I have tried to help it often enough since his recovery, to be able to speak positively on that point."

This disappointed me; and I owned it.

"I confess you led me to hope for a less discouraging answer than that," I said.

Ezra Jennings smiled. "It may not, perhaps, be a final answer, Mr. Blake. It may be possible to trace Mr. Candy's lost recollection, without the necessity of appealing to Mr. Candy himself."

"Indeed? Is it an indiscretion, on my part, to ask: how?"

"By no means. My only difficulty in answering your question, is the difficulty of explaining myself. May I trust to your patience, if I refer once more to Mr. Candy's illness: and if I speak of it this time without sparing you certain professional details?"

"Pray go on! You have interested me already in hearing the details."

My eagerness seemed to amuse – perhaps, I might rather say, to please him. He smiled again. We had by this time left the last houses in the town behind us. Ezra Jennings stopped for a moment, and picked some wild flowers from the hedge by the roadside. "How beautiful they are!" he said, simply, showing his little nosegay to me. "And how few people in England seem to admire them as they deserve!"

"You have not always been in England?" I said.

"No. I was born, and partly brought up, in one of our colonies. My father was an Englishman; but my mother — We are straying away from our subject, Mr. Blake; and it is my fault. The truth is, I have associations with these modest little hedgeside flowers — It doesn't matter; we were speaking of Mr. Candy. To Mr. Candy let us return."

Connecting the few words about himself which thus reluctantly escaped him, with the melancholy view of life which led him to place the conditions of human happiness in complete oblivion of the past, I felt satisfied that the story which I had read in his face was, in two particulars at least, the story that it really told. He had suffered as few men suffer; and there was the mixture of some foreign race in his English blood.

"You have heard, I dare say, of the original cause of Mr. Candy's illness?" he resumed. "The night of Lady Verinder's dinner-party was a night of heavy rain. My employer drove home through it in his gig, and reached the house, wetted to the skin. He found an urgent message from a patient, waiting for him; and he most unfortunately went at once to visit the sick person, without stopping to change his clothes. I was myself professionally detained, that night, by a case at some distance from Frizinghall. When I got back the next morning, I found Mr. Candy's groom waiting in great alarm to take me to his master's room. By that time the mischief was done; the illness had set in."

"The illness has only been described to me, in general terms, as a fever," I said.

"I can add nothing which will make the description more accurate," answered Ezra Jennings. "From first to last the fever assumed no specific form. I sent at once to two of Mr. Candy's medical friends in the town, both physicians, to come and give me their opinion of the case. They agreed with me that it looked serious; but they both strongly dissented from the view I took of the treatment. We differed entirely in the conclusions which we drew from the patient's pulse.

The two doctors, arguing from the rapidity of the beat, declared that a lowering treatment was the only treatment to be adopted. On my side, I admitted the rapidity of the pulse, but I also pointed to its alarming feebleness as indicating an exhausted condition of the system, and as showing a plain necessity for the administration of stimulants. The two doctors were for keeping him on gruel, lemonade, barley-water, and so on. I was for giving him champagne, or brandy, ammonia, and quinine. A serious difference of opinion, as you see! – a difference between two physicians of established local repute, and a stranger who was only an assistant in the house. For the first few days, I had no choice but to give way to my elders and betters; the patient steadily sinking all the time. I made a second attempt to appeal to the plain, undeniably plain, evidence of the pulse. Its rapidity was unchecked, and its feebleness had increased. The two doctors took offence at my obstinacy. They said, 'Mr. Jennings, either we manage this case, or you manage it. Which is it to be?' I said, 'Gentlemen, give me five minutes to consider, and that plain question shall have a plain reply.' When the time expired, I was ready with my answer. I said, 'You positively refuse to try the stimulant treatment?' They refused in so many words. 'I mean to try it at once, gentlemen.' – 'Try it, Mr. Jennings, and we withdraw from the case.' I sent down to the cellar for a bottle of champagne; and I administered half a tumbler-full of it to the patient with my own hand. The two physicians took up their hats in silence, and left the house."

"You had assumed a serious responsibility," I said. "In your place, I am afraid I should have shrunk from it."

"In my place, Mr. Blake, you would have remembered that Mr. Candy had taken you into his employment, under circumstances which made you his debtor for life. In my place, you would have seen him sinking, hour by hour; and you would have risked anything, rather than let the one man on earth who had befriended you, die before your eyes. Don't suppose that I had no sense of the terrible position in which I had placed myself! There were moments when I felt all the misery of my friendlessness, all the peril of my dreadful responsibility. If I had been a happy man, if I had led a prosperous life, I believe I should have sunk under the task I had imposed on myself. But *I* had no happy time to look back at, no past peace of mind to force itself into contrast with my present anxiety and suspense – and I held firm to my resolution through it all. I took an interval in the middle of the day, when my patient's condition was at its best, for the repose I needed. For the rest of the four and twenty hours, as long as his life was in danger, I never left his bedside. Towards sunset, as usual in such cases, the delirium incidental to the fever came on. It lasted more or less through the night; and then intermitted, at that terrible time in the early morning – from two o'clock to five – when the vital energies even of the healthiest of us are at their lowest. It is then that Death gathers in his human harvest most abundantly. It was then that Death and I fought our fight over the bed, which should have the man who lay on it. I never hesitated in pursuing the treatment on which I had staked everything. When wine failed, I tried brandy. When the other stimulants lost their influence, I doubled the dose. After an interval of suspense – the like of which I hope to God I shall never feel again – there came a day when the rapidity of the pulse slightly, but appreciably, diminished; and, better still, there came also a change in the beat – an unmistakable change to steadiness and strength. *Then*, I knew that I had saved him; and then I own I broke down. I laid the poor fellow's wasted hand back on the bed, and burst out crying. An hysterical relief, Mr. Blake – nothing more! Physiology says, and says truly, that some men are born with female constitutions – and I am one of them!"

He made that bitterly professional apology for his tears, speaking quietly and unaffectedly, as he had spoken throughout. His tone and manner, from beginning to end, showed him to be especially, almost morbidly, anxious not to set himself up as an object of interest to me.

"You may well ask, why I have wearied you with all these details?" he went on. "It is the only way I can see, Mr. Blake, of properly introducing to you what I have to say next. Now you know exactly what my position was, at the time of Mr. Candy's illness, you will the more readily understand the sore need I had of lightening the burden on my mind by giving it, at intervals, some sort of relief. I have had the presumption to occupy my leisure, for some years past, in writing a book, addressed to the members of my profession – a book on the intricate and delicate subject of the brain and the nervous system. My work will probably never be finished; and it will certainly never be published. It has none the less been the friend of many lonely hours; and it helped me to while away the anxious time – the time of waiting, and nothing else – at Mr. Candy's bedside. I told you he was delirious, I think? And I mentioned the time at which his delirium came on?"

"Yes."

"Well, I had reached a section of my book, at that time, which touched on this same question of delirium. I won't trouble you at any length with my theory on the subject – I will confine myself to telling you only what it is your present interest to know. It has often occurred to me in the course of my medical practice, to doubt whether we can justifiably infer – in cases of delirium – that the loss of the faculty of speaking connectedly, implies of necessity the loss of the faculty of thinking connectedly as well. Poor Mr. Candy's illness gave me an opportunity of putting this doubt to the test. I understand the art of writing in shorthand; and I was able to take down the patient's 'wanderings,' exactly as they fell from his lips. – Do you see, Mr. Blake, what I am coming to at last?"

I saw it clearly, and waited with breathless interest to hear more.

"At odds and ends of time," Ezra Jennings went on, "I reproduced my shorthand notes, in the ordinary form of writing – leaving large spaces between the broken phrases, and even the single words, as they had fallen disconnectedly from Mr. Candy's lips. I then treated the result thus obtained, on something like the principle which one adopts in putting together a child's 'puzzle.' It is all confusion to begin with; but it may be all brought into order and shape, if you can only find the right way. Acting on this plan, I filled in each blank space on the paper, with what the words or phrases on either side of it suggested to me as the speaker's meaning; altering over and over again, until my additions followed naturally on the spoken words which came before them, and fitted naturally into the spoken words which came after them. The result was, that I not only occupied in this way many vacant and anxious hours, but that I arrived at something which was (as it seemed to me) a confirmation of the theory that I held. In plainer words, after putting the broken sentences together I found the superior faculty of thinking going on, more or less connectedly, in my patient's mind, while the inferior faculty of expression was in a state of almost complete incapacity and confusion."

"One word!" I interposed eagerly. "Did my name occur in any of his wanderings?"

"You shall hear, Mr. Blake. Among my written proofs of the assertion which I have just advanced — or, I ought to say, among the written experiments, tending to put my assertion to the proof — there *is* one, in which your name occurs. For nearly the whole of one night Mr. Candy's mind was occupied with *something* between himself and you. I have got the broken words, as they dropped from his lips, on one sheet of paper. And I have got the links of my own discovering which connect those words together, on another sheet of paper. The product (as the arithmeticians would say) is an intelligible statement — first, of something actually done in the past; secondly, of something which Mr. Candy contemplated doing in the future, if his illness had not got in the way, and stopped him. The question is whether this does, or does not, represent the lost recollection which he vainly attempted to find when you called on him this morning?"

"Not a doubt of it!" I answered. "Let us go back directly, and look at the papers!"

"Quite impossible, Mr. Blake."

"Why?"

"Put yourself in my position for a moment," said Ezra Jennings. "Would *you* disclose to another person what had dropped unconsciously from the lips of your suffering patient and your helpless friend, without first knowing that there was a necessity to justify you in opening your lips?"

I felt that he was unanswerable, here; but I tried to argue the question, nevertheless.

"My conduct in such a delicate matter as you describe," I replied, "would depend greatly on whether the disclosure was of a nature to compromise my friend or not."

"I have disposed of all necessity for considering that side of the question, long since," said Ezra Jennings. "Wherever my notes included anything which Mr. Candy might have wished to keep secret, those notes have been destroyed. My manuscript experiments at my friend's bedside, include nothing, now, which he would have hesitated to communicate to others, if he had recovered the use of his memory. In your case, I have every reason to suppose that my notes contain something which he actually wished to say to you —"

"And yet, you hesitate?"

"And yet, I hesitate. Remember the circumstances under which I obtained the information which I possess! Harmless as it is, I cannot prevail upon myself to give it up to you, unless you first satisfy me that there is a reason for doing so. He was so miserably ill, Mr. Blake! and he was so helplessly dependent upon Me! Is it too much to ask, if I request you only to hint to me what your interest is in the lost recollection – or what you believe that lost recollection to be?"

To have answered him with the frankness which his language and his manner both claimed from me, would have been to commit myself to openly acknowledging that I was suspected of the theft of the Diamond. Strongly as Ezra Jennings had intensified the first impulsive interest which I had felt in him, he had not overcome my unconquerable reluctance to disclose the degrading position in which I stood. I took refuge once more in the explanatory phrases with which I had prepared myself to meet the curiosity of strangers.

This time I had no reason to complain of a want of attention on the part of the person to whom I addressed myself. Ezra Jennings listened patiently, even anxiously, until I had done.

"I am sorry to have raised your expectations, Mr. Blake, only to disappoint them," he said. "Throughout the whole period of Mr. Candy's illness, from first to last, not one word about the Diamond escaped his lips. The matter with which I heard him connect your name has, I can assure you, no discoverable relation whatever with the loss or the recovery of Miss Verinder's jewel."

We arrived, as he said those words, at a place where the highway along which we had been walking branched off into two roads. One led to Mr. Ablewhite's house; and the other to a moorland village some two or three miles off. Ezra Jennings stopped at the road which led to the village.

"My way lies in this direction," he said. "I am really and truly sorry, Mr. Blake, that I can be of no use to you."

His voice told me that he spoke sincerely. His soft brown eyes rested on me for a moment with a look of melancholy interest. He bowed, and went, without another word, on his way to the village.

For a minute or more I stood and watched him, walking farther and farther away from me; carrying farther and farther away with him what I now firmly believed to be the clue of which I was in search. He turned, after walking on a little way, and looked back. Seeing me still standing at the place where we had parted, he stopped, as if doubting whether I might not wish to speak to him again. There was no time for me to reason out my own situation – to remind myself that I was losing my opportunity, at what might be the turning-point of my life, and all to flatter nothing more important than my own self-esteem! There was only time to call him back first, and to think afterwards. I suspect I am one of the rashest of existing men. I called him back – and then I said to myself, "Now there is no help for it. I must tell him the truth!"

He retraced his steps directly. I advanced along the road to meet him.

"Mr. Jennings," I said, "I have not treated you quite fairly. My interest in tracing Mr. Candy's lost recollection is not the interest of recovering the Moonstone. A serious personal matter is at the bottom of my visit to Yorkshire. I have but one excuse for not having dealt frankly with you in this matter. It is more painful to me than I can say, to mention to anybody what my position really is."

Ezra Jennings looked at me with the first appearance of embarrassment which I had seen in him yet.

"I have no right, Mr. Blake, and no wish," he said, "to intrude myself into your private affairs. Allow me to ask your pardon, on my side, for having (most innocently) put you to a painful test."

"You have a perfect right," I rejoined, "to fix the terms on which you feel justified in revealing what you heard at Mr. Candy's bedside. I understand and respect the delicacy which influences you in this matter. How can I expect to be taken into your confidence if I decline to admit you into mine? You ought to know, and you shall know, why I am interested in discovering what Mr. Candy wanted to say to me. If I turn out to be mistaken in my anticipations, and if you prove unable to help me when you are really aware of what I want, I shall trust to your honour to keep my secret – and something tells me that I shall not trust in vain."

"Stop, Mr. Blake. I have a word to say, which must be said before you go any farther." I looked at him in astonishment. The grip of some terrible emotion seemed to have seized him, and shaken him to the soul. His gipsy complexion had altered to a livid greyish paleness; his eyes had suddenly become wild and glittering; his voice had dropped to a tone – low, stern, and resolute – which I now heard for the first time. The latent resources in the man, for good or for evil – it was hard, at that moment, to say which – leapt up in him and showed themselves to me, with the suddenness of a flash of light.

"Before you place any confidence in me," he went on, "you ought to know, and you *must* know, under what circumstances I have been received into Mr. Candy's house. It won't take long. I don't profess, sir, to tell my story (as the phrase is) to any man. My story will die with me. All I ask, is to be permitted to tell you what I have told Mr. Candy. If you are still in the mind, when you have heard that, to say what you have proposed to say, you will command my attention and command my services. Shall we walk on?"

The suppressed misery in his face silenced me. I answered his question by a sign. We walked on.

After advancing a few hundred yards, Ezra Jennings stopped at a gap in the rough stone wall which shut off the moor from the road, at this part of it.

"Do you mind resting a little, Mr. Blake?" he asked. "I am not what I was – and some things shake me."

I agreed of course. He led the way through the gap to a patch of turf on the heathy ground, screened by bushes and dwarf trees on the side nearest to the road, and commanding in the opposite direction a grandly desolate view over the broad brown wilderness of the moor. The clouds had gathered, within the last half-hour. The light was dull; the distance was dim. The lovely face of Nature met us, soft and still colourless – met us without a smile.

We sat down in silence. Ezra Jennings laid aside his hat, and passed his hand wearily over his forehead, wearily through his startling white and black hair. He tossed his little nosegay of wild flowers away from him, as if the remembrances which it recalled were remembrances which hurt him now.

"Mr. Blake!" he said, suddenly. "You are in bad company. The cloud of a horrible accusation has rested on me for years. I tell you the worst at once. I am a man whose life is a wreck, and whose character is gone."

I attempted to speak. He stopped me.

"No," he said. "Pardon me; not yet. Don't commit yourself to expressions of sympathy which you may afterwards wish to recall. I have mentioned an accusation which has rested on me for years. There are circumstances in connexion with it that tell against me. I cannot bring myself to acknowledge what the accusation is. And I am incapable, perfectly incapable, of proving my innocence. I can only assert my innocence. I assert it, sir, on my oath, as a Christian. It is useless to appeal to my honour as a man."

He paused again. I looked round at him. He never looked at me in return. His whole being seemed to be absorbed in the agony of recollecting, and in the effort to speak.

"There is much that I might say," he went on, "about the merciless treatment of me by my own family, and the merciless enmity to which I have fallen a victim. But the harm is done; the wrong is beyond all remedy. I decline to weary or distress you, sir, if I can help it. At the outset of my career in this country, the vile slander to which I have referred struck me down at once and for ever. I resigned my aspirations in my profession – obscurity was the only hope left for me. I parted with the woman I loved – how could I condemn her to share my disgrace? A medical assistant's place offered itself, in a remote corner of England. I got the place. It promised me peace; it promised me obscurity, as I thought. I was wrong. Evil report, with time and chance to help it, travels patiently, and travels far. The accusation from which I had fled followed me. I got warning of its approach. I was able to leave my situation voluntarily, with the testimonials that I had earned. They got me another situation in another remote district. Time passed again; and again the slander that was death to my character found me out. On this occasion I had no warning. My employer said, 'Mr. Jennings, I have no complaint to make against you; but you must set yourself right, or leave me.' I had but one choice – I left him. It's useless to dwell on what I suffered after that. I am only forty years old now. Look at my face, and let it tell for me the story of some miserable years. It ended in my drifting to this place, and meeting with Mr. Candy. He wanted an assistant. I referred him, on the question of capacity, to my last employer. The question of character remained. I told him what I have told you – and more. I warned him that there were difficulties in the way, even if he believed me. 'Here, as elsewhere,' I said, 'I scorn the guilty evasion of living under an assumed name: I am no safer at Frizinghall than at other places from the cloud that follows me, go where I may.' He answered, 'I don't do things by halves – I believe you, and I pity you. If *you* will risk what may happen, *I* will risk it too.' God Almighty bless him! He has given me shelter, he has given me employment, he has given me rest of mind – and I have the certain conviction (I have had it for some months past) that nothing will happen now to make him regret it."

"The slander has died out?" I said.

"The slander is as active as ever. But when it follows me here, it will come too late."

"You will have left the place?"

"No, Mr. Blake – I shall be dead. For ten years past I have suffered from an incurable internal complaint. I don't disguise from you that I should have let the agony of it kill me long since, but for one last interest in life, which makes my existence of some importance to me still. I want to provide for a person – very dear to me – whom I shall never see again. My own little patrimony is hardly sufficient to make her independent of the world. The hope, if I could only live long enough, of increasing it to a certain sum, has impelled me to resist the disease by such palliative means as I could devise. The one effectual palliative in my case, is – opium. To that all-potent and all-merciful drug I am indebted for a respite of many years from my sentence of death. But even the virtues of opium have their limit. The progress of the disease has gradually forced me from the use of opium to the abuse of it. I am feeling the penalty at last. My nervous system is shattered; my nights are nights of horror. The end is not far off now. Let it come – I have not lived and worked in vain. The little sum is nearly made up; and I have the means of completing it, if my last reserves of life fail me sooner than I expect. I hardly know how I have wandered into telling you this. I don't think I am mean enough to appeal to your pity. Perhaps, I fancy you may be all the readier to believe me, if you know that what I have said to you, I have said with the certain knowledge in me that I am a dying man. There is no disguising, Mr. Blake, that you interest me. I have attempted to make my poor friend's loss of memory the means of bettering my acquaintance with you. I have speculated on the chance of your feeling a passing curiosity about what he wanted to say, and of my being able to satisfy it. Is there no excuse for my intruding myself on you? Perhaps there is some excuse. A man who has lived as I have lived has his bitter moments when he ponders over human destiny. You have youth, health, riches, a place in the world, a prospect before you. You, and such as you, show me the sunny side of human life, and reconcile me with the world that I am leaving, before I go. However this talk between us may end, I shall not forget that you have done me a kindness in doing that. It rests with you, sir, to say what you proposed saying, or to wish me good-morning."

I had but one answer to make to that appeal. Without a moment's hesitation I told him the truth, as unreservedly as I have told it in these pages.

He started to his feet, and looked at me with breathless eagerness as I approached the leading incident of my story.

"It is certain that I went into the room," I said; "it is certain that I took the Diamond. I can only meet those two plain facts by declaring that, do what I might, I did it without my own knowledge —"

Ezra Jennings caught me excitedly by the arm.

"Stop!" he said. "You have suggested more to me than you suppose. Have *you* ever been accustomed to the use of opium?"

"I never tasted it in my life."

"Were your nerves out of order, at this time last year? Were you unusually restless and irritable?"

"Yes."

"Did you sleep badly?"

"Wretchedly. Many nights I never slept at all."

"Was the birthday night an exception? Try and remember. Did you sleep well on that one occasion?"

"I do remember! I slept soundly."

He dropped my arm as suddenly as he had taken it — and looked at me with the air of a man whose mind was relieved of the last doubt that rested on it.

"This is a marked day in your life, and in mine," he said, gravely. "I am absolutely certain, Mr. Blake, of one thing — I have got what Mr. Candy wanted to say to you this morning, in the notes that I took at my patient's bedside. Wait! that is not all. I am firmly persuaded that I can prove you to have been unconscious of what you were about, when you entered the room and took the Diamond. Give me time to think, and time to question you. I believe the vindication of your innocence is in my hands!"

"Explain yourself, for God's sake! What do you mean?"

In the excitement of our colloquy, we had walked on a few steps, beyond the clump of dwarf trees which had hitherto screened us from view. Before Ezra Jennings could answer me, he was hailed from the high-road by a man, in great agitation, who had been evidently on the look-out for him.

"I am coming," he called back; "I am coming as fast as I can!" He turned to me. "There is an urgent case waiting for me at the village yonder; I ought to have been there half an hour since – I must attend to it at once. Give me two hours from this time and call at Mr. Candy's again – and I will engage to be ready for you."

"How am I to wait!" I exclaimed, impatiently. "Can't you quiet my mind by a word of explanation before we part?"

"This is far too serious a matter to be explained in a hurry, Mr. Blake. I am not wilfully trying your patience – I should only be adding to your suspense, if I attempted to relieve it as things are now. At Frizinghall, sir, in two hours' time!"

The man on the high-road hailed him again. He hurried away, and left me.

★

CHAPTER X

How the interval of suspense to which I was now condemned might have affected other men in my position, I cannot pretend to say. The influence of the two hours' probation upon *my* temperament was simply this. I felt physically incapable of remaining still in any one place, and morally incapable of speaking to any one human being, until I had first heard all that Ezra Jennings had to say to me.

In this frame of mind, I not only abandoned my contemplated visit to Mrs. Ablewhite – I even shrank from encountering Gabriel Betteredge himself.

Returning to Frizinghall, I left a note for Betteredge, telling him that I had been unexpectedly called away for a few hours, but that he might certainly expect me to return towards three o'clock in the afternoon. I requested him, in the interval, to order his dinner at the usual hour, and to amuse himself as he pleased. He had, as I well knew, hosts of friends in Frizinghall; and he would be at no loss how to fill up his time until I returned to the hotel.

This done, I made the best of my way out of the town again, and roamed the lonely moorland country which surrounds Frizinghall, until my watch told me that it was time, at last, to return to Mr. Candy's house.

I found Ezra Jennings ready and waiting for me.

He was sitting alone in a bare little room, which communicated by a glazed door with a surgery. Hideous coloured diagrams of the ravages of hideous diseases decorated the barren buff-coloured walls. A bookcase filled with dingy medical works, and ornamented at the top with a skull, in place of the customary bust; a large deal table copiously splashed with ink; wooden chairs of the sort that are seen in kitchens and cottages; a threadbare drugget[1] in the middle of the floor; a sink of water, with a basin and waste-pipe roughly let into the wall, horribly suggestive of its connexion with surgical operations – comprised the entire furniture of the room. The bees were humming among a few flowers placed in pots outside the window; the birds were singing in the garden, and the faint intermittent jingle of a tuneless piano in some neighbouring house forced itself now and again on the ear. In any other place, these everyday sounds might have spoken pleasantly of the everyday world outside. Here, they came in as intruders on a silence which nothing but human suffering had the privilege to disturb. I looked at the mahogany instrument case, and at the huge roll of lint, occupying places of their own on the bookshelves, and shuddered inwardly as I thought of the sounds, familiar and appropriate to the everyday use of Ezra Jennings's room.

"I make no apology, Mr. Blake, for the place in which I am receiving you," he said. "It is the only room in the house, at this hour of the day, in which we can feel quite sure of being left undisturbed. Here are my papers ready for you; and here are two books to which we may have occasion to refer, before we have done. Bring your chair to the table, and we shall be able to consult them together."

I drew up to the table; and Ezra Jennings handed me his manuscript notes. They consisted of two large folio leaves of paper. One leaf contained writing which only covered the surface at intervals.

---

1   The contents of the room are modest. The deal table that Blake mentions is a table made of rough pine planks, and the drugget is a coarse rug of wool or cotton, often, coincidentally, made in India.

The other presented writing, in red and black ink, which completely filled the page from top to bottom. In the irritated state of my curiosity, at that moment, I laid aside the second sheet of paper in despair.

"Have some mercy on me!" I said. "Tell me what I am to expect, before I attempt to read this."

"Willingly, Mr. Blake! Do you mind my asking you one or two more questions?"

"Ask me anything you like!"

He looked at me with the sad smile on his lips, and the kindly interest in his soft brown eyes.

"You have already told me," he said, "that you have never – to your knowledge – tasted opium in your life."

"To my knowledge," I repeated.

"You will understand directly why I speak with that reservation. Let us go on. You are not aware of ever having taken opium. At this time, last year, you were suffering from nervous irritation, and you slept wretchedly at night. On the night of the birthday, however, there was an exception to the rule – you slept soundly. Am I right, so far?"

"Quite right."

"Can you assign any cause for the nervous suffering, and your want of sleep?"

"I can assign no cause. Old Betteredge made a guess at the cause, I remember. But that is hardly worth mentioning."

"Pardon me. Anything is worth mentioning in such a case as this. Betteredge attributed your sleeplessness to something. To what?"

"To my leaving off smoking."

"Had you been an habitual smoker?"

"Yes."

"Did you leave off the habit suddenly?"

"Yes."

"Betteredge was perfectly right, Mr. Blake. When smoking is a habit a man must have no common constitution who can leave it off suddenly without some temporary damage to his nervous system. Your sleepless nights are accounted for, to my mind.

My next question refers to Mr. Candy. Do you remember having entered into anything like a dispute with him – at the birthday dinner, or afterwards – on the subject of his profession?"

The question instantly awakened one of my dormant remembrances in connexion with the birthday festival. The foolish wrangle which took place, on that occasion, between Mr. Candy and myself, will be found described at much greater length than it deserves in the tenth chapter of Betteredge's Narrative. The details there presented of the dispute – so little had I thought of it afterwards – entirely failed to recur to my memory. All that I could now recall, and all that I could tell Ezra Jennings, was that I had attacked the art of medicine at the dinner-table with sufficient rashness and sufficient pertinacity to put even Mr. Candy out of temper for the moment. I also remembered that Lady Verinder had interfered to stop the dispute, and that the little doctor and I had "made it up again," as the children say, and had become as good friends as ever, before we shook hands that night.

"There is one thing more," said Ezra Jennings, "which it is very important I should know. Had you any reason for feeling any special anxiety about the Diamond, at this time last year?"

"I had the strongest reasons for feeling anxiety about the Diamond. I knew it to be the object of a conspiracy; and I was warned to take measures for Miss Verinder's protection, as the possessor of the stone."

"Was the safety of the Diamond the subject of conversation between you and any other person immediately before you retired to rest on the birthday night?"

"It was the subject of a conversation between Lady Verinder and her daughter –"

"Which took place in your hearing?"

"Yes."

Ezra Jennings took up his notes from the table, and placed them in my hands.

"Mr. Blake," he said, "if you read those notes now, by the light which my questions and your answers have thrown on them, you will make two astounding discoveries concerning yourself. You will find:
– First, that you entered Miss Verinder's sitting-room and took the Diamond, in a state of trance, produced by opium. Secondly, that the opium was given to you by Mr. Candy – without your own knowledge – as a practical refutation of the opinions which you had expressed to him at the birthday dinner."

I sat with the papers in my hand completely stupefied.

"Try and forgive poor Mr. Candy," said the assistant gently. "He has done dreadful mischief, I own; but he has done it innocently. If you will look at the notes, you will see that – but for his illness – he would have returned to Lady Verinder's the morning after the party, and would have acknowledged the trick that he had played you. Miss Verinder would have heard of it, and Miss Verinder would have questioned him – and the truth which has laid hidden for a year would have been discovered in a day."

I began to regain my self-possession. "Mr. Candy is beyond the reach of my resentment," I said angrily. "But the trick that he played me is not the less an act of treachery, for all that. I may forgive, but I shall not forget it."

"Every medical man commits that act of treachery, Mr. Blake, in the course of his practice. The ignorant distrust of opium (in England) is by no means confined to the lower and less cultivated classes. Every doctor in large practice finds himself, every now and then, obliged to deceive his patients, as Mr. Candy deceived you. I don't defend the folly of playing you a trick under the circumstances. I only plead with you for a more accurate and more merciful construction of motives."

"How was it done?" I asked. "Who gave me the laudanum[1] without my knowing it myself?"

"I am not able to tell you. Nothing relating to that part of the matter dropped from Mr. Candy's lips, all through his illness. Perhaps your own memory may point to the person to be suspected?"

"No."

"It is useless, in that case, to pursue the inquiry. The laudanum was secretly given to you in some way. Let us leave it there, and go on to matters of more immediate importance. Read my notes, if you can.

---

1   When it comes to any discussion of laudanum, it is safe to assume that Collins was quite the expert. He became addicted to laudanum in the 1850s, when his physician, Francis Carr Beard, first prescribed it for gout, and he remained addicted, despite several attempts to break the habit, until his death in 1889. By 1868, he was, like his creation Ezra Jennings, regularly taking large amounts of the drug, daily doses that he boasted could kill most men. And *The Moonstone* was not the first Collins novel in which laudanum played a role. In *No Name* Magdalen Vanstone contemplates suicide by laudanum, and in *Armadale* the beautiful and fiery villainess Lydia Gwilt writes in her journal: "Who was the man who invented laudanum? I thank him from the bottom of my heart, whoever he was" (Book the Fourth, Chapter X).

Familiarize your mind with what has happened in the past. I have something very bold and very startling to propose to you, which relates to the future."

Those last words roused me.

I looked at the papers, in the order in which Ezra Jennings had placed them in my hands. The paper which contained the smaller quantity of writing was the uppermost of the two. On this, the disconnected words, and fragments of sentences, which had dropped from Mr. Candy in his delirium, appeared as follows:

"... Mr. Franklin Blake ... and agreeable ... down a peg ... medicine ... confesse ... sleep at night ... tell him ... out of order ... medicine ... he tells me ... and groping in the dark mean one and the same thing ... all the company at the dinner-table... I say ... groping after sleep ... nothing but medicine ... he says ... leading the blind ... know what it means ... witty ... a night's rest in spite of his teeth ... wants sleep ... Lady Verinder's medicine chest ... five-and-twenty minims[1] ... without his knowing it ... to-morrow morning ... Well, Mr. Blake ... medicine to-day ... never ... without it ... out, Mr. Candy ... excellent ... without it ... down on him ... truth ... something besides ... excellent ... dose of laudanum, sir ... bed ... what ... medicine now."

There, the first of the two sheets of paper came to an end. I handed it back to Ezra Jennings.

"That is what you heard at his bedside?" I said.

"Literally and exactly what I heard," he answered – "except that the repetitions are not transferred here from my shorthand notes. He reiterated certain words and phrases a dozen times over, fifty times over, just as he attached more or less importance to the idea which they represented. The repetitions, in this sense, were of some assistance to me in putting together those fragments. Don't suppose," he added, pointing to the second sheet of paper, "that I claim to have reproduced the expressions which Mr. Candy himself would have used if he had been capable of speaking connectedly. I only say that I have penetrated through the obstacle of the disconnected expression, to

---

1 A minim is a unit of fluid measure equal to 1/480 of a fluid ounce.

the thought which was underlying it connectedly all the time. Judge for yourself."

I turned to the second sheet of paper, which I now knew to be the key to the first.

Once more, Mr. Candy's wanderings appeared, copied in black ink; the intervals between the phrases being filled up by Ezra Jennings in red ink. I reproduce the result here, in one plain form; the original language and the interpretation of it coming close enough together in these pages to be easily compared and verified.

"…Mr. Franklin Blake is clever and agreeable, but he wants taking down a peg when he talks of medicine. He confesses that he has been suffering from want of sleep at night. I tell him that his nerves are out of order, and that he ought to take medicine. He tells me that taking medicine and groping in the dark mean one and the same thing. This before all the company at the dinner-table. I say to him, you are groping after sleep, and nothing but medicine can help you to find it. He says to me, I have heard of the blind leading the blind, and now I know what it means. Witty – but I can give him a night's rest in spite of his teeth. He really wants sleep; and Lady Verinder's medicine chest is at my disposal. Give him five-and-twenty minims of laudanum to-night, without his knowing it; and then call to-morrow morning. 'Well, Mr. Blake, will you try a little medicine to-day? You will never sleep without it.' – 'There you are out, Mr. Candy: I have had an excellent night's rest without it.' Then, come down on him with the truth! 'You have had something besides an excellent night's rest; you had a dose of laudanum, sir, before you went to bed. What do you say to the art of medicine, now?'"

Admiration of the ingenuity which had woven this smooth and finished texture out of the ravelled skein was naturally the first impression that I felt, on handing the manuscript back to Ezra Jennings. He modestly interrupted the first few words in which my sense of surprise expressed itself, by asking me if the conclusion which he had drawn from his notes was also the conclusion at which my own mind had arrived.

"Do you believe as I believe," he said, "that you were acting under the influence of the laudanum in doing all that you did, on the night of Miss Verinder's birthday, in Lady Verinder's house?"

"I am too ignorant of the influence of laudanum to have an opinion of my own," I answered. "I can only follow your opinion, and feel convinced that you are right."

"Very well. The next question is this. You are convinced; and I am convinced – how are we to carry our conviction to the minds of other people?"

I pointed to the two manuscripts, lying on the table between us. Ezra Jennings shook his head.

"Useless, Mr. Blake! Quite useless, as they stand now, for three unanswerable reasons. In the first place, those notes have been taken under circumstances entirely out of the experience of the mass of mankind. Against them, to begin with! In the second place, those notes represent a medical and metaphysical theory. Against them, once more! In the third place, those notes are of *my* making; there is nothing but *my* assertion to the contrary, to guarantee that they are not fabrications. Remember what I told you on the moor – and ask yourself what my assertion is worth. No! my notes have but one value, looking to the verdict of the world outside. Your innocence is to be vindicated; and they show how it can be done. We must put our conviction to the proof – and You are the man to prove it!"

"How?" I asked.

He leaned eagerly nearer to me across the table that divided us.

"Are you willing to try a bold experiment?"

"I will do anything to clear myself of the suspicion that rests on me now."

"Will you submit to some personal inconvenience for a time?"

"To any inconvenience, no matter what it may be."

"Will you be guided implicitly by my advice? It may expose you to the ridicule of fools; it may subject you to the remonstrances of friends whose opinions you are bound to respect –"

"Tell me what to do!" I broke out impatiently. "And, come what may, I'll do it."

"You shall do this, Mr. Blake," he answered. "You shall steal the Diamond, unconsciously, for the second time, in the presence of witnesses whose testimony is beyond dispute."

I started to my feet. I tried to speak. I could only look at him.

"I believe it *can* be done," he went on. "And it *shall* be done – if you will only help me. Try to compose yourself – sit down, and hear what I have to say to you. You have resumed the habit of smoking; I have seen that for myself. How long have you resumed it?"

"For nearly a year."

"Do you smoke more or less than you did?"

"More."

"Will you give up the habit again? Suddenly, mind! – as you gave it up before."

I began dimly to see his drift. "I will give it up, from this moment," I answered.

"If the same consequences follow, which followed last June," said Ezra Jennings – "if you suffer once more as you suffered then, from sleepless nights, we shall have gained our first step. We shall have put you back again into something assimilating to your nervous condition on the birthday night. If we can next revive, or nearly revive, the domestic circumstances which surrounded you, and if we can occupy your mind again with the various questions concerning the Diamond which formerly agitated it, we shall have replaced you, as nearly as possible, in the same position, physically and morally, in which the opium found you last year. In that case we may fairly hope that a repetition of the dose will lead, in a greater or lesser degree, to a repetition of the result. There is my proposal, expressed in a few hasty words. You shall now see what reasons I have to justify me in making it."

He turned to one of the books at his side, and opened it at a place marked by a small slip of paper.

"Don't suppose that I am going to weary you with a lecture on physiology," he said. "I think myself bound to prove, in justice to both of us, that I am not asking you to try this experiment in deference to any theory of my own devising. Admitted principles, and recognised authorities, justify me in the view that I take. Give me five minutes of your attention; and I will undertake to show you that Science sanctions my proposal, fanciful as it may seem. Here, in the first place, is the physiological principle on which I am acting, stated by no less a person than Dr. Carpenter.[1] Read it for yourself."

---

1 The Dr. Carpenter mentioned here was William Benjamin Carpenter (1813-85), a renowned physiologist and professor of forensic medicine at University College London. His most famous work was *The Principles of General and Comparative Physiology* (1839).

He handed me the slip of paper which had marked the place in the book. It contained a few lines of writing, as follows: –

"There seems much ground for the belief, that every sensory impression which has once been recognised by the perceptive consciousness, is registered (so to speak) in the brain, and may be reproduced at some subsequent time, although there may be no consciousness of its existence in the mind during the whole intermediate period."

"Is that plain, so far?" asked Ezra Jennings.

"Perfectly plain."

He pushed the open book across the table to me, and pointed to a passage marked by pencil lines.

"Now," he said, "read that account of a case, which has – as I believe – a direct bearing on your own position, and on the experiment which I am tempting you to try. Observe, Mr. Blake, before you begin, that I am now referring you to one of the greatest of English physiologists. The book in your hand is Doctor Elliotson's *Human Physiology*; and the case which the doctor cites rests on the well-known authority of Mr. Combe."[1]

The passage pointed out to me was expressed in these terms: –

"Dr. Abel informed me," says Mr. Combe, "of an Irish porter to a warehouse, who forgot, when sober, what he had done when drunk; but, being drunk, again recollected the transactions of his former state of intoxication. On one occasion, being drunk, he had lost a parcel of some value, and in his sober moments could give no account of it. Next time he was intoxicated, he recollected that he had left the par-

---

1 The Dr. John Elliotson (1791-1868) to whom Jennings here refers was a famous though quite controversial and eccentric physiologist Collins had come to know through Dickens and whom Collins consulted for help with his rheumatic gout. Elliotson also interested Collins as a pioneer in mesmerism, having published the controversial book *Numerous Cases of Surgical Operation without Pain in the Mesmeric State* in 1843. The *Human Physiology* (1840), directly quoted here by Ezra Jennings, was perhaps Elliotson's best-known work. Mr. Combe was George Combe (1788-1858), a physiologist and phrenologist whose wildly popular "Essay on the Constitution of Man" (1828, 1835) sold over fifty thousand copies between 1835 and 1838. Mention of Carpenter, Elliotson, and Combe allows Collins to concretize some of his claims about somnambulism and mesmerism.

cel at a certain house, and there being no address on it, it had remained there safely, and was got on his calling for it."

"Plain again?" asked Ezra Jennings.

"As plain as need be."

He put back the slip of paper in its place, and closed the book. "Are you satisfied that I have not spoken without good authority to support me?" he asked. "If not, I have only to go to those book-shelves and you have only to read the passages which I can point out to you."

"I am quite satisfied," I said, "without reading a word more."

"In that case, we may return to your own personal interest in this matter. I am bound to tell you that there is something to be said against the experiment as well as for it. If we could, this year, exactly reproduce, in your case, the conditions as they existed last year, it is physiologically certain that we should arrive at exactly the same result. But this – there is no denying it – is simply impossible. We can only hope to approximate to the conditions; and if we don't succeed in getting you nearly enough back to what you were, this venture of ours will fail. If we do succeed – and I am myself hopeful of success – you may at least so far repeat your proceedings on the birthday night, as to satisfy any reasonable person that you are guiltless, morally speaking, of the theft of the Diamond. I believe, Mr. Blake, I have now stated the question, on both sides of it, as fairly as I can, within the limits that I have imposed on myself. If there is anything that I have not made clear to you, tell me what it is – and if I can enlighten you, I will."

"All that you have explained to me," I said, "I understand perfectly. But I own I am puzzled on one point, which you have not made clear to me yet."

"What is the point?"

"I don't understand the effect of the laudanum on me. I don't understand my walking downstairs, and along corridors, and my opening and shutting the drawers of a cabinet, and my going back again to my own room. All these are active proceedings. I thought the influence of opium was first to stupefy you, and then to send you to sleep."

"The common error about opium, Mr. Blake! I am, at this moment, exerting my intelligence (such as it is) in your service, under the influence of a dose of laudanum, some ten times larger than the dose Mr. Candy administered to you. But don't trust to my authority – even on a question which comes within my own personal experience. I anticipated the objection you have just made: and I have again provided myself with independent testimony which will carry its due weight with it in your own mind and in the minds of your friends."

He handed me the second of the two books which he had by him on the table.

"There," he said, "are the far-famed *Confessions of an English Opium-Eater!* Take the book away with you, and read it. At the passage which I have marked, you will find that when De Quincey[1] had committed what he calls 'a debauch of opium,' he either went to the gallery at the Opera to enjoy the music, or he wandered about the London markets on Saturday night, and interested himself in observing all the little shifts and bargainings of the poor in providing their Sunday's dinner. So much for the capacity of a man to occupy himself actively, and to move about from place to place under the influence of opium."

"I am answered so far," I said; "but I am not answered yet as to the effect produced by the opium on myself."

"I will try to answer you in a few words," said Ezra Jennings. "The action of opium is comprised, in the majority of cases, in two influences – a stimulating influence first, and a sedative influence afterwards. Under the stimulating influence, the latest and most vivid impressions left on your mind – namely, the impressions relating to the Diamond – would be likely, in your morbidly sensitive nervous condition, to become intensified in your brain, and would subordinate to themselves your judgment and your will – exactly as an ordinary dream subordinates to itself your judgment and your will. Little by little, under this action, any apprehensions about the safety of the Diamond which you might have felt during the day, would be liable

---

1 Thomas De Quincey (1785-1859) published his *Confessions of an English Opium Eater* in 1822. In the chapter titled "The Pleasures of Opium," he wrote, "The late Duke of Norfolk used to say, 'Next Friday, by the blessing of Heaven, I purpose to be drunk'; and in like manner I used to fix beforehand how often, within a given time, and when, I would commit a debauch of opium."

to develop themselves from the state of doubt to the state of certainty – would impel you into practical action to preserve the jewel – would direct your steps, with that motive in view, into the room which you entered – and would guide your hand to the drawers of the cabinet, until you had found the drawer which held the stone. In the spiritualised intoxication of opium, you would do all that. Later, as the sedative action began to gain on the stimulant action, you would slowly become inert and stupefied. Later still you would fall into a deep sleep. When the morning came, and the effect of the opium had been all slept off, you would wake as absolutely ignorant of what you had done in the night as if you had been living at the Antipodes. – Have I made it tolerably clear to you so far?"

"You have made it so clear," I said, "that I want you to go farther. You have shown me how I entered the room, and how I came to take the Diamond. But Miss Verinder saw me leave the room again, with the jewel in my hand. Can you trace my proceedings from that moment? Can you guess what I did next?"

"That is the very point I was coming to," he rejoined. "It is a question with me whether the experiment which I propose as a means of vindicating your innocence, may not also be made a means of recovering the lost Diamond as well. When you left Miss Verinder's sitting-room, with the jewel in your hand, you went back in all probability to your own room –"

"Yes! And what then?"

"It is possible, Mr. Blake – I dare not say more – that your idea of preserving the Diamond led, by a natural sequence, to the idea of hiding the Diamond, and that the place in which you hid it was somewhere in your bedroom. In that event, the case of the Irish porter may be your case. You may remember, under the influence of the second dose of opium, the place in which you hid the Diamond under the influence of the first."

It was my turn, now, to enlighten Ezra Jennings. I stopped him, before he could say any more.

"You are speculating," I said, "on a result which cannot possibly take place. The Diamond is, at this moment, in London."

He started, and looked at me in great surprise.

"In London?" he repeated. "How did it get to London from Lady Verinder's house?"

"Nobody knows."

"You removed it with your own hand from Miss Verinder's room. How was it taken out of your keeping?"

"I have no idea how it was taken out of my keeping."

"Did you see it, when you woke in the morning?"

"No."

"Has Miss Verinder recovered possession of it?"

"No."

"Mr. Blake! there seems to be something here which wants clearing up. May I ask how you know that the Diamond is, at this moment, in London?"

I had put precisely the same question to Mr. Bruff, when I made my first inquiries about the Moonstone, on my return to England. In answering Ezra Jennings, I accordingly repeated what I had myself heard from the lawyer's own lips – and what is already familiar to the readers of these pages.

He showed plainly that he was not satisfied with my reply.

"With all deference to you," he said, "and with all deference to your legal adviser, I maintain the opinion which I expressed just now. It rests, I am well aware, on a mere assumption. Pardon me for reminding you, that your opinion also rests on a mere assumption as well."

The view he took of the matter was entirely new to me. I waited anxiously to hear how he would defend it.

"*I* assume," pursued Ezra Jennings, "that the influence of the opium – after impelling you to possess yourself of the Diamond, with the purpose of securing its safety – might also impel you, acting under the same influence and the same motive, to hide it somewhere in your own room. *You* assume that the Hindoo conspirators could by no possibility commit a mistake. The Indians went to Mr. Luker's house after the Diamond – and, therefore, in Mr. Luker's possession the Diamond must be! Have you any evidence to prove that the Moonstone was taken to London at all? You can't even guess how, or by whom, it was removed from Lady Verinder's house! Have you any evidence that the jewel was pledged to Mr. Luker? He declares that he never heard of the Moonstone; and his bankers' receipt acknowledges nothing but the deposit of a valuable of great price. The Indians assume that Mr. Luker is lying – and you assume again that the

Indians are right. All I say, in differing with you, is – that my view is possible. What more, Mr. Blake, either logically or legally, can be said for yours?"

It was put strongly; but there was no denying that it was put truly as well.

"I confess you stagger me," I replied. "Do you object to my writing to Mr. Bruff, and telling him what you have said?"

"On the contrary, I shall be glad if you will write to Mr. Bruff. If we consult his experience, we may see the matter under a new light. For the present, let us return to our experiment with the opium. We have decided that you leave off the habit of smoking from this moment?"

"From this moment."

"That is the first step. The next step is to reproduce, as nearly as we can, the domestic circumstances which surrounded you last year."

How was this to be done? Lady Verinder was dead. Rachel and I, so long as the suspicion of theft rested on me, were parted irrevocably. Godfrey Ablewhite was away, travelling on the Continent. It was simply impossible to reassemble the people who had inhabited the house, when I had slept in it last. The statement of this objection did not appear to embarrass Ezra Jennings. He attached very little importance, he said, to reassembling the same people – seeing that it would be vain to expect them to reassume the various positions which they had occupied towards me in the past times. On the other hand, he considered it essential to the success of the experiment, that I should see the same objects about me which had surrounded me when I was last in the house.

"Above all things," he said, "you must sleep in the room which you slept in, on the birthday night, and it must be furnished in the same way. The stairs, the corridors, and Miss Verinder's sitting-room, must also be restored to what they were when you saw them last. It is absolutely necessary, Mr. Blake, to replace every article of furniture in that part of the house which may now be put away. The sacrifice of your cigars will be useless, unless we can get Miss Verinder's permission to do that."

"Who is to apply to her for permission?" I asked.

"Is it not possible for *you* to apply?"

"Quite out of the question. After what has passed between us on the subject of the lost Diamond, I can neither see her, nor write to her, as things are now."

Ezra Jennings paused, and considered for a moment.

"May I ask you a delicate question?" he said.

I signed to him to go on.

"Am I right, Mr. Blake, in fancying (from one or two things which have dropped from you) that you felt no common interest in Miss Verinder, in former times?"

"Quite right."

"Was the feeling returned?"

"It was."

"Do you think Miss Verinder would be likely to feel a strong interest in the attempt to prove your innocence?"

"I am certain of it."

"In that case, *I* will write to Miss Verinder – if you will give me leave."

"Telling her of the proposal that you have made to me?"

"Telling her of everything that has passed between us to-day."

It is needless to say that I eagerly accepted the service which he had offered to me.

"I shall have time to write by to-day's post," he said, looking at his watch. "Don't forget to lock up your cigars, when you get back to the hotel! I will call to-morrow morning and hear how you have passed the night."

I rose to take leave of him; and attempted to express the grateful sense of his kindness which I really felt.

He pressed my hand gently. "Remember what I told you on the moor," he answered. "If I can do you this little service, Mr. Blake, I shall feel it like a last gleam of sunshine, falling on the evening of a long and clouded day."

We parted. It was then the fifteenth of June. The events of the next ten days – every one of them more or less directly connected with the experiment of which I was the passive object – are all placed on record, exactly as they happened, in the Journal habitually kept by Mr. Candy's assistant. In the pages of Ezra Jennings, nothing is concealed, and nothing is forgotten. Let Ezra Jennings tell how the venture with the opium was tried, and how it ended.

★

FOURTH NARRATIVE

Extracted from the Journal of Ezra Jennings

1849. – *June 15th*. . . . With some interruption from patients, and some interruption from pain, I finished my letter to Miss Verinder in time for to-day's post. I failed to make it as short a letter as I could have wished. But I think I have made it plain. It leaves her entirely mistress of her own decision. If she consents to assist the experiment, she consents of her own free will, and not as a favour to Mr. Franklin Blake or to me.

June 16th. – Rose late, after a dreadful night; the vengeance of yesterday's opium, pursuing me through a series of frightful dreams. At one time, I was whirling through empty space with the phantoms of the dead, friends and enemies together. At another, the one beloved face which I shall never see again, rose at my bedside, hideously phosphorescent in the black darkness, and glared and grinned at me. A slight return of the old pain, at the usual time in the early morning, was welcome as a change. It dispelled the visions – and it was bearable because it did that.

My bad night made it late in the morning, before I could get to Mr. Franklin Blake. I found him stretched on the sofa, breakfasting on brandy and soda-water, and a dry biscuit.

"I am beginning, as well as you could possibly wish," he said. "A miserable, restless night; and a total failure of appetite this morning. Exactly what happened last year, when I gave up my cigars. The sooner I am ready for my second dose of laudanum, the better I shall be pleased."

"You shall have it on the earliest possible day," I answered. "In the meantime, we must be as careful of your health as we can. If we allow you to become exhausted, we shall fail in that way. You must get an appetite for your dinner. In other words, you must get a ride or a walk this morning, in the fresh air."

"I will ride, if they can find me a horse here. By-the-bye, I wrote to Mr. Bruff, yesterday. Have you written to Miss Verinder?"

"Yes – by last night's post."

"Very good. We shall have some news worth hearing, to tell each other to-morrow. Don't go yet! I have a word to say to you. You appeared to think, yesterday, that our experiment with the opium was not likely to be viewed very favourably by some of my friends. You were quite right. I call old Gabriel Betteredge one of my friends; and you will be amused to hear that he protested strongly when I saw him yesterday. 'You have done a wonderful number of foolish things in the course of your life, Mr. Franklin, but this tops them all!' There is Betteredge's opinion! You will make allowance for his prejudices, I am sure, if you and he happen to meet?"

I left Mr. Blake, to go my rounds among my patients; feeling the better and the happier even for the short interview that I had had with him.

What is the secret of the attraction that there is for me in this man? Does it only mean that I feel the contrast between the frankly kind manner in which he has allowed me to become acquainted with him, and the merciless dislike and distrust with which I am met by other people? Or is there really something in him which answers to the yearning that I have for a little human sympathy – the yearning, which has survived the solitude and persecution of many years; which seems to grow keener and keener, as the time comes nearer and nearer when I shall endure and feel no more? How useless to ask these questions! Mr. Blake has given me a new interest in life. Let that be enough, without seeking to know what the new interest is.

June 17th. – Before breakfast, this morning, Mr. Candy informed me that he was going away for a fortnight, on a visit to a friend in the south of England. He gave me as many special directions, poor fellow, about the patients, as if he still had the large practice which he possessed before he was taken ill. The practice is worth little enough now! Other doctors have superseded *him*; and nobody who can help it will employ *me*.

It is perhaps fortunate that he is to be away just at this time. He would have been mortified if I had not informed him of the experiment which I am going to try with Mr. Blake. And I hardly know what undesirable results might not have happened, if I had taken him into my confidence. Better as it is. Unquestionably, better as it is.

The post brought me Miss Verinder's answer, after Mr. Candy had left the house.

A charming letter! It gives me the highest opinion of her. There is no attempt to conceal the interest that she feels in our proceedings. She tells me, in the prettiest manner, that my letter has satisfied her of Mr. Blake's innocence, without the slightest need (so far as she is concerned) of putting my assertion to the proof. She even upbraids herself – most undeservedly, poor thing! – for not having divined at the time what the true solution of the mystery might really be. The motive underlying all this, proceeds evidently from something more than a generous eagerness to make atonement for a wrong which she has innocently inflicted on another person. It is plain that she has loved him, throughout the estrangement between them. In more than one place the rapture of discovering that he has deserved to be loved, breaks its way innocently through the stoutest formalities of pen and ink, and even defies the stronger restraint still of writing to a stranger. Is it possible (I ask myself, in reading this delightful letter) that I, of all men in the world, am chosen to be the means of bringing these two young people together again? My own happiness has been trampled underfoot; my own love has been torn from me. Shall I live to see a happiness of others, which is of my making – a love renewed, which is of my bringing back? Oh merciful Death, let me see it before your arms enfold me, before your voice whispers to me, "Rest at last!"

There are two requests contained in the letter. One of them prevents me from showing it to Mr. Franklin Blake. I am authorised to tell him that Miss Verinder willingly consents to place her house at our disposal; and, that said, I am desired to add no more.

So far, it is easy to comply with her wishes. But the second request embarrasses me seriously.

Not content with having written to Mr. Betteredge, instructing him to carry out whatever directions I may have to give, Miss Verinder asks leave to assist me, by personally superintending the restoration of her own sitting-room. She only waits a word of reply from me to make the journey to Yorkshire, and to be present as one of the witnesses on the night when the opium is tried for the second time.

Here, again, there is a motive under the surface; and, here again, I fancy that I can find it out.

What she has forbidden me to tell Mr. Franklin Blake, she is (as I interpret it) eager to tell him with her own lips, *before* he is put to the test which is to vindicate his character in the eyes of other people. I understand and admire this generous anxiety to acquit him, without waiting until his innocence may, or may not, be proved. It is the atonement that she is longing to make, poor girl, after having innocently and inevitably wronged him. But the thing cannot be done. I have no sort of doubt that the agitation which a meeting between them would produce on both sides – reviving dormant feelings, appealing to old memories, awakening new hopes – would, in their effect on the mind of Mr. Blake, be almost certainly fatal to the success of our experiment. It is hard enough, as things are, to reproduce in him the conditions as they existed, or nearly as they existed, last year. With new interests and new emotions to agitate him, the attempt would be simply useless.

And yet, knowing this, I cannot find it in my heart to disappoint her. I must try if I can discover some new arrangement, before post-time, which will allow me to say Yes to Miss Verinder, without damage to the service which I have bound myself to render to Mr. Franklin Blake.

Two o'clock. – I have just returned from my round of medical visits; having begun, of course, by calling at the hotel.

Mr. Blake's report of the night is the same as before. He has had some intervals of broken sleep, and no more. But he feels it less to-day, having slept after yesterday's dinner. This after-dinner sleep is the result, no doubt, of the ride which I advised him to take. I fear I shall have to curtail his restorative exercise in the fresh air. He must not be too well; he must not be too ill. It is a case (as a sailor would say) of very fine steering.

He has not heard yet from Mr. Bruff. I found him eager to know if I had received any answer from Miss Verinder.

I told him exactly what I was permitted to tell, and no more. It was quite needless to invent excuses for not showing him the letter. He told me bitterly enough, poor fellow, that he understood the delicacy which disinclined me to produce it. "She consents, of course, as a matter of common courtesy and common justice," he said. "But she keeps her own opinion of me, and waits to see the result." I was sorely tempted to hint that he was now wronging her as she had wronged him. On reflection, I shrank from forestalling her in the double luxury of surprising and forgiving him.

My visit was a very short one. After the experience of the other night, I have been compelled once more to give up my dose of opium. As a necessary result, the agony of the disease that is in me has got the upper hand again. I felt the attack coming on, and left abruptly, so as not to alarm or distress him. It only lasted a quarter of an hour this time, and it left me strength enough to go on with my work.

Five o'clock. – I have written my reply to Miss Verinder.

The arrangement I have proposed reconciles the interests on both sides, if she will only consent to it. After first stating the objections that there are to a meeting between Mr. Blake and herself, before the experiment is tried, I have suggested that she should so time her journey as to arrive at the house privately, on the evening when we make the attempt. Travelling by the afternoon train from London, she would delay her arrival until nine o'clock. At that hour, I have undertaken to see Mr. Blake safely into his bedchamber; and so to leave Miss Verinder free to occupy her own rooms until the time comes for administering the laudanum. When that has been done, there can be no objection to her watching the result, with the rest of us. On the next morning, she shall show Mr. Blake (if she likes) her correspondence with me, and shall satisfy him in that way that he was acquitted in her estimation, before the question of his innocence was put to the proof.

In that sense, I have written to her. This is all that I can do to-day. To-morrow I must see Mr. Betteredge, and give the necessary directions for re-opening the house.

June 18th. – Late again, in calling on Mr. Franklin Blake. More of that horrible pain in the early morning; followed, this time, by complete prostration, for some hours. I foresee, in spite of the penalties which it exacts from me, that I shall have to return to the opium for the hundredth time. If I had only myself to think of, I should prefer the sharp pains to the frightful dreams. But the physical suffering exhausts me. If I let myself sink, it may end in my becoming useless to Mr. Blake at the time when he wants me most.

It was nearly one o'clock before I could get to the hotel to-day. The visit, even in my shattered condition, proved to be a most amusing one – thanks entirely to the presence on the scene of Gabriel Betteredge.

I found him in the room, when I went in. He withdrew to the window and looked out, while I put my first customary question to my patient. Mr. Blake had slept badly again, and he felt the loss of rest this morning more than he had felt it yet.

I asked next if he had heard from Mr. Bruff.

A letter had reached him that morning. Mr. Bruff expressed the strongest disapproval of the course which his friend and client was taking under my advice. It was mischievous – for it excited hopes that might never be realised. It was quite unintelligible to *his* mind, except that it looked like a piece of trickery, akin to the trickery of mesmerism, clairvoyance, and the like. It unsettled Miss Verinder's house, and it would end in unsettling Miss Verinder herself. He had put the case (without mentioning names) to an eminent physician; and the eminent physician had smiled, had shaken his head, and had said – nothing. On these grounds, Mr. Bruff entered his protest, and left it there.

My next inquiry related to the subject of the Diamond. Had the lawyer produced any evidence to prove that the jewel was in London?

No, the lawyer had simply declined to discuss the question. He was himself satisfied that the Moonstone had been pledged to Mr. Luker. His eminent absent friend, Mr. Murthwaite (whose consummate knowledge of the Indian character no one could deny), was satisfied also. Under these circumstances, and with the many demands already made on him, he must decline entering into any disputes on the subject of evidence. Time would show; and Mr. Bruff was willing to wait for time.

It was quite plain – even if Mr. Blake had not made it plainer still by reporting the substance of the letter, instead of reading what was actually written – that distrust of *me* was at the bottom of all this. Having myself foreseen that result, I was neither mortified nor surprised. I asked Mr. Blake if his friend's protest had shaken him. He answered emphatically, that it had not produced the slightest effect on his mind. I was free after that to dismiss Mr. Bruff from consideration – and I did dismiss him accordingly.

A pause in the talk between us followed – and Gabriel Betteredge came out from his retirement at the window.

"Can you favour me with your attention, sir?" he inquired, addressing himself to me.

"I am quite at your service," I answered.

Betteredge took a chair and seated himself at the table. He produced a huge old-fashioned leather pocket-book, with a pencil of dimensions to match. Having put on his spectacles, he opened the pocket-book, at a blank page, and addressed himself to me once more.

"I have lived," said Betteredge, looking at me sternly, "nigh on fifty years in the service of my late lady. I was page-boy before that, in the service of the old lord, her father. I am now somewhere between seventy and eighty years of age – never mind exactly where! I am reckoned to have got as pretty a knowledge and experience of the world as most men. And what does it all end in? It ends, Mr. Ezra Jennings, in a conjuring trick being performed on Mr. Franklin Blake, by a doctor's assistant with a bottle of laudanum – and by the living jingo, I'm appointed, in my old age, to be conjurer's boy!"

Mr. Blake burst out laughing. I attempted to speak. Betteredge held up his hand, in token that he had not done yet.

"Not a word, Mr. Jennings!" he said. "It don't want a word, sir, from you. I have got my principles, thank God. If an order comes to me, which is own brother to an order come from Bedlam,[1] it don't matter. So long as I get it from my master or mistress, as the case may be, I obey it. I may have my own opinion, which is also, you will please to remember, the opinion of Mr. Bruff – the Great Mr. Bruff!" said Betteredge, raising his voice, and shaking his head at me solemnly. "It don't matter; I withdraw my opinion, for all that. My young lady says, 'Do it.' And I say, 'Miss, it shall be done.' Here I am, with my book and my pencil – the latter not pointed so well as I could wish; but when Christians take leave of their senses, who is to expect that pencils will keep their points? Give me your orders, Mr. Jennings. I'll have them in writing, sir. I'm determined not to be behind 'em, or before 'em, by so much as a hair's-breadth. I'm a blind agent – that's what I am. A blind agent!" repeated Betteredge, with infinite relish of his own description of himself.

"I am very sorry," I began, "that you and I don't agree –"

"Don't bring *me* into it!" interposed Betteredge. "This is not a

---

1   Betteredge refers colloquially to the Hospital of St. Mary of Bethlehem, an insane asylum in Lambeth (as of 1815) run by the City of London. Bedlam is a contraction of Bethlehem.

matter of agreement, it's a matter of obedience. Issue your directions, sir – issue your directions!"

Mr. Blake made me a sign to take him at his word. I "issued my directions" as plainly and as gravely as I could.

"I wish certain parts of the house to be re-opened," I said, "and to be furnished, exactly as they were furnished at this time last year."

Betteredge gave his imperfectly pointed pencil a preliminary lick with his tongue. "Name the parts, Mr. Jennings!" he said loftily.

"First, the inner hall, leading to the chief staircase."

"'First, the inner hall,'" Betteredge wrote. "Impossible to furnish that, sir, as it was furnished last year – to begin with."

"Why?"

"Because there was a stuffed buzzard, Mr. Jennings, in the hall last year. When the family left, the buzzard was put away with the other things. When the buzzard was put away – he burst."

"We will except the buzzard then."

Betteredge took a note of the exception. "'The inner hall to be furnished again, as furnished last year. A burst buzzard alone excepted.' Please go on, Mr. Jennings."

"The carpet to be laid down on the stairs, as before."

"'The carpet to be laid down on the stairs, as before.' Sorry to disappoint you, sir. But that can't be done either."

"Why not?"

"Because the man who laid that carpet down is dead, Mr. Jennings – and the like of him for reconciling together a carpet and a corner, is not to be found in all England, look where you may."

"Very well. We must try the next best man in England."

Betteredge took another note; and I went on issuing my directions.

"Miss Verinder's sitting-room to be restored exactly to what it was last year. Also, the corridor leading from the sitting-room to the first landing. Also, the second corridor, leading from the second landing to the best bedrooms. Also, the bedroom occupied last June by Mr. Franklin Blake."

Betteredge's blunt pencil followed me conscientiously, word by word. "Go on, sir," he said, with sardonic gravity. "There's a deal of writing left in the point of this pencil yet."

I told him that I had no more directions to give. "Sir," said Betteredge, "in that case, I have a point or two to put on my own behalf." He opened his pocket-book at a new page, and gave the inexhaustible pencil another preliminary lick.

"I wish to know," he began, "whether I may, or may not, wash my hands –"

"You may decidedly," said Mr. Blake. "I'll ring for the waiter."

"– of certain responsibilities," pursued Betteredge, impenetrably declining to see anybody in the room but himself and me. "As to Miss Verinder's sitting-room, to begin with. When we took up the carpet last year, Mr. Jennings, we found a surprising quantity of pins.[1] Am I responsible for putting back the pins?"

"Certainly not."

Betteredge made a note of that concession, on the spot.

"As to the first corridor next," he resumed. "When we moved the ornaments in that part, we moved a statue of a fat naked child – profanely described in the catalogue of the house[2] as 'Cupid, god of Love.' He had two wings last year, in the fleshy part of his shoulders. My eye being off him, for the moment, he lost one of them. Am I responsible for Cupid's wing?"

I made another concession, and Betteredge made another note.

"As to the second corridor," he went on. "There having been nothing in it last year, but the doors of the rooms (to every one of which I can swear, if necessary), my mind is easy, I admit, respecting that part of the house only. But, as to Mr. Franklin's bedroom (if *that* is to be put back to what it was before), I want to know who is responsible for keeping it in a perpetual state of litter, no matter how often it may be set right – his trousers here, his towels there, and his French novels everywhere.[3] I say, who is responsible for untidying the tidiness of Mr. Franklin's room, him or me?"

---

1 Carpet pins were tacks placed beneath the carpet to secure it to the wood flooring. Sue Lonoff mentions the carpet pins to support her claim that Collins "rendered the texture of domestic life ... with accuracy and conviction" (184).

2 A well-run Victorian estate like the Verinders's kept various and detailed inventories on the premises. As we have already seen, an itemized laundry list plays a crucial role in the mystery of the theft.

3 The English generally believed all contemporary French fiction – even that of such masters as Flaubert, Dumas, Zola, all of whom Collins admired – to be sexually explicit, making Betteredge's discovery of Blake's reading material an off-hand indication of Franklin's bachelor status.

Mr. Blake declared that he would assume the whole responsibility with the greatest pleasure. Betteredge obstinately declined to listen to any solution of the difficulty, without first referring it to my sanction and approval. I accepted Mr. Blake's proposal; and Betteredge made a last entry in the pocket-book to that effect.

"Look in when you like, Mr. Jennings, beginning from to-morrow," he said, getting on his legs. "You will find me at work, with the necessary persons to assist me. I respectfully beg to thank you, sir, for overlooking the case of the stuffed buzzard, and the other case of the Cupid's wing – as also for permitting me to wash my hands of all responsibility in respect of the pins on the carpet, and the litter in Mr. Franklin's room. Speaking as a servant, I am deeply indebted to you. Speaking as a man, I consider you to be a person whose head is full of maggots, and I take up my testimony against your experiment as a delusion and a snare. Don't be afraid, on that account, of my feelings as a man getting in the way of my duty as a servant! You shall be obeyed. The maggots notwithstanding, sir, you shall be obeyed. If it ends in your setting the house on fire, Damme if I send for the engines, unless you ring the bell and order them first!"

With that farewell assurance, he made me a bow, and walked out of the room.

"Do you think we can depend on him?" I asked.

"Implicitly," answered Mr. Blake. "When we go to the house, we shall find nothing neglected, and nothing forgotten."

June 19th. – Another protest against our contemplated proceedings! From a lady this time.

The morning's post brought me two letters. One, from Miss Verinder, consenting, in the kindest manner, to the arrangement that I have proposed. The other from the lady under whose care she is living – one Mrs. Merridew.

Mrs. Merridew presents her compliments, and does not pretend to understand the subject on which I have been corresponding with Miss Verinder, in its scientific bearings. Viewed in its social bearings, however, she feels free to pronounce an opinion. I am probably, Mrs. Merridew thinks, not aware that Miss Verinder is barely nineteen years of age. To allow a young lady, at her time of life, to be present (without a "chaperon") in a house full of men among whom a medical experiment is being carried on, is an outrage on propriety which Mrs. Merridew cannot possibly permit. If the matter is allowed to proceed, she will feel it to be her duty – at a serious sacrifice of her own personal convenience – to accompany Miss Verinder to Yorkshire. Under these circumstances, she ventures to request that I will kindly reconsider the subject; seeing that Miss Verinder declines to be guided by any opinion but mine. Her presence cannot possibly be necessary; and a word from me, to that effect, would relieve both Mrs. Merridew and myself of a very unpleasant responsibility.

Translated from polite commonplace, into plain English, the meaning of this is, as I take it, that Mrs. Merridew stands in mortal fear of the opinion of the world. She has unfortunately appealed to the very last man in existence who has any reason to regard that opinion with respect. I won't disappoint Miss Verinder; and I won't delay a reconciliation between two young people who love each other, and who have been parted too long already. Translated from plain English into polite commonplace, this means that Mr. Jennings presents his compliments to Mrs. Merridew, and regrets that he cannot feel justified in interfering any farther in the matter.

Mr. Blake's report of himself, this morning, was the same as before. We determined not to disturb Betteredge by overlooking him at the house to-day. To-morrow will be time enough for our first visit of inspection.

June 20th. – Mr. Blake is beginning to feel his continued restlessness at night. The sooner the rooms are refurnished, now, the better.

On our way to the house, this morning, he consulted me, with some nervous impatience and irresolution, about a letter (forwarded to him from London) which he had received from Sergeant Cuff.

The Sergeant writes from Ireland. He acknowledges the receipt (through his housekeeper) of a card and message which Mr. Blake left at his residence near Dorking, and announces his return to England as likely to take place in a week or less. In the meantime, he requests to be favoured with Mr. Blake's reasons for wishing to speak to him (as stated in the message) on the subject of the Moonstone. If Mr. Blake can convict him of having made any serious mistake, in the course of his last year's inquiry concerning the Diamond, he will consider it a duty (after the liberal manner in which he was treated by the late

Lady Verinder) to place himself at that gentleman's disposal. If not, he begs permission to remain in his retirement, surrounded by the peaceful floricultural attractions of a country life.

After reading the letter, I had no hesitation in advising Mr. Blake to inform Sergeant Cuff, in reply, of all that had happened since the inquiry was suspended last year, and to leave him to draw his own conclusions from the plain facts.

On second thoughts I also suggested inviting the Sergeant to be present at the experiment, in the event of his returning to England in time to join us. He would be a valuable witness to have, in any case; and, if I proved to be wrong in believing the Diamond to be hidden in Mr. Blake's room, his advice might be of great importance, at a future stage of the proceedings over which I could exercise no control. This last consideration appeared to decide Mr. Blake. He promised to follow my advice.

The sound of the hammer informed us that the work of refurnishing was in full progress, as we entered the drive that led to the house.

Betteredge, attired for the occasion in a fisherman's red cap, and an apron of green baize, met us in the outer hall. The moment he saw me, he pulled out the pocket-book and pencil, and obstinately insisted on taking notes of everything that I said to him. Look where we might, we found, as Mr. Blake had foretold, that the work was advancing as rapidly and as intelligently as it was possible to desire. But there was still much to be done in the inner hall, and in Miss Verinder's room. It seemed doubtful whether the house would be ready for us before the end of the week.

Having congratulated Betteredge on the progress that he had made (he persisted in taking notes every time I opened my lips; declining, at the same time, to pay the slightest attention to anything said by Mr. Blake); and having promised to return for a second visit of inspection in a day or two, we prepared to leave the house, going out by the back way. Before we were clear of the passages downstairs, I was stopped by Betteredge, just as I was passing the door which led into his own room.

"Could I say two words to you in private?" he asked, in a mysterious whisper.

I consented of course. Mr. Blake walked on to wait for me in the garden, while I accompanied Betteredge into his room. I fully anticipated a demand for certain new concessions, following the precedent already established in the cases of the stuffed buzzard, and the Cupid's wing. To my great surprise, Betteredge laid his hand confidentially on my arm, and put this extraordinary question to me:

"Mr. Jennings, do you happen to be acquainted with *Robinson Crusoe?*"

I answered that I had read *Robinson Crusoe* when I was a child.

"Not since then?" inquired Betteredge.

"Not since then."

He fell back a few steps, and looked at me with an expression of compassionate curiosity, tempered by superstitious awe.

"He has not read *Robinson Crusoe* since he was a child," said Betteredge, speaking to himself – not to me. "Let's try how *Robinson Crusoe* strikes him now!"

He unlocked a cupboard in a corner, and produced a dirty and dog's-eared book, which exhaled a strong odour of stale tobacco as he turned over the leaves. Having found a passage of which he was apparently in search, he requested me to join him in the corner; still mysteriously confidential, and still speaking under his breath.

"In respect to this hocus-pocus of yours, sir, with the laudanum and Mr. Franklin Blake," he began. "While the workpeople are in the house, my duty as a servant gets the better of my feelings as a man. When the workpeople are gone, my feelings as a man get the better of my duty as a servant. Very good. Last night, Mr. Jennings, it was borne in powerfully on my mind that this new medical enterprise of yours would end badly. If I had yielded to that secret Dictate, I should have put all the furniture away again with my own hand, and have warned the workmen off the premises when they came the next morning."

"I am glad to find, from what I have seen upstairs," I said, "that you resisted the secret Dictate."

"Resisted isn't the word," answered Betteredge. "Wrostled is the word. I wrostled, sir, between the silent orders in my bosom pulling me one way, and the written orders in my pocket-book pushing me the other, until (saving your presence) I was in a cold sweat. In that dreadful perturbation of mind and laxity of body, to what remedy did I apply? To the remedy, sir, which has never failed me yet for the last thirty years and more – to This Book!"

He hit the book a sounding blow with his open hand, and struck out of it a stronger smell of stale tobacco than ever.

"What did I find here," pursued Betteredge, "at the first page I opened? This awful bit, sir, page one hundred and seventy-eight, as follows: – 'Upon these, and many like Reflections, I afterwards made it a certain rule with me, That whenever I found those secret Hints or Pressings of my Mind, to doing, or not doing any Thing that presented; or to going this Way, or that Way, I never failed to obey the secret Dictate.' – As I live by bread, Mr. Jennings, those were the first words that met my eye, exactly at the time when I myself was setting the secret Dictate at defiance! You don't see anything at all out of the common in that, do you, sir?"

"I see a coincidence – nothing more."

"You don't feel at all shaken, Mr. Jennings, in respect to this medical enterprise of yours?"

"Not the least in the world."

Betteredge stared hard at me, in dead silence. He closed the book with great deliberation; he locked it up again in the cupboard with extraordinary care; he wheeled round, and stared hard at me once more. Then he spoke.

"Sir," he said gravely, "there are great allowances to be made for a man who has not read *Robinson Crusoe*, since he was a child. I wish you good-morning."

He opened his door with a low bow, and left me at liberty to find my own way into the garden. I met Mr. Blake returning to the house.

"You needn't tell me what has happened," he said. "Betteredge has played his last card: he has made another prophetic discovery in *Robinson Crusoe*. Have you humoured his favourite delusion? No? You have let him see that you don't believe in *Robinson Crusoe*? Mr. Jennings! you have fallen to the lowest possible place in Betteredge's estimation. Say what you like, and do what you like, for the future. You will find that he won't waste another word on you now."

June 21st. – A short entry must suffice in my journal to-day.

Mr. Blake has had the worst night that he has passed yet. I have been obliged, greatly against my will, to prescribe for him. Men of his sensitive organization are fortunately quick in feeling the effect of remedial measures. Otherwise, I should be inclined to fear that he will be totally unfit for the experiment when the time comes to try it.

As for myself, after some little remission of my pains for the last two days, I had an attack this morning, of which I shall say nothing but that it has decided me to return to the opium. I shall close this book, and take my full dose – five hundred drops.

June 22nd. – Our prospects look better to-day. Mr. Blake's nervous suffering is greatly allayed. He slept a little last night. My night, thanks to the opium, was the night of a man who is stunned. I can't say that I woke this morning; the fitter expression would be, that I recovered my senses.

We drove to the house to see if the refurnishing was done. It will be completed to-morrow – Saturday. As Mr. Blake foretold, Betteredge raised no further obstacles. From first to last, he was ominously polite, and ominously silent.

My medical enterprise (as Betteredge calls it) must now, inevitably, be delayed until Monday next. To-morrow evening the workmen will be late in the house. On the next day, the established Sunday tyranny[1] which is one of the institutions of this free country, so times the trains as to make it impossible to ask anybody to travel to us from London. Until Monday comes, there is nothing to be done but to watch Mr. Blake carefully, and to keep him, if possible, in the same state in which I find him to-day.

In the meanwhile, I have prevailed on him to write to Mr. Bruff, making a point of it that he shall be present as one of the witnesses. I especially choose the lawyer, because he is strongly prejudiced against us. If we convince *him*, we place our victory beyond the possibility of dispute.

Mr. Blake has also written to Sergeant Cuff; and I have sent a line to Miss Verinder. With these, and with old Betteredge (who is really a person of importance in the family), we shall have witnesses enough for the purpose – without including Mrs. Merridew, if Mrs. Merridew persists in sacrificing herself to the opinion of the world.

---

1   Betteredge expresses here Collins's own opinions. In an article he wrote for G.H. Lewes's *Leader*, "A Plea for Sunday Reform" (September 27, 1851: 925-26), Collins wonders why the decent working poor have to slave six days a week at their job and then suffer the burden of long hours in church every Sunday. He spells out his belief the these people, not normally disposed to spending their day off in worship, might benefit by being exposed to what he calls "the humanizing powers" of the arts.

June 23rd. – The vengeance of the opium overtook me again last night. No matter; I must go on with it now till Monday is past and gone.

Mr. Blake is not so well again to-day. At two this morning, he confesses that he opened the drawer in which his cigars are put away. He only succeeded in locking it up again by a violent effort. His next proceeding, in case of temptation, was to throw the key out of window. The waiter brought it in this morning, discovered at the bottom of an empty cistern – such is Fate! I have taken possession of the key until Tuesday next.

June 24th. – Mr. Blake and I took a long drive in an open carriage. We both felt beneficially the blessed influence of the soft summer air. I dined with him at the hotel. To my great relief – for I found him in an over-wrought, over-excited state, this morning – he had two hours' sound sleep on the sofa after dinner. If he has another bad night, now – I am not afraid of the consequence.

June 25th, Monday. – The day of the experiment! It is five o'clock in the afternoon. We have just arrived at the house.

The first and foremost question, is the question of Mr. Blake's health.

So far as it is possible for me to judge, he promises (physically speaking) to be quite as susceptible to the action of the opium tonight as he was at this time last year. He is, this afternoon, in a state of nervous sensitiveness which just stops short of nervous irritation. He changes colour readily; his hand is not quite steady; and he starts at chance noises, and at unexpected appearances of persons and things.

These results have all been produced by deprivation of sleep, which is in its turn the nervous consequence of a sudden cessation in the habit of smoking, after that habit has been carried to an extreme. Here are the same causes at work again, which operated last year; and here are, apparently, the same effects. Will the parallel still hold good, when the final test has been tried? The events of the night must decide.

While I write these lines, Mr. Blake is amusing himself at the billiard table in the inner hall, practising different strokes in the game, as he was accustomed to practise them when he was a guest in this house in June last. I have brought my journal here, partly with a view to occupying the idle hours which I am sure to have on my hands between this and to-morrow morning; partly in the hope that something may happen which it may be worth my while to place on record at the time.

Have I omitted anything, thus far? A glance at yesterday's entry shows me that I have forgotten to note the arrival of the morning's post. Let me set this right before I close these leaves for the present, and join Mr. Blake.

I received a few lines then, yesterday, from Miss Verinder. She has arranged to travel by the afternoon train, as I recommended. Mrs. Merridew has insisted on accompanying her. The note hints that the old lady's generally excellent temper is a little ruffled, and requests all due indulgence for her, in consideration of her age and her habits. I will endeavour, in my relations with Mrs. Merridew, to emulate the moderation which Betteredge displays in his relations with me. He received us to-day, portentously arrayed in his best black suit, and his stiffest white cravat. Whenever he looks my way, he remembers that I have not read *Robinson Crusoe* since I was a child, and he respectfully pities me.

Yesterday, also, Mr. Blake had the lawyer's answer. Mr. Bruff accepts the invitation – under protest. It is, he thinks, clearly necessary that a gentleman possessed of the average allowance of common sense, should accompany Miss Verinder to the scene of, what he will venture to call, the proposed exhibition. For want of a better escort, Mr. Bruff himself will be that gentleman. – So here is poor Miss Verinder provided with two "chaperons." It is a relief to think that the opinion of the world must surely be satisfied with this!

Nothing has been heard of Sergeant Cuff. He is no doubt still in Ireland. We must not expect to see him to-night.

Betteredge has just come in, to say that Mr. Blake has asked for me. I must lay down my pen for the present.

* * * * *

Seven o'clock. – We have been all over the refurnished rooms and staircases again; and we have had a pleasant stroll in the shrubbery which was Mr. Blake's favourite walk when he was here last. In this way, I hope to revive the old impressions of places and things as vividly as possible in his mind.

We are now going to dine, exactly at the hour at which the birthday dinner was given last year. My object, of course, is a purely medical one in this case. The laudanum must find the process of digestion, as nearly as may be, where the laudanum found it last year.

At a reasonable time after dinner I propose to lead the conversation back again – as inartificially as I can – to the subject of the Diamond, and of the Indian conspiracy to steal it. When I have filled his mind with these topics, I shall have done all that it is in my power to do, before the time comes for giving him the second dose.

★   ★   ★   ★   ★

Half-past eight. – I have only this moment found an opportunity of attending to the most important duty of all; the duty of looking in the family medicine chest, for the laudanum which Mr. Candy used last year.

Ten minutes since, I caught Betteredge at an unoccupied moment, and told him what I wanted. Without a word of objection, without so much as an attempt to produce his pocket-book, he led the way (making allowances for me at every step) to the store-room in which the medicine chest is kept.

I discovered the bottle, carefully guarded by a glass stopper tied over with leather. The preparation which it contained was, as I had anticipated, the common Tincture of Opium. Finding the bottle still well filled, I have resolved to use it, in preference to employing either of the two preparations with which I had taken care to provide myself, in case of emergency.

The question of the quantity which I am to administer presents certain difficulties. I have thought it over, and have decided on increasing the dose.

My notes inform me that Mr. Candy only administered twenty-five minims. This is a small dose to have produced the results which followed – even in the case of a person so sensitive as Mr. Blake. I think it highly probable that Mr. Candy gave more than he supposed himself to have given – knowing, as I do, that he has a keen relish of the pleasures of the table, and that he measured out the laudanum on the birthday, after dinner. In any case, I shall run the risk of enlarging the dose to forty minims. On this occasion, Mr. Blake knows beforehand that he is going to take the laudanum – which is equivalent, physiologically speaking, to his having (unconsciously to himself) a certain capacity in him to resist the effects. If my view is right, a larger quantity is therefore imperatively required, this time, to repeat the results which the smaller quantity produced, last year.

*   *   *   *   *

Ten o'clock. – The witnesses, or the company (which shall I call them?) reached the house an hour since.

A little before nine o'clock I prevailed on Mr. Blake to accompany me to his bedroom; stating, as a reason, that I wished him to look round it, for the last time, in order to make quite sure that nothing had been forgotten in the refurnishing of the room. I had previously arranged with Betteredge, that the bedchamber prepared for Mr. Bruff should be the next room to Mr. Blake's, and that I should be informed of the lawyer's arrival by a knock at the door. Five minutes after the clock in the hall had struck nine, I heard the knock; and, going out immediately, met Mr. Bruff in the corridor.

My personal appearance (as usual) told against me. Mr. Bruff's distrust looked at me plainly enough out of Mr. Bruff's eyes. Being well used to producing this effect on strangers, I did not hesitate a moment in saying what I wanted to say, before the lawyer found his way into Mr. Blake's room.

"You have travelled here, I believe, in company with Mrs. Merridew and Miss Verinder?" I said.

"Yes," answered Mr. Bruff, as drily as might be.

"Miss Verinder has probably told you, that I wish her presence in the house (and Mrs. Merridew's presence of course), to be kept a secret from Mr. Blake, until my experiment on him has been tried first?"

"I know that I am to hold my tongue, sir!" said Mr. Bruff, impatiently. "Being habitually silent on the subject of human folly, I am all the readier to keep my lips closed on this occasion. Does that satisfy you?"

I bowed, and left Betteredge to show him to his room. Betteredge gave me one look at parting, which said, as if in so many words, "You have caught a Tartar,[1] Mr. Jennings – and the name of him is Bruff."

---

1   The Tartars were the fierce Mongolians who, under Ghengis Khan, overran much of central and western Asia and eastern Europe in the 13th century.

It was next necessary to get the meeting over with the two ladies. I descended the stairs – a little nervously, I confess – on my way to Miss Verinder's sitting-room.

The gardener's wife (charged with looking after the accommodation of the ladies) met me in the first-floor corridor. This excellent woman treats me with an excessive civility which is plainly the offspring of downright terror. She stares, trembles, and curtseys whenever I speak to her. On my asking for Miss Verinder, she stared, trembled, and would no doubt have curtseyed next, if Miss Verinder herself had not cut that ceremony short, by suddenly opening her sitting-room door.

"Is that Mr. Jennings?" she asked.

Before I could answer, she came out eagerly to speak to me in the corridor. We met under the light of a lamp on a bracket. At the first sight of me, Miss Verinder stopped, and hesitated. She recovered herself instantly, coloured for a moment – and then, with a charming frankness, offered me her hand.

"I can't treat you like a stranger, Mr. Jennings," she said. "Oh, if you only knew how happy your letters have made me!"

She looked at my ugly wrinkled face, with a bright gratitude so new to me in *my* experience of my fellow-creatures, that I was at a loss how to answer her. Nothing had prepared me for her kindness and her beauty. The misery of many years has not hardened my heart, thank God. I was as awkward and as shy with her, as if I had been a lad in my teens.

"Where is he now?" she asked, giving free expression to her one dominant interest – the interest in Mr. Blake. "What is he doing? Has he spoken of me? Is he in good spirits? How does he bear the sight of the house, after what happened in it last year? When are you going to give him the laudanum? May I see you pour it out? I am so interested; I am so excited – I have ten thousand things to say to you, and they all crowd together so that I don't know what to say first. Do you wonder at the interest I take in this?"

"No," I said. "I venture to think that I thoroughly understand it."

She was far above the paltry affectation of being confused. She answered me as she might have answered a brother or a father.

"You have relieved me of indescribable wretchedness; you have given me a new life. How can I be ungrateful enough to have any concealments from *you*? I love him," she said simply, "I have loved him from first to last – even when I was wronging him in my own thoughts; even when I was saying the hardest and the cruellest words to him. Is there any excuse for me, in that? I hope there is – I am afraid it is the only excuse I have. When to-morrow comes, and he knows that I am in the house, do you think – ?"

She stopped again, and looked at me very earnestly.

"When to-morrow comes," I said, "I think you have only to tell him what you have just told me."

Her face brightened; she came a step nearer to me. Her fingers trifled nervously with a flower which I had picked in the garden, and which I had put into the button-hole of my coat.

"You have seen a great deal of him lately," she said. "Have you, really and truly, seen *that*?"

"Really and truly," I answered. "I am quite certain of what will happen to-morrow. I wish I could feel as certain of what will happen to-night."

At that point in the conversation, we were interrupted by the appearance of Betteredge with the tea-tray. He gave me another significant look as he passed on into the sitting-room. "Aye! aye! make your hay while the sun shines. The Tartar's upstairs, Mr. Jennings – the Tartar's upstairs!"

We followed him into the room. A little old lady, in a corner, very nicely dressed, and very deeply absorbed over a smart piece of embroidery, dropped her work in her lap, and uttered a faint little scream at the first sight of my gipsy complexion and my piebald hair.

"Mrs. Merridew," said Miss Verinder, "this is Mr. Jennings."

"I beg Mr. Jennings's pardon," said the old lady, looking at Miss Verinder, and speaking at *me*. "Railway travelling always makes me nervous. I am endeavouring to quiet my mind by occupying myself as usual. I don't know whether my embroidery is out of place, on this extraordinary occasion. If it interferes with Mr. Jennings's medical views, I shall be happy to put it away, of course."

I hastened to sanction the presence of the embroidery, exactly as I had sanctioned the absence of the burst buzzard and the Cupid's wing. Mrs. Merridew made an effort – a grateful effort – to look at my hair. No! it was not to be done. Mrs. Merridew looked back again at Miss Verinder.

"If Mr. Jennings will permit me," pursued the old lady, "I should like to ask a favour. Mr. Jennings is about to try a scientific experiment to-night. I used to attend scientific experiments when I was a girl at school. They invariably ended in an explosion. If Mr. Jennings will be so very kind, I should like to be warned of the explosion this time. With a view to getting it over, if possible, before I go to bed."

I attempted to assure Mrs. Merridew that an explosion was not included in the programme on this occasion.

"No," said the old lady. "I am much obliged to Mr. Jennings – I am aware that he is only deceiving me for my own good. I prefer plain dealing. I am quite resigned to the explosion – but I *do* want to get it over, if possible, before I go to bed."

Here the door opened, and Mrs. Merridew uttered another little scream. The advent of the explosion? No: only the advent of Betteredge.

"I beg your pardon, Mr. Jennings," said Betteredge, in his most elaborately confidential manner. "Mr. Franklin wishes to know where you are. Being under your orders to deceive him, in respect to the presence of my young lady in the house, I have said I don't know. That you will please to observe, was a lie. Having one foot already in the grave, sir, the fewer lies you expect me to tell, the more I shall be indebted to you, when my conscience pricks me and my time comes."

There was not a moment to be wasted on the purely speculative question of Betteredge's conscience. Mr. Blake might make his appearance in search of me, unless I went to him at once in his own room. Miss Verinder followed me out into the corridor.

"They seem to be in a conspiracy to persecute you," she said. "What does it mean?"

"Only the protest of the world, Miss Verinder – on a very small scale – against anything that is new."

"What are we do with Mrs. Merridew?"

"Tell her the explosion will take place at nine to-morrow morning."

"So as to send her to bed?"

"Yes – so as to send her to bed."

Miss Verinder went back to the sitting-room, and I went upstairs to Mr. Blake.

To my surprise I found him alone; restlessly pacing his room, and a little irritated at being left by himself.

"Where is Mr. Bruff?" I asked.

He pointed to the closed door of communication between the two rooms. Mr. Bruff had looked in on him, for a moment; had attempted to renew his protest against our proceedings; and had once more failed to produce the smallest impression on Mr. Blake. Upon this, the lawyer had taken refuge in a black leather bag, filled to bursting with professional papers. "The serious business of life," he admitted, "was sadly out of place on such an occasion as the present. But the serious business of life must be carried on, for all that. Mr. Blake would perhaps kindly make allowance for the old-fashioned habits of a practical man. Time was money – and, as for Mr. Jennings, he might depend on it that Mr. Bruff would be forthcoming when called upon." With that apology, the lawyer had gone back to his own room, and had immersed himself obstinately in his black bag.

I thought of Mrs. Merridew and her embroidery, and of Betteredge and his conscience. There is a wonderful sameness in the solid side of the English character – just as there is a wonderful sameness in the solid expression of the English face.

"When are you going to give me the laudanum?" asked Mr. Blake impatiently.

"You must wait a little longer," I said. "I will stay and keep you company till the time comes."

It was then not ten o'clock. Inquiries which I had made, at various times, of Betteredge and Mr. Blake, had led me to the conclusion that the dose of laudanum given by Mr. Candy could not possibly have been administered before eleven. I had accordingly determined not to try the second dose until that time.

We talked a little; but both our minds were preoccupied by the coming ordeal. The conversation soon flagged – then dropped altogether. Mr. Blake idly turned over the books on his bedroom table. I had taken the precaution of looking at them, when we first entered the room. *The Guardian*; *The Tatler*; Richardson's *Pamela*; Mackenzie's *Man of Feeling*; Roscoe's *Lorenzo de' Medici*; and Robertson's *Charles the Fifth* – all classical works;[1] all (of course) immeasurably superior to

---

1   The *Guardian* was a short-lived political periodical founded and run by Sir Richard Steele (1672-1729) from March to October 1713; the *Tatler* was another of Steele's

anything produced in later times; and (from my present point of view) possessing the one great merit of enchaining nobody's interest, and exciting nobody's brain. I left Mr. Blake to the composing influence of Standard Literature, and occupied myself in making this entry in my journal.

My watch informs me that it is close on eleven o'clock. I must shut up these leaves once more.

★   ★   ★   ★   ★

Two o'clock A.M. – The experiment has been tried. With what result, I am now to describe.

At eleven o'clock, I rang the bell for Betteredge, and told Mr. Blake that he might at last prepare himself for bed.

I looked out of the window at the night. It was mild and rainy, resembling, in this respect, the night of the birthday – the twenty-first of June, last year. Without professing to believe in omens, it was at least encouraging to find no direct nervous influences – no stormy or electric perturbations – in the atmosphere. Betteredge joined me at the window, and mysteriously put a little slip of paper into my hand. It contained these lines:

"Mrs. Merridew has gone to bed, on the distinct understanding that the explosion is to take place at nine to-morrow morning, and that I am not to stir out of this part of the house until she comes and sets me free. She has no idea that the chief scene of the experiment is my sitting-room – or she would have remained in it for the whole night! I am alone, and very anxious. Pray let me see you measure out the laudanum; I want to have something to do with it, even in the unimportant character of a mere looker-on. – R.V."

I followed Betteredge out of the room, and told him to remove the medicine-chest into Miss Verinder's sitting-room.

The order appeared to take him completely by surprise. He looked as if he suspected me of some occult medical design on Miss Verinder! "Might I presume to ask," he said, "what my young lady and

---

periodicals, running between April 1709 and January 1711; *Pamela, or Virtue Rewarded* (1740-41) is Samuel Richardson's (1689-1761) best-known work; the *Man of Feeling* (1771) is Scotsman Henry MacKenzie's (1745-1831) most influential novel; the *Life of Lorenzo de' Medici* (1795) is William Roscoe's (1753-1831) principal work; and *Charles the Fifth* (1769) was one of several histories written by William Robertson (1721-93).

the medicine-chest have got to do with each other?"

"Stay in the sitting-room, and you will see."

Betteredge appeared to doubt his own unaided capacity to super-intend me effectually, on an occasion when a medicine-chest was included in the proceedings.

"Is there any objection, sir," he asked, "to taking Mr. Bruff into this part of the business?"

"Quite the contrary! I am now going to ask Mr. Bruff to accompany me downstairs."

Betteredge withdrew to fetch the medicine-chest, without another word. I went back into Mr. Blake's room, and knocked at the door of communication. Mr. Bruff opened it, with his papers in his hand – immersed in Law; impenetrable to Medicine.

"I am sorry to disturb you," I said. "But I am going to prepare the laudanum for Mr. Blake; and I must request you to be present, and to see what I do."

"Yes?" said Mr. Bruff, with nine-tenths of his attention riveted on his papers, and with one-tenth unwillingly accorded to me. "Anything else?"

"I must trouble you to return here with me, and to see me administer the dose."

"Anything else?"

"One thing more. I must put you to the inconvenience of remaining in Mr. Blake's room, and of waiting to see what happens."

"Oh, very good!" said Mr. Bruff. "My room, or Mr. Blake's room – it doesn't matter which; I can go on with my papers anywhere. Unless you object, Mr. Jennings, to my importing *that* amount of common sense into the proceedings?"

Before I could answer, Mr. Blake addressed himself to the lawyer, speaking from his bed.

"Do you really mean to say that you don't feel any interest in what we are going to do?" he asked. "Mr. Bruff, you have no more imagination than a cow!"[1]

---

[1] This comment, coming as it does in the midst of the experiment with opium, brings to mind another passage from De Quincey's *Confessions of an English Opium Eater*. In a section of the work titled "Preliminary Confessions," De Quincey wrote, "If a man 'whose talk is of oxen,' should become an opium-eater, the probability is, that (if he is not too dull to dream at all) – he will dream about oxen."

"A cow is a very useful animal, Mr. Blake," said the lawyer. With that reply he followed me out of the room, still keeping his papers in his hand.

We found Miss Verinder, pale and agitated, restlessly pacing her sitting-room from end to end. At a table in a corner stood Betteredge, on guard over the medicine-chest. Mr. Bruff sat down on the first chair that he could find, and (emulating the usefulness of the cow) plunged back again into his papers on the spot.

Miss Verinder drew me aside, and reverted instantly to her one all-absorbing interest – her interest in Mr. Blake.

"How is he now?" she asked. "Is he nervous? Is he out of temper? Do you think it will succeed? Are you sure it will do no harm?"

"Quite sure. Come, and see me measure it out."

"One moment! It is past eleven now. How long will it be before anything happens?"

"It is not easy to say. An hour perhaps."

"I suppose the room must be dark, as it was last year?"

"Certainly."

"I shall wait in my bedroom – just as I did before. I shall keep the door a little way open. It was a little way open last year. I will watch the sitting-room door; and the moment it moves, I will blow out my light. It all happened in that way, on my birthday night. And it must all happen again in the same way, mustn't it?"

"Are you sure you can control yourself, Miss Verinder?"

"In *his* interests, I can do anything!" she answered fervently.

One look at her face told me that I could trust her. I addressed myself again to Mr. Bruff.

"I must trouble you to put your papers aside for a moment," I said.

"Oh, certainly!" He got up with a start – as if I had disturbed him at a particularly interesting place – and followed me to the medicine-chest. There, deprived of the breathless excitement incidental to the practice of his profession, he looked at Betteredge – and yawned wearily.

Miss Verinder joined me with a glass jug of cold water, which she had taken from a side-table. "Let me pour out the water," she whispered. "I *must* have a hand in it!"

I measured out the forty minims from the bottle, and poured the laudanum into a medicine glass. "Fill it till it is three parts full," I said, and handed the glass to Miss Verinder. I then directed Betteredge to lock up the medicine-chest; informing him that I had done with it now. A look of unutterable relief overspread the old servant's countenance. He had evidently suspected me of a medical design on his young lady!

After adding the water as I had directed, Miss Verinder seized a moment – while Betteredge was locking the chest, and while Mr. Bruff was looking back at his papers – and slyly kissed the rim of the medicine-glass. "When you give it to him," said the charming girl, "give it to him on that side!"

I took the piece of crystal which was to represent the Diamond from my pocket, and gave it to her.

"You must have a hand in this, too," I said. "You must put it where you put the Moonstone last year."

She led the way to the Indian cabinet, and put the mock Diamond into the drawer which the real Diamond had occupied on the birthday night. Mr. Bruff witnessed this proceeding, under protest, as he had witnessed everything else. But the strong dramatic interest which the experiment was now assuming, proved (to my great amusement) to be too much for Betteredge's capacity of self-restraint. His hand trembled as he held the candle, and he whispered anxiously, "Are you sure, miss, it's the right drawer?"

I led the way out again, with the laudanum and water in my hand. At the door, I stopped to address a last word to Miss Verinder.

"Don't be long in putting out the lights," I said.

"I will put them out at once," she answered. "And I will wait in my bedroom, with only one candle alight."

She closed the sitting-room door behind us. Followed by Mr. Bruff and Betteredge, I went back to Mr. Blake's room.

We found him moving restlessly from side to side of the bed, and wondering irritably whether he was to have the laudanum that night. In the presence of the two witnesses, I gave him the dose, and shook up his pillows, and told him to lie down again quietly and wait.

His bed, provided with light chintz curtains, was placed, with the head against the wall of the room, so as to leave a good open space on either side of it. On one side, I drew the curtains completely – and in the part of the room thus screened from his view, I placed Mr. Bruff and Betteredge, to wait for the result. At the bottom of the bed I half drew the curtains – and placed my own chair at a little distance, so that I might let him see me or not see me, speak to me or not speak to me, just as the circumstances might direct. Having already been informed that he always slept with a light in the room, I placed one of the two lighted candles on a little table at the head of the bed, where the glare of the light would not strike on his eyes. The other candle I gave to Mr. Bruff; the light, in this instance, being subdued by the screen of the chintz curtains. The window was open at the top, so as to ventilate the room. The rain fell softly, the house was quiet. It was twenty minutes past eleven, by my watch, when the preparations were completed, and I took my place on the chair set apart at the bottom of the bed.

Mr. Bruff resumed his papers, with every appearance of being as deeply interested in them as ever. But looking towards him now, I saw certain signs and tokens which told me that the Law was beginning to lose its hold on him at last. The suspended interest of the situation in which we were now placed was slowly asserting its influence even on *his* unimaginative mind. As for Betteredge, consistency of principle and dignity of conduct had become, in his case, mere empty words. He forgot that I was performing a conjuring trick on Mr. Franklin Blake; he forgot that I had upset the house from top to bottom; he forgot that I had not read *Robinson Crusoe* since I was a child. "For the Lord's sake, sir," he whispered to me, "tell us when it will begin to work."

"Not before midnight," I whispered back. "Say nothing, and sit still."

Betteredge dropped to the lowest depth of familiarity with me, without a struggle to save himself. He answered by a wink!

Looking next towards Mr. Blake, I found him as restless as ever in his bed; fretfully wondering why the influence of the laudanum had not begun to assert itself yet. To tell him, in his present humour, that the more he fidgeted and wondered, the longer he would delay the result for which we were now waiting, would have been simply useless. The wiser course to take was to dismiss the idea of the opium from his mind, by leading him insensibly to think of something else.

With this view, I encouraged him to talk to me; contriving so to direct the conversation, on my side, as to lead it back again to the subject which had engaged us earlier in the evening – the subject of the

Diamond. I took care to revert to those portions of the story of the Moonstone, which related to the transport of it from London to Yorkshire; to the risk which Mr. Blake had run in removing it from the bank at Frizinghall; and to the unexpected appearance of the Indians at the house, on the evening of the birthday. And I purposely assumed, in referring to these events, to have misunderstood much of what Mr. Blake himself had told me a few hours since. In this way, I set him talking on the subject with which it was now vitally impor tant to fill his mind – without allowing him to suspect that I was making him talk for a purpose. Little by little, he became so interested in putting me right that he forgot to fidget in the bed. His mind was far away from the question of the opium, at the all-important time when his eyes first told me that the opium was beginning to lay its hold on his brain.

I looked at my watch. It wanted five minutes to twelve, when the premonitory symptoms of the working of the laudanum first showed themselves to me.

At this time, no unpractised eyes would have detected any change in him. But, as the minutes of the new morning wore away, the swift-ly-subtle progress of the influence began to show itself more plainly. The sublime intoxication of opium gleamed in his eyes; the dew of a stealthy perspiration began to glisten on his face. In five minutes more, the talk which he still kept up with me, failed in coherence. He held steadily to the subject of the Diamond; but he ceased to com-plete his sentences. A little later, the sentences dropped to single words. Then, there was an interval of silence. Then, he sat up in bed. Then, still busy with the subject of the Diamond, he began to talk again – not to me, but to himself. That change told me that the first stage in the experiment was reached. The stimulant influence of the opium had got him.

The time, now, was twenty-three minutes past twelve. The next half-hour, at most, would decide the question of whether he would, or would not, get up from his bed, and leave the room.

In the breathless interest of watching him – in the unutterable tri-umph of seeing the first result of the experiment declare itself in the manner, and nearly at the time, which I had anticipated – I had utter-ly forgotten the two companions of my night vigil. Looking towards them now, I saw the Law (as represented by Mr. Bruff's papers) lying unheeded on the floor. Mr. Bruff himself was looking eagerly through a crevice left in the imperfectly-drawn curtains of the bed. And Betteredge, oblivious of all respect for social distinctions, was peeping over Mr. Bruff's shoulder.

They both started back, on finding that I was looking at them, like two boys caught out by their schoolmaster in a fault. I signed to them to take off their boots quietly, as I was taking off mine. If Mr. Blake gave us the chance of following him, it was vitally necessary to follow him without noise.

Ten minutes passed – and nothing happened. Then, he suddenly threw the bed-clothes off him. He put one leg out of bed. He waited.

"I wish I had never taken it out of the bank," he said to himself. "It was safe in the bank."

My heart throbbed fast; the pulses at my temples beat furiously. The doubt about the safety of the Diamond was, once more, the dominant impression in his brain! On that one pivot, the whole success of the experiment turned. The prospect thus suddenly opened before me was too much for my shattered nerves. I was obliged to look away from him – or I should have lost my self-control.

There was another interval of silence.

When I could trust myself to look back at him he was out of his bed, standing erect at the side of it. The pupils of his eyes were now contracted; his eyeballs gleamed in the light of the candle as he moved his head slowly to and fro. He was thinking; he was doubting – he spoke again.

"How do I know?" he said. "The Indians may be hidden in the house."

He stopped, and walked slowly to the other end of the room. He turned – waited – came back to the bed.

"It's not even locked up," he went on. "It's in the drawer of her cabinet. And the drawer doesn't lock."

He sat down on the side of the bed. "Anybody might take it," he said.

He rose again restlessly, and reiterated his first words.

"How do I know? The Indians may be hidden in the house."

He waited again. I drew back behind the half-curtain of the bed. He looked about the room, with a vacant glitter in his eyes. It was a breathless moment. There was a pause of some sort. A pause in the action of the opium? A pause in the action of the brain? Who could tell? Everything depended, now, on what he did next.

He laid himself down again on the bed!

A horrible doubt crossed my mind. Was it possible that the sedative action of the opium was making itself felt already? It was not in my experience that it should do this. But what is experience, where opium is concerned? There are probably no two men in existence on whom the drug acts in exactly the same manner. Was some constitutional peculiarity in him feeling the influence in some new way? Were we to fail on the very brink of success?

No! He got up again abruptly. "How the devil am I to sleep," he said, "with *this* on my mind?"

He looked at the light, burning on the table at the head of his bed. After a moment, he took the candle in his hand.

I blew out the second candle, burning behind the closed curtains. I drew back, with Mr. Bruff and Betteredge, into the farthest corner by the bed. I signed to them to be silent, as if their lives had depended on it.

We waited – seeing and hearing nothing. We waited, hidden from him by the curtains.

The light which he was holding on the other side of us moved suddenly. The next moment he passed us, swift and noiseless, with the candle in his hand.

He opened the bedroom door, and went out.

We followed him along the corridor. We followed him down the stairs. We followed him along the second corridor. He never looked back; he never hesitated.

He opened the sitting-room door, and went in, leaving it open behind him.

The door was hung (like all the other doors in the house) on large old-fashioned hinges. When it was opened, a crevice was opened between the door and the post. I signed to my two companions to look through this, so as to keep them from showing themselves. I placed myself – outside the door also – on the opposite side. A recess in the wall was at my left hand, in which I could instantly hide myself, if he showed any signs of looking back into the corridor.

He advanced to the middle of the room, with the candle still in his hand: he looked about him – but he never looked back.

I saw the door of Miss Verinder's bedroom standing ajar. She had put out her light. She controlled herself nobly. The dim white outline of her summer dress was all that I could see. Nobody who had not known it beforehand would have suspected that there was a living creature in the room. She kept back, in the dark: not a word, not a movement escaped her.

It was now ten minutes past one. I heard, through the dead silence, the soft drip of the rain and the tremulous passage of the night air through the trees.

After waiting irresolute, for a minute or more, in the middle of the room, he moved to the corner near the window, where the Indian cabinet stood.

He put his candle on the top of the cabinet. He opened, and shut, one drawer after another, until he came to the drawer in which the mock Diamond was put. He looked into the drawer for a moment. Then he took the mock Diamond out with his right hand. With the other hand, he took the candle from the top of the cabinet.

He walked back a few steps towards the middle of the room, and stood still again.

Thus far, he had exactly repeated what he had done on the birthday night. Would his next proceeding be the same as the proceeding of last year? Would he leave the room? Would he go back now, as I believed he had gone back then, to his bedchamber? Would he show us what he had done with the Diamond, when he had returned to his own room?

His first action, when he moved once more, proved to be an action which he had *not* performed, when he was under the influence of the opium for the first time. He put the candle down on a table, and wandered on a little towards the farther end of the room. There was a sofa here. He leaned heavily on the back of it, with his left hand – then roused himself, and returned to the middle of the room. I could now see his eyes. They were getting dull and heavy; the glitter in them was fast dying out.

The suspense of the moment proved too much for Miss Verinder's self-control. She advanced a few steps – then stopped again. Mr. Bruff and Betteredge looked across the open doorway at me for the first time. The prevision of a coming disappointment was impressing itself on their minds as well as on mine.

Still, so long as he stood where he was, there was hope. We waited, in unutterable expectation, to see what would happen next.

The next event was decisive. He let the mock Diamond drop out of his hand.

It fell on the floor, before the doorway – plainly visible to him, and to everyone. He made no effort to pick it up: he looked down at it vacantly, and, as he looked, his head sank on his breast. He staggered – roused himself for an instant – walked back unsteadily to the sofa – and sat down on it. He made a last effort; he tried to rise, and sank back. His head fell on the sofa cushions. It was then twenty-five minutes past one o'clock. Before I had put my watch back in my pocket, he was asleep.

It was all over now. The sedative influence had got him; the experiment was at an end.

I entered the room, telling Mr. Bruff and Betteredge that they might follow me. There was no fear of disturbing him. We were free to move and speak.

"The first thing to settle," I said, "is the question of what we are to do with him. He will probably sleep for the next six or seven hours, at least. It is some distance to carry him back to his own room. When I was younger, I could have done it alone. But my health and strength are not what they were – I am afraid I must ask you to help me."

Before they could answer, Miss Verinder called to me softly. She met me at the door of her room, with a light shawl, and with the counterpane[1] from her own bed.

"Do you mean to watch him while he sleeps?" she asked.

"Yes, I am not sure enough of the action of the opium in his case to be willing to leave him alone."

She handed me the shawl and the counterpane.

"Why should you disturb him?" she whispered. "Make his bed on the sofa. I can shut my door, and keep in my room."

It was infinitely the simplest and the safest way of disposing of him for the night. I mentioned the suggestion to Mr. Bruff and Betteredge – who both approved of my adopting it. In five minutes I had laid him comfortably on the sofa, and had covered him lightly with the

---

1   A counterpane is a bedspread or a quilt.

counterpane and the shawl. Miss Verinder wished us good night, and closed the door. At my request, we three then drew round the table in the middle of the room, on which the candle was still burning, and on which writing materials were placed.

"Before we separate," I began, "I have a word to say about the experiment which has been tried to-night. Two distinct objects were to be gained by it. The first of these objects was to prove, that Mr. Blake entered this room, and took the Diamond, last year, acting unconsciously and irresponsibly, under the influence of opium. After what you have both seen, are you both satisfied, so far?"[1]

They answered me in the affirmative, without a moment's hesitation.

"The second object," I went on, "was to discover what he did with the Diamond, after he was seen by Miss Verinder to leave her sitting-room with the jewel in his hand, on the birthday night. The gaining of this object depended, of course, on his still continuing exactly to repeat his proceedings of last year. He has failed to do that; and the purpose of the experiment is defeated accordingly. I can't assert that I am not disappointed at the result – but I can honestly say that I am not surprised by it. I told Mr. Blake from the first, that our complete success in this matter depended on our completely reproducing in him the physical and moral conditions of last year – and I warned him that this was the next thing to a downright impossibility. We have only partially reproduced the conditions, and the experiment has been only partially successful in consequence. It is also possible that I may have administered too large a dose of laudanum. But I myself look upon the first reason that I have given, as the true reason why we have to lament a failure, as well as to rejoice over a success."

After saying those words, I put the writing materials before Mr. Bruff, and asked him if he had any objection – before we separated for the night – to draw out, and sign, a plain statement of what he had

---

1   A tongue-in-cheek review of Collins's dramatic adaptation of *The Moonstone* offered the following comment: "The lesson to be gained from *The Moonstone* is, don't give up smoking, or you will walk in your sleep, and steal the jewels of your lover. But what will the Anti-Tobacco Society say to Mr. Wilkie Collins? The Havana merchants ought to send him a splendid box of cigars. No one will dream of leaving off smoking after this, for a prime Partaga is better than a night in the lock-up, and a position in the felon's dock." See Appendix G, 4 for the full text of this review.

seen. He at once took the pen, and produced the statement with the fluent readiness of a practised hand.

"I owe you this," he said, signing the paper, "as some atonement for what passed between us earlier in the evening. I beg your pardon, Mr. Jennings, for having doubted you. You have done Franklin Blake an inestimable service. In our legal phrase, you have proved your case."

Betteredge's apology was characteristic of the man.

"Mr. Jennings," he said, "when you read *Robinson Crusoe* again (which I strongly recommend you to do), you will find that he never scruples to acknowledge it, when he turns out to have been in the wrong. Please to consider me, sir, as doing what *Robinson Crusoe* did, on the present occasion." With those words he signed the paper in his turn.

Mr. Bruff took me aside, as we rose from the table.

"One word about the Diamond," he said. "Your theory is that Franklin Blake hid the Moonstone in his room. My theory is, that the Moonstone is in the possession of Mr. Luker's bankers in London. We won't dispute which of us is right. We will only ask, which of us is in a position to put his theory to the test?"

"The test, in my case," I answered, "has been tried to-night, and has failed."

"The test, in my case," rejoined Mr. Bruff, "is still in process of trial. For the last two days I have had a watch set for Mr. Luker at the bank; and I shall cause that watch to be continued until the last day of the month. I know that he must take the Diamond himself out of his banker's hands – and I am acting on the chance that the person who has pledged the Diamond may force him to do this by redeeming the pledge. In that case I may be able to lay my hand on the person. If I succeed, I clear up the mystery, exactly at the point where the mystery baffles us now! Do you admit that, so far?"

I admitted it readily.

"I am going back to town by the morning train," pursued the lawyer. "I may hear, when I return, that a discovery has been made – and it may be of the greatest importance that I should have Franklin Blake at hand to appeal to, if necessary. I intend to tell him, as soon as he wakes, that he must return with me to London. After all that has happened, may I trust to your influence to back me?"

"Certainly!" I said.

Mr. Bruff shook hands with me, and left the room. Betteredge followed him out.

I went to the sofa to look at Mr. Blake. He had not moved since I had laid him down and made his bed – he lay locked in a deep and quiet sleep.

While I was still looking at him, I heard the bedroom door softly opened. Once more, Miss Verinder appeared on the threshold, in her pretty summer dress.

"Do me a last favour?" she whispered. "Let me watch him with you."

I hesitated – not in the interests of propriety; only in the interest of her night's rest. She came close to me, and took my hand.

"I can't sleep; I can't even sit still, in my own room," she said. "Oh, Mr. Jennings, if you were me, only think how you would long to sit and look at him. Say, yes! Do!"

Is it necessary to mention that I gave way? Surely not!

She drew a chair to the foot of the sofa. She looked at him in a silent ecstasy of happiness, till the tears rose in her eyes. She dried her eyes, and said she would fetch her work. She fetched her work, and never did a single stitch of it. It lay in her lap – she was not even able to look away from him long enough to thread her needle. I thought of my own youth; I thought of the gentle eyes which had once looked love at *me*. In the heaviness of my heart I turned to my Journal for relief, and wrote in it what is written here.

So we kept our watch together in silence. One of us absorbed in his writing; the other absorbed in her love.

Hour after hour he lay in his deep sleep. The light of the new day grew and grew in the room, and still he never moved.

Towards six o'clock, I felt the warning which told me that my pains were coming back. I was obliged to leave her alone with him for a little while. I said I would go upstairs, and fetch another pillow for him out of his room. It was not a long attack, this time. In a little while I was able to venture back, and let her see me again.

I found her at the head of the sofa, when I returned. She was just touching his forehead with her lips. I shook my head as soberly as I could, and pointed to her chair. She looked back at me with a bright smile, and a charming colour in her face. "You would have done it," she whispered, "in my place!"

★   ★   ★   ★   ★

It is just eight o'clock. He is beginning to move for the first time.

Miss Verinder is kneeling by the side of the sofa. She has so placed herself that when his eyes first open, they must open on her face.

Shall I leave them together?

Yes!

★   ★   ★   ★   ★

Eleven o'clock. – The house is empty again. They have arranged it among themselves; they have all gone to London by the ten o'clock train. My brief dream of happiness is over. I have awakened again to the realities of my friendless and lonely life.

I dare not trust myself to write down the kind words that have been said to me – especially by Miss Verinder and Mr. Blake. Besides, it is needless. Those words will come back to me in my solitary hours, and will help me through what is left of the end of my life. Mr. Blake is to write, and tell me what happens in London. Miss Verinder is to return to Yorkshire in the autumn (for her marriage, no doubt); and I am to take a holiday, and be a guest in the house. Oh me, how I felt, as the grateful happiness looked at me out of her eyes, and the warm pressure of her hand said, "This is your doing!"

My poor patients are waiting for me. Back again, this morning, to the old routine! Back again, to-night, to the dreadful alternative between the opium and the pain!

God be praised for His mercy! I have seen a little sunshine – I have had a happy time.

★

FIFTH NARRATIVE

The Story Resumed by FRANKLIN BLAKE

CHAPTER I

BUT few words are needed, on my part, to complete the narrative that has been presented in the Journal of Ezra Jennings.

Of myself, I have only to say that I awoke on the morning of the twenty-sixth, perfectly ignorant of all that I had said and done under the influence of the opium – from the time when the drug first laid its hold on me, to the time when I opened my eyes, in Rachel's sitting-room.

Of what happened after my waking, I do not feel called upon to render an account in detail. Confining myself merely to results, I have to report that Rachel and I thoroughly understood each other, before a single word of explanation had passed on either side. I decline to account, and Rachel declines to account, for the extraordinary rapidity of our reconciliation. Sir and Madam, look back at the time when you were passionately attached to each other – and you will know what happened, after Ezra Jennings had shut the door of the sitting-room, as well as I know it myself.

I have, however, no objection to add, that we should have been certainly discovered by Mrs. Merridew, but for Rachel's presence of mind. She heard the sound of the old lady's dress in the corridor, and instantly ran out to meet her. I heard Mrs. Merridew say, "What is the matter?" and I heard Rachel answer, "The explosion!" Mrs. Merridew instantly permitted herself to be taken by the arm, and led into the garden, out of the way of the impending shock. On her return to the house, she met me in the hall, and expressed herself as greatly struck by the vast improvement in Science, since the time when she was a girl at school. "Explosions, Mr. Blake, are infinitely milder than they were. I assure you, I barely heard Mr. Jennings's explosion from the garden. And no smell afterwards, that I can detect, now we have come back to the house. I must really apologise to your medical friend. It is only due to him to say, that he has managed it beautifully!"

So, after vanquishing Betteredge and Mr. Bruff, Ezra Jennings vanquished Mrs. Merridew herself. There is a great deal of undeveloped liberal feeling in the world, after all!

At breakfast, Mr. Bruff made no secret of his reasons for wishing that I should accompany him to London by the morning train. The watch kept at the bank, and the result which might yet come of it, appealed so irresistibly to Rachel's curiosity, that she at once decided (if Mrs. Merridew had no objection) on accompanying us back to town – so as to be within reach of the earliest news of our proceedings.

Mrs. Merridew proved to be all pliability and indulgence, after the truly considerate manner in which the explosion had conducted itself; and Betteredge was accordingly informed that we were all four to travel back together by the morning train. I fully expected that he would have asked leave to accompany us. But Rachel had wisely provided her faithful old servant with an occupation that interested him. He was charged with completing the refurnishing of the house, and was too full of his domestic responsibilities to feel the "detective-fever" as he might have felt it under other circumstances.

Our one subject of regret, in going to London, was the necessity of parting, more abruptly than we could have wished, with Ezra Jennings. It was impossible to persuade him to accompany us. I could only promise to write to him – and Rachel could only insist on his coming to see her when she returned to Yorkshire. There was every prospect of our meeting again in a few months – and yet there was something very sad in seeing our best and dearest friend left standing alone on the platform, as the train moved out of the station.

On our arrival in London, Mr. Bruff was accosted at the terminus by a small boy, dressed in a jacket and trousers of threadbare black cloth, and personally remarkable in virtue of the extraordinary prominence of his eyes. They projected so far, and they rolled about so loosely, that you wondered uneasily why they remained in their sockets. After listening to the boy, Mr. Bruff asked the ladies whether they would excuse our accompanying them back to Portland Place. I had barely time to promise Rachel that I would return, and tell her everything that had happened, before Mr. Bruff seized me by the arm, and hurried me into a cab. The boy with the ill-secured eyes took his place on the box by the driver, and the driver was directed to go to Lombard-street.

"News from the bank?" I asked, as we started.

"News of Mr. Luker," said Mr. Bruff. "An hour ago, he was seen to leave his house at Lambeth, in a cab, accompanied by two men, who were recognised by *my* men as police officers in plain clothes. If Mr. Luker's dread of the Indians is at the bottom of this precaution, the inference is plain enough. He is going to take the Diamond out of the bank."

"And we are going to the bank to see what comes of it?"

"Yes – or to hear what has come of it, if it is all over by this time. Did you notice my boy – on the box, there?"

"I noticed his eyes."

Mr. Bruff laughed. "They call the poor little wretch 'Gooseberry,' at the office," he said. "I employ him to go on errands – and I only wish my clerks who have nicknamed him were as thoroughly to be depended on as he is. Gooseberry is one of the sharpest boys in London, Mr. Blake, in spite of his eyes."

It was twenty minutes to five when we drew up before the bank in Lombard Street. Gooseberry looked longingly at his master, as he opened the cab door.

"Do you want to come in too?" asked Mr. Bruff kindly. "Come in then, and keep at my heels till further orders. He's as quick as lightning," pursued Mr. Bruff, addressing me in a whisper. "Two words will do with Gooseberry, where twenty would be wanted with another boy."

We entered the bank. The outer office – with the long counter, behind which the cashiers sat – was crowded with people; all waiting their turn to take money out, or to pay money in, before the bank closed at five o'clock.

Two men among the crowd approached Mr. Bruff, as soon as he showed himself.

"Well," asked the lawyer. "Have you seen him?"

"He passed us here half an hour since, sir, and went on into the inner office."

"Has he not come out again yet?"

"No, sir."

Mr. Bruff turned to me. "Let us wait," he said.

I looked round among the people about me for the three Indians. Not a sign of them was to be seen anywhere. The only person present with a noticeably dark complexion was a tall man in a pilot coat, and a round hat, who looked like a sailor. Could this be one of them in disguise? Impossible! The man was taller than any of the Indians; and his face, where it was not hidden by a bushy black beard, was twice the breadth of any of their faces at least.

"They must have their spy somewhere," said Mr. Bruff, looking at the dark sailor in his turn. "And he may be the man."

Before he could say more, his coat-tail was respectfully pulled by his attendant sprite with the gooseberry eyes. Mr. Bruff looked where the boy was looking. "Hush!" he said. "Here is Mr. Luker!"

The money-lender came out from the inner regions of the bank, followed by his two guardian policemen in plain clothes.

"Keep your eye on him," whispered Mr. Bruff. "If he passes the Diamond to anybody, he will pass it here."

Without noticing either of us, Mr. Luker slowly made his way to the door – now in the thickest, now in the thinnest part of the crowd. I distinctly saw his hand move, as he passed a short, stout man, respectably dressed in a suit of sober grey. The man started a little, and looked after him. Mr. Luker moved on slowly through the crowd. At the door, his guard placed themselves on either side of him. They were all three followed by one of Mr. Bruff's men – and I saw them no more.

I looked round at the lawyer, and then looked significantly towards the man in the suit of sober grey. "Yes!" whispered Mr. Bruff, "I saw it too!" He turned about, in search of his second man. The second man was nowhere to be seen. He looked behind him for his attendant sprite. Gooseberry had disappeared.

"What the devil does it mean?" said Mr. Bruff angrily. "They have both left us at the very time when we want them most."

It came to the turn of the man in the grey suit to transact his business at the counter. He paid in a cheque – received a receipt for it – and turned to go out.

"What is to be done?" asked Mr. Bruff. "*We* can't degrade ourselves by following him."

"*I* can!" I said. "I wouldn't lose sight of that man for ten thousand pounds!"

"In that case," rejoined Mr. Bruff, "I wouldn't lose sight of *you*, for twice the money. A nice occupation for a man in my position," he muttered to himself, as we followed the stranger out of the bank.

"For Heaven's sake don't mention it. I should be ruined if it was known."

The man in the grey suit got into an omnibus, going westward. We got in after him. There were latent reserves of youth still left in Mr. Bruff. I assert it positively – when he took his seat in the omnibus, he blushed!

The man with the grey suit stopped the omnibus, and got out in Oxford Street. We followed him again. He went into a chemist's shop.[1]

Mr. Bruff started. "My chemist!" he exclaimed. "I am afraid we have made a mistake."

We entered the shop. Mr. Bruff and the proprietor exchanged a few words in private. The lawyer joined me again, with a very crest-fallen face.

"It's greatly to our credit," he said, as he took my arm, and led me out– "that's one comfort!"

"What is to our credit?" I asked.

"Mr. Blake! you and I are the two worst amateur detectives that ever tried their hands at the trade. The man in the grey suit has been thirty years in the chemist's service. He was sent to the bank to pay money to his master's account – and he knows no more of the Moonstone than the babe unborn."

I asked what was to be done next.

"Come back to my office," said Mr. Bruff. "Gooseberry, and my second man, have evidently followed somebody else. Let us hope that *they* had their eyes about them at any rate!"

When we reached Gray's Inn Square, the second man had arrived there before us. He had been waiting for more than a quarter of an hour.

"Well?" asked Mr. Bruff. "What's your news?"

"I am sorry to say, sir," replied the man, "that I have made a mistake. I could have taken my oath that I saw Mr. Luker pass something

---

1   Just northeast of Hyde Park, Oxford Street was minutes from Collins's birthplace and several of the homes in which he lived in the 1850s and 1860s. Some of the theatres that Collins frequented – the Princess's, the Pantheon, and the Oxford – were located on Oxford Street. The chemist's shop – a chemist was a druggist – into which the man in grey walks seems part of a quiet joke on Collins's part, for he knew from reading his De Quincey that the chemist from whom the famous opium eater first purchased laudanum had his shop on Oxford Street.

to an elderly gentleman, in a light-coloured paletot.[1] The elderly gentleman turns out, sir, to be a most respectable master ironmonger in Eastcheap."[2]

"Where is Gooseberry?" asked Mr. Bruff resignedly.

The man stared. "I don't know, sir. I have seen nothing of him since I left the bank."

Mr. Bruff dismissed the man. "One of two things," he said to me. "Either Gooseberry has run away, or he is hunting on his own account. What do you say to dining here, on the chance that the boy may come back in an hour or two? I have got some good wine in the cellar, and we can get a chop from the coffee-house."

We dined at Mr. Bruff's chambers. Before the cloth was removed, "a person" was announced as wanting to speak to the lawyer. Was the person, Gooseberry? No: only the man who had been employed to follow Mr. Luker when he left the bank.

The report, in this case, presented no feature of the slightest interest. Mr. Luker had gone back to his own house, and had there dismissed his guard. He had not gone out again afterwards. Towards dusk, the shutters had been put up, and the doors had been bolted. The street before the house, and the alley behind the house, had been carefully watched. No signs of the Indians had been visible. No person whatever had been seen loitering about the premises. Having stated these facts, the man waited to know whether there were any further orders. Mr. Bruff dismissed him for the night.

"Do you think Mr. Luker has taken the Moonstone home with him?" I asked.

"Not he," said Mr. Bruff. "He would never have dismissed his two policemen, if he had run the risk of keeping the Diamond in his own house again."

We waited another half-hour for the boy, and waited in vain. It was then time for Mr. Bruff to go to Hampstead, and for me to return to Rachel in Portland Place. I left my card, in charge of the porter at the chambers, with a line written on it to say that I should be at my lodgings at half-past ten, that night. The card was to be given to the boy, if the boy came back.

---

1   A paletot is a loose outer garment, a cloak, a coat for men or women.
2   An ironmonger was, in essence, a hardware merchant. Eastcheap lies between London Bridge and the Tower of London, just north of the Thames.

Some men have a knack of keeping appointments; and other men have a knack of missing them. I am one of the other men. Add to this, that I passed the evening at Portland Place, on the same seat with Rachel, in a room forty feet long, with Mrs. Merridew at the farther end of it. Does anybody wonder that I got home at half-past twelve instead of half-past ten? How thoroughly heartless that person must be! And how earnestly I hope I may never make that person's acquaintance!

My servant handed me a morsel of paper when he let me in. I read in a neat legal handwriting, these words: – "If you please, sir, I am getting sleepy. I will come back to-morrow morning, between nine and ten." Inquiry proved that a boy, with very extraordinary-looking eyes, had called, and presented my card and message, had waited an hour, had done nothing but fall asleep and wake up again, had written a line for me, and had gone home – after gravely informing the servant that "he was fit for nothing unless he got his night's rest."

At nine, the next morning, I was ready for my visitor. At half-past nine, I heard steps outside my door. "Come in, Gooseberry!" I called out. "Thank you, sir," answered a grave and melancholy voice. The door opened. I started to my feet, and confronted – Sergeant Cuff.

"I thought I would look in here, Mr. Blake, on the chance of your being in town, before I wrote to Yorkshire," said the Sergeant.

He was as dreary and as lean as ever. His eyes had not lost their old trick (so subtly noticed in Betteredge's Narrative) of "looking as if they expected something more from you than you were aware of yourself." But, so far as dress can alter a man, the great Cuff was changed beyond all recognition. He wore a broad-brimmed white hat, a light shooting jacket, white trousers, and drab gaiters. He carried a stout oak stick. His whole aim and object seemed to be to look as if he had lived in the country all his life. When I complimented him on his Metamorphosis, he declined to take it as a joke. He complained, quite gravely, of the noises and the smells of London. I declare I am far from sure that he did not speak with a slightly rustic accent! I offered him breakfast. The innocent countryman was quite shocked. *His* breakfast hour was half-past six – and *he* went to bed with the cocks and hens!

"I only got back from Ireland last night," said the Sergeant, coming round to the practical object of his visit, in his own impenetrable manner. "Before I went to bed, I read your letter, telling me what has happened since my inquiry after the Diamond was suspended last year. There's only one thing to be said about the matter on my side. I completely mistook my case. How any man living was to have seen things in their true light, in such a situation as mine was at the time, I don't profess to know. But that doesn't alter the facts as they stand. I own that I made a mess of it. Not the first mess, Mr. Blake, which has distinguished my professional career! It's only in books that the offices of the detective force are superior to the weakness of making a mistake."

"You have come in the nick of time to recover your reputation," I said.

"I beg your pardon, Mr. Blake," rejoined the Sergeant. "Now I have retired from business, I don't care a straw about my reputation. I have done with my reputation, thank God! I am here, sir, in grateful remembrance of the late Lady Verinder's liberality to me. I will go back to my old work – if you want me, and if you will trust me – on that consideration, and on no other. Not a farthing of money is to pass, if you please, from you to me. This is on honour. Now tell me, Mr. Blake, how the case stands since you wrote to me last."

I told him of the experiment with the opium, and of what had occurred afterwards at the bank in Lombard-street. He was greatly struck by the experiment – it was something entirely new in his experience. And he was particularly interested in the theory of Ezra Jennings, relating to what I had done with the Diamond after I had left Rachel's sitting-room, on the birthday night.

"I don't hold with Mr. Jennings that you hid the Moonstone," said Sergeant Cuff. "But I agree with him, that you must certainly have taken it back to your own room."

"Well?" I asked. "And what happened then?"

"Have you no suspicion yourself of what happened, sir?"

"None whatever."

"Has Mr. Bruff no suspicion?"

"No more than I have."

Sergeant Cuff rose, and went to my writing-table. He came back with a sealed envelope. It was marked "Private"; it was addressed to me; and it had the Sergeant's signature in the corner.

"I suspected the wrong person, last year," he said: "and I may be suspecting the wrong person now. Wait to open the envelope, Mr. Blake, till you have got at the truth. And then compare the name of the guilty person, with the name that I have written in that sealed letter."

I put the letter into my pocket – and then asked for the Sergeant's opinion of the measures which we had taken at the bank.

"Very well intended, sir," he answered, "and quite the right thing to do. But there was another person who ought to have been looked after besides Mr. Luker."

"The person named in the letter you have just given to me?"

"Yes, Mr. Blake, the person named in the letter. It can't be helped now. I shall have something to propose to you and Mr. Bruff, sir, when the time comes. Let's wait, first, and see if the boy has anything to tell us that is worth hearing."

It was close on ten o'clock, and the boy had not made his appearance. Sergeant Cuff talked of other matters. He asked after his old friend Betteredge, and his old enemy the gardener. In a minute more, he would no doubt have got from this, to the subject of his favourite roses, if my servant had not interrupted us by announcing that the boy was below.

On being brought into the room, Gooseberry stopped at the threshold of the door, and looked distrustfully at the stranger who was in my company. I told the boy to come to me.

"You may speak before this gentleman," I said. "He is here to assist me; and he knows all that has happened. Sergeant Cuff," I added, "this is the boy from Mr. Bruff's office."

In our modern system of civilization, celebrity (no matter of what kind) is the lever that will move anything. The fame of the great Cuff had even reached the ears of the small Gooseberry. The boy's ill-fixed eyes rolled, when I mentioned the illustrious name, till I thought they really must have dropped on the carpet.

"Come here, my lad," said the Sergeant, "and let's hear what you have got to tell us."

The notice of the great man – the hero of many a famous story in every lawyer's office in London – appeared to fascinate the boy. He placed himself in front of Sergeant Cuff, and put his hands behind him, after the approved fashion of a neophyte who is examined in his catechism.

"What is your name?" said the Sergeant, beginning with the first question in the catechism.

"Octavius Guy," answered the boy. "They call me Gooseberry at the office because of my eyes."

"Octavius Guy, otherwise Gooseberry," pursued the Sergeant with the utmost gravity, "you were missed at the bank yesterday. What were you about?"

"If you please, sir, I was following a man."

"Who was he?"

"A tall man, sir, with a big black beard, dressed like a sailor."

"I remember the man!" I broke in. "Mr. Bruff and I thought he was a spy employed by the Indians."

Sergeant Cuff did not appear to be much impressed by what Mr. Bruff and I had thought. He went on catechizing Gooseberry.

"Well?" he said – "and why did you follow the sailor?"

"If you please, sir, Mr. Bruff wanted to know whether Mr. Luker passed anything to anybody on his way out of the bank. I saw Mr. Luker pass something to the sailor with the black beard."

"Why didn't you tell Mr. Bruff what you saw?"

"I hadn't time to tell anybody, sir, the sailor went out in such a hurry."

"And you ran out after him – eh?"

"Yes, sir."

"Gooseberry," said the Sergeant, patting his head, "you have got something in that small skull of yours – and it isn't cotton-wool. I am greatly pleased with you, so far."

The boy blushed with pleasure. Sergeant Cuff went on:

"Well? and what did the sailor do, when he got into the street?"

"He called a cab, sir."

"And what did you do?"

"Held on behind, and run after it."

Before the Sergeant could put his next question, another visitor was announced – the head clerk from Mr. Bruff's office.

Feeling the importance of not interrupting Sergeant Cuff's examination of the boy, I received the clerk in another room. He came with bad news of his employer. The agitation and excitement of the last two days had proved too much for Mr. Bruff. He had awoke that morning with an attack of gout; he was confined to his room at

Hampstead; and, in the present critical condition of our affairs, he was very uneasy at being compelled to leave me without the advice and assistance of an experienced person. The chief clerk had received orders to hold himself at my disposal, and was willing to do his best to replace Mr. Bruff.

I wrote at once to quiet the old gentleman's mind, by telling him of Sergeant Cuff's visit: adding that Gooseberry was at that moment under examination; and promising to inform Mr. Bruff, either personally or by letter, of whatever might occur later in the day. Having dispatched the clerk to Hampstead with my note, I returned to the room which I had left, and found Sergeant Cuff at the fireplace, in the act of ringing the bell.

"I beg your pardon, Mr. Blake," said the Sergeant. "I was just going to send word by your servant that I wanted to speak to you. There isn't a doubt on my mind that this boy – this most meritorious boy," added the Sergeant, patting Gooseberry on the head, "has followed the right man. Precious time has been lost, sir, through your unfortunately not being home at half-past ten last night. The only thing to do, now, is to send for a cab immediately."

In five minutes more, Sergeant Cuff and I (with Gooseberry on the box to guide the driver) were on our way eastward, towards the City.

"One of these days," said the Sergeant, pointing through the front window of the cab, "that boy will do great things in my late profession. He is the brightest and cleverest little chap I have met with, for many a long year past. You shall hear the substance, Mr. Blake, of what he told me while you were out of the room. You were present, I think, when he mentioned that he held on behind the cab, and ran after it?"

"Yes."

"Well, sir, the cab went from Lombard-street to the Tower Wharf.[1] The sailor with the black beard got out, and spoke to the steward of the Rotterdam steamboat, which was to start next morning. He asked if he could be allowed to go on board at once, and sleep in his berth overnight. The steward said, No. The cabins, and berths, and bedding were all to have a thorough cleaning that evening, and no passenger

1 The Wharf, which runs the length of the south side of the Tower of London, was a major docking point for ships heading to and from London.

could be allowed to come on board, before the morning. The sailor turned round, and left the wharf. When he got into the street again, the boy noticed for the first time, a man dressed like a respectable mechanic, walking on the opposite side of the road, and apparently keeping the sailor in view. The sailor stopped at an eating-house in the neighbourhood, and went in. The boy – not being able to make up his mind, at the moment – hung about among some other boys, staring at the good things in the eating-house window. He noticed the mechanic waiting, as he himself was waiting – but still on the opposite side of the street. After a minute, a cab came by slowly and stopped where the mechanic was standing. The boy could only see plainly one person in the cab, who leaned forward at the window to speak to the mechanic. He described that person, Mr. Blake, without any prompting from me, as having a dark face, like the face of an Indian."

It was plain, by this time, that Mr. Bruff and I had made another mistake. The sailor with the black beard was clearly not a spy in the service of the Indian conspiracy. Was he, by any possibility, the man who had got the Diamond?

"After a little," pursued the Sergeant, "the cab moved on slowly down the street. The mechanic crossed the road, and went into the eating-house. The boy waited outside till he was hungry and tired – and then went into the eating-house, in his turn. He had a shilling in his pocket; and he dined sumptuously, he tells me, on a black-pudding, an eel-pie, and a bottle of ginger-beer. What can a boy *not* digest? The substance in question has never been found yet!"

"What did he see in the eating-house?" I asked.

"Well, Mr. Blake, he saw the sailor reading the newspaper at one table, and the mechanic reading the newspaper at another. It was dusk before the sailor got up, and left the place. He looked about him suspiciously when he got out into the street. The boy – *being* a boy – passed unnoticed. The mechanic had not come out yet. The sailor walked on, looking about him, and apparently not very certain of where he was going next. The mechanic appeared once more, on the opposite side of the road. The sailor went on, till he got to Shore Lane, leading into Lower Thames Street.[1] There he stopped before a

---

1 Directly south of Eastcheap, Lower Thames Street runs along the river from London Bridge to the Tower of London. Shore Lane may have existed in the 1850s or 1860s, but it does not exist any longer.

public-house, under the sign of 'The Wheel of Fortune,' and, after examining the place outside, went in. Gooseberry went in too. There were a great many people, mostly of the decent sort, at the bar. 'The Wheel of Fortune' is a very respectable house, Mr. Blake; famous for its porter and porkpies."

The Sergeant's digressions irritated me. He saw it; and confined himself more strictly to Gooseberry's evidence when he went on.

"The sailor," he resumed, "asked if he could have a bed. The landlord said 'No; they were full.' The barmaid corrected him, and said 'Number Ten was empty.' A waiter was sent for to show the sailor to Number Ten. Just before that, Gooseberry had noticed the mechanic among the people at the bar. Before the waiter had answered the call, the mechanic had vanished. The sailor was taken off to his room. Not knowing what to do next, Gooseberry had the wisdom to wait and see if anything happened. Something did happen. The landlord was called for. Angry voices were heard upstairs. The mechanic suddenly made his appearance again, collared by the landlord, and exhibiting, to Gooseberry's great surprise, all the signs and tokens of being drunk. The landlord thrust him out at the door, and threatened him with the police if he came back. From the altercation between them, while this was going on, it appeared that the man had been discovered in Number Ten, and had declared with drunken obstinacy, that he had taken the room. Gooseberry was so struck by this sudden intoxication of a previously sober person, that he couldn't resist running out after the mechanic into the street. As long as he was in sight of the public-house, the man reeled about in the most disgraceful manner. The moment he turned the corner of the street, he recovered his balance instantly, and became as sober a member of society as you could wish to see. Gooseberry went back to 'The Wheel of Fortune,' in a very bewildered state of mind. He waited about again, on the chance of something happening. Nothing happened; and nothing more was to be heard, or seen, of the sailor. Gooseberry decided on going back to the office. Just as he came to this conclusion, who should appear, on the opposite side of the street as usual, but the mechanic again! He looked up at one particular window at the top of the public-house, which was the only one that had a light in it. The light seemed to relieve his mind. He left the place directly. The boy made his way back to Gray's Inn – got your card and message – called – and failed to find you. There you have the state of the case, Mr. Blake, as it stands at the present time."

"What is your own opinion of the case, Sergeant?"

"I think it's serious, sir. Judging by what the boy saw, the Indians are in it, to begin with."

"Yes. And the sailor is evidently the person to whom Mr. Luker passed the Diamond. It seems odd that Mr. Bruff, and I, and the man in Mr. Bruff's employment, should all have been mistaken about who the person was."

"Not at all, Mr. Blake. Considering the risk that person ran, it's likely enough that Mr. Luker purposely misled you, by previous arrangement between them."

"Do you understand the proceedings at the public-house?" I asked. "The man dressed like a mechanic was acting of course in the employment of the Indians. But I am as much puzzled to account for his sudden assumption of drunkenness as Gooseberry himself."

"I think I can give a guess at what it means, sir," said the Sergeant. "If you will reflect, you will see that the man must have had some pretty strict instructions from the Indians. They were far too noticeable themselves to risk being seen at the bank, or in the public-house – they were obliged to trust everything to their deputy. Very good. Their deputy hears a certain number named in the public-house, as the number of the room which the sailor is to have for the night – that being also the room (unless our notion is all wrong) which the Diamond is to have for the night, too. Under those circumstance, the Indians, you may rely on it, would insist on having a description of the room – of its position in the house, of its capability of being approached from the outside, and so on. What was the man to do, with such orders as these? Just what he did! He ran upstairs to get a look at the room, before the sailor was taken into it. He was found there, making his observations – and he shammed drunk, as the easiest way of getting out of the difficulty. That's how I read the riddle. After he was turned out of the public-house, he probably went with his report to the place where his employers were waiting for him. And his employers, no doubt, sent him back to make sure that the sailor was really settled at the public-house till the next morning. As for what happened at 'The Wheel of Fortune,' after the boy left – we ought to have discovered that last night. It's eleven in the morning, now. We must hope for the best, and find out what we can."

In a quarter of an hour more, the cab stopped in Shore Lane, and Gooseberry opened the door for us to get out.

"All right?" asked the Sergeant.

"All right," answered the boy.

The moment we entered "The Wheel of Fortune" it was plain even to my inexperienced eyes that there was something wrong in the house.

The only person behind the counter at which the liquors were served, was a bewildered servant girl, perfectly ignorant of the business. One or two customers, waiting for their morning drink, were tapping impatiently on the counter with their money. The barmaid appeared from the inner regions of the parlour, excited and preoccupied. She answered Sergeant Cuff's inquiry for the landlord, by telling him sharply that her master was upstairs, and was not to be bothered by anybody.

"Come along with me, sir," said Sergeant Cuff, coolly leading the way upstairs, and beckoning to the boy to follow him. The barmaid called to her master, and warned him that strangers were intruding themselves into the house. On the first floor we were encountered by the landlord, hurrying down, in a highly irritated state, to see what was the matter.

"Who the devil are you? and what do you want here?" he asked.

"Keep your temper," said the Sergeant quietly. "I'll tell you who I am to begin with. I am Sergeant Cuff."

The illustrious name instantly produced its effect. The angry landlord threw open the door of a sitting-room, and asked the Sergeant's pardon.

"I am annoyed and out of sorts, sir – that's the truth," he said. "Something unpleasant has happened in the house this morning. A man in my way of business has a deal to upset his temper, Sergeant Cuff."

"Not a doubt of it," said the Sergeant. "I'll come at once, if you will allow me, to what brings us here. This gentleman and I want to trouble you with a few inquiries, on a matter of some interest to both of us."

"Relating to what, sir?" asked the landlord.

"Relating to a dark man, dressed like a sailor, who slept here last night."

"Good God! that's the man who is upsetting the whole house at this moment!" exclaimed the landlord. "Do you, or does this gentleman know anything about him?"

"We can't be certain till we see him," answered the Sergeant.

"See him?" echoed the landlord. "That's the one thing that nobody has been able to do since seven o'clock this morning. That was the time when he left word, last night, that he was to be called. He *was* called – and there was no getting an answer from him, and no opening his door to see what was the matter. They tried again at eight, and they tried again at nine. No use! There was the door still locked – and not a sound to be heard in the room! I have been out this morning – and I only got back a quarter of an hour ago. I have hammered at the door myself – and all to no purpose. The potboy[1] has gone to fetch a carpenter. If you can wait a few minutes, gentlemen, we will have the door opened, and see what it means."

"Was the man drunk last night?" asked Sergeant Cuff.

"Perfectly sober, sir – or I would never have let him sleep in my house."

"Did he pay for his bed beforehand?"

"No."

"Could he leave the room in any way, without going out by the door?"

"The room is a garret," said the landlord. "But there's a trap-door in the ceiling, leading out on to the roof – and a little lower down the street, there's an empty house under repair. Do you think, Sergeant, the blackguard has got off in that way, without paying?"

"A sailor," said Sergeant Cuff, "might have done it – early in the morning, before the street was astir. He would be used to climbing, and his head wouldn't fail him on the roofs of the houses."

As he spoke, the arrival of the carpenter was announced. We all went upstairs, at once, to the top storey. I noticed that the Sergeant was unusually grave, even for *him*. It also struck me as odd that he told the boy (after having previously encouraged him to follow us), to wait in the room below till we came down again.

---

1   A potboy took orders and delivered beer to patrons in a tavern.

The carpenter's hammer and chisel disposed of the resistance of the door in a few minutes. But some article of furniture had been placed against it inside, as a barricade. By pushing at the door, we thrust this obstacle aside, and so got admission to the room. The landlord entered first; the Sergeant second; and I third. The other persons present followed us.

We all looked towards the bed, and all started.

The man had not left the room. He lay, dressed, on the bed – with a white pillow over his face, which completely hid it from view.

"What does that mean?" said the landlord, pointing to the pillow.

Sergeant Cuff led the way to the bed, without answering, and removed the pillow.

The man's swarthy face was placid and still; his black hair and beard were slightly, very slightly, discomposed. His eyes stared wide-open, glassy and vacant, at the ceiling. The filmy look and the fixed expression of them horrified me. I turned away, and went to the open window. The rest of them remained, where Sergeant Cuff remained, at the bed.

"He's in a fit!" I heard the landlord say.

"He's dead," the Sergeant answered. "Send for the nearest doctor, and send for the police."

The waiter was despatched on both errands. Some strange fascination seemed to hold Sergeant Cuff to the bed. Some strange curiosity seemed to keep the rest of them waiting, to see what the Sergeant would do next.

I turned again to the window. The moment afterwards, I felt a soft pull at my coat-tails, and a small voice whispered, "Look here, sir!"

Gooseberry had followed us into the room. His loose eyes rolled frightfully – not in terror, but in exultation. He had made a detective-discovery on his own account. "Look here, sir," he repeated – and led me to a table in the corner of the room.

On the table stood a little wooden box, open, and empty. On one side of the box lay some jewellers' cotton. On the other side, was a torn sheet of white paper, with a seal on it, partly destroyed, and with an inscription in writing, which was still perfectly legible. The inscription was in these words:

"Deposited with Messrs. Bushe, Lysaught, and Bushe, by Mr. Septimus Luker, of Middlesex Place, Lambeth, a small wooden box, sealed up in this envelope, and containing a valuable of great price. The box, when claimed, to be only given up by Messrs. Bushe and Co. on the personal application of Mr. Luker."

Those lines removed all further doubt, on one point at least. The sailor had been in possession of the Moonstone, when he had left the bank on the previous day.

I felt another pull at my coat-tails. Gooseberry had not done with me yet.

"Robbery!" whispered the boy, pointing, in high delight, to the empty box.

"You were told to wait downstairs," I said. "Go away!"

"And Murder!" added Gooseberry, pointing, with a keener relish still, to the man on the bed.

There was something so hideous in the boy's enjoyment of the horror of the scene, that I took him by the two shoulders and put him out of the room.

At the moment when I crossed the threshold of the door, I heard Sergeant Cuff's voice, asking where I was. He met me, as I returned into the room, and forced me to go back with him to the bedside.

"Mr. Blake!" he said. "Look at the man's face. It is a face disguised – and here's a proof of it!"

He traced with his finger a thin line of livid white, running backward from the dead man's forehead, between the swarthy complexion and the slightly-disturbed black hair. "Let's see what is under this," said the Sergeant, suddenly seizing the black hair, with a firm grip of his hand.

My nerves were not strong enough to bear it. I turned away again from the bed.

The first sight that met my eyes, at the other end of the room, was the irrepressible Gooseberry, perched on a chair, and looking with breathless interest, over the heads of his elders, at the Sergeant's proceedings.

"He's pulling off his wig!" whispered Gooseberry, compassionating my position, as the only person in the room who could see nothing.

There was a pause – and then a cry of astonishment among the people round the bed.

"He's pulled off his beard!" cried Gooseberry.

There was another pause – Sergeant Cuff asked for something. The landlord went to the washhand-stand, and returned to the bed with a basin of water and a towel.

Gooseberry danced with excitement on the chair. "Come up here, along with me, sir! He's washing off his complexion now!"

The Sergeant suddenly burst his way through the people about him, and came, with horror in his face, straight to the place where I was standing.

"Come back to the bed, sir!" he began. He looked at me closer, and checked himself. "No!" he resumed. "Open the sealed letter first – the letter I gave you this morning."

I opened the letter.

"Read the name, Mr. Blake, that I have written inside."

I read the name that he had written. It was *Godfrey Ablewhite.*

"Now," said the Sergeant, "come with me, and look at the man on the bed."

I went with him, and looked at the man on the bed.

GODFREY ABLEWHITE!

★

SIXTH NARRATIVE

Contributed by SERGEANT CUFF

I

DORKING, Surrey, July 30th, 1849. To Franklin Blake, Esq. Sir, – I beg to apologize for the delay that has occurred in the production of the Report, with which I engaged to furnish you. I have waited to make it a complete Report; and I have been met, here and there, by obstacles which it was only possible to remove by some little expenditure of patience and time.

The object which I proposed to myself has now, I hope, been attained. You will find, in these pages, answers to the greater part – if not all – of the questions, concerning the late Mr. Godfrey Ablewhite, which occurred to your mind when I last had the honour of seeing you.

I propose to tell you – in the first place – what is known of the manner in which your cousin met his death; appending to the statement such inferences and conclusions as we are justified (according to my opinion) in drawing from the facts.

I shall then endeavour – in the second place – to put you in possession of such discoveries as I have made, respecting the proceedings of Mr. Godfrey Ablewhite, before, during, and after the time, when you and he met as guests at the late Lady Verinder's country-house.

II

As to your cousin's death, then, first.

It appears to me to be established, beyond any reasonable doubt, that he was killed (while he was asleep, or immediately on his waking) by being smothered with a pillow from his bed – that the persons guilty of murdering him are the three Indians – and that the object contemplated (and achieved) by the crime, was to obtain possession of the Diamond, called the Moonstone.

The facts from which this conclusion is drawn, are derived partly from an examination of the room at the tavern; and partly from the evidence obtained at the Coroner's Inquest.

On forcing the door of the room, the deceased gentleman was discovered, dead, with the pillow of the bed over his face. The medical man who examined him, being informed of this circumstance, considered the post-mortem appearances as being perfectly compatible with murder by smothering – that is to say, with murder committed by some person, or persons, pressing the pillow over the nose and mouth of the deceased, until death resulted from congestion of the lungs.

Next, as to the motive for the crime.

A small box, with a sealed paper torn off from it (the paper containing an inscription) was found open, and empty, on a table in the room. Mr. Luker has himself personally identified the box, the seal, and the inscription. He has declared that the box did actually contain the diamond, called the Moonstone; and he has admitted having given the box (thus sealed up) to Mr. Godfrey Ablewhite (then concealed under a disguise), on the afternoon of the twenty-sixth of June last. The fair inference from all this is, that the stealing of the Moonstone was the motive of the crime.

Next, as to the manner in which the crime was committed.

On examination of the room (which is only seven feet high), a trap-door in the ceiling, leading out on to the roof of the house, was discovered open. The short ladder, used for obtaining access to the trap-door (and kept under the bed), was found placed at the opening, so as to enable any person, or persons, in the room, to leave it again easily. In the trap-door itself was found a square aperture cut in the wood, apparently with some exceedingly sharp instrument, just behind the bolt which fastened the door on the inner side. In this way, any person from the outside could have drawn back the bolt, and opened the door, and have dropped (or have been noiselessly lowered by an accomplice) into the room – its height, as already observed, being only seven feet. That some person, or persons, must have got admission in this way, appears evident from the fact of the aperture being there. As to the manner in which he (or they) obtained access to the roof of the tavern, it is to be remarked that the third house, lower down in the street, was empty, and under repair – that a long ladder was left by the workmen, leading from the pavement to the top of the house – and that, on returning to their work, on the morning of the 27th, the men found the plank which they had tied to the ladder, to prevent anyone from using it in their absence, removed, and lying on the ground. As to the possibility of ascending by this ladder, passing over the roofs of the houses, passing back, and descending again, unobserved – it is discovered, on the evidence of the night policeman, that he only passes through Shore Lane twice in an hour, when out on his beat. The testimony of the inhabitants also declares, that Shore Lane, after midnight, is one of the quietest and loneliest streets in London. Here again, therefore, it seems fair to infer that – with ordinary caution, and presence of mind – any man, or men, might have ascended by the ladder, and might have descended again, unobserved. Once on the roof of the tavern, it has been proved, by experiment, that a man might cut through the trap-door, while lying down on it, and that in such a position, the parapet in front of the house would conceal him from the view of anyone passing in the street.

Lastly, as to the person, or persons, by whom the crime was committed.

It is known (1) that the Indians had an interest in possessing themselves of the Diamond. (2) It is at least probable that the man looking like an Indian, whom Octavius Guy saw at the window of the cab, speaking to the man dressed like a mechanic, was one of the three Hindoo conspirators. (3) It is certain that this same man dressed like a mechanic, was seen keeping Mr. Godfrey Ablewhite in view, all through the evening of the 26th, and was found in the bedroom (before Mr. Ablewhite was shown into it) under circumstances which lead to the suspicion that he was examining the room. (4) A morsel of torn gold thread was picked up in the bedroom, which persons expert in such matters, declare to be of Indian manufacture and to be a species of gold thread not known in England. (5) On the morning of the 27th, three men, answering to the description of the three Indians, were observed in Lower Thames Street, were traced to the Tower Wharf, and were seen to leave London by the steamer bound for Rotterdam.

There is here, moral, if not legal, evidence, that the murder was committed by the Indians.

Whether the man personating a mechanic was, or was not, an accomplice in the crime, it is impossible to say. That he could have committed the murder alone, seems beyond the limits of probability. Acting by himself, he could hardly have smothered Mr. Ablewhite – who was the taller and stronger man of the two – without a struggle taking place, or a cry being heard. A servant girl, sleeping in the next room, heard nothing. The landlord, sleeping in the room below, heard nothing. The whole evidence points to the inference that more than one man was concerned in this crime – and the circumstances, I repeat, morally justify the conclusion that the Indians committed it.

I have only to add, that the verdict at the Coroner's Inquest was Wilful Murder against some person, or persons, unknown. Mr. Ablewhite's family have offered a reward, and no effort has been left untried to discover the guilty persons. The man dressed like a mechanic has eluded all inquiries. The Indians have been traced. As to the prospect of ultimately capturing these last, I shall have a word to say to you on that head, when I reach the end of the present Report.

In the meanwhile, having now written all that is needful on the subject of Mr. Godfrey Ablewhite's death, I may pass next to the narrative of his proceedings before, during, and after the time, when you and he met at the late Lady Verinder's house.

III

With regard to the subject now in hand, I may state, at the outset, that Mr. Godfrey Ablewhite's life had two sides to it.

The side turned up to the public view, presented the spectacle of a gentleman, possessed of considerable reputation as a speaker at charitable meetings, and endowed with administrative abilities, which he placed at the disposal of various Benevolent Societies, mostly of the female sort. The side kept hidden from the general notice, exhibited this same gentleman in the totally different character of a man of pleasure, with a villa in the suburbs which was not taken in his own name, and with a lady in the villa, who was not taken in his own name, either.

My investigations in the villa have shown me several fine pictures and statues; furniture tastefully selected, and admirably made; and a conservatory of the rarest flowers, the match of which it would not be easy to find in all London. My investigation of the lady has resulted in the discovery of jewels which are worthy to take rank with the flowers, and of carriages and horses which have (deservedly) produced a sensation in the Park, among persons well qualified to judge of the build of the one, and the breed of the others.

All this is, so far, common enough. The villa and the lady are such familiar objects in London life, that I ought to apologize for introducing them to notice. But what is not common and not familiar (in my experience), is that all these fine things were not only ordered, but paid for. The pictures, the statues, the flowers, the jewels, the carriages and the horses – inquiry proved, to my indescribable astonishment, that not a sixpence of debt was owing on any of them. As to the villa, it had been bought, out and out, and settled on the lady.

I might have tried to find the right reading of this riddle, and tried in vain – but for Mr. Godfrey Ablewhite's death, which caused an inquiry to be made into the state of his affairs.

The inquiry elicited these facts: –

That Mr. Godfrey Ablewhite was entrusted with the care of a sum of twenty thousand pounds – as one of two Trustees for a young gentleman, who was still a minor in the year eighteen hundred and forty-eight. That the Trust was to lapse, and that the young gentleman was to receive the twenty thousand pounds on the day when he came of age, in the month of February, eighteen hundred and fifty. That, pending the arrival of this period, an income of six hundred pounds was to be paid to him by his two Trustees, half-yearly – at Christmas and Midsummer Day. That this income was regularly paid by the active Trustee, Mr. Godfrey Ablewhite. That the twenty thousand pounds (from which the income was supposed to be derived) had, every farthing of it been sold out of the Funds,[1] at different periods, ending with the end of the year eighteen hundred and forty-seven. That the power of attorney, authorizing the bankers to sell out the stock, and the various written orders telling them what amounts to sell out, were formally signed by both the Trustees. That the signature of the second Trustee (a retired army officer, living in the country) was a signature forged, in every case, by the active Trustee – otherwise Mr. Godfrey Ablewhite.

In these facts, lies the explanation of Mr. Godfrey's honourable conduct, in paying the debts incurred for the lady and the villa – and (as you will presently see) of more besides.

---

1   Ablewhite was one of two people put in charge of a young gentleman's trust money, which had been invested in the Funds, government issued securities known as "three-per-centers" because they paid 3% interest. Ablewhite surreptitiously sold all of the securities while he was in charge of the money.

We may now advance to the date of Miss Verinder's birthday (in the year eighteen hundred and forty-eight) – the twenty-first of June. On the day before, Mr. Godfrey Ablewhite arrived at his father's house, and asked (as I know from Mr. Ablewhite, senior, himself) for a loan of three hundred pounds. Mark the sum; and remember at the same time, that the half-yearly payment to the young gentleman was due on the twenty-fourth of the month. Also, that the whole of the young gentleman's fortune had been spent by his Trustee, by the end of the year 'forty-seven.

Mr. Ablewhite, senior, refused to lend his son a farthing.

The next day Mr. Godfrey Ablewhite rode over, with you, to Lady Verinder's house. A few hours afterwards, Mr. Godfrey (as you yourself have told me) made a proposal of marriage to Miss Verinder. Here, he saw his way no doubt – if accepted – to the end of all his money anxieties, present and future. But, as events actually turned out, what happened? Miss Verinder refused him.

On the night of the birthday, therefore, Mr. Godfrey Ablewhite's pecuniary position was this. He had three hundred pounds to find on the twenty-fourth of the month, and twenty thousand pounds to find in February eighteen hundred and fifty. Failing to raise these sums, at these times, he was a ruined man.

Under those circumstances, what takes place next?

You exasperate Mr. Candy, the doctor, on the sore subject of his profession; and he plays you a practical joke, in return, with a dose of laudanum. He trusts the administration of the dose, prepared in a little phial, to Mr. Godfrey Ablewhite – who has himself confessed the share he had in the matter, under circumstances which shall presently be related to you. Mr. Godfrey is all the readier to enter into the conspiracy, having himself suffered from your sharp tongue in the course of the evening. He joins Betteredge in persuading you to drink a little brandy-and-water before you go to bed. He privately drops the dose of laudanum into your cold grog. And you drink the mixture.

Let us now shift the scene, if you please, to Mr. Luker's house at Lambeth. And allow me to remark, by way of preface, that Mr. Bruff and I, together, have found a means of forcing the money-lender to made a clean breast of it. We have carefully sifted the statement he has addressed to us; and here it is at your service.

IV

Late on the evening of Friday, the twenty-third of June ('forty-eight), Mr. Luker was surprised by a visit from Mr. Godfrey Ablewhite. He was more than surprised, when Mr. Godfrey produced the Moonstone. No such Diamond (according to Mr. Luker's experience) was in the possession of any private person in Europe.

Mr. Godfrey Ablewhite had two modest proposals to make, in relation to this magnificent gem. First, Would Mr. Luker be so good as to buy it? Secondly, Would Mr. Luker (in default of seeing his way to the purchase) undertake to sell it on commission, and to pay a sum down, on the anticipated result?

Mr. Luker tested the Diamond, weighed the Diamond, and estimated the value of the Diamond, before he answered a word. *His* estimate (allowing for the flaw in the stone) was thirty thousand pounds.

Having reached that result, Mr. Luker opened his lips, and put a question: "How did you come by this?" Only six words! But what volumes of meaning in them!

Mr. Godfrey Ablewhite began a story. Mr. Luker opened his lips again, and only said three words, this time. "That won't do!"

Mr. Godfrey Ablewhite began another story. Mr. Luker wasted no more words on him. He got up, and rang the bell for the servant to show the gentleman out.

Upon this compulsion, Mr. Godfrey made an effort, and came out with a new and amended version of the affair, to the following effect.

After privately slipping the laudanum into your brandy-and-water, he wished you good-night, and went into his own room. It was the next room to yours; and the two had a door of communication between them. On entering his own room Mr. Godfrey (as he supposed) closed his door. His money-troubles kept him awake. He sat, in his dressing-gown and slippers, for nearly an hour, thinking over his position. Just as he was preparing to get into bed, he heard you, talking to yourself, in your own room, and going to the door of communication, found that he had not shut it as he supposed.

He looked into your room to see what was the matter. He discovered you with the candle in your hand, just leaving your bedchamber. He heard you say to yourself, in a voice quite unlike your own voice,

"How do I know? The Indians may be hidden in the house."

Up to that time, he had simply supposed himself (in giving you the laudanum) to be helping to make you the victim of a harmless practical joke. It now occurred to him, that the laudanum had taken some effect on you, which had not been foreseen by the doctor, any more than by himself. In the fear of an accident happening, he followed you softly to see what you would do.

He followed you to Miss Verinder's sitting-room, and saw you go in. You left the door open. He looked through the crevice thus produced, between the door and the post, before he ventured into the room himself.

In that position, he not only detected you in taking the Diamond out of the drawer – he also detected Miss Verinder, silently watching you from her bedroom, through her open door. His own eyes satisfied him that *she* saw you take the Diamond, too.

Before you left the sitting-room again, you hesitated a little. Mr. Godfrey took advantage of this hesitation to get back again to his bedroom before you came out, and discovered him. He had barely got back, before you got back too. You saw him (as he supposes) just as he was passing through the door of communication. At any rate, you called to him in a strange, drowsy voice.

He came back to you. You looked at him in a dull sleepy way. You put the Diamond into his hand. You said to him, "Take it back, Godfrey, to your father's bank. It's safe there – it's not safe here." You turned away unsteadily, and put on your dressing-gown. You sat down in the large arm-chair in your room. You said, "*I* can't take it back to the bank. My head's like lead – and I can't feel my feet under me." Your head sank on the back of the chair – you heaved a heavy sigh – and you fell asleep.

Mr. Godfrey Ablewhite went back, with the Diamond, into his own room. His statement is, that he came to no conclusion, at that time – except that he would wait, and see what happened in the morning.

When the morning came, your language and conduct showed that you were absolutely ignorant of what you had said and done overnight. At the same time, Miss Verinder's language and conduct showed that she was resolved to say nothing (in mercy to you) on her side. If Mr. Godfrey Ablewhite chose to keep the Diamond, he might do so with perfect impunity. The Moonstone stood between him and ruin. He put the Moonstone into his pocket.

V

This was the story told by your cousin (under pressure of necessity) to Mr. Luker.

Mr. Luker believed the story to be, as to all main essentials, true – on this ground, that Mr. Godfrey Ablewhite was too great a fool to have invented it. Mr. Bruff and I agree with Mr. Luker, in considering this test of the truth of the story to be a perfectly reliable one.

The next question, was the question of what Mr. Luker would do in the matter of the Moonstone. He proposed the following terms, as the only terms on which he would consent to mix himself up with, what was (even in *his* line of business) a doubtful and dangerous transaction.

Mr. Luker would consent to lend Mr. Godfrey Ablewhite the sum of two thousand pounds, on condition that the Moonstone was to be deposited with him as a pledge. If, at the expiration of one year from that date, Mr. Godfrey Ablewhite paid three thousand pounds to Mr. Luker, he was to receive back the Diamond, as a pledge redeemed. If he failed to produce the money at the expiration of the year, the pledge (otherwise the Moonstone) was to be considered as forfeited to Mr. Luker – who would, in this latter case, generously make Mr. Godfrey a present of certain promissory notes of his (relating to former dealings) which were then in the money-lender's possession.

It is needless to say, that Mr. Godfrey indignantly refused to listen to these monstrous terms. Mr. Luker, thereupon, handed him back the Diamond, and wished him good-night.

Your cousin went to the door, and came back again. How was he to be sure that the conversation of that evening, would be kept strictly secret between his friend and himself?

Mr. Luker didn't profess to know how. If Mr. Godfrey had accepted his terms, Mr. Godfrey would have made him an accomplice, and might have counted on his silence as on a certainty. As things were, Mr. Luker must be guided by his own interests. If awkward inquiries were made, how could he be expected to compromise himself, for the sake of a man who had declined to deal with him?

Receiving this reply, Mr. Godfrey Ablewhite did, what all animals (human and otherwise) do, when they find themselves caught in a trap. He looked about him in a state of helpless despair. The day of the month, recorded on a neat little card in a box on the money-lender's chimney-piece, happened to attract his eye. It was the twenty-third of June. On the twenty-fourth, he had three hundred pounds to pay to the young gentleman for whom he was trustee, and no chance of raising the money, except the chance that Mr. Luker had offered to him. But for this miserable obstacle, he might have taken the Diamond to Amsterdam, and have made a marketable commodity of it, by having it cut up into separate stones. As matters stood, he had no choice but to accept Mr. Luker's terms. After all, he had a year at his disposal, in which to raise the three thousand pounds – and a year is a long time.

Mr. Luker drew out the necessary documents on the spot. When they were signed, he gave Mr. Godfrey Ablewhite two cheques. One, dated June 23rd, for three hundred pounds. Another, dated a week on, for the remaining balance – seventeen hundred pounds.

How the Moonstone was trusted to the keeping of Mr. Luker's bankers, and how the Indians treated Mr. Luker and Mr. Godfrey (after that had been done) you know already.

The next event in your cousin's life refers again to Miss Verinder. He proposed marriage to her for the second time – and (after having been accepted) he consented, at her request, to consider the marriage as broken off. One of his reasons for making this concession has been penetrated by Mr. Bruff. Miss Verinder had only a life interest in her mother's property – and there was no raising the twenty thousand pounds on *that*.

But you will say, he might have saved the three thousand pounds, to redeem the pledged Diamond, if he had married. He might have done so certainly – supposing neither his wife, nor her guardians and trustees, objected to his anticipating more than half of the income at his disposal, for some unknown purpose, in the first year of his marriage. But even if he got over this obstacle, there was another waiting for him in the background. The lady at the Villa had heard of his contemplated marriage. A superb woman, Mr. Blake, of the sort that are not to be trifled with – the sort with the light complexion and the Roman nose.[1] She felt the utmost contempt for Mr. Godfrey Able-

---

1 A Roman nose has a high, prominent bridge.

white. It would be silent contempt, if he made a handsome provision for her. Otherwise, it would be contempt with a tongue to it. Miss Verinder's life interest allowed him no more hope of raising the "provision" than of raising the twenty thousand pounds. He couldn't marry – he really couldn't marry, under all the circumstances.

How he tried his luck again with another lady, and how *that* marriage also broke down on the question of money, you know already. You also know of the legacy of five thousand pounds, left to him shortly afterwards, by one of those many admirers among the soft sex whose good graces this fascinating man had contrived to win. That legacy (as the event has proved) led him to his death.

I have ascertained that when he went abroad, on getting his five thousand pounds, he went to Amsterdam. There he made all the necessary arrangements for having the Diamond cut into separate stones. He came back (in disguise), and redeemed the Moonstone, on the appointed day. A few days were allowed to elapse (as a precaution agreed to by both parties) before the jewel was actually taken out of the bank. If he had got safe with it to Amsterdam, there would have been just time between July 'forty-nine and February 'fifty (when the young gentleman came of age) to cut the Diamond, and to make a marketable commodity (polished or unpolished) of the separate stones. Judge from this, what motives he had to run the risk which he actually ran. It was "neck or nothing" with him – if ever it was "neck or nothing" with a man yet.

I have only to remind you, before closing this Report, that there is a chance of laying hands on the Indians, and of recovering the Moonstone yet. They are now (there is every reason to believe) on their passage to Bombay, in an East Indiaman.[1] The ship (barring accidents) will touch at no other port on her way out; and the authorities at Bombay (already communicated with by letter, overland) will be prepared to board the vessel, the moment she enters the harbour.

I have the honour to remain, dear sir, your obedient servant, RICHARD CUFF (late sergeant in the Detective Force, Scotland Yard, London).*

---

* Note. – Wherever the report touches on the events of the birthday, or of the three days that followed it, compare with Betteredge's Narrative, chapters viii to xiii.

---

1   East Indiamen were large ships that transported passengers and cargo from England to India and back.

SEVENTH NARRATIVE

In a Letter from MR. CANDY

FRIZINGHALL, Wednesday, September 26th, 1849. – Dear Mr. Franklin Blake, you will anticipate the sad news I have to tell you, on finding your letter to Ezra Jennings returned to you, unopened, in this enclosure. He died in my arms, at sunrise, on Wednesday last.

I am not to blame for having failed to warn you that his end was at hand. He expressly forbade me to write to you. "I am indebted to Mr. Franklin Blake," he said, "for having seen some happy days. Don't distress him, Mr. Candy – don't distress him."

His sufferings, up to the last six hours of his life, were terrible to see. In the intervals of remission, when his mind was clear, I entreated him to tell me of any relatives of his to whom I might write. He asked to be forgiven for refusing anything to *me*. And then he said – not bitterly – that he would die as he had lived, forgotten and unknown. He maintained that resolution to the last. There is no hope now of making any discoveries concerning him. His story is a blank.

The day before he died, he told me where to find all his papers. I brought them to him on his bed. There was a little bundle of old letters which he put aside. There was his unfinished book. There was his Diary – in many locked volumes. He opened the volume for this year, and tore out, one by one, the pages relating to the time when you and he were together. "Give those," he said, "to Mr. Franklin Blake. In years to come, he may feel an interest in looking back at what is written there." Then he clasped his hands, and prayed God fervently to bless you, and those dear to you. He said he should like to see you again. But the next moment he altered his mind. "No," he answered, when I offered to write. "I won't distress him! I won't distress him!"

At his request I next collected the other papers – that is to say, the bundle of letters, the unfinished book, and the volumes of the Diary – and enclosed them all in one wrapper, sealed with my own seal. "Promise," he said, "that you will put this into my coffin with your own hand; and that you will see that no other hand touches it afterwards."

I gave him my promise. And the promise has been performed.

He asked me to do one other thing for him – which it cost me a hard struggle to comply with. He said, "Let my grave be forgotten. Give me your word of honour that you will allow no monument of any sort – not even the commonest tombstone – to mark the place of my burial. Let me sleep, nameless. Let me rest, unknown." When I tried to plead with him to alter his resolution, he became for the first, and only time, violently agitated. I could not bear to see it; and I gave way. Nothing but a little grass mound marks the place of his rest. In time, the tombstones will rise round it. And the people who come after us will look and wonder at the nameless grave.

As I have told you, for six hours before his death his sufferings ceased. He dozed a little. I think he dreamed. Once or twice he smiled. A woman's name, as I suppose – the name of "Ella" – was often on his lips at this time. A few minutes before the end came he asked me to lift him on his pillow, to see the sun rise through the window. He was very weak. His head fell on my shoulder. He whispered, "It's coming!" Then he said, "Kiss me!" I kissed his forehead. On a sudden he lifted his head. The sunlight touched his face. A beautiful expression, an angelic expression, came over it. He cried out three times, "Peace! peace! peace!" His head sank back again on my shoulder, and the long trouble of his life was at an end.

So he has gone from us. This was, as I think, a great man – though the world never knew him. He bore a hard life bravely. He had the sweetest temper I have ever met with. The loss of him makes me feel very lonely. Perhaps I have never been quite myself again since my illness. Sometimes, I think of giving up my practice, and going away, and trying what some of the foreign baths and waters will do for me.

It is reported here, that you and Miss Verinder are to be married next month. Please to accept my best congratulations.

The pages of my poor friend's Journal are waiting for you at my house – sealed up, with your name on the wrapper. I was afraid to trust them to the post.

My best respects and good wishes attend Miss Verinder. I remain, dear Mr. Franklin Blake, truly yours, THOMAS CANDY.

EIGHTH NARRATIVE

Contributed by GABRIEL BETTEREDGE

I AM the person (as you remember no doubt) who led the way in these pages, and opened the story. I am also the person who is left behind, as it were, to close the story up.

Let nobody suppose that I have any last words to say here concerning the Indian Diamond. I hold that unlucky jewel in abhorrence – and I refer you to other authority than mine, for such news of the Moonstone as you may, at the present time, be expected to receive. My purpose, in this place, is to state a fact in the history of the family, which has been passed over by everybody, and which I won't allow to be disrespectfully smothered up in that way. The fact to which I allude is – the marriage of Miss Rachel and Mr. Franklin Blake. This interesting event took place at our house in Yorkshire, on Tuesday, October ninth, eighteen hundred and forty-nine. I had a new suit of clothes on the occasion. And the married couple went to spend the honeymoon in Scotland.

Family festivals having been rare enough at our house, since my poor mistress's death, I own – on this occasion of the wedding – to having (towards the latter part of the day) taken a drop too much on the strength of it.

If you have ever done the same sort of thing yourself, you will understand and feel for me. If you have not, you will very likely say, "Disgusting old man! why does he tell us this?" The reason why is now to come.

Having, then, taken my drop (bless you! you have got your favourite vice, too; only your vice isn't mine, and mine isn't yours), I next applied the one infallible remedy – that remedy being, as you know, *Robinson Crusoe*. Where I opened that unrivalled book, I can't say. Where the lines of print at last left off running into each other, I know, however, perfectly well. It was at page three hundred and eighteen – a domestic bit concerning *Robinson Crusoe*'s marriage, as follows:

"With those Thoughts, I considered my new Engagement, that I had a Wife" – (Observe! so had Mr. Franklin!) – "one Child born" – (Observe again! that might yet be Mr. Franklin's case, too!) – "and my

Wife then" – What *Robinson Crusoe's* wife did, or did not do, "then," I felt no desire to discover. I scored the bit about the Child with my pencil, and put a morsel of paper for a mark to keep the place: Lie you there," I said, "till the marriage of Mr. Franklin and Miss Rachel is some months older – and then we'll see!"

The months passed (more than I had bargained for), and no occasion presented itself for disturbing that mark in the book. It was not till this present month of November, eighteen hundred and fifty, that Mr. Franklin came into my room, in high good spirits, and said, "Betteredge! I have got some news for you! Something is going to happen in the house, before we are many months older."

"Does it concern the family, sir?" I asked.

"It decidedly concerns the family," says Mr. Franklin.

"Has your good lady anything to do with it, if you please, sir?"

"She has a great deal to do with it," says Mr. Franklin, beginning to look a little surprised.

"You needn't say a word more, sir," I answered. "God bless you both! I'm heartily glad to hear it."

Mr. Franklin stared like a person thunderstruck. "May I venture to inquire where you got your information?" he asked. "I only got mine (imparted in the strictest secrecy) five minutes since."

Here was an opportunity of producing *Robinson Crusoe*! Here was a chance of reading that domestic bit about the child which I had marked on the day of Mr. Franklin's marriage! I read those miraculous words with an emphasis which did them justice, and then I looked him severely in the face. "*Now*, sir, do you believe in *Robinson Crusoe*?" I asked, with a solemnity suitable to the occasion.

"Betteredge!" says Mr. Franklin, with equal solemnity, "I'm convinced at last." He shook hands with me – and I felt that I had converted him.

With the relation of this extraordinary circumstance, my reappearance in these pages comes to an end. Let nobody laugh at the unique anecdote here related. You are welcome to be as merry as you please over everything else I have written. But when I write of *Robinson Crusoe*, by the Lord it's serious – and I request you to take it accordingly!

When this is said, all is said. Ladies and gentlemen, I make my bow, and shut up the story.

EPILOGUE

THE FINDING OF THE DIAMOND

I

THE STATEMENT OF SERGEANT CUFF'S MAN (1849)

ON the twenty-seventh of June last, I received instructions from Sergeant Cuff to follow three men; suspected of murder, and described as Indians. They had been seen on the Tower Wharf that morning, embarking on board the steamer bound for Rotterdam.

I left London by a steamer belonging to another company, which sailed on the morning of Thursday the twenty-eighth. Arriving at Rotterdam, I succeeded in finding the commander of the Wednesday's steamer. He informed me that the Indians had certainly been passengers on board his vessel – but as far as Gravesend only. Off that place, one of the three had inquired at what time they would reach Calais. On being informed that the steamer was bound to Rotterdam, the spokesman of the party expressed the greatest surprise and distress at the mistake which he and his two friends had made. They were all willing (he said) to sacrifice their passage money, if the commander of the steamer would only put them ashore. Commiserating their position, as foreigners in a strange land, and knowing no reason for detaining them, the commander signalled for a shore boat, and the three men left the vessel.

This proceeding of the Indians having been plainly resolved on beforehand, as a means of preventing their being traced, I lost no time in returning to England. I left the steamer at Gravesend, and discovered that the Indians had gone from that place to London. Thence, I again traced them as having left for Plymouth. Inquiries made at Plymouth proved that they had sailed, forty-eight hours previously, in the *Bewley Castle*, East Indiaman, bound direct to Bombay.

On receiving this intelligence, Sergeant Cuff caused the authorities at Bombay to be communicated with, overland – so that the vessel might be boarded by the police immediately on her entering the port. This step having been taken, my connexion with the matter came to an end. I have heard nothing more of it since that time.

II

THE STATEMENT OF THE CAPTAIN (1849)

I AM requested by Sergeant Cuff to set in writing certain facts, concerning three men (believed to be Hindoos) who were passengers, last summer, in the ship *Bewley Castle*, bound for Bombay direct, under my command.

The Hindoos joined us at Plymouth. On the passage out, I heard no complaint of their conduct. They were berthed in the forward part of the vessel. I had but few occasions myself of personally noticing them.

In the latter part of the voyage, we had the misfortune to be becalmed for three days and nights, off the coast of India. I have not got the ship's journal to refer to, and I cannot now call to mind the latitude and longitude. As to our position, therefore, I am only able to state generally that the currents drifted us in towards the land, and that when the wind found us again, we reached our port in twenty-four hours afterwards.

The discipline of a ship (as all seafaring persons know) becomes relaxed in a long calm. The discipline of my ship became relaxed. Certain gentlemen among the passengers got some of the smaller boats lowered, and amused themselves by rowing about, and swimming, when the sun at evening time was cool enough to let them divert themselves in that way. The boats when done with, ought to have been slung up again in their places. Instead of this they were left moored to the ship's side. What with the heat, and what with the vexation of the weather, neither officers nor men seemed to be in heart for their duty while the calm lasted.

On the third night, nothing unusual was heard or seen by the watch on deck. When the morning came, the smallest of the boats was missing – and the three Hindoos were next reported to be missing too.

If these men had stolen the boat shortly after dark (which I have no doubt they did), we were near enough to the land to make it vain to send in pursuit of them, when the discovery was made in the morning. I have no doubt they got ashore, in that calm weather (making all due allowances for fatigue and clumsy rowing), before day-break.

On reaching our port, I there learnt, for the first time, the reason these passengers had for seizing their opportunity of escaping from the ship. I could only make the same statement to the authorities which I have made here. They considered me to blame for allowing the discipline of the vessel to be relaxed. I have expressed my regret on this score to them, and to my owners. Since that time, nothing has been heard to my knowledge of the three Hindoos. I have no more to add to what is here written.

III

THE STATEMENT OF MR. MURTHWAITE (1850)

(*In a letter to* MR. BRUFF)

HAVE you any recollection, my dear sir, of a semi-savage person whom you met out at dinner, in London, in the autumn of 'forty-eight? Permit me to remind you that the person's name was Murth-waite, and that you and he had a long conversation together after dinner. The talk related to an Indian Diamond, called the Moonstone, and to a conspiracy then in existence to get possession of the gem.

Since that time, I have been wandering in Central Asia. Thence I have drifted back to the scene of some of my past adventures in the north and north-west of India. About a fortnight since, I found myself in a certain district or province (but little known to Europeans) called Kattiawar.[1]

Here an adventure befel me, in which (incredible as it may appear) you are personally interested.

In the wild regions of Kattiawar (and how wild they are, you will understand, when I tell you that even the husbandmen plough the land, armed to the teeth), the population is fanatically devoted to the old Hindoo religion – to the ancient worship of Bramah and Vishnu. The few Mahometan families, thinly scattered about the villages in

---

1   See note 3 on pages 53 and 54.

the interior, are afraid to taste meat of any kind. A Mahometan even suspected of killing that sacred animal, the cow, is, as a matter of course, put to death without mercy in these parts by the pious Hindoo neighbours who surround them. To strengthen the religious enthusiasm of the people, two of the most famous shrines of Hindoo pilgrimage are contained within the boundaries of Kattiawar. One of them is Dwarka, the birthplace of the god Krishna.[1] The other is the sacred city of Somnauth – sacked, and destroyed, as long since as the eleventh century, by the Mahometan conqueror, Mahmoud of Ghizni.

Finding myself, for the second time, in these romantic regions, I resolved not to leave Kattiawar, without looking once more on the magnificent desolation of Somnauth. At the place where I planned to do this, I was (as nearly as I could calculate it) some three days distant, journeying on foot, from the sacred city.

I had not been long on the road, before I noticed that other people – by twos and threes – appeared to be travelling in the same direction as myself.

To such of these as spoke to me, I gave myself out as a Hindoo-Boodhist, from a distant province, bound on a pilgrimage. It is needless to say that my dress was of the sort to carry out this description. Add, that I know the language as well as I know my own, and that I am lean enough and brown enough to make it no easy matter to detect my European origin – and you will understand that I passed muster with the people readily: not as one of themselves, but as a stranger from a distant part of their own country.

On the second day, the number of Hindoos travelling in my direction, had increased to fifties and hundreds. On the third day, the throng had swollen to thousands; all slowly converging to one point – the city of Somnauth.

A trifling service which I was able to render to one of my fellow-pilgrims, during the third day's journey, proved the means of introducing me to certain Hindoos of the higher caste. From these men I learnt that the multitude was on its way to a great religious ceremony, which was to take place on a hill at a little distance from Somnauth.

---

1 Dwarka is a city located on the tip of the Kattiawar Peninsula in northwestern India. Krishna is the eighth and principal avatar of Vishnu.

The ceremony was in honour of the god of the Moon; and it was to be held at night.

The crowd detained us as we drew near to the place of celebration. By the time we reached the hill, the moon was high in the heaven. My Hindoo friends possessed some special privileges which enabled them to gain access to the shrine. They kindly allowed me to accompany them. When we arrived at the place, we found the shrine hidden from our view by a curtain hung between two magnificent trees. Beneath the trees a flat projection of rock jutted out, and formed a species of natural platform. Below this, I stood, in company with my Hindoo friends.

Looking back down the hill, the view presented the grandest spectacle of Nature and Man, in combination, that I have ever seen. The lower slopes of the eminence melted imperceptibly into a grassy plain, the place of the meeting of three rivers. On one side, the graceful winding of the waters stretched away, now visible, now hidden by trees, as far as the eye could see. On the other, the waveless ocean slept in the calm of the night. People this lovely scene with tens of thousands of human creatures, all dressed in white, stretching down the sides of the hill, overflowing into the plain, and fringing the nearer banks of the winding rivers. Light this halt of the pilgrims by the wild red flames of cressets and torches, streaming up at intervals from every part of the innumerable throng. Imagine the moonlight of the East, pouring in unclouded glory over all – and you will form some idea of the view that met me when I looked forth from the summit of the hill.

A strain of plaintive music, played on stringed instruments and flutes, recalled my attention to the hidden shrine.

I turned, and saw on the rocky platform, the figures of three men. In the central figure of the three I recognized the man to whom I had spoken in England, when the Indians appeared on the terrace at Lady Verinder's house. The other two who had been his companions on that occasion, were no doubt his companions also on this.

One of the spectators, near whom I was standing, saw me start. In a whisper, he explained to me the apparition of the three figures on the platform of rock.

They were Brahmins (he said) who had forfeited their caste, in the service of the god. The god had commanded that their purification should be the purification by pilgrimage. On that night, the three men were to part. In three separate directions, they were to set forth as pilgrims to the shrines of India. Never more were they to look on each other's faces. Never more were they to rest on their wanderings, from the day which witnessed their separation, to the day which witnessed their death.

As those words were whispered to me, the plaintive music ceased. The three men prostrated themselves on the rock, before the curtain which hid the shrine. They rose – they looked on one another – they embraced. Then they descended separately among the people. The people made way for them in dead silence. In three different directions, I saw the crowd part, at one and the same moment. Slowly the grand white mass of the people closed together again. The track of the doomed men through the ranks of their fellow mortals was obliterated. We saw them no more.

A new strain of music, loud and jubilant, rose from the hidden shrine. The crowd around me shuddered, and pressed together.

The curtain between the trees was drawn aside, and the shrine was disclosed to view.

There, raised high on a throne – seated on his typical antelope, with his four arms stretching towards the four corners of the earth – there, soared above us, dark and awful in the mystic light of heaven, the god of the Moon. And there, in the forehead of the deity, gleamed the yellow Diamond, whose splendour had last shone on me in England, from the bosom of a woman's dress!

Yes! after the lapse of eight centuries, the Moonstone looks forth once more, over the walls of the sacred city in which its story first began. How it has found its way back to its wild native land – by what accident, or by what crime, the Indians regained possession of their sacred gem, may be in your knowledge, but is not in mine. You have lost sight of it in England, and (if I know anything of this people) you have lost sight of it for ever.

So the years pass, and repeat each other; so the same events revolve in the cycles of time. What will be the next adventures of the Moonstone? Who can tell?

THE END.

Appendix A: Early Reviews of The Moonstone[1]

1. Geraldine Jewsbury,[2] Unsigned review, the *Athenaeum*. July 25, 1868: 106.

When persons are in a state of ravenous hunger they are eager only for food, and utterly ignore all delicate distinctions of cookery; it is only when this savage state has been somewhat allayed that they are capable of discerning and appreciating the genius of the *chef.* Those readers who have followed the fortunes of the mysterious Moonstone for many weeks, as it has appeared in tantalizing portions, will of course throw themselves headlong upon the latter portion of the third volume, now that the end is really come, and devour it without rest or pause; to take any deliberate breathing-time is quite out of the question, and we promise them a surprise that will find the most experienced novel-reader unprepared. The unravelment of the puzzle is a satisfactory reward for all the interest out of which they have been beguiled. When, however, they have read to the end, we recommend them to read the book over again from the beginning, and they will see, what on a first perusal they were too engrossed to observe, the carefully elaborate workmanship, and the wonderful construction of the story; the admirable manner in which every circumstance and incident is fitted together, and the skill with which the secret is kept to the last; so that even when all seems to have been discovered there is a final light thrown upon people and things which give them a significance they had not before. The "epilogue" of *The Moonstone* is beautiful. It redeems the somewhat sordid detective element, by a strain of solemn and pathetic human interest. Few will read of the final destiny of the Moonstone without feeling the tears rise in their eyes as they catch the last glimpse of the three men, who have sacrificed their caste in the service of their God, when the vast crowd of worshippers opens for them, as they embrace each other and separate

---

1 Parts of these reviews, and others, appear in Norman Page's *Wilkie Collins: The Critical Heritage* (London: Routledge & Kegan Paul, 1974).

2 Geraldine Jewsbury (1812-80) was a novelist and friend of Carlyle and Dickens. John Sutherland calls her "the most accomplished all-round lady of letters of the nineteenth century" (*The Stanford Companion to Victorian Fiction*. Stanford, CA: Stanford UP, 1989, 335).

to begin their lonely and never-ending pilgrimage of expiation. The deepest emotion is certainly reserved to the last.[1]

As to the various characters of the romance, they are secondary to the circumstances. The hero and heroine do not come out very distinctly, though we are quite willing to take them upon testimony. Ezra Jennings, the doctor's assistant, is the one personage who makes himself felt by the reader. The slight sketch of his history, left purposely without details, the beautiful and noble nature developed in spite of calumny, loneliness, and the pain of a deadly malady, is drawn with a firm and masterly hand; it has an aspect of reality which none of the other personages possess though we fancy we should recognize old Betteredge if we were to meet him, even without a copy of *Robinson Crusoe* in his hand! We wish some means could have been found to save Rosanna Spearman. The cloud that hangs over her horrible death might have been lifted by a true artist, and she might have been allowed to live and recover her right mind, under the tender influence of her friend, "Limping Lucy." Mr. Godfrey Ablewhite, the distinguished philanthropist and his lady worshippers, as seen by the light thrown on him by his ardent admirer, Miss Clack, is very cleverly managed; the reader suspects him, like Sergeant Cuff and Mr. Bruff; but the reader is destined to be quite as much taken by surprise as they were.

2. Unsigned review, the *Spectator*, July 25, 1868, xli: 881–82.

The Moonstone is not worthy of Mr. Wilkie Collins's reputation as a novelist. We are no especial admirers of the department of art to which he has devoted himself, any more than we are of double acrostics, or anagrams, or any of the many kinds of puzzle on which it pleases some minds to exercise their ingenuity. Still if readers like a book containing little besides a plot, and that plot constructed solely to set them guessing, there is no particular reason why they should not be gratified. The making and guessing of conundrums are both harmless exercises of ingenuity, but when men of intellect engage in

---

1 Jewsbury was the first to comment on the implicit sympathy Collins expresses for the Indians who journey to England to retrieve the diamond. It was a sympathy that led many later critics to examine the novel as Collins's anti-imperialist manifesto.

them they ought at least to succeed. If the work is to be done at all, the better it is done the nearer does it rise to a work of genuine intellectual interest. Hitherto Mr. Wilkie Collins has done his work well, has been among the makers of conundrum-novels something more than chief, the only one whose writing was endurable by cultivated taste. Few men who could read *The Woman in White* at all read it without pleasure, or forgot its one character, the subtle, cowardly, intellectual sybarite Count Fosco. The plot of *No Name* also was worked out with rare skill, such skill as to suggest a regret that it had not been all expanded on the heroine, Magdalen Vanstone, the born actress, and the single person in the story with a character at all. Captain Wragge only appears to have one, and is obliged to tell you every five minutes what kind of villain he is. The excessive and morbid improbability of *Armadale* could not destroy all its interest, or the curiosity of its readers in the proceedings of that vulgarized Becky Sharp,[1] Miss Gwilt. In *The Moonstone*, however, we have no person who can in any way be described as a character, no one who interests us, no one who is human enough to excite even a faint emotion of dull curiosity as to his or her fate. The heroine is an impulsive girl, generally slanging somebody, whose single specialty seems to be that, believing her lover had stolen her diamond, she hates him and loves him both at once, but neither taxes him with the offence nor pardons him for committing it, a heroine who seems to have been borrowed from one of those old novels where everybody is miserable because nobody will talk common sense for five minutes. The hero has no qualities at all. In the beginning of the book Mr. Wilkie Collins had apparently an idea of describing a rather remarkable figure, a man who, educated in many countries, has so far imbibed their intellectual specialities that he by turns displays the French, German, Italian, and English side of his nature. The idea is not a bad one, for though no such human being ever existed, even a lay figure may be made interesting by carefully selected costume, but it is clumsily worked out even at first, through nonsensical talk about objective and subjective, and very soon found burdensome and abandoned; after which Franklin Blake becomes a person to whom all manner of fascinating qualities are attributed, but who does nothing remarkable except, indeed, cry when the girl he

---

1   Becky Sharp is the bold main figure in William M. Thackeray's (1811-63) *Vanity Fair* (1847-48).

loves declares that he has stolen her jewellery. Of the minor characters Miss Clack is an absurd exaggeration of the bitter evangelical type, a woman who reveals her greed and spitefulness and love of power in broad splashes, not touches, in her own letters; Godfrey Ablewhite is the most ordinary of hypocrites; Gabriel Betteredge a butler like no butler the world ever saw, now a garrulous old goose, now shrewd enough to detect the effect of several educations on his interlocutor; and Mr. Bruff is a very inferior copy of Pedgift Senior in *Armadale*. The only remaining character is introduced with this flourish of physiognomical trumpets: –

> His complexion was of a gipsy darkness; his fleshless cheeks had fallen into deep hollows, over which the bone projected like a pent-house. His nose presented the fine shape and modelling so often found among the ancient people of the East, so seldom visible among the newer races of the West. His forehead rose high and straight from the brow. His marks and wrinkles were innumerable. From this strange face, eyes, stranger still, or the softest brown – eyes dreamy and mournful, and deeply sunk in their orbits – looked out at you, and (in my case at least) took your attention captive at their will. Add to this a quantity of thick, closely curling hair, which, by some freak of nature, had lost its colour in the most startlingly partial and capricious manner. Over the top of his head it was still of the deep black which was its natural colour. Round the sides of his head – without the slightest gradation of grey to break the force of the extraordinary contrast – it had turned completely white. The line between the two colours preserved no sort of regularity. At one place the white hair ran up into the black; at another, the black hair ran down into the white.

All this description, however, and Mr. Jennings' special position as a man lying under an unjust suspicion, have no concern with the story in which he plays a part any shrewd surgeon could have played as well or better, a part in which his special character and appearance in no way assist or retard him. Such an array of dummies was never got together in any book of Mr. Wilkie Collins's before, or, we venture to say, in any book written by a man with the same literary reputation.

The plot is a little better than the characters, and very little. Mr. Wilkie Collins usually asks reviewers not to reveal the secret which is the essence of his story, and the request is too just to be disregarded, though the concession makes any criticism seem meaningless. We may, however, say that the Moonstone is a yellow diamond which once adorned an Indian idol; that three Brahmins have left India to recover it by any means – crime included; that it falls into the possession of the heroine, who wears it at a birthday party; that it is stolen either by the Indians or some one of the guests, and that the secret of the novel is the discovery of the thief. In making this discovery difficult Mr. Wilkie has shown some of his accustomed power. He has accumulated any number of persons, any one of whom may by possibility have stolen the jewel, and against each of whom the reader perceives strong circumstantial evidence, evidence arranged in two of the cases with remarkable cleverness. Nothing can be better, for example, in its way, than the mode in which the reader is compelled to doubt Mr. Godfrey Ablewhite, yet compelled to see also that he could not, from the few circumstances of crime, have taken the jewel from its resting-place. But the suspicion it is needful to throw on Rachel Verinder strikes us as clumsily managed, at least it never deceived us for a moment, though we frankly acknowledge ourselves, probably from stupidity, to have fixed on the wrong person, on whom we imagine the author never intended to throw suspicion at all. The idea of a girl like Rachel Verinder, however, stealing her own jewel, is one which, though it might by possibility have taken in the detective, cannot take in the reader. It is at once too improbable and too obtrusively put forward, to the great weakening of the only claim of its book, its merit as an elaborate conundrum. To those who enjoy the exercise of the faculty of guessing, without reference to the subject, *The Moonstone* will doubtless be readable; but Mr. Collins might, we think, have provided some enjoyment for those to whom that particular employment of time seems a wearisome waste of power. Hitherto, we do him the credit to say, he has always tried to do this, usually with some success, but *The Moonstone* gives the impression that he is weary of his own occupation, and puts together the pieces of his puzzle with little trouble and no interest. It is a pity, for even toys of that kind may as well be well made, and Mr. Wilkie Collins has it in him to be the very best puzzle-maker in the world.

3. Unsigned review, *Nation*, September 17, 1868, vii: 235.

Mr. Wilkie Collins's new book is very suggestive of a game called "button," which children used to play, and probably play now. A number of little folks being seated in a circle, each with hands placed palm to palm in front of him, one of the party, who holds a button, comes in turn to each of the others, and ostensibly drops it into his closed hands. Of course, but one of the party can receive it, but in each case the same motions are gone through with; and having made his rounds, the principal performer enquires, "Who's got the button?" Each one, including him who has it, but who intentionally misleads the rest, guesses at the puzzle, and he who guesses right carries the button at the next trial. *The Moonstone* riddle is so like in its essential features to this child's-play, that it might very well have been suggested by it. Mr. Collins's art consists, in this particular case, in converting the button into a yellow diamond, worth thirty thousand pounds; in calling the players Hindoos, detective policemen, reformed thieves, noble ladies, and so on, and in thus more effectually distracting his reader's attention from the puzzle itself, which turns out at last, like most of Mr. Collins's mysteries, to have no vital connection with his characters, considered as human beings, but to be merely an extraneous matter thrown violently into the current of his story. It would perhaps be more correct to say that there is no story at all, and that the characters are mere puppets, grouped with more or less art around the thing the conjurer wishes to conceal until the time comes for displaying it. These books of his are, in their way, curiosities of literature. The word "novel," as applied to them, is an absurd misnomer, however that word is understood. There is nothing new in Mr. Collins's stories, if the reader has ever read a book of puzzles, and they serve none of the recognized purposes of the novel. They reflect neither nature nor human life; the actors whom they introduce are nothing but more or less ingenious pieces of mechanism, and they are all alike-like each other and like nothing else. They teach no moral lessons; they are unsuggestive of thought, and they appeal to no sentiment profounder than the idlest curiosity. They are simply conundrums. It is for this reason that Mr. Collins, wise in his generation, deprecates any attempts on the part of his critics to tell the plot of his stories. One commits, however, no breach of trust in speaking of the theatrical properties which supply, in our author's case, the place of dramatic ability. He cannot create a character, unless the solitary instance of Count Fosco be an exception; he can only dress a lay-figure with more or less of skill. Take his "Moonstone," for instance – which, as far as the real business of the plot is concerned, might as well have been a black bean or a horn button – call it a yellow diamond, stolen, centuries ago, from the forehead of an Indian idol, and make its recovery a part of the religion of three mysterious, lithe, swarthy East Indians in flowing white robes, and there is a chance of awakening, in the most hardened of novel-readers, a curiosity which would assuredly have slept over the possible whereabouts of a button.

But it is hardly worth while to go on. One might say of the book, that it is like a pantomime – the characters appear to speak, but really say nothing, and are merely conventional figures, and not characters at all. Mr. Collins ventriloquizes behind each of his puppets, in order to give a sufficient number of misleading sounds. But his art is bad, and he has not art enough – his voice always betrays him, and the reader is never deceived into thinking that it is anybody but Mr. Collins that is talking. We do not know of any books of which it is truer than of Mr. Collins's to make the damaging remark, that nobody reads them twice, and that when the end of the first perusal is reached, everybody thinks his time has been wasted.

4. Unsigned review, *The Times*, October 3, 1868: 4.

[The following passages are excerpted from an extremely long and primarily positive review that is credited by many for creating an atmosphere that allowed *The Moonstone* to become a bestseller.]

It would be unjust to the memory of Edgar Poe, or perhaps – to look further back still – to Mrs Radcliffe,[1] to style Mr. Wilkie Collins the founder of the sensational school in novels, but he long ago placed himself at its head. He proved, indeed, at so early a period, his skill in the construction of a plot, that he has since been his own most formidable rival. His *Basil* displayed a more intense concentration than,

---

1   Poe (1809-49) and Ann Radcliffe (1764-1823) were both leading exponents of Gothic fiction. The reviewer believes Collins's sensationalism has its roots in their earlier works.

perhaps, any of his later tales of tragic interest, of however painful a kind, but about one or two characters only; in *The Woman in White* he evinced that he could preserve the unity and concentration of interest while multiplying his actors and circumstances; and in the present story he has shown himself a master in the art of amalgamating the most unmalleable and inconsistent of facts – fatalism and Hindoo mysticism and devotion, English squirearchy, detectives, and house-maids – and seems to have taken by choice difficulties for his resources.

[Here follows a lengthy summary of the novel's plot.]

Who took the Moonstone, where it has been, where it is, together with the virtues and failings of medical theories and opium, we have not the cruelty to explain further to our readers. Let them discover for themselves. A bubble is a very pretty thing, but a bubble which has burst is no good except to point a moral.

Mr. Wilkie Collins explains that the distinction between the present and former tales of his is that the attempt made in this is to "trace the influence of character on circumstances," and to show that the conduct of the several actors directs the course of those portions of the story in which they are concerned. We will sketch them, that the reader may exercise his ingenuity in guessing how, among persons of such characters, by what, or by whose, agency, the Moonstone could have been lost or stolen.

[Here follows a very lengthy series of descriptions of virtually every character in the novel: Lady Verinder, Rachel Verinder, Franklin Blake, Godfrey Ablewhite, Mr. Candy, Ezra Jennings, Rosanna Spearman, Septimus Luker, Mr. Bruff, Sergeant Cuff, Miss Clack, and Betteredge.]

Into and among these characters rolls and revolves the Moonstone, with its mythical burden of misfortune. All the ill attends it of which its legend told. The theft of it turns the robber into a pariah among Englishmen. The bequest of it kills his sister of a broken heart. It loses its legatee her lover and faith for a time in loyalty and honour; the mere shadow of it hurries another woman to her grave in the Shivering Sand. It brings a philanthropist to a scandalous conclusion. It rewards the devotedness of its ministers with the doom of a weary wandering to their lives' end. Yet itself is a harmless diamond enough. It works its mischief by purely natural means; every one is the voluntary agent in his or her own undoing; and, after all, the mystery is found to be due to the professional pique of one country doctor, and is solved by another. The character of each of the real actors in the story is the centre of attraction within the orbit of its own circumstances, the actions of each in conformity with such person's character becoming in their turn circumstances on which the characters of the others have to operate. The robbery of the sacred diamond is in conformity with Herncastle's sullen obstinacy and defiance of opinion, combined with his brooding imaginativeness. His sister's somewhat unbending haughtiness predisposed her to find the stigma affecting her daughter's name unbearable. Her daughter's morbid habit of reticence involved her in a maze of doubt and reproach, and postponed a general clearing up of the mystery, to the reader's signal profit, who has thereby gained Miss Clack, but to Rachel's misery, for a whole year. Rosanna's experiences as a thief render her ready to suspect that Franklin Blake is a thief too; her love makes her desire to find him one, that there may not stand between her and him "the dreadful reproach which honest people are in themselves to a woman like her;" and it makes her, in the resolution to save him from the discovery of his imagined crime, take a course which wonderfully complicates the difficulties of the plot. Finally, Franklin's own manysidedness of character, which leads him through various phases of controversy till he politely informs his antagonist, a surgeon, that medical men are all impostors, puts him up as a mark for a little medical experiment of very serious consequences to himself.

So much for Mr. Wilkie Collins's theory. His readers, probably far too soon for their retention of the scientific placidity necessary for the due weighing of the principles laid down in his preface, if they ever read it, will be caught in the vortex of his plot. The essence and secret of sensational novel-writing is to keep flashing a metaphorical bullseye up the particular dark archways where the thief is not lurking; to make the circumstances agree with one given explanation, which is not the true one; and to disguise as long as possible the fact that they agree also with a perfectly different conclusion. It is to present a real clue and a pseudo clue, and tempt the reader on to follow the pseudo clue till past the middle of the third volume. The whole school has this habit of laying eggs and hiding them. But Mr. Wilkie Collins has a complex variety of this propensity for secretiveness. He is not satisfied with one false clue, but is perpetually dropping clues, and, like a bird, by his demonstrative employment of various arts to lead his readers elsewhere, away from the spot where he originally induced them to fancy the nest was, only makes them more eagerly bent on keeping the old path. Every character in the book has his or her theory as to the mystery, and each of the theories is partly true. But then it is also partly, and that manifestly, false. So when, as often, a hint of the truth is let fall by one of them, the reader has by this time grown so suspicious that he refuses to accept it. "No one has stolen the Diamond," says Sergeant Cuff, and Sergeant Cuff is very king among detectives. But, as Sergeant Cuff says also, "Your young lady has got a travelling companion, Mr. Betteredge, and the name of it is the Moonstone," in which he is certainly wrong, the reader disbelieves the true part of his theory. The idea at the foundation of the story is the discovery by a young girl, given to act for herself and not fond of sympathy, that her lover is a thief and has robbed herself; – and the question is what her consequent conduct will be. The author's main object throughout seems to be to conceal this. For this purpose the second volume, direct and positive as are the merits of Miss Clack, is interpolated. Almost everything of materiality to the plot is given in the first and third. If all from Rosanna's suicide, and Rachel's departure from home, at the end of the first, to the discovery made by Franklin on the seashore at the end of the second, were omitted, the plot would remain whole and entire. The creation of a rival heroine to Rachel in the person of Rosanna Spearman has the same object. Rosanna and her whole story do not, in fact, advance the action of the novel one inch. It is not any reflection of her suspicion of Franklin's dishonesty, which lowers him in Rachel's eyes. It does not expose him to the suspicions of Cuff. An old intimacy which she is stated to have had with Luker leads to nothing. Her love does not make Rachel jealous. She might have gone on living without the course of this story being slackened or quickened. Franklin himself discovers what it was she had hidden; and the revelations in her posthumous letter are made to him. He uses them to force on an explanation from Rachel of her strange aversion from him. But that must have come on scarcely later of itself. She is made, perhaps, the most interesting personage in the book; and a larger space is devoted to her character and doings than to those of any one else; – and all solely for the sake of throwing the reader out, and seducing him from a too exclusive concentration of attention on the simple facts of Rachel's change of demeanor to her lover.

Mr. Wilkie Collins never once quits his hold of his reader's interest. When one part of the mystery is solved, the interest in what remains becomes still more eager. The true test of writings like this, and one which *The Moonstone* will stand, is whether at each stage and break of the story a negative answer must be returned to the question whether the final denouement be yet seen. When the Diamond is first found to be stolen the reader suspects the Indians. By the time that it is clear that it is not they, it becomes apparent that Rachel knows something, but is hiding it to shelter some one, not herself. It seems equally clear that there is knowledge, and probably, but not so certainly, not directly guilty knowledge, in Rosanna. The reader suspects, with the sergeant, that there is collusion between them though not, as the sergeant fancies, to shield Rachel. When the absence of this proved at Rosanna's death, there still lurks a doubt as in Rosanna's freedom from innocent connexion with the theft. A suspicion now also arises, and goes on gaining strength continually, that another person has, at all events, the benefit of the theft, and that either Rachel or Rosanna has known this. When Rachel's indignation at the rumour against that person exonerates her from such knowledge, there is still nothing to clear Rosanna of collusion. When the discovery on the sea shore and her letter show this is not so, but it becomes more and more certain who has the diamond, the double difficulty how it has been taken and how the possessor became such appears no nearer its solution. When the author shows his whole hand, and while he is revealing the procedure by which it was taken by the one, and, came into the hands of the other, the interest even yet does not flag, and the reader traces each step to the goal which he sees before him in eager suspense and uncertainty, up to the last page, whether the real catastrophe be not still behind. Mr. Wilkie Collins has built his plot like an iron ship with the several compartments combining perfectly, but isolated and all watertight. It is not until every one has been burst open that the plot sinks, and the reader's interest with it; – although it must be confessed, that when it does sink, it sinks, after the manner of sensational plots, utterly, and can never be weighed up again. Or, to explain our meaning by another comparison, the plot of The Moonstone has the quality which was fixed as a condition of the competition for the new law courts. One made free of the building will find all the rooms communicating with each other as soon as he gets inside; but the public, coming out of curiosity, can make their way from one court into another only by going outside and entering it by its own special door.

The book has its shortcomings. There are some petty ambiguities and flaws in the plot. It is obscure how the Indians, whose discoveries are not represented as supernatural, should have been aware of Colonel Herncastle's sealed instructions to have the Moonstone cut up if he were murdered. It is strange that it should never have occurred to Lady Verinder, who had disowned her brother for stealing the diamond, that a scrupulous conscience might even now make restitution to the State. The detective's omissions to examine the linen because Rachel excepted hers from the search, of the servants' clothes and boxes, although one of them was known by him to have been a professional thief, and the jewel to have been left at night to her knowledge in an unoccupied room, in an open drawer, and his "speechless amusement" at Lady Verinder for preferring to examine her daughter as to her acquaintance with the circumstances of the theft of which she was suspected by him, instead of intrusting the inquisition to himself, are rather curious. It seems hardly plausible that Miss Clack calling on her aunt should be left waiting in the hall; and "Good-bye, Clack!" is a curt form of address from a well brought-up young lady to her mother's guest. The general dislike, too, to Ezra Jennings, a miracle of benevolence and professional skill, on the apparent ground simply of his piebald hair, is strange. There is, again, a certain pervading high-pressure tone about the characters which is exhausting. The medical men are so very medical; the lawyers are so very legal, and peruse abstracts of title with "breathless excitement;" the politicians are so very political, and are seen "amusing" themselves "at home with the Parliamentary plaything which they call a Private Bill." "Eminent" professional personages outside the action of the book are so extremely pompous and silly, and philanthropists such hypocrites and cheats at bottom. Those who are retained for the narrative are so extremely sagacious, and, if by their special profession trained to be bitter, display for that reason natural tempers so much the more benevolent and kindly. Every character is sure to have his pet theory as to life, and to be exceedingly epigrammatic. There is a superabundance of law; and lastly, and above all, every narrator makes too much a point of giving to his simplest statements the air of depositions taken before a police magistrate.

But some of these faults are very closely allied to the merits of the book. We could not spare one item of Miss Clack's "patience" and "abstinence from judging" others, though all pious ladies are not malignant; Betteredge's frequent stumblings into epigram are none too many; and the legal tediousness and preciseness of the ordinary course of the narrative arises from the same intellectual quality whence come the minute touches (each doing its own work without projecting the smallest shadow in front), which work up the reader's interest at any important crisis to boiling point. To object again, as some ungrateful readers probably may, that there is no desire to turn back to the first volume when the last is read and con over each separate detail fondly, is to complain that the tale belongs to a class in which in proportion to the intensity of interest in the catastrophe is the suddenness of the descent into acquiescence when that is reached; it is to murmur at Mr. Wilkie Collins because his primary aims are not those of Miss Austen or even Mr. Anthony Trollope.[1] There is one positive and intrinsic defect in Mr. Wilkie Collins as a novelist. It is a want of what Mr. Matthew Arnold has called "sweetness" and "charm."[2] But those who admire the spectacle of ingenuity in the construction of a plot, and of the power of bringing home to the imagination the dreariness and terror of dreary and terrible scenes, should seek, and will find, it in *The Moonstone*.

---

1 Walter Scott's pronouncement that the novels of Jane Austen (1775-1817) showed an "exquisite touch which renders ordinary commonplace things and characters interesting" holds true for the stories of Anthony Trollope (1815-82) as well. *The Times* reviewer warns readers sympathetic with the ordinariness of Austen and Trollope not to hold Collins's novel to the same critical light.

2 Matthew Arnold (1822-88), English poet and literary critic, published six essays in *The Cornhill* between the summer of 1867 and the fall of 1868, the first under the title "Culture and Its Enemies," the last five as "Anarchy and Authority." The first of these essays ultimately became the opening section of Arnold's *Culture and Anarchy* (1869), a chapter titled "Sweetness and Light."

5. Unsigned review, *Harper's New Monthly Magazine*, October 1868, xxxvii: 712-13.

If there were such a word as "story-wright," corresponding to the term "playwright," Wilkie Collins would be styled the one great "story-wright." He indeed writes always good sound English, such as De Foe or Swift[1] might have written; but he has none of the delicacies or mannerisms of style which characterize the works of Dickens and Thackeray.[2] It would be hard to find in all his characteristic works a page which from mere form of expression any one could declare to be his rather than that of any other person who understands grammar and has at command a good store of good words. But Mr. Collins has the faculty of constructing a story in such a way that while no one when it is in progress shall even guess at its winding-up, yet when all is done the reader will wonder why he had not anticipated the end of the plot. Mr. Dickens somewhere complains that unscrupulous playwrights, taking one of his novels when half completed, "adapted it to the stage," anticipating the event which was to have formed the climax. Thackeray seems never to have had a plot in his mind. In the preface to *Pendennis* he tells humorously how, until the last chapter was to be written, he did not know how the work was to end. No one who reads Dickens's *Our Mutual Friend* will doubt that the final explanation of Mr. Boffin's strange conduct never entered into the mind of the author until long after the story was begun. More odd still is the fate of Paul Emanuel in Charlotte Brontë's *Villette*.[3] Of ten critical readers of the story, five will be sure that he was drowned, and the other five will be just as sure that he came home, married Lucy Snowe, and "lived happily ever after." No such difficulties will confront the readers of any novel by Wilkie Collins. They may not be able

---

1 Daniel Defoe (1660-1731) and Jonathan Swift (1667-1745) were, of course, giants of England's early eighteenth-century literary landscape. Defoe's *Robinson Crusoe* plays no minor role in *The Moonstone*.

2 Charles Dickens (1812-70) and William M. Thackeray (1811-63) were considered by most critics and readers of the day to be a literary tier or two above Collins.

3 *Pendennis* (1848-50) is Thackeray's rather scattered *Bildungsroman*, *Our Mutual Friend* (1864-65) is Dickens's last complete novel, and *Villette* (1853) is Brontë's (1816-55) remembrance of her life in Brussels in the early 1840s. The novel's ending is ambiguous, for Lucy Snowe refuses to tell her reader whether Emanuel has drowned on his return to Europe from the West Indies.

to even guess, while the story is in progress, how it is to turn out. If they did guess, most likely their guesses would turn out wrong. Mr. Collins possesses the faculty, almost amounting to genius, of writing a novel. In *The Moonstone* he has come nearer to success than in any of his former stories. If he has fallen short of producing a great novel, he has succeeded in making a most readable story.

6. Unsigned review, *Lippincott's Magazine*, December 1868, ii: 679–80.

"I'm sick to death of novels with an earnest purpose. I'm sick to death of outbursts of eloquence, and large-minded philanthropy, and graphic descriptions and unsparing anatomy of the human heart, and all that sort of thing. Good gracious me! Isn't it the original intention or purpose, or whatever you call it, of a work of fiction, to set out distinctly by telling a story? And how many of these books, I should like to know, do that? Why, so far as telling a story is concerned, the greater part of them might as well be sermons as novels. Oh, dear me! what I want is something that seizes hold of my interest, and makes me forget when it is time to dress for dinner – something that keeps me reading, reading, reading, in a breathless state, to find out the end."

Wilkie Collins' confession of faith as a novelist is comprised in the above speech of his sprightly heroine, Miss Jessie Yelverton, in *The Queen of Hearts*. He is emphatically a story-writer. He is unrivalled in the construction of an elaborate and intricate plot, and he certainly succeeds in making his readers "go on reading, reading, reading, in a breathless state, to find out the end."

Wilkie Collins' career has been a progressive one. There are some ardent novel-readers who will doubtless remember the publication, years ago, of *Antonina*, and a few years later of *Basil* – two books of singular power, but which, we believe, were failures; and no wonder. *Antonina*, a tale of the days of ancient Rome, was filled with ghastly pictures of famine, murder and other "onpleasantnesses," while *Basil* was a veritable literary nightmare. The very force and vigor of the author only served to add to the discomfort of the reader by making its painful pictures strangely vivid and impressive. The scarred face of the fiend, Mannion, and the fever-deathbed of Margaret Sherwin, have haunted many an imagination in persistent and uncomfortable fashion. Soon after Mr. Dickens commenced the publication of *Household Words*, there appeared in that periodical a number of short stories which were remarkable for the perfection of their style, the elaboration and originality of their plots and their general artistic finish.[1]

Wilkie Collins is, however, no mere weaver of intricate plots – no teller of elaborately constructed stories only. Few characters in modern fiction are as well drawn and sustained as that of Count Fosco, the cool, sensible, intellectual villain in *The Woman in White*, or the swindling but soft-hearted Captain Wragge in *No Name*. Collins also possesses, in common with Anthony Trollope, the power of delineating a heroine who shall be neither a dressed-up doll nor an impossible angel. Rosamond in *The Dead Secret*, Magdalen Vanstone in *No Name*, Marion Halcombe in *The Woman in White*, and Rachel Verinder in the book before us, bear witness to the truth of this assertion. Nor does his powerful mind and pencil fail when called upon to depict scenes of purer and gentler emotion. Rosamond, revealing the "dead secret" to her blind husband, and the vigil of Rachel Verinder beside her sleeping lover, are pictures drawn with a touch truthful, delicate and tender as that of a woman.

The novel that now lies before us is the best that Mr. Collins has of late years given to the world, and we are inclined to consider it, with the one exception of *The Woman in White*, the best he has ever written. The story is singularly original; and when we remember the force and extent of Hindoo superstition, we can scarcely venture to pronounce it improbable. And how admirably is the story told! Clear, lucid and forcible in style, never straying into the alluring but pernicious paths of description or dissertation, the narrative moves onward

---

1   The half-dozen or so titles just ticked off by the reviewer represent much of Collins's early work as a writer of fiction. "A Terribly Strange Bed," "Sister Rose," and "The Yellow Mask" are all short stories originally published in Dickens's *Household Words* between 1852 and 1855. Collins re-issued them as part of the collection *After Dark* in 1856. *The Queen of Hearts* (1859) is also a collection of shorter material published in the mid-1850s. *The Dead Secret* (1857), serialized in Dickens's *Household Words*, is Collins's fourth novel. *The Woman in White* (1859-60), Collins's fifth novel, ran as the second novel serialized in Dickens's *All the Year Round* (behind *A Tale of Two Cities*). *No Name* (1862-63), Collins's sixth novel, was also serialized in Dickens's *All the Year Round*, and *Armadale* (1864-66), Collins's seventh novel, was serialized in *The Cornhill*.

in its unbroken and entrancing course. Let the impatient reader, hurrying to reach the denouement, skip half a dozen pages. Instantly the thread of the story is broken, the tale becomes incomprehensible, the incidents lose their coherence. *The Moonstone* is a perfect work of art, and to remove any portion of the cunningly constructed fabric destroys the completeness and beauty of the whole. We will not attempt to give any sketch of the plot or resume of the incidents. Suffice it to say that the story turns on the fortunes of an Indian diamond (which gives its name to the book), stolen from the shrine of a Hindoo idol, and bequeathed, with sinister purpose, by a vindictive uncle to his unloved niece.

It would be well if some of the New England writers, who look upon a novel as a mere vehicle for the introduction of morbid and unwholesome metaphysical and psychological studies, or long dissertations on Art – well enough in their way perhaps, but strangely out of place in a story – would study the elements of their art from Wilkie Collins. Then would the words "American novel" cease to by synonymous with the weariness of the reader; and arguments for amalgamation would be placed before the public in their naked deformity, instead of under the thin disguise of novels possessing little plot and less probability.

Appendix B: Excerpts from Newspaper Accounts of the Constance Kent/Road-house Murder Case of 1860

[The following excerpts from newspaper coverage of the crime, the investigation, the confession, the trial, and the trial's aftermath provide some interesting background on the case which so fascinated Collins that he wove much of it into the fabric of his novel.]

1. From *The Times*, July 3, 1860: 12.

The following article marked the first announcement of the murder of young Francis Saville Kent.

Barbarous Murder

A shocking murder was perpetrated at Road, a village about four miles from Frome,[1] on Saturday morning last. Mr. S.S. Kent, a gentleman holding a lucrative situation as inspector of factories for the district, lives in a house standing in its own grounds at Road. On Saturday morning, about 7 o'clock, it was found that one of his sons, a fine lad just four years of age, was missing from his cot in the nurse's room, in which he usually slept, and after an hour's search his body was found stuffed down the seat of a privy on the premises, the throat being cut so as almost to sever the head from the body, and a large stab being apparent near the heart, evidently inflicted after death, as no blood had flowed from it. The body was wrapped in a blanket belonging to its bed, and he appears to have been killed while still asleep. The perpetrator is as yet undiscovered, but, of course, the most diligent inquiries are being made. It is evident that the guilty person must have been in the house over night, for all the fastenings were exactly as they had been left the previous night, when Mr. Kent himself saw they were secure, except the drawing-room window which

---

1 Frome is a small town in Somerset, a county in southwestern England. Along with Trowbridge and Devizes, also mentioned in many of these accounts, it lies just a few miles southeast of Bath.

opens on to the lawn; this was a little way open and the shutters unfastened, but no violence had been used either there or at the drawing-room door. The wounds were apparently inflicted with a large table knife, but no such weapon nor any clothes stained with blood have as yet been found on the premises. The knife it is supposed was wiped on a piece of paper, which has been found. The family consisted of Mr. and Mrs. Kent and seven children, three girls and one boy being children by the first wife, and two little girls and the deceased by the present Mrs. Kent. It is a singular fact that nearly three years ago the two younger children of Mr. Kent's first wife – Constance and William – considering themselves to be ill-treated, started off, both dressed in male attire, and were not found for two days. They have now recently returned from school. It seems almost beyond belief that the child could have been abducted from the nurse's room without her knowledge; nevertheless no suspicion attaches to her.

2. From *The Times*, July 4, 1860: 9.

The following report describes a baffled investigative committee.

The Frome Murder

The inquest on the body of Francis Saville Kent, aged four years, the victim of the atrocious outrage which has so astounded the locality, was held on Monday at the Temperance-hall Road, before Mr. Sylvester, the coroner for Wilts. The large room was crowded to excess. Mr. Rodway, solicitor, of Trowbridge, attended to watch the case on behalf of the family. The nursemaid, out of whose room the child was taken; the housemaid, who examined the fastenings of the drawing-room the night before and found them undone in the morning; and the persons who discovered the dead body in the water-closet, were examined, but no fresh facts were elicited, and the barbarous affair still is involved in the same inexplicable obscurity. Constance and William Kent, half brother and sister of deceased, were also examined, but no new information was gained. The superintendents of police from Frome, Trowbridge, and Devizes, and the chief constable of the Wilts constabulary were in attendance. The jury returned a verdict of "Wilful murder against some person or persons unknown."

3. From *The Times*, July 11, 1860: 5.

The following article shows a reporter for *The Times* both making the remarkably bold claim that the murderer *had* to be a family member and calling for professional investigators to take over for the outwitted local constabulary.[1]

The Recent Murder at Road

A crime has just been committed which for mystery, complication of probabilities, and hideous wickedness is without parallel in our criminal records. A family retires to bed at night with the usual sense of peace and security, yet before the time for rising next morning one of the children has been seized and murdered, and not a soul in the place can give the slightest evidence on the subject. The house, it is said, was locked and secured as usual by the housemaid, but it was found in the morning opened; and a way had evidently been taken through the drawing-room. The murderer or murderers had certainly stolen into the nurse's bedroom, where the child slept in a little cot, and had taken off the coverlet and folded it tidily down, had then taken the bright little creature, scarcely four years old, wrapped him in the under blanket, carried him downstairs through the drawing-room on to the lawn, through the back premises, where a watch-dog was running loose, to the water-closet, there cut his throat to the very vertebrae, and then thrust him down head first. The act is so dreadful that we would spare our readers the recital of it if we could, but it is not for the press to pass over these atrocities in silence. We must speak, and do our part in inquiring who is guilty of this foul deed. Every effort, say the local papers, has been made to detect the murderer, but hitherto without effect. Perhaps so, but we are of opinion that many efforts yet untried may be made, and that in due time the murderer

---

1   The press of the day enjoyed, as Richard Altick states, an "uninhibited freedom to comment on criminal cases both before and after they became formal legal actions. . . . Trial by newspaper was a fact of Victorian life" (*Deadly Encounters*, Philadelphia, U of Pennsylvania Press, 1986, 28).

will be brought to justice. Without intending any disrespect to the coroner or his jury, we take the liberty of saying that the circumstances demand a much more searching investigation than they have received at the hands of these functionaries. The Secretary of State must take it up, and the case must be sifted by a commission under his authority. As far as we can understand the story, it seems that the house was thoroughly closed up on the night preceding the murder. In the morning the house was partly open; but it does not appear to have been opened by violence from without. Therefore the inference is plain that the secret lies with some one who was within. This seems so plain that we do not hesitate for an instant to say that, however painful such a proceeding may be, and however for a while the innocent may seem to suffer with the guilty, yet it must be held that the persons who composed the household must collectively be responsible for this mysterious and dreadful event. Not one of them ought to be at large till the whole mystery is cleared up. Let a *cordon judiciare* be drawn round the house, and let parents and nurse, master and servants, be confined within it until the truth is found. We cannot divest ourselves of the belief that the child suffered death at the hands of some one belonging to the house....

The extraordinary circumstances of the case require the employment by authority of the acutest discerners of probabilities and the most experienced of detectives....

It is clear to us that the solution of the question turns upon very delicate points, which, in their nicety, lie far beyond the powers and skill of a country coroner's jury. The case must be put into higher hands, and, we repeat, the investigation must proceed upon the presumption that one (or more) of the parties in the family is guilty....

4. From *The Times*, July 14, 1860: 5.

The mystery deepened when the Kent's nursemaid, Elizabeth Gough, was briefly held under suspicion of murder.

The Late Mysterious Child Murder at Road

As stated in *The Times* of Thursday, Elizabeth Gough, the nursemaid in the service of Mr. Kent, the father of the murdered child, was taken into custody on Tuesday, on suspicion of being implicated in this foul outrage, and was remanded till yesterday. Our Bristol correspondent proceeded to Road on that day, but was informed by the magistrates engaged in the investigation of the case that for the present they were of opinion that the ends of justice would be frustrated by the publication of evidence....

Up to the present time the magistrates have taken the statements of every inmate of Mr. Kent's house, with the exception of Mrs. Kent and one of the daughters of Mr. Kent by his former wife. The reason for these exceptions is stated to be that in the opinion of the medical attendant of the family an examination of Mrs. Kent, who is at present near her confinement, might endanger her life and that of her offspring, and in the case of Miss Kent she is said to be of so exceedingly nervous a temperament as to be unable to undergo the ordeal of a judicial examination on this distressingly painful subject.

5. From *The Times*, July 17, 1860: 12.

Gough was cleared almost as soon as Inspector Jonathan Whicher reached Trowbridge after having been assigned to the case. Suspicion began to shift to Constance Kent.

The Child Murder at Road

Sir G.C. Lewis, Home Secretary,[1] has despatched Inspector Whicher, of the metropolitan detective police, to Road, for the purpose of endeavouring to dissipate the mystery which still hangs over the murder of the child of Mr. Kent. The inspector reached Trowbridge from London on Sunday evening, and proceeded yesterday morning to Road, where he had an interview with the magistrates by whom the inquiry has been conducted. In the course of the conference Elizabeth Gough, the nursemaid, was brought before the Bench and liberated....

---

1   The home secretary was a secretary of state for home affairs. He was in charge of law and order, running the prisons and Scotland Yard. George Cornewall Lewis (1806-63) was the Home Secretary for Lord Palmerston's second administration between 1859 and 1863.

6. From *The Times*, July 21, 1860: 5.

A few days after his arrival, Inspector Whicher swore out a warrant for Constance Kent's arrest and informed the magistrates of his opinions concerning her role in the crime. The following passage from *The Times* article offers the first indication that Whicher believed a missing nightdress might be the key to the crime's solution.

Apprehension of Miss Constance Kent, Road, Friday Evening

Inspector Whicher sworn. – From many inquiries that I have made, and from information received, I sent for Constance Kent on Monday last to her bed room, having previously examined her drawers and found a list of her linen which I now produce, in which were enumerated, among other things, three night dresses as belonging to her. I said to her, "Is this a list of your linen?" She replied, "Yes." I said, "In whose writing is it?" She said, "It is my own writing." I said, "Here are three night dresses; where are they?" She said, "I have two; the other was lost at the wash the week after the murder." She then brought me the two which I now produce. I also saw a night dress and cap on her bed, and asked whose they were. She said, "They are my sister's. The two she brought me had been worn. This afternoon I again proceeded to the house and sent for the prisoner into the dining-room. I said, "I am a police officer, and I hold a warrant for your apprehension, charging you with the murder of your brother Francis Saville Kent, which I will read to you." I then read the warrant to her, and she commenced crying, and said, "I am innocent!" which she repeated several times. I then accompanied her to her bedroom, where she put on her bonnet and mantle, and brought her to this place. She made no further remark to me. I now ask for a remand for a few days, and on the next occasion I believe I shall be able to show the animus which existed between the prisoner and the deceased and to search for the missing nightgown, which, if in existence, may possibly be found. To Wednesday or Thursday next I think will be ample time.

After some further consultation the prisoner was remanded till Friday next, and was removed to Devizes Gaol in custody of Inspector Whicher and Superintendent Woolf.

7. From the *Somerset and Wilts Journal*, July 21, 1860 (quoted in John Rhode, *The Case of Constance Kent*. New York: Scribner's, 1928: 73).

The "extraordinary occurrence" described below suggests a degree of ineptitude on the part of local police officials that is difficult to imagine. It also imbues the tale with a certain macabre comicality.

An extraordinary occurrence seems to have taken place on the night after the murder. Two policemen were put on duty inside the house and proposed to remain in the lobby at the foot of the stairs all night. By some means, however, they found their way into the kitchen, and while there they were locked in by someone, where they remained about an hour, when, awaking to a sense of their position, they began hammering on the door, which after twenty minutes was opened by Mr. Kent! Surely this implies negligence in someone.

8. From *The Times*, July 23, 1860: 12.

The following excerpt shows the initial respect held for Whicher, a respect that dwindled when he was unable to produce the nightdress on which his case hinged.

The Road Child Murder

Mr. Inspector Whicher is pursuing the inquiry with his wonted sagacity, and at the adjourned investigation evidence will be produced showing the animus that existed in the prisoner's mind towards the deceased child, and it is hoped that, if still in existence, the missing bedgown of Miss Constance Kent will be discovered, together with other facts tending to throw light on this mysterious affair.

9. From *The Times*, July 26, 1860: 9.

Nearly a month after the murder, the police called for assistance from the general public, as the following article reports.

Sergeant Williamson, of the metropolitan detective force, has arrived at Road, and is actively engaged with Mr. Inspector Whicher, Captain Meredith, chief constable, and other officers of the county police in investigating this tragic affair....

Every possible exertion is being made by the police to collect further evidence, and to find, if possible, the missing nightdress belonging to Miss Constance Kent. It is believed that, if not burnt, it is secreted somewhere in the vicinity of the house, and, with the view of inducing the inhabitants of the village to assist in the search, a placard has been issued, offering a reward of £5 to any person finding the nightdress and delivering it to the police....

10. From *The Times*, July 28 1860: 12.

Near the end of a long, four-column article devoted to the public inquiry of the case, the reporter for *The Times* recorded the following remarkable scene in which Constance Kent's solicitor, at the expense of Inspector Whicher's professionalism, urged that charges be dropped. By managing to recruit the public's sympathy for their client, Kent's solicitors played a large role in turning the public against Whicher. By the end of 1860 even the press taunted him for having bullied Miss Kent.[1] Whicher retired in 1863.

The Late Mysterious Child Murder at Road

Mr. Edlin then asked the Bench instantly to liberate the accused, and restore her to her friends. There was not a tittle of evidence against her, not one word on which the finger of infamy could be pointed against her. Although a most atrocious murder had been committed, it had been followed by a judicial murder no less atrocious. If the mur-

---

1 The *Annual Register* for 1860 castigates as follows: "The grounds on which [Whicher's] accusation was made were so frivolous, and the evidence by which it was attempted to be supported so childish, that the proceeding can only be described as absurd and cruel" (101). The report goes on to suggest that the police detective's "repeated failures [to solve the case] ... cast an imputation upon the capacity of the magistrates and the acuteness of the police" (102).

derer were never discovered, it would never be forgotten that this young lady had been dragged like a common felon to Devizes gaol. The fact alone was quite sufficient to insure the sympathy of every man in the country and the kingdom. The steps which had been taken must blast her hopes and prospects for life, and those steps had been taken solely on the suspicion of an inspector of police, acting under the influence of the reward which had been offered. The fact respecting the missing bedgown had been cleared up to the satisfaction of every one who had heard the evidence that day, and no doubt could remain that this little peg, upon which this fearful charge had been grounded, had fallen to the ground. He asked the magistrates, therefore, to pause and say whether for one moment longer this young lady should be kept in custody. Without reproaching Inspector Which for what he had done, he must say that the hunting up the schoolfellows of Miss Constance Kent reflected ineffable disgrace upon those who had been the means of bringing them there. Nothing that had been elicited from those young ladies showed anything like animus on the part of the prisoner towards the deceased child, nor had any motive been established which would induce the prisoner to imbrue her hands in the blood of the poor little child. He appealed to the Bench, therefore, the case for the prosecution being exhausted – and a weaker one he had never heard – to perform their duty to the country and to the prisoner by at once saying that the evidence adduced satisfied them that the charge was groundless, and that Miss Constance Kent should be at once discharged. A fearful responsibility would rest upon the magistrates if they should again remand the prisoner. No evidence to warrant a remand had been adduced upon the first occasion: but if, now the young lady should be again sent back to gaol, he hesitated not to say that great injustice would be failing in the discharge of the duties they were sworn to perform. He besought the magistrates, therefore, immediately to liberate the young lady, and to restore her to her friends and her home.

Some applause followed the address of the learned counsel, which was instantly suppressed.

The Magistrates, after a brief consultation, announced that they had decided on discharging the prisoner, on her father entering into recognizances of £200, for her appearance if called upon.

The prisoner was discharged.

11. From *The Times*, November 10, 1860: 12.

In early November 1860, T.B. Saunders, a Wiltshire magistrate, took it upon himself to open his own public re-investigation of the case. Though not officially sanctioned, the proceedings lasted about a week and brought to light some interesting new information. In particular, as reported below, Londoners learned for the first time that Superintendent Foley and the local authorities had found a bloody nightdress, or shift, hidden in a boiler-flue at the Kent house on the morning after the murder but had, incredibly, dismissed the finding as unimportant. The testimony of Sergeant James Watts, followed by comments from a befuddled Mr. Foley, suggests a conspiracy of dunces unwilling to or incapable of making appropriate decisions concerning potentially important evidence. Inspector Whicher refers to this episode in his letter to Mr. Hancock, reprinted in *The Times*, July 24, 1865. (See below, no. 14, for the text of Whicher's letter.)

The Road Child Murder. Road, Friday

Mr. Saunders reopened his inquiry at Road this afternoon, in the presence of the smallest audience which has yet assembled....

Sergeant James Watts, of the Frome division of the Somersetshire constabulary. – I went to Road-hill house on the morning of the 30th of June. I found men engaged in emptying the cesspool of the place where the body of the child was found; this was about 2 o'clock p.m. I went into the kitchen and scullery, and on searching about in the scullery and opening the door of the boiler-furnace, I saw something wrapped up there. I pulled it out, and found what appeared to me to be a shift wrapped up in a piece of brown paper, I believe. I took it out into the stable to examine it, and called the attention of police-constable Dallimore to it. I think Urch was also present. On opening the bundle in the stable I found it to contain a shift in a very dirty state; it was very bloody. It was dry then, but I should not think the stains had been on it a long time. It did not appear to have been partially washed. Some of the blood was on the front and some on the back. I wrapped up the shift again, and as I was coming out I saw Mr. Kent just outside the stable door in the yard. He asked me what I had found, and said he must have it seen, and that Dr. Parsons must see it.

I did not let Mr. Kent see it, but handed it over to Mr. Foley. I believe Foley was in the front part of the house when I found the shift, and he was at the back when I handed it over to him. Dallimore was present at the time. Mr. Foley took possession of the bundle containing the shift, and I have not seen anything more of it from that day to this....

Mr. Superintendent Foley declined to ask Sergeant Watts any questions, or to add any statement of his own in reference to what had transpired this morning. In reply to Mr. Saunders, Mr. Foley stated that when the shift was handed to him he shuddered to think the man that found it was so foolish as to expose it. By his (Foley's) directions it was afterwards shown to Mr. Stapleton, surgeon, of Trowbridge; before doing so he was perfectly satisfied that the shift had nothing to do with the murder.

12. From *The Times*, April 26, 1865: 9.

Over four years after the crime, Constance Kent returned from France, where she had spent time in a convent, to confess to the murder. The following account reports the news to a shocked London.

The Road-Hill Murder.
Voluntary Confession and Surrender of Constance Kent

Yesterday afternoon Sir Thomas Henry, the chief magistrate of Bow-street, received information that Miss Constance Kent, formerly of Road-hill-house, near Frome, had arrived in London from Brighton for the purpose of surrendering herself to officers of justice as the perpetrator of the above memorable crime.

The charge having been taken in the usual form, Sir Thomas Henry, addressing the prisoner, said, – Am I to understand, Miss Kent, that you have given yourself up of your own free act and will on this charge?

Miss Kent. – Yes, Sir.

Sir Thomas Henry. – Anything you may say here will be written down, and may be used against you. Do you quite understand that?

Miss Kent. – Yes, Sir.

Sir Thomas Henry. – Is this paper, now produced before me, in your own handwriting, and written of your own free will?

Miss Kent. – It is, Sir.

Sir Thomas Henry. – Then, let the charge be entered in her own words.

The charge was then entered as follows: – "Miss Constance Emilie Kent, of 2, Queen-square, Brighton, is charged upon her own confession with having, alone and unaided, on the night of the 29th of June, 1860, murdered at Road-hill-house, Wiltshire, one Francis Saville Kent...."

The confession was then read by Mr. Burnaby, the chief clerk. It was as follows: –

"I, Constance Emilie Kent, alone and unaided, on the night of the 29th of June, 1860, murdered at Road-hill-house, Wiltshire, one Francis Saville Kent. Before the deed was done no one knew of my intention, nor afterwards of my guilt. No one assisted me in the crime, nor in the evasion of discovery."

13. From *The Times*, July 22, 1865: 10.

Nearly three months after her startling confession, Constance Kent went to trial for the murder of her brother. The report below is remarkable for the description of the emotional courtroom scene during sentencing.

The Trial of Constance Kent. (From Our Own Reporter). Western Circuit. Crown Side (Before Mr. Justice Willes).[1] Salisbury, July 21

Constance Emilie Kent was indicted for the wilful murder of Francis Saville Kent, at Road-hill-house, on the 29th of June, 1860....

Mr. Justice Willes having taken his seat, the governor of the gaol was desired to put up Constance Emilie Kent. In a few minutes the prisoner came upstairs into the dock, dressed in deep mourning, and

---

1 Willes was Sir James Shaw Willes (1814–72). His emotional pronouncement of sentence upon Constance Kent, recounted here by *The Times*'s court reporter, strengthens the *Dictionary of National Biography* claim that "His duties as a criminal judge added to the strain upon a mind naturally emotional and equally anxious to do justice and show mercy." He committed suicide seven years after the trial.

having on a thick veil. She first went to the back of the dock and had some conversation with her solicitor, Mr. Rodway. She then put up her veil and came to the front of the dock.

The Clerk of Assize[1] then stated the nature of the indictment, and asked the prisoner, – How say you, Constance Emilie Kent, are you guilty or not guilty?

The prisoner, in a mild voice, said, "Guilty."

Mr. Justice Willes. – Are you aware that you are charged with having wilfully, intentionally murdered your brother? Do you plead guilty to that?

The prisoner uttered something which could not be understood.

The Judge. – What is your answer? I will repeat it. You are charged with having intentionally and with malice killed and murdered your brother. Are you guilty, or not guilty?

Prisoner. – Guilty.

The Judge. – Let the plea be recorded.

Mr. Coleridge then rose and addressed the Court in the following terms: – As counsel for the prisoner, and noting on her behalf and by her direct instructions, I desire to say two things before the sentence of the Court is passed. In the first place the prisoner solemnly, in the presence of Almighty God, and as a person who values her own soul, desires me to say that the guilt is hers alone, and that her father and others, who have so long suffered most unjust and cruel suspicions, are wholly and absolutely innocent. Next, she desires me to say that she was not driven to this act, as has been asserted, by any unkind treatment in her home. She met nothing there but tender and for-bearing love, and I hope I may add not improperly that it gives me a melancholy pleasure to be made the organ of these statements, because on my honour I believe them to be true.

The Clerk of Assize then addressed the prisoner. – Constance Emilie Kent, you have confessed yourself guilty of the wilful murder of Francis Saville Kent. What have you to say why sentence of death should not be passed upon you according to law?

Mr. Justice Willes, having put on the black cap, then said, with manifest emotion, – Constance Emilie Kent, you have pleaded

---

1 An assize was a periodic court session held in each of the counties of England for the trial of civil or criminal court cases.

'Guilty' to the indictment charging you with the wilful murder of your brother, Francis Saville Kent, on the 29th of June, 1860. It is my duty to receive that plea, which you have deliberately put forward, and it is a satisfaction to know that it was not pleaded until after having had the advice of counsel who would have freed you from this dreadful charge if you could have been freed from it. I can entertain no doubt, after having read the evidence, and considering it in connexion with your three confessions of the crime, that your plea is the plea of a guilty person. The murder was one committed under circumstances of great deliberation and cruelty. You appear to have allowed feelings of jealousy and anger to have worked in your breast, until at last they assumed over you the influence and power of the evil one. [Here the learned judge was deeply affected, and spoke in accents broken by emotion. The prisoner was likewise completely overcome by her feelings, and almost turning round in the dock sobbed audibly.] The learned Judge proceeded, – Whether Her Majesty, with whom the prerogative of mercy rests, may be advised to exercise that prerogative in your case on account of the fact of your youth at the time when the murder was committed, the fact that you are convicted on your own confession, and the fact that the confession removes suspicion from others, is a question which it would be presumptuous in me to answer. It now well behoves you to live what is left to you of life as one about to die, and to seek a more enduring mercy by sincere and deep contrition, and by a reliance on the holy redemption, propitiation, and satisfaction for all sins. It remains for me to discharge the duty which the law imposes on the Court without alternative, and that is to pass on you the sentence which the law adjudges to all murderers. The learned Judge then, in the usual terms, passed the awful sentence of the law upon the prisoner, who, after standing for a short time in the dock, covered her face with her veil, and was conducted out of the court.

14. From *The Times*, July 24, 1865: 9.

The following article not only vindicates the beleaguered Inspector Whicher but documents the bungling and seemingly criminal negligence committed by local constabularies, Mr. Foley chief among them, before Whicher took over the Kent case. Collins clearly modeled his inept Superintendent Seegrave after Foley.

The Road Murder

The following letter was addressed by Mr. Inspector Whicher, the detective engaged in the above case, to Mr. Handcock, chief superintendent of the Bristol police, and formerly an officer of the A division of the Metropolitan force. It is dated November 23, 1860, and, read by the light of subsequent events, strongly corroborates the theory which was at first formed by the inspector regarding this mysterious case: –

"I have been on several occasions about addressing a few lines to you relative to the above case, as I have not had the pleasure of seeing you since the discharge of Miss Constance, for whose arrest I had such severe castigation from all quarters. Although I admit that there was not sufficient [evidence] for her further detention, still I believe that had there been counsel for the prosecution to have opened the case and examined the witnesses properly, it would have assumed a somewhat different shape in public opinion....

"Again, whoever did this deed no doubt did it in their night clothes. When Constance Kent went to bed that night she had three night dresses belonging to her in the house. After the murder she had but two. What, then, became of the third? It was not lost at the wash, as it was so craftily endeavoured to make it appear, but was got rid of in some other way. Where is it, then, and what became of it...?

"I want to draw your particular attention to a most important fact which oozed out the other day at Mr. Saunders's inquiry, which was stifled in its birth by the police concerned, or at least they attempted to do so by pooh-poohing it. It now appears that on the day of the murder, on searching the house, the police found a blood-stained night-shift secreted in the boiler-hole in the back kitchen. Now, up to the time of Mr. Saunders's inquiry this all-important fact had been kept a perfect secret, and it would not have come out then had it not been for a Sergeant Watts, of the Somerset constabulary, letting it out in some way, and he does not appear to have been compromised in the losing of it. I see that the matter was passed over very lightly by Foley and Dallimore (of the Wilts police) telling Mr. Saunders that they did not take the trouble to find out who it belonged to, as they showed it to the surgeon, Mr. Stapleton, who said the stains arose from natural causes, and that they put it back in the boiler-hole again, or down by the side of it, and that was all they knew about it. As regards their having shown the dress to Mr. Stapleton, it turns out to be an untruth, as the one they showed him was one belonging to the elder Miss Kent, which was found in her bedroom. Mr. Stapleton says they never showed him the one found in the boiler-hole, nor did they ever name the circumstance to me or to any of the magistrates. The real truth of the matter is, I have no doubt, that by some careless-ness they lost possession of it either by putting it out of their hands and Constance got possession of it again, or they put it back in the boiler-hole to try to catch the owner coming to take it away, and it having been got away without their knowledge a compact of secrecy was entered into in reference to it which was well kept, for, as said before, not one word was said to me or the magistrates, or in fact to any one, about the finding of this dress or shift, and it would not have come out now if it had not been for Watts who found it, but who was not compromised in the losing of it. Where it was must now, through this bungling, like the other part of the case, remain a mystery. The magistrates (one of whom has been up to see me about it) are making an investigation into the matter; and I am told that on finding the statement that the dress or shift was shown to Mr. Stapleton was denied by him, the police said it had been found to belong to the cook, but on inquiry this also turns out to be untrue. Now, just imag-ine a blood-stained garment being found in a house where a murder had just been committed by 5 p.m. on the same day, supposing the account first given to be true, to put it back into the hiding-place again without further inquiry would hardly be believed. I have, how-ever, little doubt that it was let slip in the way I have described, and that would account for what I never could get an explanation to – viz., why the men were secreted in the kitchen the same night. Foley never would explain that to me, but Mr. Kent said in his evidence that Foley told him that it was to see if anyone got up to destroy anything, but they did not tell him what they found."

15. From *The Times*, August 23, 1865: 12.

The following article documents the commutation of Kent's death sentence by Queen Victoria, suggesting that sympathy for Kent extended to the highest reaches of the Kingdom.

The Case of Constance Kent

Yesterday morning, Mr. Dowding, the Governor of the Wilts County Gaol, received an official communication from Mr. Chitty, Clerk of Assize for the Western Circuit, announcing that the sentence of death recently passed on Constance Emilie Kent, for the murder of her half-brother, Francis Saville Kent, at Road-hill-house in June, 1860, had been commuted by Her Majesty into one of penal servitude for life. In the course of the day, the result was made known to the prisoner, who received the announcement with the same calmness which has characterized her throughout. The statement that she has written a history of her life while in prison is without the slightest foundation.

16. From *The Times*, October 2, 1865: 4.

The following excerpt records Constance Kent's transfer to Millbank where she spent twenty years of her sentence before being quietly released and disappearing from sight.

The Road Murder

Constance Emilie Kent has been removed by order of Sir George Grey,[1] the Home Secretary, from the Wilts county gaol, at Fisherton, Salisbury, to the convict prison at Millbank,[2] to undergo her sentence of penal servitude for life.

---

1   Grey (1799-82) was chosen by Lord John Russell as Home Secretary in 1846, in which position he remained, with occasional interruption, for nearly twenty years.
2   Millbank Penitentiary, which was located where the Tate Gallery sits today, was built in 1821 based on a modified version of plans drawn up by Jeremy Bentham in 1791. After nearly seventy years of service, it closed its gates in 1890 and was demolished.

Appendix C: Excerpts from The Times *Accounts of the Major Murray / Northumberland Street Case of 1861.*

[The following excerpts from *The Times* coverage of the incident and the investigation provide some interesting background on this case. A thorough account of the case can be found in Richard Altick's *Deadly Encounters: Two Victorian Sensations.* Philadelphia: U of Pennsylvania Press, 1986.]

1. From *The Times,* July 13, 1861: 12.

The following is the initial report of the "fearful scene" in Northumberland Street, a scene that both puzzled and intrigued Londoners.

Frightful Encounter in Northumberland-Street

Between 11 and 12 o'clock yesterday a fearful scene took place at Northumberland-chambers, 16, Northumberland-street, Strand, in the apartments of Mr. J. Roberts,[1] a soldier and bill discounter, who occupies the first floor of that house. A deadly struggle had taken place between Mr. Roberts and Mr. Murray, late a Major in the 10th Hussars.[2] At about half-past 11 o'clock several pistol shots were heard in Mr. Roberts's chambers, after which the back window was thrown open, and Major Murray leaped out into the back yard. He then scaled the wall and entered the garden of the next house, occupied by Mr. Ransom, who, finding that Major Murray, a stranger to him, was bleeding from the neck and forehead, assisted him to the Charing-cross Hospital, and sent a messenger to the police-office in Scotland-yard, whence constables were sent to examine the premises. In the meantime information was sent from the hospital to the police-station, Bow-street, whereupon Superintendent Durkin and Inspector Mackenzie proceeded to the spot, and undertook the investigation. The doors of the apartments being locked, a ladder was procured, and

---

1   The man's full name was William John Roberts.
2   Murray was a Major in the light cavalry.

an entry effected by the windows. In the back room they found traces of a recent struggle. The furniture was disordered, pictures and frames smashed, and great pools of blood were on the floor. Several pistols were found about the room, one pair of which had been discharged. In the front room they found Mr. Roberts, much hurt about the head and face, huddled up against the wall near the door almost insensible. He was removed to the hospital. He has not yet been able to give any account of the transaction. Major Murray states that he knows nothing of Mr. Roberts, and had never seen him till that day, but had been invited by him to his chambers to speak of some pecuniary matters relating to a company with which Major Murray is connected; that Roberts fired upon him twice; and that he defended himself with the firetongs until he had disabled Roberts. Major Murray is not so much injured but that hopes may be entertained of his recovery. Both now lie in the hospital under the care of Dr. Canton, and are guarded by police....

As to the cause of the attempted murder, nothing of a very reliable character has as yet transpired. Our reporter was last night told that Major Murray had volunteered a statement, and that his words were substantially as follows: –

"Yesterday morning, shortly before 12 o'clock, I was walking down Northumberland-street, Strand, when I was accosted by a person whom I had never seen before. He said 'Are you not Major Murray?' I replied that I was; and he then said he wished to make a communication to me, and invited me into his house. I followed him upstairs to the first floor and went into a room. Almost immediately afterwards he fired a pistol at me, the ball of which only grazed my temple. He then fired another, and I felt I was wounded in the neck. I thought he had another pistol, and I fell down and pretended to be dead, trying not to breathe. He came and stood over me, carefully scanning my face to see whether I was alive, and when he turned from me, believing that he was going to attack me again, I jumped up, seized the poker, and struck him down. When he was on the floor I made my escape through the window, and made my way into the next house."

There is great reason to believe that the above is all true, with the exception of the statement as to Major Murray and Mr. Roberts being strangers to each other.

2. From *The Times*, July 15, 1861: 5.

The following story relates in greater detail Major Murray's account of the crime. The reporter also takes it upon himself to cast doubt on Murray's veracity.

The Encounter in Northumberland-Street

Very little additional information concerning this inexplicable encounter has been obtained since the publication of the first narrative on Saturday. A few facts have, however, been added to the statement volunteered by Major Murray.

It appears that this gentleman is a chief shareholder and also a director of a large hotel company. It was while walking through Hungerford-market towards the Strand that he was accosted by his assailant. The stranger asked him if his name was Major Murray, and whether he was not a director of an hotel company, which he named. To these questions the major replied in the affirmative, and the man continuing to address him, said, – "I believe you are desirous to complete the capital of that undertaking, and if so, I think that I can introduce you to a mode of accomplishing it." Major Murray replied that some addition to the capital of the company was required, but that he himself was only one of the body of directors, and that he could say nothing to a proposition from a stranger to himself, but that if his questioner would give him his name and address he would take care to make his proposition known to his co-directors. The stranger thereupon remarked that his chambers were close at hand, and that if Mr. Murray would accompany him thither he would at once give him the outlines of what he desired to lay before his Board. Major Murray consented to accompany him, and was led by the stranger to a house let out in offices, and know as Northumberland-chambers, Nos. 15 and 16, in a well-known street, leading off the Strand. Ascending to the first floor, the stranger introduced Major Murray to the back room of some chambers, upon which the name of Mr. John Francis Walker, solicitor, appeared. Here he requested Major Murray to be seated. Major Murray states that he sat down while, as he supposed, the stranger was looking for some papers. In a few moments he observed the stranger approaching him from behind, and the next instant he experienced a stunning sensation, and fell forward on the floor. He had been struck by a bullet. His consciousness was not destroyed by the concussion, but his limbs were powerless for action, and his instinct led him to keep silent. A lapse of time, brief though terrible, occurred at this juncture, and before his limbs recovered their power of motion he heard another shot fired, and felt the concussion of a severe blow upon his cheek-bone. At this horrible moment he states he considered his only safety was to remain motionless and simulate death. The paralyzed sensation caused by the first bullet, for such it was, that had entered the back of his neck and actually rested in the vertebral bones, passed off in a short time, and Major Murray, still lying on the floor, every moment expecting some blow that would prove fatal, took advantage of an instant when he perceived his antagonist's back to be turned towards him to seize the tongs, and, springing to his feet, to deal the fellow a blow on the back of his head which felled him to the ground. The stranger, a sturdy and thick-built man, was up again in an instant; and now a fierce struggle arose for the possession of the tongs. Major Murray, badly wounded and bleeding profusely, was scarcely a match for his desperate opponent, and at length, feeling his hold on the tongs relaxing, he caught up an empty beer-bottle. With this weapon he dealt his antagonist so severe a blow on the forehead as once more to fell him to the ground. Snatching the tongs from his grasp, Major Murray now, in the natural excitement of his situation, belaboured the wretched man with such force as effectually to render him powerless for further mischief, as he lay crouched up and bleeding on the floor. Major Murray next endeavoured to effect his escape from the trap into which he felt himself to have fallen. For this purpose he tried the door of the room, which to his astonishment and dismay he found locked and without a key. Anxious to obtain an exit from the murderous den, he raised the sash of a window opening into the rear of the house, and leaped into the yard below, where two workmen were engaged in repairing a closet....

The house-surgeons at Charing-cross Hospital, Messrs. Skegg and Short, state that there is no sign of delirium about Major Murray. He persists in his statement that he never knew Mr. Roberts until he met him on Friday morning, and accompanied him home, but he has not given any explanation either as to the origin of his acquaintance with Roberts, the motive he had for accompanying him home, or of the circumstances which provoked the assault. It is, however, generally supposed that Major Murray, instead of meeting Roberts in the street and accompanying him home, called upon him "in the way of business." What that business may have been is known but to the two unfortunate men themselves, but it is pretty certain that it in some way related to documents or correspondence, for Mr. Roberts's escritoire was found broken open, and the papers which it contained scattered in fragments over the floor in a pool of blood and wine. This circumstance throws some discredit upon the account which Major Murray has given of the transaction, that there had been no altercation in the room previous to Roberts firing a pistol at him.

All through yesterday crowds of people were led by curiosity to view the scene of this unaccountable occurrence, but as the police inspector had locked up Mr. Roberts's office, they were denied the opportunity of gratifying their morbid taste for the horrible. At first the two patients were placed in the same room, but they have since been separated....

3. From *The Times*, July 16, 1861: 9.

The reporter, having been allowed to visit the scene of the crime, provides lurid details in the following article.

The Encounter in Northumberland-Street

There is, apparently, some inexplicable mystery enveloping the circumstances connected with this fearful affray. The police are vigilant and incessant in their efforts to clear it up, and, we believe we may say, have now a clue which is likely to lead to important disclosures. More than this it would be imprudent to state, except that it is expected a few days, at most, will suffice to explain much of what now appears so utterly incomprehensible, and that a woman will, it is said, be found to be the true cause of quarrel on one side or the other. Major Murray still adheres to his original statement that he never knew Mr. Roberts before; that the latter accosted him in the street, and offered to advance him money for a company of which the Major was a director; that on this offer he accompanied Mr. Roberts to his chambers, and was there shot down; that on recovering his senses he seized the tongs, struck down his assailant and made his escape by jumping from the back window. On the face of it this is an extraordinary and most improbable statement, and it appears to be contradicted by the state in which the room was found when the police did at last effect an entry. Mr. Roberts's chambers are on the first floor, and consist of a front and back drawing-room, communicating by folding doors.

A description of these rooms would read almost like a chapter from a French novel. The front room has originally been furnished in the most luxurious and costly style. On the walls are five watercolour drawings, and between them handsome brackets, supporting statuettes and copies from the antique. Round the room are ranged costly buhl cabinets and inlaid tables, on which are all sorts of ornaments under large glass shades....

If two wild beasts had been turned loose to kill each other in this apartment it could not have presented traces of a more prolonged or deadly contest than it does. The furniture is broken and overturned in hideous confusion; the walls, the gilded tables, backs of chairs, and sides of dirty inlaid cabinets are streaked and smeared about with bloody fingers. One may almost trace where blows were struck by the star-shaped splashes of blood along the walls, while over the glass shades of the ornaments and doors of the cabinets it has fallen like rain, as if a bloody mop had been trundled round and round there....

Mr. Roberts, on his removal to the hospital, was found to have sustained three distinct fractures of the skull and a bad fracture of the cheek bone, as well as terrible lacerated face and scalp wounds. At first his life was quite despaired of, but after a time he regained his consciousness, and, though still in the most imminent danger, continues to progress favourably....

Major Murray, though far from being out of danger, is still going on well. His account of the attack is so far borne out by the fact that the worst and most dangerous wound he received was from a bullet which entered the back of the neck, and which, therefore, must have been fired from behind. Mr. Roberts's clothes have been carefully searched, and all the papers found in them secured. We are not aware that this precaution was taken or thought necessary with Major Murray. Both the wounded men are in the custody of the police at the hospital.

4. From *The Times*, July 19, 1861: 12.

When Roberts died of his wounds on July 18th, the police suddenly had a potential murder investigation.

The Fatal Encounter in Northumberland-Street

Yesterday evening Mr. Roberts, one of the principals in this most mysterious encounter, died of his injuries at Charing-cross Hospital. When this unfortunate gentleman was first admitted little if any hopes were entertained of his recovery, or even of his surviving through the night. The fearful nature of his wounds and the nervous shock which followed on them made his death appear almost certain....

In the meantime the police, under Mr. Superintendent Durkin and Inspector Mackenzie, are busied night and day in endeavouring to elucidate this affair. The greater part of the immense mass of documents, notes, and papers in the deceased's room have been carefully examined, and we believe we are now justified in saying that from these and other sources a clue to this mystery has been obtained. It is not likely, however, that the nature of the suspicions entertained will transpire even at the inquest to be held on the body of Mr. Roberts.

It was not thought advisable last night to inform Major Murray of the death of his antagonist or assailant.

5. From *The Times*, July 24, 1861: 5.

Excerpts from this long, four-column article bring into focus for the first time the driving force behind Roberts's attack on Murray, one Anne Maria Moodie, who lived with the Major as "Mrs. Murray." Also revealed in this excerpt is a small bit of detective work, accomplished by Inspector Robert Mackenzie, that would have made Wilkie Collins proud.

Fatal Encounter in Northumberland-Street. The Inquest on Mr. Roberts

Yesterday the adjourned inquiry into the mysterious circumstances connected with this most desperate affray was resumed at Charing-cross Hospital before Mr. Bedford, the coroner....

Mr. Robert Mackenzie, Inspector of the F division of police, said that, from information he received at noon on Friday, the 12th, he went at once to the rooms occupied by the deceased....

In a kind of basket or hamper in the front room he found three shirts, a handkerchief, and a towel. One shirt, the towel, and the hand-kerchief were stained with blood. They were stuffed into the hamper like dirty clothes. (The articles were handed in, and, with the exception of the spots of blood on them, they were perfectly clean, and had evidently not been worn.) Continuing his search of the room, the witness said he found on the table a sheet of white blotting-paper. It was much stained with blood. In a clean corner were the words –

"Mrs. Murray, Elm Lodge, Talbot-road, Tottenham...."

[Inspector Mackenzie] had found the blotting-paper on the table. He had been to the address on it, and found that a lady calling herself Mrs. Murray did live there. Her Christian name was Anne Maria.

Mr. Humphreys said he intended to tender that lady as a witness at a future stage of the proceedings....

6. From *The Times*, July 26, 1861: 5.

Excerpts from this long, four-column account of the final day of the inquest reveal much drama and excitement as a nervous and occasionally hysterical "Mrs. Murray" is questioned about her relationship with both Roberts and Murray.

Fatal Encounter in Northumberland-Street. The Inquest on Mr. Roberts

Mrs. Murray was accordingly called upon, and the excitement among the crowded audience to hear and see her became more intense. She was brought into court by a friend, and was given a seat at the foot of the table. She was dressed plainly but very well, in the ordinary walking dress which would be worn by a lady of means and position. She wore a thick black veil over her face, and appeared to be in such a dreadful state of nervous agitation as with difficulty to keep herself from fainting or going into hysterics. Her distress was so deep that it was quite painful to look at her....

When all eyes were directed on her she began to cry, and became still more agitated. One of the medical gentleman connected with the hospital stood by her, and when overcome, as she frequently was in giving her evidence, administered *sal volatile* and water, or gave her salts to smell. She gave her evidence in a low tone of voice, but with an evident effort to be clearly understood. At times, however, when referring to Major Murray, her hysterical attacks overtook her, and she made an effort to conclude her statement in gasps that were almost unintelligible, till she entirely broke down. Her statement was exactly as follows: – My name Anne Marie Moodie, and I live at Elm Lodge, Tottenham. I am a single woman – that is, I mean that I have never been married. [The witness concluded this last remark with difficulty, and cried bitterly when it was made.] I have known the deceased between three and four years. I have often been to his rooms in Northumberland-street. I was last there on the Wednesday before this affair took place....

By the Coroner. – Do you know any motive that the deceased had for wishing to get rid of the Major?

Witness. – Oh, yes! He wanted me. I, however, never heard him express any threat....

I first went to him on business, and latterly I used to go to him only in fear that, if I did not go, he would tell the Major that I had been there, and then the Major would have been angry at my going there for money. I first went to deceased on business only, and I constantly went to him on money business. Latterly he held such awe over me that I was fearful to displease him, lest he should make my home unhappy. I went first to borrow money of him....

My debt to him was for a small amount, only £15. I used to go to him to pay him the interest. I had £15 of him, and my acceptance was given for £20. I never owed him more than £20....

When I tried to save up the money to pay him I found I could not do it, and I could only pay him the quarter's interest of it – £5. I went to him, and told him so, and the deceased replied not to make myself unhappy about it, and if I would be his he would forgive me the whole of it. (It was with the utmost difficulty that the witness was able to gasp out this statement, and when she had done so she became fainting and hysterical for some time. The windows of the court as before were opened, and after a short while the witness recovered, and continued her answers to Mr. Sleigh, who put them with the utmost kindness and delicacy.) I told him I had come to pay him honourably, that I was honourable myself, and he must treat me so. I never took any present from him; never....

At the conclusion of the witness's examination, and as she rose to leave the court, there were repeated manifestations of applause which the officers were unable to suppress. The witness, however, took not the least notice of them, but dropped her veil and hurried away as quickly as she could. The inquiry adjourned for half an hour....

There being no further evidence to offer, the Coroner proceeded to sum up, when, commencing to read Mr. Canton's evidence as to the cause of death, the Jury intimated that they were then almost entirely agreed upon their verdict.

The Coroner, upon this, only explained under what circumstances they would be justified in returning a verdict of justifiable homicide, if they considered that the Major had killed the deceased in the effort to save his own life. He read over at length the whole statement of Major Murray, and at its conclusion asked the jury if they wished to retire to consider their verdict.

The foreman replied that it was not necessary, and, after conferring with his colleagues for a minute, said, "We find a verdict of justifiable homicide, and that Major Murray slew the deceased to save his own life."

The verdict was received by applause in the Court....

Thus ended the proceedings in this most extraordinary case.

Appendix D: Collins on Indians

Wilkie Collins's "A Sermon for Sepoys." From Charles Dickens's *Household Words: A Weekly Journal*, no. 414, Saturday, February 27, 1858, 244-47.

While we are still fighting for the possession of India, benevolent men of various religious denominations are making their arrangements for taming the human tigers in that country by Christian means. Assuming that this well-meant scheme is not an entirely hopeless one, it might, perhaps, not be amiss to preach to the people of India, in the first instance, out of some of their own books – or, in other words, to begin the attempt to purify their minds by referring them to the excellent moral lessons which they may learn from their own Oriental literature. Such lessons exist in the shape of ancient parables, once addressed to the ancestors of the sepoys, and still quite sufficient for the purpose of teaching each man among them his duty towards his neighbour, before he gets on to higher things. Here is a specimen of one of these Oriental apologues. Is there any reason why it should not be turned to account, as a familiar introduction to the first Christian sermon addressed to a pacified native congregation in the city of Delhi?

In the seventeenth century of the Christian era, the Emperor Shah Jehan – the wise, the bountiful, the builder of the new city of Delhi – saw fit to appoint the pious Vizir, Gazee Ed Din, to the government of all the district of Morodabad.

The period of the Vizir's administration was gratefully acknowledged by the people whom he governed as the period of the most-precious blessings they had ever enjoyed. He protected innocence, he honoured learning, he rewarded industry. He was an object for the admiration of all eyes, – a subject for the praise of all tongues. But the grateful people observed, with grief, that the merciful ruler who made them all happy, was himself never seen to smile. His time, in the palace, was passed in mournful solitude. On the few occasions when he appeared in the public walks, his face was gloomy, his gait was slow, his eyes were fixed on the ground. Time passed, and there was no change in him for the better. One morning the whole population was astonished and afflicted by news that he had resigned the reins of government and had gone to justify himself before the emperor at Delhi.

Admitted to the presence of Shah Jehan, the Vizir made his obeisance, and spoke these words: –

"Wise and mighty Ruler, condescend to pardon the humblest of your servants if he presumes to lay at your feet the honours which you have deigned to confer on him in the loveliest country on the earth. The longest life, oh bountiful Master, hardly grants time enough to man to prepare himself for death. Compared with the performance of that first of duties, all other human employments are vain as the feeble toil of an ant on the highway, which the foot of the first traveller crushes to nothing! Permit me, then, to prepare myself for the approach of eternity. Permit me, by the aid of solitude and silence, to familiarise my mind with the sublime mysteries of religion; and to wait reverently for the moment when eternity unveils itself to my eyes, and the last summons calls me to my account before the Judgment Seat."

The Vizir said these words, knelt down, laid his forehead on the earth, and was silent. After a minute of reflection, the emperor answered him in these terms: –

"Faithful servant! Your discourse has filled my mind with perplexity and fear. The apprehensions which you have caused in me are like those felt by a man who finds himself standing, unawares, on the edge of a precipice. Nevertheless, I cannot decide whether the sense of trouble that you have awakened within me is justified by sound reason or not. My days, like yours, however long they may be, are but an instant compared with eternity. But, if I thought as you do; if all men capable of doing good followed your example, who would remain to guide the faithful? Surely the duties of government would then fall to the share of those men only who are brutally careless of the future that awaits them beyond the grave – who are insensible to all feelings which are not connected with their earthly passions and their earthly interests? In that case, should I not be – should you not be – responsible before the Supreme Being for the miseries, without number, which would then be let loose on the world? Ponder that well, Vizir! And while I, on my side, consider the same subject attentively, depart in peace to the abode which I have prepared to receive you, since your arrival in this city. May Heaven direct us both into the way which it is safest and best to take!"

The Vizir withdrew. For three days he remained in his retirement, and received no message from the emperor. At the end of the third day, he sent to the palace to beg for a second audience. The request was immediately granted. When he again appeared in the presence of his sovereign, his countenance expressed the tranquillity of his mind. He drew a letter from his bosom, kissed it, and presented it to the emperor on his knees. Shah Jehan having given him permission to speak, he expressed himself, thereupon, in these words: –

"Sovereign lord and master! The letter which you have deigned to take from my hands has been addressed to me by the sage, Abbas, who now stands with me in the light of your presence, and who has lent me the assistance of his wisdom to unravel the scruples and perplexities which have beset my mind. Thanks to the lesson I have learned from him, I can now look back on my past life with pleasure, and contemplate the future with hope. Thanks to the wisdom which I have imbibed from his teaching, I can now conscientiously bow my head before the honours which your bounty showers on me, and can gladly offer myself again to be the shadow of your power in the province of Morodabad."

Shah Jehan, who had listened to the Vizir with amazement and curiosity, directed that the letter should be given to the sage, Abbas, and ordered him to read aloud the words of wisdom that he had written to Gazee Ed Din. The venerable man stood forth in the midst of the Court, and, obeying the Emperor, read these lines: –

"May the pious and merciful Vizir, to whom the wise generosity of our sovereign lord and master has entrusted the government of a province, enjoy to the end of his days the blessing of perfect health!

"I was grieved in my inmost heart when I heard that you had deprived the millions of souls who inhabit Morodabad of the advantages which they enjoyed under your authority. Modesty and respect prevented me from combating your scruples of conscience while you were describing them in the presence of the Emperor. I hasten, therefore, to write the words which I could not venture to speak. My purpose is to clear your mind of the doubts which now darken it, by relating to you the history of my own youth. The anxious thoughts which now trouble you, were once the thoughts which troubled me also. May your soul be relieved of the burden that oppresses it, as mine was relieved in the byegone time!

"My early manhood was passed in studying the science of medicine. I learnt all the secrets of my art, and practised it for the benefit of my species. In time, however, the fearful scenes of suffering and death which perpetually offered themselves to my eyes, so far affected my mind as to make me tremble for my own life. Wherever I went, my grave seemed to be yawning at my feet. The awful necessity of preparing myself for eternity, impressed itself upon my soul, and withdrew my thoughts from every earthly consideration. I resolved to retire from the world, to despise the acquisition of all mortal knowledge, and to devote my remaining days to the severest practices of a purely religious life. In accordance with this idea, I resolved to humble myself by suffering the hardship of voluntary poverty. After much consideration, I came to the conclusion that those who stood in need of my money were the persons who were least worthy of being benefited by it: and that those who really deserved the exercise of my charity were too modest, or too high-minded, to accept my help. Under the influence of this delusion, I buried in the earth all the treasure that I possessed; and took refuge from human society in the wildest and most inaccessible mountains of my native country. My abode was in the darkest corner of a huge cavern; my drink was the running water; my food consisted of the herbs and fruits that I could gather in the woods. To add to the severe self-restraint which had now become the guiding principle of my life, I frequently passed whole nights in watching – on such occasions, keeping my face turned towards the East, and waiting till the mercy of the Prophet should find me out, and unveil the mysteries of Heaven to my mortal view.

"One morning, after my customary night of watching, exhaustion overpowered me, at the hour of sunrise; and I sank prostrate in spite of myself, on the ground at the entrance of my cave.

"I slept, and a vision appeared to me.

"I was still at the mouth of the cave, and still looking at the rays of the rising sun. Suddenly a dark object passed between me and the morning light. I looked at it attentively, and saw that it was an eagle, descending slowly to the earth. As the bird floated nearer and nearer to the ground, a fox dragged himself painfully out of a thicket near at hand. Observing the animal, as he sank exhausted close by me, I discovered that both his fore legs were broken. While I was looking at him, the eagle touched the earth, laid before the crippled fox a morsel of goat's flesh that he carried in his talons, flapped his huge wings, and, rising again into the air, slowly disappeared from sight.

"On coming to my senses again, I bowed my forehead to the earth, and addressed my thanksgivings to the Prophet for the vision which he had revealed to me. I interpreted it, in this manner. 'The divine Power,' I said to myself, 'accepts the sacrifice that I have made in withdrawing myself from the contaminations of the world; but reveals to me, at the same time, that there is still some taint of mortal doubt clinging to my mind, and rendering the trust which it is my duty to place in the mercy of Heaven less absolute and unconditional than it ought to be. So long as I waste even the smallest portion of my time in the base employment of providing for my own daily wants, so long will my confidence in Providence be imperfect, and my mind be incapable of wholly abstracting itself from earthly cares. This is what the vision is designed to teach me. If the bounty of Heaven condescends to employ an eagle to provide for the wants of a crippled fox, how sure I may feel that the same mercy will extend the same benefits to me! Let me wholly devote myself, then, to the service of my Creator, and commit the preservation of my life to the means which His wisdom is sure to supply.'

"Strong in this conviction, I searched the woods no more for the herbs and fruits which had hitherto served me for food. I sat at the mouth of my cavern, and waited through the day, and no heavenly messenger appeared to provide for my wants. The night passed; and I was still alone. The new morning came; and my languid eyes could hardly lift themselves to the light, my trembling limbs failed to sustain me when I strove to rise. I lay back against the wall of my cavern, and resigned myself to die.

"The consciousness of my own existence seemed to be just passing from me, when the voice of an invisible being sounded close at my ear. I listened, and heard myself addressed in these words: –

" 'Abbas,' said the supernatural voice, 'I am the Angel whose charge it is to search out and register your inmost thoughts. I am sent to you on a mission of reproof. Vain man! do you pretend to be wiser than the wisdom which is revealed to you? The blindness of your vision and the vainglory of your heart have together perverted a lesson which was mercifully intended to teach you the duties that your Creator expects you to perform. Are you crippled like the fox? Has not nature, on the contrary, endowed you with the strength of an eagle? Rise, and bestir yourself! Rise, and let the example of the eagle guide you, henceforth, in the right direction. Go back to the city from which you have fled. Be, for the future, the messenger of health and life to those who groan on the hard bed of sickness. Ill-judging mortal! the virtue that dies in this solitude, lives in the world from which you have withdrawn. Prove your gratitude to your Creator by the good that you do among his helpless and afflicted creatures. There is the way that leads you from earth to Heaven. Rise, Abbas – rise humbly, and take it!'

"An unseen hand lifted me from the ground, an unseen hand guided me back to the city. Humbled, repentant, enlightened at last, I drew my treasure from its hiding place, and employed it in helping the poor. Again I devoted all my energies to the blessed work of healing the sick. Years passed and found me contented and industrious in my vocation. As the infirmities of age approached, I assumed the sacred robe, and comforted the souls of my fellow-creatures, as I had formerly comforted their bodies. Never have I forgotten the lesson that I learnt in my hermitage on the mountain. You see me now, high in the favour of my Sovereign – Know that I have deserved my honours, because I have done good in my generation, among the people over whom he rules.

"Such, oh, pious Vizir, is the story of my youth. May the lesson which enlightened me, do the same good office for you. I make no pretensions to wisdom: I speak only of such things as I know. Believe me, all wisdom which extends no farther than yourself is unworthy of you. A life sacrificed to subtle speculations is a life wasted. Let the eagle be the object of your emulation as he was of mine. The more gifts you have received, the better use it is expected you will make of them. Although the All-Powerful alone can implant virtue in the human heart, it is still possible for you, as the dreaded representative of authority, to excite to deeds of benevolence, even those who may have no better motive for doing good, than the motive of serving their own interests. With time, you may teach them the knowledge of higher things. Meanwhile, it will matter little to the poor who are succoured, whether it is mere ostentation or genuine charity that relieves them. Spread the example, therefore, of your own benevolence, beyond the circle of those only who are wise and good. Widen the sphere of your usefulness among your fellow-creatures, with every day; and fortify your mind with the blessed conviction that the life you will then lead, will be of all lives the most acceptable in the eyes of the Supreme Being.

"Farewell. May the blessings of a happy people follow you wherever you go. May your name, when you are gathered to your fathers, be found written in the imperishable page – in the Volume of the Book of Life!"

Abbas ceased. As he bowed his head, and folded up the scroll, the emperor beckoned him to the foot of the throne, and thanked the sage for the lesson that he had read to his Sovereign and to all the Court. The next day, the Vizir was sent back to his government at Morodabad. Shah Jehan also caused copies of the letter to be taken, and ordered them to be read to the people in the high places of the city. When that had been done, he further commanded that this inscription should be engraved on the palace gates, in letters of gold, which men could read easily, even from afar off: –

THE LIFE THAT IS MOST ACCEPTABLE TO THE
SUPREME BEING, IS THE LIFE THAT IS MOST
USEFUL TO THE HUMAN RACE.

Surely not a bad Indian lesson, to begin with, when Betrayers and Assassins are the pupils to be taught?

Appendix E: Letters by Wilkie Collins Concerning The Moonstone (the Novel and the Play)

The following seven letters, all published courtesy of Harry Ransom Research Center, University of Texas, Austin, Texas, offer a number of interesting insights into Collins's professional and familial concerns at the time he was writing *The Moonstone*. Though all are addressed to Collins's publishers – six of the letters are to his American publishers, Harper and Brothers, and the seventh is to Tinsley's, who printed the first edition of *The Moonstone* in England – they are much livelier than one would expect letters of business and discussions of contracts to be.

1. To Harper Brothers.[1]

18 June 1867
From *All the Year Round* Office
26 Wellington Street

Dear Sirs,

I am beginning a new serial work of fiction – and I offer to your firm the first opportunity of making me a proposal for the "advance sheets" for publication in America.

My new novel will be published (in the first instance) in England, in *All the Year Round*. The first weekly number will appear – so far as I know now – towards the close of the present year.

The work will extend – so far as I can now calculate – from 26 to 30 weekly parts.

Will you kindly let me know, at your earliest convenience, what sum you will offer (in English money) for the advance weekly proofs

---

1   Collins had been paid £5000 for *No Name* in 1862 and £3000 for *Armadale* in 1864, so he knew by 1867 that he could play publishers against one another in a bidding war if need be. As it turns out, he accepted Harper Brothers offer for serial and volume-form publication. This letter also indicates how carefully Collins planned his work in advance. *The Moonstone*, which he speculated might reach thirty weekly parts, was completed in thirty-two weekly parts more than a year after Collins wrote this letter.

of this new story, and in what form you propose to pay the money?

I must request that you will be so good as to communicate with me in this matter, *directly*, and not through your London agents. Circumstances have occurred which prevent me from renewing any literary business relation with the firm of Mssrs. Sampson Low, Son and Co.[1] In the event of our agreeing upon terms, if there is any difficulty in your transmitting the necessary remittance directly to me in England, I shall be happy to refer you to a firm in New York, the members of which will receive whatever money is due to me, on my account.

I remain,
Faithfully yours,
Wilkie Collins

2. To Harper Brothers.[2]

From *All the Year Round* Office
26 Wellington Street
20 July 1867

Dear Sirs,

I accept the second of the proposals with which you favour me in your letter dated the 2nd of this month – choosing, of the two alternatives contained in that proposal, the alternative of sending you a copy of the original MS of my forthcoming story in two halves.

I understand that I am to send you from London the first of those halves, containing (say) from 13 to 14 weekly portions, forty days before the first weekly portion is published in England. This, allowing the average of ten days of transmission, would place the first half of the MS in your hands in New York, one month before any part of it is

---

1   Of the seeming fallout with Sampson, Low and Co., little is known. Collins severed his business relations with the company, which had exclusive rights to his fiction at the time, in early 1867. Smith, Elder and later Chatto and Windus bought subsequent rights to various of Collins's novels.

2   This letter indicates that Collins had begun writing his novel early enough in 1867 to be comfortable in the belief he would be half finished by the end of 1867. As it turns out, he was wise to begin work early, for early 1868 brought severe illness and his mother's death, both of which nearly interrupted the novel's serialization.

published there. The second half is to be sent, according to the same arrangement, forty days before the 14th or 15th number (as the case may be) is published in England.

For the MS, divided into these two halves, I am to receive seven hundred and fifty pounds sterling (£750).[1] £375, payable in a bill of exchange to my order on Barings,[2] on receipt of the first half of MS – and £375, payable in the same manner, on receipt of the second half. I suggest, as the sum is thus halved, that the period for which the bill of exchange is to be drawn should be, if possible, 30 days, instead of the 60 days which you propose, if I sent the whole MS at once, and receive the whole sum at once.

I have one condition to add to my side. It is this: – that you shall only print and publish the periodical instalments of the story from the printed proofs, which I will send to you regularly. The copy of the MS is only to be used by you for the purpose of illustrating the story – and, except in the event of miscarriage of the proofs, it is not to be printed from.

I make this stipulation in your interests, as well as mine – for it enables you to publish my story with my last corrections. These corrections will not affect the scene which your artist may choose for illustration, but they will very often, by apparently trifling means, assist the influence of the story on the reader's mind.

On the MS, as on the proofs, the weekly dates of publication in England will be indicated at the beginning of each weekly number, so that there may be no mistake made, in any case, about the dates of publication and the weekly quantity published in America – which are, of course, exactly to follow the dates of publication and the quantity published in England.

I shall be obliged if you will acknowledge the receipt of this letter, and inform me that you interpret, as I interpret, the arrangement entered into between us for my new story.

Believe me, Dear Sirs,
Faithfully yours,
Wilkie Collins

---

1 The £750 fee for serialization was slightly less than the £850 payment he received from Dickens for the English serial rights.
2 Barings is the oldest merchant bank in London, established by John and Francis Baring in Queen Street in 1763.

3. To Harper Brothers.

20 Gloucester Place
Portman Square W.
London
12 November 1867

THE MOONSTONE[1] A NEW SERIAL STORY
BY WILKIE COLLINS

Dear Sirs,
I send you above a proof of the title. It has only just been decided on, and it has not yet been advertised in England. So far as I know, your advertisement of the title will appear simultaneously with the advertisement here.

The first weekly part of the story will be published in *All the Year Round*, on *Wednesday January 1st, 1868*. We shall therefore appear on both sides of the Atlantic on New Year's Day.

I send you (under another cover) by this mail – Tuesday November 12th – a first portion of the first half of the MS copy of the story. This instalment leaves England fifty clear days before the first weekly part is published in England. The quantity of MS now sent comprises at least seven weekly parts of the story. The remainder of the first half of the complete MS copy shall follow as rapidly as possible. It proceeds more slowly than I had anticipated from two causes. My own MS for the press here is so altered and interlined as to be very difficult to read – and the literary necessities of this story force me to correct and re-correct the first half, with a special view to what is to come in the second. If I am a few days later than the thirty days advance with what is to come, I hope you will take into consideration that I have been a few days earlier with what is already sent.

With regard to the printed proofs, I hope to begin sending them to you in a week's time or less. The alterations which you will find, here and there, between the proofs and the MS – though important

---

1 Collins had at one time anticipated calling his upcoming novel *The Serpent's Eye*, but he seems rather pleased with himself in this letter as he announces the name upon which he had recently decided.

in a literary point of view – are not likely to embarrass the illustrator. They are alteration in the form only. The substance of the book (as presenting subjects for illustration) will remain the same in MS as in print.

Mr. Charles Dickens (who left for America by the steamer of the 9th Nov.) will call on you while he is in New York – and will kindly say for me anything I may have omitted to say here.[1]

Please acknowledge the receipt of this portion of MS copy, and the receipt of this letter.

Faithfully yours,
Wilkie Collins

4. To Harper Brothers.[2]

Bentham Hill Cottage
near Tunbridge Wells
England
30 January 1868

Dear Sirs,

Your kind letter has reached me at a time of painful domestic anxiety. The dangerous illness of my mother has called me to her cottage in the country – and I am working at my story, as best I can, in the intervals of my attendance at her bedside. Mr. Dickens has already written to tell me of the liberal manner in which you had met my proposal. And now your your letter comes, telling me of an additional concession to my convenience, at a time when your consideration for me speaks with special friendship, and when I assure you I feel encouraged in no ordinary degree by the kindness of my American publishers.

You will receive with this a corrected revise of the twelfth weekly part of *The Moonstone*, and a portion of the thirteenth weekly part.

---

1 On his last trip to America, Dickens sailed on the *Cuba* to Boston; he stayed in the States into April 1868, returning to England on May 1.

2 This letter provides the first indication of the trouble that plagued Collins for the first half of 1868. His mother's illness – she would die on March 19 – had taken him away from London and a consistent work schedule. Though he seems doggedly determined to work on the novel whenever possible, he also seems anxious about falling behind.

The completion of the thirteenth weekly part will follow, I hope, by Tuesday's mail. But for the inevitable delay in transmitting the manuscript and receiving the proof by post, caused by my absence from London, you would have received the whole weekly part by mail of February 1st. I will arrange to send slips (for the convenience of your artist) by every mail, so long as my mother's critical condition obliges me to remain here. And I will be careful – as I have hitherto been careful – to forward the duplicates regularly, in case of accidents by the post. After the next two or three weekly portions, I shall hope to be able to send you beforehand a list of subjects for the artist, referring to a part of the story which is already settled in detail, and in relation to which he may feel secure against any after-alterations when I am writing for press.

The two numbers of the *Weekly* have reached me safely. The illustrations to the first number are very picturesque – the three Indians and the boy being especially good, as I think. In the second number there is a mistake (as we should call it in England) of presenting Gabriel Betteredge in *livery*. As head-servant, he would wear plain black clothes and would look, with his white cravat and grey hair, like an old clergyman. I only mention this for future illustration – and because I see the dramatic effect of the story (in the first number) conveyed with such real intelligence by the artist that I want to see him taking the right direction, even in the smallest technical details.[1]

You may rely on my sparing no effort to study *your* convenience, after the readiness that you have shown to consider mine. I am very glad to hear that you like the story, so far. There are some effects to come, which – unless I am altogether mistaken – have never been tried in fiction before.

> Believe me, dear Sirs,
> With sincere esteem
> and regard,
> Truly yours,
> Wilkie Collins

---

1 Another fascinating element of this letter appears in the admonition to Harper Brothers that their artist, William Jewett, had misrepresented Gabriel Betteredge in a sketch in the American journal's second number. An insistence on accuracy, even with seemingly minor details, was a Collinsian trademark.

5. To Harper Brothers.[1]

90 Gloucester Place
Portman Square W.
London
Saturday,
22 February 1868

Dear Sirs,

You will, I hope, receive with this a carefully-corrected proof (for the artist) of weekly portion 15 of *The Moonstone*. Receiving this – you will receive, so far as I can now calculate, one full half of the book.

This weekly part, and the last, have been partly dictated, partly written by me, in intervals of severe pain from a rheumatic attack – which has tortured my eyes this time as well as the rest of my body. I am now getting better – with little to contend against but the weakness caused by the suffering – and by the action of the remedies employed. Rather better accounts of my mother have, I am glad to say, cheered me on my sick bed. Assuming that I have had *my* share for the present of the afflictions of human life – I shall hope to get on faster into the second half of *The Moonstone* than with the first. "Miss Clack's" narrative will be finished in one or two more weekly parts. And "Franklin Blake's narrative" will follow it. In *this* part of the story, I hope to be able to send the artist some subjects beforehand.

I send with part 15, duplicate of revised part 14 – and a duplicate of the corrected slip in part 13. You now have all my latest corrections – and the American and the English publications of *The Moonstone* are literally the same.

Depend – barring accidents – on my steadily doing my best to increase the present advance [i.e. sheets]. I have declined all new proposals made to me here – I am to work uninterrupted at *The Moonstone* until it is done.

> Believe me, Dear Sirs,
> Faithfully yours,
> Wilkie Collins

---

1   The weekly numbers discussed in this and the next letter – numbers 15 and 16 – are the shortest in the serial, primarily because Collins had fallen behind his writing schedule due to his mother's illness and his own battle with the gout.

6. To Harper Brothers.

20 Gloucester Place
Portman Square W.
London
29 February 1868

Dear Sirs,

Your letter of the 19th reached me this evening – too late for acknowledgment by today's mail.

I am not only gratified – I may really say I am affected by the generous interpretation of the relations between us which has given me more than my due, after I have given you less than *yours*. I acknowledged the receipt of the five-hundred pounds which I have this day received from you "on account," not only with a sincere sense of your liberality, but with sincere pleasure in accepting an obligation which I owe to your friendly regard for *me*, and to your sympathetic appreciation of the merits of my *story*. Thank you heartily – I say no more.

I have sent you by today's mail, a revise of weekly part 15 – and the great part of weekly portion 16. A severe return of the rheumatism for the past two days, stopped my pen altogether. Today, I am a little better, and in better working trim. Tuesday's mail will, I hope, bring you the complete weekly part 16, to print from.

Many thanks for the number of the Weekly – which I have looked at with great interest. Before this letter goes on Tuesday, I will add to it, for the assistance of the artists, such subjects for future illustrations as I can be sure of at this moment.

Believe me, Dear Sirs,
Most truly yours,
Wilkie Collins

7. To Tinsley's.

90 Gloucester Place
Portman Square West
6 June 1868[1]

Dear Sir,

I have only a moment before post to say that I hope to finish *The Moonstone* at the 32nd or 33rd weekly part. Also, that I send you with the usual proofs, a recorrected portion, of the first part of the story – which will be followed here in the reprint in book-form, which you will do well to follow also in your reprint. The remaining part of the story – by far the larger part as you will see – remains unaltered and will be reprinted as it now stands in the periodical form.

Faithfully yours
Wilkie Collins

★   ★   ★   ★   ★

Two letters to American actress Fanny Davenport[2] indicate that Collins's adaptation of the novel was finished and printed well before the play was performed for the first time on September 17, 1877. Both letters appear courtesy of Harry Ransom Research Center, University of Texas, Austin, Texas.

1. To Miss Davenport

90 Gloucester Place
Portman Square West
28 July 1877

My dear Miss Davenport,

I am indeed sorry to hear that you are obliged to hurry your departure – but I see the necessity, and deplore it.

---

1   Though his novel was due to be published in book form in just over five weeks from the date of this hurried letter to London publisher, Collins seems still a bit uncertain as to when he would finish writing his story.

2   The Miss Davenport to whom the letters are addressed was Fanny Lily Gipsy Davenport (1850-98), daughter of Edward Loomis Davenport (1815-77). She was on

Collins's September 8th 1877 letter to Fanny Davenport, with Collins's sketch of the stage design as he envisioned it for a performance of *The Moonstone*. Courtesy the Harry Ransom Research Center, University of Texas at Austin.

The best likeness of me is unfortunately not on card-board. I enclose it, as a temporary offering, until I can send something more durable. Thank you most sincerely, for the charming photographs which have accompanied your kind letter. The make-up in *Posthumia*[1] is really marvelous – quite as true to nature, and quite as effective in a dramatic point of view as the make-up of the French actress.

I must ask you to let me send the piece [*The Moonstone*] after you. The printers have not got more than half way through it – and the manuscript is in their hands.[2] You shall have the proofs. If I address to the Fifth Avenue Theatre, N.Y.[3] I suppose my letter will reach you.

Whatever I *can* do, *shall* be done, rely on it, when you return to us. In the meantime, I will keep *The Moonstone* piece free, *so far as America is concerned*, until you have kindly sent me a line to say whether the principal part *is* "a part for Miss Davenport" – or not. We begin here on the 1st or 8th of September next.[4]

My rheumatism keeps me terribly dependent on the weather. But I will try hard to get to you on Monday just to say goodbye, and then to run away again, a few minutes before six. If the damp cripples me as it crippled me today – then I must put up with my disappointment, and heartily wish you and your fellow travellers, the most peaceful and prosperous of all possible voyages (in this letter).

Your most truly,
Wilkie Collins

---

the stage as a child in her father's company, making her adult début in Tom Taylor's *Still Waters Run Deep* in 1865. She was New York playwright Augustin Daly's leading lady between 1869 and 1877.

1   The play to which Collins refers remains unidentified.

2   The printer, Crystal Palace Press, was an operation run by Charles Dickens's son Charley (1837-96). Upon inheriting his father's weekly magazine *All the Year Round* in 1870, Charley incorporated it as part of the Dickens and Evans (of Bradbury and Evans) printing firm, where Collins had the play privately printed.

3   The Fifth Avenue Theatre was Augustin Daly's theatre at Broadway and 28th Street, New York. Daly had opened it in 1874 after the original Fifth Avenue Theatre – four blocks away on 24th Street – burned in 1873. Daly left the theatre in 1878, after which it went through many management changes until it was demolished in 1908.

4   The play opened on September 17, 1877 at the Olympic Theatre. For whatever reason, the stage version of *The Moonstone* did not reach the American stage.

2. To Miss Davenport.[1]

90 Gloucester Place
Portman Square West
8 September 1877

My dear Miss Davenport,
    Here is the piece [*The Moonstone*]. I have only time to send it off by today's mail. Next week, I will write more at length on the subject.

Always but yours,
Wilkie Collins

P.S.
It may be as well to add (on the question of protecting the piece in America) that many of the chief scenes and situations are not in the novel at all, and are now first invented by me.[2]

1   This letter was accompanied by a quickly drawn sketch of the stage as Collins envisioned it for a performance of his play. See page 603.
2   Collins was always cautious about copyright questions, and he was particularly wary of American publishers, who relentlessly pirated his works. For more on Collins's opinions of the issue of copyright, see his "Considerations on the Copyright Question: Addressed to an American Friend," published as a sixteen-page pamphlet in 1889 by Trübner & Company.

Appendix F: Collins's Stage Adaptation of The Moonstone

Introduction

In 1972, George Rowell, attempting to explain the almost total absence of contemporary editions of Victorian drama, wrote, "[I]f any drama was intended to be acted, and acted by professionals steeped in their craft, it was the Victorian drama. Written for actors – as opposed to companies – often rewritten by actors, and always dominated by actors, it existed as a text for the stage, not a text for the written page...."[1] In one respect, Rowell's comment remains correct today, for even giants of the period and some of their most popular and successful works are now long forgotten, appearing only as occasional footnotes in modern textbooks. At the same time, though, Rowell did not distinguish between works by those professional dramatists who wrote solely for the stage (in a time when the drama was entertainment, not art, and when theatre was not yet quite socially acceptable[2]) and those by artists whose primary medium was fiction but who felt also the call of the theatre. It is a distinction that should be made. The dramatic works of Victorian novelists-turned-occasional-playwrights – Charles Dickens, Wilkie Collins, Edward Bulwer Lytton, and Charles Reade to name just a few – deserve a renewed critical attention for at least two reasons: they may offer the modern reader easier access into the neglected and shadowy world of the Victorian theatre and drama, but more importantly, they may shed some light on the broader literary motivations of the artists themselves. With that in mind, this edition provides the reader with an opportunity to explore a never-before published work by Wilkie Collins, a play that he

---

1   This passage comes from Rowell's introduction to his edition titled *Nineteenth Century Plays* (Oxford: Oxford UP, 1972, viii).

2   Collins addressed the problem of popular prejudice against the theatre in an article he wrote for Dickens's *Household Words* in October 1858. "Highly Proper!" (October 2, 1858, Volume XVIII, Number 445, 361-63) condemns certain private schools for refusing to enrol the children of certain London theatre managers.

adapted for the stage from his most popular novel, *The Moonstone*. Before turning to the play, though, we should place Collins's interest in drama against a backdrop of the theatrical community for which he was writing.

Wilkie Collins as Dramatist

Collins had a lifelong love of the theatre and of drama, a love that he nourished at every turn throughout his career, and one that he expressed often in his writing. Drama became a part of his life early on, as he accompanied his father to Italian theatres in Sorrento, Rome, and Naples during the Collins family visit to the continent between 1836 and 1838, when Wilkie was a boy. Collins nurtured this passion for drama, and beginning in 1844, when he was twenty, he made almost annual pilgrimages to Paris primarily to frequent the French theatres, whose fare he always believed to be more palatable than that found in their English counterparts.[1] As early as 1849, as he was beginning to cut his teeth as a writer,[2] Collins and his friends often amused themselves with amateur theatricals produced at his mother's Blandford Square home, dubbed by the group the "Theatre Royal, Back Drawing-Room." Such small scale entertainments were done for the simple pleasure they brought to friends and family, of course, but they also served to convince Collins, who eagerly took command of their production and always charged headlong into the roles he provided for himself, that his passion for drama might extend to the role of playwright. In early 1850 he tried his hand at drama by translating into English a French melodrama, one he titled *A Court Duel*, by the playwrights Joseph Phillippe

---

1   Collins went so far as to write, "If I had been a Frenchman, with such a public to write for, such rewards to win, and such actors to interpret for me, as the French stage presents, all the stories I have written from *Antonina* to *The Woman in White* would have been told in dramatic form." For more of Collins's comparisons of French and English theatre, see his *Household Words* article "The Dramatic Grub Street. Explored in Two Letters" (March 6, 1858, Volume XVII, Number 415, 265–70).

2   Collins's earliest publication was the brief short story "The Last Stage Coachman," which appeared in *The Illuminated Magazine* in 1843. His next published work was the massive two-volume biography of his father, *Memoirs of the Life of William Collins, Esq., R.A.*, which Longmans published in 1848.

Simon and Edmond Badon.[1] Performed at the Miss Kelly's Theatre in Soho to benefit The Female Emigration Fund, the play marked Collins's debut as a dramatist as well as his first appearance on a public stage.

Within a few days of the opening performance of *A Court Duel*, though, the publication and modestly successful reception of his first novel, *Antonina* (1850), compelled Collins to turn his professional attention to fiction writing, a craft he realized would bring him a far better income than playwriting;[2] but even though he did not write another drama for nearly five years, his passion for the theatre did not wane. In fact, by early 1851, his interest in drama and amateur acting led to his meeting Charles Dickens, who shared Collins's intense passion for anything theatrical. The two men met when Collins eagerly agreed, at the request of mutual friend Augustus Egg, to participate in Dickens's elaborate amateur production of Bulwer Lytton's pastiche *Not So Bad As We Seem*. Thereafter, and until Dickens's death in 1870, the two novelists remained best of friends, often acting together in various amateur productions, more often spending evenings together at the theatre, and even collaborating on two popular dramas, *The Frozen Deep* (1857) and *No Thoroughfare* (1867).[3] Also during the first

1   International copyright laws were nonexistent in the mid-nineteenth century, and it was very common practice for English writers to "translate and adapt," with little or no credit to the original author, continental dramas for the London stage. Moses Montrose argued that the lack of a copyright law contributed to what he saw to be "the poverty of the British stage" during the mid-nineteenth century. He reasons that without a meaningful copyright law, "British theatre managers ... translated freely whatever they like of current French productions. The native dramatist could find no encouragement for original work, but had to sink his talents to the level of a hack translator. There was a great demand for the tried French successes, and thus many a British play cost the manager a mere pittance, but cost the English playwright his artistic soul" (*Representative British Dramas: Victorian and Modern*, Boston: Little, Brown, 1929, viii-ix). Including *A Court Duel*, Wilkie Collins wrote fifteen plays during his life, more than half of them dramatic interpretations of his own novels.

2   Collins complained bitterly about how little money the playwright received from the production of one of his plays. In his *Household Words* article "A Breach of British Privilege" (March 19, 1859, Volume XIX, Number 469, 361-64), he calculates at length and very meticulously what he considers to be the unfair advantage enjoyed by theatre owners and actors when it came to the money made by a successful drama.

3   Collins and Dickens had written a story of the same title for the 1867 Christmas number of Dickens's weekly magazine *All the Year Round*. The two decided to col-

half of the 1850s Collins became a regular contributor of theatre reviews to Thornton Leigh Hunt and George Henry Lewes's new politically radical weekly paper *The Leader*. His assignments took him frequently to London's theatre district, where he not only honed his skills as a drama critic but also developed strong opinions about the virtues and failings of various London playhouses, opinions that eventually became material for several theatre articles that he contributed to Dickens's weekly magazine *Household Words* near the end of the 1850s.

The popular success of the first four of Collins's novels, *Antonina, Basil, Hide and Seek*, and *The Dead Secret*, all written and published during the 1850s, established his reputation as an important young novelist of the day, and though he remained an industrious writer of fiction for the rest of his life, publishing nearly twenty-five novels during his thirty-five year career, he also realized that as a professional novelist he need not abandon his passion for drama. Indeed, an 1862 preface to his second novel, *Basil*, spelled out his belief that the two forms are in fact related, that "the Novel and the Play are twin-sisters in the family of Fiction; that the one is a drama narrated, as the other is a drama acted; and that all the strong and deep emotions which the Play-writer is privileged to excite, the Novel-writer is privileged to excite also...."[1] He was, it seems, well aware of the role his fascination with drama played in his fiction, for many of his novels have a distinctly dramatic, even theatrical, flavour.

This theatricality is sometimes apparent in his novel's characters, who often have to assume unfamiliar roles, costume themselves in elaborate disguises, and practice the actor's art of deception to gain their ends. Lydia Gwilt of *Armadale* and Magdalen Vanstone and Captain Wragge of *No Name* come immediately to mind here. Occasionally, as in *No Name*, the most theatrically melodramatic of Collins's novels — whose sections Collins went so far as to divide into dramatic "Scenes" — the novels contain wonderfully vivid descriptions of actors, actresses, theatres, and performances. But more noticeably, his fiction often *reads* like drama. Most of Collins's fiction was serialized,

---

laborate as well on its dramatization, but Dickens eventually let Collins and Charles Fechter, who was to play the lead when the play was performed at the Adelphi Theatre, do most of the writing.

1 The passage appears in *Basil*'s introductory "Letter of Dedication," addressed to Collins's friend Charles J. Ward and dated July 1862.

and he was a master of the suspenseful serial ending, using the ends of chapters much as a playwright uses the curtain to bring a scene to a memorable conclusion. Serialization also allowed Collins to create vivid and memorable individual episodes or scenes in his fiction, scenes in many ways similar to the *tableaux* employed by dramatists of the period. And finally, perhaps because of his interest in the theatre, Collins more often than not chose in his fiction to establish and develop his characters through dramatic dialogue rather than with lengthy narrative description. The long expository conversations between Marian Halcombe and Count Fosco over the course of *The Woman in White*, or between Franklin Blake and Gabriel Betteredge or Ezra Jennings in *The Moonstone* offer examples of such dialogic characterization.

The 1860s established Collins as a novelist of the first rank. He published the wildly popular *The Woman in White* in 1859-60; *No Name* in 1862; *Armadale*, for which he was paid £5000 by *The Cornhill*, in 1864-66, and *The Moonstone*, whose sales and popularity eclipsed all the others, in 1868. As his income and his fame as a novelist increased, he began to feel more comfortable indulging his passion for the drama, going so far as to write, in 1862, "[I]f I know anything of my own faculty, it is a dramatic one."[1] He turned to drama more frequently than he had done before, writing or co-writing a dozen plays over the last twenty years of his life. And he realized that he had ready material for his dramatic efforts, for he began in the mid-1860s to take the fiction that had made him his fortune and adapt it for the stage. In fact, between 1867 and 1877 Collins turned often to his fiction for the subjects of his plays, adapting during that time six of his novels for performance on the stage.[2]

The 1870s, which many Collins scholars mark as the period during which his powers as a novelist began to waver,[3] mark the high-

---

1   This passage may be found in a letter dated March 1862 in the Morris L. Parrish Collection at Princeton University Library. It may also be found quoted in Nuel Pharr Davis's biography of Collins, *The Life of Wilkie Collins* (Urbana, Illinois: Illinois UP, 1956, 79).

2   One of the novels, *Armadale*, became two separate dramas, *Armadale* (1870) and *Miss Gwilt* (1875).

3   Some scholars suggest that Dickens's death played some role in what they perceive to be Collins's decline as a novelist, arguing that without his primary mentor, he turned to another friend, the irascible novelist/playwright Charles Reade, for liter-

point of his secondary career as a playwright. In 1871 he adapted *The Woman in White* for the stage, oversaw its production, and basked in the glory of its nearly five-month run at the Olympic Theatre. *The Woman in White* played often to capacity houses, earning its author over fifty pounds a week through the fall and winter of 1871-72. Two years later, Collins enjoyed two more great successes as a dramatist, the first when his adaptation of his novel *Man and Wife* ran for twenty-three weeks at Squire Bancroft's Prince of Wales's Theatre (grossing over one hundred pounds a night during the run), and the second, later in 1873, when he recruited the famed actress Ada Cavendish for the title role in his dramatic version of his novel *The New Magdalen*. The drama played four months to packed houses at the Olympic before touring the provinces, after which it was performed throughout Europe and revived in England several times over the course of the next decade. In 1876, *Miss Gwilt*, Collins's dramatic version of his novel *Armadale*, ran successfully (again the title role was given to Ada Cavendish) for twelve weeks in London before being taken to New York, where it ran for less than a month to American audiences who apparently thought less of it than their English counterparts.[1] It is not surprising that these popular dramatic successes led Collins inevitably to construct a play from the plot of his most popular success, *The Moonstone*. But *The Moonstone*, which opened at the Olympic Theatre in the fall of 1877 to favourable reviews from several critics, slowed Collins's dramatic momentum, for it proved not to be the success that many had predicted. It ran for nine weeks before being withdrawn in favour of a Tom Taylor melodrama, *Henry Dunbar*.

Perhaps a bit daunted by the lukewarm public reception of the stage version of his most successful novel, Collins turned away from the theatre and returned to novel writing at the end of the decade. Between 1879 and 1883 he wrote five novels before assuming the role of playwright once again, and when he did, with his melodrama *Rank and Riches* in 1883, he suffered humiliation. The first-night audience

---

ary direction. Perhaps, then, Dickens's death steered Collins even more directly toward the role of playwright, for in many ways Reade influenced Collins to work with his novels as material for the stage.

1   Robert Ashley offers a fascinating look at Collins's relationship with the American theatre in his article "Wilkie Collins and the American Theater" *(Nineteenth-Century Fiction* 8, March 1954, 241-55).

jeered and hooted the actors off the stage of the Adelphi Theatre and nearly broke into a riot when G. W. Anson, one of the play's leads, shouted from the stage that they were a "lot of damned cads." Collins closed the play within the week. Two years after this disaster, in 1885, Collins wrote his final play, *The Evil Genius*, at the same time he was writing and publishing the novel of the same name. The dramatic version of *The Evil Genius* was performed only once, at the Vaudeville Theatre, for the purpose of securing copyright; after this single performance, and after various London and New York theatre managers refused to accept the play for production, Collins relinquished the role of dramatist and became content to remain quietly diligent as a novelist, writing and publishing fiction until his death in September 1889.

Those of Collins's dramatic adaptations that found their way onto the stage were usually well received by Victorian theatregoers, but they remained without exception less popular with his audiences than the novels that had inspired them. In 1879, reviewer for the *New York Times* wrote of Collins's dramas: "Transplanted from the book to the play, a story by Mr. Collins naturally loses its one strong claim to our admiration – the presentation through innumerable and closely-linked details of a coherent and absorbing plot."[1] Still, the plays speak to Collins's resolve as a playwright as well as to his skill as a craftsman, suggesting that he often wrote his fiction with an eye toward the stage, but most impressively giving the modern reader some inkling of his tremendous ability to distil from his often huge novels and their labyrinthine plots a condensed yet entertaining tale for the stage.

The adaptation of *The Moonstone* included in this volume affords readers an intriguing opportunity to speculate about Collins's motivations as a playwright as well as about his dual role as novelist/playwright. Readers familiar with the novel from which the play derived may also explore interesting comparisons concerning Collins's manipulations of plot and character as he manoeuvered his material from the pages of his novel to the boards of a London theatre. Indeed, those familiar with the novel may be surprised by its dramatic counterpart, for in many ways the play is quite distinct from its fictional

---

1   This passage appears in a review of a New York performance of *Miss Gwilt* in the summer of 1879 (*New York Times*, June 6, 1879, 5).

predecessor. In it Collins depended on his audience's knowledge of his novel's story, but rather than attempting to duplicate the novel, which would probably have been disastrous – if not impossible to accomplish – on the stage, he chose to manipulate his audience's expectations through bold departures from the formulas that had proven successful in the fiction, thus adding a tension to the drama that might not have existed otherwise.[1]

The most notable changes in the play resulted from Collins's recognition that his original story had been an elaborate mystery whose secrets had already been revealed to most who would make up his theatre audience. With that in mind, he concentrated on substituting expectation for surprise in the stage version of The Moonstone, which led to some quite striking and radical manipulations of chronology. In the stage version, instead of spreading the action over fifty years as he did in the novel, Collins chose to observe the dramatic unities, telescoping the story into one twenty-four hour period during which the action never strays from the main room of Rachel Verinder's summer house in Kent. Such a collapsing of time demanded that Collins substitute expectation for the mystery that unfolded over the course of a year in the novel, so he allows the play's audience to witness Franklin Blake steal the diamond at the end of the play's first act. Collins then uses the rest of the play to reconstruct the somnambulistic solution to the theft.

Some of the differences apparent in the play are less than satisfying to a modern reader familiar with the novel. For instance, many of the minor characters – and some of the major ones – that make up the rich fabric of the novel have disappeared from the play. In the stage

---

1　Upon the production of The Woman in White in 1871, fearing that his audience might not welcome some of the changes, he used the cover of the Olympic Theatre programme to explain some of his tactics. He wrote: "[The dramatist] has not hesitated, while preserving the original story in substance, materially to alter it in form. Scenes which he dismissed, when writing as a novelist, in a few lines, he has developed, when writing as a dramatist, into situations which more than once occupy an entire act. On the other hand, passages carefully elaborated in the book have been in some cases abridged and in others omitted altogether, as unsuitable to the play. This method of treatment has necessarily resulted in much that is entirely new in the invention of incident and in the development of character; the object contemplated, in either case, being the presentation of the story of the novel in a purely dramatic form."

adaptation of *The Moonstone*, the enigmatic Indian traveller Mr. Murthwaite, the pathetic Rosanna Spearman and her provocative companion, Limping Lucy Yolland, and even the novel's recondite puzzle solver, Ezra Jennings, are all absent. Of the characters who remain from the novel, certain changes are noteworthy. Franklin Blake and Rachel Verinder seem most like their counterparts in the novel, but the villain Godfrey Ablewhite has in the play become a somewhat watered-down version of himself. His simpering hypocrisy is overwrought, and his fate – there are no Indians to murder him in his bed – is rather disappointingly prosaic. The two characters who seem to have undergone the most noticeable modifications are Miss Drusilla Clack and Gabriel Betteredge. Clack, the cloying and comical fundamentalist Christian who plays a relatively small role in the action of the novel has become what one may safely call a major player in the drama. The reviewer for *The Spirit of the Times* pronounced her role "tediously elaborate."[1] She dominates several scenes in the play with her aggressive Christianity, but she serves primarily as a comic counterpart to Gabriel Betteredge, the Sam Weller-esque butler of the novel who has sadly become a mere buffoon in the play, a clown of sorts who teams with Clack to provide low humour in the form of slapstick, sight gags, comical asides, and overdone soliloquies. Their base humour, and it is unclear why Collins felt the need to include so much of it, wears a bit thin by the play's final scenes.

It is easy to say that the play suffers from such emendations, or that it seems somewhat austere when placed side by side with its luxurious fictional predecessor.[2] But such claims are hardly fair. Instead, one should judge the play on its own merits, for there are many, and resist the temptation to force a competition with what most have long recognized as Collins's masterpiece. Nuel Pharr Davis, one of Collins's early biographers, reinforces this admonition by noting that the

---

1   For the full text of this review, see Appendix G, 4.

2   Some early critics of the plays, *The Moonstone* in particular, said precisely that. The critic for the *Athenaeum* was most severe, writing of *The Moonstone*, "That a work so ambitious in aim, and so composite in nature, could not without some sacrifice of character and of story be brought within the compass of a play, was obvious from the first. There must surely, however, have been some means of obtaining the desired result at a sacrifice less damaging than that of the whole character and conception of the novel." (For the entire text of this and other reviews of the staged version of *The Moonstone*, see Appendix G, 1-4.)

dramatic version of *The Moonstone*, even with its "tight script," seems unsatisfying, but only when compared with the "perfection of the novel."[1]

Victorian Theatre and Drama in the 1860s and 1870s

Those who made their living acting on the stages of London's theatres in the 1870s comprised a relatively small and extremely close knit and hale community. Though theirs was not yet an entirely respectable or socially accepted profession, they were beginning to enjoy a prosperity that some of the older members of the circle had looked forward to from 1843, when the Theatres Act granted any properly licensed private theatres the right to perform original serious drama. For more than a century until 1843, the crown had strictly regulated London's theatres, creating a monopoly that allowed only the companies of the Theatres Royal – Covent Garden and Drury Lane – to perform "legitimate" drama; all other theatre companies, deemed "minor" by the crown, were limited to providing public entertainments in the form of musicals, song and dance performances, circus and equestrian shows, and the like. Though a few of the minor theatres rivaled the sanctioned theatres in terms of size and resplendence, most were incapacious, very uncomfortable, and ultimately unpleasant places to view a play.[2] Such legal restrictions and attendant problems served to stunt the growth of legitimate theatre in England at the time, though often company managers would exploit loopholes in the law in an effort to attract audiences. For instance, to skirt the Lord Chamberlain's[3] pronouncement that a minor theatre might produce a play only if during the performance at least six songs

---

1   This passage may be found in Davis's biography of Collins, *The Life of Wilkie Collins* (Urbana, Illinois: Illinois UP, 1956, 284).

2   Collins wrote often of the unpleasantnesses of the Victorian theatre experience. Three articles in particular – "Strike!," "Dramatic Grub Street. Explored in Two Letters," (both appearing in Dickens's *Household Words* in 1858) and "'The Use of Gas In Theatres' or 'The Air and the Audience: Considerations on the Atmospheric Influences of Theatres'" (written in 1885) – present long tirades against the horrid conditions through which London theatregoers suffered when seeing a play.

3   The Lord Chamberlain's office, the crown's official Examiner of Plays, licensed, regulated, and censored plays, which had to be submitted for scrutiny before they could be performed anywhere in Great Britain. The office remained intact until the Theatres Act of 1968 took theatrical matters out of its hands.

were sung, theatre owners took to creating what came to be known as burlettas, serious dramas into which were injected often ridiculously out-of-place musical numbers. Musical versions of Shakespeare's tragedies – unimaginable today – were not uncommon in London's minor theatres before 1843.

Perhaps used to working within the restrictions that had existed for so long, London's minor theatre companies were slow to change after being granted relative freedom[1] by the 1843 Act. No new theatres were constructed in London until the 1860s, and the existing companies remained content throughout the 1850s to continue catering to the lower classes with cheap amusements in the form of burlesques, burlettas, melodramas, and farces. Montrose Moses argued that the freeing of the theatres in 1843 merely led to a "wildcat competition ... which resulted in the cheapening of theatrical performances, and in the unthinking exploitation of the French drama."[2]

Change began to take place in the mid-1860s, when innovative theatre managers such as Squire and Marie Bancroft saw the need for and the opportunity to reform. Taking over the management of the old and run-down Queen's Theatre (popularly known as the "Dust Hole"), Marie Wilton – who married Squire Bancroft, an actor in her company, in 1867 – refurbished the interior and opened it in 1865 as the Prince of Wales's Theatre with the intention of producing only first-rate dramas by recognized playwrights. The Bancrofts teamed often with Tom Robertson, a skilled and popular dramatist of the period, and with him and a set company of actors, they turned their theatre into a success, often playing host to royalty and thus helping to legitimize theatre for all. The Bancrofts gambled successfully when they chose to abandon the long-standing custom of offering playgoers a mélange of short plays over the course of an exhausting (sometimes six-hour) evening in favour of one well-rehearsed, well-produced, well-acted drama. But perhaps their most radical innovation resulted from a keen eye for naturalistic detail – in terms of realistic sets, costumes, acting – that was new to the theatre world.

---

1   The companies could perform what they chose, but their choices were still subject to censorship by the office of the Lord Chamberlain.
2   This passage may be found in Moses Montrose's edition, *Representative British Dramas: Victorian and Modern* (Boston: Little, Brown, 1929, vii).

Shortly after they produced Robertson's hugely popular *Caste* in 1867, other companies and theatres began to imitate their formula, and London's theatre scene began flourish in earnest. Between 1866 and 1880 twelve new theatres,[1] each it seemed attempting to outdo the others in terms of splendour, came into existence in London alone, and with them came an increasingly intelligent and more demanding playgoing public, an increase in competition, better conditions and pay for members of the various companies, and, ultimately, better drama.

This is not to say, though, that the drama of the period shook the foundations of the halls of literature. In fact, works considered to be the best and most popular English plays of the 1860s – Dion Boucicault's domestic drama *The Colleen Bawn* (Royal Adelphi Theatre, 1860), Tom Taylor's melodrama *The Ticket-of-Leave Man* (Olympic Theatre, 1863), and T. W. Robertson's light comedy *Caste* (Prince of Wales's Theatre, 1867) – seem tedious to today's readers. They are replete with overwrought melodrama and often startling sensationalism,[2] suggesting that the playwrights of the sixties and seventies were still slave to the demands of the masses at the time and that the masses wanted entertainment more than edification. As a result, more often than not playwrights and theatre managers spent less time worrying about the content of a drama than about attracting theatregoers by dressing plays up with elaborate stage properties and spectacular machinery. J. O. Bailey writes of theatrical extravaganzas that employed "mists (made of gauze), agitated seas, waterfalls, raging fires (of gas, lycopodium, and blowers), snow storms, fire engines, and railroad engines,"[3] all of which indicated that theatre managers and producers were more than willing to spend much time and money to insure the notoriety that accompanied such ostentatiousness.

---

1 Among the theatres that opened during this period were the Gaiety, the Globe, the New Royal Amphitheatre, the Royal Aquarium, the Royal Opera Comique, the New Oxford, the New Queen's theatre, and St. George's Hall. Many existing theatres underwent remodeling during the same period, including the Olympic, where Collins's dramas were performed.

2 Sensation novels were the rage in 1860s Victorian England, and it should not be surprising to any student of the period that what was popular in fiction became popular in drama. In fact, many of the most popular sensation novels of the 1860s found their way onto the stage.

3 This passage appears in the introduction to J. O. Bailey's anthology *British Plays of the Nineteenth Century* (New York: Odyssey, 1976, 6).

W. S. Gilbert remarked sardonically that "every play which contains a house on fire, a sinking steamer, a railway accident, and a dance in a casino, will ... succeed in spite of itself. In point of fact, nothing could wreck such a piece but carefully written dialogue and strict attention to probability."[1] George Rowell argues that in light of these "Entertain us or be gone" edicts of the Victorian theatre audiences in the sixties and seventies, "it is perhaps more surprising that the playwrights achieved what they did than that their achievement was so slight."[2]

Though the changes initiated by the Bancrofts and other theatre managers caused an initial upheaval, they eventually served to stabilize the theatre scene. More often than not, the playhouses came to be under the control of actor/managers who secured loyal patrons by consistently offering them dramas performed by companies of actors who performed together in many different plays and for long stretches of time. Though theatre-jumping did exist, most actors established formal affiliations with single theatre companies to whom they remained loyal for several seasons. In fact, it is not uncommon to find on Victorian playbills and in theatre programmes of the period the names of actors and actresses who performed together for years on end. Often, also, playbills will reveal the names of husbands and wives, parents and children, brothers and sisters who teamed to act for the same companies for years. The Patemans, Robert and Bella, who appeared in Collins's *The Moonstone*, were one such husband and wife team who often appeared on stage at the Olympic, and Frederick Robson, Jr., who played Pesca in the 1871 stage version of *The Woman in White*, was the son of the famous comic actor who had single-handedly popularized the Olympic during the 1860s.[3]

---

1 This statement is quoted by J. O. Bailey in his introduction to the anthology *British Plays of the Nineteenth Century* (New York: Odyssey, 1976, 7).

2 This passage comes from Rowell's introduction to his edition titled *Nineteenth Century Plays* (Oxford: Oxford UP, 1972, viii).

3 In fact, many of the players who appeared in Collins's dramas were members of acting families. Ada Dyas, who played the dual-role of Laura Fairlie and Anne Catherick in *The Woman in White*, was the daughter of a well-known husband and wife team; Edmund Garden, who played Kyrle in *The Woman in White*, occasionally teamed with his son, who also achieved moderate success on the stage; Mrs. Irving, who played the Matron of the Asylum in *The Woman in White*, was the wife of actor

It was into this atmosphere of change that Collins entered with some exuberance in the 1870s, and his entrance seems to have been one welcomed by the acting world. He was befriended by all of the theatre managers with whom he worked, establishing a deep friendship with the Bancrofts when they successfully produced his *Man and Wife* at their Prince of Wales's Theatre in 1873, and working closely with W.H. Liston on the Olympic Theatre production of *The Woman in White* in 1871, as well as with Henry Neville on the production of *The Moonstone* at the same venue in 1877. Collins also seemed to have an easy ability to work well with the actors to whom he entrusted his plays. Wybert Reeve, who played Walter Hartright (and later Count Fosco) in the 1871 performance of *The Woman in White*, became one of Collins's closest friends in his later years, and it is Reeve to whom we are indebted for what seems to be the only written account of the behind-the-scenes preparations for the production of the play. His recollections provide some interesting insights into Collins's character, as well as some intriguing information about the play, which Reeve pronounced "a decided success," and its players:

> The rehearsals of the play were tiresome and very annoying – from ten o'clock in the morning until five o'clock in the afternoon, sometimes from six or seven o'clock in the evening to one and two o'clock in the morning. Endless arguments arose about crossing the stage, the position of the several characters, of a chair, a sofa, or a table, chiefly attributed to the indecision of Mr. George Vining, who was playing 'Fosco' and arranging the production of the play. Wilkie Collins attended often, and looked through it all 'perplexed in the extreme;' but he was gentlemanly, patient, and good-tempered, always ready with a smile if a chance offered itself, or a peaceful word kindly sug-

---

Joseph Irving and mother of actress Ethel Irving; John Billington, who played Percival Glyde, often appeared beside his wife on London stages; Mrs. Viner, who played Marian Halcombe, was married twice, each time to a well-known actor; George Vining, Collins's first Count Fosco, was a third-generation London actor; and Henry Neville, who played the lead in *The Moonstone*, was also from a family of actors.

gesting when a point was to be gained. I marvelled at him, for authors as a rule are naturally the reverse of patient when attending rehearsals of piece they have written.[1]

Such kind words serve to remind us of Collins's conscientious and quiet enthusiasm for drama, the theatre, and acting, and of his devotion to that which he considered most important to him, his written work. That work reminds us also of Collins's skills as a conscientious craftsman and artist.

The Olympic Theatre[2]

The Olympic Theatre, in which *The Moonstone* was first performed, stood at 6-10 Wych Street, Strand, just off Drury Lane. The original structure, under the ownership/management of Philip Astley (1742-1814),[3] opened on September 18, 1806 as the Olympic Pavilion and was home primarily to circus acts and equestrian performances. Astley, who steadily lost money with the theatre, sold it to the flamboyant entrepreneur Robert Elliston (1774-1831) in 1813. Elliston, attempting to make his new theatre a London showpiece capable of competing for patrons with the patent theatres, Drury Lane and Covent Garden, re-named the building the Olympic Theatre, re-modeled in 1813, and installed gas in 1815, making the Olympic among the first theatres in London to have such lighting.[4] The theatre during this

---

1 This passage appears in Wybert Reeve's "Recollections of Wilkie Collins" (*Chambers's Journal*, Volume IX, June 1906, 458). Reeve devotes an entire chapter of his 1895 reminiscence *From Life* to recollections of his friendship with Collins.
2 Perhaps the best accounts of the life of the Olympic Theatre appear in Erroll Sherson's astonishingly detailed work *London's Lost Theatres of the Nineteenth Century: With Notes on Plays and Players Seen There* (London: John Lane, 1925); in H. Barton Baker's *History of the London Stage and Its Famous Players 1576-1903* (1904, reprinted New York: Benjamin Blom, 1969); and in Raymond Mander and Joe Mitchenson's *The Lost Theatres of London* (New York: Taplinger, 1968).
3 Astley was a horse-breaker/equestrian retired from the military, and it was this background that led him to combine equestrianism and clown/tumbling acts at his theatres in Dublin and London.
4 Gas had only been available for two or three years, since the London Gaslight and Coke Company incorporated in 1812.

time was usually home to a variety of farces, burlettas, burlesques, and melodramas, and it immediately turned a nice profit for its owner, who refurbished the interior in 1818.[1] Elliston's success with the Olympic allowed him to buy the lesseeship of Drury Lane Theatre in 1819, after which he leased the Olympic to a number of different managers until mid-1826, when he sold the theatre to John Scott, then the owner of the Adelphi Theatre.

Madame Eliza Vestris (1797-1856) leased the Olympic from Scott in 1830 and ran the theatre quite successfully for the next nine years. She quickly established a reputation for presenting genteel and socially acceptable light entertainment. Her company, unrivalled as a comic troupe, included James Robinson Planché (1797-1880), John Liston (1776-1846), the Keeleys (Mary Ann, 1806-99, and Robert, 1793-1869) and Vestris's husband, Charles James Mathews (1803-78). When Vestris left to join the Covent Garden company in 1839, she seems to have taken many of her theatre's patrons with her, for the Olympic quickly lost its fashionable audience and sank into relative obscurity until it burned to the ground on March 29, 1849. The fire, according to *The Illustrated London News* account, "resulted in the entire demolition of the Olympic Theatre, and the partial destruction of upwards of a dozen other buildings." The report claims that the blaze had begun in the late afternoon well before the theatre opened for the evening performances, and had been "occasioned by the carelessness of a boy in lighting the gas at the first wing. The lamps at that time being turned towards the stage, and the curtain at the same time being withdrawn, and the overhanging lamps, the curtain took fire, and instantly communicated it to the wing."[2]

Despite the total destruction, the structure was quickly rebuilt, with an expanded auditorium that held nearly two thousand, and the theatre re-opened on Boxing Day 1849. Its interior, much like a modern theatre's, resembled nearly every other theatre in London at the time with its auditorium horseshoe-shaped and its stage framed

---

1   The first fifteen years established for the theatre a reputation it would have throughout its existence, as a playhouse that provided theatregoers with light entertainment – farces, burlettas, burlesques, melodramas.

2   From *The Illustrated London News* account of the blaze, (March 31, 1849, 216).

by the proscenium arch and boxed by canvas flats. Trouble arose again within a few months, though, when the Olympic's new manager, Walter Watts, was found to have financed the reconstruction with part of the nearly £80,000 he had embezzled from the Globe Insurance Company. In July 1850 Watts committed suicide in his jail cell rather than face transportation, and the Olympic closed its doors again for several months before opening for a short season under the management of George Bolton (1825-68).

Bolton's stint as manager lasted less than a year; in fact, between 1851 and 1869, the Olympic was home for seven different managers.[1] During this period, managers William Farren (1825-1908) and Alfred Wigan (1818-78) introduced and cultivated the talents of Frederick Robson, whose comic genius made him the theatre's star attraction for ten years until his death in 1864. It was with Robson that the Olympic re-gained its reputation as a place for popular light comedies and burlesques. Along with its reputation, it regained its audience. In 1868 Wigan also oversaw extensive interior alterations and improvements that reduced the theatre's seating capacity from somewhere near two thousand to just under nine hundred.[2]

William Henry Liston (1830-76) and his wife, Maria (1834-79), who managed the theatre between 1869 and 1872, were in charge when Collins brought *The Woman in White* to the Olympic stage, where it ran, during the fall and winter of 1871-72, for nineteen weeks (October 9-February 24) before taking to the provincial the-

---

1 After Bolton resigned as manager, William Farren, Alfred Wigan, Frederick Robson, William Emden, Horace Wigan, Benjamin Webster, and William Henry Liston managed the theatre, the last named overseeing the production of *The Woman in White*.

2 The renovated auditorium held 889 patrons: 136 in stalls, 161 in the pit, 209 in the dress and upper circles, 335 in the amphitheatre and gallery, and 48 in the boxes. From 1849 until 1869, the theatre held upwards of two thousand customers, 38 in the stalls, 800 to 850 in the pit, about 200 in the boxes, and 700 to 750 in the gallery. A final renovation, a complete reconstruction, in 1890 brought the capacity back up to near three thousand.

The prices for admission to the theatre for the 1877 showing of *The Moonstone* were as follows: Stalls, 7s. 6d.; Dress Circle, 5s.; Boxes (with Bonnets), 4s. Pit, 2s.; Amphitheatre, 1s. 6d.; Gallery, 1s.; Private Boxes, one to three guineas. Patrons had the option of securing tickets either at the theatre itself or at any of London's private circulating libraries.

atres for a run of over five hundred nights. Famed actress Ada Cavendish (1847-95), who would in 1873 receive great acclaim for her portrayal of Mercy Merrick in Collins's dramatic version of *The New Magdalen*, replaced the Listons in December 1872 and managed the theatre for a single season before being replaced by Henry G. Neville, an actor/manager/producer who provided some stability for the Olympic by remaining in charge for the next six years. It was under Neville's management that Collins produced *The Moonstone* in late 1877 (September 17- November 17). After Neville retired from management, the Olympic once again found itself home to a string of short-term managers,[1] among the last of whom was Wilson Barrett (1846-1904), who completely rebuilt the theatre in 1890 to accommodate nearly three thousand patrons. Barrett's venture was unsuccessful, though, and he gave up tenancy in 1891, after which the theatre saw several more one-season managers until it closed, after the ninety-performance run of the bizarre *A Trip to Midget Town*, whose castmembers were all midgets, in November 1897. The Olympic stood derelict thereafter until it its demolition in 1904, along with the nearby Globe, Gaiety, and Opera Comique Theatres, to make way for the widening of the Strand.

A Note on the Text of the Dramatic Version of *The Moonstone*:

The text of this play comes from an edition that Collins had printed privately for his own use and convenience by the Dickens and Evans printing house, run by the son of Charles Dickens, who became a partner, after a fashion, with John Evans's publishing firm by marrying his daughter, Bessie. Collins entered the play at Stationers' Hall to secure copyrights, though the copyright system at the time did little if anything to protect the author. Letters written by Collins suggest that this version of the play was printed before the theatre productions

---

1   These managers included, among others Fanny Josephs, Charles Baker, Mrs. Anna Georgian Harriet Conover, Grace Hawthorne, Agnes Hewitt, Charles Wilmot, Wilson Barrett, Charlotte Wilmot, and Theodore Rosenfeld. In the mid-1880s, when Conover, Hawthorne, and Hewitt managed the Olympic, it came to be called a "Woman's Theatre."

took place, and there is evidence that the texts for the stage play differed slightly from the texts which appears here.

Acts II and III of *The Moonstone*, along with Henry Neville's prompt copy, are held at Harvard University's Berg Library. A transcript of the play, revised by Collins, is held at the British Library.

THE

MOONSTONE:

A Dramatic Story, in Three Acts.[1]

ALTERED FROM THE NOVEL FOR PERFORMANCE ON
THE STAGE.

BY

WILKIE COLLINS.

[*This Play is not published. It is privately printed for the
convenience of the Author.*]

CHARLES DICKENS & EVANS, CRYSTAL PALACE PRESS.[2]
1877

---

1 Victorian scripts often changed from performance to performance, depending on audience reaction or written critical reception. Though the present version of the play is divided into three acts, the original performance, according to the programme, contained four acts: Act I, The Loss: Rachel Doubts Him; Act II, The Search: Rachel Screens Him; Act III, The Surprise: Rachel Hates Him; and Act IV, The Discovery: Rachel Loves Him.

2 The Charles Dickens mentioned here is the son of the novelist. In 1861 Charley (1837-96) had, against his father's wishes, married Elizabeth Matilda Moule (Bessie) Evans, daughter of Frederick Evans, of Bradbury and Evans Publishers, with whom the elder Dickens had had a falling out. Upon inheriting his father's weekly magazine *All the Year Round* in 1870, Charley incorporated it as part of the Dickens and Evans printing firm, where Collins had the play privately printed.

PERSONS OF THE DRAMA [The Original Cast of The Olympic
Theatre Performance of *The Moonstone*][1]

Miss Beaumont[2] (Miss Verinder's Maid, Penelope) [Of Miss Beaumont, nothing is known.]
Mr. Daniels (A Policeman in Plain Clothes) [Of Daniels, nothing is
known.]
Miss Kate Gerard (Penelope, Miss Clack) [Gerard was, according
to Sherson, "a very clever actress who had gained much experience in

---

1   Not a great deal is known about the players who acted in the original Olympic
Theatre performance of *The Moonstone*. The original play programmes offer the
names of the players, and most of the available biographical information has been
gathered from the following sources: the *Dictionary of National Biography*; William
Davenport Adams's *A Dictionary of the Drama: A Guide to the Plays, Playwrights, Players, and Playhouses of the United Kingdom and America from the Earliest Times to the Present* (London: Chatto & Windus, 1904); Wybert Reeve's "Recollections of Wilkie
Collins," (*Chambers's Journal*, June 1906, 458-61); Squire Bancroft's *The Bancrofts: Rec-
ollections of Sixty Years* (London: John Murray, 1909); Erroll Sherson's *London's Lost
Theatres of the Nineteenth Century* (London: John Lane, 1925); Henry Morley's *Jour-
nal of a London Playgoer* (1866, reprinted by Leceister UP, 1974); Frank Archer's *An
Actor's Notebook* (London: Stanley Paul, 1912); Charles E. Pascoe's *The Dramatic List:
A Record of the Performances of Living Actors and Actresses of the British Stage*, 2nd ed.
(London: David Bogue, 1889); Albert Douglass's *Memories of Mummers and the Old
Standard Theatre* (London: The "Era," 1924); and Felix Morris's *Reminiscences* (New
York: International Telegram, 1892).
    The play programs also provide interesting information about the original pro-
duction:
a. Each evening performance commenced at 8:30 p.m. following a presentation of
the J. B. Buckstone farce *Good for Nothing* (1851), which included several members of the cast of *The Moonstone*. There was at least one "Morning Performance," on Saturday, October 27, "in consequence of numerous inquiries, and
for the convenience of families residing at a distance." For this performance, the
theatre opened at eleven, and the play commenced at 2:30 p.m.;
b. The Olympic Theatre's "Refreshment Department" was under the management of one Mr. H. Harvey;
c. Mr. Henry Neville was the "Actual and Responsible Manager," while Mr.
George Coleman was "Acting Manager." Mr. Walter Hann, as he did six years
earlier for *The Woman in White*, prepared the scenery. The play's "Musical Con-
ductor" was Mr. Victor Buziau.
2   A program printed near the end of *The Moonstone's* nine-week run at the Olympic
marks a few changes in *dramatis personæ*: Miss Beaumont, who had played one of
Miss Verinder's maids, assumed the role of Penelope; Miss Gerard, who had played
the role of Penelope, assumed the role of Miss Clack; and Laura Seymour, who had
played Miss Clack, was removed (for reasons unknown) from the cast. Also, Johnston Forbes-Robertson replaced Henry Neville as Franklin Blake, supposedly to
"give Henry Neville a few day's rest."

the provinces as leading lady in *Caste*" and other T. W. Robertson comedies. Apparently, she retired from the stage early in life and married Henry Abbey, an American impresario. Sherson called her interpretation of Ophelia in 1880 at the Princess's Theatre "one of the best ever seen." At least one reviewer enjoyed her performance in *The Moonstone*, suggesting that she "made a sprightly and pleasant little lady's maid."]

Mr. Charles Harcourt (Godfrey Ablewhite) [Harcourt (1838-80), whose real name was Charles Parker Hillier, was described by Sherson as "a refined West End actor." He first appeared on stage in London in 1863 and for the next seventeen years played such roles as Robert Audley in a dramatic version of M.E. Braddon's *Lady Audley's Secret*, Frank Rochdale in George Colman's *John Bull*, Captain Absolute in R.B. Sheridan's *The Rivals*, and Mercutio in *Romeo and Juliet*. He is described in the *Dictionary of National Biography* as having been "an able, vigorous, and conscientious actor." He died in October 1880, ten days after suffering a fall while rehearsing for the role of Horatio at the Haymarket Theatre. His performance as Godfrey Ablewhite drew little attention from audiences and critics alike.]

Mr. Heathcote (Andrew)[Of Heathcote, nothing is known.]

Mr. W.J. Hill (Gabriel Betteredge) [Though not much is known about Hill (1834-88), whose real name was William Hill Jones, he seems to have had a reputation as a comedic actor (a reviewer for the American weekly *The Spirit of the Times* called him a "comedian of great intelligence") who enjoyed roles in many farces. He played the role of Dixon in T. W. Robertson's *Caste* at the Prince of Wales's Theatre in 1867. Of his performance in *The Moonstone*, Sherson called him "an excellent doddering Betteredge," and the reviewer for *The Times* claimed he was "very good."]

Miss MacMahon (Miss Verinder's Maid) [Of MacMahon, nothing is known.]

Miss McGill (Miss Verinder's Maid) [Of McGill, nothing is known.]

Mr. Henry Garstide Neville (Franklin Blake) [Neville (1836-1910), born into an acting family, was the forty-one year old manager of the Olympic Theatre when he agreed to Collins's request that he play Franklin Blake in *The Moonstone*. He had first acted at the

Olympic in 1861, had managed there since 1873, and would remain there until he retired from management altogether in 1879. Neville was an esteemed mainstay on the London stage for nearly fifty years, though according to Sherson, his "best days ... were ... in the sixties and seventies." Frank Archer, who called him "all that was pleasant and agreeable," maintained that he "was one of the few actors of romantic and chivalric parts in melodrama that London could boast of." Neville was trusted by Collins and worked with him in other of Wilkie's dramas, performing as Richard Wardour in the 1866 Olympic Theatre presentation of *The Frozen Deep* and as Vendale in the 1867 Adelphi Theatre production of *No Thoroughfare*. Of his role as Franklin Blake, the critics agreed that he played the part with "judgment and force," that he "was, as he always is, manly and effective," though the reviewer for *The Times* tempered his praise, writing, "Neville ... plays his part very much better than most we have seen him in of late." For reasons that are not clear today, Neville gave up his role as Franklin Blake to Johnston Forbes-Robertson for a least some of *The Moonstone*'s final performances at the Olympic Theatre.]

Miss Bella Pateman (Rachel Verinder) [Bella Pateman (1843-1908), Robert Pateman's wife, enjoyed a long run on the London stage. She also seemed to enjoy acting with many of the same people through much of her career. After honing her skills as an actress in provincial theatres and in the United States, she made her London stage debut at the Olympic Theatre in an 1876 production of Tom Taylor's *Lady Clancarty*, where she played opposite Henry Neville (who played Franklin Blake to her Rachel Verinder in the 1877 production of *The Moonstone*). She played opposite Neville once again in the 1889 Princess's Theatre production of Pettit and Sims's *Master and Man*. Albert Douglass suggested that he had "never seen an actress who could equal Miss Pateman's performance of Lady Isabel in *East Lynne*." Of her role in *The Moonstone*, one critic claimed that she showed "much force and breadth of style" in the role of Rachel Verinder, while another paid her a rather back-handed compliment by suggesting that her acting was "by many degrees the best she has as yet shown" but that it was "still ... disfigured by ... affectations of voice and gesture." The same reviewers criticized her for what one called her "grotesque affectation in dress."]

Mr. Robert Pateman (Mr. Candy) [Pateman (1843-1924), Bella Pateman's husband, was another journeyman of the London stage, playing for many years in the acting company at the Olympic Theatre, where, in 1876, he made his début, a month before his wife, as Carrigue in *The Duke's Device*. American actor Felix Morris proclaimed Pateman "an excellent comedian and character actor," while Sherson described him as a "forcible actor of grotesque and semitragic parts, something in the style of Robson but far behind him in power and genius." Albert Douglass claimed, "I never remember an actor working harder to obtain the success he never failed to achieve." Of his role as Mr. Candy, *The Times* critic suggested he "showed an agreeable diminution of a somewhat exuberant style."]

Mr. Johnston Forbes-Robertson (Franklin Blake) [Forbes-Robertson (1853-1937), knighted in 1913, first appeared on the London stage in 1874, which marked the beginning a nearly forty-year acting career. He appeared as Hamlet in 1897 and was judged by many to be the finest player of that part of his generation. He seems to have stood in for Henry Neville for a few performances near the end of *The Moonstone*'s 1877 run at the Olympic, for scribbled by someone onto a copy of an extant programme is the following explanation of his replacement of Henry Neville as Franklin Blake: "Played to give Henry Neville a rest for a few days." He is not mentioned by the play's reviewers.]

Mrs. Laura Seymour (Miss Clack) [Seymour (née Allison, 1820-1879) was a close friend of Collins and the housekeeper for the well-known novelist/playwright Charles Reade. She was a part of the London theatre scene from the 1830s until her death, co-managing the St. James's Theatre, along with Reade, during the 1854 season. Her role as Miss Clack was to be her last appearance on the stage, for she fell ill in the winter of 1877 with cancer and died just over a year later. The reviewer for *The Times* seemed not to like the part she played but was careful to add that Seymour was not at fault, that she had been "burdened with an ungrateful part, and one, too, that is from the first seen to be an unnecessary part." For reasons that are unclear today, perhaps because of her illness, perhaps because of tepid reviews, she was replaced as Miss Clack by Kate Gerard near the end of *The Moonstone*'s run.]

Mr. Thomas Swinbourne (Sergeant Cuff) [Swinbourne, who died in 1895, was in the 1860s a member of the acting company that played at Drury Lane. Perhaps his most famous role was as Claudius (alongside Edwin Booth's Hamlet) at the Princess's Theatre production of *Hamlet* in 1880. His performance as Cuff seems to have been unremarkable, the reviewer for *The Times* going so far as to condemn it.]

SCENE: KENT[1]
PERIOD: THE PRESENT TIME[2]

The action of the drama extends over twenty-four hours, and passes entirely in the inner hall of MISS VERINDER's *country-house.[3] At the back of the hall is a long gallery, approached by a flight of stairs, and supposed to lead to the bed-chambers of the house. The stairs must be so built that persons can pass backwards and forwards behind them, in the part of the hall which is situated under the gallery. Two of the bedchamber doors, leading respectively into the rooms occupied by* FRANKLIN BLAKE *and* GODFREY ABLEWHITE, *are visible to the audience. The other rooms are supposed to be continued off the stage on the left. The entrances are three in number. One, under the gallery, at the back, supposed to lead to the staircase in the outer hall and to the house door. One on the left, at the front of the stage, supposed to lead to* RACHEL's *boudoir and bedroom. And one opposite, formed by a large window, which opens to the floor, and which is supposed to lead into a rose-garden. The fireplace is on the left, just above the door leading into* RACHEL's *room. The stage directions refer throughout to the right and left of the actors as they front the audience.*

---

1   Kent is a coastal county in southeast England. In the novel, of course, the Verinder estate was located on the Yorkshire coast in northern England.

2   The present, 1848-1850 in the novel, is now 1877. Since the play is less dependent on the Verinder family history than the novel, Collins could set it in "the present" without difficulty.

3   By telescoping the action into twenty-four hours at Rachel's country-house, Collins observes the dramatic unities of time, place, and action. He also offers himself the means to cut many of the complexities of the novel, complexities that he felt were simply too unwieldy for a dramatic version of his work.

THE FIRST ACT

At the rise of the curtain, the lamps hanging from the ceiling are lit in the hall. The time is between eight and nine o'clock in the evening. BETTEREDGE *is discovered arranging cold refreshments on a table at the back. He leaves the table and takes a telegram out of his pocket.*

Betteredge. There is one great misfortune in the lives of young ladies in general – they have nothing to do. As a natural consequence, their minds shift about like a weathercock; and every change in the wind blows a new botheration in the way of their unfortunate servants. (*He opens a telegram.*) Here is a proof of it! A week ago, my young mistress telegraphed to me as follows: (*He reads the telegram.*) "Miss Rachel Verinder, London, to Gabriel Betteredge, House Steward, Crowmarsh Hall, Kent. I have made up my mind to pass the rest of the year in town. Cover up the furniture, and set the painters at work." (*He speaks.*) Very good. I covered up the furniture, and I set the painters to work. (*He folds up the telegram, and produces another.*) An hour ago comes another telegram. "Miss Rachel Verinder," as before, "to Gabriel Betteredge," as before. "Uncover the furniture, and turn the painters out. I have made up my mind to pass the rest of the year in the country. Expect me by the seven-forty train from London. I shall bring Miss Clack, and my cousin, Mr. Godfrey Ablewhite. Send to Mr. Candy, and ask him to sup with us." (*He folds up the second telegram.*) Turn out the painters? All very well! Can I turn out the stink the painters have left behind them? There (*he points to an open space under the cabinet*) are their pots and brushes not cleared away yet. "Invite Mr. Candy?" Well, there's some sense in inviting *him*. He's the doctor at our town here – and he'll be nice and handy when the smell of the paint has given the whole party the colic. I've sent for Mr. Candy! (PENELOPE *hurries in excitedly by the hall door. She is smartly dressed, with gay cap ribbons.*) Here's a whirlwind in petticoats! What's wrong now, Penelope?[1]

---

1 At least one critic, writing for *The Athenaeum*, objected to what he saw to be Collins's "preposterous" overuse of some rather creaky soliloquizing for the sake of exposition. (See Appendix G, 3 for the full text of this review.)

Penelope (breathlessly). Oh, father, such news! A fly[1] has just driven up to the door – and who do you think has come in it? Mr. Franklin Blake!

Betteredge. Mr. Franklin Blake? I remember Master Franklin, the nicest boy that ever spun a top or broke a window. Nonsense, Penelope! It's too good to be true! (FRANKLIN's *voice is heard outside.*)

Franklin. Betteredge!

Betteredge. That's his voice, sure enough. This way, Mr. Franklin, this way! (FRANKLIN BLAKE *enters by the hall door.*)

Franklin. Dear old Betteredge, give me your hand! You don't look a day older since I borrowed seven and sixpence of you the last time I was home for the holidays –

Betteredge. Which seven and sixpence you never *have* paid me back, Master Franklin, and never *will*. Welcome home, sir, from foreign parts!

Franklin (noticing PENELOPE). Who's this? Not Penelope?

Penelope (simpering). I thought you didn't remember me, sir.

Franklin. Remember you! You promised to be a pretty girl when I remember you, and you have kept your promise. Virtue claims its own reward. (*He kisses her.*) Betteredge, I am devoured by anxiety. I left the Dover train at Tunbridge[2] on the chance that my cousin Rachel might be here. Have I made a mistake? Is she in London?

Betteredge. You have fallen on your legs, sir. Miss Rachel is coming here to-night.

Franklin. One more question, and my mind will be at ease again. Rachel isn't married yet, is she?

Penelope (answering before her father can speak). Oh no, sir.

Franklin. Do you think she is waiting for my return? I am much obliged to you, Penelope. You encourage me. (*He kisses her again.* BET-TEREDGE *shakes his head.*) Don't look sour, Betteredge. It's only a way I have of expressing my gratitude.

Betteredge. There's a limit to everything, sir. My girl has got as much of your gratitude as is good for her. Penelope, go and get Mr. Franklin Blake's room ready for him. (PENELOPE *curtsies to* FRANKLIN, *ascends*

---

1   See note 1 on page 141 of the novel.
2   Franklin, just back from Italy, has ridden the train from the port city of Dover to Tunbridge Wells, a town in the western part of the county of Kent.

the stairs to the gallery, and enters one of the bedrooms.) Your old room, sir – up in the gallery. What have they done with your luggage?

Franklin. One of the servants took my portmanteau. By-the-bye, has a foreign letter been received here, addressed to Rachel?

Betteredge. Yes, sir: only two days since.

Franklin. Did you forward it to London?

Betteredge. Miss Rachel has been veering about in her own mind, sir, betwixt staying in London and staying in the country. I was told to forward no letters until further orders. (*He opens a table drawer, takes out some letters waiting for* RACHEL, *and chooses one.*) Is this the letter you mean, sir?

Franklin (*looking at the post-mark*). That's it! – an official letter from the consul at Rome, informing Rachel of a legacy coming to her from foreign parts. (*He returns the letter to* BETTEREDGE.) A legacy of ten thousand pounds, Betteredge – and I've got it here in my pocket. (*He touches his breast-pocket.*)

Betteredge. Mercy preserve use! In bank-notes, sir?

Franklin (*producing a jeweller's box*). No; in this. The ten thousand pounds, Betteredge, is the estimated value of a prodigious diamond. (BETTEREDGE *holds up his hands in amazement.*) And the prodigious diamond is a legacy left to Rachel by her uncle the Colonel.

Betteredge (*in alarm*). Not the Moonstone?

Franklin. Yes, the Moonstone. (*He hands the box to* BETTEREDGE, *who receives it with marked aversion, and refuses to open it.*) Don't be afraid. It isn't an infernal machine – it won't blow your brains out.

Betteredge (*sternly*). This is no joking matter, Master Franklin. The wicked Colonel sent you on a wicked errand when he sent you here with his diamond. Is he really dead, sir?

Franklin. Dead and buried – at Rome. I was with him in his last moments. In my judgment, the worst thing you could say about him was that he was mad. What did he do, Betteredge, to be called "the wicked Colonel"?

Betteredge. Do? I shouldn't get through the catalogue of the Colonel's misdeeds if I was to talk till tomorrow. My late lady, Miss Rachel's mother, was (as you know) the Colonel's sister. She refused to see him or to speak to him. She held him, rightly, to be a disgrace to the family. He was as proud as Lucifer, and his sister wounded him in his one tender place. "You have publicly shut your door in my face," he wrote to her. "Sooner or later I'll be even with you for doing that." Here (*he holds up the box*) is the proof that he was as good as his word. He knew by his own bitter experience that the Moonstone carried a curse with it; and he has left it to Miss Rachel in revenge.[1]

Franklin. I wish *I* had offended the Colonel.

Betteredge. If you knew how he got this diamond, sir, you would wish nothing of the sort! It was in the Indian wars. The Moonstone was an ornament on one of their heathen images in those parts. The last place they defended against the English troops was their temple. The Colonel was the first of the storming party to get in. He killed the two priests who defended their idol, and he cut the diamond out of the wooden head of the image with his sword. "Loot" they call it in the army; *I* call it murder and robbery. And the curse of murder and robbery goes with the diamond. You are almost as fond of Miss Rachel, sir, as I am. While we have the chance, let's go out into the yard and chuck the Moonstone into the well!

Franklin. Stop a minute, Betteredge! Have you got ten thousand pounds anywhere about you?

Betteredge. I, Master Franklin!

Franklin. We can't afford the luxury of drowning the Moonstone. Say no more about it. It's Rachel's property. Give it back to me. (*He takes the box from* BETTEREDGE, *puts it back in his pocket, and looks round him.*) Ah! here's the great hall looking just as splendid as ever! Time that makes changes everywhere else makes no changes here. (*He notices an old cabinet placed near the foot of the gallery stairs.*) What have they been doing with this cabinet? It's shamefully neglected. It ought to be varnished.

Betteredge. It *is* to be varnished, sir. But Miss Rachel's sudden arrival has stopped the painters' work till further orders.

---

1   One of the complaints leveled at the dramatic version of *The Moonstone* was that it had very little of the mysterious charm of the novel. Here is a case in point. Betteredge and Franklin hint at some curse related to the diamond, but there is nothing like the mystique surrounding the stone and its Indian protectors that we find in the original. In fact, there are no Indians in the play. Ezra Jennings and Rosanna Spearman, two of the novel's most colourful figures, are also absent from the drama. Even the exotica of the smeared paint on the door (it becomes a rather prosaic varnish on a cabinet in the play) and Mr. Candy's laudanum (Franklin is upset by dinner and grog in the play) are missing.

Franklin (noticing the painters' utensils). I see! Here are their pots and brushes. What's this? (*He takes up a tin pot with a label on it.*)

Betteredge. Don't you touch those things, sir! I'll take them out of the way.

Franklin (stopping him). Wait a minute. (*He reads the label.*) "The original Dutch polish. Restores old furniture, and is warranted to dry in five hours." This *is* the varnish! Betteredge, I have nothing to do till Rachel comes; *I'll* varnish the cabinet. (*He pulls off his coat and chooses a brush.*)

Betteredge. Mercy on us, Master Franklin! You don't mean it, do you? Think of the wet varnish and the ladies' dresses, sir, when the company come.

Franklin. The varnish dries in five hours. (*He looks at the clock.*) It's nine o'clock now. By two in the morning the cabinet will be as dry as a bone. (*He begins to varnish.*) You talked of company coming here. Who does Rachel bring with her?

Betteredge. She brings Miss Clack, sir, for one.

Franklin (varnishing). What! my old enemy? She will never forgive me. I once called her a Rampant Spinster. Does Miss Clack still go about the world reforming everybody? And when she is particularly spiteful does she open her bag and say: "Permit me to offer you a tract"?

Betteredge (dryly). Come, come, Master Franklin! Do the lady justice. She has a pretty taste in wine. Likes her champagne dry – and plenty of it.

Franklin (varnishing). Who else is expected?

Betteredge. Your other cousin, sir, Mr. Godfrey Ablewhite.

Franklin (varnishing). Worse and worse! A professional philanthropist and a ladies' man, both in one! Officially attached to half the female Societies in London. Wherever there is a table with a council of ladies sitting round it, there is Mr. Treasurer Ablewhite keeping the accounts of the committee, and leading the dear creatures along the thorny ways of business hat in hand! (*He suddenly leaves off varnishing and looks round at* BETTEREDGE.) I say, Betteredge! has Godfrey Ablewhite any particular motive for coming here? You don't think he is after Rachel, do you?

Betteredge. He *has* been after her, sir, and he's just the man to try it again at the first opportunity. Don't be alarmed! Miss Rachel has said

"No" to him once, and now you're here she'll say "No" again.

Franklin (returning to his varnishing). Dear good girl, how I enjoy varnishing her cabinet! She wouldn't give me a definite answer, Betteredge, when I asked her to marry me before I left England. Do you think she has any serious objection to me?

Betteredge. You have been all your life in debts and difficulties, sir, and you take it as easy as if you had paid your way honestly from your birth upwards. Miss Rachel objects to that. In her way of thinking, a man who doesn't pay his creditors commits a dishonourable action. Be a little more careful in money matters, and Miss Rachel's objections to you will melt away like snow off a dyke. *(He starts.)* What's that I hear? Carriage wheels outside? *(The door bell rings.)* There's Miss Rachel! Leave it to me, Master Franklin, I'll tell her you're here! *(He goes out by the hall door.)*

Franklin (looking about him). Where's my coat? *(He hurriedly puts on his coat.)* Do I smell of varnish, I wonder? Is there time to get to my room and brush myself up? (RACHEL *enters by the hall door, followed by* MISS CLACK, *carrying her black bag of tracts, and by* GODFREY ABLEWHITE. MISS CLACK *looks about her at the different objects in the hall, with an over-acted appearance of humility and admiration.*)

Rachel (heartily). My dear Franklin! this is a pleasure I never hoped for. (FRANKLIN *advances as if to kiss her. After a momentary hesitation, she offers him her cheek.*) Oh, yes – you are my cousin – you may kiss me. Turn to the light, Franklin. Do you know that you are not looking at all well? What is the matter with you?

Franklin. I have given up smoking, Rachel, and I have not had a good night's rest since I left off my cigars.

Rachel. Why have you given up smoking?

Franklin (whispering). You dislike tobacco. I have given up smoking to please you. (GODFREY *jealously approaches, as if to interrupt them, and speaks aside with* RACHEL. *She listens to him for a moment, and then turns away to take off her hat and cloak.* FRANKLIN *notices* GODFREY'S *jealousy when he approaches* RACHEL, *and speaks aside*).[1] Jealous of my whispering to Rachel! Mercenary humbug! *(He addresses* GODFREY *coldly.)* How do you do, Godfrey?)

---

1   This is the first of dozens of rather intrusive asides employed by Collins primarily for exposition and humour. They serve to illustrate some of the difficulties he had preparing what had been a serial mystery for the stage.

Godfrey (with excessive cordiality). Delighted to see you again, dear Franklin! *(Aside.)* He has designs on Rachel! Fortune-hunting vagabond!

Rachel (returning). Where is Miss Clack? *(Aside to* FRANKLIN*).* I am obliged to have a chaperon, and I have taken poor Miss Clack. Do be civil to her! *(She looks round, and discovers* MISS CLACK*.)* My dear Drusilla! what are you looking at so very attentively?

Miss Clack (mournfully).[1] I am renewing my acquaintance, Rachel, with the objects of beauty in this luxurious house. Wealth always has a dazzling effect on me at first. I shall soon get used to it, dear. You will excuse a poor relation, I am sure. *(She notices* FRANKLIN, *and speaks to him with spiteful humility.)* Mr. Franklin Blake, I believe? I beg your pardon, sir, for not having spoken to you before.

Franklin. Miss Clack, your politeness overwhelms me. How many tracts have you scattered, and how many obdurate persons have you converted, since I saw you last?

Miss Clack (innocently). Am I expected to laugh? Dearest Rachel, is this what the world calls wit? It is quite thrown away, Mr. Blake, on poor me. You don't offend me, sir, by sneering at my humble efforts in the good cause. (FRANKLIN *looks at* RACHEL *with a smile.* MISS CLACK *observes him.)* I can even put up with your openly disbelieving what I say. *(She turns to* GODFREY*.)* Dear Mr. Godfrey?

Godfrey. Dear Miss Clack!

Miss Clack. You are our charitable hero. Will *you* tell Mr. Blake that it is quite useless to attempt to offend us?

Godfrey (returning the compliment). You are our Dorcas[2] of modern

---

1   Miss Clack's part in this drama seems to be overdone; she exists in the play as a far more important figure than she is in the novel. The critic for *The Times* identified the likeliest cause of her expanded role when he wrote that Clack's "undue prominence is perhaps to be explained by the necessity Mr. Collins may have felt himself to be under of providing a part for Mrs. Seymour." See Appendix G, 1 for the entire text of this review. Laura Seymour, the house-mate of novelist Charles Reade since 1856, was a close friend of Collins, who might have felt obliged to give her more prominence than the role called for. This was to be Seymour's last role, for shortly after the play closed, she fell ill with the cancer that killed her two years later in September 1879.

2   Dorcas was a Christian disciple mentioned in the following passage from the New Testament: "Now there was at Joppa a certain disciple named Tabitha, which by interpretation is called Dorcas: this woman was full of good works and almsdeeds which she did" (Acts 9:36). Dorcas Societies were women's auxiliary groups, often sponsored by a church, that provided clothes for the poor.

times! Will Mr. Blake believe me, if he won't believe Dorcas? (MISS CLACK *opens her bag of tracts.*)

Franklin (eyeing the bag). I'll do anything to be agreeable to Dorcas and the hero – I'll even accept a tract!

Miss Clack (changing her mind). We will wait, Mr. Blake, till you are in a fitter frame of mind. Dear Rachel has remarked on the state of your health. On the first occasion when sickness lays you low – if the place is within an easy railway fare of my residence at the time – you will find me at your bedside with a choice of tracts. (*With sudden spitefulness.*) And may those tracts sound like a blast of trumpets in your obdurate ears!

Rachel (interfering). Come, come! there is a time for everything. It's supper-time now. Drusilla, take off your travelling-wraps, and be comfortable after your journey.

Miss Clack. My room is upstairs, Rachel, is it not?

Rachel. Nonsense! You needn't go all the way upstairs to take off your hat and cloak. Come into my room here.

Miss Clack. Thank you, dearest. Always so thoughtful in temporal matters! Well, well; the higher thoughtfulness will follow. (*She puts her hand to her head.*) My poor head!

Rachel. Have you still got the headache? Try my smelling-bottle.

Miss Clack. Thank you, dear. Oh, how nice! What might be the value of *this* object of luxury, Rachel?

Rachel (impatiently). Five shillings – ten shillings. How should I know?

Miss Clack (amazed). Ten shillings! (*She mentally calculates on her fingers.*) Forty basins of charitable soup – twelve basketfuls of missionary buns – all locked up in this futile little thing! (*She shows it to* GODFREY *with a groan.*) Oh, Mr. Godfrey!

Godfrey. Oh, Miss Clack!

Miss Clack. Take it back, Rachel. Your smelling-bottle saddens me. After you, dear – after you.

Franklin. Don't be long, Rachel. (RACHEL *and* MISS CLACK *go out on the left.*)

Godfrey. You don't like being left, Franklin, in such poor company as I am?

Franklin. Nonsense, Godfrey! How are you getting on with your ladies and their charities – maternal societies for doctoring poor women; Magdalen societies for rescuing poor women; strong-minded societies for putting poor women into poor men's places, and leaving the men to shift for themselves – are they all flourishing under your sympathetic superintendence?

Godfrey (aside). He is as insolent as ever! (*to* FRANKLIN.) Thank you for your kind inquiries, Franklin. You speak flippantly, but I daresay you mean well. And how are *you* prospering?

Franklin. Prospering! I don't know which way to turn next for want of money. I say, Godfrey! Is your father still head partner at the bank in the neighbouring town here?

Godfrey. Certainly! I shall go to Frizinghall tomorrow to see my father.

Franklin. Ah, yes! Frizinghall – that's the name of the town. I have been so long away I had almost forgotten it. Do me a service, Godfrey – ask your father to lend me two hundred pounds.

Godfrey. Oh, Franklin!

Franklin. Nobody else will lend me a farthing. My credit is at an end – even with old Luker himself.

Godfrey (innocently). Who is Mr. Luker?

Franklin. Enchanting innocence! Did you really never hear of the famous London money-lender – Luker, of Clement's Inn?[1] (GODFREY *shakes his head.*) Such is fame! Look here, Godfrey, if I write to your father, will you take the letter?

Godfrey. Quite useless, Franklin. I once asked my dear father for a loan of five pounds. He buttoned up his pockets, and he said: "Do as I did at your age – go and earn it!"

Franklin. I should have answered that. I should have said: "Do as *I* do at *my* age – come and spend it!" Forgive me for boring you with my affairs. I daresay you're worried enough about money matters yourself.

Godfrey (surprised). What do you mean?

Franklin. As treasurer to those charitable societies of yours, do you never have hard work of it to make both ends meet?

Godfrey (relieved). Ah! yes, yes! Quite true, Franklin – quite true! (RACHEL *appears at the door on the left; neither* FRANKLIN *nor* GODFREY *observes her.*)

---

1 One of the Inns of Chancery, Clement's Inn was, by the mid-nineteenth century, a place inhabited by London's solicitors and attorneys.

Franklin (continuing). Speaking generally, my debts don't trouble me the least in the world. But there's one of my creditors who won't be pacified – a little hunchbacked Frenchman who keeps a restaurant in Paris. (*He goes on more and more carelessly – laughing as he speaks.*) His wife is in bed, and his child has got the whooping-cough, and little crook-back wants his money. I only borrowed two hundred pounds of him, and he writes furious letters to me, and calls me a thief!

Rachel (advancing). Godfrey!

Franklin (speaking aside). She has heard me!

Godfrey (approaching her). Yes, dear Rachel?

Rachel. Leave me with Franklin for five minutes. (FRANKLIN *draws back, and looks guiltily at* RACHEL.)

Godfrey (aside). In five minutes he may make her an offer! I'll put an obstacle in his way. (*He whispers to Rachel.*) One word in private, dear Rachel. Beware of Franklin if he tries to borrow money of you. His debts have utterly degraded him. (*He goes out by the hall door.*)

Rachel (to FRANKLIN *very earnestly).* Franklin, I heard what you said to Godfrey a moment since. Have you no principle? Have you no feeling?

Franklin. My dear Rachel – !

Rachel. A poor struggling man who has trusted you – and who finds in the hour of his distress that your promise to pay him back his money is a mockery and a delusion! And you speak of it lightly! In your place, I would have sold the watch out of my pocket, and the rings off my fingers, rather than be dishonoured as you are dishonoured now.

Franklin. Strong language, Rachel!

Rachel. I speak strongly, because I feel strongly. I have a true interest in you – I hope great things from you in the future. If you begin with this shocking carelessness about obligations which you have bound yourself to respect, how will you end? Who can say to what degradation you may not descend the next time you want money, and the next, and the next?

Franklin. May I say a word in my own defence?

Rachel. No. You may occupy your time in doing better than that. This poor man with his sick wife and child – I can't bear to think of it! Wait, Franklin. I have something more to say to you. Wait! (*She goes to the writing-table and writes a cheque.* FRANKLIN *speaks to himself.*)

Franklin (aside). She feels a "true interest in me!" Is that interest strong enough to stand my friend, if I own that I love her — if I ask her to be my wife? She is prettier than ever; and I am fonder of her than ever; and she refused Godfrey the last time he asked her. I think I'll risk it!

Rachel (rising, and giving FRANKLIN *the cheque).* Send that to my banker's, with your creditor's address in Paris. *I* am your creditor now. (FRANKLIN *attempts to speak.*) No! I want no thanks. I want amendment; I want you — oh, Franklin, I do really want you to be worthy of yourself!

Franklin (earnestly). It is in your power, Rachel, to make me all that you could wish.

Rachel (relenting). I don't understand you.

Franklin. I have loved you for years. (RACHEL *tries to interrupt him.*) Absence has only made you dearer to me than ever. Grant me the one aspiration of my life! I will answer for living worthily, if I may only live to be worthy of *you.*

Rachel (aside). He is making love to me! (*To* FRANKLIN). How dare you make love to me, when I am so angry with you?

Franklin (taking her hand). I have travelled night and day; I have returned to England only to see *you.* Don't I deserve a little indulgence? Am I not worthy of one kind look?

Rachel (aside). What a contemptible creature I am! Why don't I tell him to leave the room? (*To* FRANKLIN.) Have you got my hand?

Franklin. Yes, I've got your hand.

Rachel. Let go of it!

Franklin (kissing her hand). Say you forgive me.

Rachel (yielding). Oh, where is Miss Clack? where is Miss Clack?

Franklin. I am truly penitent, I am honestly desirous of being worthy of you. Don't cast me off! Say: "Franklin, you may hope."

Rachel. Will you let me go, if I do?

Franklin (still holding her hand). Yes, I will even make that sacrifice.

Rachel (yielding). "Franklin, you may hope."

Franklin (as before). May I hope that you love me?

Rachel (in a whisper). Yes!

Franklin. My darling Rachel. (*He is on the point of taking her into his arms. The door on the left opens.* MISS CLACK *appears.*) The devil take her!

Miss Clack. Oh, dear! dear! Have I come in at the wrong time?

Shall I go back again, Rachel, and wait till you ring?

Rachel. Drusilla, you are perfectly insufferable! Don't stand there talking nonsense. Come and have some supper. (GODFREY *enters by the hall door.*)

Godfrey. I am not in the way, Rachel, am I?

Rachel. Good heavens! here is another modest person who is afraid of disturbing me! Make yourself of some use, Godfrey; open that bottle of wine. Betteredge seems to have deserted us. Franklin, ring the bell. (FRANKLIN *rings.* GODFREY *and* RACHEL *busy themselves at the table.* MISS CLACK *approaches* FRANKLIN *with an expression of extreme penitence.*)

Miss Clack. I am *so* sorry. I came in at the wrong time. It must be *so* unpleasant to be caught in a ridiculous position, with your arms like this. (*She imitates* FRANKLIN's *attempt to embrace* RACHEL. FRANKLIN *turns away angrily, and withdraws to the back, jealously watching* GODFREY *and* RACHEL *at the supper-table.* BETTEREDGE *enters by the hall door, answering the bell.*)

Rachel (*to* BETTEREDGE). Where is Mr. Candy? I told you to invite him to sup with us.

Betteredge. The doctor has just arrived, miss. (*He draws back from the hall door, and announces the doctor's name as he enters.*) Mr. Candy! (*As* MR. CANDY *approaches* RACHEL, ANDREW *enters by the hall door with a bottle of champagne.* BETTEREDGE *takes it from him, and points to the painters' utensils under the cabinet.* ANDREW *collects them and carries them out.* BETTEREDGE *opens the bottle of champagne, takes a glass, and approaches* MISS CLACK, *while* RACHEL *and* MR. CANDY *are speaking.*)

Rachel (*advancing to shake hands with him*). I am glad to see you, Mr. Candy. Have you any news for me? How are you getting on in the neighbourhood?

Mr. Candy. Much as usual, Miss Rachel. The population employs the doctor freely, and only hesitates when it comes to the questions of paying him. (*He notices* GODFREY.) Mr. Godfrey Ablewhite! (MR. CANDY *and* GODFREY *shake hands cordially. They remain in conversation with* RACHEL.)

Betteredge (*to* MISS CLACK, *speaking after* MR. CANDY). I think you like it dry, miss? (*Aside, looking at the bottle in his hand.*) And plenty of it!

Miss Clack (*modestly*). I am so little used to luxuries, Mr. Betteredge. Do you really think it will do me good?

Betteredge (confidentially). That is my deliberate opinion, miss. (*He fills the glass.* MISS CLACK *receives it with humble gratitude, takes a sip, discovers that it is really dry, and finishes the glass at a draught.* GODFREY, *leaving* MR. CANDY *and* RACHEL, *approaches* BETTEREDGE *and takes the bottle from him.* BETTEREDGE *relieves* MISS CLACK *of her empty glass.*)

Godfrey. We will help ourselves, my good Betteredge. Don't you think you had better get another bottle?

Betteredge (looking at MISS CLACK's *empty glass).* Yes, sir, I think I had. (*He goes out by the hall door.* GODFREY *escorts* MISS CLACK *to the supper-table, where they join* RACHEL. MR. CANDY *discovers* FRANKLIN *and greets him cordially.*)

Mr. Candy. Mr. Franklin Blake! Delighted to see you again, sir, after your long absence in foreign parts. (*Shaking hands.*) Excuse a professional remark. How feverish your hand is!

Franklin. I have been travelling a good deal lately, and I haven't recovered it yet.

Rachel (overhearing them). He has given up his cigars, Mr. Candy, and he has not had a good night's rest since. Is it because he has left off smoking?

Mr. Candy (speaking seriously). Unquestionably, Miss Rachel. (*To Franklin.*) You should have dropped your cigars gradually, Mr. Blake. It's a serious trial to a man's nervous system to give up the habitual use of tobacco at a moment's notice. Take care what you eat and drink, sir, in the present state of your health. (*He turns away to the supper-table.*)

Franklin (to RACHEL*).* A medical consultation for nothing! (RACHEL *goes to the supper-table.* FRANKLIN *speaks to himself.*) I suspect he is right about my nerves. (*He looks at his hand as he holds it out.*) It trembles like the hand of an old man!

Rachel. Come and have some supper, Franklin! The doctor doesn't condemn you to absolute starvation, I am sure. (*She addresses* MR. CANDY.) Let *me* prescribe for him, Mr. Candy. Give Mr. Blake some of that game pie.

Franklin. Thank you, Rachel, I never eat supper.

Rachel. It's never too late to mend, Franklin. Begin now.

Mr. Candy (passing a plate with some pie on it to FRANKLIN, *and speaking to him in a whisper).* Take my advice, don't eat it.

Franklin (looking at Mr. Candy, who is enjoying his pie). You eat it yourself! (*He examines the pie.*) It looks delicious. How softly the truffles repose on their gamy bed! How persuasively they say: "Why don't you eat us?" (*He tastes the pie.* GODFREY *has attended to* RACHEL *and* MISS CLACK *in the meantime.* MISS CLACK *addresses* MR. CANDY. *As the conversation proceeds,* FRANKLIN *finishes his pie, and helps himself to wine.*)

Miss Clack (*severely*). Mr. Candy!

Mr. Candy. Yes, Miss Clack?

Miss Clack. Miss Rachel was speaking of the neighbourhood just now. I have my doubts of the neighbourhood. (*Taking up her glass.*) I thought I saw a beer-shop on our way from the station.

Mr. Candy (filling his glass). If you had known where to look, you might have seen a dozen.

Miss Clack (finishing her champagne). How unspeakably dreadful! Rachel! Do you hear that? A neighbourhood of beer-drinkers all round this beautiful house. And that neighbourhood your property!

Rachel. What am *I* to do?

Miss Clack (with enthusiasm). Establish branch connections with our London institutions. Grapple with beer-drinking in its domestic results! Set up a Mothers'-Small-Clothes-Conversion-Society!

(RACHEL, FRANKLIN, *and* MR. CANDY *look at each other.*)

Godfrey (softly rattling his knife-handle on the table). Hear! hear!

Franklin (looking up from his plate). What does the Society do, Miss Clack?

Miss Clack (severely). The Mothers'-Small-Clothes-Conversion-Society, sir, rescues unredeemed fathers' trousers from the pawnbroker, and prevents their resumption on the part of the irreclaimable parent, by abridging them to suit the proportions of the innocent son. (GODFREY *applauds again with his knife-handle.*)

Franklin. What becomes of the trouserless fathers, Miss Clack?

Miss Clack (sternly). A properly-constituted mind doesn't dwell, Mr. Blake, on a trouserless father. Dear Mr. Godfrey, use your eloquence to persuade Rachel! The Mothers'-Small-Clothes is particularly rich in material just now. I may truly describe our struggling sisterhood as being quite overwhelmed with trousers!

Godfrey (pathetically). Too true! too true!

Rachel. My dear Drusilla, I don't understand these things. If *you* like to start the institution, you have my full permission to do so.

Miss Clack (clapping her hands). Oh, thank you, dearest! Oh, how happy you have made me! (BETTEREDGE *enters with the second bottle of champagne, and makes straight for* MISS CLACK.) Yes, Mr. Betteredge. One more little glass to drink success to the new institution.

Betteredge (confidentially). Dry, as before, miss. (*He fills her glass, and then fills the glasses of the rest of the company.*)

Miss Clack. May I propose a toast? May I, without impropriety, place myself, for one little moment, in a public position? Success to the Branch-Mothers'-Small-Clothes-Conversion-Society!

Franklin (repeating the toast). Success to the Branch-Mothers'-Small-Clothes-Conversion-Society! (*aside.*) And may the wind be tempered to the shorn fathers! (BETTEREDGE, *who has been waiting his opportunity of speaking to* FRANKLIN, *now approaches him, and speaks confidentially.*)

Betteredge. I say, Mr. Franklin, when are you going to show Miss Rachel the Moonstone?

Franklin (starting). Good heavens, I had completely forgotten it! Rachel! (RACHEL *approaches him.*) Prepare yourself for a great surprise. You have heard of your uncle, the Colonel?

Rachel. I have some vague remembrance of his behaving badly to my poor mother, and of his being celebrated as the possessor of a famous diamond.

Franklin. The Colonel is dead, Rachel, and the famous Moonstone is left to *you* by his will. The official announcement of it is among your letters in that drawer. And here is the diamond itself. (*He offers the box to* RACHEL.)

Rachel (amazed). What!

Betteredge (very earnestly, aside to RACHEL). Don't take it, miss!

Rachel (taking the jewel-box from FRANKLIN). Not take it? (*To* FRANKLIN.) What does he mean?

Franklin. Betteredge is superstitious –

Betteredge (indignantly interrupting him). I'm nothing of the sort, Mr. Franklin! I only say the wicked Colonel's diamond will bring ill-luck to Miss Rachel and to everybody in the house. Is that superstition? It's nothing of the sort – it's reason founded on experience! (*They all laugh.* RACHEL *opens the box.* GODFREY, MISS CLACK, *and* MR. CANDY *all look at the diamond.*)

Rachel. Oh, heavens! the lovely thing!

Godfrey (softly). Exquisite! exquisite!

Miss Clack. Vanity! vanity!

Mr. Candy. Carbon – mere carbon!

Rachel. How shall I have it set? As a bracelet or as a brooch? Look at the wonderful light in it – the lovely radiant glow, like the light of the harvest moon![1]

Franklin (showing her how to hold it). It takes its name from that light, Rachel. Bring it here, into the dark corner, and hold it as I tell you, and the glow will be brighter still.

Rachel (delighted). Come, Drusilla! Betteredge, *you* may see it too. (RACHEL *and* MISS CLACK *follow* FRANKLIN *to the back of the hall.*)

Betteredge (alone, in front). I am much obliged to you, miss. A little of that unlucky jewel goes a long way with *me!* (*In a lower tone.*) I'll mark it on my almanac. The wicked Colenel's vengeance begins tonight. (*He goes out.*) (MR. CANDY *and* GODFREY *are left together in front.* MR. CANDY *looks at his watch.* GODFREY *observes him.*)

Godfrey. You are not going yet?

Mr. Candy. I must go soon. I have an interesting case in the town. A London doctor has heard of it, and is coming to see the patient by the night express.

Godfrey. Is the malady serious? (*Shrinking from* MR. CANDY.) Nothing infectious, I hope?

Mr. Candy. Make your mind easy. It's a case of somnambulism. A lad, who has never been known before to walk in his sleep, has surprised everybody by turning sleep-walker at the age of seventeen.

Godfrey. Very remarkable! Have you discovered the cause?

Mr. Candy. I think so. Like Mr. Blake there, my patient was not accustomed to eating supper, and he was tempted to try the experiment by some friends. He eat[2] heartily, and he afterwards drank spirits, which he was not in the habit of doing either. There was no drunkenness, mind! After one glass of grog each the party rose from table, and adjourned to another room for a little music. The lad followed them, and sang too. Some strangers were present at the concert. He was introduced to them, and made his bow with perfect

---

1   The Harvest Moon is the full moon that occurs nearest the autumnal equinox.

2   The present tense of this word was at the time often used to mean "ate."

politeness. Conversation followed the music. Our young fellow joined in, and began to talk in an odd, absent way, mixing up his own affairs with the subject under discussion. Most of the party thought the poor wretch must be a little tipsy. One of them, rougher than the rest, gave him a shake, by way of sobering him, I suppose. He jumped up with a scream of terror, and looked about him in the wildest confusion. In plain English, he woke!

Godfrey. What! had he been asleep all the time?

Mr. Candy. Fast asleep and dreaming, with his eyes open!

Godfrey. After only eating supper?

Mr. Candy. No! no! after eating when he was not accustomed to eat, and drinking what he was not accustomed to drink. That makes all the difference. When he recovered his composure, he was asked if he remembered singing with the company, and being presented to the strangers. He stared in astonishment; he no more knew what he had been doing than you did before I told you of the circumstances.

Godfrey. You astonish me!

Mr. Candy. Oh! the thing has happened before. A case of sleep-walking, under similar circumstances, occurred in the last century – the case of Dr. Blacklock, the poet.[1] A morbid condition of the stomach produced in Dr. Blacklock. A morbid condition of the stomach produced in my young man. The brain affected by it in both cases. There's the explanation, to *my* mind! We shall hear what the London doctor says. If you'll excuse me, I'll just tell them to put my horse to in the gig.[2] (*He goes out by the hall door.* RACHEL *leads the way back to the front of the stage, followed by* FRANKLIN. MISS CLACK *stops at the library-table, and takes up an illustrated newspaper.*)

Rachel (to GODFREY). Oh Godfrey! you don't know what you have missed! A perfectly unearthly light shines out of the diamond in the dark! (*She turns to* FRANKLIN.) What shall I do with it? (*She looks round.*) I'll put it in the cabinet.

Franklin. Don't go near the cabinet! I have been varnishing it, and it's not dry yet.

Rachel. You put it away for me. (*She gives the diamond to* FRANKLIN. GODFREY *retires, and talks with* MISS CLACK *at the library-table.*)

---

1 Thomas Blacklock (1721-1791), a minor Scottish poet of the eighteenth century, was known as "the blind bard," having lost his sight as an infant.

2 See note 2 on page 133 in the novel.

Franklin (going to the cabinet). I wonder whether the door locks? (*He tries the key.*) Like all old cabinets, the lock is out of order, of course. Rachel! the lock's rusty, and won't act.

Rachel. What does that matter?

Franklin. Are you aware that the Moonstone is valued at ten thousand pounds? Seriously, Rachel, am I to put such a valuable jewel as this in a place that won't lock up?

Rachel. You won't find a place that *does* lock up, belonging to me. I hate the worry of keeping keys! What use are they here? Is my house an hotel? Are my faithful old servants thieves? Don't make a fuss about nothing! Do as I tell you!

Franklin (opening the drawer in the cabinet). There it is, in the third drawer from the top. (*Aside.*) I must find a safer place for it than this – Betteredge will help me. (*He closes the drawer and shuts the door of the cabinet, then examines the varnish carefully.*) I haven't smeared the varnish, have I? No! The surface is as smooth as glass, and the effect will be beautiful to-morrow. (MR. CANDY *re-enters.*)

Rachel. Have you been ordering your gig, Mr. Candy? You are not going already?

Mr. Candy. It's late, Miss Rachel.

Rachel (looking at her watch). So it is! (*calling to* MISS CLACK). Drusilla, shall we say good-night?

Miss Clack. Certainly, Rachel. (*She takes leave of* GODFREY, *who remains at the library-table, looking over an album of photographs.* RACHEL *shakes hands with* FRANKLIN *and* MR. CANDY. *At the same time* BETTEREDGE *enters with a kettle and a spirit-lamp.*[1] *He is followed by* PENELOPE *with the bedroom candles.* PENELOPE *lights the candles at a side-table.*)

Rachel (shaking hands with MR. CANDY). Mr. Candy, take something before you go.

Mr. Candy. Thank you, Miss Rachel. Good-night, Miss Clack.

Miss Clack. Good-night, Mr. Candy. I shall be at the town the first thing to-morrow, to start the new institution. (MR. CANDY *goes to the supper-table and stands there mixing and sipping his grog.* PENELOPE *hands* MISS CLACK *her candle.* MISS CLACK *fixes her eyes sternly on* PENELOPE'S *smart cap ribbons.*) Thank you, Penelope. Don't suppose I am admiring your cap ribbons – far from it! (*She turns to* RACHEL.) Good-night,

---

1 A spirit-lamp used alcohol or other liquid fuel.

love. (*She kisses* RACHEL, *who wishes her good-night, and enters her room on the left.* PENELOPE *has previously gone out at the back, offended by* MISS CLACK's *remarks on her ribbons.* MISS CLACK, *with a dignified bend of her head to* FRANKLIN, *ascends the stairs which lead to the gallery.*)

Franklin. Good-night, Miss Clack! (*Speaking to himself.*) Oh, dear, how tired I am! (*He drops wearily into an arm-chair on the right near the back of the stage, and calls to* BETTEREDGE.) Betteredge, I want to speak to you.

Betteredge (*approaching Franklin*). Yes, sir.

Franklin. Rachel insisted on my putting the diamond in the cabinet-drawer. It isn't safe there; the doors won't lock.

Miss Clack (*stopping at the top of the gallery stairs*). Mr. Betteredge!

Betteredge (*aside, taking the bottle*). More champagne? (*He steps out, so as to be seen by* MISS CLACK *from the gallery.*) Yes, miss!

Miss Clack. Tell Penelope I have a tract for her on vanity in dress. She is to read it to-morrow. You may mention the title – "A Word with You on Your Cap Ribbons." (*She goes out by the gallery on the left.*)

Betteredge. Thank you, miss! (*To himself, as he returns to* FRANKLIN.) My daughter's cap ribbons will be smarter than ever to-morrow! (*To* FRANKLIN.) Excuse me for remarking it, sir, you're a cup too low: you want rousing a bit. Try a drop of grog.

Franklin. I never tasted spirits in my life.

Betteredge. Lord, sir! what a pleasure you have got to come!

Mr. Candy. Mr. Blake, a little while since I warned you not to eat supper when you were not used to it.

Franklin. And I eat the supper, nevertheless.

Mr. Candy. I warn you again. In the present state of your health, don't drink grog if you are not used to it.

Franklin. More advice gratis! With a glass of grog in his own hand all the time! (*Enter* ANDREW *by the hall door.*)

Andrew (*to* MR. CANDY). Your gig is ready, sir.

Mr. Candy. Good-night, Mr. Blake, and don't forget my advice, though it *is* gratis! I have a patient in the town who never took supper and never tasted spirits, like you. He has reason now to regret having tried the experiment. Ask Mr. Ablewhite. (*He turns to* GODFREY.) Good-night, Mr. Ablewhite! (*He takes leave of* GODFREY, *who is still occupied with the photographs at the library-table, and goes out, followed by* ANDREW.)

Franklin. Mr. Candy is a little too fond of his profession. Why can't he leave it with his hat in the hall? Betteredge, you are the best doctor of the two. I feel wretchedly uncomfortable. Mix me some grog.

Betteredge. That's right, sir! Stick to your brandy-and-water, and never mind about the Moonstone! (*He mixes the grog.*)

Franklin (*impatiently*). But I *do* mind about the Moonstone! Other people put their jewels in the strong room at their banker's. Why shouldn't Rachel? (*He calls.*) Godfrey! (GODFREY *rises and approaches* FRANKLIN.) You are going to Frizinghall in the morning to see your father. I'm uneasy about the safety of the diamond. Take the Moonstone to-morrow to your father's bank.

Godfrey. With pleasure, dear Franklin, if Rachel will allow it.

Franklin. I will undertake to get Rachel's permission.

Betteredge (*to* FRANKLIN). Here is your nightcap, sir.

Franklin (*drinking, and setting down his glass*). Grog is an acquired taste, I suppose? I don't much like it.

Betteredge. Try again, sir, and you will find it grow on you. Shall I give you your candle?

Franklin. Thank you. (*He rises.*) My head feels heavy. I really believe I shall sleep to-night.

Godfrey. If you are in want of anything that I can do for you, don't forget there's a door of communication between your room and mine.

Franklin. All right. We will leave the door open, and talk if I can't sleep. (*He looks back at the cabinet.*) I don't like leaving the Moonstone there even for one night. (*He turns away, and follows* GODFREY *up the gallery stairs.* BETTEREDGE *goes to the hall door and calls* ANDREW.)

Betteredge. Now then, Andrew. Clear away, and put out the lamps. (ANDREW *enters and begins to clear the supper-table.* BETTEREDGE *watches him.* FRANKLIN *and* GODFREY *shake hands as they part at their bedroom doors.* BETTEREDGE *looks up at them.*) There they go to their beds! I shan't be sorry when I follow their example. (*He seats himself wearily, and speaks, partly to himself, partly to* ANDREW, *while the man goes on clearing the supper-table.*) Which of the two is the man for Miss Rachel? All things considered, *I* back Mr. Franklin. Andrew! have you noticed our two young gentlemen? Which of them should *you* say has the best chance of taking Miss Rachel's fancy?

Andrew. I should say Mr. Godfrey, sir. He has such a beautiful head of hair.

Betteredge (gravely). There's something in that. And he's a public character too. Such a speaker, Andrew, at charitable meetings! The last time I was in London, my young lady gave me two treats. She sent me to the theatre to see a dancing woman who was all the rage; and she sent me to Exeter Hall[1] to hear Mr. Godfrey. The lady did it with a band of music. The gentleman did it with a white handkerchief and a glass of water. Crowds at the performance with the legs. Ditto at the performance with the tongue. And which of the two charmed most money out of the pockets of the public is more than I can say. Have you cleared the table, Andrew? Now put out the lamps, my man; and then come along with me, and lock up for the night. (ANDREW *gets the steps to put out the lamps hanging from the ceiling.* BETTEREDGE *rises, and looks at the cabinet disapprovingly.*) Ah, you're a shiny cabinet enough to look at, now you're varnished. Not a speck or smear on you anywhere. (ANDREW *begins to put out the lamps.*) Who would think you had got the devil himself inside you, in the shape of the Moonstone? Who knows what turn the Colonel's vengeance will take before another day is over our heads? Gently, Andrew, gently. A fine lamp is like a fine lady. They both of them want delicate handling. (*He leads the way to the door at the back.*) Come away! Time to lock up! Time to lock up! (*He goes out, followed by* ANDREW, *and is heard to lock the hall door. A pause, marked by low music. The solitary hall is dimly lit by the last red embers of the fire.* BETTEREDGE *is just heard, speaking outside.*)

Betteredge. Have you locked up in the outer hall?

Andrew (outside). Yes, sir.

Betteredge. Fasten the back door next.

Andrew. All right, sir! (*Another pause.* RACHEL's *door opens. She appears in her dressing-gown.*)

Rachel. I am so restless, the limits of my own room won't hold me! I feel as if I should never sleep again. What sort of night is it? (*She crosses to the window and draws one of the curtains. The high window, reaching to the cornice, is seen protected by a broad iron-sheathed shutter, which covers two-thirds of it from the floor upwards. Through the uncovered glass at the top, the moon appears. Its light streams into the room over the place occupied*

---

1   See note 3 on page 111 of the novel.

by the cabinet.) Oh, the beautiful moonlight! How peaceful! how pure! What does my wakefulness mean? Am I thinking of the diamond? or thinking of Franklin? (*She glances at the cabinet.*) No! I won't look at the Moonstone. There's something evil in the unearthly light that shines out of it in the dark. Ridiculous! I am as superstitious as poor old Betteredge himself! (*She pauses, lost in thought.*) Franklin! I wish he hadn't spoken in that cruel way of the poor deformed man who lent him the money in Paris. It wouldn't matter if I didn't love him. But I do love him — dearly! And I can't bear to feel that he has disappointed me. I almost doubt him! (*Another pause.*) I won't think any more of Franklin — at least, not to-night! I'll get a book, and read myself to sleep. (*She approaches the bookcase. The door of* FRANKLIN'*s room opens. She hears it and looks up.* FRANKLIN *appears, in his dressing-gown and slippers.* RACHEL *starts, and makes for her own door.*) What does he want? Why is he out of his bed? Is *he* sleepless, too? Is *he* coming down for a book? (FRANKLIN *slowly descends the stairs.*) I can't let him find me here alone, at this time of night! (*She hurriedly enters her room, then looks out again cautiously into the hall, keeping the door in her hand.* FRANKLIN *descends the stairs, with slow measured steps.* RACHEL *watches him, ready to enter her room if he moves her way. Arrived near the cabinet, he pauses in the slanting ray of the moonlight, not looking towards Rachel, but looking straight before him.* RACHEL *speaks to herself.*) What is he waiting for? Is he listening? Is he frightened? What *does* it mean? (FRANKLIN *slowly approaches the cabinet; he mutters to himself.*)

Franklin (*in low vacant tones*). It's not safe in the cabinet. What's to be done with the Moonstone?

Rachel (*barely hearing the last word*). I can't hear what he says. Did he speak of the Moonstone? (FRANKLIN *opens the doors of the cabinet and pauses, looking round him suspiciously.* RACHEL *watches him, hiding herself behind her half-opened door.*) What is he doing? He seems afraid of being discovered! (FRANKLIN *opens the drawer in which the diamond is placed, and looks round him again.* RACHEL *lifts her hands in horror.*) Is he going to take the diamond? By stealth? In the dead of night? (*She turns her head away, shuddering.*) Is Godfrey right? Have his debts utterly degraded him? (*She looks at him again.* FRANKLIN *takes the diamond out of the drawer, and turns to re-ascend the stairs.*)[1] He *has* taken the dia-

---

1 Collins realized that his audience knew the story of his novel so well that any attempt at keeping Franklin Blake's theft of the diamond a mystery would be

mond! (*She calls to him faintly.*) Franklin! (*She shudders, and takes a step to re-enter her room.*) Oh, I can't speak to him! I can't look at him! A thief! a thief! (RACHEL's *voice sinks to a whisper. She hurries back horror-stricken to her room.* FRANKLIN *reaches his own door, opens it, enters, and closes it after him.*

The First Act ends without the fall of the curtain. During the whole interval between the First and Second Acts, the stage is left empty in the view of the audience. Low music from the orchestra marks the lapse of time until the action of the piece is renewed. Changes also occur in the aspect of the scene. The moonlight gradually fades and disappears. The fire next dies away by degrees. There is pitch-darkness in the hall. A long pause follows, after which the faint light of dawn just begins to show itself through the uncovered top of the window, strengthens, and leads to the sunrise of the new day. The music in the orchestra modulates to a brighter melody while these changes proceed. The Second Act begins.[1]

THE END OF THE FIRST ACT

———

THE SECOND ACT

Footsteps and voices of servants, followed by the unbarring of the house door, are audible outside. BETTEREDGE *is next heard to unlock the hall door. He enters, followed by* ANDREW, *and by two housemaids. Under* BETTEREDGE's *direction,* ANDREW *folds back the shutters, and lets the full daylight into the hall through the window. The women begin to put the hall tidy.* PENELOPE *enters next, and offers her morning greeting to her father.* BETTEREDGE *speaks as he kisses her.*

Betteredge. Good-morning, my dear! Are you going to wake Miss Rachel?

Penelope. Yes, father. I had Miss Rachel's orders to wake her early this morning. (*She crosses to* RACHEL's *door, knocks, and enters.* BETTEREDGE *observes the cabinet, and approaches it.*)

Betteredge. I may as well see that the Moonstone's safe before I go

———

ludicrous. With fair results, he chose to substitute expectation for mystery and surprise.

1 Collins, a master of serialized fiction, used the ends of his drama's Acts in much the same way he used the ends of his novel's serial numbers, to build suspense and anticipation.

to Mr. Franklin's room. (*He opens the drawer, and starts back.*) Nothing in it! Have I mistaken the drawer? (*He opens all the other drawers.*) Lord bless us and save us! – the Moonstone's gone! (ANDREW *and the* HOUSEMAIDS *hurry to* BETTEREDGE, *exclaiming together:* "GONE!")

Betteredge. Down with you on your knees, you young ones, and see if the diamond has dropped behind the cabinet, or on the floor! It's in a jeweller's box – a little white card-box. Well, have you found it?

Andrew and the Servants. No, sir!

Betteredge (*bewildered*). Gone! A diamond worth ten thousand pounds, gone! This is the most dreadful thing that has happened in my time. Who can have taken it? We are all honest people in this house.

Andrew (*to Betteredge*). Will the servants be suspected, sir?

Betteredge (*still bewildered*). The servants? I locked the hall door last night, and took the key into my own room. Don't bother me with questions – I want time to think. (*To himself*). Only yesterday I marked it down on my almanac: "The wicked Colonel's vengeance begins to-night." The morning comes, and I find myself a true prophet! (*He pauses, and looks about him in perplexity.*) What is it my duty to do?

The Housemaids (*hearing him*). To speak up for the servants' characters!

Betteredge. Hold your tongues! (*Recovering himself.*) My duty is plain. I must report what has happened to Miss Rachel, and I must send to Frizinghall for the police. (*He crosses to* RACHEL's *room door and knocks.* PENELOPE *appears.*) Penelope, is Miss Rachel up?

Penelope (*observing his agitation*). Lord bless us, father! what's the matter?

Betteredge (*impatiently*). Answer my question! Is Miss Rachel up?

Penelope. Up and dressed, before I knocked at her door. I don't know what has happened to her. She looks shockingly ill this morning.

Betteredge. Ill or well, I must see her directly. (*He enters.* PENELOPE *follows him, closing the door.* ANDREW *and the* HOUSEMAIDS *are left alone on the stage.*)

First Housemaid (*speaking firmly*). I'm glad he means to send for the police. The police will clear our characters.

Andrew. That's true, miss. I quite agree with you.

Second Housemaid (*timidly*). Will the police search our boxes?

First Housemaid. We are innocent people – what does it matter if they do? (BETTEREDGE *reappears with a note in his hand.*)

Betteredge (to Andrew). The groom is to ride to the police-station at Frizinghall, and he is to give that note to the Inspector. (ANDREW *hurries out with the note.* BETTEREDGE *reflects.*) I don't know what to make of Miss Rachel. She flatly refused to let me send for the police. I was all but obliged to go on my knees before I could get her consent. I suppose I'd better tell Mr. Franklin about it next. Go on with your work, you girls – go on with your work. (*He ascends to* FRANKLIN'S *room.*)

Second Housemaid. I'm in such a flutter, I don't know what my work *is*.

First Housemaid. If you stand shivering and shaking like that, you'll be suspected of the robbery. Pull yourself together and sweep the carpet.

Second Housemaid (taking the broom). Oh, my poor nerves!

First Housemaid (dusting a chair). Your nerves, indeed! If I chose to give way like you, I should go into hysterics in this chair. (FRANKLIN *appears in morning dress and speaks as he descends the stairs, followed by* BETTEREDGE. *The* HOUSEMAIDS *seeing him, go out with their brooms and dusters.*)

Franklin. It's no use appealing to me, Betteredge; I am as completely puzzled as you are. I can't realise it. I can't believe it. No doors have been forced open. Nobody has broken into the house. Who *can* have taken the diamond? *is* it stolen, or is it only lost? The mystery is simply impenetrable; I can't find the slightest clue to it, think as I may.

Betteredge. Let's hope the police will enlighten us, sir.

Franklin (abruptly). What police?

Betteredge. The police from Frizinghall.

Franklin. They will be of no use! The case is beyond the reach of the local police. We shall only lose time and have to send to London after all. (*He pauses and considers.*) I have it! I know the very man who will help us. Give me a form, I'll telegraph to London at once!

Betteredge (giving him the form). What for, sir?

Franklin. For the famous detective, Sergeant Cuff.

Betteredge. That's a good notion, Mr. Franklin. Shall I tell Miss Rachel?

Franklin (writing). No, no! I'll tell Rachel myself. (ANDREW *enters by the hall door.*)

Andrew (to Betteredge). Where am I to lay the breakfast, sir?

Betteredge. Lord bless me, I forgot the breakfast! Not in here; we may have the police in here. In the morning room, Andrew. (ANDREW *turns to go out.*)

Franklin (finishing his telegram). Stop! send this to the railway station directly.

Andrew. Yes, sir. (*He goes out with the telegram.*)

Betteredge. When will Sergeant Cuff be here, sir?

Franklin. He will start the instant he gets my telegram. How long is the railway journey from London?

Betteredge. Barely an hour by a quick train. (GODFREY *appears at his room door.* BETTEREDGE *looks up.*) Here's Mr. Godfrey, sir. Perhaps he's got something to propose?

Franklin (while GODFREY *descends the stairs).* Not he! When did you ever know a ladies' man who was of any use in an emergency?

Godfrey. Well, dear Franklin, what have you done about this dreadful business?

Franklin. I've done the best I can – I have telegraphed for Sergeant Cuff.

Godfrey (starting). The famous detective?

Franklin. Yes; and just the man we want to find the diamond.

Godfrey. You know him?

Franklin. Perfectly well. The last time I was in town I had a look at the vagabond side of London life – the tramps and thieves, you know – and Sergeant Cuff was my guide. The queerest fellow you ever saw. Looks more like a Methodist parson than a detective. Has a taste for flowers, absolutely dotes on roses. Think of that for a policeman!

Godfrey. Does Rachel know you have sent for this man?

Franklin. I am going to tell her the moment she comes out of her room. (ANDREW *appears at the door.*)

Andrew. Breakfast, gentlemen!

Franklin (taking GODFREY's *arm).* Come along, Godfrey! (*He stops as they pass the cabinet.*) If Rachel hadn't forced me to put the diamond in that infernal cabinet – let's go to breakfast! (*They go out.*)

Betteredge (alone). Aye! aye! go to your coffee and cutlets. Whatever happens in a house, whether it's robbery or murder, you must have your breakfast! (PENELOPE *enters from* RACHEL's *room.*) Well, Penelope? What news of Miss Rachel?

Penelope. You will see for yourself, father. Miss Rachel is coming to speak to you. Do you know if Miss Clack has gone out yet?

Betteredge. Half-an-hour ago. I met her coming down the back staircase on her way to the town, to worry everybody about that new "Beer-and-Breeches-Society." What do you want with her, Penelope?

Penelope. Miss Clack had the impudence to give me a tract about my cap ribbons when I woke her this morning! I shall give it to her back again at the first opportunity. (*She goes out by the hall door.*)

Betteredge (alone). I should chuck it into the fire and think no more about it. There's the difference between a man and a woman! (*He looks towards* RACHEL's *door.*) What does Miss Rachel want with me, I wonder? (RACHEL *enters suddenly from her room.*)

Rachel (in great agitation). Betteredge! have you sent for the police?

Betteredge. Yes, miss.

Rachel. Send directly and countermand the order. I won't have the police in the house!

Betteredge. For the servants' sakes – for my sake, miss, don't say that! The police must be sent for. Ask Mr. Franklin (RACHEL *starts*), if you won't believe me.

Rachel (with a sudden change). Where is Mr. Franklin?

Betteredge. At breakfast, miss. Do you wish to see him?

Rachel (in confusion). Yes – no – go away! (BETTEREDGE *turns to go out.*) Stop! Tell Mr. Franklin Blake I want to speak to him.

Betteredge (speaking aside, puzzled and alarmed). What on earth is the matter with Miss Rachel? (*He goes out by the hall door.*)

Rachel (alone). The meanness of this detestable theft – the longer I think, the more keenly I feel the revolting meanness of it! He daren't make away with the diamond on the journey to England – the consul's letter to me would have pointed at him as the thief. No, he waits till the Moonstone is safe in my house! He can calculate on my poor servants being suspected of the theft; he can sell the jewel abroad, and cheat me as he has cheated his creditors! And this is the man I love? This is the hero of my secret thoughts, for years past? (*She pauses and reflects.*) What am I to say to him? Now I have sent for him, what am I to say? Can I tell him, in plain words, what I saw last night? (*Recoiling from the idea.*) Oh, no! no! I degrade myself, if I degrade *him.* Only yesterday I owned that I loved him. Can I tell him, after that, that he is a thief? Oh, never! never! I should die under the shame of it! (*She pauses again.*) Is it possible that I have judged him rashly? Am I hard on him, poor fellow? He may have been almost beside himself last night with his debts and difficulties. If I only give him a hint, and then leave him here by himself, he may take the opportunity; he may put the diamond back in the drawer. Shall I try it? I will! (FRANKLIN *enters by the hall door.* RACHEL *starts, and composes herself.*)

Franklin (in his usual manner). Betteredge says you wish to see me, Rachel.

Rachel (trying to assume indifference). How did you sleep last night, Franklin?

Franklin (aside). Is that all she wants me for? (*To* RACHEL.) I had a perfect night's rest; I never once woke till the sun looked in at my window. Pardon me for remarking it, Rachel – you don't look well this morning.

Rachel (confusedly). I was restless last night. (*She again eyes* FRANKLIN *attentively.*) I was walking about – here, in the hall.

Franklin (with sudden interest). After everybody was in bed?

Rachel (with her eye on him). Why are you so anxious to know?

Franklin. To get information for the police, to be sure. Did you look at your diamond? Did you see it safe in the drawer?

Rachel (aside, disgusted by his apparent duplicity). He speaks of it first! (*to* FRANKLIN.) I did *not* look at the diamond. (*She pauses, and suddenly makes up her mind what to say next.*) I had a dream about it.

Franklin (quietly). A dream that it was stolen?

Rachel (aside – with a burst of indignation). Oh! (*To* FRANKLIN.) Stolen – and restored. I dreamed that the thief repented, and privately put the diamond back in its place, and trusted the rest to my mercy. (*She timidly places her hand on* FRANKLIN's *arm, and speaks with great tenderness.*) And I made allowances for the temptation, Franklin; I forgave him with all my heart!

Franklin (smiling). Your dream won't help us to find the diamond, Rachel. Suppose we get back to realities? I have something to say to you about the police.

Rachel (turning away from him indignantly). I don't want to hear it! (*She approaches the window on the right.*)

Franklin (looking after her in amazement). What have I done to offend her?

Rachel (to herself). If I stay here a moment longer, I shall accuse him of the theft. And what would he do if I did accuse him? Lie to me again, as he has lied to me already. (*She advances nearer to the window*.)

Franklin (following her a step and stopping). Are you going into the rose-garden?

Rachel (still pursuing her own thoughts). And he knows that I would forgive him. He knows that his shameful secret is safe with *me*!

Franklin (approaching her). May I go with you, Rachel?

Rachel (furiously). No! (*She goes out on the right*.)

Franklin (alone, looking after her in extreme astonishment). In all my experience of women, I never met with the like of this. Her manner to me is absolutely insulting! It almost looks as if the loss of the Moonstone had turned her brain. (GODFREY *and* MR. CANDY *enters by the hall door*. MR. CANDY *has a book under his arm*.)

Godfrey. Franklin! Mr. Candy has called to inquire after you.

Mr. Candy. Good-morning, Mr. Blake. How did the experiment of the supper and the grog succeed last night?

Franklin. Wonderfully well. I haven't had such a night's sleep for weeks past. (MR. CANDY *looks astonished*.) I evidently surprise you?

Mr. Candy. You agreeably surprise me, sir. Any news yet of the lost diamond?

Franklin. No news.

Mr. Candy. Sorry to hear it. (*To* GODFREY.) Tell Miss Rachel I have brought back the book I borrowed from the library some time since.

Godfrey (looking at the book). Ah, yes. Combe's famous work on Phrenology.[1] Some curious things in that book.

Mr. Candy. Very curious. (*He goes to the bookcase to put the volume away*.)

Godfrey (to FRANKLIN). I am going to Frizinghall. I suppose I can be of no use here?

Franklin (impatiently). Use? We are all in the dark together.

Godfrey. My dear Franklin, you talk as if there was no hope. The local police have arrived (BETTEREDGE *appears at the hall door*), and the Inspector has begun his inquiries.

---

1 See note on page 459 of the novel.

Betteredge (speaking at the hall door). The Inspector has made a complete mess of it already.

Franklin. What is he doing?

Betteredge (approaching FRANKLIN). He has set up the backs of all the women servants in the house. Talks of examining their bedrooms. The cook looks as if she could grill him alive, and the rest of the women are ready to eat him afterwards – underdone. (GODFREY *laughs, and joins* MR. CANDY *at the bookcase.)*

Franklin. Just what I feared. We'll dismiss the Inspector before he does any more mischief. Come along. (*He goes out with* BETTEREDGE *by the hall door.)*

Godfrey (returning to the front with MR. CANDY). What news of your sleep-walking patient, Mr. Candy? What does the London doctor say?

Mr. Candy. The London doctor, after hearing my opinion, put it to the proof on a plan of his own – and the proof disappointed us both. I'll tell you about it when I have a little more time. (*He looks at his watch.*) My patients are waiting, and my only errand here was to inquire after Mr. Blake.

Godfrey (confidentially). I doubt if Mr. Blake passed quite so quiet a night as he supposes. I thought I heard him moving.

Mr. Candy. Quite likely. In his state of health he *must* have been restless after that supper last night. He had dreams, you may rely on it.

Godfrey. He seems to have entirely forgotten his dreams.

Mr. Candy. There is nothing wonderful in that. Recollect what my patient in the town did when he was asleep and dreaming, and how absolutely unconscious of it *he* was when he woke. My respects to Miss Rachel, and I hope she will soon recover the diamond. Good-morning.

Godfrey. Good-morning. (MR. CANDY *goes out by the hall door.* GODFREY *looks at the clock on the mantelpiece, and speaks a little anxiously.*) I have some time to spare. Shall I risk proposing to Rachel while I have the chance? I should like to feel sure of my charming cousin before I leave her – with Franklin in the house! She was in the rose-garden when I last heard of her. (*He approaches the window, and is met by* SERGEANT CUFF, *entering from the garden.*)

Cuff. Mr. Godfrey Ablewhite, I believe?

Godfrey (a little surprised). You know me?

Cuff. Everybody knows you, sir.

Godfrey (rather suspiciously). May I ask to whom I have the pleasure of speaking? (CUFF *takes a card out of his pocket-book, and silently hands it to* GODFREY. GODFREY *starts as he reads the name.*) "Sergeant Cuff, Detective Police Force." (*He turns to* CUFF, *speaking rather confusedly*). How is it, Sergeant, that you – I mean, why are you left to find your way in here, without a servant to announce you?

Cuff. It's a habit of mine, in cases of theft, to slip in quietly, and take the place, as it were, by surprise.

Godfrey (recovering himself). You have taken us all by surprise, Sergeant. We never expected to see you so soon.

Cuff (with his eye on GODFREY). I met the servant at the station here, sir, and got my telegram before it went to London.

Godfrey. A strange coincidence! What brought you to the station here?

Cuff. Another case, sir, confided to my care. I left it to one of my colleagues, and came on here directly I read Mr. Blake's message.

Godfrey. May I venture to ask what interested you so greatly in Mr. Blake's message?

Cuff (as before). I think it must have been the dulness of the other case, sir, and the hope of meeting with something pleasanter to my feelings here. The other case, you see, was so dreadfully common. (*Watching* GODFREY's *face.*) The old story! False entries detected in a cash-book; a sum of money embezzled; private inquiries into the lives and habits of the persons suspected, and nothing positive discovered up to this time. (*He walks back to the window, and stands with his hands in his pockets, looking through it.*)

Godfrey. Ah, indeed? Just so – just so! To return to our case here. (*He follows* CUFF. *The Sergeant keeps his back turned on* GODFREY, *as if absorbed in the view from the window.* As a practical man, what is your opinion – ?

Cuff (indignantly). Just look at that rose-garden! (*He points through the window, still keeping his back turned on* GODFREY.)

Godfrey (persisting). What is your opinion of the loss of the diamond?

Cuff (as before, pretending not to hear him). Just look at it! I should like to punch the head of the man who laid that garden out! The walks between the rose-beds are made of gravel. It's enough to turn one sick to look at them! (*Suddenly addressing* GODFREY.) Grass walks between your roses, Mr. Ablewhite! nice, soft, velvety grass walks! Gravel's too hard for them, pretty creatures! (*He turns away again up the stage on the right, and notices the roses ranged between the window and the back of the hall.*)

Godfrey (*aside, distrustfully*). He has got on his favourite subject already. Is that an excuse for not answering me?

Cuff (*admiring the roses*). Ah, here's something worth looking at, if you like! Here's a sweet pretty lot of white and blush roses! They always mix well together, don't they? Here's the white musk-rose, Mr. Ablewhite – our old English rose – holding up its head along with the best and the newest of them. Pretty dear! (*He fondles the rose with his hand.*)

Godfrey (*looking at him distrustfully*). A taste for flowers, Sergeant, is rather a strange taste for a man in your line of life.

Cuff. If you will look about you, sir – which most people won't do – you will see that the nature of a man's taste is, nine times out of ten, as opposite as possible from the nature of a man's business. I began my life among the roses in my father's nursery-garden, and I shall end my life among them if I can. Yes; one of these days I shall retire from catching thieves, and try my hand at growing roses. There will be grass walks in my rose-garden, Mr. Ablewhite – no gravel! no gravel! (*Suddenly changing his tone.*) Can I see Mr. Franklin Blake, sir?

Godfrey. Mr. Blake is engaged, at present, with the Inspector of police at our town here.

Cuff. Mr. Blake may dismiss the Inspector whenever he wishes. It's another of my queer tastes to prefer working single-handed. Who first discovered the loss of the jewel?

Godfrey. Mr. Betteredge, the house steward. A most intelligent man – a most reliable witness. You will to examine Betteredge, of course? Allow me to ring the bell! (*He goes to the fireplace and rings the bell.*)

Cuff (*to himself*). Allow him to ring the bell! The most obliging gentleman I ever met with. (He takes a turn in the room and whistles to himself softly the first few notes of "The Last Rose of Summer.")

Godfrey (*looking after him in surprise*). Somebody whistling?

Cuff. I beg your pardon, sir. It's a bad habit of mine to whistle when I'm in good spirits – when I see my way, you know, to something pleasant and encouraging. You won't find my whistling much of a nuisance – I only know one tune.

Godfrey. And that is, "The Last Rose of Summer"?

Cuff. Yes, sir. It must be something about the roses, or it wouldn't do for me. (*He looks towards the hall door.* ANDREW *appears.*) Here's the servant, sir.

Godfrey (*to* ANDREW). Send Mr. Betteredge here directly. Stop! (*He turns to* CUFF.) A point for your consideration, Sergeant. The Inspector is attended by a policeman in plain clothes. In small matters of detail now – matters that are beneath your notice – the policeman might perhaps be of use to you.

Cuff (*aside*). First he rings the bell, and now he provides me with a policeman! (*To* GODFREY.) I'll try the man, sir, out of respect for your opinion.

Godfrey (*to* ANDREW). Send the policeman here with Mr. Betteredge! (ANDREW *goes out.* GODFREY *continues to* CUFF.) I am going this morning to Frizinghall, our town here.

Cuff. Shall you be long away, sir?

Godfrey. Only a few hours. If you decide to search the house before I come back (*he points to his room*), there is my room entirely at your service.

Cuff (*aside*). Another delicate attention! Here's his room at my service, now! (*He looks towards the hall door.*) There's somebody at the door, sir.

Godfrey (*turning*). This way, Betteredge – this way. (BETTEREDGE *enters, followed by the policeman in plain clothes.* GODFREY *presents* BETTEREDGE.) Betteredge, this is Sergeant Cuff. Sergeant, this is the policeman.

Cuff. Take a seat, Mr. Policeman. (*He turns to* BETTEREDGE.) Proud to be introduced, sir, to the witness who discovered the loss of the diamond.

Betteredge. Your most obedient servant, Sergeant. (*They shake hands.* GODFREY *looks at his watch.*)

Godfrey. Betteredge, is Miss Rachel still in the garden?

Rachel (*entering by the window*). Miss Rachel is here. (CUFF *joins the policeman at the back, without being noticed by* RACHEL, *speaks to him in dumb show, and then watches* GODFREY *while he and* RACHEL *are speaking.* BETTEREDGE *crosses to the fireplace on the left and makes up the fire.* RACHEL *continues to* GODFREY.) Not gone yet! Mind, I expect you back before dinner-time.

Godfrey (tenderly, in an undertone). Do you really feel any interest in my return?

Rachel (to Godfrey). Your father will be wondering what has become of you? Go to Frizinghall!

Godfrey. Have you forgotten what I said to you the last time we were together?

Rachel. My memory is not to be trusted, Godfrey! (*She turns aside to the roses.* GODFREY *tries vainly to persuade her to listen to him.* CUFF *speaks to the policeman in a low tone.*)

Cuff. Now, do what I told you! Now is your time. (*The policeman goes out by the hall door.* GODFREY *speaks to* RACHEL.)

Godfrey (kissing her hand). Rachel! my faithful heart still worships you, and still hopes!

Rachel (leaving him). Go to Frizinghall!

Godfrey (aside). I'll try her again, when I come back! (*To* CUFF.) Good-morning, Sergeant. (*He checks himself as he goes out, and looks round the room.*) Where is the policeman?

Cuff. I've found him useful already, sir. I've sent him on a little errand. (GODFREY *goes out by the hall door.* RACHEL *looks suspiciously at* CUFF.)

Rachel. Betteredge, who is that?

Betteredge. Sergeant Cuff, miss, of the detective police.

Rachel (aside). The very sight of a policeman is hateful to me! (*She approaches her own room.* CUFF *advances to stop her.*)

Cuff. Be so very good, miss, as not to leave the room. I may have some questions to ask you.

Rachel (contemptuously). I decline to answer your questions.

Betteredge (scandalised by RACHEL's *want of politeness).* In the interest of the servants' characters, Miss Rachel, don't treat the Sergeant so harshly. I am your old servant, and I ask it as a favour.

Rachel (frankly offering him her hand). More than my old servant – my old friend! (BETTEREDGE *kisses her hand.*) I will wait, Betteredge, to please you. (*She seats herself, turning her back on* CUFF, *and takes up a newspaper.*)

Betteredge (aside, with immense relief). Ah, now I know Miss Rachel again! (*He turns a little pompously to* CUFF, *proud of* RACHEL's *compliment to him.*) Ask your questions, Mr. Sergeant; ask your questions.

Cuff. When the diamond was put away for the night, where was it put?

Betteredge (pointing to the cabinet). In that drawer.

Cuff (examining the cabinet). Were the cabinet doors locked? (*He tries the lock.*) I see! The lock won't act. (*He looks again at the cabinet, and puts his nose to it.*) Has this cabinet been varnished lately? (RACHEL *suddenly puts down the paper and listens.*)

Betteredge. Varnished by Mr. Franklin Blake no later than yesterday evening.

Cuff (still examining the cabinet). Where is Mr. Blake?

Betteredge. He heard you had come, Sergeant, and like the rest of us, he didn't know where to find you. When last I saw him he was off to the stables to question the man who drove you.

Cuff (pointing to a place at the lower part of the cabinet). Hullo! here's a smear on the varnish!

Betteredge. Lord bless us, so there is ! I saw no smear there when I locked up the house close on twelve o'clock last night.

Cuff (looking at the smear through a magnifying glass). Was the varnish dry then?

Betteredge. No, sir. Mr. Franklin told me it would not be dry before two in the morning.

Cuff (to himself). Aha! (*He looks again through the magnifying glass, and, while he looks, whistles the first notes of his favourite air.*)

Betteredge (to himself). What's he whistling for?

Cuff (hearing him). Do you never whistle yourself, Mr. Betteredge?

Betteredge. I have done such a thing, sir, when I had reason to feel particularly well pleased with myself.

Cuff. My case exactly! I whistle when I think I've got the clue in my hand. I think I've got it now.

Betteredge (eagerly). Where?

Cuff (pointing). Here! The clue to the missing diamond begins at this smear on the varnish.

Betteredge (To RACHEL*).* Do you hear that, Miss Rachel?

Rachel (coldly). No. I am reading the newspaper.

Cuff (continuing). To the best of my judgment, the smear has been made by a loose article of dress that has swept over the wet varnish.

Betteredge. Do you mean a woman's petticoat, sergeant?

Cuff. Yes. Or, may be, the tail of a man's dressing-gown. (RACHEL *starts. The newspaper drops from her hand.* CUFF *observes her.*) Anything wrong, miss?

Rachel (coldly). I don't understand you.

Cuff (aside). She knows something about it! (*to* RACHEL.) Sorry to trouble you, miss. After what I have discovered on this cabinet, I must examine the things for the wash.

Betteredge (admiring CUFF). Wonderful man! He's going to find the thief in the dirty-linen bag.

Cuff (to RACHEL, *continuing*). You see, miss, the reason's plain enough. If it's a petticoat that has made the smear, the woman that petticoat belongs to must be able to tell me what she was doing here between midnight and two in the morning. If it's a dressing-gown –

Rachel (impatiently). What do you want?

Cuff. Your authority, miss, to give my orders to the laundry-maid.

Rachel (as before). Give your orders.

Cuff. Now, Mr. Betteredge. Introduce me to the laundry-maid.

Betteredge. With pleasure, Mr. Sergeant. (*He whispers in* CUFF's *ear.*) She's a nice plump young girl – you couldn't begin with a better one. (*They go out at the hall door.*)

Rachel (springing to her feet). He wore his dressing-gown last night! His room will be searched – the stain will be discovered – he will be exposed as a thief before every creature in the house! (*She walks distractedly to and fro.*) After all I have suffered, to see him publicly disgraced – ruined, ruined for life! It's maddening to think of it! (*She pauses, reflecting.*) The dressing-gown may be in his room at this moment; the one chance of saving him is to destroy it before the search begins! (*She looks round her.*) Franklin is at the stables – I heard Betteredge say so. Miss Clack has not returned yet. There is nobody to see me. Can I – dare I – risk it? Oh, Franklin! Franklin! (*She rushes up the stairs. As she enters* FRANKLIN's *room,* MISS CLACK *appears below at the hall door, with her bag on her arm, returning from the town.*)

Miss Clack. In all my experience, I have never met with anything so disheartening to an earnest worker as the worldly tone of mind which pervades this household. Nobody is interested in the progress of the Branch-Mothers'-Small-Clothes-Conversion-Society. They are all absorbed in vain regret for the loss of the diamond. Ah! If we *are* to mourn, let it be over our obdurate fellow-creatures – our lost human diamonds by the wayside! (*She places her bag of tracts on a chair.*) How I miss dear Mr. Godfrey's ready sympathy! I fancy his manner has been more than usually affectionate towards me of late. I wonder where he is? (*She calls off at the hall door.*) Penelope! (PENELOPE *enters sulkily.*) Has Mr. Godfrey Ablewhite gone out?

Penelope. Yes, miss.

Miss Clack. You don't know when he will return?

Penelope. No, miss. (*Aside.*) I believe she's sweet on Mr. Godfrey – at her time of life!

Miss Clack. Is Miss Rachel in her room?

Penelope. I suppose so. (*Aside.*) How many more questions, I wonder!

Miss Clack (*eyeing* PENELOPE's *cap ribbons*). Have you read your tract, Penelope? Are you aware of the enormity of your cap ribbons?

Penelope. No, miss. (*She produces the tract.*) If this "Word with Me on my Cap Ribbons" is written by a man, he is an impudent fellow, and he knows nothing about it! If it's written by a woman, I know what is going on in *her* mind – she would be only too glad to wear the ribbons herself! (*She offers the tract back.*) Please to take it back, miss.

Miss Clack (*receiving the tract in her sweetest manner*). You will ask me for it again before I have done with you.

Penelope. I shan't!

Miss Clack. Oh, yes, you will. It's no use being impudent to *me.* The more impudent you are, my poor girl, the more interested I feel in you. (PENELOPE *attempts to speak.*) No, you young castaway, you don't offend me! You present plenty of obstructive material to work upon.

Penelope. I won't be called names! I'm not an Obstructive Material! I shall complain to my mistress! (*She goes out indignantly.*)

Miss Clack (*alone, in high triumph*). A thoroughly bad girl – how very encouraging! – a thoroughly bad girl. (*She goes to* RACHEL's *door, and knocks.*) Rachel! Rachel, dear! (*No answer.*) Perhaps she is asleep? I'll go in and see. (MISS CLACK *opens the door and enters* RACHEL's *room.* RACHEL *appears in the gallery, at* FRANKLIN's *door, and sees that the hall is empty, and descends the stairs, with* FRANKLIN's *dressing-gown over her arm.*)

Rachel. The stain *is* on his dressing-gown! I have saved from exposure a degraded wretch who is unworthy of my interest – unworthy of my pity. Oh, how ashamed of myself I feel! I never knew how meanly I could behave until now. (*She looks at the dressing-gown.*) How am I to destroy it! I might burn it when the house is quiet for the night. In the meantime, where can I find a safe place for it? Nobody will venture to search *my* room – I can hide it there. (*She advances to her room, and is met by* MISS CLACK *coming out.*)

Miss Clack. I have been looking for you, dearest. I am just back from my mission in the town. (*She notices the dressing-gown, which* RACHEL *tries vainly to conceal.*) Dear me! What have you got hanging over your arm? (CUFF *enters by the hall door, and stops, seeing* RACHEL *in the company of a lady who is a stranger to him.* MISS CLACK *goes on.*) It looks like a dressing-gown!

Cuff (*to himself, hearing* MISS CLACK's *last words*). A dressing-gown?

Rachel (*impatiently*). Never mind what it looks like! (*She tries to pass to her room.*) Let me by!

Cuff (*to himself, struck by* RACHEL's *manner*). Hullo!

Miss Clack. I meant no offence, Rachel. It was only natural I should notice the dressing-gown hanging over your arm. Why are you angry with me?

Rachel (*pushing by her*). Don't talk nonsense! (*She enters her room, and closes the door sharply.*)

Miss Clack. First insulted by Penelope, and now insulted by Rachel! Two trials to pass through – two offences to forgive. Oh, what a happy day! (*She turns, sees* CUFF, *and starts.*) Who is this? (*To* CUFF.) Are you a clergyman, sir?

Cuff (*to himself*). There's a compliment! (*To* MISS CLACK.) I am only a police-officer, ma'am.

Miss Clack (*modestly*). Not "ma'am," if you please. I am not married – yet.

Cuff. I beg your pardon, miss.

Miss Clack. Are you here about the diamond, sir?

Cuff. Yes, miss. I'm to find out who has stolen the diamond.

Miss Clack (*resignedly, speaking to herself*). I am quite prepared to be suspected! (*To* CUFF.) Is there any harm, Mr. Policeman, in my going to take off my bonnet in my own room?

Cuff. Not in the least, miss!

Miss Clack (*humbly*). Thank you, sir! (*She ascends to the gallery, and goes off on the left.* CUFF *walks thoughtfully to and fro, whistling the first notes of his favourite air. As* MISS CLACK *disappears, he speaks.*)

Cuff. The linen for the wash has wasted my time, and has told me nothing. Thanks to that extraordinary female, I know what article of clothing to examine next. Miss Rachel's own conduct associates the dressing-gown with the smear on the varnish. Why was she so angry when that polite spinster noticed the dressing-gown? And what was she doing with a dressing-gown at this time of day? (FRANKLIN *and* BETTEREDGE *enter by the hall door.*)

Betteredge (to CUFF). I have found Mr. Franklin, sir. Here he is!

Franklin. I have been looking for you in all the wrong places, Sergeant. What are you doing here? What about the missing diamond?

Cuff. I have failed to find the diamond, so far, sir; and I came here to ask for a minute's conversation with Miss Rachel.

Franklin. Where is she? In her own room? (*He knocks at the door.*) Rachel!

Rachel (suddenly opening the door, and speaking eagerly). Franklin's voice! (*She sees* CUFF *and* BETTEREDGE, *and drawing back, speaks aside.*) I thought he had come to confess everything! (*To* FRANKLIN, *sharply.*) Why am I disturbed?

Cuff (interposing). It is my duty to inform you, miss, that the examination of the linen has led to nothing. I have made up my mind to look at the servants' wardrobes next.

Rachel. I won't allow it! It's an insult to my honest servants.

Betteredge. Thank you kindly, Miss Rachel! But it had better be done, for all that.

Cuff. I am as anxious to consult the servants' feelings as you are, miss. I propose that you and the gentlefolks staying in the house should set the example, and offer your wardrobes to be examined first.

Franklin. An excellent notion! The servants can't complain if we do that.

Rachel (with a furious look at FRANKLIN). I refuse to let my wardrobe be examined! I refuse to let this shameful farce go on any longer.

Cuff. Please reflect, miss, before you decide. I have undertaken to conduct this inquiry, and I have a duty to perform to my employer here. (*He indicates* FRANKLIN.)

Rachel (suddenly stepping up to CUFF). Your employer? Do you mean to tell me Mr. Franklin Blake sent for you?

Franklin. Certainly, Rachel, I sent for him.

Rachel. You sent to London for Sergeant Cuff?

Franklin. Why are you angry with me? I have sent for the right man to recover your diamond.

Rachel (with a burst of indignation). Oh! this is more than even my endurance can bear. (*She rings the bell furiously.* ANDREW *appears.*) Order the carriage – I am going back to London by the next train. (*She takes her garden hat off a table.* FRANKLIN *looks at her in amazement.* CUFF *smiles to himself.*)

Franklin. My dear Rachel – !

Rachel. Not a word. Don't speak to me – don't look at me! The very air of the house is hateful to me while *you* are in it!

Franklin. What do you mean, Rachel? Do you know that you are insulting me before these men?

Rachel. Insult you? *You?* Franklin Blake, you're beneath being insulted, and you know it! (FRANKLIN *stands petrified.* RACHEL *continues, pointing to* CUFF.) Betteredge! pay that man his fee, and don't let me find him here when I come back! (*She goes out on the right.*)

Cuff (looking after her). She knows who took the diamond! (*To* FRANKLIN.) We've found the clue, sir.

Franklin (in great surprise). Where is the clue?

Cuff (pointing to RACHEL's *room).* In that room.

Betteredge (scandalised). Miss Rachel's room! You're not going in there without Miss Rachel's leave?

Cuff. It's my duty to search the room, Mr. Betteredge. And I mean to search it while I have the chance.

Betteredge (furiously). Your duty? Damn you, you have some suspicion of Miss Rachel! (*He seizes* CUFF *by the collar of his coat.* CUFF *shows no surprise, and makes no resistance.*)

Franklin (interfering). Betteredge! (*He forces* BETTEREDGE *to release* CUFF.) The Sergeant is right. Rachel's own conduct justifies him. (*He retires with a gesture of despair, seats himself at a table, and hides his face in his hands.* BETTEREDGE *stands petrified by what* FRANKLIN *has just said to him.*)

Cuff (as quietly as usual). If it's any comfort to you, Mr. Betteredge, collar me again. You don't in the least know how to do it. But I'll overlook your awkwardness in consideration of your feelings.

Betteredge (strongly agitated). I ask your pardon, Sergeant. Please to remember as some excuse for me that I've served the family for fifty years. Many and many a time Miss Rachel's climbed on my knees when she was a child – (*His voice fails him – he turns away to hide his tears.*)

Cuff. Don't distress yourself, Mr. Betteredge. I've hushed up worse cases than this in my time. (*He goes into* RACHEL'*s room.*)

Betteredge (bewildered and distressed). Master Franklin! You have a clear head – you can see farther than I can. What *does* this mean?

Franklin (without moving). It means that I have done my best to help Rachel to find her diamond, and that she has grossly insulted me in return. It means that Rachel is the one person in the house who refuses to let her wardrobe be examined. Who is to blame Sergeant Cuff if he suspects her after that?

Betteredge (sternly). Suspects her of what, sir?

Franklin. Of knowing who stole the Moonstone, and of concealing the scoundrel who took it for some reason of her own.

Betteredge (indignantly). It's a lie – it's an infernal lie! I wish I had throttled the Sergeant when I had hold of him. (CUFF *appears at the door with the dressing-gown in his hand.* BETTEREDGE *turns on him with renewed anger.*) Well! now you've searched her room, what have you got there? (*He points to the dressing-gown.*)

Cuff (quietly). I've got the thief.

Franklin (starting up and joining them). Who is the thief? (CUFF *opens the dressing-gown.* FRANKLIN *recognises it as his own, and starts back, like a man thunderstruck.*)

Cuff (pointing to it). Who wore this dressing-gown last night? Here is the stain of the varnish as plain as can be, to sight and smell. (*He looks up and notices* FRANKLIN.) Mr. Blake, you know something about this.

Betteredge (also noticing him, in alarm). Master Franklin! Master Franklin! What's come to you? (FRANKLIN *tries vainly to speak. His eyes are fixed, horror-struck, on the dressing-gown.* CUFF *approaches* FRANKLIN *suspiciously, with the dressing-gown still in his hand.*)

Cuff. I rely on your honour, sir, to speak the truth – no matter how painful it may be. (*He holds up the dressing-gown.*) Whose dressing-gown is this?

Franklin (wildly). Mine! ! ! (*As* FRANKLIN *gives his answer,* RACHEL *enters from the garden. She sees the dressing-gown – a faint cry escapes her –*

she stops, rooted to the spot. The three men all turn, and look at her in silence. BETTEREDGE *is the first to speak.*)

Betteredge (*pointing to the dressing-gown*). Miss Rachel! do you know anything about this? (RACHEL *remains immovably silent, with her eyes fixed on* FRANKLIN.)

Cuff. Innocent people may be suspected, miss, unless you tell us what you know. (RACHEL *still keeps silence.*)

Franklin (*appealing to her in despair*). Rachel! Rachel! (RACHEL *shudders at his voice. Her head sinks upon her breast. With a motion of her hand she signs sternly to* BETTEREDGE *and to* CUFF, *who stand between her and the door of her room, to let her pass. They obey. She slowly crosses the stage to the door.* CUFF *makes a last appeal to her.*)

Cuff. For the last time, miss, have you nothing to tell us?

Rachel (*coldly and sternly*). I have nothing to tell you.

Betteredge. Oh, Miss Rachel! surely you have something to say?

Rachel (*to* BETTEREDGE). I have this to say. I supposed my room to be sacred from intrusion, especially while *you* were here. For the future I shall lock my door. (*She enters her room, and is heard to double-lock her door.*)

Franklin (*wildly*). Am I the thief? (BETTEREDGE *vainly attempts to compose him.*) Do your duty, Sergeant! On my word as an honest man, on my oath as a Christian, I know no more how that stain came on my dressing-gown than you do. I can't expect you to believe me. Do your duty.

Cuff (*firmly*). Compose yourself, sir. I know my trade a little better than to trust to appearances. (*He throws the dressing-gown across a chair.*) As matters stand, I grant you, the right reading of the riddle seems hard to guess. Patience, Mr. Blake! Time will do for us what we can't do for ourselves.

Franklin. Patience? There is the dressing-gown accusing me on the plainest evidence of being a thief! Who can be patient under that?

Betteredge (*angrily*). The dressing-gown's a liar!

Cuff. Gently, Mr. Betteredge. The dressing-gown is only a witness that can't speak. (*To* FRANKLIN.) There's one awkward difficulty in our way, sir. Miss Rachel has given me my dismissal from the house.

Franklin (*passionately*). Neither you nor I can leave the house until my innocence is established! In the frightful position in which I am placed I want all your experience to help me. (*He walks to and fro excit-*

edly.) Rachel's conduct is simply inhuman! "I have nothing to tell you – " that is all she has to say; with my dressing-gown found in her room, and with my reputation at stake. I will make her explain herself. (*He approaches the door on the left.* CUFF *and* BETTEREDGE *stop him.*)

Cuff. You were good enough to say just now, sir, that you wanted my experience to help you. If you speak a word to Miss Rachel as things are at present, you force me to throw up the case.

Betteredge. Don't do that, Master Franklin! Just let me give you a word of advice. There's a mine of hidden perversity in the best woman that ever lived. (FRANKLIN *shows impatience.*) Wait a bit, sir; I have something to propose. You keep out of Miss Rachel's way for the present, and let me tell her, when she next inquires after you, that you have left the house.

Cuff (*To* FRANKLIN). Not a bad notion! What the young lady won't say before your face, she *may* say behind your back.

Betteredge (*scandalised*). That's not my notion, Mr. Sergeant! When I set a trap for my young lady, it's baited with love. (*to* FRANKLIN.) This is what I speculate on, Mr. Franklin! When Miss Rachel thinks that you have left her, take my word for it she will be sorry she treated you so ill. Then show yourself, and catch her unawares, with her heart softened towards you and the tear in her eye!

Cuff. Follow his advice, Mr. Blake. An hour's rest will do you no harm. You're looking sadly upset, sir.

Franklin (*giving way*). I am broken by this dreadful discovery, and I can't hide it any longer! Take me away, Betteredge.

Betteredge. Come into my little sitting-room, Master Franklin; you will be in safe hiding there. (*He puts* FRANKLIN'S *arm in his, turns to lead him out, sees the dressing-gown thrown on the chair and apostrophises it.*) As for you, you scandal-mongering, mischief-making, varnish-stinking, substitute-bed-gown – come along! (*He angrily snatches up the dressing-gown with his free hand, and leads* FRANKLIN *out by the hall door.*)

Cuff (*alone*). Now I have got rid of them I can think a little. Two roads to discovery lie before me: a long road that starts from the dressing-gown, and a short cut that starts from the first suspicion I had in my mind when I entered this house. If I follow the long road I travel in the dark, and lose time by the way. If I try the short cut, I know where *that* is likely to lead me before the next train takes Miss Rachel to London. My choice: Try the short cut. (*He looks at his watch.*) Why hasn't the policeman come back from his errand? Why doesn't he send in his report? (*He rings the bell, and then glances at* RACHEL's *door.*) I suppose I have time to make an inquiry before Miss Rachel turns me out of the house! (ANDREW *enters by the hall door with a letter in his hand.*)

 Andrew. A letter for you, sir.

 Cuff. Who brought it?

 Andrew. The policeman, sir.

 Cuff. Is he waiting?

 Andrew. Yes, sir. (CUFF *leaves* ANDREW, *so as turn his back on the servant, and speaks while he reads the letter.*)

 Cuff. The policeman's written report! After the errand I sent him on, it wouldn't do to risk his being found here in private conversation with me. (*He reads the report, and then, looking up, whistles the first notes of his favourite air.*) My suspicion has hit the mark! There are one or two people in this house who will be rather surprised when the truth comes out. (*He turns towards* ANDREW.) Are there any telegraph forms on the writing-table there?

 Andrew (*producing the forms*). Here they are, sir.

 Cuff (*seating himself at the table*). Wait, while I write. (ANDREW *waits at the back.* CUFF *writes his telegram, and reads what he has written, to himself.*) "Have you seen or heard anything of a large yellow diamond, now missing from this house? Answer immediately. All expenses paid." That will do! (*He seals the telegram in an envelope, writes on the envelope, and hands it to* ANDREW.) Give that to the policeman at once. Has he got a fly at the door?

 Andrew. Yes, sir – the fly he came in.

 Cuff. Tell him to go at a gallop to the station. He is to wait there for the telegram reply, and to bring it to me, as fast as a fresh horse and carriage can take him. (ANDREW *goes out with the telegram.* CUFF *rises, puzzled by his own symptoms.*) What's the matter with me? Is my heart beating faster than usual? I declare I am excited for the first time in my life! This will never do! I must compose my mind – I'll have a look at the roses. (*He crosses to the flowers.*) Ah, my darlings! It takes the dirty taste of a thief out of one's mind only to look at you! (*He glances out of the window into the garden.*) I can't endure the sight of those gravel walks in the rose-garden. Grass walks among your roses, Miss Rachel – grass walks next time. I beg and pray of you! (*He looks round sharply at the hall door, and sees* GODFREY *entering.*) Fine day for a walk, sir. I hope you have enjoyed it.

Godfrey. Any news, Sergeant?

Cuff. No news, sir.

Godfrey (carelessly). What are you going to do next? (*He walks to the library table and takes up a newspaper.*)

Cuff (aside, looking towards RACHEL's *door.*) As things are now, I'd better keep out of Miss Rachel's way till I get my telegram (*To* GODFREY.) I am going to take a turn in the garden, sir.

Godfrey (satirically). Do you expect to find the Moonstone there?

Cuff (very quietly and emphatically). Perhaps I may surprise you, sir, by finding the Moonstone sooner than you think. (*He goes out on the right.*)

Godfrey (alone). What does he mean? He is evidently at his wits' end. Sergeant Cuff is a highly overrated man. (*He looks towards* RACHEL's *door.*) Where is my charming cousin, I wonder? (*He goes to the door and speaks.*) Are you in your room, Rachel?

Rachel (speaking inside). Is that Godfrey?

Godfrey. Yes, dear Rachel!

Rachel (unlocking the door, and appearing). I am glad to see you back again. (*Aside.*) Oh, what a relief it is to find somebody whom I can still respect! (*To* GODFREY.) Have you seen anything – ? (*She stops short.*)

Godfrey. Yes?

Rachel. Have you seen anything of Franklin?

Godfrey. Nothing. I have only this moment returned.

Rachel (aside). What has become of that miserable wretch?

Godfrey (aside). She's thinking of Franklin. I had better make haste. (*To* RACHEL.) May I ask a bold question, dear Rachel?

Rachel (absorbed in her own thoughts). I beg your pardon. (*She rings the bell.*) I want Betteredge for a moment. (BETTEREDGE *enters by the hall door.*)

Betteredge. Did you ring, miss?

Rachel (speaking to him apart from GODFREY).* Where is Mr. Franklin Blake?

Betteredge. Mr. Franklin Blake has left the house, miss. (*Aside.*) I've told my lie, and now I'm comfortable! (*He goes out.*)

Rachel (sadly, to herself). Gone! (*She turns away to the fireplace, and stands there looking sadly at the bright flame.* MISS CLACK *appears in the gallery.*)

Godfrey (*looking at* RACHEL *from the other side of the stage*). Has Franklin proposed? and has she refused him?

Miss Clack (*gaily, as she descends the stairs*). Mr. Godfrey! I thought you would be back by this time!

Godfrey (*to himself*). The devil take Miss Clack!

Miss Clack (*advancing*). Have you been to Frizinghall?

Godfrey (*sullenly*). Yes, Miss Clack.

Miss Clack. So have I! How unfortunate that we never met! (GOD-FREY *is silent.* MISS CLACK *looks at him with interest.*) Excuse me for remarking it, dear Mr. Godfrey, your walk appears to have fatigued you.

Godfrey (*absently*). Very likely; I used to be a better walker than I am now. (*He glances at* RACHEL, *still standing thoughtfully by the fire.*) There she is, ready to listen to me – if I could only get rid of Miss Clack! (*He turns away.* MISS CLACK *follows him, and tenderly resumes the conversation.*)

Miss Clack. I have sometimes thought, Mr. Godfrey, that your charitable business is perhaps a little too much for you. Why not employ a devoted person in the capacity of assistant? (*She looks down in modest confusion.*) Speaking as a true friend, I sometimes think you might find that devoted person in a wife. (GODFREY *starts and looks alarmed.*) She is to be found – yes, dear Mr. Godfrey (though you look as if you doubted it), the right woman – the woman worthy of you – *is* to be found.)

Rachel (*rousing herself*). Godfrey, do you mind inquiring if the carriage is at the door?

Godfrey (*eagerly*). With the greatest pleasure! (*He hurries out at the back.* MISS CLACK *looks after him as if he had a little disappointed her.*)

Miss Clack (*to herself*). Politeness is certainly a virtue. Mr. Godfrey is perhaps a little *too* polite. (*She looks at* RACHEL.) Dearest Rachel, how unhappy you look!

Rachel. I look what I am. Do you know what it is to reproach yourself when reproach comes too late?

Miss Clack (*aside*). At last she feels the want of Me! (*Looking about her.*) Where is my bag? (*She discovers the bag where she had placed it on entering the room, takes it, and returns to* RACHEL, *holding up the bag.*)

Here, dearest, is the remedy for all your sorrows!

Rachel. I daresay you mean well, Drusilla, but your idea of consolation is not mine. Forgive me, I shall be better if I keep quiet till the carriage comes. (*She retires to a sofa at the back, and reclines on it with her face turned away on the cushion.*)

Miss Clack (*in confidence to herself*). In all my experience, I never met with a more promising case for tracts! The one question is how to direct her attention to the inestimable blessings in this bag? She must go back to her room to put on her bonnet when the carriage comes. I know what I'll do! When she leaves that sofa, she shall find one of my precious tracts waiting for her in every part of the hall! (MISS CLACK *trips softly to and fro, depositing tracts on the different articles of furniture as she names them.*) A tract on her favourite chair, if she happens to look that way! Another on her work-table! Another at the fireplace! Another among the roses! And one more pinned to the curtain, to catch her eye if she goes out by the garden. (*While* MISS CLACK *is pinning her tract on the outer side of the window curtain, so that she is hidden by it from the observation of anyone entering the room,* GODFREY *returns from his errand.*)

Godfrey (*advancing*). I have been to the stables, Rachel. (*He looks round him, and continues, aside.*) We are alone again!

Rachel (*raising herself to a sitting position*). Is the carriage ready?

Godfrey. It will be ready in ten minutes. (RACHEL *rises, and advances a few steps as if to return to her room to get ready.* GODFREY *follows, and stops her.*) Dearest Rachel! (MISS CLACK, *hearing him, suddenly checks herself on the point of returning to the room.*)

Miss Clack (*aside*). "Dearest Rachel"?

Rachel (*looking at* GODFREY *in surprise*). What do you want?

Godfrey. One word with you. There is nobody to hear us. We are relieved of the everlasting presence of Miss Clack.

Miss Clack (*to herself*). My everlasting presence!

Godfrey (*continuing*). May I speak? (RACHEL *understands him. Her head droops on her bosom.* GODFREY *leads her to her chair. She sees the tract in it, and checks herself.*)

Rachel. What is that in the chair?

Godfrey (*taking it up*). A book of yours? (*He reads the title.*) "Man the Deceiver, by the author of Woman the Dupe!"

Miss Clack (*to herself*). How perfectly appropriate!

Godfrey (*throwing the tract aside*). Miss Clack and her ridiculous tracts!

Miss Clack (*to herself*). My ridiculous tracts!

Godfrey. Be seated, dear Rachel. Your charming kindness since I have been here has once more emboldened me to hope. Am I mad to dream of some future day when your heart may soften to me? (*He places his hand on the table while he speaks, and knocks off the tract which* MISS CLACK *has put there. It falls on* RACHEL's *lap. She takes it up.*)

Rachel. Another book that doesn't belong to me? (*She reads.*) "Soft Soap. By a Converted Laundress."

Miss Clack (*to herself*). Mr. Godfrey's own language, exactly described!

Godfrey (*continuing*). I have lost every interest in life, Rachel, but my interest in you. My charitable business has become an unendurable nuisance to me. When I see a ladies' committee, I wish them all at the uttermost ends of the earth!

Miss Clack (*to herself*). The "Mothers'-Small-Clothes" a nuisance! He wishes us all at the uttermost ends of the earth! (*She shakes her fist at* GODFREY.) Apostate! (*In her anger she has spoken the last word just loud enough for* RACHEL *to hear her voice, while* GODFREY *is still pleading with her.*)

Rachel (*starting*). Is there somebody at the window? (GODFREY *turns towards the window.* MISS CLACK *sees him, and instantly feigns to be entering the room, after a walk in the garden.*)

Miss Clack (*innocently*). You can't imagine how delightful the air is in the garden! (*She looks round her.*) Oh, dear! Have I come in again at the wrong time? I'll go back to the garden directly!

Godfrey (*with formal politeness*). You will excuse me, I am sure, Miss Clack, if I own that I have something to say in confidence to Rachel.

Miss Clack (*spitefully*). Ah, Mr. Godfrey, I can guess what it is! You good man! You are trying to interest Rachel in that charitable business which is the delight of your life. You are bent on persuading her to join those ladies' committees to which you are so unselfishly and so devotedly attached. Forgive my innocent intrusion. Good-morning! (*She goes out again on the right, angrily tearing away the tract pinned to the curtain as she passes.*)

Godfrey (*aside*). Has she been listening? (*He returns to* RACHEL, *who has remained absorbed in her own thoughts during the dialogue between* MISS

CLACK *and* GODFREY.) Rachel, you are not annoyed by this trifling interruption? Will you recall what I have said to you? Will you favour me, dearest, with a word of reply?

Rachel (sadly). You have made your confession, Godfrey. Would it cure you of your unhappy attachment to me if I made mine? I am the wretchedest woman living.

Godfrey. Rachel! Rachel!

Rachel. What greater wretchedness can there be than to live degraded in your own estimation? After what you have said, Godfrey, I owe it to you to speak as plainly as I can. Forget for a moment your favourable opinion of me. Suppose you were in love with some other woman?

Godfrey. Yes?

Rachel. Suppose you discovered the woman to be utterly unworthy of you – a false, shameless, degraded creature. And suppose your faithful heart still clung, in spite of you, to that first object of your love? Suppose – (*She stops, despairing of herself.*) Oh, how can I make a *man* understand that a feeling which horrifies me at myself can be a feeling which fascinates me at the same time? Godfrey, it's the breath of my life, and it's the poison that kills me – both in one! Don't ask me any more. I will never see him again – let that be enough. Oh, my heart! my heart! I feel as if I was stifling for want of breath! (*She tries to speak lightly.*) Is there a form of hysterics, Godfrey, that bursts into words instead of tears? What does it matter? You will get over your love for me now. I have dropped to my right place in your estimation, haven't I? (*The hysterical passion returns and overpowers her.*) Don't notice me! don't pity me! For God's sake, go! (*She bursts into tears.*)

Godfrey (to himself). Franklin Blake! – I see my way. (*He drops on one knee, and takes* RACHEL's *hand.*) Rachel, you have spoken of your place in my estimation. Judge what that place is, when I implore you on my knees to let the cure of your poor wounded heart be my care!

Rachel (looking at him in amazement). You can't have listened to what I said to you.

Godfrey. Not a word of it has been lost on me!

Rachel (sadly). You are speaking under a generous impulse. I am generous enough, on my side, not to take advantage of it.

Godfrey. I am speaking in the full possession of my reason. Rachel, it is your duty to yourself to forget this ill-placed attachment. At your age, and with your attractions, can you sentence yourself to a single life? Impossible ! You may marry some other man some years hence. Or you may marry the man who now pleads with you, and who asks of heaven no purer joy than to make you his wife.

Rachel (struggling against herself). Say no more! You are trying to reconcile me to reasons which have been in my mind already. When I have tried to find my way back to my own self-respect, I confess I have thought of another marriage. I confess I have remembered your expressions of attachment to me. (GODFREY *attempts to speak.*) Don't tempt me, Godfrey! I am wretched enough and reckless enough, if you press me, to marry you on your own terms. Take the warning, and say no more!

Godfrey. I won't rise from my knees until you have said "Yes."

Rachel (beginning to yield). You will repent, and I shall repent, when it is too late.

Godfrey. We shall both bless the day when I pressed and you yielded.

Rachel (still yielding). You won't hurry me, Godfrey?

Godfrey. My time shall be yours.

Rachel. You won't ask me for more than I can give.

Godfrey. My angel! I only ask you to give me yourself.

Rachel (faintly). Take me! (*Her head drops.* GODFREY *puts his arm round her. She submits for a moment, then draws back with a start.*) Leave me for a little while. I am dreadfully agitated. Let me compose myself.

Godfrey. When may I see you again?

Rachel. Wait for me in the garden. I will join you in a few minutes.

Godfrey. Till then – (*He kisses his hand to her, turns away to the window with an air of relief, and speaks aside.*) The best day's work I ever did in my life! (*He goes out on the right.*)

Rachel (confusedly). Have I given him my promise? Am I engaged to be his wife? Why not? What have I done that is not wise and right? He is a good man – he is a true man; he will help me forget. (*She pauses thoughtfully.* BETTEREDGE *appears at the hall door and looks in.*)

Betteredge (in a whisper to himself). Nobody with her! Now for Mr. Franklin! (*He disappears again.* RACHEL *continues.*)

Rachel (pursuing her thoughts). I don't expect to be happy, but surely I ought to feel contented, at least? Who could wish for truer devotion than Godfrey's? (*She pauses again, and suddenly starts to her feet.*)

Franklin! I'm thinking of Franklin again! Oh, how base I am – how hatefully, shamefully weak! Will nothing shake that man's fatal influence over me? (FRANKLIN *appears at the hall door.* RACHEL, *standing with her back turned on him, walks angrily to the right.*) I *will* forget him! I *will* be true to Godfrey, if I break my heart in doing it! (*She turns to walk back again and sees* FRANKLIN. *She stops instantly, in dead silence, rooted to the spot.* FRANKLIN, *in silence on his side, slowly advances a few steps towards her and pauses. They look at each other.*)

 Franklin (softly). Rachel!

 Rachel (rousing herself, and looking at him with contemptuous surprise). Another lie? More treachery?

 Franklin (louder). Rachel!

 Rachel (with bitter deliberation). You have even degraded my honest old servant. Betteredge told me you had left the house. And now you steal your way in here, when I am alone. (*She speaks her next words, not angrily but with contemptuous calmness.*) You coward. You mean, miserable, heartless coward.

 Franklin (controlling himself). I remember the time, Rachel, when you could have told me that I had offended you in a worthier way than that. I regret that I permitted Betteredge to deceive you. I ask your pardon.

 Rachel (with ironical humility). I suppose *I* ought to ask *your* pardon? Perhaps there is some excuse for me. After what you have done, it does seem a cowardly action to try the experiment of taking me by surprise. But that is only a woman's view. I should have done better if I had controlled myself, and said nothing.

 Franklin (stung by her tone). If my honour were not in your hands, I would leave you this instant, and never see you again. (*He pauses, overcome by his agitation, and supports himself by resting his hand on a chair; then continues, in faint, sad tones.*) I am weak and ill; I am not able to control myself as I ought. Be just to me, Rachel; I only ask you to be just. You speak of what I have done. What have I done?

 Rachel (with rising anger). You ask that question of *me*?

 Franklin. I ask more. I ask why you insulted me before Betteredge and the police-officer. I ask what was in your mind when you said: "Franklin Blake, you are beneath being insulted, and you know it."

 Rachel (pointing to the door). Leave the room!

 Franklin. Not until you have answered me!

Rachel. You refuse?

Franklin. I refuse!

Rachel (in violent exasperation). There is one last degradation left for you – you shall be turned out by the servants. *(She approaches the table on which the bell is placed.* FRANKLIN *takes her by the hand, as she tries to touch the bell.)*

Franklin (firmly). Look at me!

Rachel (feeling the influence of his eye and his touch). Let me go!

Franklin (tenderly, still holding her hand). Rachel, you once loved me.

Rachel (struggling more and more feebly against his influence over her). Let me go!

Franklin (more and more tenderly). Remember the happy old times when we were children together. Let the memory of your mother plead for me. I was her favourite; she could hardly have been fonder of me if I had been her own son!

Rachel (melting into tears). Don't speak of it, Franklin! You break my heart! Why do you come here to humiliate yourself? Why do you come here to humiliate me? Are you afraid I shall expose you? Have you not seen for yourself that I can't expose you? I can't tear you out of my heart! No matter how falsely I may be suspected, no matter how vilely I may be wronged, the secret of your infamy is safe in my keeping! *(FRANKLIN draws back from her slowly, overwhelmed by her last words.)*

Franklin (in low tones of horror). My infamy?

Rachel (with a sudden outbreak of despair). Be content with the confession that you have wrung from me. Go!

Franklin (as before). My infamy?

Rachel (drawing back from him on her side). He looks as if *I* had injured *him*! *(She turns again, appealing to him for the last time.)* I gave you one opportunity after another of owning the truth, or of making reparation in secret. I left unsaid nothing that I could say; I left undone nothing that I could do. *(Her anger begins to rise.)* And all the return you made was to look at me with your heartless pretence of innocence, as you are looking now!

Franklin (suddenly rising to indignation on his side). Of what infamy do you believe me guilty? Say it in plain words, or *I* will ring the bell, and call every soul in the house to judge between you and me!

Rachel (roused to passion). Oh! is there another man like this in the world? After seeing his dressing-gown in the policeman's hands! After hearing me refuse to give any explanation, for *his* sake! You villain, you mean villain, I would rather have lost fifty diamonds, than see your face lying to me as it lies now!

Franklin (passionately). What do you mean?

Rachel (more passionately on her side). What I say!

Franklin (staggering back). You believe that I stole the diamond?

Rachel (following him up furiously). Believe? I *saw* you steal the diamond with my own eyes! ! ! (FRANKLIN *throws up his hands with a faint cry, and drops in a swoon at her feet.* RACHEL *starts back with a cry of horror.*) Oh God! have I killed him? Help! help! (BETTEREDGE *and* CUFF *enter together by the hall door.* RACHEL *appeals to them distractedly.*) Look! oh, look at him!

Betteredge (kneeling by FRANKLIN, *raising his head, and feeling his heart).* Compose yourself, Miss Rachel. It's only a fainting-fit. (*While* BETTEREDGE *is speaking,* CUFF *goes to a side-table, on which a bottle of water and some tumblers are placed, and returns to* BETTEREDGE *with a glass of water.* RACHEL, *at the same moment, pushes* BETTEREDGE *aside, and takes his place by* FRANKLIN.)

Rachel (answering BETTEREDGE). Leave him to Me! Nobody shall touch him but Me! (*She kneels over* FRANKLIN, *resting his head on her knee, and sprinkling his forehead with water from the tumbler which* BETTEREDGE *receives from* CUFF, *and holds for her.* Oh Betteredge, he doesn't move, his colour doesn't come back! (ANDREW *appears at the hall door, followed by the* POLICEMAN *with a telegram in his hand.*)

Andrew (entering the room). The carriage is at the door, miss.

Rachel. Send the carriage to the town for the doctor. Instantly! Instantly!

Andrew. Yes, miss! (*He hurries out.* RACHEL *resumes her efforts to revive* FRANKLIN. BETTEREDGE *remains with her.* CUFF *notices the telegram in the* POLICEMAN's *hands.*)

Cuff (to the POLICEMAN). For me?

The Policeman. For you. (*He hands the telegram to* CUFF, *and waits.*)

Cuff (snapping his fingers in triumph, after a glance at the telegram). I've found the Moonstone! (*The curtain falls.*)

THE END OF THE SECOND ACT

―――

THE THIRD ACT

Scene: as before. Time: evening, on the same day. The lamps are lit again, and the curtains are drawn over the window on the right, as in Act I. At the rise of the curtain, FRANKLIN, BETTEREDGE, and MR. CANDY are discovered. FRANKLIN is seated at a table, hiding his face in his hands. MR. CANDY stands on one side of him, and BETTEREDGE on the other.

Mr. Candy. Are you quite sure of the facts, Mr. Blake? You have not long recovered from a fainting fit, and your mind may still be a little confused.

Franklin. My mind is perfectly clear. Put me to the test in any way you like.

Mr. Candy. Repeat what you said to me about Miss Rachel just now.

Franklin (repeating it). Rachel told me, with her own lips, that she saw me take the diamond out of the cabinet drawer. And my dressing-gown has the stain of the wet varnish on it to prove that she spoke the truth.

Mr. Candy. And you know absolutely nothing about it yourself?

Franklin. Absolutely nothing. (MR. CANDY *pauses and considers with himself.* BETTEREDGE *addresses him.*)

Betteredge. What do you say to *that*, sir? Solomon himself would be at a loss to put the pieces of the puzzle together!

Mr. Candy (to BETTEREDGE). Was Mr. Blake at all anxious about the safe keeping of the diamond before he went to bed?

Betteredge. Anxious isn't the word, sir. Bothered is the word. Impossible to persuade him that the diamond was safe in the cabinet drawer.

Mr. Candy (suddenly turning to FRANKLIN). Are you composed enough to hear me patiently, Mr. Blake, if I venture on a bold guess?

Franklin (despondently). Say what you like!

Mr. Candy. I say this. You were dreaming of the Moonstone last night, and you took the diamond while you were walking in your sleep.

Franklin (starting up). Walking in my sleep! ! !

Betteredge (indignantly). He never did such a thing in his life!

Mr. Candy (quietly). He did it for the first time last night, Mr. Betteredge. I defy you to explain what has happened in any other way.

Franklin. Have you any reason for what you say?

Mr. Candy. I have three reasons. First, the disordered condition of your nervous system. Second, your supper and your grog. Third, a case of somnambulism in my practice, which is in many respects like your case – as I believe it to be.

Franklin. Suppose you are right. What then?

Mr. Candy. If you will assist me, sir, I think I can *prove* that I am right.

Franklin. Can you find the lost diamond? Can you prove that I took it without knowing what I was about at the time? I am disgraced for life, and through no fault of mine. Betteredge! pack my portmanteau, I shall leave by the night express.

Betteredge. Don't say that, sir! What's the use of leaving us? Where are you going to?

Franklin (irritably). I am going to the devil!

Betteredge. God bless you, sir, go where you may!

Mr. Candy (to FRANKLIN*).* Decide nothing rashly, Mr. Blake. Let me say to Miss Rachel what I have just said to you. And let her tell us if she saw anything strange in your looks and your movements last night.

Betteredge. I'll fetch her, Master Franklin! She's only giving some orders in the servants'-hall. (*He attempts to go out at the back.* FRANKLIN *stops him.*)

Franklin. Rachel has deliberately charged me with stealing her diamond. Nothing will induce me to see her again until my innocence of the theft is a proved fact.

Betteredge. Leave it to me, sir, to tell her what Mr. Candy has said. Let me be the first to ease my dear young mistress's mind!

Franklin (impatiently). Tell your mistress what I have just said, and tell her anything else you like.

Betteredge. Thank you, sir, thank you. (*Aside to* MR. CANDY.) Make the most of your time with him before Miss Rachel comes in. (*He goes out by the hall door.*)

Mr. Candy. Your position is not so hopeless as you seem to think it, sir. Will you hear what I have to say?

Franklin. Tell me one thing first. What am I to expect in the future? Am I never to sleep quietly in my bed for the rest of my life?

Mr. Candy. You have only to recover your health, and I will answer for your sleeping as quietly as any man living. Let us return to the other question, which you put to me just now. You have asked if I can find the lost diamond?

Franklin. Yes.

Mr. Candy. You have asked if I can prove your innocence of the theft?

Franklin. Well!

Mr. Candy. I may be able to do both the one and the other, if you will consent to be guided by *me.* (RACHEL's *voice is heard outside.*)

Rachel (*speaking in great agitation*). I don't want to hear any more! I insist on seeing him!

Franklin (*quietly to* MR. CANDY). If you wish to speak further with me, you will find me in my room. (*He ascends the stairs deliberately, careless whether* RACHEL *sees him or not.*)

Mr. Candy (*following and remonstrating with him*). Mr. Blake – !

Rachel (*outside*). Let me go! How dare you stand between me and the door. (*She appears at the hall door, hurriedly entering the room*). Where is he? (MR. CANDY *returns to* RACHEL. FRANKLIN *reaches the top of the stairs.*) Mr. Candy, I *must* see him! I must ask his pardon on my knees!

Mr. Candy. You can't see him now, Miss Rachel. He has just gone upstairs.

Rachel (*seeing* FRANKLIN *open his bedroom door*). To avoid me! (*She calls entreatingly.*) Franklin! (FRANKLIN *enters his room, and closes the door.* RACHEL *turns in tears to* MR. CANDY.) Not a word of answer! Not even a look! I deserve it.

Mr. Candy (*surprised*). You deserve it?

Rachel (*with the keenest self-reproach*). I was alone in the hall last night, when the house was shut up, and there was not light but the moon. I saw him take the diamond, and I put the vilest construction on what I saw!

Mr. Candy. My dear young lady, how could you possibly suspect that he was sleeping and dreaming, when you couldn't see him plainly, and when you never heard of such a thing as his walking in his sleep?

Rachel. I don't care! I have treated him cruelly – I who love him with all my heart and soul! Oh Mr. Candy, I have lost him! He will never forgive me – he will never forget what I said to him!

Mr. Candy (*earnestly*). Miss Rachel, he may yet forgive and forget! He may yet be nearer and dearer to you than ever! (RACHEL *starts.*)

Compose yourself, and tell me one thing. After he had taken the Moonstone, what did he do with it?

Rachel. He took it upstairs with him to his own room.

Mr. Candy. It is at least possible that he has hidden it there in his sleep – dreaming, of course, that he was putting it in a place of safety. You follow me, so far?

Rachel. I don't follow you at all! I want to hear about the happy time you have promised me – the time when Franklin is to be nearer and dearer to me than ever. Get on to that!

Mr. Candy. A moment's patience, Miss Rachel. I am getting to it now. (BETTEREDGE *enters by the hall door.*)

Rachel (to BETTEREDGE). What do you want? Don't interrupt us! Go away!

Betteredge. I beg your pardon, miss. I have got a message for you, and I must indeed deliver it.

Rachel. Go away!

Mr. Candy (to RACHEL). One moment! (*To* BETTEREDGE.) Does your message relate to the Moonstone?

Betteredge. Knowing the person who gave me the message, sir, I haven't a doubt of it.

Mr. Candy. Let him speak, Miss Rachel. (RACHEL *signs to* BET-TEREDGE *to speak.*)

Betteredge. I won't be long, miss. Since you left me I have been having a little talk with a person in the grounds.

Rachel. Who is the person?

Betteredge. You will be angry if I mention his name.

Rachel. Sergeant Cuff?

Betteredge. Right, miss, at the first guess.

Rachel. That man still in the house! What does he mean? What is he doing? What does he want?

Betteredge. That's exactly what I've been trying to tell you, miss, ever since I came into the room. As to what he means, he keeps it to himself. As to what he is doing, he has just had a long private conversation behind the stables with a strange gentleman who came from the railway in a fly. As to what he wants, he wants two minutes' talk immediately, Miss Rachel, with you.

Rachel. I refuse to see him! I insist on his leaving the house. (CUFF *appears at the hall door.* RACHEL *points to him indignantly.*) Mr. Candy!

Betteredge! do you see that man? This is a downright insult. I appeal to your protection.

Betteredge. Don't be angry, miss. I'll take him away. (*He attempts to approach* CUFF, *and is stopped by* MR. CANDY.)

Mr. Candy. Wait a minute! (*To* CUFF.) You will find pen and ink in the servants' hall. Tell Miss Rachel, in writing, what you want.

Cuff. Might I whisper one word in your ear, sir? (*He whispers.* MR. CANDY *starts back with a cry of astonishment.*)

Rachel (*observing him*). What is it?

Mr. Candy (*excitedly*). Something that you *must* hear, Miss Rachel! Something that makes the Sergeant's presence at our conference indispensable. Take a seat, Sergeant Cuff.

Cuff (*looking at* BETTEREDGE). I have an order to give, sir, to the policeman who is waiting outside. (*To* RACHEL.) Might I ask Mr. Betteredge to take another message for me?

Rachel. Certainly! Betteredge, take the message!

Betteredge (*coming forward unwillingly*). Yes, miss. (*Aside.*) Just as I wanted to hear what they're going to say next! Just as my curiosity is thirsting as it were for a drop more!

Cuff (*to* BETTEREDGE). You will find the policeman on the drive in front of the house. He is on no account to go back to the town before I have seen him again. The man is hungry and tired, Mr. Betteredge. Will you please see that he has some supper?

Betteredge (*aside*). I wish his supper may choke him! (*He goes out by the hall door.*)

Rachel. Now, Mr. Candy, what does this mean?

Mr. Candy. Ask Sergeant Cuff.

Rachel (*to* CUFF). You wish to speak to me? What do you want?

Cuff (*quietly*). A little matter of business, miss. I only want to give you back your diamond.

Rachel (*thunderstruck*). What! ! !

Cuff. There is the Moonstone. (*He hands it to* RACHEL. RACHEL *stands petrified.* CUFF, *smiling grimly, waits to hear what she will say to him.* RACHEL, *recovering herself, turns to* MR. CANDY, *and shows him the diamond.*)

Rachel. Can I believe my own eyes!

Cuff (*to* RACHEL). I won't intrude on you any longer, miss. I'll be off by the next train.

Rachel. Don't talk of going away (*suddenly changing to perfect amiability.*) I owe you an apology, Mr. Cuff. Pray excuse the hasty words I said to you earlier in the day – and, for Heaven's sake, tell me how the Moonstone found its way into your hands!

Cuff. You will please keep it a secret, miss, from every soul in the house; Mr. Betteredge, in particular, must know nothing about it. That good man is of too liberal a nature to keep anything to himself. (*To* MR. CANDY.) He told me, sir, of your notion about Mr. Blake, and the diamond, within hearing of all the men at the stables.

Rachel (impatiently). We quite understand you. Go on! go on!

Cuff. Very good, miss. Thus it happened: Earlier in the day I received information of a visit paid by a money-*borrowing* person, to a money-*lending* person in London.

Rachel. What are their names?

Cuff. Sorry to disappoint you, miss. For the present, I am not at liberty to mention their names. Having my own reasons for suspecting that I was on the trace of the diamond, I telegraphed to the money-*lending* person –

Rachel (impatiently). Do give him a name!

Cuff. All right, miss! We will give him a number, as they do in the prisons. We will call the money-*lending* person Number One. I telegraphed to Number One, inquiring if he had seen or heard anything of the lost Moonstone. His answer informed me that the money-*borrowing* person – shall we give *him* a number, miss? Shall we call him Number Two?

Rachel. Yes! yes!

Cuff. The answer informed me that Number Two had this very day offered your diamond as security for a loan.

Rachel (eagerly). How did he get my diamond?

Cuff. That's exactly what I want to find out!

Mr. Candy (eagerly). You really don't know?

Cuff. I know no more than you do.

Mr. Candy. I may be able to help you.

Cuff (surprised). You, sir!

Rachel (to MR. CANDY). How can you help him?

Mr. Candy. You will hear, when I return to what I was saying, before Betteredge interrupted us. Let the Sergeant finish his story first.

Cuff. My story is done, sir. The money-*lending* person, otherwise Number One, received my telegram in time to stop the loan. Half-an-hour since, miss, he handed the diamond over to me in your stable-yard. (*To* MR. CANDY.) Now, sir, about the money-*borrowing* person, otherwise Number Two? How do you propose to trace the Moonstone into his hands?

Mr. Candy. Just as I proposed to find the Moonstone when I thought it was lost. Has Betteredge told you of my sleep-walking patient in the town?

Cuff. Yes, sir.

Mr. Candy. A London doctor came to consult with me on the case last night. I made the lad eat and drink (at the same hour) exactly what he eat and drank on the night when he walked in his sleep –

Rachel. And what came of it?

Mr. Candy. He never even moved in his chair. The experiment was a complete failure. I don't care – I am not satisfied yet. What fails with one patient succeeds with another. I mean to try the experiment again with Mr. Franklin Blake.

Rachel. Are you speaking seriously? Do you really believe you can make Franklin take the Moonstone in his sleep for the second time?

Mr. Candy. Do people never have the same dream for the second time? It's a common thing in everybody's experience.

Rachel. I admit that. But dreaming is not sleep-walking.

Mr. Candy. I beg your pardon – sleep-walking is simply putting a dream in action, nothing more. (*He rises.*) I am going to make Mr. Blake repeat the supper to which he is not accustomed, and the drink that he doesn't like, on the chance that last night's cause may once more produce last night's effect. Has his health altered in the interval? His nerves are just as irritable as ever. Does he feel no further anxiety about the diamond? He is more anxious about it than ever. And, to crown it all, he is a far more sensitive subject than my patient in the town. Is there no hope of success, with all these chances in favour?

Rachel. I can't argue with you, Mr. Candy. But I believe you will fail.

Mr. Candy. What do *you* say, Sergeant?

Cuff. Ditto to Miss Rachel, sir.

Mr. Candy. Public opinion! Nothing is probable unless it appeals to our own trumpery experience. I am driven to my last resources. I must refer to the only unanswerable authority – authority that is printed in a book. (*He goes to the bookshelves.* RACHEL *and* CUFF *both rise.*)

Rachel. What are you about?

Mr. Candy. I have borrowed books enough from this library, Miss Rachel, to know what I am about. (*He takes the book which he brought with him in the Second Act, opens it, and hands it to* RACHEL.) There is the famous case of the Irish porter, quoted by Mr. Combe, the great phrenologist.[1]

Cuff. Read it out, miss, if you please.

Rachel (reading). "There was a certain Irish porter in a shop in Dublin, who was a little too fond of his native whisky. One day, he was sent to a house with a parcel. He got drunk on the way, and left his parcel at the wrong place. The next morning, when he was sober, he had no idea of where he had left it. In a day or two after, the Irish porter was drunk again. And what did he do? Went back straight to the house that he couldn't remember when he was sober, and got the parcel."

Mr. Candy (with enthusiasm). That is what I call a case in point!

Rachel (contemptuously). An Irish porter!

Mr. Candy. My confidence in the Irish porter is not to be expressed in words! What the drink did with *him*, I expect the supper and the glass of grog to do with Mr. Blake. I grant you it all depends on his dreaming of the diamond again. Let him only do that – and I believe he will lead us, in his sleep, straight to the person who took the Moonstone to London.

Rachel. I begin to feel interested! When may I order the supper to be sent in?

Cuff (interposing). Not in here, miss, if the doctor will allow me to interfere. (*To* MR. CANDY.) Let the supper be sent up to Mr. Blake in his room, by the back staircase which is used by the servants only.

Mr. Candy. You have your reasons, I suppose?

Cuff. The hall is open to everybody, sir. If you try your experiment here, suspicion may be excited in a certain quarter, which I won't particularly mention just yet. Tell me what is to be sent upstairs, and I will see that it gets to Mr. Blake without being discovered by anybody.

Mr. Candy. The game pie, Sergeant, the champagne, and the brandy-and-water. We shall see you again, I suppose?

Cuff. Certainly, sir – when I have said one more word to the policeman outside. (*He goes out by the hall door.* RACHEL *approaches* MR. CANDY *in her most winning manner.*)

Rachel. Dear Mr. Candy. Let me go with you when you go to Franklin!

Mr. Candy. Impossible, Miss Rachel!

Rachel. Don't be hard upon me! I am heartbroken about Franklin. Let me go with you?

Mr. Candy (*taking her hand gently*). I appeal to your own good sense, Miss Rachel. It is of the utmost importance to the success of our experiment that Mr. Blake's mind should be fixed on the Moonstone. By talking on that subject, and no other, we may help him to dream of it for the second time. Judge by your own feelings, how your presence would agitate him now!

Rachel. If I consent to wait, how shall I know when I may see Franklin?

Mr. Candy. I will ring the bell in Mr. Blake's bedroom. Can you hear it down here, or in your own room?

Rachel. Yes, if there is no noise at the time. (*She pauses, considers a moment, and speaks to herself.*) I will say something to Franklin – somehow! (*She takes an ornamental drinking-glass from the curiosities placed on the cheffonier,*[1] *turns it till she sees a flower painted outside near the rim, kisses the rim there, and approaches* MR. CANDY.) Please, Mr. Candy, let him have this glass at his supper, and turn it so that he drinks on that side, where the flower is. I hope I have not done anything that looks unladylike in your eyes. It will comfort me to think that I have given him a kiss, even in that way!

Mr. Candy (*smiling*). He shall take your kiss, Miss Rachel, as certainly as he takes his brandy-and-water. (*Aside.*) A charming girl! I wish I was Mr. Franklin Blake! (*He ascends the stairs, and enters* FRANKLIN'S *room.* RACHEL *watches him until he disappears.*)

Rachel (*alone*). He is with Franklin now. He is speaking to Franklin at this moment. And I am left down here by myself! A doctor has no

---

1   This was a chest of drawers or a bureau, often with an attached mirror.

feeling; Mr. Candy is a hateful man! (BETTEREDGE *appears at the hall door.*)

Betteredge. Miss Rachel –

Rachel. What is it?

Betteredge. Mr. Godfrey's compliments –

Rachel (with a cry of horror). Oh! I had forgotten Godfrey! (*She pauses, terror-struck by the remembrance of her engagement to* GODFREY. BETTEREDGE *approaches her in alarm.*)

Betteredge. You're not ill, miss, are you?

Rachel. No! no! (*Aside.*) Godfrey has my promise! Godfrey is engaged to marry me! It's like a frightful dream. What *am* I to do?

Betteredge (aside, watching her). Miss Rachel as pale as ashes; Mr. Candy nowhere to be seen; Sergeant Cuff and the policeman whispering together in a corner! There's something serious on foot; and I am kept out of it!

Rachel (rallying her courage, and returning to BETTEREDGE*).* Where is Mr. Godfrey?

Betteredge. In the morning room. He wants to know when you can conveniently see him.

Rachel (to herself). I can't see him! I daren't see him! Drusilla must speak to him for me. (*To* BETTEREDGE.) Go up to Miss Clack's room. Knock at the door, and say I want to speak to her instantly.

Betteredge (aside, as he approaches the stairs). Even Miss Clack is in the conspiracy. Everybody but me! (*He goes out by the gallery on the left.*)

Rachel (alone). Oh, what fools women are! We are always saying what we ought *not* to say. We are always doing the wrong thing at the wrong time, and then repenting when it is too late! I don't care. If I can't marry Franklin, I will marry nobody else. What right had Godfrey to take advantage of me when I was half mad with misery? Shameful! shameful! Where *is* Drusilla? (*She looks round.* MISS CLACK *appears in the gallery, followed by* BETTEREDGE.) Be quick! You walk as if you were following a funeral. Be quick! (MISS CLACK *deliberately descends the stairs. She has a quill-pen behind her ear, and letters and papers in her hand. Her manner towards* RACHEL *is cold and dignified, as if still resenting the interview which she overheard in the Second Act.*)

Miss Clack (aside). I hope I am incapable of using unladylike language. But, if she ventures to speak of her marriage to Mr. Godfrey – !

(*To* RACHEL.) Be as brief as you can, Rachel. I am immersed in correspondence with my Societies. The public interests must not suffer on account of any little personal troubles of yours, my dear.

Rachel (to herself). What have I done to offend her? (*To* MISS CLACK.) My dear Drusilla, I am going to appeal to your long-tried friendship – (*She observes* BETTEREDGE *listening eagerly, and addresses him sharply.*) Go to Mr. Godfrey, and say that I will receive him here in five minutes' time.

Betteredge. I beg your pardon, miss. As an old servant, may I say a word relative to what is going on in this house – ?

Rachel. As an old servant, do what I tell you.

Betteredge (offended). After fifty years' service, miss, it's a little hard to be cut short –

Rachel. Will you go? or must I ring for Andrew?

Betteredge (aside). I shall give warning to leave at the end of the month! (*He goes out indignantly by the hall door.*)

Rachel. Drusilla! I am in dreadful trouble, and I have no friend to help me but you.

Miss Clack. My humble advice has been offered again and again, and has been repelled again and again in the rudest manner.

Rachel. I beg your pardon, Drusilla –

Miss Clack. Pray don't mention it!

Rachel. I will always take your advice for the future.

Miss Clack. No, Rachel, no! I feel that I took a liberty, in my humble position, when I offered advice to a lady who hires me at a salary – paid by the quarter, I hasten to acknowledge, punctually when it's due.

Rachel (seizing her by the arm). Don't drive me mad! I am half mad already! I am engaged to be married to Godfrey Ablewhite.

Miss Clack (solemnly). May you be happy! Heaven knows I don't expect it!

Rachel (throwing her arms round DRUSILLA's *neck).* Oh, you darling! The very thing I wanted you to say! I don't expect it either. I hate Godfrey! When I said "Yes," I meant "No." I would rather throw myself out of the window than marry him. Get me off the engagement, Drusilla, and you will be the dearest friend I ever had in my life.

Miss Clack (eagerly). You really mean it?

Rachel. Yes! yes! yes!

Miss Clack (*embracing* RACHEL). My beloved Rachel is restored to me! (*With a burst of enthusiasm.*) *I'll* give him his dismissal, my dear. Your life shall not be sacrificed to a man who is, to my certain knowledge, quite unworthy of you. He shall find an immovable obstacle in his way. And the name of that obstacle is Drusilla Clack. (*Hurrying her to the left.*) Go to your room, dearest. Not a word of thanks; this is a labour of love. Go to your room! (*She hurries* RACHEL *into her room, and closes the door on her.*)

Miss Clack (*alone*). Now, Mr. Godfrey, the Mothers'-Small-Clothes-Conversion-Society will be even with *you*! How do I look? (*She goes to the glass.*) A pen behind my ear! (*She throws it into the fire.*) These tiresome papers are of no use! (*She throws them into the fire. Then arranges her hair and smooths out her dress.*) I should like to put on my best black silk dress, in honour of the occasion. Would it take too long? (GODFREY *appears at the hall door.*) Yes! Here he is!

Godfrey (*to himself*). Miss Clack! (*He advances and addresses* MISS CLACK.) Do you know where Rachel is? I expected to find her here.

Miss Clack (*with extreme politeness*). Pray take a seat.

Godfrey. I beg your pardon; I have an appointment with Rachel.

Miss Clack (*mysteriously*). I beg *your* pardon, Mr. Godfrey. You have an appointment with *me*. Dear Rachel is not well enough to see you. I am the chosen representative of her views and wishes. Her inmost secrets are lodged in my bosom. Pray sit down.

Godfrey (*aside, seating himself*). What does this mean?

Miss Clack (*seating herself, with the highest relish of the pain she is about to inflict*). Mr. Godfrey, as an affectionate well-wisher and friend, as one long accustomed to arouse, convince, prepare, enlighten, and fortify others, permit me to take the liberty of composing your mind.

Godfrey (*coldly*). Be good enough to state your business with me plainly.

Miss Clack. Quite impossible, without preparing your mind first. My precious friend, I know your sensitive nature – I know how unequal you are to sustain a sudden shock. I have undertaken to scatter all your fondest hopes to the winds, but I have *not* undertaken to see you rolling on the floor in hysterics at my feet.

Godfrey (*rising*). You have something to say to me from Rachel. I presume you know that we are engaged to be married?

Miss Clack. Oh, don't! don't! You go through me like a knife! Engaged to be married to Rachel? Poor Mr. Godfrey! poor Mr. Godfrey!

Godfrey (impatiently). Once for all, Miss Clack, will you deprive yourself of the pleasure of hearing your own voice? Will you speak briefly, and speak out?

Miss Clack (irritated into speaking out abruptly, and with the greatest rapidity). Your engagement with Rachel is at an end, Mr. Godfrey. Is that brief enough for you?

Godfrey (thunderstruck). What! ! !

Miss Clack (as before). Rachel regrets her rash acceptance of your proposal. Rachel respects, but can never love you. Rachel withdraws her promise, and positively refuses to be your wife. Is that plain enough, Mr. Godfrey?

Godfrey. Miss Clack, I have nothing to say to *you.* I insist on seeing Rachel immediately. (*He approaches* RACHEL's *door.* MISS CLACK *places herself before the door.*) Let me pass, if you please.

Miss Clack. Are you prepared, sir, to employ brute force with a woman?

Godfrey (calling). Rachel!

Miss Clack (calling). Don't answer him, dear Rachel! (*To* GODFREY.) Tear me, by brute force, from the spot I stand on! You don't approach Rachel in any other way.

Godfrey (yielding). Take advantage, Miss Clack, of your privilege as a woman. Sooner or later Rachel must come out. (*He returns to his chair.*) If I wait all night, here I sit till she leaves her room.

Miss Clack (setting down her chair with a bang). And here *I* sit, Mr. Godfrey, until I have sat you out! (*A momentary silence. A bell is heard to ring outside the hall door from* FRANKLIN's *room.* RACHEL *suddenly opens her door and appears.* MISS CLACK *and* GODFREY *both start up together.*)

Miss Clack. My dear! why do you leave your room?

Rachel (looking at the gallery). Hush! the bell! (BETTEREDGE *enters to answer the bell.* MR. CANDY *appears in the gallery, closing* FRANKLIN's *door behind him.*)

Godfrey. Rachel! I must have a word in private with you immediately.

Rachel (impatiently). Not now! Not now! (*She draws back from him. He follows, remonstrating with her.* BETTEREDGE *addresses* MR. CANDY *from the bottom of the gallery stairs.*)

Betteredge. Am I wanted upstairs, sir?

Mr. Candy. Stay where you are. You are wanted in the hall. Turn down the lamps.

Godfrey (hearing him). Turn down the lamps?

Betteredge (aside). Turn down the lamps? Here's the doctor in the secret now! Everybody but me!

Rachel (to BETTEREDGE). Betteredge, do as Mr. Candy tells you.

Betteredge (sulkily). Very well, miss. If you prefer being in the dark, very well. (*He gets the steps, and puts out the lamps. The dialogue proceeds.*)

Miss Clack (startled). What does this mean, Rachel?

Godfrey (surprised). Why are they darkening the room?

Rachel (drawing back once more from GODFREY). Wait, and you will see. (*Aside.*) The experiment has succeeded! He is darkening the room to make it the same as last night! (GODFREY *is about to follow* RACHEL, *when* MR. CANDY's *voice, still speaking from the gallery, stops him.*)

Mr. Candy. Mr. Betteredge, is there a moon tonight?

Betteredge (to himself, still putting out the lamps). The moon is in it, too! (*To* MR. CANDY.) Yes, sir. (CUFF *shows himself at the hall door.*)

Mr. Candy. Draw back the curtains from the garden window.

Betteredge (aside). The curtains are in the conspiracy!

Cuff (advancing). Don't hurry yourself, Mr. Betteredge – I'll open the curtains. (*He pulls the string that draws back the curtains. The moonlight streams in across the place occupied by the cabinet. The room is also partially lit, as in the First Act, by the firelight.* CUFF *locks the window, after opening the curtains, and puts the key in his pocket.* BETTEREDGE, *after putting back the steps, joins* CUFF *at the window.* MR. CANDY *watches* FRANKLIN's *door.* RACHEL, MISS CLACK, *and* GODFREY *all observe* MR. CANDY, *with the varying emotions which agitate them. During this interval of by-play,* GOD-FREY *continues the dialogue.*)

Godfrey (calling from the hall). Mr. Candy!

Mr. Candy (turning round). Yes?

Godfrey. Is there anything the matter with Franklin Blake?

Mr. Candy. There is nothing the matter with Franklin Blake.

Godfrey. What do these extraordinary proceedings mean?

Mr. Candy. Hush! (*He descends the stairs and approaches* RACHEL, *to whom he speaks aside.*) Mr. Blake is asleep, and stirring in his bed. He is dreaming, if ever I saw a man dreaming yet. Wait a little, and (*speaking his next words emphatically*) don't forget the case of the Irish porter!

Betteredge (*whispering to* CUFF). I saw you lock the window. What for?

Cuff (*whispering*). Use your eyes and ears, and do as I tell you. Stand before the hall door, and let nobody pass out until I give the word. (*A pause.* BETTEREDGE, *completely puzzled, places himself at the hall door.* CUFF, *after looping up the curtains, joins* Mr. CANDY, *passing from right to left under the gallery.* FRANKLIN's *door slowly opens. He appears in his dressing-gown, as in the First Act, pausing before he descends the stairs.*)

Rachel (*softly to herself*). Dear! dear Franklin!

Mr. Candy (*taking* RACHEL *aside*). Don't speak to him! Have you got the Moonstone?

Rachel. Yes.

Mr. Candy. Put it back in the cabinet drawer. (RACHEL *obeys, passing under the gallery.* MISS CLACK *follows her, in alarm.* GODFREY's *attention is riveted on* FRANKLIN. FRANKLIN *begins to descend the stairs slowly.*)

Miss Clack. Rachel! I'm frightened.

Rachel (*drawing back under the gallery*). Keep with me, and I'll tell you what it means. (*She speaks in dumb show to* MISS CLACK. BETTEREDGE, *behind them, on guard at the hall door, listens eagerly.* ANDREW *and the other servants are just seen, assembled outside the hall door.* MR. CANDY *and* CUFF *are together, having withdrawn under the gallery.* GODFREY, *left by himself, standing with his back to the audience, opposite the staircase, suddenly turns as* FRANKLIN *descends the stairs step by step, and shows his face, disturbed by guilty terror. He makes first for the hall door.* RACHEL *and* MISS CLACK *draw aside from him.*)

Betteredge (*to* GODFREY *in a whisper*). You can't pass! (*The servants block up the doorway.* GODFREY *retreats to the window on the right, and tries it.*)

Godfrey (*to himself in a whisper*). Locked! (*He draws back again, passing under the gallery.* FRANKLIN *has by this time advanced into the hall, and stops, looking straight before him, as in the First Act.* GODFREY, *passing behind him, tries to escape by the gallery stairs.* CUFF *has placed himself there on guard, at the moment when* FRANKLIN *advanced into the hall. He signs to* GODFREY *to stand back.* GODFREY *retreats, panic-stricken, to the front, between the fireplace and* RACHEL's *door, and stands there, watching* FRANKLIN, *as he slowly moves towards the cabinet, turning his back on* GODFREY. *At the same time,* MR. CANDY *joins* RACHEL *and* MISS CLACK *under the gallery.* FRANKLIN *speaks to himself, as he spoke in the First Act.*)

Franklin (in his sleep). It's not safe in the cabinet. What's to be done with the Moonstone? (*He hesitates, then opens the folding-doors of the cabinet.*)

Godfrey (to himself, in a whisper). What is he doing? (*He advances a few steps on tip-toe towards the middle of the hall, as if impelled by some irresistible impulse to discover what* FRANKLIN *is about.* FRANKLIN *opens the cabinet drawer, takes the Moonstone out of it, turns and approaches* GODFREY, *holding out the diamond.*)

Godfrey (recognising the Moonstone with a start of horror). The diamond! (*He slowly retreats towards the fireplace. Step by step* FRANKLIN *follows him, till* GODFREY *is brought to a stand-still by the fireplace. The other persons present –* CUFF *included – all eagerly advance on the right, watching the same.* FRANKLIN *speaks to* GODFREY *as he spoke to him towards the close of the First Act.*)

Franklin (in his sleep). Godfrey! I'm uneasy about the safety of the diamond. Take the Moonstone to your father's bank. (*He hands the diamond to* GODFREY. *A faint cry of indignation escapes* RACHEL *– suppressed so that it is just audible, and no more.* GODFREY's *hands fall helplessly at his sides. The diamond drops on the carpet at his feet.* FRANKLIN *turns away, slowly and warily, towards the stairs. Instead of ascending them, as before, he stops, lays his arm on one of the carved pillars by which the balusters of the stairs are terminated on either side, and languidly rests his head on it. The persons present all watch him intently.* RACHEL *approaches him.* MR. CANDY *stops her.*)

Mr. Candy (whispering). Don't disturb him! His dream is passing away. He feels the approach of the deeper sleep. (MR. CANDY, *assisted by* RACHEL, *wheels an arm-chair towards the middle of the stage.* FRANKLIN *is placed in the chair, and reclines, sleeping peacefully.* MR. CANDY *and* RACHEL *stand on either side of the chair, watching him.* GODFREY *moves as if to leave the hall.* CUFF, *followed by* BETTEREDGE *and* MISS CLACK, *advances, so as to stand in the way of his departure, and speaks to him.*)

Cuff. Stop a minute, sir! We may as well understand each other before you go. Mr. Blake offered you the Moonstone last night, walking in his sleep, just as he has offered it to you now. Last night, you were alone with him upstairs, and you took it. Down here, there are witnesses present, and you let it drop. (*He picks up the diamond, and shows it to* GODFREY.) Don't you know it again?

Godfrey. I don't understand you.

Cuff. Oh yes, you do! Didn't I tell you of that commonplace case of mine, that I left in London? It was a Charitable Society, sir, that employed me to recover the stolen money, and you, being treasurer, were one of the officers privately reckoned up by the police. I made the necessary inquiries myself. I found out your private villa in the suburbs, and your contraband lady with the carriage and jewels –

Godfrey (taking out his white handkerchief). Oh! ! ! *(He hides his face in his handkerchief.* RACHEL *and* MISS CLACK, *both listening, both express indignation and disgust.)*

Cuff (pointing to GODFREY*).* Lord! what virtue there is in a white handkerchief! I was also informed, sir, through your servant, of your visit to Miss Rachel's house. I was on my way here to arrest you on suspicion of embezzlement, when I got Mr. Blake's telegram. The society's audit-day was close at hand, you know; and the Moonstone offered you a chance of replacing the stolen money, if you were really the man who had taken it. I believed you *were* the man, when I found you so devilish anxious to assist me. It was cleverly intended, sir, but you overdid it. Thanks to your interference, I had the policeman ready to follow you. He traced you from Frizinghall to London; and he followed you to Mr. Luker, the money-lender. The telegraph did the rest. Is it all pretty clear now, sir? Don't you think you had better get away while you have the chance? *(*GODFREY *stands irresolute.* CUFF *turns to* RACHEL, *standing behind him, and offers her the Moonstone.)* Your diamond, miss. *(*RACHEL *refuses to take it.* CUFF *offers the diamond to* BETTEREDGE *next.* BETTEREDGE *draws back from it in horror.* CUFF *places the Moonstone on the writing-table.)*

Godfrey (turning to RACHEL, *with his white handkerchief to his eyes).* Rachel! *(*RACHEL *recoils from him in disgust. He appeals next to* MISS CLACK*.)* Miss Clack! *(*MISS CLACK *turns away like* RACHEL. GODFREY *walks slowly towards the hall door, then turns to say his last words.)*

Godfrey (in his oratorical manner). The poet has said: "To err is human, to forgive divine."[1] My defence, ladies and gentlemen, is entirely comprised in that grand line. Properly understood, I am that essentially pardonable person, the victim of circumstances. Farewell!

---

1 The poet is Alexander Pope (1688-1744); the line is from *An Essay on Criticism* (1709).

(*He bows and goes out.*)

Betteredge (*to* CUFF). Sergeant, you're not going to let that damned rogue escape scot-free?

Cuff. Don't alarm yourself, Mr. Betteredge. The policeman is outside. (*He looks at* FRANKLIN *sleeping in the chair, with* RACHEL *and* MR. CANDY *on either side of him*). Still fast asleep, sir?

Mr. Candy. Yes. (CUFF *walks away, and takes a last look at the roses near the garden window.* MR. CANDY *turns to* RACHEL.) I will keep watch, Miss Rachel, till he wakes.

Rachel. Nobody shall watch him but me! Leave me, all of you, to be the first who sees him and speaks to him when he opens his eyes. My heart is set on it – pray indulge me! (MR. CANDY *and* BETTEREDGE *approach to take leave of* RACHEL. *She is absorbed in* FRANKLIN, *and answers by signs only.* CUFF *remains near the roses.* MISS CLACK *goes to the writing-table, lights a candle standing on it, and writes a telegram, very slowly, as if it costs her considerable thought.*)

Mr. Candy. Miss Rachel, has the Irish porter justified my confidence in him? (RACHEL *gives* MR. CANDY *her hand – he kisses it.*) Accept my congratulations. Good-night! {*He goes out by the hall door.*)

Betteredge. I have only one remark to make, miss, in wishing you good-night in my turn. As an old servant of the family, you might have let me into the secret a little sooner. My duty to Mr. Franklin when he wakes, and Heaven grant you a speedy marriage! {*He follows* MR. CANDY.)

Cuff (*approaching* RACHEL). Might I ask a great favour before I go back to London? Might I take one cutting from the roses there? (RACHEL *smiles, and bows her head.*) Thank you, miss. (*He takes the cutting, and holds it up in triumph.*) My rose-garden shall begin with this! And – excuse me, Miss Rachel – there will be grass walks between *my* flower-beds. No gravel! no gravel! (*He follows* BETTEREDGE.)

Miss Clack (*rising from the table*). All blessings attend you, dear Rachel! I have a telegram to send to London the first thing in the morning. May I give it to the servants over-night? (RACHEL *assents.* MISS CLACK *reads her telegram over to herself.*) Have I been sufficiently explicit? Let me see. (*She reads*). "Miss Clack, to the Mothers'-Small-Clothes-Conversion-Society. Beware of Mr. Godfrey. He is perfectly capable of stealing our trousers." (*She goes out by the hall door.*)

Rachel (*alone with* FRANKLIN). How peacefully he sleeps! How pale and worn he looks! My love! my love! if ever a woman made a man happy, your life shall be a happy one with me! (*She rises, and looks towards the hall door, which is left open*). Why have they left the door open? He may feel the draught. (*She goes to the hall door and closes it. Returning to him, she passes the writing-table, and notices the gleam of the diamond in the light of the candle which* MISS CLACK *has left burning.*) You hateful Moonstone, you shall never be an ornament of mine! I'll sell you to-morrow; and the money shall be a fund for the afflicted and the poor. (*She returns to* FRANKLIN, *and leans over the back of the chair, looking down at him.*) This is *my* jewel! Shall I disturb him if I kiss him? I *must* kiss him! (*Still standing behind the chair, she stoops over and touches his forehead with her lips. He starts, and opens his eyes.*)

    Rachel (*starting back*). Oh, I've woke him!

    Franklin (*looking up, bewildered*). Who is it?

    Rachel (*bending over him again*). Only your wife! (*The curtain falls slowly.*)

THE END

Appendix G: Reviews of the Olympic Theatre Performances of Wilkie Collins's The Moonstone

1. *The Times*, Friday, September 21, 1877: 4.

Rarely, we think, has Mr. Wilkie Collins displayed more ingenuity and more knowledge of scenic effect than in the version of *The Moonstone* which was played for the first time on Monday night. But he has not quite succeeded. Yet we cannot call to mind any living writer for our stage who would have been more successful, and we very much doubt whether any one else would have been as successful. He has exhibited a self-denial rarely found in those novelists who are allowed to prepare their own works for representation. Many of his characters he has altogether eliminated, and many of his most striking scenes – characters and scenes described and elaborated with many happy touches and much graphic power, with which it must have been hard indeed to part, and which a less practised hand would probably have refused to leave. The Indians, who by the unbending laws of their religion are sworn to follow the sacred jewel from generation to generation till it shine once more in the forehead of their god, have no place in the play, and though one cannot doubt the practical wisdom of the omission, all the charm of mystery and vague foreboding of evil which belonged to them disappears with them. Rosanna Spearman, too, the poor deformed girl, whose hopeless passion for Franklin Blake is so ingeniously employed to complicate the fable, we neither hear of nor see. Godfrey Ablewhite owns but the smallest share in the action. His romantic end – one of the most striking scenes in the book – is altogether lost, and his motive for the theft of the diamond merely hinted at, while of all the ingenious complications to which that theft gives rise we know absolutely nothing. He has, in short, no part of his own to play, but merely serves incidentally to bring the fortunes of the lovers to a happy close. Of the few characters that are preserved, Franklin Blake himself, and Miss Clack are the only two, perhaps, that retain their identity in any degree of completeness. Rachel Verinder, though she is still the kind-hearted, self-willed, and impulsive Rachel of the book, is placed in a somewhat different atmosphere; Betteredge, the family butler, to whom the pages of *Robinson Crusoe* are as the Sibylline Leaves,[1] is much curtailed both in speech and action; and so, too, is his daughter Penelope; while Mr. Candy, the village doctor, now plays in the discovery the share allotted originally to his mysterious assistant. These, with Cuff, the detective, and some servants, complete the list of characters. The traits of Franklin Blake and Rachel, the hero and heroine, are well preserved, in accordance with the book; nor have the necessary curtailments prevented the author from distinguishing and defining their separate individualities as well on the stage as in the novel. The Betteredge of the play is a decided improvement on his prototype, who was apt to press rather too much at times. Cuff, the detective, was, as detectives in books are generally wont to be, rather a fabulous sort of being, and the compound of shrewdness and simplicity had a savour rather of the circulating library than of Scotland-yard. He is much the same now, though both his cunning and his pastoral innocence are somewhat lopped of their full proportions, and the indications of the latter, which consist of disjointed and rather *mal à propos* sentences, seem somewhat out of place. Mr. Swinbourne, too, invests the part with a solemn air of high tragedy, which, save on the supposition that it is his natural manner, is somewhat difficult to account for. Godfrey Ablewhite, too – so much, that is, as we see of him – is easily to be recognized, and Mr. Charles Harcourt finishes the picture well, and would make it still better if he would modify some few peculiarities of dress, which are evidently meant to indicate the pretentious nature of Godfrey's assumed piety, but in reality create rather a suspicion of burlesque. Miss Clack, as we have already said, is also fairly like the original – in one respect, indeed, too like. This sour-tempered old maid, with her tracts and her charitable societies, was the weak point of the novel, and she is the weak point of the play. She does nothing to promote, and she not unfrequently does a good deal to retard, the action. In the book, to be sure, she annoys us chiefly through the medium of her diary, but in the play she annoys us in her person. The lady who represents the part does so with so unnecessary an effusion

---

1 Prophetic sayings or collections of sayings written usually in Greek and attributed to the Cumæn sybil, who was consulted by Æneas before his descent into Hades.

of manner as first to weary and then to irritate the spectator. Of all the characters in the book this one might best have been spared; that it has been retained, and invested, indeed, with an undue prominence, is perhaps to be explained by the necessity Mr. Collins may have felt himself to be under of providing a part for Mrs. Seymour.[1]

But the characters are all that remain. The charm of the story is gone. That which is but an episode in the book is the play itself. This drama of *The Moonstone* only shows how in his sleep Franklin Blake took the diamond from the cabinet, and how, by repeating in his sleep once more the same act, his innocence is established. The play, by a spectator ignorant of the book, might, indeed, be almost taken for the illustration of some popular cure for somnambulism. The four acts in which the action is presented are all ingeniously managed. The last two are, perhaps, unduly prolonged beyond the catastrophe, but the "situations" are for the most part artistically contrived, and arise naturally out of the chain of events. It is the story of the play itself that disappoints. The actions of Blake and Rachel are intelligible enough, but all the rest is vague and unsatisfactory. The impression made is that of a story left but half told because it was found impossible to complete it. There are hints of something more, allusions to what is supposed to have happened elsewhere, or what is, as it seems, to happen; half explanations of motives, but nothing definite, nothing substantial. Excepting the hero and heroine, the characters seem to owe their existence merely to the fact that they exist in the novel. Even the doctor, who is no unimportant instrument in the catastrophe, scarcely appears to have any proper place in the play. Indeed, had not Mr. Collins been hampered by having written his novel, it is possible that he might have placed upon the stage a far better illustration of an ingenious theory concerning somnambulism.

The general tone of the representation is good. The actors, on the whole, act the characters that the author has drawn, and act them well. Of some we have already spoken. Mr. Swinbourne and Mrs. Seymour we cannot indeed praise, but for the latter it must be said that she is burdened with an ungrateful part, and one, too, that is from

---

1   Mrs. Laura Seymour, née Alison (1820–79), with whom novelist Charles Reade lived for nearly twenty-five years, was Collins's good friend. See Appendix F, pages 626–30, for more biographical information on other members of the original cast.

the first seen to be an unnecessary part. If she could have made this fact less obvious it would have been better, but in any circumstances "Miss Clack" must remain, if she is suffered to remain, the blot of the piece. Mr. Harcourt, save for the little extravagancies of costume we have mentioned, very well realizes the Ablewhite of the novel – that the substance of the novel is but a shadow in the play is no fault of his. Mr. Hill is very good indeed as Betteredge – a little more humourous and a little less pompous, perhaps, than Mr. Collins's butler would seem to have been, but very good for all that, and much more quiet in his humour than he sometimes is. Miss Gerard made a sprightly and pleasant little lady's maid, and Mr. Pateman's Doctor Candy showed an agreeable diminution of a somewhat exuberant style. Mr. Neville, too, plays his part very much better than most we have seen him in of late. The careless, sunny, happy-go-lucky nature of the hero exactly suits his style, and at the same time he gets now and again a chance of turning aside for a moment from that beaten track in which he has travelled so long. There are moments when Franklin Blake almost makes us forget Bob Brierly.[1] We should question, however, whether his emotion at the close of the third act, where Rachel reveals to him her supposed knowledge of the robber is not a little exaggerated. Susceptible and impulsive as Blake was, an excess of feeling so violent as to cast him in a swoon upon the floor hardly, we should think, belongs to the character. In other respects this scene is a good one. Miss Pateman's acting is by many degrees the best she has as yet shown. She has caught the spirit of the character well, a wayward, impetuous, and yet loving girl. In the more emotional scenes, too, she displays strong feeling with far less tendency to violence than she has hitherto displayed in similar circumstances. Her acting, however, is still, though in a less degree, disfigured by what in an older actress would be called mannerisms, but what with her may be call affectations, of voice and gesture, of which she may be counselled to get rid as soon as possible. Another affectation, too, she has, no less promptly and much more easily, perhaps, to discard, and this is a grotesque affectation in dress. There was a time when to comment on an actor's or an actress's dress would in itself have been considered a piece of affectation. But those times have long passed away. On the

---

1 Neville played the lead, Robert Brierly, in Tom Taylor's (1817-80) popular *The Ticket-of-Leave Man* (1863), also at the Olympic Theatre.

modern stage "Quin's high plume and Oldfield's petticoat"[1] often play parts scarcely less prominent than those assumed by the wearers of petticoats and plumes. Our stage must mirror not only the manners but the fashions of the day. How it fulfils the first requisition we need not now discuss, but that it prides itself on its fulfilment of the second is very obvious. But Miss Pateman's dress was on Monday not the fashion, but the burlesque of the fashion. Moreover, it seriously incommoded not only the other actors, but herself. She was at times, and those, too, important times, so much busied with Miss Pateman's skirts as to have too little leisure to think of Miss Verinder's feelings. Indeed, it is scarcely too much to say that the most prominent faults of her acting were very considerably increased by the faults of her dress. This is a mistake so easily to be remedied that it will be more than a pity if it is repeated.

None of those accessories which are so highly appreciated at the present day were forgotten. The scene – all the four acts were laid in one scene, a hall in Miss Verinder's house – was very complete. There were stained glass windows, gorgeous curtains, china vases, a big fireplace, comfortable chairs, a staircase, a gallery, a supper table, and a supper. Nothing had been spared to please the eye, and the actors did their best to gratify the higher sense.

2. *The Illustrated London News*, Saturday, September 22, 1877: 290.

On Monday, at the Olympic, an adaptation of Mr. Wilkie Collins's *The Moonstone* was performed for the first time. All novel readers are well acquainted with the incidents of this clever story, and appreciate the mesmeric interest which it contains. The adaptation for the stage has the advantage of having been prepared by the novelist himself. Mr. Collins has arranged it upon a safe plan. He has successfully resisted the temptation to found his plot upon the principle of surprise, and has substituted for it that of expectation. This is the true dramatic principle, as the reader will perceive who takes the trouble to peruse what Coleridge wrote upon it so long ago in his *Biographia Literaria*.[2]

---

1   Quin is James Quin (1693-1766), and Oldfield is Anne Oldfield (1683-1730) both well-known London actors at the beginning of the eighteenth century.

2   Samuel Taylor Coleridge (1772-1834), best known as a poet, published his two-volume *Biographia Literaria* in July 1817.

By the observance of this principle, much pain is spared the spectator of the play, when the perplexed agents in the action are placed in situations of moral difficulty. When Miss Bella Pateman, as Rachel, shows her conviction that Franklin is guilty, and is irritated by the calmness which he maintains, the spectator is relieved by the knowledge of circumstances which the latter feels assured will in the end produce a right understanding between the lovers. Mr. Henry Neville in this scene acts with equal judgment and force. The acting, indeed, throughout is marked by the constant excellence which attends the prosperous efforts of competent artists. The humorous characters, in particular, were well filled, and thoroughly appreciated by the audience. The sustained interest, however, was too intense to admit of frequent and noisy applause; but in the end the general approbation was vehemently expressed.

3. *The Athenaeum* Saturday, September 22, 1877: 381.

Mr. Wilkie Collins cannot be congratulated on the manner in which he has dramatized his novel of *The Moonstone*. That a work so ambitious in aim, and so composite in nature, could not without some sacrifice of character and of story be brought within the compass of a play, was obvious from the first. There must surely, however, have been some means of obtaining the desired result at a sacrifice less damaging than that of the whole character and conception of the novel. The extravagance and impossibility of portions of *The Moonstone* are forgotten by the reader who finds himself steeped in a rich glow of Oriental colour. In its way, *The Moonstone* is a species of "Monte Christo,"[1] a work in which you are content to admit what you know to be inconceivable, and allow full scope to an invention which supplies so fully every detail of the life it creates; you accept as true what might have been, even though it is not. There is something impressive in the conception of the circumstances under which the jewel is stolen from an Indian idol; the magic power with which it is supposed to be invested and the sort of curse attached to its possession

---

1   The reviewer may be referring to Alexandre Dumas's (1802-70) novel *Le Comte de Monte Cristo* (1844-45), or to any of a number of British stage adaptations that were flourishing at the time in London theatres.

flatter that love of the supernatural which lurks within our nature; and the figures of the three Indians dogging the possessors of the sacred emblem, though they lend themselves easily to ludicrous associations, are not without an element of absolute terror. In the dramatic version this is entirely lost. Some slight attempt is made to attach to the possession of the stone a species of curse. The panic, however, of an imbecile old servant, which is unshared by any other character, forms but a poor substitute for the weird qualities with which in the original the gem is invested; and the declaration of the heroine at the end, that she will sell the stone and build with the money thus obtained a hospital, strikes us only as unreasonable. In degrading the moonstone, Mr. Collins degrades his story. Thus, though he has framed an interesting and successful play, we cannot help wishing he had called it something else.

The entire story consists in the theft of the moonstone by Franklin Blake while he is in a state of somnambulism, and the solution of the mystery thus begotten by means of a surgeon, who, placing Blake in conditions exactly the same as those in which he has formerly been, causes him to repeat his previous action. There is, in addition, a rivalry for the hand of Rachel Verinder between the unconscious perpetrator of the theft and Godfrey Ablewhite, the pseudo-philanthropist, who endeavours to turn the action to this own profit. Now, putting on one side the question of the inadequacy of the cause which brings about the tendency to sleep-walking – though this, which is in the play merely the effect of supper and a glass of hot brandy-and-water upon a man who is in a nervous condition and is unused to such indulgence, does, in fact, by its frivolity, shock the spectator – it is obvious there is no need, in the case of so simple a plot, to call in the agency of the moonstone. Any article of value enough to tempt a man who is needy would do as well as this for the purpose, and the play would be to the full as effective. It would, indeed, be in all respects more satisfactory to substitute bank-notes for the diamond, seeing that Ablewhite might, under such circumstances, be more easily tempted to the crime he commits, inasmuch as he could scarcely hope, without encountering some extreme risk, to dispose of a stone of the splendour and size of the moonstone. If it is urged against this that the play would thus be reduced to the level of an ordinary drama suggested by the opera of "La Sonnambula,"[1] the answer is that this is already done, and that the substitution we recommend would do nothing to lower the tone of the work.

Thus, though the play is interesting and successful, and needs only slight alterations to obtain a success equal to that of its author's former dramas, it is disappointing from the standpoint of Mr. Collins's previous accomplishment. The only other fault we are inclined to find is, that some of the characters undergo a distinct process of deterioration. Rachel Verinder, Betteredge, and Penelope remain pretty much the same as they appear in the book, though Betteredge has lost his habit of referring everything to *Robinson Crusoe*, after the fashion formerly adopted in the Sortes Homericæ or Virgilianæ.[2] Rosanna Spearman, like the three Indians, has entirely disappeared. Franklin Blake seems at first a heartless adventurer, his anxiety to espouse the heiress at a time when he is absolutely penniless exposing him to the worst suspicion. Godfrey Ablewhite becomes a species of transparent hypocrite, and Miss Clack's sanctimony and meddlesomeness, seen from without and not from within, are far less telling. Some strong situations are obtained, the strongest being that when the hero is openly taxed with theft by the woman he loves. The play is curiously conformable to old ideas, the unities of time and place being rigorously observed. The action thus passes in one scene, the breakfast-room in the house of Miss Verinder, and the entire time it occupies is little more than twenty-four hours. A respectable interpretation was afforded. Mr. Neville marked with distinctness the different phases of shame and indignation through which the hero passed, and was, as he always is, manly and effective. Miss Pateman showed much force and breadth of style as Rachel. It is to be regretted that her costume suggested burlesque rather than serious drama. A lady appearing at breakfast time in her own house in a dress with a train extending half way across the stage is an almost unpardonable absurdity. Mr. Hill was

---

1 This is Henry James Byron's (1835-84) *La Sonnambula!, or, the supper, the sleeper, and the merry Swiss boy: an original operatic burlesque* (1865). Byron's version is a burlesque of Vincenzo Bellini's (1801-35) opera of the same name.

2 This refers to a type of divination practised in ancient Rome where advice was sought by opening a copy of Homer or Virgil at random and acting on whatever information appeared. Betteredge's inspiration, at least in the novel, often comes from Daniel Defoe's (1660-1731) novel *Robinson Crusoe* (1719).

Betteredge, a part thoroughly fitted to him; Mr. Pateman Mr. Candy, Mr. Harcourt Mr. Ablewhite, and Mr. Swinbourne Sergeant Cuff. The interpretation of these characters was competent, without being in any respect remarkable.

4. *The Spirit of the Times, New York*. Saturday, October 6, 1877: 261.

At the Olympic, Mr. Wilkie Collins has dramatized his novel called *The Moonstone*, with considerable cleverness. So simply and explicitly has he told the story, and so successfully has he cut away the leaves and branches that interfered with the view, that, as old as the story is, and simple as the plot may be, still a serious and sincere interest was created purely by the arrangement and skill of the dramatist. For once Mr. Collins has observed the unities of "time" and "place." He has arranged so as to make the whole action of the play take place in the space of twenty-four hours, and one complete scene suffices for all the four acts. Thus arranged, the story stands somewhat as follows: In the first act Franklin Blake (Mr. Harry Neville) has arrived with the famous yellow diamond, called the Moonstone, to hand it over to his cousin Rachel, with whom he is in love. He has a not very formidable rival in Rachel's affection in Godfrey Ablewhite, a smooth-tongued and oily hypocrite. Everyone appears to be well and happy in the house of Rachel the heiress, except Franklin, who is depressed, melancholy, and out of spirits. He has given up smoking, of which pleasure he was passionately fond, and he has been induced, on this occasion, to eat a heavy supper of game pie, to drink freely of dry champagne, and to wind up with a steaming glass of hot grog. The doctor, who is present, declares that this is enough to make anyone walk in his sleep. And the doctor is right, for Franklin, who has all the evening been anxious about the safety of the wonderful diamond, not only walks in his sleep, but descends to an old oak cabinet, pockets the diamond, and takes it up to bed with him. The fair Rachel, who has been wandering about at night in search of a book, sees with her own eyes this mysterious proceeding, and takes her own lover for a common thief. The detectives are called in, much against the wish of Rachel, to find out who stole the diamond, and a certain clue to the robber is found in the fact that the cabinet, which had been recently varnished, had been rubbed by a garment of some description.

Rachel, anxious to screen her guilty cousin, much as she despises him, steals his dressing-gown from his room, and as she finds on it deliberate traces of the varnish, is eager to destroy it. But the detectives are too keen on the scent, and Franklin is publicly accused of the robbery.

The third act owes its great interest to a very powerful scene between Rachel and Franklin, admirably acted at all points by Mr. Neville and Miss Bella Pateman. The woman is in a furious passion at her lover's assumption of injured innocence. The man is proud and dignified under the woman's taunts. The battle of conflicting impulse is carried on to the final point, where Rachel declares she believes her lover to be a common thief, and Franklin falls in a swoon on the floor. This is reversing the order of things. On the stage, the woman invariably faints, and the man comforts her. Here it is exactly the other way, and Rachel's love returns in full force as she caresses, with tears, the prostrate form of her adored, but, apparently guilty cousin. This one scene is really very finely acted. Miss Pateman threw away her little mannerisms and crudeness of style, and abandoned herself well to the tempest of the situation. Mr. Neville acted with manliness and excellent effect. Nothing could well have been better on either side, and the scene aroused the house to enthusiasm. How then is it to be made clear that Franklin did not take the Moonstone in order that he may marry Rachel and live happily ever afterwards. The doctor solves the difficulty in a purely scientific and somewhat comical fashion. He makes Franklin eat another supper of game pie, drink more dry champagne, and swallow another jorum of hot brandy and water. Strange to say, he again walks in his sleep, and once more steals the Moonstone. Happily, he does more, for he gives the stolen diamond into the safe custody of the hypocritical Godfrey, who is acknowledged to be, if not the actual thief, at least the willing receiver of stolen goods. So the play ends to the satisfaction of everybody, and with only slight discontent over the somewhat tediously-elaborated comicalities of Miss Clack, one of the author's favorite comic characters. The low comedy part of Betteredge, the faithful butler, was very cleverly acted by Mr. W. J. Hill, a comedian of great intelligence. It is strange that many of the plays of Mr. Wilkie Collins contain a curious and instructive lesson in physical science. The moral of *Man and Wife* was don't take too much muscular exercise, or you will die of heart disease. This is what Geoffrey Delamaine did, as we all saw. The lesson to be gained from *The Moonstone* is, don't give up smoking, or you will walk in your sleep, and steal the jewels of your lover. But what will the Anti-Tobacco Society say to Mr. Wilkie Collins? The Havana merchants ought to send him a splendid box of cigars. No one will dream of leaving off smoking after this, for a prime Partaga[1] is better than a night in the lock-up, and a position in the felon's dock.

---

1 Partagas, founded in 1845, is one of the oldest Havana brands of cigars.

Select Bibliography

Bibliographies

Andrew, R.V. "A Wilkie Collins Check-List." *English Studies in Africa* 3 (March 1960): 79-98.

Ashley, Robert. "Wilkie Collins." *Victorian Fiction: A Second Guide to Research.* Ed. George H. Ford, New York: Modern Language Association, 1978.

Beetz, Kirk H. *Wilkie Collins: An Annotated Bibliography, 1889-1976.* Metuchen, NJ: Scarecrow, 1976.

———. "Wilkie Collins Studies, 1972-83." *Dickens Studies Annual* 13 (1984): 333-55.

Gasson, Andrew. "Wilkie Collins: A Collector's and Bibliographer's Challenge." *The Private Library* (Summer 1980): 51-77.

Parrish, M.L. *Wilkie Collins and Charles Reade: First Editions, Described with Notes.* London: Constable, 1940.

Wolff, Robert L. "Wilkie Collins." *Nineteenth-Century Fiction: A Bibliographical Catalogue,* Vol. 1. New York: Garland, 1981. 254-72.

Biographies

Ashley, Robert. *Wilkie Collins.* London: Arthur Barker, 1952.

Clarke, William. *The Secret Life of Wilkie Collins.* London: Allison & Busby, 1988.

Davis, Nuel Pharr. *The Life of Wilkie Collins.* Urbana, Illinois: U of Illinois P, 1956.

Marshall, William. *Wilkie Collins.* New York: Twayne, 1970.

Peters, Catherine. *The King of Inventors: A Life of Wilkie Collins.* London: Secker & Warburg, 1991.

Robinson, Kenneth. *Wilkie Collins: A Biography.* London: Bodley Head, 1951.

Sayers, Dorothy. *Wilkie Collins: A Biographical and Critical Study.* Ed. E.R. Gregory. Toledo, Ohio: Friends of the U of Toledo Libraries, 1977.

Critical Studies, General Studies, Letters

Andrew, R.V. *Wilkie Collins: A Critical Survey of His Prose Fiction, With a Bibliography.* New York: Garland, 1979.

Brashear, Barbara. "Wilkie Collins: From Novel to Play." Diss. Case Western Reserve, 1972.

Coleman, Ronald, ed. "The University of Texas Collections of the Letters of

Wilkie Collins, Victorian Novelist." Diss. University of Texas, 1975.

de la Mare, Walter. "The Early Novels of Wilkie Collins." *The Eighteen Sixties*. Ed. J. Drinkwater, London: Cambridge UP, 1931: 51-101.

Ellis, S.M. *Wilkie Collins, Le Fanu, and Others*. London: Constable, 1931.

Gasson, Andrew. *Wilkie Collins.: An Illustrated Guide*. Oxford: Oxford UP, 1998.

Heller, Tamar. *Dead Secrets: Wilkie Collins and the Female Gothic*. New Haven, CT: Yale UP, 1992.

Lonoff, Sue. *Wilkie Collins and His Victorian Readers: A Study in the Rhetoric of Authorship*. New York: AMS, 1982.

Milley, H.J.W. "The Achievement of Wilkie Collins and His Influence on Dickens and Trollope." Diss. Yale, 1941.

Nayder, Lillian. *Wilkie Collins Revisited*. New York: Twayne, 1997.

O'Neill, Philip. *Wilkie Collins: Women, Property and Propriety*. London: Macmillan, 1988.

Page, Norman, ed. *Wilkie Collins: The Critical Heritage*. London: Routledge & Kegan Paul, 1974.

Phillips, W.C. *Dickens, Reade and Collins: Sensation Novelists*. New York: Columbia UP, 1919.

Rance, Nicholas. *Walking the Moral Hospital: Wilkie Collins and other Sensation Novelists*. New York: Macmillan, 1991.

Smith, Nelson, and R.C. Terry, eds. *Wilkie Collins to the Forefront: Some Reassessments*. New York: AMS, 1995.

Swinburne, Algernon. "Wilkie Collins." *Studies in Prose and Poetry*. London: Chatto and Windus, 1894.

Taylor, Jenny Bourne. *In the Secret Theatre of Home: Wilkie Collins, Sensation Narrative and Nineteenth-Century Psychology*. London: Routledge, 1988.

Thoms, Peter. *The Windings of the Labyrinth: Quest and Structure in the Major Novels of Wilkie Collins*. Athens, OH: Ohio UP, 1992.

The Moonstone

Altick, Richard. *Victorian Studies in Scarlet: Murders and Manners in the Age of Victoria*. New York: W.W. Norton, 1970.

———. *Deadly Encounters: Two Victorian Sensations*. Philadelphia: U of Pennsylvania P, 1986.

Ashley, Robert. "Wilkie Collins and the Detective Story." *Nineteenth-Century Fiction* 6 (June 1951): 47-60.

Booth, Bradford. "Collins and the Art of Fiction." *Nineteenth-Century Fiction* 6 (September 1951): 131-43.

Burgan, William. "Masonic Symbolism in *The Moonstone* and *The Mystery of Edwin Drood.*" *Dickens Studies Annual* 16 (1987): 257-303.

Burgess, Anthony. "Introduction" to *The Moonstone.* London: Pan, 1967.

Cole, G.D.H., and Margaret Cole. "Introduction" to *The Moonstone.* London: Collins, 1953.

Duncan, Ian. "*The Moonstone,* the Victorian Novel, and Imperialist Panic." *Modern Language Quarterly* 55 (September 1994): 297-319.

Eliot, T.S. "Wilkie Collins and Dickens." *Selected Essays.* London: Faber and Faber, 1932.

———. "Introduction" to *The Moonstone.* London: Oxford UP, 1928.

Elwin, Malcolm. "Wilkie Collins: The Pioneer of the Thriller," *London Mercury,* April 1931: 574-84.

———. "Introduction" to *The Moonstone.* London: Heron, 1969.

Frick, Patricia Miller. "Wilkie Collins's 'Little Jewel': The Meaning of *The Moonstone.*" *Philological Quarterly* 63 (Summer 1984): 313-21.

Gregory, E.R. "Murder in Fact: Wilkie Collins." *The New Republic* July 22, 1978, 33-34.

Hartman, Mary S. *Victorian Murderesses: A True History of Thirteen Respectable French and English Women Accused of Unspeakable Crimes.* New York: Schocken, 1977.

Hayter, Alethea. *Opium and the Romantic Imagination.* Faber and Faber, 1968.

Hennelly, Mark. "Detecting Collins' Diamond: From Serpentstone to Moonstone." *Nineteenth-Century Fiction* 39:1 (June 1984): 25-47.

Hughes, Winifred. *The Maniac in the Cellar: Sensation Novels of the 1860s.* Princeton, NJ: Princeton UP, 1980.

Hutter, Albert D. "Dreams, Transformations, and Literature: The Implications of Detective Fiction." *Victorian Studies* 19 (December 1975): 181-209.

Laidlaw, R. P. "'Awful Images and Associations': A Study of Wilkie Collins's *The Moonstone.*" *Southern Review: An Australian Journal of Literary Studies* 9 (November 1976): 211-27.

Lane, Lauriat. "Introduction" to *The Moonstone.* New York: Airmont, 1965.

Lawson, Lewis. "Wilkie Collins and *The Moonstone.*" *American Imago* 20 (Spring 1963): 61-79.

Lonoff, Sue. "Charles Dickens and Wilkie Collins." *Nineteenth-Century Fiction* 35 (September 1980): 150-70.

Mead, Harry. "On the Trail of Yorkshire's *Moonstone*." *Yorkshire Journal* (Fall 1994): 26-31.

Meckier, Jerome. "Undoing by Outdoing Continued: *Great Expectations. The Moonstone*." *Hidden Rivalries in Victorian Fiction*. Lexington, KY: UP of Kentucky, 1987: 122-52.

Miller, D.A. "From 'roman policier' to 'roman-police': Wilkie Collins's *The Moonstone*." *Novel* 13 (Winter 1980): 153-70.

Milley, H.J.W. "*The Eustace Diamonds* and *The Moonstone*." *Studies in Philology* 36 (October 1939): 651-63.

Milligan, Barry. "'Accepting a Matter of Opium as a Matter of Fact': *The Moonstone*, Opium, and Hybrid Anglo-Indian Culture." *Pleasure and Pains: Opium and the Orient in Nineteenth-Century British Culture*. Charlottesville: UP of Virginia, 1995: 69-82.

Murfin, Ross C. "The Art of Representation: Collins' *The Moonstone* and Dickens' Example." *ELH: A Journal of English Literary History* 49 (1982): 653-72.

Nadel, Ira Bruce. "Science and *The Moonstone*." *Dickens Studies Annual*, 12 (1983): 239-59.

Nayder, Lillian. "Robinson Crusoe and Friday in Victorian Britain: 'Discipline,' 'Dialogue,' and Collins's Critique of Empire in *The Moonstone*." *Dickens Studies Annual* 21 (1992): 213-31.

Newman, Hilary. "The Narrators in Wilkie Collins's *The Moonstone*." *The Wilkie Collins Society Newsletter* (Winter/Spring 1997): 3-6.

Ousby, Ian. *Bloodhounds of Heaven*. Cambridge, MA: Harvard UP, 1976.

Peters, Catherine. "Introduction" to *The Moonstone*. New York: Knopf, 1992.

Peterson, Audrey. *Victorian Masters of Mystery: From Wilkie Collins to Conan Doyle*. New York: Frederick Ungar, 1984.

Reed, J.R. "English Imperialism and the Unacknowledged Crime of *The Moonstone*." *Clio* 2 (1973): 281-90.

———. "The Stories of *The Moonstone*." *Wilkie Collins to the Forefront: Some Reassessments*. Eds. Nelson Smith and R.C. Terry. New York: AMS, 1995: 91-100.

Rhode, John. *The Case of Constance Kent*. New York: Scribner's, 1928.

Roy, Ashish. "The Fabulous Imperialist Semiotic of Wilkie Collins's *The Moonstone*." *New Literary History* 24 (Summer 1993): 657-81.

Rycroft, Charles. "A Detective Story: Psychoanalytic Observations." *Psychoanalytic Quarterly* 26 (1957): 229-45.

Sayers, Dorothy L. "Introduction" to *The Moonstone*. London: Dent, 1944.

Shaw, W. David. "The Critic as Detective: Mystery and Method in *The Moonstone*." *Victorians and Mystery: Crises in Representation*. Ithaca: Cornell UP, 1990: 288-99.

Siegel, Shepard. "Psychopharmacology and the Mystery of *The Moonstone*." *American Psychologist* 40 (May 1985): 580-81.

Smith, Muriel. "'Everything to My Wife': the Inheritance Theme in *The Moonstone* and *Sense and Sensibility*." *Wilkie Collins Society Journal* 7 (1987): 13-18.

Stewart, J.I.M. "Introduction" to *The Moonstone*. Harmondsworth: Penguin, 1966.

Symons, Julian. *Bloody Murder: from the Detective Story to the Crime Novel*. London: Faber and Faber, 1972.

Thomas, Ronald R. "The Policing of Dreams: Nineteenth-Century Detection." *Dreams of Authority: Freud and the Fictions of the Unconscious*. Ithaca: Cornell UP, 1990: 193-253.

Trodd, Anthea. "Introduction" to *The Moonstone*. Oxford: Oxford UP, 1982.

———. *Domestic Crime in the Victorian Novel*. New York: Macmillan, 1989.

Webster, Lucille Jones. "Introduction" to *The Moonstone*. New York: Harper, 1965.

Welsh, Alexander. "Collins's Setting for a Moonstone." *Strong Representations: Narrative and Circumstantial Evidence in England*. Baltimore: The Johns Hopkins UP, 1992: 215-36.

Wolfe, Peter. "Point of View and Characterization in Wilkie Collins's *The Moonstone*." *Forum* (Houston) 4 (Summer 1965): 27-29.

Victorian Theatre

Archer, Frank. *An Actor's Notebook, Being Some Memories, Friendships, Criticisms and Experiences of Frank Archer*. London: Stanley Paul, 1901.

Bailey, J.O., ed. *British Plays of the Nineteenth Century: An Anthology to Illustrate the Evolution of Drama*. New York: Odyssey, 1966.

Bancroft, Squire and Marie Bancroft. *The Bancrofts: Recollections of Sixty Years*. London: John Murray, 1909.

Booth, Michael R. *Theatre in the Victorian Age*. Cambridge: Cambridge UP, 1991.

Caine, Hall. *My Story*. London: William Heinemann, 1908.

Cook, E. Dutton. *Nights at the Play*. London: Chatto and Windus, 1883.

Fitzball, Edward. *Thirty-Five Years of a Dramatic Author's Life.* 2 vols. London: T. C. Newby, 1859.

Fitzgerald, Percy. *Memoirs of an Author.* 2 viols. London: Richard Bentley and Sons, 1895.

Jackson, Russell, ed. *Victorian Theatre: The Theatre in Its Time.* New York: New Amsterdam, 1989.

Jenkins, Anthony. *The Making of Victorian Drama.* Cambridge: Cambridge UP, 1991.

Johnson, Claudia, and Vernon Johnson: *Nineteenth-Century Theatrical Memoirs.* Westport, CT: Greenwood, 1982.

Mander, Raymond, and Joe Mitchenson. *The Lost Theatres of London.* New York: Taplinger, 1968.

Morley, Henry. *The Journal of a London Playgoer.* 1866. Leicester: Leicester UP, 1974.

Mullin, Donald, ed. *Victorian Actors and Actresses in Review: A Dictionary of Contemporary Views of Representative British and American Actors and Actresses, 1837-1901.* Westport, CT: Greenwood, 1983.

——, ed. *Victorian Plays: A Record of Significant Productions on the London Stage, 1837-1901.* New York: Greenwood, 1987.

Neville, Henry Garston. *The Stage: Its Past and Present in Relation to Fine Art.* London: Richard Bentley, 1875.

Reeve, Wybert. *From Life.* Melbourne: George Robertson, 1895.

Rowell, George. *Victorian Theatre, 1792-1914: A Survey.* 2nd ed. Cambridge: Cambridge UP, 1978.

Rowell, George, and Anthony Jackson. *The Repertory Movement: A History of Regional Theatre in Britain.* Cambridge: Cambridge UP, 1984.

Sherson, Erroll. *London's Lost Theatres of the Nineteenth Century: With Notes on Plays and Players Seen There.* London: John Lane, 1925.

Stephens, John Russell. *The Censorship of English Drama, 1824-1901.* Cambridge: Cambridge UP, 1980.

——. *The Profession of the Playwright: British Theatre 1800-1900.* Cambridge: Cambridge UP, 1992.

Taylor, George. *Players and Performances in the Victorian Theatre.* Manchester: Manchester UP, 1989.

broadview literary texts

"This is a series in which the editing is something of an art form."
The Washington Post

"Broadview's format is inviting. Clearly printed on good paper, with distinctive photographs on the covers, the books provide the physical pleasure that is so often a component of enticing one to pick up a book in the first place....And, by providing a broad context, the editors have done us a great service."
Eighteenth-Century Fiction

"These editions *[Frankenstein, Hard Times, Heart of Darkness]* are top-notch—far better than anything else in the market today."
Craig Keating, Langara College

The Broadview Literary Texts series represents an important effort to see the ever-changing canon of English literature from new angles. The series brings together texts that have long been regarded as classics with lesser-known texts that offer a fresh light—and that in many cases may also claim to be of real importance in our literary tradition.

Each volume in the series presents the text together with a variety of documents from the period, enabling readers to get a fuller, richer sense of the world out of which it emerged. Samples of the science available for Mary Shelley to draw on in writing *Frankenstein,* stark reports from the Congo in the late nineteenth century that help to illuminate Conrad's *Heart of Darkness;* late eighteenth-century statements on the proper roles for women and men that help contextualize the feminist themes of the late eighteenth-century novels *Millenium Hall* and *Something New*—these are the sorts of fascinating background materials that round out each Broadview Literary Texts edition.

Each volume also includes a full introduction, chronology, bibliography, and explanatory notes. Newly typeset and produced on high-quality paper in an attractive Trade paperback format, Broadview Literary Texts are a delight to handle as well as to read.

The distinctive cover images for the series are also designed (like the duotone process itself) to combine two slightly different perspectives. Early photographs inevitably evoke a sense of pastness, yet the images for most volumes in the series involve a conscious use of anachronism. The covers are thus designed to draw attention to social and temporal context, while suggesting that the works themselves may also relate to periods other than that from which they emerged—including our own era.